C[illegible]RD

and

SELECTED SHORT STORIES

CRANFORD

&

Selected Short Stories

MR HARRISON'S CONFESSIONS
THE DOOM OF THE GRIFFITHS
LOIS THE WITCH, CURIOUS, IF TRUE
SIX WEEKS AT HEPPENHEIM
COUSIN PHILLIS

Elizabeth C. Gaskell

Introduction and Notes by
JOHN CHAPPLE

WORDSWORTH CLASSICS

In loving memory of
MICHAEL TRAYLER
the founder of Wordsworth Editions

2

Readers who are interested in other titles from Wordsworth Editions are invited to visit our website at www.wordsworth-editions.com

For our latest list and a full mail-order service, contact Bibliophile Books, 5 Thomas Road, London E14 7BN
TEL: +44 (0)20 7515 9222 FAX: +44 (0)20 7538 4115
E-MAIL: orders@bibliophilebooks.com

This edition published 1998 by Wordsworth Editions Limited
8B East Street, Ware, Hertfordshire SG12 9HJ

ISBN 978-1-84022-451-1

Typeset in Great Britain by Antony Gray
Printed and bound by Clays Ltd, St Ives plc

Contents

GENERAL INTRODUCTION

Wordsworth Classics are inexpensive editions designed to appeal to the general reader and students. We commissioned teachers and specialists to write wide ranging, jargon-free introductions and to provide notes that would assist the understanding of our readers rather than interpret the stories for them. In the same spirit, because the pleasures of reading are inseparable from the surprises, secrets and revelations that all narratives contain, we strongly advise you to enjoy this book before turning to the Introduction.

Editorial Adviser
KEITH CARABINE
Rutherford College
The University of Kent at Canterbury

INTRODUCTION TO *CRANFORD*

Cranford began as a series of sketches in *Household Words*, a weekly family magazine established in 1850 by Charles Dickens. Mrs Gaskell claimed much later that she had not intended to write more than one paper, and certainly the appearance of the others between 1851 and 1853 was very irregular.[1] Nevertheless, the charm and humour with which the narrator Mary Smith observes genteel society in the little country town of Cranford continues throughout and her tone deepens as she responds ever more perceptively to the pathos of the life of one character in particular, Miss Matty Jenkyns. The early episodes were pretty well self-contained, but in the course of further composition they became more and more interlinked to form what may be regarded as a short novel. Moreover, *Cranford*

1 Chapple and Pollard (eds), *Letters*, pp. 174 and 748 (henceforth, *Letters*). The Bibliography at the end of this Introduction gives details of *Cranford*'s magazine publication and full titles of secondary works.

has been popular ever since its first appearance as a sixteen-chapter book in June 1853, and has been translated into several languages and reprinted hundreds of times in England and America since the author's death.

It grew slowly in her imagination. Its origins are found in an anonymous descriptive article, 'The Last Generation in England', which appeared in an American magazine in July 1849. Inspired by Southey's idea of writing a 'history of English domestic life', Elizabeth Gaskell had set herself to record what she knew first-hand or had been told of divisions of rank, individual eccentricities just kept in check by custom, and the curious and innocent ways in which ladies on a low income managed to keep up appearances in Knutsford. Not long afterwards she turned from fact to fiction, contributing to the *Ladies' Companion* between February and April 1851 a story entitled 'Mr Harrison's Confessions', again based on her close knowledge of Knutsford. For this story she adopted the device of a male narrator, an outsider joining an existing practice in a little country town as a medical apprentice.[2] Mr Harrison finds, somewhat to his surprise, that personal and social relations with his patients seem to be every bit as important as medical skill, and that his appearance as a marriageable young man in a largely female society has predictable consequences. Here was an opportunity for Elizabeth Gaskell to display her versatility as an author. She could evoke the terrors of a child dying of croup, or dramatise the behaviour of Mr Harrison's impudent friend mimicking his 'professional way of mousing about a room, and mewing and purring according as [his] patients were ill or well', or devise comically romantic traps laid for him by determined matrons with unmarried sisters and daughters.

'Our Society at Cranford' begins in December 1851 with the famous assertion that the town was 'in possession of the Amazons; all the holders of houses above a certain rent are women'. Such lives must have been utterly familiar to this author. Aunt Hannah Lumb, her 'more than mother', had private money and a good annual income derived from a separation settlement. She lived in one of the best houses in Knutsford, associating with her Holland sisters and nieces rather older than Elizabeth herself. Mrs Gaskell received seventy-six pounds from *Household Words* for the eight Cranford papers; their publication and republication as a book would earn her yet further

2 Her uncle Peter Holland (1766–1855), surgeon of Knutsford, lived there for well over half a century. He used to take medical apprentices.

sums.[3] She had not been brought up to consider money beneath her dignity. Indeed, Victorian realist fiction in her hands constantly recurs to the subject. Towards the climax of *Cranford*, Miss Matty's finances assume a special importance and are precisely itemised.

Cranford is a treasury of detail and local colour. How did individuals look, dress, decorate their homes, entertain friends, travel about the town, behave towards each other? Elizabeth Gaskell was observant and endlessly curious, writing to a friend in her youth, 'Remember every little, leetle particular about yourself, and your concerns, and gossipry, and scandal, are most welcome to me . . . '[4] Oral history and traditions fascinated her, too. Thus 'Disappearances', a short piece she sent to *Household Words* in 1851, is a mosaic of stories told to her by other people, anecdotes and reminiscences heard in Knutsford and elsewhere. She is the chronicler of Knutsford in particular, a little community united by gossip and a habit of stories, but she did not hesitate to draw from any source and remodel as she thought fit.[5] More examples are to be found in the notes below.

For all its shifting basis in real life, Cranford is a fiction, always engaging, sometimes incredible. Her verisimilitude could be highly selective, choosing the freakish as well as the humdrum. She told John Ruskin that she herself used to read it when she felt low, for 'I have seen the cow that wore the grey flannel jacket – and I know the cat that swallowed the lace, that belonged to the lady that sent for the doctor, that gave the emetic &c !!!' As a kind of proof she gave him another anecdote, about a neat maidservant who 'performed a sort of "pas-de-basque", hopping & sliding with more grace than security to the dishes she held', in order to avoid stepping on the white parts in the design of a carpet newly laid for her employers. In 1854 she sent John Forster a joke too late to be included, actually calling it a 'Cranfordism'. An old lady had said to one of her cousins, 'I have never been able to spell since I lost my teeth'![6]

The striking and famous term in the first chapter, 'elegant

3 Dorothy W. Collin, 'The Composition and Publication of Elizabeth Gaskell's *Cranford*', *Bulletin of John Rylands University Library of Manchester*, 69 (Autumn 1986), p. 70; *Letters*, p. 967

4 To Harriet Carr, 31 August 1831; Chapple and Shelston (eds), *Further Letters*, p. 6

5 Sharps (*Mrs Gaskell's Observation and Invention*, pp. 128–9) notes that Charlotte Brontë's belief that she could not sleep after drinking green tea on a visit to the Gaskells finds parallels in *Cranford*. See pp. 116–17 and 139–40 below.

6 *Letters*, pp. 290 and 748. Cf. pp. 15 and 44 below.

economy', crystallises a great deal. Most of the genteel spinsters and widows of Cranford could not afford to be other than frugal. Evening card parties are at the centre of their social life, but only if organised with great discretion. Everything needed – tables with green baize tops, candles and clean packs of cards at each one – is prepared by daylight. As the hour approaches, the ladies of the house stand ready, dressed in their best, each holding a candle-lighter, 'ready to dart at the candles as soon as the first knock came'. Delicate egg-shell china is set out, old-fashioned silver highly polished – but the eatables are 'of the slightest description'. That a little charity-school maid in the tiny drawing-room of one of the poorest ladies, Miss Forrester, should disturb 'the ladies on the sofa by a request that she might get the tea-tray out from underneath' might sound simply amusing, but in the circumstances it is both touching and psychologically plausible. The guests happily collude. They take 'this novel proceeding as the most natural thing in the world' and talk on as if their hostess were mistress of a large establishment with 'a regular servants' hall'.

Mrs Gaskell's narrator, Mary Smith, at first without a name, is important as a relatively detached observer from Drumble, the booming industrial city nearby, with knowledge of driven lives outside Cranford's static female society. Younger than the ladies she observes so keenly (Miss Pole's appearance in morning costume, for example, 'the principal feature of which was her being without teeth, and wearing a veil to conceal the deficiency'), her common sense combined with loving intelligence make her the perfect register of Cranford life. She is portrayed as sensitive and sympathetic, aware like her creator of accelerating forces for change in a larger world, but more and more drawn back into an affectionate understanding of the thoughts and feelings of the little town she gets to know over so many years. It is a finely maintained and subtly changing balance.

The first paper (Chapters 1 and 2) is self-contained but proves to be a model for the whole work. The Cranford ladies' emphasis upon ladylike behaviour, and their associated view that money is vulgar 'because that subject savoured of commerce and trade', are quite upset when Captain Brown comes to live amongst them. Retired from active service on half-pay, and in some way connected with a neighbouring 'obnoxious railroad', he openly proclaims his poverty (two pounds per annum was 'a large sum in Captain Brown's annual disbursements') in a loud military voice. But on Mary Smith's next visit, months later, she discovers that he has become a general favourite, even with ladies who had almost persuaded themselves that merely to be a man was 'vulgar'. Oblivious to slights and sarcasm, his masculine common sense and readiness to help everybody, whatever their status, are exemplary. Only Miss Jenkyns, elder daughter of the deceased rector of Cranford and therefore high in the local hierarchy, cannot be brought to approve of him.[7] Symbolically, as one of the principal Amazons of the neighbourhood, she crosses swords with him in a dramatic scene, reading the formal sentences of *Rasselas* 'in a high-pitched, majestic voice' to counteract his infinitely livelier rendering of Sam Weller's 'swarry' in *Pickwick Papers*. The attitudes and values of two centuries are juxtaposed. The 'great Doctor' Samuel Johnson is opposed to Dickens, whom Ruskin once called 'a pure modernist – a leader of the steam-whistle party *par excellence*'.[8]

Yet beneath the Cranford ladies' attachment to outmoded forms and strict sense of propriety, Mary Smith discovers, there is true humanity. When it is found that the older of Captain Brown's two daughters suffers from an incurable, lingering illness, the whole community delicately attempts to alleviate her suffering. Even Miss Jenkyns sends an apple full of cloves to be heated and smell pleasantly by the sick-bed – though as she stuck in each clove she could not resist uttering a sonorous Johnsonian sentence. Mary Smith is shown losing her early detachment as an outsider, realising that what she had thought was an expression of 'unmitigated crossness' on Miss Brown's face was mostly caused by pain, and that Miss Jessie Brown's 'singing out of tune, and juvenility of dress' must be forgiven in the light of the patient tenderness she displayed whenever her sister became querulous and complaining.

These gradual softenings in Cranford's spirit and attitude are sensationally interrupted by news of Captain Brown's death on 'them nasty cruel railroads'.[9] This is perhaps a reminder that the modern world is inescapable. The shock certainly releases Miss

7 Miss Jenkyns is supposed to reflect cousin Mary Holland, probably the sister whom Maria Edgeworth the novelist thought good and sensible, but possessing 'a forbidding countenance and a manner reserved till it is *gruff*'. See Christina Colvin (ed.), *Maria Edgeworth: Letters from England 1813–1844*, Clarendon Press, Oxford, 1971, p. 20.

8 Quoted by Philip Collins (ed.), *Dickens: The Critical Heritage*, Routledge and Kegan Paul, 1971, p. 443

9 The politician William Huskisson had been accidentally killed by a Manchester–Liverpool train in 1830. The railway accident soon became a fictional convention, as in Dickens's *Dombey and Son* (1846–8), Ch. 55.

Jenkyns from her bondage to the antiquated values of her father the rector. She helps care for the dying Miss Brown and accompanies Miss Jessie Brown to their father's funeral, though Mary Smith's feelings are mixed when she sees Miss Jenkyns's alterations to her little black silk bonnet: 'I was full of sorrow, but, by one of those whimsical thoughts which come unbidden into our heads, in times of deepest grief, I no sooner saw the bonnet than I was reminded of a helmet; and in that hybrid bonnet, half-helmet, half-jockey-cap, did Miss Jenkyns attend Captain Brown's funeral.' For Elizabeth Gaskell, humour and compassion can lie close together. When Major Gordon, who had once been the lover of Miss Jessie Brown, reappears, a transformed Miss Jenkyns has the tact to leave them alone together in her own sacred drawing-room. And when a terrified Miss Matty reports that he is sitting with his arm round her waist, the former 'model of feminine decorum' utters an astonishing snub: 'The most proper place in the world for his arm to be in. Go away, Matilda, and mind your own business'!

After Miss Jenkyns's own death, Miss Matty (Matilda for a while) strives to live up to and beyond her sister's once rigid standards, but a visit from a cousin, Major Jenkyns, returning after years in India, sadly flusters her. Years of subservient spinsterhood have given her no idea how a gentleman should be entertained. Soon after this Elizabeth Gaskell craftily introduces an old man, Thomas Holbrook, object of Miss Matty's failed 'love affair of long ago'. Always honest and loud-speaking (often in dialect), he is dressed as a prosperous yeoman in a 'blue coat with brass buttons, drab breeches, and gaiters'. Never 'enough of a gentleman' for a rector's daughter, evidently. There is a visit to his idyllic farm, where he surprises Mary Smith with his 'apt and beautiful quotations' of poetry, ranging from George Herbert to Byron and Goethe, 'as naturally as if he were thinking aloud'. A homely meal passes so well that Miss Matty hopes dining with a bachelor was not improper, as 'so many pleasant things are!' Any romantic developments are prevented by his death, however. Miss Matty, who like Viola in *Twelfth Night* had never told her love, leaves off the best cap she had taken to wearing every day and asks the little milliner in the town to make her something in the style of the widow's cap worn by the Honourable Mrs Jamieson. Sentimentally, she relaxes the antiquated Cranford rule forbidding servants to have 'followers' and allows her faithful Martha to receive her young man's visits openly. Miss Matty submits to 'Fate and Love'. Martha takes on a less abstract entity: 'Jem Hearn, and he's a joiner, making three and sixpence a day, and six foot one in his stocking feet'.

Time shifts in *Cranford* now become increasingly subtle and unexpected, as if mirroring the random processes of the author's recollections, like birds gliding and swooping in invisible currents of air. In Chapter 5, Miss Matty and Mary Smith look through bundles of old family letters, some full of vivid life and hope, others of loss and misery.[10] Their perusal revives the layered family past – the tender if ridiculous love between Matty's grandparents in 1774, the fear of a French invasion felt about 1805 by a much younger Deborah Jenkyns in Newcastle and her sister Matty at home.[11] From one letter, quite unexpectedly, as if Mrs Gaskell had at last been suddenly struck by an idea for a plot-development, we learn that they had once had a brother. Details of his past history are cleverly delayed for several pages into Chapter 6, and they prove to be strangely troubling.

'Poor Peter', specifically said to be like dear Captain Brown in his readiness to help old and young, used to be far too fond of 'hoaxing', Matty remembers. Whilst his sister Deborah was away on a visit, he put on her garments to make fun of her and of old ladies in Cranford who would believe anything, walking about with a pillow as a pretend baby. This sarcastic cross-dressing is not entirely inappropriate, for Deborah had always criticised him and been a firm upholder of their stern father's patriarchal codes. Matty rather implausibly asserts that Peter did not intend to hurt her, it was just 'to make something to talk about in the town'. If Peter's behaviour was a mere joke, Deborah's, we might think today, points to a kind of unnatural repression of her womanly self. Such matters, however, are not spelt out by a novelist who is otherwise so expert in penetrating human opacities and juxtaposing different perceptions. Thus, after their father's merciless and public flogging of his son when he arrives upon the scene, Matty's later feeble comment, 'I don't know what he thought he saw', must mask unendurable thoughts about male atavism.

Why include an episode that so agonisingly rends the gentle

10 In December 1852, Mrs Gaskell offered her sister-in-law 'odd bundles of old letters', which might well have been these, to read during her confinement (*Letters*, p. 218).

11 Mary Holland was in Newcastle 1802–3, when the city raised an armed home guard of nearly twelve hundred men. See Chapple, *Elizabeth Gaskell: The Early Years*, pp. 149 and 361 (henceforth, *EGEY*).

narrative fabric? One clue might lie in its melodramatic sequel. Peter runs away to sea, joins the navy and sends home an Indian shawl for his mother. But it does not arrive until after her death from grief; sadly, it is the sort she had wanted in her youth but her own mother had never given her. Similarly, Elizabeth Gaskell's sailor brother John Stevenson had once brought her a piece of tartan silk for a gown from India, which her stepmother had considered her too young to have, though she was not far off eighteen years of age. Soon after this John sailed again to India for good, never to return, his fate unknown. Aunt Lumb in Knutsford had surrounded her niece with love, but this painful loss, contemporary with the debts, overwork and illness she knew were afflicting her father and stepmother in Chelsea, from not long after their marriage in 1814 to his death in 1829, had made her acutely unhappy. Though we have no knowledge of a flogging, and Elizabeth Gaskell hardly ever alludes to these traumas, she is for once allowing herself to revive in symbolic form the agonies of her teens.[12]

The dread voice passes. In Chapters 7 and 8, Elizabeth Gaskell reverts to her customary shrewd, sunny 'Knutsford' self, with much delicious satire of pretension. We meet the snobbish gentleman whose name began with 'two little ffs – ffoulkes', and who looked like dying a bachelor till he met with a rich and widowed Mrs ffaringdon at a spa. There is the card table, animated by four whispering 'ladies' niddle-noddling caps, all nearly meeting over the middle'; the brooches, 'some that were like small picture frames with mausoleums and weeping willows neatly executed in hair inside'; and Miss Jamieson's wonderfully imposing butler, Mr Mulliner, who even in 'his pleasantest and most gracious moods' looked like 'a sulky cockatoo'. Change is irresistible. The ladies, fearful that their numbers are falling, admit the sister of the coarsely named surgeon, Mr Hoggins, to their circle. Another outsider, awaited with nervous delight because she is a member of the nobility, the Scottish Lady Glenmire, turns out to be a brisk, unpretentious and 'sharp, stirring sort of a body', a female version of Captain Brown. The once strictly 'separate spheres' of rank and gender in Cranford are interlocking more and more.

Chapter 9, begun after a long pause in 1852 needed to finish *Ruth*, marks a new phase of structural integration. Old plots are renewed

12 Her Elizabeth Stevenson self for a brief moment revives in the misery of recollection. See *EGEY*, pp. 314–21, 330–3 and 339–40, and Uglow (*Elizabeth Gaskell*, pp. 293–4), who suggests a pattern that psychotherapists would recognise.

and concluded, new plot lines begin. And, of all things, turbans are foregrounded in a way that picks out themes and incidents. Miss Matty's cousin in Chapter 3 had brought with him a fascinating Hindu servant with 'white turban and brown complexion'. She now expresses an innocent desire for a fashionable sea-green turban to impress certain county families expected to visit Knutsford, but Mary Smith disappointingly buys her a 'pretty, neat, middle-aged cap'. The arrival of the conjuror Signor Brunoni in magnificent Turkish costume causes Miss Matty to say in sorrowful tone, 'You see, my dear, turbans *are* worn.' His dazzling stage performance in the Cranford assembly rooms brings us into a realm of magic, disguise and transformation, fortunately sanctioned by the presence of the 'tall, thin, dry, dusty' but smiling old bachelor rector, 'sitting surrounded by National School boys, guarded by troops of his own sex from any approach of the many Cranford spinsters', as Mary Smith puts it.

Reports of robberies and mysterious crimes in the district become absurdly associated with the Signor in Chapter 10. Cranford people, claims Mrs Forrester, are 'too grateful to the aristocracy who were so kind as to live near the town' ever to disgrace themselves in such ways, so the criminals must be strangers, most likely foreigners – and who 'so likely as the French?' Signor Brunoni speaks in broken English and though he wears a turban like a Turk, she has 'seen a print of Madame de Staël with a turban on'. We can sense a recovery of Mrs Gaskell's artistic *joie de vivre* as she entertains herself as well as us. She makes Miss Pole ludicrously transform two passing men and an Irish beggar-woman into stage villains: a man with black hair hanging in elf-locks, another with red hair, 'which deepened into carroty', a hump and a decided squint, and a masculine woman with glaring eyes – probably a man in disguise. The account of Mrs Forrester's party at Over Place, two hundred fearful and scurrying yards up a dark and lonely lane, is a characteristic triumph. It is impossible to read the passages in which they then recount their private precautions against imaginary robbers without laughing aloud – especially at the thought of a younger and active Miss Matty taking a flying leap into bed from a distance, terrified that a man concealed beneath it might seize her last leg. (Did Edward Lear ever draw this?) She gave up this feat of athleticism because it annoyed Deborah, so now she rolls a penny ball under the bed every night, taking care to have her hand on the bell rope, ready to call on an imaginary John and Harry if the ball did not come out the other side.

The comedy of errors (there is even a twin brother as well as fear and magic) continues. Signor Brunoni, who has terrified the neighbourhood for six weeks, suffers an accident and is cured by the skill of Cranford's doctor, Mr Hoggins, assisted by Lady Glenmire, and nourished by Mrs Forrester's famous bread-jelly, from a secret recipe, 'bequeathed, as her executors would find, to Miss Matty'. Brunoni, as his name suggests, turns out to be plain Samuel Brown. Mary Smith discovers that he knows 'the proper sit of a turban' because, unlike his twin, he had actually been in India. For a time we listen to the voice of tragi-comedy as his wife tells their pathetic story – the deaths of six of their children, her desperate journey on foot, carrying her new baby, to Calcutta in order to get a passage home, and the help she received from kind natives. The baby fell ill, but fortune changed; they are saved by a Englishman, whose name is delayed for a page – Aga Jenkyns. Could he be the lost Peter, Mary Smith asks herself?

This highly speculative but not irrational question is at once followed in Chapter 12 by a joyously batty set of puns and misunderstandings. Miss Pole's belief that Peter might have been elected Great Lama of Tibet soon turns into a 'dispute whether llamas were carnivorous animals or not', whereat Miss Forrester admits that she always confused carnivorous and gramnivorous, as well as horizontal and perpendicular. The atmosphere of misrule continues with the startling news that Lady Glenmire is to be married to Mr Hoggins the surgeon, who, Miss Pole has reason to believe, 'sups on bread and cheese and beer every night'. How much a year did *he* have? Had *she* married for an establishment? Would she drop the use of her title? Would the absent Mrs Jamieson ('dull, and inert, and pompous, and tiresome') allow them to be visited? Could they be congratulated before her return, or should the engagement be seen 'in the same light as the Queen of Spain's legs – facts which certainly existed, but the less said about the better'?

A last ordeal awaits Miss Matty. The bank in which her small fortune of £149 13*s*. 4*d*. a year was invested fails. She is left with only thirteen pounds a year. Yet beneath her defeated aspirations for a husband and child, and her attempts to retain social status, lies dogged moral courage if not a financial brain. She gives the five gold sovereigns she had saved for a new gown to a farmer whose worthless banknote had been refused in a shop. The ladies of Cranford, superficially so ignorant and slaves to decorum, band together to help support her financially; and, with perfect delicacy, anonymously.[13] Her servant Martha makes a wonderful pudding in the shape of a lion *couchant* and then drags in her Jem Hearn, 'crimson with shyness', announcing to *his* surprise that he wants to marry her offhand and take one quiet lodger.[14] This community solidarity extends to Drumble, when Mary Smith enlists her father's help. He is so decisive and businesslike that he baffles them; nevertheless, he is another caring male in the line of Captain Brown, Mr Hoggins and Peter Jenkyns. *Cranford*, Jenny Uglow rightly argues, is not 'a separatist Utopia, but an appeal *against* separate spheres'.[15]

Miss Matty opens a small shop, a perfectly realistic thing to do in the circumstances,[16] but Mary Smith had secretly sent a letter to Aga Jenkyns in far-away India, with the forlorn hope that he was in fact the long-lost brother. We at once guess there will be a happy ending. Sure enough, Peter Jenkyns, deeply bronzed, with snow-white hair, eventually returns. He, like Captain Brown, becomes a general favourite with the Cranford ladies, whose quiet lives are 'astonishingly stirred up' by his wonderful stories. If his audience swallow a tallish anecdote one week, they have 'the dose considerably increased the next'. *Cranford* is enriched by the roles that men and women play in each other's company, charged with the sex attraction and antagonism that lighten our lives and animate so much comic drama. He even tells the Honourable Mrs Jamieson, haughtiest of the haughty, that when hunting in the Himalayas he had shot 'a cherubim' by mistake. Miss Jamieson is appalled: 'But, Mr Peter, shooting a cherubim – don't you think – I am afraid that was sacrilege!' He at once acknowledges her judgement, mimics a sober look and begs for understanding on the grounds that he has been living for many years amongst savages and heathens – 'some of them, he was afraid, were downright Dissenters'. For readers this is sheer delight. We respond to Elizabeth Gaskell's creation of a little community in which such joyful irony can flourish – at the expense

13 The Misses Byerley of Elizabeth Stevenson's Avonbank school (where they tried to teach everything without masters) concealed the fact that they were paying their widowed mother's pension (*EGEY*, p. 240).

14 The Gaskells' life-long friend and servant was called Ann Hearn.

15 Uglow, *Elizabeth Gaskell*, p. 288

16 Elizabeth Gaskell had recently written to the Royal Literary Fund on 3 June 1850 for a Mrs Granville of Knutsford: 'Her sole dependence, a very precarious one, is on a small shop, the rent of which is 8£ a year, and on an annuity of 10£.' See Chapple and Shelston (eds), *Further Letters*, pp. 49–50, 67–8 and 109.

of men, too, for we should not forget Mary Smith's reflection that her own father, despite his commercial virtuosity, 'lost upwards of a thousand pounds by roguery only last year'.

Wives and Daughters, a major novel of her full maturity, can be regarded as an extended version of *Cranford*, far wider in scope but dealing with much the same material in a very similar way. How she could at the same time be the author of deeply serious social-problem novels has puzzled critics since their rediscovery some forty-five years ago. Her first novel, the passionately felt *Mary Barton* of 1848, dramatises the sufferings of cotton workers in Manchester, the 'shock city' of the age, torn by industrial disputes between 'masters' and 'hands'. The 'Manchester' side of her writing self is rooted in the common life of working people and determined to engage in humanitarian crusades, whatever the cost in personal terms. Her vehemence rises to a climax of intensity as she struggles to finish her next controversial novel, *Ruth*, tackling dangerous topics like sweated labour, the 'fallen woman' and concealed illegitimacy. In November 1852 she even wrote from Manchester in a spasm of anxiety to a friend who mentioned that she had seen an advertisement for it, 'I had hoped to have come over to Knutsford before this subject of pain to me was broached. Now I shall not come, because morbid or not morbid I can't bear to be talked to about it.'[17]

The renunciation, if more than rhetorical, was very temporary. She could never deny her 'Knutsford' self, returning in life and in art to the little community that was an inalienable part of her own experience and whose existence in time she found it so easy to revive. She is also utterly sure of her paradoxical ground as a married citizen of Manchester, knowing that there it was impossible to avoid living by and amongst irreconcileables. She does her best to recreate these in *North and South*, a truly remarkable novel of personal growth and development, in which the heroine finds herself stranded amongst the perplexing sex, class, cultural and religious conflicts of a great industrial city. But *Cranford* should not therefore be dismissed as a largely escapist text, an indulgent satire of the little female eccentricities she could capture so well. There is a depth of feeling that can break through its comic surface, and it encapsulates some of the same historical forces for change as her social-problem novels, though in a minor, subdued and more private manner. She

17 To Mary Green, ?20 November 1852; Chapple and Shelston (eds), *Further Letters*, p. 74

successfully blends comedy and pathos, tradition and change, loss and gain. We may still wonder at the diversity of character and incident in such a short work – much, it would seem, discovered and instinctively shaped as she wrote away in her fast, well-formed hand. Her fiction dances on the page, stirring the emotions and lifting the spirits of generations of readers from Dickens and Charlotte Brontë onwards.

JOHN CHAPPLE

BIOGRAPHICAL NOTE ON THE AUTHOR

Elizabeth Cleghorn Gaskell was born in Chelsea on 29 September 1810, the daughter of Elizabeth and William Stevenson. Her mother was a Holland of Sandlebridge in Cheshire, her father from Berwick. Successively a Unitarian minister, a tutor in classics, a farmer and a learned contributor to major reviews, he became in 1806 Keeper of the Papers at the Treasury in London. His wife died a year after Elizabeth's birth. A son John, born on 27 November 1798, became a mate in the merchant marine. Elizabeth was sent to her mother's sister, Hannah Lumb, a widow living at Knutsford in comfortable circumstances. In 1821 she sent Elizabeth for five years to a first-class private school for girls in Warwickshire, enabling her to lead the typical life of a young lady.

In 1832 she married William Gaskell, junior minister of a very important Unitarian chapel at Cross Street in Manchester. They had seven children between 1833 and 1846. Four girls only survived, the greatest loss being that of a son who almost reached his first birthday. Both William and Elizabeth wrote verse, but it was Elizabeth Gaskell who became known after 1847 for accomplished novels, stories and articles of various kinds.

Her circle of acquaintance widened dramatically. In 1850 she made friends with Charlotte Brontë, of whom, after her unexpected death, she swiftly wrote a major biography, *The Life of Charlotte Brontë* (1857). This, like *Cranford*, has never fallen out of favour. The revival of Elizabeth Gaskell's reputation in the last few decades has meant that works like *Mary Barton* (1848), *Ruth* (1853), *North and South* (1855), *Sylvia's Lovers* (1863) and *Cousin Phillis* (1864) can now be found in a number of editions, together with selections from her short stories and a collected edition of her brilliant letters (1966, 1997). *Wives and Daughters*, which many regard as her masterpiece, was not quite finished at her death on 12 November 1865.

BIBLIOGRAPHY

First appearance in *Household Words*, Vols 4–7:

13 December 1851	'Our Society at Cranford' (Chs 1–2)
3 January 1852	'A Love Affair at Cranford' (Chs 3–4)
13 March 1852	'Memory at Cranford' (Chs 5–6)
3 April 1852	'Visiting at Cranford' (Chs 7–8)
8 & 15 January 1853	'The Great Cranford Panic' (Chs 9–11)
2 April 1853	'Stopped Payment at Cranford' (Chs 12–13)
7 May 1853	'Friends in Need, at Cranford' (Ch. 14)
21 May 1853	'A Happy Return to Cranford' (Chs 15–16)

General

Elizabeth Gaskell: The Critical Heritage, Angus Easson (ed.), Routledge, London and New York, 1991; a substantial collection of reviews, opinions and significant judgements up to 1910

John Geoffrey Sharps, *Mrs Gaskell's Observation and Invention: A Study of Her Non-Biographic Works*, Linden Press, Fontwell, Sussex, 1970; a detailed Introduction to each work in turn, based on extensive and original research

Amanda Vickery, *The Gentleman's Daughter: Women's Lives in Georgian England*, Yale University Press, New Haven and London, 1998; based upon many eighteenth- and early-nineteenth-century primary sources (letters, diaries and account books)

Nancy S. Weyant, *Elizabeth Gaskell: An Annotated Bibliography of English-Language Sources, 1976–1991*, Scarecrow Press, Metuchen, NJ and London, 1994; *Guide 1992–2001*, Lanham (Maryland), Toronto, Oxford, 2004

Graham Handley, *Elizabeth Gaskell: A Chronology*, Palgrave Macmillan, 2005

Letters

The Letters of Mrs Gaskell, J. A. V. Chapple and Arthur Pollard (eds), Manchester University Press, 1966; Mandolin, 1997

Further Letters of Mrs Gaskell, John Chapple and Alan Shelston (eds), Manchester University Press, 2000

J. A. V. Chapple (assisted by J. G. Sharps), *Elizabeth Gaskell: A Portrait in Letters*, Manchester University Press, 1980; a selection of letters with interlinking commentary

Selected Biography and Criticism (in chronological order)

A. B. Hopkins, *Elizabeth Gaskell: Her Life and Work*, John Lehmann, 1952; an early and well-researched study

Arthur Pollard, *Mrs Gaskell: Novelist and Biographer*, Manchester University Press, 1965; introduction to the life and works by a pioneer in the modern appraisal of Elizabeth Gaskell

Winifred Gérin, *Elizabeth Gaskell: A Biography*, Clarendon Press, Oxford, 1976; fluent and readable

Angus Easson, *Elizabeth Gaskell*, Routledge and Kegan Paul, London, Boston and Henley, 1979; an acute and independent survey of the works as well as of Gaskell's life and times

Pauline Nestor, *Female Friendships and Communities: Charlotte Brontë, George Eliot, Elizabeth Gaskell*, Clarendon Press, Oxford 1985; very useful, for the servant–mistress bond, etc.

Patsy Stoneman, *Elizabeth Gaskell*, Harvester Press, Brighton, 1987; an exceptionally clear and informative feminist analysis

Felicia Bonaparte, *The Gipsy Bachelor of Manchester: The Life of Mrs Gaskell's Demon*, Virginia University Press, Charlottesville and London, 1992; unusual but engaging study of Gaskell's life and art as a single imaginative enterprise.

Hilary M. Schor, *Scheherezade in the Market Place: Elizabeth Gaskell and the Victorian Novel*, Oxford University Press, 1992

Jenny Uglow, *Elizabeth Gaskell: A Habit of Stories*, Faber and Faber, London and Boston, 1993; the most stimulating book to date; a fresh and substantial account of Gaskell's life and times, accompanied by fine criticism of her works

Terence Wright, *Elizabeth Gaskell 'We are not angels': Realism, Gender, Values*, Macmillan, Basingstoke, 1995; close, sensitive textual analysis and criticism

John Chapple, *Elizabeth Gaskell: The Early Years*, Manchester University Press, Manchester and New York, 1997; contains much new information

Shirley Foster, *Elizabeth Gaskell: A Literary Life*, Palgrave Macmillan, 2002; a very useful introduction

Knutsford

Edward Hall, typescript in Manchester Central Reference Library, entitled '*Cranford* Again: The Knutsford Letters, 1809–1824': lengthy selections from the extensive correspondence of the Whittaker family

Henry Green, *Knutsford, Its Traditions and History: With Reminiscences, Anecdotes, and Notices of the Neighbourhood* (1859), Introduction by E. L. Burney, E. J. Morten, Didsbury, 1969; by Knutsford's Unitarian minister from 1827, a close friend of the Gaskells

George A. Payne, *Mrs Gaskell and Knutsford*, 2nd edn, Clarkson & Griffiths, Manchester, and Mackie & Co., London (1905); amiable survey by a successor of Green

K. Goodchild, P. Ikin and J. Leach, *Looking Back at Knutsford*, Willow Publishing, Timperley, 1984; contains many illustrations

The Works of Elizabeth Gaskell, Joanne Shattock (general editor), Pickering and Chatto, London, 10 vols – in progress. Five volumes of this scholarly, collected edition have been published (2005).

The Gaskell Society Journal and *The Gaskell Society Newsletter* contain critical articles and new information.

Mitsuharu Matsuoka's 'The Gaskell Web' on the Internet is very useful. It contains 'A Cranford Walk Around Knutsford, Past and Present' – http://lang.nagoya-u.ac.jp/~matsuoka/Gaskell.html. This is a virtual tour he prepared with the Honorary Secretary of the Gaskell Society, Mrs Joan Leach; it also has a digital map and many illustrations.

CRANFORD

CHAPTER I

Our Society

In the first place, Cranford is in possession of the Amazons;[1] all the holders of houses above a certain rent are women. If a married couple come to settle in the town, somehow the gentleman disappears; he is either fairly frightened to death by being the only man in the Cranford evening parties, or he is accounted for by being with his regiment, his ship, or closely engaged in business all the week in the great neighbouring commercial town of Drumble,[2] distant only twenty miles on a railroad. In short, whatever does become of the gentlemen, they are not at Cranford. What could they do if they were there? The surgeon has his round of thirty miles, and sleeps at Cranford; but every man cannot be a surgeon.[3] For keeping the trim gardens full of choice flowers without a weed to speck them; for frightening away little boys who look wistfully at the said flowers through the railings; for rushing out at the geese[4] that occasionally venture in to the gardens if the gates are left open; for deciding all questions of literature and politics without troubling themselves with unnecessary reasons or arguments; for obtaining clear and correct knowledge of everybody's affairs in the parish; for keeping their neat maidservants in admirable order; for kindness (somewhat dictatorial) to the poor, and real tender good offices to each other whenever they are in distress, the ladies of Cranford are quite sufficient. 'A man,' as one of them observed to me once, 'is *so* in the way in the house!' Although the ladies of Cranford know all each other's proceedings, they are exceedingly indifferent to each other's opinions. Indeed, as each has her own individuality, not to say eccentricity, pretty strongly developed, nothing is so easy as verbal retaliation; but, somehow, goodwill reigns among them to a considerable degree.

The Cranford ladies have only an occasional little quarrel, spirted out in a few peppery words and angry jerks of the head; just enough to prevent the even tenor of their lives from becoming too flat. Their dress is very independent of fashion; as they observe, 'What does it signify how we dress here at Cranford, where everybody knows us?' And if they go from home, their reason is equally cogent, 'What does it signify how we dress here, where nobody knows us?' The materials of their clothes are, in general, good and plain, and most of them are nearly as scrupulous as Miss Tyler, of cleanly memory;[5] but I will answer for it, the last gigot,[6] the last tight and scanty petticoat in wear in England, was seen at Cranford – and seen without a smile.

I can testify to a magnificent family red silk umbrella, under which a gentle little spinster, left alone of many brothers and sisters, used to patter to church on rainy days. Have you any red silk umbrellas in London? We had a tradition of the first that had ever been seen in Cranford; and the little boys mobbed it, and called it 'a stick in petticoats'. It might have been the very red silk one I have described, held up by a strong father over a troop of little ones; the poor little lady – the survivor of all – could scarcely carry it.

Then there were rules and regulations for visiting and calls; and they were announced to any young people who might be staying in the town, with all the solemnity with which the old Manx laws were read once a year on the Tinwald Mount.[7]

'Our friends have sent to inquire how you are after your journey tonight, my dear' (fifteen miles in a gentleman's carriage); 'they will give you some rest tomorrow, but the next day, I have no doubt, they will call; so be at liberty after twelve – from twelve to three are our calling hours.'

Then, after they had called: 'It is the third day; I dare say your mamma has told you, my dear, never to let more than three days elapse between receiving a call and returning it; and also, that you are never to stay longer than a quarter of an hour.'

'But am I to look at my watch? How am I to find out when a quarter of an hour has passed?'

'You must keep thinking about the time, my dear, and not allow yourself to forget it in conversation.'

As everybody had this rule in their minds, whether they received or paid a call, of course no absorbing subject was ever spoken about. We kept ourselves to short sentences of small talk, and were punctual to our time.

I imagine that a few of the gentlefolks of Cranford were poor, and had some difficulty in making both ends meet; but they were like the Spartans,[8] and concealed their smart under a smiling face. We none of us spoke of money, because that subject savoured of commerce and trade, and though some might be poor, we were all aristocratic. The Cranfordians had that kindly *esprit de corps*[9] which made them overlook all deficiencies in success when some among them tried to conceal their poverty. When Mrs Forrester, for instance, gave a party in her baby-house of a dwelling, and the little maiden disturbed the ladies on the sofa by a request that she might get the tea-tray out from underneath, everyone took this novel proceeding as the most natural thing in the world, and talked on about household forms and ceremonies as if we all believed that our hostess had a regular servants' hall, second table, with housekeeper and steward, instead of the one little charity-school maiden, whose short ruddy arms could never have been strong enough to carry the tray upstairs, if she had not been assisted in private by her mistress, who now sat in state, pretending not to know what cakes were sent up, though she knew, and we knew, and she knew that we knew, and we knew that she knew that we knew, she had been busy all the morning making tea-bread and sponge-cakes.

There were one or two consequences arising from this general but unacknowledged poverty, and this very much acknowledged gentility, which were not amiss, and which might be introduced into many circles of society to their great improvement. For instance, the inhabitants of Cranford kept early hours, and clattered home in their pattens,[10] under the guidance of a lantern-bearer, about nine o'clock at night; and the whole town was abed and asleep by half-past ten. Moreover, it was considered 'vulgar' (a tremendous word in Cranford) to give anything expensive, in the way of eatable or drinkable, at the evening entertainments. Wafer bread-and-butter and sponge-biscuits were all that the Honourable Mrs Jamieson gave; and she was sister-in-law to the late Earl of Glenmire, although she did practise such 'elegant economy'.[11]

'Elegant economy!' How naturally one falls back into the phraseology of Cranford! There, economy was always 'elegant', and money-spending always 'vulgar and ostentatious'; a sort of sour-grapeism which made us very peaceful and satisfied. I never shall forget the dismay felt when a certain Captain Brown came to live at Cranford, and openly spoke about his being poor – not in a whisper to an intimate friend, the doors and windows being previously closed, but in the public street! in a loud military voice! alleging his poverty as a reason for not taking a particular house. The ladies of Cranford were already rather moaning over the invasion of their territories by a man and a gentleman. He was a half-pay captain, and had obtained some situation on a neighbouring railroad, which had been vehemently petitioned against by the little town; and if, in addition to his masculine gender, and his connection with the obnoxious railroad, he was so brazen as to talk of being poor – why, then, indeed, he must be sent to Coventry. Death was as true and as common as poverty; yet people never spoke about that, loud out in the streets. It was a word not to be mentioned to ears polite. We had tacitly agreed to ignore that any with whom we associated on terms of visiting equality could ever be prevented by poverty from doing anything that they wished. If we walked to or from a party, it was because the night was *so* fine, or the air *so* refreshing, not because sedan-chairs were expensive. If we wore prints, instead of summer silks, it was because we preferred a washing material; and so on, till we blinded ourselves to the vulgar fact that we were, all of us, people of very moderate means. Of course, then, we did not know what to make of a man who could speak of poverty as if it was not a disgrace. Yet, somehow, Captain Brown made himself respected in Cranford, and was called upon, in spite of all resolutions to the contrary. I was surprised to hear his opinions quoted as authority at a visit which I paid to Cranford about a year after he had settled in the town. My own friends had been among the bitterest opponents of any proposal to visit the Captain and his daughters, only twelve months before; and now he was even admitted in the tabooed hours before twelve. True, it was to discover the cause of a smoking chimney, before the fire was lighted; but still Captain Brown walked upstairs, nothing daunted, spoke in a voice too large for the room, and joked quite in the way of a tame man about the house. He had been blind to all the small slights, and omissions of trivial ceremonies, with which he had been received. He had been friendly, though the Cranford ladies had been cool; he had answered small sarcastic compliments in good faith; and with his manly frankness had overpowered all the shrinking which met him as a man who was not ashamed to be poor. And, at last, his excellent masculine common sense, and his facility in devising expedients to overcome domestic dilemmas, had gained him an extraordinary place as an authority among the Cranford ladies. He himself went on in his course, as unaware of his popularity as he had been of the reverse; and I am sure he was startled one day when he found his advice so highly esteemed as to make some counsel which he had given in jest to be taken in sober, serious earnest.

It was on this subject: an old lady had an Alderney cow,[12] which she looked upon as a daughter. You could not pay the short quarter of an hour call without being told of the wonderful milk or wonderful intelligence of this animal. The whole town knew and kindly regarded Miss Betsy Barker's Alderney; therefore great was the sympathy and regret when, in an unguarded moment, the poor cow tumbled into a lime-pit.[13] She moaned so loudly that she was soon heard and rescued; but meanwhile the poor beast had lost most of her hair, and came out looking naked, cold, and miserable, in a bare skin. Everybody pitied the animal, though a few could not restrain their smiles at her droll appearance. Miss Betsy Barker absolutely cried with sorrow and dismay; and it was said she thought of trying a bath of oil. This remedy, perhaps, was recommended by someone of the number whose advice she asked; but the proposal, if ever it was made, was knocked on the head by Captain Brown's decided 'Get her a flannel waistcoat and flannel drawers, ma'am, if you wish to keep her alive. But my advice is, kill the poor creature at once.'

Miss Betsy Barker dried her eyes, and thanked the Captain heartily; she set to work, and by and by all the town turned out to see the Alderney meekly going to her pasture, clad in dark grey flannel. I have watched her myself many a time. Do you ever see cows dressed in grey flannel in London?

Captain Brown had taken a small house on the outskirts of the town, where he lived with his two daughters. He must have been upwards of sixty at the time of the first visit I paid to Cranford after I had left it as a residence. But he had a wiry, well-trained, elastic figure, a stiff military throw-back of his head, and a springing step, which made him appear much younger than he was. His eldest daughter looked almost as old as himself, and betrayed the fact that his real was more than his apparent age. Miss Brown[14] must have been forty; she had a sickly, pained, careworn expression on her face, and looked as if the gaiety of youth had long faded out of sight. Even when young she must have been plain and hard-featured. Miss Jessie Brown was ten years younger than her sister, and twenty shades prettier. Her face was round and dimpled. Miss Jenkyns once said, in a passion against Captain Brown (the cause of which I will tell you presently), 'that she thought it was time for Miss Jessie to leave off her dimples, and not always to be trying to look like a child'. It was true there was something childlike in her face; and there will be, I think, till she dies, though she should live to a hundred. Her eyes were large blue wondering eyes, looking straight at you; her nose was unformed and snub, and her lips were red and dewy; she wore her hair, too, in little rows of curls, which heightened this appearance. I do not know whether she was pretty or not; but I liked her face, and so did everybody, and I do not think she could help her dimples. She had something of her father's jauntiness of gait and manner; and any female observer might detect a slight difference in the attire of the two sisters – that of Miss Jessie being about two pounds per annum more expensive than Miss Brown's. Two pounds was a large sum in Captain Brown's annual disbursements.

Such was the impression made upon me by the Brown family when I first saw them all together in Cranford church. The Captain I had met before – on the occasion of the smoky chimney, which he had cured by some simple alteration in the flue. In church, he held his double eye-glass to his eyes during the Morning Hymn, and then lifted up his head erect and sang out loud and joyfully. He made the responses louder than the clerk – an old man with a piping feeble voice, who, I think, felt aggrieved at the Captain's sonorous bass, and quavered higher and higher in consequence.

On coming out of church, the brisk Captain paid the most gallant attention to his daughters. He nodded and smiled to his acquaintances, but he shook hands with none until he had helped Miss Brown to unfurl her umbrella, had relieved her of her prayer-book, and had waited patiently till she, with trembling nervous hands, had taken up her gown to walk through the wet roads.

I wondered what the Cranford ladies did with Captain Brown at their parties. We had often rejoiced, in former days, that there was no gentleman to be attended to, and to find conversation for, at the card-parties. We had congratulated ourselves upon the snugness of the evenings; and, in our love for gentility, and distaste of mankind, we had almost persuaded ourselves that to be a man was to be 'vulgar'; so that when I found my friend and hostess, Miss Jenkyns, was going to have a party in my honour, and that Captain and the Miss Browns were invited, I wondered much what would be the course of the evening. Card-tables, with green baize tops, were set out by daylight, just as usual; it was the third week in November, so the evenings closed in about four. Candles, and clean packs of cards, were arranged on each table. The fire was made up; the neat maidservant had received her last directions; and there we stood, dressed in our best, each with a candle-lighter in our hands, ready to dart at the candles as soon as the first knock came. Parties in Cranford were solemn festivities, making the ladies feel gravely elated as they sat together in their best dresses. As soon as three had arrived, we sat down to 'Preference',[15] I being the unlucky fourth. The next four comers were put down immediately to another table; and presently the tea-trays, which I had seen set out in the storeroom as I passed in the morning, were placed each on the middle of a card-table. The china was delicate eggshell; the old-fashioned silver glittered with polishing; but the eatables were of the slightest description. While the trays were yet on the tables, Captain and the Miss Browns came in: and I could see that, somehow or other the Captain was a favourite with all the ladies present. Ruffled brows were smoothed, sharp voices lowered at his approach. Miss Brown looked ill, and depressed almost to gloom. Miss Jessie smiled as usual, and seemed nearly as popular as her father. He immediately and quietly assumed the man's place in the room; attended to every one's wants, lessened the pretty maid-servant's labour by waiting on empty cups and bread-and-butterless ladies; and yet did it all in so easy and dignified a manner, and so much as if it were a matter of course for the strong to attend to the weak, that he was a true man throughout. He played for threepenny points with as grave an interest as if they had been pounds; and yet, in all his attention to strangers, he had an eye on his suffering daughter – for suffering I was sure she was, though to many eyes she might only appear to be irritable. Miss Jessie could not play cards: but she talked to the sitters-out, who, before her coming, had been rather inclined to be cross. She sang, too, to an old cracked piano, which I think had been a spinet in its youth. Miss Jessie sang *Jock of Hazeldean*[16] a little out of tune; but we were none of us musical, though Miss Jenkyns beat time, out of time, by way of appearing to be so.

It was very good of Miss Jenkyns to do this; for I had seen that, a little before, she had been a good deal annoyed by Miss Jessie Brown's unguarded admission (apropos of Shetland wool) that she had an uncle, her mother's brother, who was a shopkeeper in Edinburgh. Miss Jenkyns tried to drown this confession by a terrible cough – for the Honourable Mrs Jamieson was sitting at the card-table nearest Miss Jessie, and what would she say or think if she found out she was in the same room with a shopkeeper's niece! But Miss Jessie Brown (who had no tact, as we all agreed the next morning) *would* repeat the information, and assure Miss Pole she could easily get her the identical Shetland wool required, 'through my uncle, who has the best assortment of Shetland goods of any one in Edinbro' '. It was to take the taste of this out of our mouths, and the sound of this out of our ears, that Miss Jenkyns proposed music; so I say again, it was very good of her to beat time to the song.

When the trays reappeared with biscuits and wine, punctually at a quarter to nine, there was conversation, comparing of cards, and talking over tricks; but by and by Captain Brown sported a bit of literature.

'Have you seen any numbers of *The Pickwick Papers*?' said he. (They were then publishing in parts.) 'Capital thing!'

Now Miss Jenkyns was daughter of a deceased rector[17] of Cranford; and, on the strength of a number of manuscript sermons, and a pretty good library of divinity, considered herself literary, and looked upon any conversation about books as a challenge to her. So she answered and said, 'Yes, she had seen them; indeed, she might say she had read them.'

'And what do you think of them?' exclaimed Captain Brown. 'Aren't they famously good?'

So urged, Miss Jenkyns could not but speak.

'I must say, I don't think they are by any means equal to Dr Johnson. Still, perhaps, the author is young. Let him persevere, and who knows what he may become if he will take the great Doctor for his model?' This was evidently too much for Captain Brown to take placidly; and I saw the words on the tip of his tongue before Miss Jenkyns had finished her sentence.

'It is quite a different sort of thing, my dear madam,' he began.

'I am quite aware of that,' returned she. 'And I make allowances, Captain Brown.'

'Just allow me to read you a scene out of this month's number,' pleaded he. 'I had it only this morning, and I don't think the company can have read it yet.'

'As you please,' said she, settling herself with an air of resignation. He read the account of the 'swarry'[18] which Sam Weller gave at Bath. Some of us laughed heartily. *I* did not dare, because I was staying in the house. Miss Jenkyns sat in patient gravity. When it was ended, she turned to me, and said with mild dignity: 'Fetch me *Rasselas*,[19] my dear, out of the book-room.'

When I had brought it to her, she turned to Captain Brown.

'Now allow *me* to read you a scene, and then the present company can judge between your favourite, Mr Boz,[20] and Dr Johnson.'

She read one of the conversations between Rasselas and Imlac, in a high-pitched, majestic voice; and when she had ended, she said: 'I imagine I am now justified in my preference of Dr Johnson as a writer of fiction.' The Captain screwed his lips up, and drummed on the table, but he did not speak. She thought she would give him a finishing blow or two.

'I consider it vulgar, and below the dignity of literature, to publish in numbers.'

'How was the *Rambler*[21] published, ma'am?' asked Captain Brown in a low voice, which I think Miss Jenkyns could not have heard.

'Dr Johnson's style is a model for young beginners. My father recommended it to me when I began to write letters – I have formed my own style upon it; I recommend it to your favourite.'

'I should be very sorry for him to exchange his style for such pompous writing,' said Captain Brown.

Miss Jenkyns felt this as a personal affront, in a way of which the Captain had not dreamed. Epistolary writing she and her friends considered as her *forte*.[22] Many a copy of many a letter have I seen written and corrected on the slate, before she 'seized the half-hour just previous to post-time to assure' her friends of this or of that; and Dr Johnson was, as she said, her model in these compositions. She drew herself up with dignity, and only replied to Captain Brown's last remark by saying, with marked emphasis on every syllable: 'I prefer Dr Johnson to Mr Boz.'

It is said – I won't vouch for the fact – that Captain Brown was heard to say, *sotto voce*,[23] 'Damn Dr Johnson!' If he did, he was penitent afterwards, as he showed by going to stand near Miss Jenkyns's armchair, and endeavouring to beguile her into conversation on some more pleasing subject. But she was inexorable. The next day she made the remark I have mentioned about Miss Jessie's dimples.

CHAPTER 2

The Captain

It was impossible to live a month at Cranford and not know the daily habits of each resident; and long before my visit was ended I knew much concerning the whole Brown trio. There was nothing new to be discovered respecting their poverty; for they had spoken simply and openly about that from the very first. They made no mystery of the necessity for their being economical. All that remained to be discovered was the Captain's infinite kindness of heart, and the various modes in which, unconsciously to himself, he manifested it. Some little anecdotes were talked about for some time after they occurred. As we did not read much, and as all the ladies were pretty well suited with servants, there was a dearth of subjects for conversation. We therefore discussed the circumstance of the Captain taking a poor old woman's dinner out of her hands one very slippery Sunday. He had met her returning from the bakehouse[24] as he came from church, and noticed her precarious footing; and, with the grave dignity with which he did everything, he relieved her of her burden, and steered along the street by her side, carrying her baked mutton and potatoes safely home. This was thought very eccentric; and it was rather expected that he would pay a round of calls, on the Monday morning, to explain and apologise to the Cranford sense of propriety: but he did no such thing: and then it was decided that he was ashamed, and was keeping out of sight. In a kindly pity for him, we began to say: 'After all, the Sunday morning's occurrence showed great goodness of heart,' and it was resolved that he should be comforted on his next appearance amongst us; but, lo! he came down upon us, untouched by any sense of shame, speaking loud and bass as ever, his head thrown back, his wig as jaunty and well-curled as usual, and we were obliged to conclude he had forgotten all about Sunday.

Miss Pole and Miss Jessie Brown had set up a kind of intimacy on the strength of the Shetland wool and the new knitting stitches; so it happened that when I went to visit Miss Pole I saw more of the Browns than I had done while staying with Miss Jenkyns, who had never got over what she called Captain Brown's disparaging remarks upon Dr Johnson as a writer of light and agreeable fiction. I found that Miss Brown was seriously ill of some lingering, incurable complaint, the pain occasioned by which gave the uneasy expression to her face that I had taken for unmitigated crossness. Cross, too, she was at times, when the nervous irritability occasioned by her disease became past endurance. Miss Jessie bore with her at these times, even more patiently than she did with the bitter self-upbraidings by which they were invariably succeeded. Miss Brown used to accuse herself, not merely of hasty and irritable temper, but also of being the cause why her father and sister were obliged to pinch, in order to allow her the small luxuries which were necessaries in her condition. She would so fain have made sacrifices for them, and have lightened their cares, that the original generosity of her disposition added acerbity to her temper. All this was borne by Miss Jessie and her father with more than placidity – with absolute tenderness. I forgave Miss Jessie her singing out of tune, and her juvenility of dress, when

I saw her at home. I came to perceive that Captain Brown's dark Brutus wig[25] and padded coat (alas! too often threadbare) were remnants of the military smartness of his youth, which he now wore unconsciously. He was a man of infinite resources, gained in his barrack experience. As he confessed, no one could black his boots to please him except himself; but, indeed, he was not above saving the little maidservant's labours in every way – knowing, most likely, that his daughter's illness made the place a hard one.

He endeavoured to make peace with Miss Jenkyns soon after the memorable dispute I have named, by a present of a wooden fire-shovel (his own making), having heard her say how much the grating of an iron one annoyed her. She received the present with cool gratitude, and thanked him formally. When he was gone, she bade me put it away in the lumber room; feeling, probably, that no present from a man who preferred Mr Boz to Dr Johnson could be less jarring than an iron fire-shovel.

Such was the state of things when I left Cranford and went to Drumble. I had, however, several correspondents, who kept me *au fait*[26] as to the proceedings of the dear little town. There was Miss Pole, who was becoming as much absorbed in crochet as she had been once in knitting, and the burden of whose letter was something like: 'But don't you forget the white worsted at Flint's'[27] of the old song; for at the end of every sentence of news came a fresh direction as to some crochet commission which I was to execute for her. Miss Matilda Jenkyns (who did not mind being called Miss Matty, when Miss Jenkyns was not by) wrote nice, kind, rambling letters, now and then venturing into an opinion of her own; but suddenly pulling herself up, and either begging me not to name what she had said, as Deborah thought differently, and *she* knew; or else putting in a postscript to the effect that, since writing the above, she had been talking over the subject with Deborah, and was quite convinced that, etc. – (here probably followed a recantation of every opinion she had given in the letter). Then came Miss Jenkyns – *Debörah* as she liked Miss Matty to call her, her father having once said that the Hebrew name ought to be so pronounced. I secretly think she took the Hebrew prophetess for a model in character; and, indeed, she was not unlike the stern prophetess in some ways, making allowance, of course, for modern customs and difference in dress. Miss Jenkyns wore a cravat, and a little bonnet like a jockey-cap, and altogether had the appearance of a strong-minded woman; although she would have despised the modern idea of women being equal to men.[28]

Equal, indeed! she knew they were superior. But to return to her letters. Everything in them was stately and grand like herself. I have been looking them over (dear Miss Jenkyns, how I honoured her!) and I will give an extract, more especially because it relates to our friend Captain Brown:

> The Honourable Mrs Jamieson has only just quitted me; and, in the course of conversation, she communicated to me the intelligence that she had yesterday received a call from her revered husband's quondam[29] friend, Lord Mauleverer. You will not easily conjecture what brought his lordship within the precincts of our little town. It was to see Captain Brown, with whom, it appears, his lordship was acquainted in the 'plumed wars',[30] and who had the privilege of averting destruction from his lordship's head when some great peril was impending over it, off the misnomered Cape of Good Hope. You know our friend the Honourable Mrs Jamieson's deficiency in the spirit of innocent curiosity, and you will therefore not be so much surprised when I tell you she was quite unable to disclose to me the exact nature of the peril in question. I was anxious, I confess, to ascertain in what manner Captain Brown, with his limited establishment, could receive so distinguished a guest; and I discovered that his lordship retired to rest, and, let us hope, to refreshing slumbers, at the Angel Hotel;[31] but shared the Brunonian meals during the two days that he honoured Cranford with his august presence. Mrs Johnson, our civil butcher's wife, informs me that Miss Jessie purchased a leg of lamb; but, besides this, I can hear of no preparation whatever to give a suitable reception to so distinguished a visitor. Perhaps they entertained him with 'the feast of reason and the flow of soul';[32] and to us, who are acquainted with Captain Brown's sad want of relish for 'the pure wells of English undefiled',[33] it may be matter for congratulation that he has had the opportunity of improving his taste by holding converse with an elegant and refined member of the British aristocracy. But from some mundane failings who is altogether free?

Miss Pole and Miss Matty wrote to me by the same post. Such a piece of news as Lord Mauleverer's visit was not to be lost on the Cranford letter-writers: they made the most of it. Miss Matty humbly apologised for writing at the same time as her sister, who was so much more capable than she to describe the honour done to Cranford; but in spite of a little bad spelling, Miss Matty's account gave me the best idea of the commotion occasioned by his lordship's visit, after it had occurred; for, except the people at the Angel, the Browns, Mrs Jamieson, and a little lad his lordship had sworn at for driving a dirty hoop against the aristocratic legs, I could not hear of anyone with whom his lordship had held conversation.

My next visit to Cranford was in the summer. There had been neither births, deaths, nor marriages since I was there last. Everybody lived in the same house, and wore pretty nearly the same well-preserved, old-fashioned clothes. The greatest event was, that Miss Jenkyns had purchased a new carpet for the drawing-room. Oh, the busy work Miss Matty and I had in chasing the sunbeams, as they fell in an afternoon right down on this carpet through the blindless window! We spread newspapers over the places and sat down to our book or our work; and, lo! in a quarter of an hour the sun had moved, and was blazing away on a fresh spot; and down again we went on our knees to alter the position of the newspapers. We were very busy, too, one whole morning, before Miss Jenkyns gave her party, in following her directions, and in cutting out and stitching together pieces of newspaper so as to form little paths to every chair set for the expected visitors, lest their shoes might dirty or defile the purity of the carpet. Do you make paper paths for every guest to walk upon in London?

Captain Brown and Miss Jenkyns were not very cordial to each other. The literary dispute, of which I had seen the beginning, was a 'raw', the slightest touch on which made them wince. It was the only difference of opinion they had ever had; but that difference was enough. Miss Jenkyns could not refrain from talking *at* Captain Brown; and, though he did not reply, he drummed with his fingers, which action she felt and resented as very disparaging to Dr Johnson. He was rather ostentatious in his preference of the writings of Mr Boz; would walk through the streets so absorbed in them that he all but ran against Miss Jenkyns; and though his apologies were earnest and sincere, and though he did not, in fact, do more than startle her and himself, she owned to me she had rather he had knocked her down, if he had only been reading a higher style of literature. The poor, brave Captain! he looked older, and more worn, and his clothes were very threadbare. But he seemed as bright and cheerful as ever, unless he was asked about his daughter's health.

'She suffers a great deal, and she must suffer more: we do what we can to alleviate her pain – God's will be done!' He took off his hat at these last words. I found, from Miss Matty, that everything had been done, in fact. A medical man, of high repute in that country neighbourhood, had been sent for, and every injunction he had given was attended to, regardless of expense. Miss Matty was sure they denied themselves many things in order to make the invalid comfortable; but they never spoke about it; and as for Miss Jessie! – 'I really think she's an angel,' said poor Miss Matty, quite overcome. 'To see her way of bearing with Miss Brown's crossness, and the bright face she puts on after she's been sitting up a whole night and scolded above half of it, is quite beautiful. Yet she looks as neat and as ready to welcome the Captain at breakfast-time as if she had been asleep in the Queen's bed all night. My dear! you could never laugh at her prim little curls or her pink bows again if you saw her as I have done.' I could only feel very penitent, and greet Miss Jessie with double respect when I met her next. She looked faded and pinched; and her lips began to quiver, as if she was very weak, when she spoke of her sister. But she brightened, and sent back the tears that were glittering in her pretty eyes, as she said: 'But, to be sure, what a town Cranford is for kindness! I don't suppose anyone has a better dinner than usual cooked, but the best part of all comes in a little covered basin for my sister. The poor people will leave their earliest vegetables at our door for her. They speak short and gruff, as if they were ashamed of it; but I am sure it often goes to my heart to see their thoughtfulness.' The tears now came back and overflowed; but after a minute or two she began to scold herself, and ended by going away the same cheerful Miss Jessie as ever.

'But why does not this Lord Mauleverer do something for the man who saved his life?' said I.

'Why, you see, unless Captain Brown has some reason for it, he never speaks about being poor; and he walked along by his lordship looking as happy and cheerful as a prince; and as they never called attention to their dinners by apologies, and as Miss Brown was better that day, and all seemed bright, I dare say his lordship never knew how much care there was in the background. He did send game in the winter pretty often, but now he is gone abroad.'

I had often occasion to notice the use that was made of fragments and small opportunities in Cranford; the rose-leaves that were gathered ere they fell to make into a pot-pourri for someone who had no garden; the little bundles of lavender flowers sent to strew the drawers of some town-dweller, or to burn in the chamber of some invalid. Things that many would despise, and actions which it seemed scarcely worthwhile to perform, were all attended to in Cranford. Miss Jenkyns stuck an apple full of cloves, to be heated and smell pleasantly in Miss Brown's room; and as she put in each clove she uttered a Johnsonian sentence. Indeed, she never could think of the Browns without talking Johnson; and, as they were seldom absent from her thoughts just then, I heard many a rolling, three-piled sentence.[34]

Captain Brown called one day to thank Miss Jenkyns for many little kindnesses, which I did not know until then that she had rendered. He had suddenly become like an old man; his deep bass voice had a quavering in it, his eyes looked dim, and the lines on his face were deep. He did not – could not – speak cheerfully of his daughter's state, but he talked with manly, pious resignation, and not much. Twice over he said: 'What Jessie has been to us, God only knows!' and after the second time, he got up hastily, shook hands all round without speaking, and left the room.

That afternoon we perceived little groups in the street, all listening with faces aghast to some tale or other. Miss Jenkyns wondered what could be the matter for some time before she took the undignified step of sending Jenny out to enquire.

Jenny came back with a white face of terror. 'Oh, ma'am! Oh, Miss Jenkyns, ma'am! Captain Brown is killed by them nasty cruel railroads!' and she burst into tears. She, along with many others, had experienced the poor Captain's kindness.

'How? – where – where? Good God! Jenny, don't waste time in crying, but tell us something.' Miss Matty rushed out into the street at once, and collared the man who was telling the tale.

'Come in – come to my sister at once, Miss Jenkyns, the rector's daughter. Oh, man, man! say it is not true,' she cried, as she brought the affrighted carter, sleeking down his hair, into the drawing-room, where he stood with his wet boots on the new carpet, and no one regarded it.

'Please, mum, it is true. I seed it myself,' and he shuddered at the recollection. 'The Captain was a-reading some new book as he was deep in, a-waiting for the down train; and there was a little lass as wanted to come to its mammy, and gave its sister the slip, and came toddling across the line. And he looked up sudden, at the sound of the train coming, and seed the child, and he darted on the line and cotched it up, and his foot slipped, and the train came over him in no time. O Lord, Lord! Mum, it's quite true, and they've come over to tell his daughters. The child's safe, though, with only a bang on its shoulder as he threw it to its mammy. Poor Captain would be glad of that, mum, wouldn't he? God bless him!' The great rough carter puckered up his manly face, and turned away to hide his tears. I turned to Miss Jenkyns. She looked very ill, as if she were going to faint, and signed to me to open the window.

'Matilda, bring me my bonnet. I must go to those girls. God pardon me, if ever I have spoken contemptuously to the Captain!'

Miss Jenkyns arrayed herself to go out, telling Miss Matilda to give the man a glass of wine. While she was away, Miss Matty and I huddled over the fire, talking in a low and awestruck voice. I know we cried quietly all the time.

Miss Jenkyns came home in a silent mood, and we durst not ask her many questions. She told us that Miss Jessie had fainted, and that she and Miss Pole had had some difficulty in bringing her round; but that, as soon as she recovered, she begged one of them to go and sit with her sister.

'Mr Hoggins says she cannot live many days, and she shall be spared this shock,' said Miss Jessie, shivering with feelings to which she dared not give way.

'But how can you manage, my dear?' asked Miss Jenkyns; 'you cannot bear up, she must see your tears.'

'God will help me – I will not give way – she was asleep when the news came; she may be asleep yet. She would be so utterly miserable, not merely at my father's death, but to think of what would become of me; she is so good to me.' She looked up earnestly in their faces with her soft true eyes, and Miss Pole told Miss Jenkyns afterwards she could hardly bear it, knowing, as she did, how Miss Brown treated her sister.

However, it was settled according to Miss Jessie's wish. Miss Brown was to be told her father had been summoned to take a short journey on railway business. They had managed it in some way – Miss Jenkyns could not exactly say how. Miss Pole was to stop with Miss Jessie. Mrs Jamieson had sent to enquire. And this was all we heard that night; and a sorrowful night it was. The next day a full account of the fatal accident was in the county paper which Miss Jenkyns took in. Her eyes were very weak, she said, and she asked me to read it. When I came to the 'gallant gentleman was deeply engaged in the perusal of a number of *Pickwick*, which he had just received', Miss Jenkyns shook her head long and solemnly, and then sighed out: 'Poor, dear, infatuated man!'

The corpse was to be taken from the station to the parish church, there to be interred. Miss Jessie had set her heart on following it to the grave; and no dissuasives could alter her resolve. Her restraint upon herself made her almost obstinate; she resisted all Miss Pole's entreaties and Miss Jenkyns's advice. At last Miss Jenkyns gave up the point; and after a silence, which I feared portended some deep displeasure against Miss Jessie, Miss Jenkyns said she should accompany the latter to the funeral.

'It is not fit for you to go alone. It would be against both propriety and humanity were I to allow it.'

Miss Jessie seemed as if she did not half like this arrangement; but her obstinacy, if she had any, had been exhausted in her determination to go to the interment. She longed, poor thing, I have no doubt, to cry alone over the grave of the dear father to whom she had been all in all, and to give way, for one little half-hour, uninterrupted by sympathy and unobserved by friendship. But it was not to be. That afternoon Miss Jenkyns sent out for a yard of black crape, and employed herself busily in trimming the little black silk bonnet I have spoken about. When it was finished she put it on, and looked at us for approbation – admiration she despised. I was full of sorrow, but, by one of those whimsical thoughts which come unbidden into our heads, in times of deepest grief, I no sooner saw the bonnet than I was reminded of a helmet; and in that hybrid bonnet, half-helmet, half-jockey-cap, did Miss Jenkyns attend Captain Brown's funeral, and, I believe, supported Miss Jessie with a tender, indulgent firmness which was invaluable, allowing her to weep her passionate fill before they left.

Miss Pole, Miss Matty, and I, meanwhile attended to Miss Brown: and hard work we found it to relieve her querulous and never-ending complaints. But if we were so weary and dispirited, what must Miss Jessie have been! Yet she came back almost calm, as if she had gained a new strength. She put off her mourning dress, and came in, looking pale and gentle, thanking us each with a soft long pressure of the hand. She could even smile – a faint, sweet, wintry smile – as if to reassure us of her power to endure; but her look made our eyes fill suddenly with tears, more than if she had cried outright.

It was settled that Miss Pole was to remain with her all the watching livelong night; and that Miss Matty and I were to return in the morning to relieve them, and give Miss Jessie the opportunity for a few hours of sleep. But when the morning came, Miss Jenkyns appeared at the breakfast-table, equipped in her helmet-bonnet, and ordered Miss Matty to stay at home, as she meant to go and help to nurse. She was evidently in a state of great friendly excitement, which she showed by eating her breakfast standing, and scolding the household all round.

No nursing – no energetic strong-minded woman could help Miss Brown now. There was that in the room as we entered which was stronger than us all, and made us shrink into solemn awestruck helplessness. Miss Brown was dying. We hardly knew her voice, it was so devoid of the complaining tone we had always associated with it. Miss Jessie told me afterwards that it, and her face too, were just what they had been formerly, when her mother's death left her the young anxious head of the family, of whom only Miss Jessie survived.

She was conscious of her sister's presence, though not, I think, of ours. We stood a little behind the curtain: Miss Jessie knelt with her face near her sister's, in order to catch the last soft awful whispers.

'Oh, Jessie! Jessie! How selfish I have been! God forgive me for letting you sacrifice yourself for me as you did! I have so loved you – and yet I have thought only of myself. God forgive me!'

'Hush, love! hush!' said Miss Jessie, sobbing.

'And my father, my dear, dear father! I will not complain now, if God will give me strength to be patient. But, oh, Jessie! tell my father how I longed and yearned to see him at last, and to ask his forgiveness. He can never know now how I loved him – oh! if I might but tell him, before I die! What a life of sorrow his has been, and I have done so little to cheer him!'

A light came into Miss Jessie's face. 'Would it comfort you, dearest, to think that he does know? – would it comfort you, love, to know that his cares, his sorrows – ' Her voice quivered, but she steadied it into calmness – 'Mary! he has gone before you to the place where the weary are at rest.[35] He knows now how you loved him.'

A strange look, which was not distress, came over Miss Brown's face. She did not speak for some time, but then we saw her lips form the words, rather than heard the sound – 'Father, mother, Harry, Archy – ' then, as if it were a new idea throwing a filmy shadow over her darkened mind – 'But you will be alone, Jessie!'

Miss Jessie had been feeling this all during the silence, I think; for the tears rolled down her cheeks like rain, at these words, and she could not answer at first. Then she put her hands together tight, and lifted them up, and said – but not to us – 'Though He slay me, yet will I trust in Him.'

In a few moments more Miss Brown lay calm and still – never to sorrow or murmur more.

After this second funeral, Miss Jenkyns insisted that Miss Jessie should come to stay with her rather than go back to the desolate house, which, in fact, we learned from Miss Jessie, must now be given up, as she had not wherewithal to maintain it. She had something above twenty pounds a year, besides the interest of the money for which the furniture would sell; but she could not live upon that: and so we talked over her qualifications for earning money.

'I can sew neatly,' said she, 'and I like nursing. I think, too, I could manage a house, if anyone would try me as housekeeper; or I would go into a shop as saleswoman, if they would have patience with me at first.'

Miss Jenkyns declared, in an angry voice, that she should do no such thing; and talked to herself about 'some people having no idea of their rank as a captain's daughter', nearly an hour afterwards, when she brought Miss Jessie up a basin of delicately-made arrowroot, and stood over her like a dragoon until the last spoonful was finished: then she disappeared. Miss Jessie began to tell me some more of the plans which had suggested themselves to her, and insensibly fell into talking of the days that were past and gone, and interested me so much I neither knew nor heeded how time passed. We were both startled when Miss Jenkyns reappeared, and caught us crying. I was afraid lest she would be displeased, as she often said that crying hindered digestion, and I knew she wanted Miss Jessie to get strong; but, instead, she looked queer and excited, and fidgeted round us without saying anything. At last she spoke.

'I have been so much startled – no, I've not been at all startled – don't mind me, my dear Miss Jessie – I've been very much surprised – in fact, I've had a caller, whom you knew once, my dear Miss Jessie – '

Miss Jessie went very white, then flushed scarlet, and looked eagerly at Miss Jenkyns.

'A gentleman, my dear, who wants to know if you would see him.'

'Is it? – it is not – ' stammered out Miss Jessie – and got no farther.

'This is his card,' said Miss Jenkyns, giving it to Miss Jessie; and while her head was bent over it, Miss Jenkyns went through a series of winks and odd faces to me, and formed her lips into a long sentence, of which, of course, I could not understand a word.

'May he come up?' asked Miss Jenkyns at last.

'Oh, yes! certainly!' said Miss Jessie, as much as to say, this is your house, you may show any visitor where you like. She took up some knitting of Miss Matty's and began to be very busy, though I could see how she trembled all over.

Miss Jenkyns rang the bell, and told the servant who answered it to show Major Gordon upstairs; and, presently, in walked a tall, fine, frank-looking man of forty or upwards. He shook hands with Miss Jessie; but he could not see her eyes, she kept them so fixed on the ground. Miss Jenkyns asked me if I would come and help her to tie up the preserves in the storeroom; and though Miss Jessie plucked at my gown, and even looked up at me with begging eye, I durst not refuse to go where Miss Jenkyns asked. Instead of tying up preserves in the storeroom, however, we went to talk in the dining-room; and there Miss Jenkyns told me what Major Gordon had told her; how he had served in the same regiment with Captain Brown, and had become acquainted with Miss Jessie, then a sweet-looking, blooming girl of eighteen; how the acquaintance had grown into love on his part, though it had been some years before he had spoken; how, on becoming possessed, through the will of an uncle, of a good estate in Scotland, he had offered and been refused, though with so much agitation and evident distress that he was sure she was not indifferent to him; and how he had discovered that the obstacle was the fell disease which was, even then, too surely threatening her sister. She had mentioned that the surgeons foretold intense suffering; and there was no one but herself to nurse her poor Mary, or cheer and comfort her father during the time of illness. They had had long discussions; and on her refusal to pledge herself to him as his wife when all should be over, he had grown angry, and broken off entirely, and gone abroad, believing that she was a cold-hearted person whom he would do well to forget. He had been travelling in the East, and was on his return home when, at Rome, he saw the account of Captain Brown's death in *Galignani*.[36]

Just then Miss Matty, who had been out all the morning, and had only lately returned to the house, burst in with a face of dismay and outraged propriety.

'Oh, goodness me!' she said. 'Deborah, there's a gentleman sitting in the drawing-room with his arm round Miss Jessie's waist!' Miss Matty's eyes looked large with terror.

Miss Jenkyns snubbed her down in an instant.

'The most proper place in the world for his arm to be in. Go away, Matilda, and mind your own business.' This from her sister, who had hitherto been a model of feminine decorum, was a blow for poor Miss Matty, and with a double shock she left the room.

The last time I ever saw poor Miss Jenkyns was many years after this. Mrs Gordon had kept up a warm and affectionate intercourse with all at Cranford. Miss Jenkyns, Miss Matty, and Miss Pole had all been to visit her, and returned with wonderful accounts of her house, her husband, her dress, and her looks. For, with happiness, something of her early bloom returned; she had been a year or two younger than we had taken her for. Her eyes were always lovely, and, as Mrs Gordon, her dimples were not out of place. At the time to which I have referred, when I last saw Miss Jenkyns, that lady was old and feeble, and had lost something of her strong mind. Little Flora Gordon was staying with the Misses Jenkyns, and when I came in she was reading aloud to Miss Jenkyns, who lay feeble and changed on the sofa. Flora put down the *Rambler* when I came in.

'Ah!' said Miss Jenkyns, 'you find me changed, my dear. I can't see as I used to do. If Flora were not here to read to me, I hardly know how I should get through the day. Did you ever read the *Rambler*? It's a wonderful book – wonderful! and the most improving reading for Flora' (which I dare say it would have been, if she could have read half the words without spelling, and could have understood the meaning of a third), 'better than that strange old book, with the queer name, poor Captain Brown was killed for reading – that book by Mr Boz, you know – "Old Poz";[37] when I was a girl – but that's a long time ago – I acted Lucy in "Old Poz".' She babbled on long enough for Flora to get a good long spell at the *Christmas Carol*,[38] which Miss Matty had left on the table.

CHAPTER 3

A Love Affair of Long Ago

I THOUGHT that probably my connection with Cranford would cease after Miss Jenkyns's death; at least, that it would have to be kept up by correspondence, which bears much the same relation to personal intercourse that the books of dried plants I sometimes see (*Hortus Siccus*,[39] I think they call the thing) do to the living and fresh flowers in the lanes and meadows. I was pleasantly surprised, therefore, by receiving a letter from Miss Pole (who had always come in for a supplementary week after my annual visit to Miss Jenkyns) proposing that I should go and stay with her; and then, in a couple of days after my acceptance came a note from Miss Matty, in which, in a rather circuitous and very humble manner, she told me how much pleasure I should confer if I could spend a week or two with her, either before or after I had been at Miss Pole's; 'for', she said, 'since my dear sister's death I am well aware I have no attractions to offer; it is only to the kindness of my friends that I can owe their company'.

Of course I promised to come to dear Miss Matty as soon as I had ended my visit to Miss Pole; and the day after my arrival at Cranford I went to see her, much wondering what the house would be like without Miss Jenkyns, and rather dreading the changed aspect of things. Miss Matty began to cry as soon as she saw me. She was evidently nervous from having anticipated my call. I comforted her as well as I could; and I found the best consolation I could give was the honest praise that came from my heart as I spoke of the deceased. Miss Matty slowly shook her head over each virtue as it was named and attributed to her sister; and at last she could not restrain the tears which had long been silently flowing, but hid her face behind her handkerchief and sobbed aloud.

'Dear Miss Matty,' said I, taking her hand – for indeed I did not know in what way to tell her how sorry I was for her, left deserted in the world. She put down her handkerchief and said: 'My dear, I'd rather you did not call me Matty. *She* did not like it; but I did many a thing she did not like, I'm afraid – and now she's gone! If you please, my love, will you call me Matilda?'

I promised faithfully, and began to practise the new name with Miss Pole that very day; and, by degrees, Miss Matilda's feeling on the subject was known through Cranford, and we all tried to drop the more familiar name, but with so little success that by and by we gave up the attempt.

My visit to Miss Pole was very quiet. Miss Jenkyns had so long taken the lead in Cranford that now she was gone, they hardly knew how to give a party. The Honourable Mrs Jamieson, to whom Miss Jenkyns herself had always yielded the post of honour, was fat and inert, and very much at the mercy of her old servants. If they chose that she should give a party, they reminded her of the necessity for so doing: if not, she let it alone. There was all the more time for me to hear old-world stories from Miss Pole, while she sat knitting, and I making my father's shirts.[40] I always took a quantity of plain sewing to Cranford; for, as we did not read much, or walk much, I found it a capital time to get through my work. One of Miss Pole's stories related to a shadow of a love affair that was dimly perceived or suspected long years before.

Presently, the time arrived when I was to remove to Miss Matilda's house. I found her timid and anxious about the arrangements for my comfort. Many a time, while I was unpacking, did she come backwards and forwards to stir the fire which burned all the worse for being so frequently poked.

'Have you drawers enough, dear?' asked she. 'I don't know exactly how my sister used to arrange them. She had capital methods. I am sure she would have trained a servant in a week to make a better fire than this, and Fanny has been with me four months.'

This subject of servants was a standing grievance, and I could not wonder much at it; for if gentlemen were scarce, and almost unheard of in the 'genteel society' of Cranford, they or their counterparts – handsome young men – abounded in the lower classes. The pretty neat servant-maids had their choice of desirable 'followers'; and their mistresses, without having the sort of mysterious dread of men and matrimony that Miss Matilda had, might well feel a little anxious lest the heads of their comely maids should be turned by the joiner, or the butcher, or the gardener, who were obliged, by their callings, to come to the house, and who, as ill luck would have it, were generally handsome and unmarried. Fanny's lovers, if she had any – and Miss Matilda suspected her of so many flirtations that, if she had not been very pretty, so I should have doubted her having one – were a constant anxiety to her mistress. She was forbidden, by the articles of her engagement, to have 'followers'; and though she had answered, innocently enough, doubling up the hem of her apron as she spoke, 'Please, ma'am, I never had more than one at a time,' Miss Matty prohibited that one. But a vision of a man seemed to haunt the kitchen. Fanny assured me that it was all fancy, or else I should have said myself that I had seen a man's coat-tails whisk into the scullery once, when I went on an errand into the storeroom at night; and another evening, when, our watches having stopped, I went to look at the clock, there was a very odd appearance, singularly like a young man squeezed up between the clock and the back of the open kitchen door: and I thought Fanny snatched up the candle very hastily, so as to throw the shadow on the clock face, while she very positively told me the time half an hour too early, as we found out afterwards by the church clock. But I did not add to Miss Matty's anxieties by naming my suspicions, especially as Fanny said to me, the next day, that it was such a queer kitchen for having odd shadows about it, she really was almost afraid to stay; 'for you know, miss', she added, 'I don't see a creature from six o'clock tea, till Missus rings the bell for prayers at ten'.

However, it so fell out that Fanny had to leave; and Miss Matilda begged me to stay and 'settle her' with the new maid; to which I consented, after I had heard from my father that he did not want me at home. The new servant was a rough, honest-looking, country girl, who had only lived in a farm place before; but I liked her looks when she came to be hired; and I promised Miss Matilda to put her in the ways of the house. The said ways were religiously such as Miss Matilda thought her sister would approve. Many a domestic rule and regulation had been a subject of plaintive whispered murmur to me during Miss Jenkyns's life; but now that she was gone, I do not think that even I, who was a favourite, durst have suggested an alteration. To give an instance: we constantly adhered to the forms which were observed, at meal-times, in 'my father, the rector's house'. Accordingly, we had always wine and dessert; but the decanters were only filled when there was a party, and what remained was seldom touched, though we had two wine glasses apiece every day after dinner, until the next festive occasion arrived, when the state of the remainder wine was examined into in a family council. The dregs were often given to the poor: but occasionally, when a good deal had been left at the last party (five months ago, it might be), it was added to some of a fresh bottle, brought up from the cellar. I fancy poor Captain Brown did not much like wine, for I noticed he never finished his first glass, and most military men take several. Then, as to our dessert, Miss Jenkyns used to gather currants and gooseberries for it herself, which I sometimes thought would have tasted better fresh from the trees; but then, as Miss Jenkyns observed, there would have been nothing for dessert in summertime. As it was, we felt very genteel with our two glasses apiece, and a dish of gooseberries at the top, of currants and biscuits at the sides, and two decanters at the bottom. When oranges came in, a curious proceeding was gone through. Miss Jenkyns did not like to cut the fruit; for, as she observed, the juice all ran out nobody knew where; sucking (only I think she used some more recondite word) was in fact the only way of enjoying oranges; but then there was the unpleasant association with a ceremony frequently gone through by little babies; and so, after dessert, in orange season, Miss Jenkyns and Miss Matty used to rise up, possess themselves each of an orange in silence, and withdraw to the privacy of their own rooms to indulge in sucking oranges.

I had once or twice tried, on such occasions, to prevail on Miss

Matty to stay, and had succeeded in her sister's lifetime. I held up a screen,[41] and did not look, and, as she said, she tried not to make the noise very offensive; but now that she was left alone, she seemed quite horrified when I begged her to remain with me in the warm dining-parlour, and enjoy her orange as she liked best. And so it was in everything. Miss Jenkyns's rules were made more stringent than ever, because the trainer of them was gone where there could be no appeal. In all things else Miss Matilda was meek and undecided to a fault. I have heard Fanny turn her round twenty times in a morning about dinner, just as the little hussy chose; and I sometimes fancied she worked on Miss Matilda's weakness in order to bewilder her, and to make her feel more in the power of her clever servant. I determined that I would not leave her till I had seen what sort of a person Martha was; and, if I found her trustworthy, I would tell her not to trouble her mistress with every little decision.

Martha was blunt and plain-spoken to a fault; otherwise she was a brisk, well-meaning, but very ignorant girl. She had not been with us a week before Miss Matilda and I were astounded one morning by the receipt of a letter from a cousin of hers, who had been twenty or thirty years in India, and who had lately, as we had seen by the *Army List*, returned to England, bringing with him an invalid wife[42] who had never been introduced to her English relations. Major Jenkyns wrote to propose that he and his wife should spend a night at Cranford, on his way to Scotland – at the inn, if it did not suit Miss Matilda to receive them into her house; in which case they should hope to be with her as much as possible during the day. Of course it *must* suit her, as she said; for all Cranford knew that she had her sister's bedroom at liberty; but I am sure she wished the major had stopped in India and forgotten his cousins out and out.

'Oh! how must I manage?' asked she helplessly. 'If Deborah had been alive she would have known what to do with a gentleman-visitor. Must I put razors in his dressing-room? Dear! dear! and I've got none. Deborah would have had them. And slippers, and coat-brushes?' I suggested that probably he would bring all these things with him. 'And after dinner, how am I to know when to get up and leave him to his wine? Deborah would have done it so well; she would have been quite in her element. Will he want coffee, do you think?' I undertook the management of the coffee, and told her I would instruct Martha in the art of waiting – in which it must be owned she was terribly deficient – and that I had no doubt Major and Mrs Jenkyns would understand the quiet mode in which a lady lived by herself in a country town. But she was sadly fluttered. I made her empty her decanters and bring up two fresh bottles of wine. I wished I could have prevented her from being present at my instructions to Martha, for she frequently cut in with some fresh direction, muddling the poor girl's mind as she stood open-mouthed, listening to us both.

'Hand the vegetables round,' said I (foolishly, I see now – for it was aiming at more than we could accomplish with quietness and simplicity); and then, seeing her look bewildered, I added, 'Take the vegetables round to people, and let them help themselves.'

'And mind you go first to the ladies,' put in Miss Matilda. 'Always go to the ladies before gentlemen when you are waiting.'

'I'll do it as you tell me, ma'am,' said Martha; 'but I like lads best.'

We felt very uncomfortable and shocked at this speech of Martha's, yet I don't think she meant any harm; and, on the whole, she attended very well to our directions, except that she 'nudged' the major when he did not help himself as soon as she expected to the potatoes, while she was handing them round.

The major and his wife were quiet, unpretending people enough when they did come; languid, as all East Indians are, I suppose. We were rather dismayed at their bringing two servants with them, a Hindu body-servant for the major, and a steady elderly maid for his wife; but they slept at the inn, and took off a good deal of the responsibility by attending carefully to their master's and mistress's comfort. Martha, to be sure, had never ended her staring at the East Indian's white turban and brown complexion, and I saw that Miss Matilda shrunk away from him a little as he waited at dinner. Indeed, she asked me, when they were gone, if he did not remind me of Blue Beard?[43] On the whole, the visit was most satisfactory, and is a subject of conversation even now with Miss Matilda; at the time it greatly excited Cranford, and even stirred up the apathetic and honourable Mrs Jamieson to some expression of interest, when I went to call and thank her for the kind answers she had vouchsafed to Miss Matilda's enquiries as to the arrangement of a gentleman's dressing-room – answers which I must confess she had given in the wearied manner of the Scandinavian prophetess: 'Leave me, leave me to repose.'[44]

And *now* I come to the love affair.

It seems that Miss Pole had a cousin, once or twice removed, who had offered to Miss Matty long ago. Now this cousin lived four or five miles from Cranford on his own estate; but his property was not large enough to entitle him to rank higher than a yeoman;[45] or rather, with something of the 'pride which apes humility',[46] he had refused to push himself on, as so many of his class had done, into the ranks of the squires. He would not allow himself to be called Thomas Holbrook,[47] *Esq*.; he even sent back letters with this address, telling the postmistress at Cranford that his name was *Mr* Thomas Holbrook, yeoman. He rejected all domestic innovations; he would have the house door stand open in summer and shut in winter, without knocker or bell to summon a servant. The closed fist or the knob of a stick did this office for him if he found the door locked. He despised every refinement which had not its root deep down in humanity. If people were not ill, he saw no necessity for moderating his voice. He spoke the dialect of the country in perfection, and constantly used it in conversation; although Miss Pole (who gave me these particulars) added, that he read aloud more beautifully and with more feeling than anyone she had ever heard, except the late rector.

'And how came Miss Matilda not to marry him?' asked I.

'Oh, I don't know. She was willing enough, I think; but you know Cousin Thomas would not have been enough of a gentleman for the rector and Miss Jenkyns.'

'Well! but they were not to marry him,' said I, impatiently.

'No; but they did not like Miss Matty to marry below her rank. You know she was the rector's daughter, and somehow they are related to Sir Peter Arley: Miss Jenkyns thought a deal of that.'

'Poor Miss Matty!' said I.

'Nay, now, I don't know anything more than that he offered and was refused. Miss Matty might not like him – and Miss Jenkyns might never have said a word – it is only a guess of mine.'

'Has she never seen him since?' I enquired.

'No, I think not. You see Woodley, Cousin Thomas's house, lies halfway between Cranford and Misselton;[48] and I know he made Misselton his market-town very soon after he had offered to Miss Matty; and I don't think he has been into Cranford above once or twice since – once, when I was walking with Miss Matty, in High Street, and suddenly she darted from me, and went up Shire Lane. A few minutes after I was startled by meeting Cousin Thomas.'

'How old is he?' I asked, after a pause of castle building.

'He must be about seventy, I think, my dear,' said Miss Pole, blowing up my castle, as if by gunpowder, into small fragments.

Very soon after – at least during my long visit to Miss Matilda – I had the opportunity of seeing Mr Holbrook; seeing, too, his first encounter with his former love, after thirty or forty years' separation. I was helping to decide whether any of the new assortment of coloured silks which they had just received at the shop would do to match a grey and black *mousseline-de-laine*[49] that wanted a new breadth, when a tall, thin, Don Quixote-looking[50] old man came into the shop for some woollen gloves. I had never seen the person (who was rather striking) before, and I watched him rather attentively while Miss Matty listened to the shopman. The stranger wore a blue coat with brass buttons, drab breeches, and gaiters, and drummed with his fingers on the counter until he was attended to. When he answered the shop boy's question: 'What can I have the pleasure of showing you today, sir?' I saw Miss Matilda start, and then suddenly sit down; and instantly I guessed who it was. She had made some enquiry which had to be carried round to the other shopman.

'Miss Jenkyns wants the black sarsenet[51] two and twopence the yard'; and Mr Holbrook had caught the name, and was across the shop in two strides.

'Matty – Miss Matilda – Miss Jenkyns! God bless my soul! I should not have known you. How are you? how are you?' He kept shaking her hand in a way which proved the warmth of his friendship; but he repeated so often, as if to himself, 'I should not have known you!' that any sentimental romance which I might be inclined to build was quite done away with by his manner.

However, he kept talking to us all the time we were in the shop; and then waving the shopman with the unpurchased gloves on one side, with 'Another time, sir! another time!' he walked home with us. I am happy to say my client, Miss Matilda, also left the shop in an equally bewildered state, not having purchased either green or red silk. Mr Holbrook was evidently full with honest loud-spoken joy at meeting his old love again; he touched on the changes that had taken place; he even spoke of Miss Jenkyns as 'Your poor sister! Well, well! we have all our faults'; and bade us goodbye with many a hope that he should soon see Miss Matty again. She went straight to her room, and never came back till our early teatime, when I thought she looked as if she had been crying.

CHAPTER 4

A Visit to an Old Bachelor

A FEW DAYS AFTER, a note came from Mr Holbrook, asking us – impartially asking both of us – in a formal, old-fashioned style, to spend a day at his house – a long June day – for it was June now. He named that he had also invited his cousin, Miss Pole; so that we might join in a fly,[52] which could be put up at his house.

I expected Miss Matty to jump at this invitation; but, no! Miss Pole and I had the greatest difficulty in persuading her to go. She thought it was improper; and was even half annoyed when we utterly ignored the idea of any impropriety in her going with two other ladies to see her old lover. Then came a more serious difficulty. She did not think Deborah would have liked her to go. This took us half a day's good hard talking to get over; but, at the first sentence of relenting, I seized the opportunity, and wrote and dispatched an acceptance in her name – fixing day and hour, that all might be decided and done with.

The next morning she asked me if I would go down to the shop with her; and there, after much hesitation, we chose out three caps to be sent home and tried on, that the most becoming might be selected to take with us on Thursday.

She was in a state of silent agitation all the way to Woodley. She had evidently never been there before; and, although she little dreamt I knew anything of her early story, I could perceive she was in a tremor at the thought of seeing the place which might have been her home, and round which it is probable that many of her innocent girlish imaginations had clustered. It was a long drive there, through paved jolting lanes. Miss Matilda sat bolt upright, and looked wistfully out of the windows as we drew near the end of our journey. The aspect of the country was quiet and pastoral. Woodley stood among fields; and there was an old-fashioned garden where roses and currant-bushes touched each other, and where the feathery asparagus formed a pretty background to the pinks and gilly flowers; there was no drive up to the door. We got out at a little gate, and walked up a straight box-edged path.

'My cousin might make a drive, I think,' said Miss Pole, who was afraid of earache, and had only her cap on.

'I think it is very pretty,' said Miss Matty, with a soft plaintiveness in her voice, and almost in a whisper; for just then Mr Holbrook appeared at the door, rubbing his hands in very effervescence of hospitality. He looked more like my idea of Don Quixote than ever, and yet the likeness was only external. His respectable housekeeper stood modestly at the door to bid us welcome; and, while she led the elder ladies upstairs to a bedroom, I begged to look about the garden. My request evidently pleased the old gentleman, who took me all round the place and showed me his six-and-twenty cows, named after the different letters of the alphabet. As we went along, he surprised me occasionally by repeating apt and beautiful quotations from the poets, ranging easily from Shakespeare and George Herbert[53] to those of our own day. He did this as naturally as if he were thinking aloud, and their true and beautiful words were the best expression he could find for what he was thinking or feeling. To be sure he called Byron 'my Lord Byrron', and pronounced the name of Goethe[54] strictly in accordance with the English sound of the letters – 'As Goethe says, "Ye ever-verdant palaces",' etc. Altogether, I never met with a man, before or since, who had spent so long a life in a secluded and not impressive country, with ever-increasing delight in the daily and yearly change of season and beauty.

When he and I went in, we found that dinner was nearly ready in the kitchen – for so I suppose the room ought to be called, as there were oak dressers and cupboards all round, all over by the side of the fireplace, and only a small Turkey carpet[55] in the middle of the flag floor.[56] The room might have been easily made into a handsome dark oak dining-parlour by removing the oven and a few other appurtenances of a kitchen, which were evidently never used, the real cooking-place being at some distance. The room in which we were expected to sit was a stiffly furnished, ugly apartment; but that in which we did sit was what Mr Holbrook called the counting-house, where he paid his labourers their weekly wages at a great desk near the door. The rest of the pretty sitting-room – looking into the orchard, and all covered over with dancing tree-shadows – was filled with books. They lay on the ground, they covered the walls, they strewed the table. He was evidently half ashamed and half proud of his extravagance in this respect. They were of all kinds – poetry and wild weird tales prevailing. He evidently chose his books in accordance with his own tastes, not because such and such were classical or established favourites.

'Ah!' he said, 'we farmers ought not to have much time for reading; yet somehow one can't help it.'

'What a pretty room!' said Miss Matty, *sotto voce.*

'What a pleasant place!' said I, aloud, almost simultaneously.

'Nay! if you like it,' replied he; 'but can you sit on these great, black leather, three-cornered chairs? I like it better than the best parlour; but I thought ladies would take that for the smarter place.'

It was the smarter place, but, like most smart things, not at all pretty, or pleasant, or homelike; so, while we were at dinner, the servant-girl dusted and scrubbed the counting-house chairs, and we sat there all the rest of the day.

We had pudding before meat; and I thought Mr Holbrook was going to make some apology for his old-fashioned ways, for he began: 'I don't know whether you like new-fangled ways.'

'Oh, not at all!' said Miss Matty.

'No more do I,' said he. 'My housekeeper *will* have these in her new fashion; or else I tell her that, when I was a young man, we used to keep strictly to my father's rule: "No broth, no ball; no ball, no beef"; and always began dinner with broth. Then we had suet puddings, boiled in the broth with the beef: and then the meat itself. If we did not sup our broth, we had no ball, which we liked a deal better; and the beef came last of all, and only those had it who had done justice to the broth and the ball. Now folks begin with sweet things, and turn their dinners topsy-turvy.'

When the ducks and green peas came, we looked at each other in dismay; we had only two-pronged, black-handled forks. It is true the steel was as bright as silver; but what were we to do? Miss Matty picked up her peas, one by one, on the point of the prongs, much as Aminé ate her grains of rice after her previous feast with the Ghoul.[57] Miss Pole sighed over her delicate young peas as she left them on one side of her plate untasted, for they *would* drop between the prongs. I looked at my host: the peas were going wholesale into his capacious mouth, shovelled up by his large round-ended knife. I saw, I imitated, I survived! My friends, in spite of my precedent, could not muster up courage enough to do an ungenteel thing; and, if Mr Holbrook had not been so heartily hungry, he would probably have seen that the good peas went away almost untouched.

After dinner, a clay pipe was brought in, and a spittoon; and, asking us to retire to another room, where he would soon join us, if we disliked tobacco smoke, he presented his pipe to Miss Matty, and requested her to fill the bowl. This was a compliment to a lady in his youth; but it was rather inappropriate to propose it as an honour to Miss Matty, who had been trained by her sister to hold smoking of every kind in utter abhorrence. But if it was a shock to her refinement, it was also a gratification to her feelings to be thus selected; so she daintily stuffed the strong tobacco into the pipe, and then we withdrew.

'It is very pleasant dining with a bachelor,' said Miss Matty softly, as we settled ourselves in the counting-house. 'I only hope it is not improper; so many pleasant things are!'

'What a number of books he has!' said Miss Pole, looking round the room. 'And how dusty they are!'

'I think it must be like one of the great Dr Johnson's rooms,' said Miss Matty. 'What a superior man your cousin must be!'

'Yes!' said Miss Pole, 'he's a great reader; but I am afraid he has got into very uncouth habits with living alone.'

'Oh! uncouth is too hard a word. I should call him eccentric; very clever people always are!' replied Miss Matty.

When Mr Holbrook returned, he proposed a walk in the fields; but the two elder ladies were afraid of damp, and dirt, and had only very unbecoming calashes[58] to put on over their caps; so they declined, and I was again his companion in a turn which he said he was obliged to take to see after his men. He strode along, either wholly forgetting my existence, or soothed into silence by his pipe – and yet it was not silence exactly. He walked before me with a stooping gait, his hands clasped behind him; and, as some tree or cloud, or glimpse of distant upland pastures, struck him, he quoted poetry to himself, saying it out loud in a grand sonorous voice, with just the emphasis that true feeling and appreciation give. We came upon an old cedar tree, which stood at one end of the house: 'The cedar spreads his dark-green layers of shade.'[59]

'Capital term – "layers"! Wonderful man!' I did not know whether he was speaking to me or not; but I put in an assenting 'wonderful', although I knew nothing about it, just because I was tired of being forgotten, and of being consequently silent.

He turned sharp round. 'Ay! you may say "wonderful". Why, when I saw the review of his poems in *Blackwood*,[60] I set off within an hour, and walked seven miles to Misselton (for the horses were not in the way) and ordered them. Now, what colour are ash-buds in March?'

Is the man going mad? thought I. He is very like Don Quixote.

'What colour are they, I say?' repeated he vehemently.

'I am sure I don't know, sir,' said I, with the meekness of ignorance.

'I knew you didn't. No more did I – an old fool that I am! – till this young man comes and tells me. "Black as ash-buds in March." And I've lived all my life in the country; more shame for me not to know. Black: they are jet-black, madam.' And he went off again, swinging along to the music of some rhyme he had got hold of.

When we came back, nothing would serve him but he must read us the poems he had been speaking of; and Miss Pole encouraged him in his proposal, I thought, because she wished me to hear his beautiful reading, of which she had boasted; but she afterwards said it was because she had got to a difficult part of her crochet, and wanted to count her stitches without having to talk. Whatever he had proposed would have been right to Miss Matty; although she did fall sound asleep within five minutes after he had begun a long poem, called *Locksley Hall*, and had a comfortable nap, unobserved, till he ended; when the cessation of his voice wakened her up, and she said, feeling that something was expected, and that Miss Pole was counting: 'What a pretty book!'

'Pretty, madam! it's beautiful! Pretty, indeed!'

'Oh yes! I meant beautiful!' said she, fluttered at his disapproval of her word. 'It is so like that beautiful poem of Dr Johnson's my sister used to read – I forget the name of it; what was it, my dear?' turning to me.

'Which do you mean, ma'am? What was it about?'

'I don't remember what it was about, and I've quite forgotten what the name of it was; but it was written by Dr Johnson, and was very beautiful, and very like what Mr Holbrook has just been reading.'

'I don't remember it,' said he reflectively. 'But I don't know Dr Johnson's poems well. I must read them.'

As we were getting into the fly to return, I heard Mr Holbrook say he should call on the ladies soon, and enquire how they got home; and this evidently pleased and fluttered Miss Matty at the time he said it; but after we had lost sight of the old house among the trees her sentiments towards the master of it were gradually absorbed into a distressing wonder as to whether Martha had broken her word, and seized on the opportunity of her mistress's absence to have a 'follower'. Martha looked good, and steady, and composed enough, as she came to help us out; she was always careful of Miss Matty, and tonight she made use of this unlucky speech: 'Eh! dear ma'am, to think of your going out in an evening in such a thin shawl! It's no better than muslin. At your age, ma'am, you should be careful.'

'My age!' said Miss Matty, almost speaking crossly, for her, for she was usually gentle – 'My age! Why, how old do you think I am, that you talk about my age?'

'Well, ma'am, I should say you were not far short of sixty: but folks' looks is often against them – and I'm sure I meant no harm.'

'Martha, I'm not yet fifty-two!' said Miss Matty, with grave emphasis; for probably the remembrance of her youth had come very vividly before her this day, and she was annoyed at finding that golden time so far away in the past.

But she never spoke of any former and more intimate acquaintance with Mr Holbrook. She had probably met with so little sympathy in her early love, that she had shut it up close in her heart; and it was only by a sort of watching, which I could hardly avoid since Miss Pole's confidence, that I saw how faithful her poor heart had been in its sorrow and its silence.

She gave me some good reason for wearing her best cap every day, and sat near the window, in spite of her rheumatism, in order to see, without being seen, down into the street.

He came. He put his open palms upon his knees, which were far apart, as he sat with his head bent down, whistling, after we had replied to his enquiries about our safe return. Suddenly he jumped up.

'Well, madam! have you any commands for Paris? I am going there in a week or two.'

'To Paris!' we both exclaimed.

'Yes, madam! I've never been there, and always had a wish to go; and I think if I don't go soon, I mayn't go at all; so as soon as the hay is got in I shall go, before harvest time.'

We were so much astonished that we had no commissions.

Just as he was going out of the room, he turned back, with his favourite exclamation: 'God bless my soul, madam! but I nearly forgot half my errand. Here are the poems for you you admired so much the other evening at my house.' He tugged away at a parcel in his coat-pocket. 'Goodbye, miss,' said he; 'goodbye, Matty! take care of yourself.' And he was gone. But he had given her a book, and he had called her Matty, just as he used to do thirty years ago.

'I wish he would not go to Paris,' said Miss Matilda anxiously. 'I don't believe frogs will agree with him; he used to have to be very careful what he ate, which was curious in so strong-looking a young man.'

Soon after this I took my leave, giving many an injunction to Martha to look after her mistress, and to let me know if she thought that Miss Matilda was not so well; in which case I would volunteer a visit to my old friend, without noticing Martha's intelligence to her.

Accordingly I received a line or two from Martha every now and then; and, about November, I had a note to say her mistress was 'very low and sadly off her food'; and the account made me so uneasy that, although Martha did not decidedly summon me, I packed up my things and went.

I received a warm welcome, in spite of the little flurry produced by my impromptu visit, for I had only been able to give a day's notice. Miss Matilda looked miserably ill; and I prepared to comfort and cosset her.

I went down to have a private talk with Martha.

'How long has your mistress been so poorly?' I asked, as I stood by the kitchen fire.

'Well! I think it's better than a fortnight; it is, I know; it was one Tuesday, after Miss Pole had been, that she went into this moping way. I thought she was tired, and it would go off with a night's rest; but no! she has gone on and on ever since, till I thought it my duty to write to you, ma'am.'

'You did quite right, Martha. It is a comfort to think she has so faithful a servant about her. And I hope you find your place comfortable.'

'Well, ma'am, missus is very kind, and there's plenty to eat and drink, and no more work but what I can do easily – but – ' Martha hesitated.

'But what, Martha?'

'Why, it seems so hard of missus not to let me have any followers; there's such lots of young fellows in the town; and many a one has as much as offered to keep company with me; and I may never be in such a likely place again, and it's like wasting an opportunity. Many a girl as I know would have 'em unbeknownst to missus; but I've given my word, and I'll stick to it; or else this is just the house for missus never to be the wiser if they did come: and it's such a capable kitchen – there's such dark corners in it – I'd be bound to hide anyone. I counted up last Sunday night – for I'll not deny I was crying because I had to shut the door in Jem Hearn's face, and he's a steady young man, fit for any girl; only I had given missus my word.' Martha was all but crying again; and I had little comfort to give her, for I knew, from old experience, of the horror with which both the Miss Jenkynses looked upon 'followers'; and in Miss Matty's present nervous state this dread was not likely to be lessened.

I went to see Miss Pole the next day, and took her completely by surprise, for she had not been to see Miss Matilda for two days.

'And now I must go back with you, my dear, for I promised to let her know how Thomas Holbrook went on; and, I'm sorry to say, his housekeeper has sent me word today that he hasn't long to live. Poor Thomas! that journey to Paris was quite too much for him. His housekeeper says he has hardly ever been round his fields since, but just sits with his hands on his knees in the counting-house, not reading or anything, but only saying what a wonderful city Paris was! Paris has much to answer for if it's killed my cousin Thomas, for a better man never lived.'

'Does Miss Matilda know of his illness?' asked I – a new light as to the cause of her indisposition dawning upon me.

'Dear! to be sure, yes! Has not she told you? I let her know a fortnight ago, or more, when first I heard of it. How odd she shouldn't have told you!'

Not at all, I thought; but I did not say anything. I felt almost guilty of having spied too curiously into that tender heart, and I was not going to speak of its secrets – hidden, Miss Matty believed, from all the world. I ushered Miss Pole into Miss Matilda's little drawing-room, and then left them alone. But I was not surprised when Martha came to my bedroom door, to ask me to go down to dinner alone, for that missus had one of her bad headaches. She came into the drawing-room at teatime, but it was evidently an effort to her; and, as if to make up for some reproachful feeling against her late sister, Miss Jenkyns, which had been troubling her all the afternoon, and for which she now felt penitent, she kept telling me how good and how clever Deborah was in her youth; how she used to settle what gowns they were to wear at all the parties (faint, ghostly ideas of grim parties, far away in the distance, when Miss Matty and Miss Pole were young!); and how Deborah and her mother had started the benefit society[61] for the poor, and taught girls cooking and plain sewing; and how Deborah had once danced with a lord; and how she used to visit at Sir Peter Arley's, and tried to remodel the quiet rectory establishment on the plans of Arley Hall,[62] where they kept thirty servants; and how she had nursed Miss Matty through a long, long illness, of which I had never heard before, but which I now dated in my own mind as following the dismissal of the suit of Mr Holbrook. So we talked softly and quietly of old times through the long November evening.

The next day Miss Pole brought us word that Mr Holbrook was

dead. Miss Matty heard the news in silence; in fact, from the account of the previous day, it was only what we had to expect. Miss Pole kept calling upon us for some expression of regret, by asking if it was not sad that he was gone, and saying: 'To think of that pleasant day last June, when he seemed so well! And he might have lived this dozen years if he had not gone to that wicked Paris, where they are always having revolutions.'[63]

She paused for some demonstration on our part. I saw Miss Matty could not speak, she was trembling so nervously; so I said what I really felt; and after a call of some duration – all the time of which I have no doubt Miss Pole thought Miss Matty received the news very calmly – our visitor took her leave.

Miss Matty made a strong effort to conceal her feelings – a concealment she practised even with me, for she has never alluded to Mr Holbrook again, although the book he gave her lies with her Bible on the little table by her bedside. She did not think I heard her when she asked the little milliner of Cranford to make her caps something like the Honourable Mrs Jamieson's, or that I noticed the reply: 'But she wears widows' caps,[64] ma'am!'

'Oh! I only meant something in that style; not widows', of course, but rather like Mrs Jamieson's.'

This effort at concealment was the beginning of the tremulous motion of head and hands which I have seen ever since in Miss Matty.

The evening of the day on which we heard of Mr Holbrook's death, Miss Matilda was very silent and thoughtful; after prayers she called Martha back and then she stood uncertain what to say.

'Martha!' she said, at last, 'you are young' – and then she made so long a pause that Martha, to remind her of her half-finished sentence, dropped a curtsey, and said: 'Yes, please, ma'am; two-and-twenty last third of October, please, ma'am.'

'And, perhaps, Martha, you may some time meet with a young man you like, and who likes you. I did say you were not to have followers; but if you meet with such a young man, and tell me, and I find he is respectable, I have no objection to his coming to see you once a week. God forbid!' said she in a low voice, 'that I should grieve any young hearts.' She spoke as if she were providing for some distant contingency, and was rather startled when Martha made her ready eager answer: 'Please, ma'am, there's Jem Hearn, and he's a joiner making three and sixpence a day, and six foot one in his stocking feet, please, ma'am; and if you'll ask about him tomorrow morning, everyone will give him a character for steadiness; and he'll be glad enough to come tomorrow night, I'll be bound.'

Though Miss Matty was startled, she submitted to Fate and Love.[65]

CHAPTER 5

Old Letters

I HAVE OFTEN NOTICED that almost everyone has his own individual small economies – careful habits of saving fractions of pennies[66] in some one peculiar direction – any disturbance of which annoys him more than spending shillings or pounds on some real extravagance. An old gentleman of my acquaintance, who took the intelligence of the failure of a Joint-Stock Bank,[67] in which some of his money was invested, with stoical mildness, worried his family all through a long summer's day because one of them had torn (instead of cutting) out the written leaves of his now useless bankbook; of course, the corresponding pages at the other end came out as well, and this little unnecessary waste of paper (his private economy) chafed him more than all the loss of his money. Envelopes fretted his soul terribly when they first came in;[68] the only way in which he could reconcile himself to such waste of his cherished article was by patiently turning inside out all that were sent to him, and so making them serve again. Even now, though tamed by age, I see him casting wistful glances at his daughters when they send a whole inside of a half-sheet of note paper, with the three lines of acceptance to an invitation, written on only one of the sides. I am not above owning that I have this human weakness myself. String is my foible. My pockets get full of little hanks of it, picked up and twisted together, ready for uses that never come. I am seriously annoyed if anyone cuts the string of a parcel instead of patiently and faithfully undoing it fold by fold. How people can bring themselves to use india-rubber rings, which are a sort of deification of string, as lightly as they do, I cannot imagine. To me an india-rubber ring is a precious treasure. I have one which is not new – one that I picked up off the floor nearly six years ago. I have really tried to use it, but my heart failed me, and I could not commit the extravagance.

Small pieces of butter grieve others. They cannot attend to

conversation because of the annoyance occasioned by the habit which some people have of invariably taking more butter than they want. Have you not seen the anxious look (almost mesmeric) which such persons fix on the article? They would feel it a relief if they might bury it out of their sight by popping it into their own mouths and swallowing it down; and they are really made happy if the person on whose plate it lies unused suddenly breaks off a piece of toast (which he does not want at all) and eats up his butter. They think that this is not waste.

Now Miss Matty Jenkyns was chary of candles. We had many devices to use as few as possible. In the winter afternoons she would sit knitting for two or three hours – she could do this in the dark, or by firelight – and when I asked if I might not ring for candles to finish stitching my wristbands, she told me to 'keep blind man's holiday'.[69] They were usually brought in with tea; but we only burnt one at a time. As we lived in constant preparation for a friend who might come in any evening (but who never did), it required some contrivance to keep our two candles of the same length, ready to be lighted, and to look as if we burnt two always. The candles took it in turns; and, whatever we might be talking about or doing, Miss Matty's eyes were habitually fixed upon the candle, ready to jump up and extinguish it and to light the other before they had become too uneven in length to be restored to equality in the course of the evening.

One night, I remember this candle economy particularly annoyed me. I had been very much tired of my compulsory 'blind man's holiday', especially as Miss Matty had fallen asleep, and I did not like to stir the fire and run the risk of awakening her; so I could not even sit on the rug, and scorch myself with sewing by firelight, according to my usual custom. I fancied Miss Matty must be dreaming of her early life; for she spoke one or two words in her uneasy sleep bearing reference to persons who were dead long before. When Martha brought in the lighted candle and tea, Miss Matty started into wakefulness, with a strange, bewildered look around, as if we were not the people she expected to see about her. There was a little sad expression that shadowed her face as she recognised me; but immediately afterwards she tried to give me her usual smile. All through teatime her talk ran upon the days of her childhood and youth. Perhaps this reminded her of the desirableness of looking over all the old family letters, and destroying such as ought not to be allowed to fall into the hands of strangers; for she had often spoken of the necessity of this task, but had always shrunk from it, with a timid dread of something painful. Tonight, however, she rose up after tea and went for them – in the dark; for she piqued herself on the precise neatness of all her chamber arrangements, and used to look uneasily at me when I lighted a bed-candle to go to another room for anything. When she returned there was a faint, pleasant smell of Tonquin beans[70] in the room. I had always noticed this scent about any of the things which had belonged to her mother; and many of the letters were addressed to her – yellow bundles of love-letters, sixty or seventy years old. Miss Matty undid the packet with a sigh; but she stifled it directly, as if it were hardly right to regret the flight of time, or of life either. We agreed to look them over separately, each taking a different letter out of the same bundle and describing its contents to the other before destroying it. I never knew what sad work the reading of old letters was before that evening, though I could hardly tell why. The letters were as happy as letters could be – at least those early letters were. There was in them a vivid and intense sense of the present time, which seemed so strong and full, as if it could never pass away, and as if the warm, living hearts that so expressed themselves could never die, and be as nothing to the sunny earth. I should have felt less melancholy, I believe, if the letters had been more so. I saw the tears stealing down the well-worn furrows of Miss Matty's cheeks, and her spectacles often wanted wiping. I trusted at last that she would light the other candle, for my own eyes were rather dim, and I wanted more light to see the pale, faded ink; but no, even through her tears, she saw and remembered her little economical ways.

The earliest set of letters were two bundles tied together, and ticketed (in Miss Jenkyns's handwriting) 'Letters interchanged between my ever-honoured father and my dearly beloved mother, prior to their marriage, in July 1774.' I should guess that the rector of Cranford was about twenty-seven years of age when he wrote those letters; and Miss Matty told me that her mother was just eighteen at the time of her wedding. With my idea of the rector, derived from a picture in the dining-parlour, stiff and stately, in a huge full-bottomed wig, with gown, cassock, and bands,[71] and his hand upon a copy of the only sermon he ever published – it was strange to read these letters. They were full of eager, passionate ardour; short homely sentences, right fresh from the heart (very different from the grand Latinised, Johnsonian style of the printed sermon, preached before some judge at assize time).[72] His letters were a curious contrast to those of his girl-bride. She was evidently rather annoyed at his demands upon her for expressions of love, and could not quite understand what he meant by repeating the same thing over in so many different ways; but what she was quite clear about was a longing for a white 'Paduasoy'[73] – whatever that might be; and six or seven letters were principally occupied in asking her lover to use his influence with her parents (who evidently kept her in good order) to obtain this or that article of dress, more especially the white 'Paduasoy'. He cared nothing how she was dressed; she was always lovely enough for him, as he took pains to assure her, when she begged him to express in his answers a predilection for particular pieces of finery, in order that she might show what he said to her parents. But at length he seemed to find out that she would not be married till she had a 'trousseau' to her mind; and then he sent her a letter, which had evidently accompanied a whole box full of finery, and in which he requested that she might be dressed in everything her heart desired. This was the first letter, ticketed in a frail, delicate hand, 'From my dearest John.' Shortly afterwards they were married, I suppose, from the intermission in their correspondence.

'We must burn them, I think,' said Miss Matty, looking doubtfully at me. 'No one will care for them when I am gone.' And one by one she dropped them into the middle of the fire, watching each blaze up, die out, and rise away, in faint, white, ghostly semblance, up the chimney, before she gave another to the same fate. The room was light enough now; but I, like her, was fascinated into watching the destruction of those letters, into which the honest warmth of a manly heart had been poured forth.

The next letter, likewise docketed by Miss Jenkyns, was endorsed, 'Letter of pious congratulation and exhortation from my venerable grandfather to my beloved mother, on occasion of my own birth. Also some practical remarks on the desirability of keeping warm the extremities of infants, from my excellent grandmother.'

The first part was, indeed, a severe and forcible picture of the responsibilities of mothers, and a warning against the evils that were in the world, and lying in ghastly wait for the little baby of two days old. His wife did not write, said the old gentleman, because he had forbidden it, she being indisposed with a sprained ankle, which (he said) quite incapacitated her from holding a pen. However, at the foot of the page was a small 't.o.', and on turning it over, sure enough, there was a letter to 'my dear, dearest Molly', begging her, when she left her room, whatever she did, to go *up* stairs before going *down*: and telling her to wrap her baby's feet up in flannel, and keep it warm by the fire, although it was summer, for babies were so tender.

It was pretty to see from the letters, which were evidently exchanged with some frequency between the young mother and the grandmother, how the girlish vanity was being weeded out of her heart by love for her baby. The white 'Paduasoy' figured again in the letters, with almost as much vigour as before. In one, it was being made into a christening cloak for the baby. It decked it when it went with its parents to spend a day or two at Arley Hall. It added to its charms, when it was 'the prettiest little baby that ever was seen. Dear mother; I wish you could see her! Without any parshality, I do think she will grow up a regular bewty!' I thought of Miss Jenkyns, grey, withered, and wrinkled, and I wondered if her mother had known her in the courts of heaven: and then I knew that she had, and that they stood there in angelic guise.

There was a great gap before any of the rector's letters appeared. And then his wife had changed her mode of her endorsement. It was no longer from 'My dearest John'; it was from 'My honoured Husband'. The letters were written on occasion of the publication of the same sermon which was represented in the picture. The preaching before 'My Lord Judge', and the 'publishing by request', was evidently the culminating point – the event of his life. It had been necessary for him to go up to London to superintend it through the press. Many friends had to be called upon and consulted before he could decide on any printer fit for so onerous a task; and at length it was arranged that J. and J. Rivingtons[74] were to have the honourable responsibility. The worthy rector seemed to be strung up by the occasion to a high literary pitch, for he could hardly write a letter to his wife without cropping out into Latin. I remember the end of one of his letters ran thus: 'I shall ever hold the virtuous qualities of my Molly in remembrance, *dum memor ipse mei*, *dum spiritus regit artus*',[75] which, considering that the English of his correspondent was sometimes at fault in grammar, and often in spelling, might be taken as a proof of how much he 'idealised his Molly'; and, as Miss Jenkyns used to say: 'People talk a great deal about idealising nowadays, whatever that may mean.' But this was nothing to a fit of writing classical poetry which soon seized him, in which his Molly figured away as 'Maria'. The letter containing the *carmen*[76] was endorsed by her: 'Hebrew verses sent me by my honoured husband. I thowt to have had a letter about killing the pig, but must wait. Mem., to send the poetry to Sir Peter Arley, as my husband desires.' And in a post-scriptum note in his handwriting it was stated that the Ode had appeared in the *Gentleman's Magazine*,[77] December 1782.

Her letters back to her husband (treasured as fondly by him as if they had been *M. T. Ciceronis Epistolae*)[78] were more satisfactory to an absent husband and father than his could ever have been to her. She told him how Deborah sewed her seam very neatly every day, and read to her in the books he had sent her; how she was a very 'forrard', good child, but *would* ask questions her mother could not answer, but how she did not let herself down by saying she did not know, but took to stirring the fire, or sending the 'forrard' child on an errand. Matty was now the mother's darling, and promised (like her sister at her age) to be a great beauty. I was reading this aloud to Miss Matty, who smiled and sighed a little at the hope, so fondly expressed, that 'little Matty might not be vain, even if she were a bewty'.

'I had very pretty hair, my dear,' said Miss Matilda; 'and not a bad mouth.' And I saw her soon afterwards adjust her cap and draw herself up. But to return to Mrs Jenkyns's letters. She told her husband about the poor in the parish; what homely domestic medicines she had administered; what kitchen physic she had sent. She had evidently held his displeasure as a rod in pickle over the heads of all the ne'er-do-wells. She asked for his directions about the cows and pigs; and did not always obtain them, as I have shown before.

The kind old grandmother was dead when a little boy was born, soon after the publication of the sermon; but there was another letter of exhortation from the grandfather, more stringent and admonitory than ever, now that there was a boy to be guarded from the snares of the world. He described all the various sins into which men might fall, until I wondered how any man ever came to a natural death. The gallows seemed as if it must have been the termination of the lives of most of the grandfather's friends and acquaintances; and I was not surprised at the way in which he spoke of this life being 'a vale of tears'.[79]

It seemed curious that I should never have heard of this brother before; but I concluded that he had died young, or else surely his name would have been alluded to by his sisters.

By and by we came to packets of Miss Jenkyns's letters. These Miss Matty did regret to burn. She said all the others had been only interesting to those who loved the writers, and that it seemed as if it would have hurt her to allow them to fall into the hands of strangers, who had not known her dear mother, and how good she was, although she did not always spell quite in the modern fashion; but Deborah's letters were so very superior! Anyone might profit by reading them. It was a long time since she had read Mrs Chapone,[80] but she knew she used to think that Deborah could have said the same things quite as well; and as for Mrs Carter! people thought a deal of her letters, just because she had written *Epictetus*,[81] but she was quite sure Deborah would never have made use of such a common expression as 'I canna be fashed!'[82]

Miss Matty did grudge burning these letters, it was evident. She would not let them be carelessly passed over with any quiet reading, and skipping, to myself. She took them from me, and even lighted the second candle in order to read them aloud with a proper emphasis, and without stumbling over the big words. Oh dear! how I wanted facts instead of reflections, before those letters were concluded! They lasted us two nights; and I won't deny that I made use of the time to think of many other things, and yet I was always at my post at the end of each sentence.

The rector's letters, and those of his wife and mother-in-law, had all been tolerably short and pithy, written in a straight hand, with the lines very close together. Sometimes the whole letter was contained on a mere scrap of paper. The paper was very yellow, and the ink very brown: some of the sheets were (as Miss Matty made me observe) the old original post, with the stamp in the corner representing a post-boy riding for life and twanging his horn.[83] The letters of Mrs Jenkyns and her mother were fastened with a great round red wafer;[84] for it was before Miss Edgeworth's *Patronage* had banished wafers from polite society. It was evident, from the tenor of what was said, that franks were in great request, and were even used as a means of paying debts by needy members of Parliament.[85] The rector sealed his epistles with an immense coat of arms, and showed by the care with which he had performed this ceremony that he expected they should be cut open, not broken by any thoughtless or impatient hand. Now, Miss Jenkyns's letters were of a later date in form and writing. She wrote on the square sheet which we have learned to call old-fashioned. Her hand was admirably calculated, together with her use of many-syllabled words, to fill up a sheet, and then came the pride and delight of crossing.[86] Poor Miss Matty got sadly puzzled with this, for the words gathered size like snowballs, and towards the end of her letter Miss Jenkyns used to become quite sesquipedalian. In one to her father, slightly theological and controversial in its tone, she had spoken of Herod, Tetrarch of Idumea. Miss Matty read it 'Herod Petrarch of Etruria', and was just as well pleased as if she had been right.

I can't quite remember the date, but I think it was in 1805 that Miss Jenkyns wrote the longest series of letters – on occasion of her absence on a visit to some friends near Newcastle-upon-Tyne.[87] These friends were intimate with the commandant of the garrison there, and heard from him of all the preparations that were being made to repel the invasion of Buonaparte, which some people imagined might take place at the mouth of the Tyne. Miss Jenkyns was evidently very much alarmed; and the first part of her letters was often written in pretty intelligible English, conveying particulars of the preparations which were made in the family with whom she was residing against the dreaded event; the bundles of clothes that were packed up ready for a flight to Alston Moor (a wild hilly piece of ground between Northumberland and Cumberland); the signal that was to be given for this flight, and for the simultaneous turning out of the volunteers under arms – which said signal was to consist (if I remember rightly) in ringing the church bells in a particular and ominous manner. One day, when Miss Jenkyns and her hosts were at a dinner party in Newcastle, this warning summons was actually given (not a very wise proceeding, if there be any truth in the moral attached to the fable of the Boy and the Wolf; but so it was), and Miss Jenkyns, hardly recovered from her fright, wrote the next day to describe the sound, the breathless shock, the hurry and alarm; and then, taking breath, she added: 'How trivial, my dear father, do all our apprehensions of the last evening appear, at the present moment, to calm and enquiring minds!' And here Miss Matty broke in with: 'But, indeed, my dear, they were not at all trivial or trifling at the time. I know I used to wake up in the night many a time and think I heard the tramp of the French entering Cranford. Many people talked of hiding themselves in the salt mines[88] – and meat would have kept capitally down there, only perhaps we should have been thirsty. And my father preached a whole set of sermons on the occasion; one set in the mornings, all about David and Goliath, to spirit up the people to fighting with spades or bricks, if need were; and the other set in the afternoons, proving that Napoleon (that was another name for Bony, as we used to call him) was all the same as an Apollyon and Abaddon.[89] I remember my father rather thought he should be asked to print this last set; but the parish had, perhaps, had enough of them with hearing.'

Peter Marmaduke Arley Jenkyns ('poor Peter!' as Miss Matty began to call him) was at school at Shrewsbury by this time. The rector took up his pen, and rubbed up his Latin once more, to correspond with his boy. It was very clear that the lad's were what are called show letters.[90] They were of a highly mental description, giving an account of his studies, and his intellectual hopes of various kinds, with an occasional quotation from the classics; but, now and then, the animal nature broke out in such a little sentence as this, evidently written in a trembling hurry, after the letter had been inspected: 'Mother dear, do send me a cake, and put plenty of citron in.' The 'mother dear' probably answered her boy in the form of cakes and 'goody', for there were none of her letters among this set; but a whole collection of the rector's, to whom the Latin in his boy's letters was like a trumpet to the old war-horse. I do not know much about Latin, certainly, and it is, perhaps, an ornamental language, but not very useful, I think – at least to judge from the bits I remember out of the rector's letters. One was: 'You have not got that town in your map of Ireland; but *Bonus Bernardus non videt omnia*,[91] as the Proverbia say.' Presently it became very evident that 'poor Peter' got himself into many scrapes. There were letters of stilted penitence to his father, for some wrongdoing; and among them all was a badly written, badly sealed, badly directed, blotted note: 'My dear, dear, dear, dearest mother, I will be a better boy; I will, indeed; but don't, please, be ill for me; I am not worth it; but I will be good, darling mother.'

Miss Matty could not speak for crying, after she had read this note. She gave it to me in silence, and then got up and took it to her sacred recesses in her own room, for fear, by any chance, it might get burnt. 'Poor Peter!' she said; 'he was always in scrapes; he was too easy. They led him wrong, and then left him in the lurch. But he was too fond of mischief. He could never resist a joke. Poor Peter!'

CHAPTER 6

Poor Peter

POOR PETER'S CAREER lay before him rather pleasantly mapped out by kind friends, but *Bonus Bernardus non videt omnia*, in this map too. He was to win honours at the Shrewsbury School, and carry them thick to Cambridge, and after that, a living[92] awaited him, the gift of his godfather, Sir Peter Arley. Poor Peter! his lot in life was very different to what his friends had hoped and planned. Miss Matty told me all about it, and I think it was a relief when she had done so.

He was the darling of his mother, who seemed to dote on all her children, though she was, perhaps, a little afraid of Deborah's superior acquirements. Deborah was the favourite of her father, and when Peter disappointed him, she became his pride. The sole honour Peter brought away from Shrewsbury was the reputation of being the best good fellow that ever was, and of being the captain of the school in the art of practical joking. His father was disappointed, but set about remedying the matter in a manly way. He could not afford to send Peter to read with any tutor, but he could read with him himself; and Miss Matty told me much of the awful preparations in the way of dictionaries and lexicons that were made in her father's study the morning Peter began.

'My poor mother!' said she. 'I remember how she used to stand in the hall, just near enough the study door to catch the tone of my father's voice. I could tell in a moment if all was going right, by her face. And it did go right for a long time.'

'What went wrong at last?' said I. 'That tiresome Latin, I dare say.'

'No! it was not the Latin. Peter was in high favour with my father, for he worked up well for him. But he seemed to think that the Cranford people might be joked about, and made fun of, and they did not like it; nobody does. He was always hoaxing them; "hoaxing" is not a pretty word, my dear, and I hope you won't tell your father I used it, for I should not like him to think that I was not choice in my language, after living with such a woman as Deborah. And be sure you never use it yourself. I don't know how it slipped out of my mouth, except it was that I was thinking of poor Peter and it was always his expression. But he was a very gentlemanly boy in many things. He was like dear Captain Brown in always being ready to help any old person or a child. Still, he did like joking and making fun; and he seemed to think the old ladies in Cranford would believe anything. There were many old ladies living here then; we are principally ladies now, I know, but we are not so old as the ladies used to be when I was a girl. I could laugh to think of some of Peter's jokes. No, my dear, I won't tell you of them, because they might not shock you as they ought to do, and they were very shocking. He even took in my father once, by dressing himself up as a lady that was passing through the town and wished to see the rector of Cranford, "who had published that admirable Assize Sermon". Peter said he was awfully frightened himself when he saw how my father took it all in, and even offered to copy out all his Napoleon Buonaparte sermons for her – him, I mean – no, her, for Peter was a lady then. He told me he was more terrified than he ever was before, all the time my father was speaking. He did not think my father would have believed him; and yet if he had not, it would have been a sad thing for Peter. As it was, he was none so glad of it, for my father kept him hard at work copying out all those twelve Buonaparte sermons for the lady – that was for Peter himself, you know. He was the lady. And once when he wanted to go fishing, Peter said: "Confound the woman!" – very bad language, my dear, but Peter was not always so guarded as he should have been; my father was so angry with him, it nearly frightened me out of my wits: and yet I could hardly keep from laughing at the little curtseys Peter kept making, quite slyly, whenever my father spoke of the lady's excellent taste and sound discrimination.'

'Did Miss Jenkyns know of these tricks?' said I.

'Oh, no! Deborah would have been too much shocked. No, no one knew but me. I wish I had always known of Peter's plans; but sometimes he did not tell me. He used to say the old ladies in the town wanted something to talk about; but I don't think they did. They had the *St James's Chronicle* three times a week, just as we have now, and we have plenty to say; and I remember the clacking noise there always was when some of the ladies got together. But, probably, schoolboys talk more than ladies. At last there was a terrible, sad thing happened.' Miss Matty got up, went to the door, and opened it; no one was there. She rang the bell for Martha, and when Martha came, her mistress told her to go for eggs to a farm at the other end of the town.

'I will lock the door after you, Martha. You are not afraid to go, are you?'

'No, ma'am, not at all; Jem Hearn will be only too proud to go with me.'

Miss Matty drew herself up, and as soon as we were alone, she wished that Martha had more maidenly reserve.

'We'll put out the candle, my dear. We can talk just as well by firelight, you know. There! Well, you see, Deborah had gone from home for a fortnight or so; it was a very still, quiet day, I remember, overhead; and the lilacs were all in flower, so I suppose it was spring. My father had gone out to see some sick people in the parish; I recollect seeing him leave the house with his wig and shovel-hat[93] and cane. What possessed our poor Peter I don't know; he had the sweetest temper, and yet he always seemed to like to plague Deborah. She never laughed at his jokes, and thought him ungenteel, and not careful enough about improving his mind; and that vexed him.

'Well! he went to her room, it seems, and dressed himself in her old gown, and shawl, and bonnet; just the things she used to wear in Cranford, and was known by everywhere; and he made the pillow into a little – you are sure you locked the door, my dear, for I should not like anyone to hear – into – into a little baby, with white long clothes. It was only, as he told me afterwards, to make something to talk about in the town; he never thought of it as affecting Deborah. And he went and walked up and down in the Filbert walk – just half hidden by the rails, and half seen; and he cuddled his pillow, just like a baby, and talked to it all the nonsense people do. Oh dear! and my father came stepping stately up the street, as he always did; and what should he see but a little black crowd of people – I dare say as many as twenty – all peeping through his garden rails. So he thought, at first, they were only looking at a new rhododendron[94] that was in full bloom, and that he was very proud of; and he walked slower, that they might have more time to admire. And he wondered if he could make out a sermon from the occasion, and thought, perhaps, there was some relation between the rhododendrons and the lilies of the field. My poor father! When he came nearer, he began to wonder that they did not see him; but their heads were all so close together, peeping and peeping! My father was amongst them, meaning, he said, to ask them to walk into the garden with him, and admire the beautiful vegetable production, when – oh, my dear, I tremble to think of it – he looked through the rails himself, and saw – I don't know what he thought he saw, but old Clare told me his face went quite grey-white with anger, and his eyes blazed out under his frowning black brows; and he spoke out – oh, so terribly! – and bade them all stop where they were – not one of them to go, not one of them to stir a step; and, swift as light, he was in at the garden door, and down the Filbert walk, and seized hold of poor Peter, and tore his clothes off his back – bonnet, shawl, gown, and all – and threw the pillow among the people over the railings: and then he was very, very angry indeed, and before all the people he lifted up his cane and flogged Peter!

'My dear, that boy's trick, on that sunny day, when all seemed going straight and well, broke my mother's heart, and changed my father for life. It did, indeed. Old Clare said, Peter looked as white as my father; and stood as still as a statue to be flogged; and my father struck hard! When my father stopped to take breath, Peter said: "Have you done enough, sir?" quite hoarsely, and still standing quite quiet. I don't know what my father said – or if he said anything. But old Clare said, Peter turned to where the people outside the railing were, and made them a low bow, as grand and as grave as any gentleman; and then walked slowly into the house. I was in the storeroom helping my mother to make cowslip wine. I cannot abide the wine now, nor the scent of the flowers; they turn me sick and faint, as they did that day, when Peter came in, looking as haughty as any man – indeed, looking like a man, not like a boy. "Mother!" he said, "I am come to say, God bless you for ever." I saw his lips quiver as he spoke; and I think he durst not say anything more loving, for the purpose that was in his heart. She looked at him rather frightened, and wondering, and asked him what was to do. He did not smile or speak, but put his arms round her and kissed her as if he did not know how to leave off; and before she could speak again, he was gone. We talked it over, and could not understand it, and she bade me go and seek my father, and ask what it was all about. I found him walking up and down, looking very highly displeased.

' "Tell your mother I have flogged Peter, and that he richly deserved it."

'I durst not ask any more questions. When I told my mother, she sat down, quite faint, for a minute. I remember, a few days after, I saw the poor, withered cowslip flowers thrown out to the leaf heap, to decay and die there. There was no making of cowslip wine that year at the rectory – nor, indeed, ever after.

'Presently my mother went to my father. I know I thought of Queen Esther and King Ahasuerus;[95] for my mother was very pretty and delicate-looking, and my father looked as terrible as King Ahasuerus. Some time after they came out together; and then my mother told me what had happened, and that she was going up to Peter's room at my father's desire – though she was not to tell Peter this – to talk the matter over with him. But no Peter was there. We looked over the house; no Peter was there! Even my father, who had not liked to join in the search at first, helped us before long. The rectory was a very old house – steps up into a room, steps down into a room, all through. At first, my mother went calling low and soft, as if to reassure the poor boy: "Peter! Peter, dear! it's only me"; but, by and by, as the servants came back from the errands my father had sent them, in different directions, to find where Peter was – as we found he was not in the garden, nor the hayloft, nor anywhere about – my mother's cry grew louder and wilder: "Peter! Peter, my darling! where are you?" for then she felt and understood that that long kiss meant some sad kind of "goodbye". The afternoon went on – my mother never resting, but seeking again and again in every possible place that had been looked into twenty times before, nay, that she had looked into over and over again herself. My father sat with his head in his hands, not speaking except when his messengers came in, bringing no tidings; then he lifted up his face, so strong and sad, and told them to go again in some new direction. My mother kept passing from room to room, in and out of the house, moving noiselessly, but never ceasing. Neither she nor my father durst leave the house, which was the meeting-place for all the messengers. At last (and it was nearly dark) my father rose up. He took hold of my mother's arm as she came with wild, sad pace through one door, and quickly towards another. She started at the touch of his hand, for she had forgotten all in the world but Peter.

' "Molly!" said he, "I did not think all this would happen." He looked into her face for comfort – her poor face all wild and white; for neither she nor my father had dared to acknowledge – much less act upon – the terror that was in their hearts, lest Peter should have made away with himself. My father saw no conscious look in his wife's hot, dreary eyes, and he missed the sympathy that she had always been ready to give him – strong man as he was, and at the dumb despair in her face his tears began to flow. But when she saw this, a gentle sorrow came over her countenance, and she said: "Dearest John! don't cry; come with me, and we'll find him," almost as cheerfully as if she knew where he was. And she took my father's great hand in her little soft one, and led him along, the tears dropping as he walked on that same unceasing, weary walk, from room to room, through house and garden.

'Oh, how I wished for Deborah! I had no time for crying, for now all seemed to depend on me. I wrote for Deborah to come home. I sent a message privately to that same Mr Holbrook's house – poor Mr Holbrook – you know who I mean. I don't mean I sent a message to him, but I sent one that I could trust to know if Peter was at his house. For at one time Mr Holbrook was an occasional visitor at the rectory – you know he was Miss Pole's cousin – and he had been very kind to Peter, and taught him how to fish – he was very kind to everybody, and I thought Peter might have gone off there. But Mr Holbrook was from home, and Peter had never been seen. It was night now; but the doors were all wide open, and my father and mother walked on and on; it was more than an hour since he had joined her, and I don't believe they had ever spoken all that time. I was getting the parlour fire lighted, and one of the servants was preparing tea, for I wanted them to have something to eat and drink and warm them, when old Clare asked to speak to me.

' "I have borrowed the nets from the weir, Miss Matty. Shall we drag the ponds tonight, or wait for the morning?"

'I remember staring in his face to gather his meaning; and when I did, I laughed out loud. The horror of that new thought – our bright, darling Peter, cold, and stark, and dead! I remember the ring of my own laugh now.

'The next day Deborah was at home before I was myself again. She would not have been so weak as to give way as I had done; but my screams (my horrible laugh had ended in crying) had roused my sweet dear mother, whose poor wandering wits were called back and collected as soon as a child needed her care. She and Deborah sat by my bedside; I knew by the looks of each that there had been no news of Peter – no awful, ghastly news, which was what I most had dreaded in my dull state between sleeping and waking.

'The same result of all the searching had brought something of the same relief to my mother, to whom, I am sure, the thought that Peter might even then be hanging dead in some of the familiar home places had caused that never-ending walk of yesterday. Her soft eyes never were the same again after that; they had always a restless, craving look, as if seeking for what they could not find. Oh! it was an awful time; coming down like a thunderbolt on the still sunny day when the lilacs were all in bloom.'

'Where was Mr Peter?' said I.

'He had made his way to Liverpool; and there was war then; and some of the king's ships lay off the mouth of the Mersey; and they were only too glad to have a fine likely boy such as him (five foot nine he was) come to offer himself. The captain wrote to my father, and Peter wrote to my mother. Stay! those letters will be somewhere here.'

We lighted the candle, and found the captain's letter and Peter's too. And we also found a little simple begging letter from Mrs Jenkyns to Peter, addressed to him at the house of an old school-fellow, whither she fancied he might have gone. They had returned it unopened; and unopened it had remained ever since, having been inadvertently put by among the other letters of that time. This is it:

> My dearest Peter – You did not think we should be so sorry as we are, I know, or you would never have gone away. You are too good. Your father sits and sighs till my heart aches to hear him. He cannot hold up his head for grief; and yet he only did what he thought was right. Perhaps he has been too severe, and perhaps I have not been kind enough; but God knows how we love you, my dear only boy. Don[96] looks so sorry you are gone. Come back, and make us happy, who love you so much. I *know* you will come back.

But Peter did not come back. That spring day was the last time he ever saw his mother's face. The writer of the letter – the last – the only person who had ever seen what was written in it, was dead long ago; and I, a stranger, not born at the time when this occurrence took place, was the one to open it.

The captain's letter summoned the father and mother to Liverpool instantly, if they wished to see their boy; and, by some of the wild chances of life, the captain's letter had been detained somewhere, somehow.

Miss Matty went on: 'And it was race time,[97] and all the post-horses at Cranford were gone to the races; but my father and mother set off in our own gig – and oh! my dear, they were too late – the ship was gone! And now read Peter's letter to my mother!'

It was full of love, and sorrow, and pride in his new profession, and a sore sense of his disgrace in the eyes of the people at Cranford; but ending with a passionate entreaty that she would come and see him before he left the Mersey: 'Mother; we may go into battle. I hope we shall, and lick those French; but I must see you again before that time.'

'And she was too late,' said Miss Matty; 'too late!'

We sat in silence, pondering on the full meaning of those sad, sad words. At length I asked Miss Matty to tell me how her mother bore it.

'Oh!' she said, 'she was patience itself. She had never been strong, and this weakened her terribly. My father used to sit looking at her: far more sad than she was. He seemed as if he could look at nothing else when she was by; and he was so humble – so very gentle now. He would, perhaps, speak in his old way – laying down the law, as it were – and then, in a minute or two, he would come round and put his hand on our shoulders, and ask us in a low voice, if he had said anything to hurt us. I did not wonder at his speaking so to Deborah, for she was so clever; but I could not bear to hear him talking so to me.

'But, you see, he saw what we did not – that it was killing my mother. Yes! killing her (put out the candle, my dear; I can talk better in the dark), for she was but a frail woman, and ill fitted to stand the fright and shock she had gone through; and she would smile at him and comfort him, not in words, but in her looks and tones, which were always cheerful when he was there. And she would speak of how she thought Peter stood a good chance of being admiral very soon – he was so brave and clever; and how she thought of seeing him in his navy uniform, and what sort of hats admirals wore; and how much more fit he was to be a sailor than a clergyman; and all in that way, just to make my father think she was quite glad of what came of that unlucky morning's work, and the flogging which was always in his mind, as we all knew. But oh, my dear! the bitter, bitter crying she had when she was alone; and at last, as she grew weaker, she could not keep her tears in when Deborah or me was by, and would give us message after message for Peter (his ship had gone to the Mediterranean, or somewhere down there, and then he was ordered off to India,[98] and there was no overland route then); but she still said that no one knew where their death lay in wait, and that we were not to think hers was near. We did not think it, but we knew it, as we saw her fading away.

'Well, my dear, it's very foolish of me, I know, when in all likelihood I am so near seeing her again.

'And only think, love! the very day after her death – for she did not live quite a twelvemonth after Peter went away – the very day after – came a parcel for her from India – from her poor boy. It was a large, soft, white Indian shawl, with just a little narrow border all round; just what my mother would have liked.

'We thought it might rouse my father, for he had sat with her hand in his all night long; so Deborah took it in to him, and Peter's letter to her, and all. At first, he took no notice; and we tried to make a kind of light careless talk about the shawl, opening it out and admiring it. Then, suddenly, he got up, and spoke. "She shall be buried in it," he said; "Peter shall have that comfort; and she would have liked it."

'Well, perhaps it was not reasonable, but what could we do or say? One gives people in grief their own way. He took it up and felt it: "It is just such a shawl as she wished for when she was married, and her mother did not give it her. I did not know of it till after, or she should have had it – she should; but she shall have it now."

'My mother looked so lovely in her death! She was always pretty, and now she looked fair, and waxen, and young – younger than Deborah, as she stood trembling and shivering by her. We decked her in the long soft folds; she lay smiling, as if pleased; and people came – all Cranford came – to beg to see her, for they had loved her dearly, as well they might; and the country-women brought posies; old Clare's wife brought some white violets and begged they might lie on her breast.

'Deborah said to me, the day of my mother's funeral, that if she had a hundred offers she never would marry and leave my father. It was not very likely she would have so many – I don't know that she had one; but it was not less to her credit to say so. She was such a daughter to my father as I think there never was before or since. His eyes failed him, and she read book after book, and wrote, and copied, and was always at his service in any parish business. She could do many more things than my poor mother could; she even once wrote a letter to the bishop for my father. But he missed my mother sorely; the whole parish noticed it. Not that he was less active; I think he was more so, and more patient in helping everyone. I did all I could to set Deborah at liberty to be with him; for I knew I was good for little, and that my best work in the world was to do odd jobs quietly, and set others at liberty. But my father was a changed man.'

'Did Mr Peter ever come home?'

'Yes, once. He came home a lieutenant; he did not get to be admiral. And he and my father were such friends! My father took him into every house in the parish, he was so proud of him. He never walked out without Peter's arm to lean upon. Deborah used to smile (I don't think we ever laughed again after my mother's death), and say she was quite put in a corner. Not but what my father always wanted her when there was letter-writing or reading to be done, or anything to be settled.'

'And then?' said I, after a pause.

'Then Peter went to sea again; and, by and by, my father died, blessing us both, and thanking Deborah for all she had been to him; and, of course, our circumstances were changed; and, instead of living at the rectory, and keeping three maids and a man, we had to come to this small house, and be content with a servant-of-all-work; but, as Deborah used to say, we have always lived genteelly, even if circumstances have compelled us to simplicity. Poor Deborah!'

'And Mr Peter?' asked I.

'Oh, there was some great war in India – I forget what they call it – and we have never heard of Peter since then. I believe he is dead myself; and it sometimes fidgets me that we have never put on mourning for him. And then again, when I sit by myself, and all the house is still, I think I hear his step coming up the street, and my heart begins to flutter and beat; but the sound always goes past – and Peter never comes.

'That's Martha back? No! I'll go, my dear; I can always find my way in the dark, you know. And a blow of fresh air at the door will do my head good, and it's rather got a trick of aching.'

So she pattered off. I had lighted the candle, to give the room a cheerful appearance against her return.

'Was it Martha?' asked I.

'Yes. And I am rather uncomfortable, for I heard such a strange noise, just as I was opening the door.'

'Where?' I asked, for her eyes were round with affright.

'In the street – just outside – it sounded like – '

'Talking?' I put in, as she hesitated a little.

'No! kissing – '

CHAPTER 7

Visiting

One morning, as Miss Matty and I sat at our work – it was before twelve o'clock, and Miss Matty had not changed the cap with yellow ribbons that had been Miss Jenkyns's best, and which Miss Matty was now wearing out in private, putting on the one made in imitation of Mrs Jamieson's at all times when she expected to be seen – Martha came up, and asked if Miss Betty Barker might speak to her mistress. Miss Matty assented, and quickly disappeared to change the yellow ribbons, while Miss Barker came upstairs; but, as she had forgotten her spectacles, and was rather flurried by the unusual time of the visit, I was not surprised to see her return with one cap on the top of the other. She was quite unconscious of it herself, and looked at us with bland satisfaction. Nor do I think Miss Barker perceived it; for, putting aside the little circumstance that she was not so young as she had been, she was very much absorbed in her errand, which she delivered herself of with an oppressive modesty that found vent in endless apologies.

Miss Betty Barker was the daughter of the old clerk at Cranford who had officiated in Mr Jenkyns's time. She and her sister had had pretty good situations as ladies' maids, and had saved money enough to set up a milliner's shop, which had been patronised by the ladies in the neighbourhood. Lady Arley, for instance, would occasionally give Miss Barkers the pattern of an old cap of hers, which they immediately copied and circulated among the *élite* of Cranford. I say the *élite*, for Miss Barkers had caught the trick of the place, and piqued themselves upon their 'aristocratic connection'. They would not sell their caps and ribbons to anyone without a pedigree. Many a farmer's wife or daughter turned away huffed from Miss Barkers' select millinery, and went rather to the universal shop, where the profits of brown soap and moist sugar enabled the proprietor to go straight to (Paris, he said, until he found his customers too patriotic and John Bullish to wear what the Mounseers wore) London, where, as he often told his customers, Queen Adelaide[99] had appeared, only the very week before, in a cap exactly like the one he showed them, trimmed with yellow and blue ribbons, and had been complimented by King William on the becoming nature of her headdress.

Miss Barkers, who confined themselves to truth, and did not approve of miscellaneous customers, throve notwithstanding. They were self-denying, good people. Many a time have I seen the eldest of them (she that had been maid[100] to Mrs Jamieson) carrying out some delicate mess to a poor person. They only aped their betters in having 'nothing to do' with the class immediately below theirs, and when Miss Barker died, their profits and income were found to be such that Miss Betty was justified in shutting up shop and retiring from business. She also (as I think I have before said) set up her cow; a mark of respectability in Cranford almost as decided as setting up a gig[101] is among some people. She dressed finer than any lady in Cranford; and we did not wonder at it; for it was understood that she was wearing out all the bonnets and caps and outrageous ribbons which had once formed her stock-in-trade. It was five or six years since she had given up shop, so in any other place than Cranford her dress might have been considered *passée*.

And now Miss Betty Barker had called to invite Miss Matty to tea at her house on the following Tuesday. She gave me also an impromptu invitation, as I happened to be a visitor – though I could see she had a little fear lest, since my father had gone to live in Drumble, he might have engaged in that 'horrid cotton trade', and so dragged his family down out of 'aristocratic society'. She prefaced this invitation with so many apologies that she quite excited my curiosity. 'Her presumption' was to be excused. What had she been doing? She seemed so overpowered by it I could only think that she had been writing to Queen Adelaide to ask for a receipt for washing lace; but the act which she so characterised was only an invitation she had carried to her sister's former mistress, Mrs Jamieson. 'Her former occupation considered, could Miss Matty excuse the liberty?' Ah! thought I, she has found out that double cap, and is going to rectify Miss Matty's headdress. No! it was simply to extend her invitation to Miss Matty and to me. Miss Matty bowed acceptance; and I wondered that, in the graceful action, she did not feel the unusual weight and extraordinary height of her headdress. But I do not think she did, for she recovered her balance, and went on talking to Miss Betty in a kind, condescending manner, very different from the fidgety way she would have had if she had suspected how singular her appearance was.

'Mrs Jamieson is coming, I think you said?' asked Miss Matty.

'Yes. Mrs Jamieson most kindly and condescendingly said she would be happy to come. One little stipulation she made, that she should bring Carlo. I told her that if I had a weakness, it was for dogs.'

'And Miss Pole?' questioned Miss Matty, who was thinking of her pool at Preference, in which Carlo would not be available as a partner.

'I am going to ask Miss Pole. Of course, I could not think of asking her until I had asked you, madam – the rector's daughter, madam. Believe me, I do not forget the situation my father held under yours.'

'And Mrs Forrester, of course?'

'And Mrs Forrester. I thought, in fact, of going to her before I went to Miss Pole. Although her circumstances are changed, madam, she was born a Tyrrell, and we can never forget her alliance to the Bigges, of Bigelow Hall.'

Miss Matty cared much more for the little circumstance of her being a very good card-player.

'Mrs Fitz-Adam – I suppose – '

'No, madam. I must draw a line somewhere. Mrs Jamieson would not, I think, like to meet Mrs Fitz-Adam. I have the greatest respect for Mrs Fitz-Adam – but I cannot think her fit society for such ladies as Mrs Jamieson and Miss Matilda Jenkyns.'

Miss Betty Barker bowed low to Miss Matty, and pursed up her mouth. She looked at me with sidelong dignity, as much as to say, although a retired milliner, she was no democrat, and understood the difference of ranks.

'May I beg you to come as near half-past six, to my little dwelling, as possible, Miss Matilda? Mrs Jamieson dines at five, but has kindly promised not to delay her visit beyond that time – half-past six.' And with a swimming curtsey Miss Betty Barker took her leave.

My prophetic soul foretold a visit that afternoon from Miss Pole, who usually came to call on Miss Matilda after any event – or indeed in sight of any event – to talk it over with her.

'Miss Betty told me it was to be a choice and select few,' said Miss Pole, as she and Miss Matty compared notes.

'Yes, so she said. Not even Mrs Fitz-Adam.'

Now Mrs Fitz-Adam was the widowed sister of the Cranford surgeon, whom I have named before. Their parents were respectable farmers, content with their station. The name of these good people was Hoggins.[102] Mr Hoggins was the Cranford doctor now; we disliked the name and considered it coarse; but, as Miss Jenkyns said, if he changed it to Piggins it would not be much better. We had hoped to discover a relationship between him and that Marchioness of Exeter whose name was Molly Hoggins; but the man, careless of his own interests, utterly ignored and denied any such relationship, although, as dear Miss Jenkyns had said, he had a sister called Mary, and the same Christian names were very apt to run in families.

Soon after Miss Mary Hoggins married Mr Fitz-Adam, she disappeared from the neighbourhood for many years. She did not move in a sphere in Cranford society sufficiently high to make any of us care to know what Mr Fitz-Adam was. He died and was gathered to his fathers without our ever having thought about him at all. And then Mrs Fitz-Adam reappeared in Cranford ('as bold as a lion', Miss Pole said), a well-to-do widow, dressed in rustling black silk, so soon after her husband's death that poor Miss Jenkyns was justified in the remark she made, that 'bombazine[103] would have shown a deeper sense of her loss'.

I remember the convocation of ladies who assembled to decide whether or not Mrs Fitz-Adam should be called upon by the old blue-blooded inhabitants of Cranford. She had taken a large rambling house, which had been usually considered to confer a patent of gentility upon its tenant, because, once upon a time, seventy or eighty years before, the spinster daughter of an earl had resided in it.[104] I am not sure if the inhabiting this house was not also believed to convey some unusual power of intellect; for the earl's daughter, Lady Jane, had a sister, Lady Anne, who had married a general officer in the time of the American war,[105] and this general officer had written one or two comedies, which were still acted on the London boards, and which, when we saw them advertised, made us all draw up, and feel that Drury Lane was paying a very pretty compliment to Cranford. Still, it was not at all a settled thing that Mrs Fitz-Adam was to be visited, when dear Miss Jenkyns died; and, with her, something of the clear knowledge of the strict code of gentility went out too. As Miss Pole observed: 'As most of the ladies of good family in Cranford were elderly spinsters, or widows without children, if we did not relax a little, and become less exclusive, by and by we should have no society at all.'

Mrs Forrester continued on the same side.

'She had always understood that Fitz meant something aristocratic; there was Fitz-Roy – she thought that some of the King's children had been called Fitz-Roy; and there was Fitz-Clarence, now – they were the children of dear good King William the Fourth.[106] Fitz-Adam! – it was a pretty name, and she thought it very probably meant "Child of Adam". No one, who had not some good blood in their veins, would dare to be called Fitz; there was a deal in a name – she had had a cousin who spelt his name with two little ffs – ffoulkes – and he always looked down upon capital letters and said they belonged to lately invented families. She had been afraid he would die a bachelor, he was so very choice. When he met with a Mrs ffarringdon, at a watering-place, he took to her immediately; and a very pretty genteel woman she was – a widow, with a very good fortune; and "my cousin", Mr ffoulkes, married her; and it was all owing to her two little ffs.'

Mrs Fitz-Adam did not stand a chance of meeting with a Mr Fitz-anything in Cranford, so that could not have been her motive for settling there. Miss Matty thought it might have been the hope of being admitted into the society of the place, which would certainly be a very agreeable rise for *ci-devant*[107] Miss Hoggins; and if this had been her hope it would be cruel to disappoint her.

So everybody called upon Mrs Fitz-Adam – everybody but Mrs Jamieson, who used to show how honourable she was by never seeing Mrs Fitz-Adam when they met at the Cranford parties. There would be only eight or ten ladies in the room, and Mrs Fitz-Adam was the largest of all, and she invariably used to stand up when Mrs Jamieson came in, and curtsey very low to her whenever she turned in her direction – so low, in fact, that I think Mrs Jamieson must have looked at the wall above her, for she never moved a muscle of her face, no more than if she had not seen her. Still Mrs Fitz-Adam persevered.

The spring evenings were getting bright and long when three or four ladies in calashes met at Miss Barker's door. Do you know what a calash is? It is a covering worn over caps, not unlike the heads fastened on old-fashioned gigs; but sometimes it is not quite so large. This kind of headgear always made an awful impression on the children in Cranford; and now two or three left off their play in the quiet sunny little street, and gathered in wondering silence round Miss Pole, Miss Matty, and myself. We were silent too, so that we could hear loud, suppressed whispers inside Miss Barker's house: 'Wait, Peggy! wait till I've run upstairs and washed my hands. When I cough, open the door; I'll not be a minute.'

And, true enough it was not a minute before we heard a noise, between a sneeze and a crow; on which the door flew open. Behind it stood a round-eyed maiden, all aghast at the honourable company of calashes, who marched in without a word. She recovered presence of mind enough to usher us into a small room, which had been the shop, but was now converted into a temporary dressing-room. There we unpinned and shook ourselves, and arranged our features before the glass into a sweet and gracious company-face; and then, bowing backwards with 'After you, ma'am,' we allowed Mrs Forrester to take precedence up the narrow staircase that led to Miss Barker's drawing-room. There she sat, as stately and composed as though we had never heard that odd-sounding cough, from which her throat must have been even then sore and rough. Kind, gentle, shabbily dressed Mrs Forrester was immediately conducted to the second place of honour – a seat arranged something like Prince Albert's near the Queen's – good, but not so good. The place of pre-eminence was, of course, reserved for the Honourable Mrs Jamieson, who presently came panting up the stairs – Carlo rushing round her on her progress, as if he meant to trip her up.

And now Miss Betty Barker was a proud and happy woman! She stirred the fire, and shut the door, and sat as near to it as she could, quite on the edge of her chair. When Peggy came in, tottering under the weight of the tea-tray, I noticed that Miss Barker was sadly afraid lest Peggy should not keep her distance sufficiently. She and her mistress were on very familiar terms in their everyday intercourse, and Peggy wanted now to make several little confidences to her, which Miss Barker was on thorns to hear, but which she thought it her duty, as a lady, to repress. So she turned away from all Peggy's asides and signs; but she made one or two very malapropos answers to what was said; and at last, seized with a bright idea, she exclaimed: 'Poor, sweet Carlo! I'm forgetting him. Come downstairs with me, poor little doggie, and it shall have its tea, it shall!'

In a few minutes she returned, bland and benignant as before; but I thought she had forgotten to give the 'poor little doggie' anything to eat, judging by the avidity with which he swallowed down chance pieces of cake. The tea-tray was abundantly loaded – I was pleased to see it, I was so hungry; but I was afraid the ladies present might think it vulgarly heaped up. I know they would have done at their own houses; but somehow the heaps disappeared here. I saw Mrs Jamieson eating seed cake, slowly and considerately, as she did everything; and I was rather surprised, for I knew she had told us, on the occasion of her last party, that she never had it in her house, it reminded her so much of scented soap. She always gave us Savoy biscuits. However, Mrs Jamieson was kindly indulgent to Miss Barker's want of knowledge of the customs of high life; and, to spare her feelings, ate three large pieces of seed cake, with a placid, ruminating expression of countenance, not unlike a cow's.

After tea there was some little demur and difficulty. We were six in number; four could play at Preference, and for the other two there was Cribbage. But all, except myself (I was rather afraid of the Cranford ladies at cards, for it was the most earnest and serious business they ever engaged in), were anxious to be of the 'pool'. Even Miss Barker, while declaring she did not know Spadille from Manille,[108] was evidently hankering to take a hand. The dilemma was soon put an end to by a singular kind of noise. If a baron's daughter-in-law could ever be supposed to snore, I should have said Mrs Jamieson did so then; for, overcome by the heat of the room, and inclined to doze by nature, the temptation of that very comfortable armchair had been too much for her, and Mrs Jamieson was nodding. Once or twice she opened her eyes with an effort, and calmly but unconsciously smiled upon us; but by and by, even her benevolence was not equal to this exertion, and she was sound asleep.

'It is very gratifying to me,' whispered Miss Barker at the card-table to her three opponents, whom, notwithstanding her ignorance of the game, she was 'basting'[109] most unmercifully – 'very gratifying indeed, to see how completely Mrs Jamieson feels at home in my poor little dwelling; she could not have paid me a greater compliment.'

Miss Barker provided me with some literature in the shape of three or four handsomely bound fashion-books ten or twelve years old, observing, as she put a little table and a candle for my especial benefit, that she knew young people liked to look at pictures. Carlo lay and snorted, and started at his mistress's feet. He, too, was quite at home.

The card-table was an animated scene to watch; four ladies' heads, with niddle-noddling caps, all nearly meeting over the middle of the table in their eagerness to whisper quick enough and loud enough: and every now and then came Miss Barker's 'Hush, ladies! if you please, hush! Mrs Jamieson is asleep.'

It was very difficult to steer clear between Mrs Forrester's deafness and Mrs Jamieson's sleepiness. But Miss Barker managed her arduous task well. She repeated the whisper to Mrs Forrester, distorting her face considerably, in order to show, by the motions of her lips, what was said; and then she smiled kindly all round at us, and murmured to herself: 'Very gratifying, indeed; I wish my poor sister had been alive to see this day.'

Presently the door was thrown wide open; Carlo started to his feet, with a loud snapping bark, and Mrs Jamieson awoke: or, perhaps, she had not been asleep – as she said almost directly, the room had been so light she had been glad to keep her eyes shut, but had been listening with great interest to all our amusing and agreeable conversation. Peggy came in once more, red with importance. Another tray! 'Oh, gentility!' thought I, 'can you endure this last shock?' For Miss Barker had ordered (nay, I doubt not, prepared, although she did say: 'Why, Peggy, what have you brought us?' and looked pleasantly surprised at the unexpected pleasure) all sorts of good things for supper – scalloped oysters, potted lobsters, jelly, a dish called 'little Cupids' (which was in great favour with the Cranford ladies, although too expensive to be given, except on solemn and state occasions – macaroons sopped in brandy, I should have called it, if I had not known its more refined and classical name). In short, we were evidently to be feasted with all that was sweetest and best; and we thought it better to submit graciously, even at the cost of our gentility – which never ate suppers in general, but which, like most non-supper-eaters, was particularly hungry on all special occasions.

Miss Barker, in her former sphere, had, I dare say, been made acquainted with the beverage they call cherry-brandy. We none of us had ever seen such a thing, and rather shrank back when she proffered it us – 'just a little, leetle glass, ladies; after the oysters and lobsters, you know. Shellfish are sometimes thought not very wholesome.' We all shook our heads like female mandarins;[110] but, at last, Mrs Jamieson suffered herself to be persuaded, and we followed her lead. It was not exactly unpalatable, though so hot and so strong that we thought ourselves bound to give evidence that we were not accustomed to such things by coughing terribly – almost as strangely as Miss Barker had done, before we were admitted by Peggy.

'It's very strong,' said Miss Pole, as she put down her empty glass; 'I do believe there's spirit in it.'

'Only a little drop – just necessary to make it keep,' said Miss Barker. 'You know we put brandy-pepper over our preserves to make them keep. I often feel tipsy myself from eating damson tart.'

I question whether damson tart would have opened Mrs Jamieson's heart as the cherry-brandy did; but she told us of a coming event, respecting which she had been quite silent till that moment.

'My sister-in-law, Lady Glenmire, is coming to stay with me.'

There was a chorus of 'Indeed!' and then a pause. Each one rapidly reviewed her wardrobe, as to its fitness to appear in the presence of a baron's widow; for, of course, a series of small festivals were always held in Cranford on the arrival of a visitor at any of our friends' houses. We felt very pleasantly excited on the present occasion.

Not long after this the maids and the lanterns were announced. Mrs Jamieson had the sedan-chair,[111] which had squeezed itself into Miss Barker's narrow lobby with some difficulty, and most literally 'stopped the way'. It required some skilful manoeuvring on the part of the old chairmen (shoemakers by day, but when summoned to carry the sedan dressed up in a strange old livery – long greatcoats, with small capes, coeval with the sedan, and similar to the dress of the class in Hogarth's pictures) to edge, and back, and try at it again, and finally to succeed in carrying their burden out of Miss Barker's front door. Then we heard their quick pit-a-pat along the quiet little street as we put on our calashes and pinned up our gowns; Miss Barker hovering about us with offers of help, which, if she had not remembered her former occupation, and wished us to forget it, would have been much more pressing.

CHAPTER 8

'Your Ladyship'

EARLY THE NEXT MORNING – directly after twelve – Miss Pole made her appearance at Miss Matty's. Some very trifling piece of business was alleged as a reason for the call; but there was evidently something behind. At last out it came.

'By the way, you'll think I'm strangely ignorant; but, do you really know, I am puzzled how we ought to address Lady Glenmire. Do you say, "Your Ladyship", where you would say "you" to a common person? I have been puzzling all morning; and are we to say "My Lady", instead of "Ma'am"? Now you knew Lady Arley – will you kindly tell me the most correct way of speaking to the peerage?'

Poor Miss Matty! she took off her spectacles and she put them on again – but how Lady Arley was addressed, she could not remember.

'It is so long ago,' she said. 'Dear! dear! how stupid I am! I don't think I ever saw her more than twice. I know we used to call Sir Peter, "Sir Peter" – but he came much oftener to see us than Lady Arley did. Deborah would have known in a minute. "My lady" – "your ladyship". It sounds very strange, and as if it was not natural. I never thought of it before; but, now you have named it, I am all in a puzzle.'

It was very certain Miss Pole would obtain no wise decision from Miss Matty, who got more bewildered every moment, and more perplexed as to etiquettes of address.

'Well, I really think,' said Miss Pole, 'I had better just go and tell Mrs Forrester about our little difficulty. One sometimes grows nervous; and yet one would not have Lady Glenmire think we were quite ignorant of the etiquettes of high life in Cranford.'

'And will you just step in here, dear Miss Pole, as you come back, please, and tell me what you decide upon? Whatever you and Mrs Forrester fix upon, will be quite right, I'm sure. "Lady Arley", "Sir Peter",' said Miss Matty to herself, trying to recall the old forms of words.

'Who is Lady Glenmire?' asked I.

'Oh, she's the widow of Mr Jamieson – that's Mrs Jamieson's late husband, you know – widow of his eldest brother. Mrs Jamieson was a Miss Walker, daughter of Governor Walker. "Your ladyship". My dear, if they fix on that way of speaking, you must just let me practise a little on you first, for I shall feel so foolish and hot saying it the first time to Lady Glenmire.'

It was really a relief to Miss Matty when Mrs Jamieson came on a very unpolite errand. I notice that apathetic people have more quiet impertinence than others; and Mrs Jamieson came now to insinuate pretty plainly that she did not particularly wish that the Cranford ladies should call upon her sister-in-law. I can hardly say how she made this clear; for I grew very indignant and warm, while with slow deliberation she was explaining her wishes to Miss Matty, who, a true lady herself, could hardly understand the feeling which made Mrs Jamieson wish to appear to her noble sister-in-law as if she only visited 'county' families.[112] Miss Matty remained puzzled and perplexed long after I had found out the object of Mrs Jamieson's visit.

When she did understand the drift of the honourable lady's call, it was pretty to see with what quiet dignity she received the intimation thus uncourteously given. She was not in the least hurt – she was of too gentle a spirit for that; nor was she exactly conscious of disapproving of Mrs Jamieson's conduct; but there was something of this feeling in her mind, I am sure, which made her pass from the subject to others in a less flurried and more composed manner than usual. Mrs Jamieson was, indeed, the more flurried of the two, and I could see she was glad to take her leave.

A little while afterwards Miss Pole returned, red and indignant. 'Well! to be sure! You've had Mrs Jamieson here, I find from Martha; and we are not to call on Lady Glenmire. Yes! I met Mrs Jamieson, halfway between here and Mrs Forrester's, and she told me; she took me so by surprise, I had nothing to say. I wish I had thought of something very sharp and sarcastic; I dare say I shall tonight. And Lady Glenmire is but the widow of a Scotch baron after all! I went on to look at Mrs Forrester's Peerage, to see who this lady was, that is to be kept under a glass case: widow of a Scotch peer – never sat in the House of Lords[113] – and as poor as Job, I dare say; and she – fifth daughter of some Mr Campbell or other. You are the daughter of a rector, at any rate, and related to the Arleys; and Sir Peter might have been Viscount Arley, everyone says.'

Miss Matty tried to soothe Miss Pole, but in vain.

That lady, usually so kind and good-humoured, was now in a full flow of anger.

'And I went and ordered a cap this morning, to be quite ready,' said she at last, letting out the secret which gave sting to Mrs Jamieson's intimation. 'Mrs Jamieson shall see if it is so easy to get me to make fourth at a pool when she has none of her fine Scotch relations with her!'

In coming out of church, the first Sunday on which Lady Glenmire appeared in Cranford, we sedulously talked together, and turned our backs on Mrs Jamieson and her guest. If we might not call on her, we would not even look at her, though we were dying with curiosity to know what she was like. We had the comfort of questioning Martha in the afternoon. Martha did not belong to a sphere of society whose observation could be an implied compliment to Lady Glenmire, and Martha had made good use of her eyes.

'Well, ma'am! is it the little lady with Mrs Jamieson, you mean? I thought you would like more to know how young Mrs Smith was dressed; her being a bride.' (Mrs Smith was the butcher's wife.)

Miss Pole said: 'Good gracious me! as if we cared about a Mrs Smith'; but was silent as Martha resumed her speech.

'The little lady in Mrs Jamieson's pew had on, ma'am, rather an old black silk, and a shepherd's plaid cloak, ma'am, and very bright black eyes she had, ma'am, and a pleasant, sharp face; not over young, ma'am, but yet, I should guess, younger than Mrs Jamieson herself. She looked up and down the church, like a bird, and nipped up her petticoats, when she came out, as quick and sharp as ever I see. I'll tell you what, ma'am, she's more like Mrs Deacon, at the Coach and Horses, nor anyone.'

'Hush, Martha!' said Miss Matty, 'that's not respectful.'

'Isn't it, ma'am? I beg pardon, I'm sure; but Jem Hearn said so as well. He said, she was just such a sharp, stirring sort of a body – '

'Lady,' said Miss Pole.

'Lady – as Mrs Deacon.'

Another Sunday passed away, and we still averted our eyes from Mrs Jamieson and her guest, and made remarks to ourselves that we thought were very severe – almost too much so. Miss Matty was evidently uneasy at our sarcastic manner of speaking.

Perhaps by this time Lady Glenmire had found out that Mrs Jamieson's was not the gayest, liveliest house in the world; perhaps Mrs Jamieson had found out that most of the county families were in London, and that those who remained in the country were not so alive as they might have been to the circumstance of Lady Glenmire being in their neighbourhood. Great events spring out of small causes; so I will not pretend to say what induced Mrs Jamieson to alter her determination of excluding the Cranford ladies, and send notes of invitation all round for a small party on the following Tuesday. Mr Mulliner himself brought them round. He *would* always ignore the fact of there being a back door to any house, and gave a louder rat-tat than his mistress, Mrs Jamieson. He had three little notes, which he carried in a large basket, in order to impress his mistress with an idea of their great weight, though they might easily have gone into his waistcoat pocket.

Miss Matty and I quietly decided that we would have a previous engagement at home: it was the evening on which Miss Matty usually made candle-lighters of all the notes and letters of the week; for on Mondays her accounts were always made straight – not a penny owing from the week before; so, by a natural arrangement, making candle-lighters fell upon a Tuesday evening, and gave us a legitimate excuse for declining Mrs Jamieson's invitation. But before our answer was written, in came Miss Pole, with an open note in her hand.

'So!' she said. 'Ah! I see you have got your note, too. Better late than never. I could have told my Lady Glenmire she would be glad enough of our society before a fortnight was over.'

'Yes,' said Miss Matty, 'we're asked for Tuesday evening. And perhaps you would just kindly bring your work across and drink tea with us that night. It is my usual regular time for looking over the last week's bills, and notes, and letters, and making candle-lighters of them; but that does not seem quite reason enough for saying I have a previous engagement at home, though I meant to make it do. Now, if you would come, my conscience would be quite at ease, and luckily the note is not written yet.'

I saw Miss Pole's countenance change while Miss Matty was speaking.

'Don't you mean to go then?' asked she.

'Oh, no!' said Miss Matty quietly. 'You don't either, I suppose?'

'I don't know,' replied Miss Pole. 'Yes, I think I do,' said she, rather briskly; and on seeing Miss Matty look surprised, she added: 'You see, one would not like Mrs Jamieson to think that anything she could do, or say, was of consequence enough to give offence; it would be a kind of letting down of ourselves, that I, for one, should not like. It would be too flattering to Mrs Jamieson if we allowed her to suppose that what she had said affected us a week, nay ten days afterwards.'

'Well! I suppose it is wrong to be hurt and annoyed so long about anything; and, perhaps, after all, she did not mean to vex us. But I must say, I could not have brought myself to say the things Mrs Jamieson did about our not calling. I really don't think I shall go.'

'Oh, come! Miss Matty, you must go; you know our friend Mrs Jamieson is much more phlegmatic than most people, and does not enter into the little delicacies of feeling which you possess in so remarkable a degree.'

'I thought you possessed them, too, that day Mrs Jamieson called to tell us not to go,' said Miss Matty innocently.

But Miss Pole, in addition to her delicacies of feeling, possessed a very smart cap, which she was anxious to show to an admiring world; and so she seemed to forget all her angry words uttered not a fortnight before, and to be ready to act on what she called the great Christian principle of 'Forgive and forget'; and she lectured dear Miss Matty so long on this head that she absolutely ended by assuring her it was her duty, as a deceased rector's daughter, to buy a new cap and go to the party at Mrs Jamieson's. So 'we were most happy to accept', instead of 'regretting that we were obliged to decline'.

The expenditure on dress in Cranford was principally in that one article referred to. If the heads were buried in smart new caps, the ladies were like ostriches, and cared not what became of their bodies. Old gowns, white and venerable collars, any number of brooches, up and down and everywhere (some with dogs' eyes painted in them; some that were like small picture frames with mausoleums and weeping willows neatly executed in hair inside; some, again, with miniatures of ladies and gentlemen sweetly smiling out of a nest of stiff muslin), old brooches for a permanent ornament, and new caps to suit the fashion of the day – the ladies of Cranford always dressed with chaste elegance and propriety, as Miss Barker once prettily expressed it.

And with three new caps, and a greater array of brooches than had ever been seen together at one time since Cranford was a town, did Mrs Forrester, and Miss Matty, and Miss Pole appear on that memorable Tuesday evening. I counted seven brooches myself on Miss Pole's dress. Two were fixed negligently in her cap (one was a butterfly made of Scotch pebbles, which a vivid imagination might believe to be the real insect); one fastened her net neckerchief; one her collar; one ornamented the front of her gown, midway between her throat and waist; and another adorned the point of her stomacher.[114] Where the seventh was I have forgotten, but it was somewhere about her, I am sure.

But I am getting on too fast, in describing the dresses of the company. I should first relate the gathering on the way to Mrs Jamieson's. That lady lived in a large house just outside the town.[115] A road which had known what it was to be a street ran right before the house, which opened out upon it without any intervening garden or court. Whatever the sun was about, he never shone on the front of that house. To be sure, the living-rooms were at the back, looking on to a pleasant garden; the front windows only belonged to kitchens and housekeepers' rooms, and pantries, and in one of them Mr Mulliner was reported to sit. Indeed, looking askance, we often saw the back of a head covered with hair powder, which also extended itself over his coat-collar down to his very waist; and this imposing back was always engaged in reading the *St James's Chronicle*, opened wide, which, in some degree, accounted for the length of time the said newspaper was in reaching us – equal subscribers with Mrs Jamieson, though, in right of her honourableness, she always had the reading of it first. This very Tuesday, the delay in forwarding the last number had been particularly aggravating; just when both Miss Pole and Miss Matty, the former more especially, had been wanting to see it, in order to coach up the Court news ready for the evening's interview with aristocracy. Miss Pole told us she had absolutely taken time by the forelock, and been dressed by five o'clock, in order to be ready if the *St James's Chronicle* should come in at the last moment – the very *St James's Chronicle* which the powdered head was tranquilly and composedly reading as we passed the accustomed window this evening.

'The impudence of the man!' said Miss Pole, in a low indignant whisper. 'I should like to ask him whether his mistress pays her quarter-share for his exclusive use.'

We looked at her in admiration of the courage of her thought; for Mr Mulliner was an object of great awe to all of us. He seemed never to have forgotten his condescension in coming to live at Cranford. Miss Jenkyns, at times, had stood forth as the undaunted champion of her sex, and spoken to him on terms of equality; but even Miss Jenkyns could get no higher. In his pleasantest and most gracious moods he looked like a sulky cockatoo. He did not speak except in gruff monosyllables. He would wait in the hall when we begged him not to wait, and then look deeply offended because we had kept him there, while, with trembling, hasty hands we prepared ourselves for appearing in company.

Miss Pole ventured on a small joke as we went upstairs, intended, though addressed to us, to afford Mr Mulliner some slight amusement. We all smiled, in order to seem as if we felt at our ease, and timidly looked for Mr Mulliner's sympathy. Not a muscle of that wooden face had relaxed; and we were grave in an instant.

Mrs Jamieson's drawing-room was cheerful; the evening sun came streaming into it, and the large square window was clustered round with flowers. The furniture was white and gold; not the later style, Louis Quatorze,[116] I think they call it, all shells and twirls; no, Mrs Jamieson's chairs and tables had not a curve or bend about them. The chair and table legs diminished as they neared the ground, and were straight and square in all their corners. The chairs were all a-row against the walls, with the exception of four or five which stood in a circle round the fire. They were railed with white bars across the back, and knobbed with gold; neither the railings nor the knobs invited to ease. There was a japanned table devoted to literature, on which lay a Bible, a Peerage, and a Prayer-Book. There was another square Pembroke table dedicated to the Fine Arts, on which were a kaleidoscope, conversation-cards, puzzle-cards[117] (tied together to an interminable length with faded pink satin ribbon), and a box painted in fond imitation of the drawings which decorate tea-chests. Carlo lay on the worsted-worked rug, and ungraciously barked at us as we entered. Mrs Jamieson stood up, giving us each a torpid smile of welcome, and looking helplessly beyond us at Mr Mulliner, as if she hoped he would place us in chairs, for, if he did not, she never could. I suppose he thought we could find our way to the circle round the fire, which reminded me of Stonehenge, I don't know why. Lady Glenmire came to the rescue of our hostess, and, somehow or other, we found ourselves for the first time placed agreeably, and not formally, in Mrs Jamieson's house. Lady Glenmire, now we had time to look at her, proved to be a bright little woman of middle age, who had been very pretty in the days of her youth, and who was even yet very pleasant-looking. I saw Miss Pole appraising her dress in the first five minutes, and I take her word when she said the next day: 'My dear! ten pounds would have purchased every stitch she had on – lace and all.'

It was pleasant to suspect that a peeress could be poor, and partly reconciled us to the fact that her husband had never sat in the House of Lords, which, when we first heard of it, seemed a kind of swindling us out of our prospects on false pretences; a sort of 'A Lord and No Lord'[118] business.

We were all very silent at first. We were thinking what we could talk about, that should be high enough to interest My Lady. There had been a rise in the price of sugar, which, as preserving-time was near, was a piece of intelligence to all our housekeeping hearts, and would have been the natural topic if Lady Glenmire had not been by. But we were not sure if the peerage ate preserves – much less knew how they were made. At last, Miss Pole, who had always a great deal of courage and *savoir faire*, spoke to Lady Glenmire, who on her part had seemed just as much puzzled to know how to break the silence as we were.

'Has your ladyship been to Court lately?' asked she; and then gave a little glance round at us, half timid and half triumphant, as much as to say: 'See how judiciously I have chosen a subject befitting the rank of the stranger.'

'I never was there in my life,' said Lady Glenmire, with a broad Scotch accent, but in a very sweet voice. And then, as if she had been too abrupt, she added: 'We very seldom went to London – only twice, in fact, during all my married life; and before I was married my father had far too large a family' (fifth daughter of Mr Campbell was in all our minds, I am sure) 'to take us often from our home, even to Edinburgh. Ye'll have been in Edinburgh, maybe?' said she, suddenly brightening up with the hope of a common interest. We had none of us been there; but Miss Pole had an uncle who once had passed a night there, which was very pleasant.

Mrs Jamieson, meanwhile, was absorbed in wonder why Mr Mulliner did not bring the tea; and at length the wonder oozed out of her mouth.

'I had better ring the bell, my dear, had not I?' said Lady Glenmire briskly.

'No – I think not – Mulliner does not like to be hurried.'

We should have liked our tea, for we dined at an earlier hour than Mrs Jamieson. I suspect Mr Mulliner had to finish the *St James's Chronicle* before he chose to trouble himself about tea. His mistress fidgeted and fidgeted, and kept saying: 'I can't think why Mulliner does not bring tea. I can't think what he can be about.' And Lady Glenmire at last grew quite impatient, but it was a pretty kind of impatience after all; and she rang the bell rather sharply, on receiving a half-permission from her sister-in-law to do so. Mr Mulliner appeared in dignified surprise. 'Oh!' said Mrs Jamieson, 'Lady Glenmire rang the bell; and I believe it was for tea.'

In a few minutes tea was brought. Very delicate was the china, very old the plate, very thin the bread and butter, and very small the lumps of sugar. Sugar was evidently Mrs Jamieson's favourite economy. I question if the little filigree sugar-tongs, made something like scissors, could have opened themselves wide enough to take up an honest, vulgar good-sized piece; and when I tried to seize two little minnikin pieces at once, so as not to be detected in too many returns to the sugar-basin, they absolutely dropped one, with a little sharp clatter, quite in a malicious and unnatural manner. But before this happened we had had a slight disappointment. In the little silver jug was cream, in the larger one was milk. As soon as Mulliner came in, Carlo began to beg, which was a thing our manners forbade us to do, though I am sure we were just as hungry; and Mrs Jamieson said she was certain we would excuse her if she gave her poor dumb Carlo his tea first. She accordingly mixed a saucerful for him, and put it down for him to lap; and then she told us how intelligent and sensible the dear little fellow was; he knew cream quite well, and constantly refused tea with only milk in it: so the milk was left for us; but we silently thought we were quite as intelligent and sensible as Carlo, and felt as if insult were added to injury when we were called upon to admire the gratitude evinced by his wagging his tail for the cream which should have been ours.

After tea we thawed down into common-life subjects. We were thankful to Lady Glenmire for having proposed some more bread and butter, and this mutual want made us better acquainted with her than we should ever have been with talking about the Court, though Miss Pole did say she had hoped to know how the dear Queen was from someone who had seen her.

The friendship begun over bread and butter extended on to cards. Lady Glenmire played Preference to admiration, and was a complete authority as to Ombre and Quadrille. Even Miss Pole quite forgot to say 'my lady', and 'your ladyship', and said 'Basto! ma'am'; 'you have Spadille, I believe', just as quietly as if we had never held the great Cranford Parliament on the subject of the proper mode of addressing a peeress.

As a proof of how thoroughly we had forgotten that we were in the presence of one who might have sat down to tea with a coronet, instead of a cap, on her head, Mrs Forrester related a curious little fact to Lady Glenmire – an anecdote known to the circle of her intimate friends, but of which even Mrs Jamieson was not aware. It related to some fine old lace, the sole relic of better days, which Lady Glenmire was admiring on Mrs Forrester's collar.

'Yes,' said that lady, 'such lace cannot be got now for either love or money; made by the nuns abroad, they tell me. They say that they can't make it now even there. But perhaps they can now they've passed the Catholic Emancipation Bill.[119] I should not wonder. But, in the meantime, I treasure up my lace very much. I daren't even trust the washing of it to my maid' (the little charity schoolgirl I have named before, but who sounded well as 'my maid'). 'I always wash it myself. And once it had a narrow escape. Of course, your ladyship knows that such lace must never be starched or ironed. Some people wash it in sugar and water, and some in coffee, to make it the right yellow colour; but I myself have a very good receipt for washing it in milk, which stiffens it enough, and gives it a very good creamy colour. Well, ma'am, I had tacked it together (and the beauty of this fine lace is that, when it is wet, it goes into a very little space), and put it to soak in milk, when, unfortunately, I left the room; on my return, I found pussy on the table, looking very like a thief, but gulping very uncomfortably, as if she was half-choked with something she wanted to swallow and could not. And, would you believe it? At first I pitied her, and said "Poor pussy! poor pussy!" till, all at once, I looked and saw the cup of milk empty – cleaned out! "You naughty cat!" said I, and I believe I was provoked enough to give her a slap, which did no good, but only helped the lace down – just as one slaps a choking child on the back. I could have cried, I was so vexed; but I determined I would not give the lace up without a struggle for it. I hoped the lace might disagree with her, at any rate; but it would have been too much for Job, if he had seen, as I did, that cat come in, quite placid and purring, not a quarter of an hour after, and almost expecting to be stroked, "No, pussy!" said I, "if you have any conscience you ought not to expect that!" And then a thought struck me; and I rang the bell for my maid, and sent her to Mr Hoggins, with my compliments, and would he be kind enough to lend me one of his top-boots for an hour? I did not think there was anything odd in the message; but Jenny said the young men in the surgery laughed as if they would be ill at my wanting a top-boot. When it came, Jenny and I put pussy in, with her forefeet straight down, so that they were fastened, and could not scratch, and we gave her a teaspoonful of currant jelly in which (your ladyship must excuse me) I had mixed some tartar emetic. I shall never forget how anxious I was for the next half-hour. I took pussy to my own room, and spread a clean towel on the floor. I could have kissed her when she returned the lace to sight, very much as it had gone down. Jenny had boiling water ready, and we soaked it and soaked it, and spread it on a lavender-bush in the sun before I could touch it again, even to put it in milk. But now your ladyship would never guess that it had been in pussy's inside.'[120]

We found out, in the course of the evening, that Lady Glenmire was going to pay Mrs Jamieson a long visit, as she had given up her apartments in Edinburgh, and had no ties to take her back there in a hurry. On the whole, we were rather glad to hear this, for she had made a pleasant impression upon us; and it was also very comfortable to find, from things which dropped out in the course of conversation, that, in addition to many other genteel qualities, she was far removed from the 'vulgarity of wealth'.

'Don't you find it very unpleasant walking?' asked Mrs Jamieson, as our respective servants were announced. It was a pretty regular question from Mrs Jamieson, who had her own carriage in the coach-house, and always went out in a sedan-chair to the very shortest distances. The answers were nearly as much a matter of course.

'Oh dear, no! it is so pleasant and still at night!' 'Such a refreshment after the excitement of a party!' 'The stars are so beautiful!' This last was from Miss Matty.

'Are you fond of astronomy?' Lady Glenmire asked.

'Not very,' replied Miss Matty, rather confused at the moment to remember which was astronomy and which was astrology – but the answer was true under either circumstance, for she read, and was slightly alarmed at, Francis Moore's astrological predictions;[121] and, as to astronomy, in a private and confidential conversation, she had told me she never could believe that the earth was moving constantly, and that she would not believe it if she could, it made her feel so tired and dizzy whenever she thought about it.

In our pattens, we picked our way home with extra care that night, so refined and delicate were our perceptions after drinking tea with 'my lady'.

CHAPTER 9

Signor Brunoni

SOON AFTER THE EVENTS of which I gave an account in my last paper, I was summoned home by my father's illness; and for a time I forgot, in anxiety about him, to wonder how my dear friends at Cranford were getting on, or how Lady Glenmire could reconcile herself to the dullness of the long visit which she was still paying to her sister-in-law, Mrs Jamieson. When my father grew a little stronger I accompanied him to the seaside, so that altogether I seemed banished from Cranford, and was deprived of the opportunity of hearing any chance intelligence of the dear little town for the greater part of that year.

Late in November – when we had returned home again, and my father was once more in good health – I received a letter from Miss Matty; and a very mysterious letter it was. She began many sentences without ending them, running them one into another, in much the same confused sort of way in which written words run together on blotting-paper. All I could make out was that, if my father was better (which she hoped he was), and would take warning and wear a great-coat from Michaelmas to Lady Day, if turbans were in fashion, could I tell her? Such a piece of gaiety was going to happen as had not been seen or known of since Wombwell's lions[122] came, when one of them ate a little child's arm; and she was, perhaps, too old to care about dress, but a new cap she must have; and, having heard that turbans were worn, and some of the county families likely to come, she would like to look tidy, if I would bring her a cap from the milliner I employed; and oh, dear! how careless of her to forget that she wrote to beg I would come and pay her a visit next Tuesday; when she hoped to have something to offer me in the way of amusement, which she would not now more particularly describe, only sea-green was her favourite colour. So she ended her letter; but in a postscript. she added, she thought she might as well tell me what was the peculiar attraction to Cranford just now; Signor Brunoni was going to exhibit his wonderful magic in the Cranford Assembly Rooms on Wednesday and Friday evenings in the following week.

I was very glad to accept the invitation from my dear Miss Matty, independently of the conjuror, and most particularly anxious to prevent her from disfiguring her small, gentle, mousy face with a great Saracen's head turban; and accordingly, I bought her a pretty, neat, middle-aged cap, which, however, was rather a disappointment to her when, on my arrival, she followed me into my bedroom, ostensibly to poke the fire, but in reality, I do believe, to see if the sea-green turban was not inside the cap-box with which I had travelled. It was in vain that I twirled the cap round on my hand to exhibit back and side fronts: her heart had been set upon a turban, and all she could do was to say, with resignation in her look and voice: 'I am sure you did your best, my dear. It is just like the caps all the ladies in Cranford are wearing, and they have had theirs for a year, I dare say. I should have liked something newer, I confess – something more like the turbans Miss Betty Barker tells me Queen Adelaide wears; but it is very pretty, my dear. And I dare say lavender will wear better than sea-green. Well, after all, what is dress, that we should care anything about it? You'll tell me if you want anything, my dear. Here is the bell. I suppose turbans have not got down to Drumble yet?'

So saying, the dear old lady gently bemoaned herself out of the room, leaving me to dress for the evening, when, as she informed me, she expected Miss Pole and Mrs Forrester, and she hoped I should not feel myself too much tired to join the party. Of course I should not; and I made some haste to unpack and arrange my dress; but, with all my speed, I heard the arrivals and the buzz of conversation in the next room before I was ready. Just as I opened the door, I caught the words: 'I was foolish to expect anything very genteel out of the Drumble shops; poor girl! she did her best, I've no doubt.' But, for all that, I had rather that she blamed Drumble and me than disfigured herself with a turban.

Miss Pole was always the person, in the trio of Cranford ladies now assembled, to have had adventures. She was in the habit of spending the morning in rambling from shop to shop, not to purchase anything (except an occasional reel of cotton or a piece of tape), but to see the new articles and report upon them, and to collect all the stray pieces of intelligence in the town. She had a way, too, of demurely popping hither and thither into all sorts of places to gratify her curiosity on any point – a way which, if she had not looked so very genteel and prim, might have been considered impertinent. And now, by the expressive way in which she cleared her throat, and waited for all minor subjects (such as caps and turbans) to be cleared off the course, we knew she had something very particular to relate, when the due pause came – and I defy any people possessed of common modesty to keep up a conversation long, where one among them sits up aloft in silence, looking down upon all the things they chance to say as trivial and contemptible compared to what they could disclose, if properly entreated. Miss Pole began: 'As I was stepping out of Gordon's shop today, I chanced to go into the George[123] (my Betty has a second cousin who is chambermaid there, and I thought Betty would like to hear how she was), and, not seeing anyone about, I strolled up the staircase, and found myself in the passage leading to the Assembly Room (you and I remember the Assembly Room, I am sure, Miss Matty! and the *minuets de la cour*!);[124] so I went on, not thinking of what I was about, when, all at once, I perceived that I was in the middle of the preparations for tomorrow night – the room being divided with great clothes-maids, over which Crosby's men were tacking red flannel; very dark and odd it seemed; it quite bewildered me, and I was going on behind the screens, in my absence of mind, when a gentleman (quite the gentleman, I can assure you) stepped forwards and asked if I had any business he could arrange for me. He spoke such pretty broken English, I could not help thinking of *Thaddeus of Warsaw*, and *The Hungarian Brothers*, and *Santo Sebastiani*;[125] and while I was busy picturing his past life to myself, he had bowed me out of the room. But wait a minute! You have not heard half my story yet! I was going downstairs, when who should I meet but Betty's second cousin. So, of course, I stopped to speak to her for Betty's sake; and she told me that I had really seen the conjuror – the gentleman who spoke broken English was Signor Brunoni himself. Just at this moment he passed us on the stairs, making such a graceful bow! in reply to which I dropped a curtsey – all foreigners have such polite manners, one catches something of it. But when he had gone downstairs, I bethought me that I had dropped my glove in the Assembly Room (it was safe in my muff all the time, but I never found it till afterwards); so I went back, and, just as I was creeping up the passage left on one side of the great screen that goes nearly across the room, who should I see but the very same gentleman that had met me before, and passed me on the stairs, coming now forwards from the inner part of the room, to which there is no entrance – you remember, Miss Matty – and just repeating, in his pretty broken English, the enquiry if I had any business there – I don't mean that he put it quite so bluntly, but he seemed very determined that I should not pass the screen – so, of course, I explained about my glove, which, curiously enough, I found at that very moment.'

Miss Pole, then, had seen the conjuror – the real, live conjuror! and numerous were the questions we all asked her. 'Had he a beard?' 'Was he young, or old?' 'Fair, or dark?' 'Did he look – ' (unable to shape my question prudently, I put it in another form) – 'How did he look?' In short, Miss Pole was the heroine of the evening, owing to her morning's encounter. If she was not the rose (that is to say the conjuror) she had been near it.[126]

Conjuration, sleight of hand, magic, witchcraft, were the subjects of the evening. Miss Pole was slightly sceptical, and inclined to think there might be a scientific solution found for even the proceedings of the Witch of Endor.[127] Mrs Forrester believed everything, from ghosts to death-watches. Miss Matty ranged between the two – always convinced by the last speaker. I think she was naturally more inclined to Mrs Forrester's side, but a desire of proving herself a worthy sister to Miss Jenkyns kept her equally balanced – Miss Jenkyns, who would never allow a servant to call the little rolls of tallow that formed themselves round candles 'winding-sheets', but insisted on their being spoken of as 'roly-polys'! A sister of hers to be superstitious! It would never do.

After tea, I was dispatched downstairs into the dining-parlour for that volume of the old Encyclopaedia which contained the nouns beginning with C, in order that Miss Pole might prime herself with scientific explanations for the tricks of the following evening. It spoilt the pool at Preference which Miss Matty and Mrs Forrester had been looking forward to, for Miss Pole became so much absorbed in her subject, and the plates by which it was illustrated, that we felt it would be cruel to disturb her otherwise than by one or two well-timed yawns, which I threw in now and then, for I was really touched by the meek way in which the two ladies were bearing their disappointment. But Miss Pole only read the more zealously, imparting to us no more information than this: 'Ah! I see; I comprehend perfectly. A represents the ball. Put A between B and D – no! between C and F, and turn the second joint of the third finger of your left hand over the wrist of your right H. Very clear indeed! My dear Mrs Forrester, conjuring and witchcraft is a mere affair of the alphabet. Do let me read you this one passage?'

Mrs Forrester implored Miss Pole to spare her, saying, from a child upwards, she never could understand being read aloud to; and I dropped the pack of cards, which I had been shuffling very audibly, and by this discreet movement I obliged Miss Pole to perceive that Preference was to have been the order of the evening, and to propose, rather unwillingly, that the pool should commence. The pleasant brightness that stole over the other two ladies' faces on this! Miss Matty had one or two twinges of self-reproach for having interrupted Miss Pole in her studies: and did not remember her cards well, or give her full attention to the game, until she had soothed her conscience by offering to lend the volume of the Encyclopaedia to Miss Pole, who accepted it thankfully, and said Betty should take it home when she came with the lantern.

The next evening we were all in a little gentle flutter at the idea of the gaiety before us. Miss Matty went up to dress betimes, and hurried me until I was ready, when we found we had an hour and a half to wait before the 'doors opened at seven precisely'. And we had only twenty yards to go! However, as Miss Matty said, it would not do to get too much absorbed in anything, and forget the time; so she thought we had better sit quietly, without lighting the candles, till five minutes to seven. So Miss Matty dozed, and I knitted.

At length we set off; and at the door under the carriageway at the George, we met Mrs Forrester and Miss Pole: the latter was discussing the subject of the evening with more vehemence than ever, and throwing A's and B's at our heads like hailstones. She had even copied one or two of the 'receipts' – as she called them – for the different tricks, on backs of letters, ready to explain and to detect Signor Brunoni's arts.

We went into the cloakroom adjoining the Assembly Room; Miss Matty gave a sigh or two to her departed youth, and the remembrance of the last time she had been there, as she adjusted her pretty new cap before the strange, quaint old mirror in the cloakroom. The Assembly Room had been added to the inn, about a hundred years before, by the different county families, who met together there once a month during the winter to dance and play at cards. Many a county beauty had first swung through the minuet that she afterwards danced before Queen Charlotte in this very room. It was said that one of the Gunnings[128] had graced the apartment with her beauty; it was certain that a rich and beautiful widow, Lady Williams, had here been smitten with the noble figure of a young artist, who was staying with some family in the neighbourhood for professional purposes, and accompanied his patrons to the Cranford Assembly. And a pretty bargain poor Lady Williams had of her handsome husband, if all tales were true.[129] Now, no beauty blushed and dimpled along the sides of the Cranford Assembly Room; no handsome artist won hearts by his bow, *chapeau bras*[130] in hand; the old room was dingy; the salmon-coloured paint had faded into a drab; great pieces of plaster had chipped off from the fine wreaths and festoons on its walls; but still a mouldy odour of aristocracy lingered about the place, and a dusty recollection of the days that were gone made Miss Matty and Mrs Forrester bridle up as they entered, and walk mincingly up the room, as if there were a number of genteel observers, instead of two little boys with a stick of toffee between them with which to beguile the time.

We stopped short at the second front row; I could hardly understand why, until I heard Miss Pole ask a stray waiter if any of the county families were expected; and when he shook his head, and believed not, Mrs Forrester and Miss Matty moved forwards, and our party represented a conversational square. The front row was soon augmented and enriched by Lady Glenmire and Mrs Jamieson. We six occupied the two front rows, and our aristocratic seclusion was respected by the groups of shopkeepers who strayed in from time to time and huddled together on the back benches. At least I conjectured so, from the noise they made, and the sonorous bumps they gave in sitting down; but when, in weariness of the obstinate green curtain that would not draw up, but would stare at me with two odd eyes, seen through holes, as in the old tapestry story,[131] I would fain have looked round at the merry chattering people behind me, Miss Pole clutched my arm, and begged me not to turn, for 'it was not the thing'. What 'the thing' was, I never could find out, but it must have been something eminently dull and tiresome. However, we all sat eyes right, square front, gazing at the tantalising curtain, and hardly speaking intelligibly, we were so afraid of being caught in the vulgarity of making any noise in a place of public amusement. Mrs Jamieson was the most fortunate, for she fell asleep.

At length the eyes disappeared – the curtain quivered – one side went up before the other, which stuck fast; it was dropped again, and, with a fresh effort, and a vigorous pull from some unseen hand, it flew up, revealing to our sight a magnificent gentleman in the Turkish costume, seated before a little table, gazing at us (I should have said with the same eyes that I had last seen through the hole in the curtain) with calm and condescending dignity, 'like a being of another sphere', as I heard a sentimental voice ejaculate behind me.

'That's not Signor Brunoni!' said Miss Pole decidedly; and so audibly that I am sure he heard, for he glanced down over his flowing beard at our party with an air of mute reproach. 'Signor Brunoni had no beard – but perhaps he'll come soon.' So she lulled herself into patience. Meanwhile, Miss Matty had reconnoitred through her eye-glass, wiped it, and looked again. Then she turned round, and said to me, in a kind, mild, sorrowful tone: 'You see, my dear, turbans *are* worn.'

But we had no time for more conversation. The Grand Turk, as Miss Pole chose to call him, arose and announced himself as Signor Brunoni.

'I don't believe him!' exclaimed Miss Pole, in a defiant manner. He looked at her again, with the same dignified upbraiding in his countenance. 'I don't!' she repeated more positively than ever. 'Signor Brunoni had not got that muffy sort of thing about his chin, but looked like a close-shaved Christian gentleman.'

Miss Pole's energetic speeches had the good effect of wakening up Mrs Jamieson, who opened her eyes wide, in sign of the deepest attention – a proceeding which silenced Miss Pole and encouraged the Grand Turk to proceed, which he did in very broken English – so broken that there was no cohesion between the parts of his sentences; a fact which he himself perceived at last, and so left off speaking and proceeded to action.

Now we *were* astonished. How he did his tricks I could not imagine; no, not even when Miss Pole pulled out her pieces of paper and began reading aloud – or at least in a very audible whisper – the separate 'receipts' for the most common of his tricks. If ever I saw a man frown and look enraged, I saw the Grand Turk frown at Miss Pole; but, as she said, what could be expected but unchristian looks from a Mussulman? If Miss Pole were sceptical, and more engrossed with her receipts and diagrams than with his tricks, Miss Matty and Mrs Forrester were mystified and perplexed to the highest degree. Mrs Jamieson kept taking her spectacles off and wiping them, as if she thought it was something defective in them which made the legerdemain; and Lady Glenmire, who had seen many curious sights in Edinburgh, was very much struck with the tricks, and would not at all agree with Miss Pole, who declared that anybody could do them with a little practice, and that she would, herself, undertake to do all he did, with two hours given to study the Encyclopaedia and make her third finger flexible.

At last Miss Matty and Mrs Forrester became perfectly awe-stricken. They whispered together. I sat just behind them, so I could not help hearing what they were saying. Miss Matty asked

Mrs Forrester 'if she thought it was quite right to have come to see such things? She could not help fearing they were lending encouragement to something that was not quite – ' A little shake of the head filled up the blank. Mrs Forrester replied, that the same thought had crossed her mind; she too was feeling very uncomfortable, it was so very strange. She was quite certain that it was her pocket-handkerchief which was in that loaf just now; and it had been in her own hand not five minutes before. She wondered who had furnished the bread? She was sure it could not be Dakin, because he was the churchwarden. Suddenly Miss Matty half-turned towards me: 'Will you look, my dear – you are a stranger in the town, and it won't give rise to unpleasant reports – will you just look round and see if the rector is here? If he is, I think we may conclude that this wonderful man is sanctioned by the Church, and that will be a great relief to my mind.'

I looked, and I saw the tall, thin, dry, dusty rector, sitting surrounded by National School[132] boys, guarded by troops of his own sex from any approach of the many Cranford spinsters. His kind face was all agape with broad smiles, and the boys around him were in chinks[133] of laughing. I told Miss Matty that the Church was smiling approval, which set her mind at ease.

I have never named Mr Hayter, the rector, because I, as a well-to-do and happy young woman, never came in contact with him. He was an old bachelor, but as afraid of matrimonial reports getting abroad about him as any girl of eighteen: and he would rush into a shop or dive down an entry, sooner than encounter any of the Cranford ladies in the street; and, as for the Preference parties, I did not wonder at his not accepting invitations to them. To tell the truth, I always suspected Miss Pole of having given very vigorous chase to Mr Hayter when he first came to Cranford; and not the less, because now she appeared to share so vividly in his dread lest her name should ever be coupled with his. He found all his interests among the poor and helpless; he had treated the National School boys this very night to the performance; and virtue was for once its own reward, for they guarded him right and left, and clung round him as if he had been the queen-bee and they the swarm. He felt so safe in their environment that he could even afford to give our party a bow as we filed out. Miss Pole ignored his presence, and pretended to be absorbed in convincing us that we had been cheated, and had not seen Signor Brunoni after all.

CHAPTER 10

The Panic

I THINK A SERIES of circumstances dated from Signor Brunoni's visit to Cranford, which seemed at the time connected in our minds with him, though I don't know that he had anything really to do with them. All at once all sorts of uncomfortable rumours got afloat in the town. There were one or two robberies – real *bona fide* robberies; men had up before the magistrates and committed for trial – and that seemed to make us all afraid of being robbed; and for a long time, at Miss Matty's, I know, we used to make a regular expedition all round the kitchens and cellars every night, Miss Matty leading the way, armed with the poker, I following with the hearth-brush, and Martha carrying the shovel and fire-irons with which to sound the alarm; and by the accidental hitting together of them she often frightened us so much that we bolted ourselves up, all three together, in the back kitchen, or storeroom, or wherever we happened to be, till, when our affright was over, we recollected ourselves and set out afresh with double valiance. By day we heard strange stories from the shopkeepers and cottagers, of carts that went about in the dead of night, drawn by horses shod with felt, and guarded by men in dark clothes, going round the town, no doubt in search of some unwatched house or some unfastened door.

Miss Pole, who affected great bravery herself, was the principal person to collect and arrange these reports so as to make them assume their most fearful aspect. But we discovered that she had begged one of Mr Hoggins's worn-out hats to hang up in her lobby, and we (at least I) had doubts as to whether she really would enjoy the little adventure of having her house broken into, as she protested she should. Miss Matty made no secret of being an arrant coward, but she went regularly through her housekeeper's duty of inspection – only the hour for this became earlier and earlier, till at last we went the rounds at half-past six, and Miss Matty adjourned to bed soon after seven, 'in order to get the night over the sooner'.

Cranford had so long piqued itself on being an honest and moral town that it had grown to fancy itself too genteel and well-bred to be otherwise, and felt the stain upon its character at this time doubly.

But we comforted ourselves with the assurance which we gave to each other that the robberies could never have been committed by any Cranford person; it must have been a stranger or strangers who brought this disgrace upon the town, and occasioned as many precautions as if we were living among the Red Indians or the French.

This last comparison of our nightly state of defence and fortification was made by Mrs Forrester, whose father had served under General Burgoyne in the American war, and whose husband had fought the French in Spain.[134] She indeed inclined to the idea that, in some way, the French were connected with the small thefts, which were ascertained facts, and the burglaries and highway robberies, which were rumours. She had been deeply impressed with the idea of French spies at some time in her life; and the notion could never be fairly eradicated, but sprang up again from time to time. And now her theory was this: the Cranford people respected themselves too much, and were too grateful to the aristocracy who were so kind as to live near the town, ever to disgrace their bringing up by being dishonest or immoral; therefore, we must believe that the robbers were strangers – if strangers, why not foreigners? – if foreigners, who so likely as the French? Signor Brunoni spoke broken English like a Frenchman; and, though he wore a turban like a Turk, Mrs Forrester had seen a print of Madame de Staël[135] with a turban on, and another of Mr Denon[136] in just such a dress as that in which the conjuror had made his appearance, showing clearly that the French, as well as the Turks, wore turbans. There could be no doubt Signor Brunoni was a Frenchman – a French spy come to discover the weak and undefended places of England, and doubtless he had his accomplices. For her part, she, Mrs Forrester, had always had her own opinion of Miss Pole's adventure at the George Inn – seeing two men where only one was believed to be. French people had ways and means which, she was thankful to say, the English knew nothing about; and she had never felt quite easy in her mind about going to see that conjuror – it was rather too much like a forbidden thing, though the rector was there. In short, Mrs Forrester grew more excited than we had ever known her before, and, being an officer's daughter and widow, we looked up to her opinion, of course.

Really I do not know how much was true or false in the reports which flew about like wildfire just at this time; but it seemed to me then that there was every reason to believe that at Mardon (a small town about eight miles from Cranford) houses and shops were entered by holes made in the walls, the bricks being silently carried away in the dead of the night, and all done so quietly that no sound was heard either in or out of the house. Miss Matty gave it up in despair when she heard of this. 'What was the use,' said she, 'of locks and bolts, and bells to the windows, and going round the house every night? That last trick was fit for a conjuror. Now she did believe that Signor Brunoni was at the bottom of it.'

One afternoon, about five o'clock, we were startled by a hasty knock at the door. Miss Matty bade me run and tell Martha on no account to open the door till she (Miss Matty) had reconnoitred through the window; and she armed herself with a footstool to drop down on the head of the visitor, in case he should show a face covered with black crape, as he looked up in answer to her enquiry of who was there. But it was nobody but Miss Pole and Betty. The former came upstairs, carrying a little hand-basket, and she was evidently in a state of great agitation.

'Take care of that!' said she to me, as I offered to relieve her of her basket. 'It's my plate. I am sure there is a plan to rob my house tonight. I am come to throw myself on your hospitality, Miss Matty. Betty is going to sleep with her cousin at the George. I can sit up here all night if you will allow me; but my house is so far from any neighbours, and I don't believe we could be heard if we screamed ever so!'

'But,' said Miss Matty, 'what has alarmed you so much? Have you seen any men lurking about the house?'

'Oh, yes!' answered Miss Pole. 'Two very bad-looking men have gone three times past the house, very slowly; and an Irish beggar-woman came not half an hour ago, and all but forced herself in past Betty, saying her children were starving, and she must speak to the mistress. You see, she said "mistress", though there was a hat hanging up in the hall, and it would have been more natural to have said "master". But Betty shut the door in her face, and came up to me, and we got the spoons together, and sat in the parlour window watching till we saw Thomas Jones going from his work, when we called to him and asked him to take care of us into the town.'

We might have triumphed over Miss Pole, who had professed such bravery until she was frightened; but we were too glad to perceive that she shared in the weaknesses of humanity to exult over her; and I gave up my room to her very willingly, and shared Miss Matty's bed for the night. But before we retired, the two ladies rummaged up, out of the recesses of their memory, such horrid stories of robbery and murder that I quite quaked in my shoes. Miss Pole was evidently anxious to prove that such terrible events had occurred within her experience that she was justified in her sudden panic; and Miss Matty did not like to be outdone, and capped every story with one yet more horrible, till it reminded me, oddly enough, of an old story I had read somewhere, of a nightingale and a musician, who strove one against the other which could produce the most admirable music, till poor Philomel dropped down dead.[137]

One of the stories that haunted me for a long time afterwards was of a girl who was left in charge of a great house in Cumberland on some particular fair-day, when the other servants all went off to the gaieties.[138] The family were away in London, and a pedlar came by, and asked to leave his large and heavy pack in the kitchen, saying he would call for it again at night; and the girl (a gamekeeper's daughter), roaming about in search of amusement, chanced to hit upon a gun hanging up in the hall, and took it down to look at the chasing; and it went off through the open kitchen door, hit the pack, and a slow dark thread of blood came oozing out. (How Miss Pole enjoyed this part of the story, dwelling on each word as if she loved it!) She rather hurried over the further account of the girl's bravery, and I have but a confused idea that, somehow, she baffled the robbers with Italian irons,[139] heated red-hot, and then restored to blackness by being dipped in grease.

We parted for the night with an awe-stricken wonder as to what we should hear of in the morning – and, on my part, with a vehement desire for the night to be over and gone: I was so afraid lest the robbers should have seen, from some dark lurking-place, that Miss Pole had carried off her plate, and thus have a double motive for attacking our house.

But until Lady Glenmire came to call next day we heard of nothing unusual. The kitchen fire-irons were in exactly the same position against the back door as when Martha and I had skilfully piled them up, like spillikins, ready to fall with an awful clatter if only a cat had touched the outside panels. I had wondered what we should all do if thus awakened and alarmed, and had proposed to Miss Matty that we should cover up our faces under bedclothes, so that there should be no danger of the robbers thinking that we could identify them; but Miss Matty, who was trembling very much, scouted this idea, and said we owed it to society to apprehend them, and that she should certainly do her best to lay hold of them and lock them up in the garret till morning.

When Lady Glenmire came, we almost felt jealous of her. Mrs

Jamieson's house had really been attacked; at least there were men's footprints to be seen on the flower borders, underneath the kitchen windows, 'where nae men should be';[140] and Carlo had barked all through the night as if strangers were abroad. Mrs Jamieson had been awakened by Lady Glenmire, and they had rung the bell which communicated with Mr Mulliner's room in the third storey, and when his night-capped head had appeared over the banisters, in answer to the summons, they had told him of their alarm, and the reasons for it; whereupon he retreated into his bedroom, and locked the door (for fear of draughts, as he informed them in the morning), and opened the window, and called out valiantly to say, if the supposed robbers would come to him he would fight them; but, as Lady Glenmire observed, that was but poor comfort, since they would have to pass by Mrs Jamieson's room and her own before they could reach him, and must be of a very pugnacious disposition indeed if they neglected the opportunities of robbery presented by the unguarded lower storeys, to go up to a garret, and there force a door in order to get at the champion of the house. Lady Glenmire, after waiting and listening for some time in the drawing-room, had proposed to Mrs Jamieson that they should go to bed; but that lady said she should not feel comfortable unless she sat up and watched; and, accordingly, she packed herself warmly up on the sofa, where she was found by the housemaid, when she came into the room at six o'clock, fast asleep; but Lady Glenmire went to bed, and kept awake all night.

When Miss Pole heard of this, she nodded her head in great satisfaction. She had been sure we should hear of something happening in Cranford that night; and we had heard. It was clear enough they had first proposed to attack her house; but when they saw that she and Betty were on their guard, and had carried off the plate, they had changed their tactics and gone to Mrs Jamieson's, and no one knew what might have happened if Carlo had not barked, like a good dog as he was!

Poor Carlo! his barking days were nearly over. Whether the gang who infested the neighbourhood were afraid of him, or whether they were revengeful enough, for the way in which he had baffled them on the night in question, to poison him; or whether, as some among the more uneducated people thought, he died of apoplexy, brought on by too much feeding and too little exercise; at any rate, it is certain that, two days after this eventful night, Carlo was found dead, with his poor legs stretched out stiff in the attitude of running, as if by such unusual exertion he could escape the sure pursuer, Death.

We were all sorry for Carlo, the old familiar friend who had snapped at us for so many years; and the mysterious mode of his death made us very uncomfortable. Could Signor Brunoni be at the bottom of this? He had apparently killed a canary with only a word of command; his will seemed of deadly force; who knew but what he might yet be lingering in the neighbourhood willing all sorts of awful things!

We whispered these fancies among ourselves in the evenings; but in the mornings our courage came back with the daylight, and in a week's time we had got over the shock of Carlo's death; all but Mrs Jamieson. She, poor thing, felt it as she had felt no event since her husband's death; indeed, Miss Pole said, that as the Honourable Mr Jamieson drank a good deal, and occasioned her much uneasiness, it was possible that Carlo's death might be the greater affliction. But there was always a tinge of cynicism in Miss Pole's remarks. However, one thing was clear and certain – it was necessary for Mrs Jamieson to have some change of scene; and Mr Mulliner was very impressive on this point, shaking his head whenever we enquired after his mistress, and speaking of her loss of appetite and bad nights very ominously; and with justice too, for if she had two characteristics in her natural state of health they were a facility for eating and sleeping. If she could neither eat nor sleep, she must be indeed out of spirits and out of health.

Lady Glenmire (who had evidently taken very kindly to Cranford) did not like the idea of Mrs Jamieson's going to Cheltenham, and more than once insinuated pretty plainly that it was Mr Mulliner's doing, who had been much alarmed on the occasion of the house being attacked, and since had said, more than once, that he felt it a very responsible charge to have to defend so many women. Be that as it might, Mrs Jamieson went to Cheltenham, escorted by Mr Mulliner; and Lady Glenmire remained in possession of the house, her ostensible office being to take care that the maidservants did not pick up followers. She made a very pleasant-looking dragon; and, as soon as it was arranged for her stay in Cranford, she found out that Mrs Jamieson's visit to Cheltenham was just the best thing in the world. She had let her house in Edinburgh, and was for the time houseless, so the charge of her sister-in-law's comfortable abode was very convenient and acceptable.

Miss Pole was very much inclined to instal herself as a heroine, because of the decided steps she had taken in flying from the two men and one woman, whom she entitled 'that murderous gang'. She described their appearance in glowing colours, and I noticed that every time she went over the story some fresh trait of villainy was added to their appearance. One was tall – he grew to be gigantic in height before we had done with him; he of course had black hair – and by and by it hung in elf-locks[141] over his forehead and down his back. The other was short and broad – and a hump sprouted out on his shoulder before we heard the last of him; he had red hair – which deepened into carroty; and she was almost sure he had a cast in the eye – a decided squint. As for the woman, her eyes glared, and she was masculine-looking – a perfect virago; most probably a man dressed in woman's clothes; afterwards, we heard of a beard on her chin, and a manly voice and a stride.

If Miss Pole was delighted to recount the events of that afternoon to all enquirers, others were not so proud of their adventures in the robbery line. Mr Hoggins, the surgeon, had been attacked at his own door by two ruffians, who were concealed in the shadow of the porch, and so effectually silenced him that he was robbed in the interval between ringing his bell and the servant's answering it. Miss Pole was sure it would turn out that this robbery had been committed by 'her men', and went the very day she heard the report to have her teeth examined, and to question Mr Hoggins. She came to us afterwards; so we heard what she had heard, straight and direct from the source, while we were yet in the excitement and flutter of the agitation caused by the first intelligence; for the event had only occurred the night before.

'Well!' said Miss Pole, sitting down with the decision of a person who has made up her mind as to the nature of life and the world (and such people never tread lightly, or seat themselves without a bump), 'well, Miss Matty! men will be men. Every mother's son of them wishes to be considered Samson and Solomon rolled into one – too strong ever to be beaten or discomfited – too wise ever to be outwitted. If you will notice, they have always foreseen events, though they never tell one for one's warning before the events happen. My father was a man, and I know the sex pretty well.'

She had talked herself out of breath, and we should have been very glad to fill up the necessary pause as chorus, but we did not exactly know what to say, or which man had suggested this diatribe against the sex; so we only joined in generally, with a grave shake of the head, and a soft murmur of 'They are very incomprehensible, certainly!'

'Now, only think,' said she. 'There, I have undergone the risk of having one of my remaining teeth drawn (for one is terribly at the mercy of any surgeon-dentist; and I, for one, always speak them fair till I have got my mouth out of their clutches), and, after all, Mr Hoggins is too much of a man to own that he was robbed last night.'

'Not robbed!' exclaimed the chorus.

'Don't tell me!' Miss Pole exclaimed, angry that we could be for a moment imposed upon. 'I believe he was robbed, just as Betty told me, and he is ashamed to own it; and, to be sure, it was very silly of him to be robbed just at his own door; I dare say he feels that such a thing won't raise him in the eyes of Cranford society, and is anxious to conceal it – but he need not have tried to impose upon me, by saying I must have heard an exaggerated account of some petty theft of a neck of mutton, which, it seems, was stolen out of the safe in his yard last week; he had the impertinence to add, he believed that that was taken by the cat. I have no doubt, if I could get at the bottom of it, it was that Irishman dressed up in woman's clothes, who came spying about my house, with the story about the starving children.'

After we had duly condemned the want of candour which Mr Hoggins had evinced, and abused men in general, taking him for the representative and type, we got round to the subject about which we had been talking when Miss Pole came in: namely, how far, in the present disturbed state of the country, we could venture to accept an invitation which Miss Matty had just received from Mrs Forrester, to come as usual and keep the anniversary of her wedding-day by drinking tea with her at five o'clock, and playing a quiet pool afterwards. Mrs Forrester had said that she asked us with some diffidence, because the roads were, she feared, very unsafe. But she suggested that perhaps one of us would not object to take the sedan, and that the others, by walking briskly, might keep up with the long trot of the chairmen, and so we might all arrive safely at Over Place,[142] a suburb of the town. (No; that is too large an expression: a small cluster of houses separated from Cranford by about two hundred yards of a dark and lonely lane.) There was no doubt but that a similar note was awaiting Miss Pole at home; so her call was a very fortunate affair, as it enabled us to consult together . . . We would all much rather have declined this invitation; but we felt that it would not be quite kind to Mrs Forrester, who would otherwise be left to a solitary retrospect of her not very happy or fortunate life. Miss Matty and Miss Pole had been visitors on this occasion for many years, and now they gallantly determined to nail their colours to the mast, and to go through Darkness Lane[143] rather than fail in loyalty to their friend.

But when the evening came, Miss Matty (for it was she who was voted into the chair, as she had a cold), before being shut down in the sedan, like jack-in-a-box, implored the chairmen, whatever might befall, not to run away and leave her fastened up there, to be murdered; and even after they had promised, I saw her tighten her features into the stern determination of a martyr, and she gave me a melancholy and ominous shake of the head through the glass. However, we got there safely, only rather out of breath, for it was who could trot hardest through Darkness Lane, and I am afraid poor Miss Matty was sadly jolted.

Mrs Forrester had made extra preparations, in acknowledgement of our exertion in coming to see her through such dangers. The usual forms of genteel ignorance as to what her servants might send up were all gone through; and harmony and Preference seemed likely to be the order of the evening, but for an interesting conversation that began I don't know how, but which had relation, of course, to the robbers who infested the neighbourhood of Cranford.

Having braved the dangers of Darkness Lane, and thus having a little stock of reputation for courage to fall back upon; and also, I dare say, desirous of proving ourselves superior to men (*videlicet*[144] Mr Hoggins) in the article of candour, we began to relate our individual fears, and the private precautions we each of us took. I owned that my pet apprehension was eyes – eyes looking at me, and watching me, glittering out from some dull, flat, wooden surface; and that if I dared to go up to my looking-glass when I was panic-stricken, I should certainly turn it round, with its back towards me, for fear of seeing eyes behind me looking out of the darkness. I saw Miss Matty nerving herself up for a confession; and at last out it came. She owned that, ever since she had been a girl, she had dreaded being caught by her last leg, just as she was getting into bed, by someone concealed under it. She said, when she was younger and more active, she used to take a flying leap from a distance, and so bring both her legs up safely into bed at once; but that this had always annoyed Deborah, who piqued herself upon getting into bed gracefully, and she had given it up in consequence. But now the old terror would often come over her, especially since Miss Pole's house had been attacked (we had got quite to believe in the fact of the attack having taken place), and yet it was very unpleasant to think of looking under a bed, and seeing a man concealed, with a great, fierce face staring out at you; so she had bethought herself of something – perhaps I had noticed that she had told Martha to buy her a penny ball, such as children play with – and now she rolled this ball under the bed every night: if it came out on the other side, well and good; if not she always took care to have her hand on the bell-rope, and meant to call out John and Harry, just as if she expected menservants to answer her ring.

We all applauded this ingenious contrivance, and Miss Matty sank back into satisfied silence, with a look at Mrs Forrester as if to ask for *her* private weakness.

Mrs Forrester looked askance at Miss Pole, and tried to change the subject a little by telling us that she had borrowed a boy from one of the neighbouring cottages and promised his parents a hundredweight of coals at Christmas, and his supper every evening, for the loan of him at nights. She had instructed him in his possible duties when he first came; and, finding him sensible, she had given him the major's sword (the major was her late husband), and desired him to put it very carefully behind his pillow at night, turning the edge towards the head of the pillow. He was a sharp lad, she was sure; for, spying out the major's cocked hat, he had said, if he might have that to wear, he was sure he could frighten two Englishmen, or four Frenchmen, any day. But she had impressed upon him anew that he was to lose no time in putting on hats or anything else; but, if he heard any noise, he was to run at it with his drawn sword. On my suggesting that some accident might occur from such slaughterous and indiscriminate directions, and that he might rush on Jenny getting up to wash, and have spitted her before he had discovered that she was not a Frenchman, Mrs Forrester said she did not think that that was likely, for he was a very sound sleeper, and generally had to be well shaken or cold-pigged[145] in a morning before they could rouse him. She sometimes thought such dead sleep must be owing to the hearty suppers the poor lad ate, for he was half-starved at home, and she told Jenny to see that he got a good meal at night.

Still this was no confession of Mrs Forrester's peculiar timidity, and we urged her to tell us what she thought would frighten her more than anything. She paused, and stirred the fire, and snuffed the candles, and then she said, in a sounding whisper: 'Ghosts!'

She looked at Miss Pole, as much as to say, she had declared it, and would stand by it. Such a look was a challenge in itself. Miss Pole came down upon her with indigestion, spectral illusions, optical delusions, and a great deal out of Dr Ferrier and Dr Hibbert[146] besides. Miss Matty had rather a leaning to ghosts, as I have mentioned before, and what little she did say was all on Mrs Forrester's side, who, emboldened by sympathy, protested that ghosts were a part of her religion; that surely she, the widow of a major in the army, knew what to be frightened at, and what not; in short, I never saw Mrs Forrester so warm either before or since, for she was a gentle, meek, enduring old lady in most things. Not all the elder-wine that ever was mulled could this night wash out the remembrance of this difference between Miss Pole and her hostess. Indeed, when the elder-wine was brought in, it gave rise to a new burst of discussion; for Jenny, the little maiden who staggered under the tray, had to give evidence of having seen a ghost with her own eyes, not so many nights ago, in Darkness Lane, the very lane we were to go through on our way home.

In spite of the uncomfortable feeling which this last consideration gave me, I could not help being amused at Jenny's position, which was exceedingly like that of a witness being examined and cross-examined by two counsel who are not at all scrupulous about asking leading questions. The conclusion I arrived at was, that Jenny had certainly seen something beyond what a fit of indigestion would have caused. A lady all in white, and without her head, was what she deposed and adhered to, supported by a consciousness of the secret sympathy of her mistress under the withering scorn with which Miss Pole regarded her. And not only she, but many others, had seen this headless lady, who sat by the roadside wringing her hands as in deep grief. Mrs Forrester looked at us from time to time with an air of conscious triumph; but then she had not to pass through Darkness Lane before she could bury herself beneath her own familiar bedclothes.

We preserved a discreet silence as to the headless lady while we were putting on our things to go home, for there was no knowing how near the ghostly head and ears might be, or what spiritual connection they might be keeping up with the unhappy body in Darkness Lane; and, therefore, even Miss Pole felt that it was as well not to speak lightly on such subjects, for fear of vexing or insulting that woebegone trunk. At least, so I conjecture; for, instead of the busy clatter usual in the operation, we tied on our cloaks as sadly as mutes at a funeral. Miss Matty drew the curtains round the windows of the chair to shut out disagreeable sights, and the men (either because they were in spirits that their labours were so nearly ended, or because they were going down hill) set off at such a round and merry pace, that it was all Miss Pole and I could do to keep up with them. She had breath for nothing beyond an imploring 'Don't leave me!' uttered as she clutched my arm so tightly that I could not have quitted her, ghost or no ghost. What a relief it was when the men, weary of their burden and their quick trot, stopped just where Headingley Causeway branches off from Darkness Lane! Miss Pole unloosed me and caught at one of the men: 'Could not you – could not you take Miss Matty round by Headingley Causeway? – the pavement in Darkness Lane jolts so, and she is not very strong.'

A smothered voice was heard from the inside of the chair: 'Oh! pray go on! What is the matter? What is the matter? I will give you sixpence more to go on very fast; pray don't stop here.'

'And I'll give you a shilling,' said Miss Pole, with tremulous dignity, 'if you'll go by Headingley Causeway.'

The two men grunted acquiescence and took up the chair, and went along the causeway, which certainly answered Miss Pole's kind purpose of saving Miss Matty's bones; for it was covered with soft, thick mud, and even a fall there would have been easy till the getting-up came, when there might have been some difficulty in extrication.

CHAPTER II

Samuel Brown

THE NEXT MORNING I met Lady Glenmire and Miss Pole setting out on a long walk to find some old woman who was famous in the neighbourhood for her skill in knitting woollen stockings. Miss Pole said to me, with a smile half-kindly and half-contemptuous upon her countenance: 'I have been just telling Lady Glenmire of our poor friend Mrs Forrester, and her terror of ghosts. It comes from living so much alone, and listening to the bug-a-boo stories of that Jenny of hers.' She was so calm and so much above superstitious fears herself that I was almost ashamed to say how glad I had been of her Headingley Causeway proposition the night before, and turned off the conversation to something else.

In the afternoon Miss Pole called on Miss Matty to tell her of the adventure – the real adventure they had met with on their morning's walk. They had been perplexed about the exact path which they were to take across the fields in order to find the knitting old woman, and had stopped to enquire at a little wayside public house, standing in the high road to London, about three miles from Cranford. The good woman had asked them to sit down and rest themselves while she fetched her husband, who could direct them better than she could; and, while they were sitting in the sanded parlour, a little girl came in. They thought that she belonged to the landlady, and began some trifling conversation with her; but, on Mrs Roberts's return, she told them that the little thing was the only child of a couple who were staying in the house. And then she began a long story, out of which Lady Glenmire and Miss Pole could only gather one or two decided facts, which were that, about six weeks ago, a light spring-cart had broken down just before their door, in which there were two men, one woman, and this child. One of the men was seriously hurt – no bones broken, only 'shaken', the landlady called it; but he had probably sustained some severe internal injury, for he had languished in their house ever since, attended by his wife, the mother of this little girl. Miss Pole had asked what he was, what he looked like. And Mrs Roberts had made answer that he was not like a gentleman, nor yet like a common person; if it had not been that he and his wife were such decent, quiet people, she could almost have thought he was a mountebank, or something of that kind, for they had a great box in the cart, full of she did not know what. She had helped to unpack it, and take out their linen and clothes, when the other man – his twin-brother, she believed he was – had gone off with the horse and cart.

Miss Pole had begun to have her suspicions at this point, and expressed her idea that it was rather strange that the box and cart and horse and all should have disappeared; but good Mrs Roberts seemed to have become quite indignant at Miss Pole's implied suggestion; in fact, Miss Pole said she was as angry as if Miss Pole had told her that she herself was a swindler. As the best way of convincing the ladies, she bethought her of begging them to see the wife; and, as Miss Pole said, there was no doubting the honest, worn, bronzed face of the woman, who at the first tender word from Lady Glenmire, burst into tears, which she was too weak to check until some word from the landlady made her swallow down her sobs, in order that she might testify to the Christian kindnesses shown by Mr and Mrs Roberts. Miss Pole came round with a swing to as vehement a belief in the sorrowful tale as she had been sceptical before; and, as a proof of this, her energy in the poor sufferer's behalf was nothing daunted when she found out that he, and no other, was our Signor Brunoni, to whom all Cranford had been attributing all manner of evil this six weeks past! Yes! his wife said his proper name was Samuel Brown – 'Sam', she called him – but to the last we preferred calling him 'the Signor'; it sounded so much better.

The end of their conversation with the Signora Brunoni was that it was agreed that he should be placed under medical advice, and for any expense incurred in procuring this Lady Glenmire promised to hold herself responsible, and had accordingly gone to Mr Hoggins to beg him to ride over to the Rising Sun[147] that very afternoon, and examine into the signor's real state; and, as Miss Pole said, if it was desirable to remove him to Cranford to be more immediately under Mr Hoggins's eye, she would undertake to seek for lodgings and arrange about the rent. Mrs Roberts had been as kind as could be all throughout, but it was evident that their long residence there had been a slight inconvenience.

Before Miss Pole left us, Miss Matty and I were as full of the morning's adventure as she was. We talked about it all the evening, turning it in every possible light, and we went to bed anxious for the morning, when we should surely hear from someone what Mr Hoggins thought and recommended; for, as Miss Matty observed, though Mr Hoggins did say 'Jack's up', 'a fig[148] for his heels', and called Preference 'Pref.' she believed he was a very worthy man and a very clever surgeon. Indeed, we were rather proud of our doctor at Cranford, as a doctor. We often wished, when we heard of Queen Adelaide or the Duke of Wellington being ill, that they would send for Mr Hoggins; but, on consideration, we were rather glad they did not, for, if we were ailing, what should we do if Mr Hoggins had been appointed physician-in-ordinary to the Royal Family?[149] As a surgeon we were proud of him; but as a man – or rather, I should say, as a gentleman – we could only shake our heads over his name and himself; and wished that he had read Lord Chesterfield's *Letters*[150] in the days when his manners were susceptible of improvement. Nevertheless, we all regarded his dictum in the signor's case as infallible, and when he said that with care and attention he might rally, we had no more fear for him.

But, although we had no more fear, everybody did as much as if there was great cause for anxiety – as indeed there was until Mr Hoggins took charge of him. Miss Pole looked out clean and comfortable, if homely, lodgings; Miss Matty sent the sedan-chair for him, and Martha and I aired it well before it left Cranford by holding a warming-pan full of red-hot coals in it, and then shutting it up close, smoke and all, until the time when he should get into it at the Rising Sun. Lady Glenmire undertook the medical department under Mr Hoggins's directions, and rummaged up all Mrs Jamieson's medicine glasses, and spoons, and bed-tables, in a free-and-easy way, that made Miss Matty feel a little anxious as to what that lady and Mr Mulliner might say, if they knew. Mrs Forrester made some of the bread jelly, for which she was so famous, to have ready as a refreshment in the lodgings when he should arrive. A present of this bread jelly was the highest mark of favour dear Mrs Forrester could confer. Miss Pole had once asked her for the receipt, but she had met with a very decided rebuff; that lady told her that she could not part with it to anyone during her life, and that after her death it was bequeathed, as her executors would find, to Miss Matty. What Miss Matty, or, as Mrs Forrester called her (remembering the clause in her will and the dignity of the occasion), Miss Matilda Jenkyns – might choose to do with the receipt when it came into her possession – whether to make it public, or to hand it down as an heirloom – she did not know, nor would she dictate. And a mould of this admirable, digestible, unique bread jelly was sent by Mrs Forrester to our poor sick conjuror. Who says that the aristocracy are proud? Here was a lady by birth a Tyrrell, and descended from the great Sir Walter that shot King Rufus,[151] and in whose veins ran the blood of him who murdered the little princes in the Tower,[152] going every day to see what dainty dishes she could prepare for Samuel Brown, a mountebank! But, indeed, it was wonderful to see what kind feelings were called out by this poor man's coming amongst us. And also wonderful to see how the great Cranford panic, which had been occasioned by his first coming in his Turkish dress, melted away into thin air on his second coming – pale and feeble, and with his heavy, filmy eyes, that only brightened a very little when they fell upon the countenance of his faithful wife, or their pale and sorrowful little girl.

Somehow we all forgot to be afraid. I dare say it was that finding out that he, who had first excited our love of the marvellous by his unprecedented arts, had not sufficient everyday gifts to manage a shying horse, made us feel as if we were ourselves again. Miss Pole came with her little basket at all hours of the evening, as if her lonely house and the unfrequented road to it had never been infested by that 'murderous gang'; Mrs Forrester said she thought that neither Jenny nor she need mind the headless lady who wept and wailed in Darkness Lane, for surely the power was never given to such beings to harm those who went about to try to do what little good was in their power, to which Jenny tremblingly assented; but the mistress's theory had little effect on the maid's practice until she had sewn two pieces of red flannel in the shape of a cross on her inner garment.

I found Miss Matty covering her penny ball – the ball that she used to roll under her bed – with gay-coloured worsted in rainbow stripes.

'My dear,' said she, 'my heart is sad for that little careworn child. Although her father is a conjuror, she looks as if she had never had a good game of play in her life. I used to make very pretty balls in this way when I was a girl, and I thought I would try if I could not make this one smart and take it to Phoebe this afternoon. I think "the gang" must have left the neighbourhood, for one does not hear any more of their violence and robbery now.'

We were all of us far too full of the signor's precarious state to talk either about robbers or ghosts. Indeed, Lady Glenmire said she never had heard of any actual robberies, except that two little boys had stolen some apples from Farmer Benson's orchard, and that some eggs had been missed on a market-day off Widow Hayward's stall. But that was expecting too much of us; we could not acknowledge that we had only had this small foundation for all our panic. Miss Pole drew herself up at this remark of Lady Glenmire's, and said 'that she wished she could agree with her as to the very small reason we had had for alarm, but with the recollection of a man disguised as a woman who had endeavoured to force himself into her house while his confederates waited outside; with the knowledge gained from Lady Glenmire herself, of the footprints seen on Mrs Jamieson's flower borders: with the fact before her of the audacious robbery committed on Mr Hoggins at his own door – ' But here Lady Glenmire broke in with a very strong expression of doubt as to whether this last story was not an entire fabrication founded upon the theft of a cat; she grew so red while she was saying all this that I was not surprised at Miss Pole's manner of bridling up, and I am certain, if Lady Glenmire had not been 'her ladyship', we should have had a more emphatic contradiction than the 'Well, to be sure!' and similar fragmentary ejaculations, which were all that she ventured upon in my lady's presence. But when she was gone Miss Pole began a long congratulation to Miss Matty that so far they had escaped marriage, which she noticed always made people credulous to the last degree; indeed, she thought it argued great natural credulity in a woman if she could not keep herself from being married; and in what Lady Glenmire had said about Mr Hoggins's robbery we had a specimen of what people came to if they gave way to such a weakness; evidently Lady Glenmire would swallow anything if she could believe the poor vamped-up story about a neck of mutton and a pussy with which he had tried to impose on Miss Pole, only she had always been on her guard against believing too much of what men said.

We were thankful, as Miss Pole desired us to be, that we had never been married; but I think, of the two, we were even more thankful that the robbers had left Cranford; at least I judge so from a speech of Miss Matty's that evening, as we sat over the fire, in which she evidently looked upon a husband as a great protector against thieves, burglars and ghosts; and said that she did not think that she should dare to be always warning young people against matrimony, as Miss Pole did continually; to be sure, marriage was a risk, as she saw, now she had had some experience; but she remembered the time when she had looked forward to being married as much as anyone.

'Not to any particular person, my dear,' said she, hastily checking herself up, as if she were afraid of having admitted too much; 'only the old story, you know, of ladies always saying, "*When* I marry", and gentlemen, "*If* I marry". ' It was a joke spoken in rather a sad tone, and I doubt if either of us smiled; but I could not see Miss Matty's face by the flickering firelight. In a little while she continued: 'But, after all, I have not told you the truth. It is so long ago, and no one ever knew how much I thought of it at the time, unless, indeed, my dear mother guessed; but I may say that there was a time when I did not think I should have been only Miss Matty Jenkyns all my life; for even if I did meet with anyone who wished to marry me now (and, as Miss Pole says, one is never too safe), I could not take him – I hope he would not take it too much to heart, but I could *not* take him – or anyone but the person I once thought I should be married to; and he is dead and gone, and he never knew how it all came about that I said "No," when I had thought many and many a time – Well, it's no matter what I thought. God ordains it all, and I am very happy, my dear. No one has such kind friends as I,' continued she, taking my hand and holding it in hers.

If I had never known of Mr Holbrook, I could have said something in this pause, but as I had, I could not think of anything that would come in naturally, and so we both kept silence for a little time.

'My father once made us,' she began, 'keep a diary, in two columns; on one side we were to put down in the morning what we thought would be the course and events of the coming day, and at night we were to put down on the other side what really had happened. It would be to some people rather a sad way of telling their lives' (a tear dropped upon my hand at these words) – 'I don't mean that mine has been sad, only so very different to what I expected. I remember, one winter's evening, sitting over our bedroom fire with Deborah – I remember it as if it were yesterday – and we were planning our future lives, both of us were planning, though only she talked about it. She said she should like to marry an archdeacon, and write his charges;[153] and you know, my dear, she never was married, and, for aught I know, she never spoke to an unmarried archdeacon in her life. I never was ambitious, nor could I have written charges, but I thought I could manage a house (my mother used to call me her right hand), and I was always so fond of little children – the shyest babies would stretch out their little arms to come to me; when I was a girl, I was half my leisure time nursing in the neighbouring cottages; but I don't know how it was, when I grew sad and grave – which I did a year or two after this time – the little things drew back from me, and I am afraid I lost the knack, though I am just as fond of children as ever, and have a strange yearning at my heart whenever I see a mother with her baby in her arms. Nay, my dear' (and by a sudden blaze which sprang up from a fall of the unstirred coals, I saw that her eyes were full of tears – gazing intently on some vision of what might have been), 'do you know I dream sometimes that I have a little child – always the same – a little girl of about two years old; she never grows older, though I have dreamt about her for many years. I don't think I ever dream of any words or sound she makes; she is very noiseless and still, but she comes to me when she is very sorry or very glad, and I have wakened with the clasp of her dear little arms round my neck. Only last night – perhaps because I had gone to sleep thinking of this ball for Phoebe – my little darling came in my dream, and put up her mouth to be kissed, just as I have seen real babies do to real mothers before going to bed. But all this is nonsense, dear! only don't be frightened by Miss Pole from being married. I can fancy it may be a very happy state, and a little credulity helps one through life very smoothly – better than always doubting and doubting and seeing difficulties and disagreeables in everything.'

If I had been inclined to be daunted from matrimony, it would not have been Miss Pole to do it; it would have been the lot of poor Signor Brunoni and his wife. And yet again, it was an encouragement to see how, through all their cares and sorrows, they thought of each other and not of themselves; and how keen were their joys, if they only passed through each other, or through the little Phoebe.

The signora told me, one day, a good deal about their lives up to this period. It began by my asking her whether Miss Pole's story of the twin-brothers were true; it sounded so wonderful a likeness, that I should have had my doubts, if Miss Pole had not been unmarried. But the signora, or (as we found out she preferred to be called) Mrs Brown, said it was quite true; that her brother-in-law was by many taken for her husband, which was of great assistance to them in their profession; 'though,' she continued, 'how people can mistake Thomas for the real Signor Brunoni, I can't conceive; but he says they do; so I suppose I must believe him. Not but what he is a very good man; I am sure I don't know how we should have paid our bill at the Rising Sun but for the money he sends; but people must know very little about art if they can take him for my husband. Why, miss, in the ball trick, where my husband spreads his fingers wide, and throws out his little finger with quite an air and a grace, Thomas just clumps up his hand like a fist, and might have ever so many balls hidden in it. Besides, he has never been in India, and knows nothing of the proper sit of a turban.'

'Have you been in India?' said I, rather astonished.

'Oh, yes! many a year, ma'am. Sam was a sergeant in the 31st; and when the regiment was ordered to India, I drew a lot to go, and I was more thankful than I can tell; for it seemed as if it would only be a slow death to me to part from my husband. But, indeed, ma'am, if I had known all, I don't know whether I would not rather have died there and then than gone through what I have done since. To be sure, I've been able to comfort Sam, and to be with him; but, ma'am, I've lost six children,' said she, looking up at me with those strange eyes that I've never noticed but in mothers of dead children – with a kind of wild look in them, as if seeking for what they never more might find. 'Yes! Six children died off, like little buds nipped untimely, in that cruel India. I thought, as each died, I never could – I never would – love a child again; and when the next came, it had not only its own love, but the deeper love that came from the thoughts of its little dead brothers and sisters. And when Phoebe was coming, I said to my husband: "Sam, when the child is born, and I am strong, I shall leave you; it will cut my heart cruel; but if this baby dies too, I shall go mad; the madness is in me now; but if you let me go down to Calcutta, carrying my baby step by step, it will, maybe, work itself off; and I will save, and I will hoard, and I will beg – and I will die, to get a passage home to England, where our baby may live!" God bless him! he said I might go; and he saved up his pay, and I saved every pice[154] I could get for washing or any way; and when Phoebe came, and I grew strong again, I set off. It was very lonely; through the thick forests, dark again with their heavy trees – along by the river's side (but I had been brought up near the Avon[155] in Warwickshire, so that flowing noise sounded like home) – from station[156] to station, from Indian village to village, I went along, carrying my child. I had seen one of the officers' ladies with a little picture, ma'am – done by a Catholic foreigner, ma'am – of the Virgin and the little Saviour, ma'am. She had him on her arm, and her form was softly curled round him, and their cheeks touched. Well, when I went to bid goodbye to this lady, for whom I had washed, she cried sadly; for she, too, had lost her children, but she had not another to save, like me; and I was bold enough to ask her would she give me that print. And she cried the more, and said *her* children were with that little blessed Jesus; and gave it me, and told me that she had heard it had been painted on the bottom of a cask, which made it have that round shape.[157] And when my body was very weary, and my heart was sick (for there were times when I misdoubted if I could ever reach my home, and there were times when I thought of my husband, and one time when I thought my baby was dying), I took out that picture and looked at it, till I could have thought the mother spoke to me, and comforted me. And the natives were very kind. We could not understand one another, but they saw my baby on my breast, and they came out to me, and brought me rice and milk, and sometimes flowers – I have got some of the flowers dried. Then, the next morning, I was so tired; and they wanted me to stay with them – I could tell that – and tried to frighten me from going into the deep woods, which, indeed, looked very strange and dark; but it seemed to me as if Death was following me to take my baby away from me; and as if I must go on, and on – and I thought how God had cared for mothers ever since the world was made, and would care for me; so I bade them goodbye, and set off afresh. And once when my baby was ill, and both she and I needed rest, He led me to a place where I found a kind Englishman lived, right in the midst of the natives.'

'And you reached Calcutta safely at last?'

'Yes, safely! Oh! when I knew I had only two days' journey more before me, I could not help it, ma'am – it might be idolatry, I cannot tell – but I was near one of the native temples, and I went into it with my baby to thank God for His great mercy; for it seemed to me that where others had prayed before to their God, in their joy or in their agony, was of itself a sacred place. And I got as servant to an invalid lady, who grew quite fond of my baby aboard-ship; and, in two years' time, Sam earned his discharge, and came home to me, and to our child. Then he had to fix on a trade; but he knew of none; and once, once upon a time, he had learnt some tricks from an Indian juggler; so he set up conjuring, and it answered so well that he took Thomas to help him – as his man, you know, not as another conjuror, though Thomas has set it up now on his own hook. But it has been a great help to us that likeness between the twins, and made a good many tricks go off well that they made up together. And Thomas is a good brother, only he has not the fine carriage of my husband, so that I can't think how he can be taken for Signor Brunoni himself, as he says he is.'

'Poor little Phoebe!' said I, my thoughts going back to the baby she carried all those hundred miles.

'Ah! you may say so! I never thought I should have reared her, though, when she fell ill at Chunderabaddad; but that good, kind Aga[158] Jenkyns took us in, which I believe was the very saving of her.'

'Jenkyns!' said I.

'Yes, Jenkyns. I shall think all people of that name are kind; for here is that nice old lady who comes every day to take Phoebe a walk!'

But an idea had flashed through my head; could the Aga Jenkyns be the lost Peter? True, he was reported by many to be dead. But, equally true, some had said that he had arrived at the dignity of Great Lama of Tibet. Miss Matty thought he was alive. I would make further enquiry.

CHAPTER 12

Engaged to be Married

WAS THE 'POOR PETER' of Cranford the Aga Jenkyns of Chunderabaddad, or was he not? As somebody says, that was the question.

In my own home, whenever people had nothing else to do, they blamed me for want of discretion. Indiscretion was my bugbear fault. Everybody has a bugbear fault, a sort of standing characteristic – a *pièce de résistance*[159] for their friends to cut at; and in general they cut and come again. I was tired of being called indiscreet and incautious; and I determined for once to prove myself a model of prudence and wisdom. I would not even hint my suspicions respecting the Aga. I would collect evidence and carry it home to lay before my father, as the family friend of the two Miss Jenkynses.

In my search after facts, I was often reminded of a description my father had once given of a ladies' committee that he had had to preside over. He said he could not help thinking of a passage in Dickens,[160] which spoke of a chorus in which every man took the tune he knew best, and sang it to his own satisfaction. So, at this charitable committee, every lady took the subject uppermost in her mind, and talked about it to her own great contentment, but not much to the advancement of the subject they had met to discuss. But even that committee could have been nothing to the Cranford ladies when I attempted to gain some clear and definite information as to poor Peter's height, appearance, and when and where he was seen and heard of last. For instance, I remember asking Miss Pole (and I thought the question was very opportune, for I put it when I met her at a call at Mrs Forrester's, and both the ladies had known Peter, and I imagined that they might refresh each other's memories) – I asked Miss Pole what was the very last thing they had ever heard about him; and then she named the absurd report to which I have alluded, about his having been elected Great Lama of Tibet; and this was a signal for each lady to go off on her separate idea. Mrs Forrester's start was made on the veiled prophet in 'Lalla Rookh'[161] – whether I thought he was meant for the Great Lama, though Peter was not so ugly, indeed rather handsome, if he had not been freckled. I was thankful to see her double upon Peter; but, in a moment, the delusive lady was off upon Rowlands' Kalydor,[162] and the merits of cosmetics and hair oils in general, and holding forth so fluently that I turned to listen to Miss Pole, who (through the llamas, the beasts of burden) had got to Peruvian bonds,[163] and the share market, and her poor opinion of joint-stock banks in general, and of that one in particular in which Miss Matty's money was invested. In vain I put in 'When was it – in what year was it that you heard that Mr Peter was the Great Lama?' They only joined issue to dispute whether llamas were carnivorous animals or not; in which dispute they were not quite on fair grounds, as Mrs Forrester (after they had grown warm and cool again) acknowledged that she always confused carnivorous and graminivorous together, just as she did horizontal and perpendicular; but then she apologised for it very prettily, by saying that in her day the only use people made of four-syllabled words was to teach how they should be spelt.

The only fact I gained from this conversation was that certainly Peter had last been heard of in India, 'or that neighbourhood'; and that this scanty intelligence of his whereabouts had reached Cranford in the year when Miss Pole had bought her Indian muslin gown, long since worn out (we washed it and mended it, and traced its decline and fall into a window-blind before we could go on); and in a year when Wombwell came to Cranford, because Miss Matty had wanted to see an elephant in order that she might the better imagine Peter riding on one; and had seen a boa constrictor too, which was more than she wished to imagine in her fancy-pictures of Peter's locality; and in a year when Miss Jenkyns had learnt some piece of poetry off by heart, and used to say, at all the Cranford parties, how Peter was 'surveying mankind from China to Peru',[164] which everybody had thought very grand, and rather appropriate, because India was between China and Peru, if you took care to turn the globe to the left instead of the right.

I suppose all these enquiries of mine, and the consequent curiosity excited in the minds of my friends, made us blind and deaf to what was going on around us. It seemed to me as if the sun rose and shone, and as if the rain rained on Cranford, just as usual, and I did not notice any sign of the times that could be considered as a prognostic of any uncommon event; and, to the best of my belief, not only Miss Matty and Mrs Forrester, but even Miss Pole herself, whom we looked upon as a kind of prophetess, from the knack she had of foreseeing things before they came to pass – although she did not like to disturb her friends by telling them her foreknowledge – even Miss Pole herself was breathless with astonishment when she came to tell us of the astounding piece of news. But I must recover myself; the contemplation of it, even at this distance of time, has taken away my breath and my grammar, and unless I subdue my emotion, my spelling will go too.

We were sitting – Miss Matty and I – much as usual, she in the blue chintz easy-chair, with her back to the light, and her knitting in her hand, I reading aloud the *St James's Chronicle*. A few minutes more, and we should have gone to make the little alterations in dress usual before calling-time (twelve o'clock) in Cranford. I remember the scene and the date well. We had been talking of the signor's rapid recovery since the warmer weather had set in, and praising Mr Hoggins's skill, and lamenting his want of refinement and manner (it seems a curious coincidence that this should have been our subject, but so it was), when a knock was heard – a caller's knock –

three distinct taps – and we were flying (that is to say, Miss Matty could not walk very fast, having had a touch of rheumatism) to our rooms, to change cap and collars, when Miss Pole arrested us by calling out, as she came up the stairs: 'Don't go – I can't wait – it is not twelve, I know – but never mind your dress – I must speak to you.' We did our best to look as if it was not we who had made the hurried movement, the sound of which she had heard; for, of course, we did not like to have it supposed that we had any old clothes that it was convenient to wear out in the 'sanctuary of home', as Miss Jenkyns once prettily called the back parlour, where she was tying up preserves. So we threw our gentility with double force into our manners, and very genteel we were for two minutes while Miss Pole recovered breath, and excited our curiosity strongly by lifting up her hands in amazement, and bringing them down in silence, as if what she had to say was too big for words, and could only be expressed by pantomime.

'What do you think, Miss Matty? What do you think? Lady Glenmire is to marry – is to be married, I mean – Lady Glenmire – Mr Hoggins – Mr Hoggins is going to marry Lady Glenmire!'

'Marry!' said we. 'Marry! Madness!'

'Marry!' said Miss Pole, with the decision that belonged to her character. 'I said marry! as you do; and I also said: "What a fool my lady is going to make of herself!" I could have said "Madness!" but I controlled myself, for it was in a public shop that I heard of it. Where feminine delicacy is gone to, I don't know! You and I, Miss Matty, would have been ashamed to have known that our marriage was spoken of in a grocer's shop, in the hearing of shopmen!'

'But,' said Miss Matty, sighing as one recovering from a blow, 'perhaps it is not true. Perhaps we are doing her injustice.'

'No,' said Miss Pole. 'I have taken care to ascertain that. I went straight to Mrs Fitz-Adam, to borrow a cookery-book which I knew she had; and I introduced my congratulations apropos of the difficulty gentlemen must have in housekeeping; and Mrs Fitz-Adam bridled up, and said that she believed it was true, though how and where I could have heard it she did not know. She said her brother and Lady Glenmire had come to an understanding at last. "Understanding"! such a coarse word! But my lady will have to come down to many a want of refinement. I have reason to believe Mr Hoggins sups on bread and cheese and beer every night.'

'Marry!' said Miss Matty once again. 'Well! I never thought of it. Two people that we know going to be married. It's coming very near!'

'So near that my heart stopped beating when I heard of it, while you might have counted twelve,' said Miss Pole.

'One does not know whose turn may come next. Here, in Cranford, poor Lady Glenmire might have thought herself safe,' said Miss Matty, with a gentle pity in her tones.

'Bah!' said Miss Pole, with a toss of her head. 'Don't you remember poor dear Captain Brown's song 'Tibbie Fowler',[165] and the line:

> 'Set her on the Tintock tap,
> The wind will blaw a man till her.'

'That was because "Tibbie Fowler" was rich, I think.'

'Well! there was a kind of attraction about Lady Glenmire that I, for one, should be ashamed to have.'

I put in my wonder. 'But how can she have fancied Mr Hoggins? I am not surprised that Mr Hoggins has liked her.'

'Oh! I don't know. Mr Hoggins is rich, and very pleasant-looking,' said Miss Matty, 'and very good-tempered and kind-hearted.'

'She has married for an establishment, that's it. I suppose she takes the surgery with it,' said Miss Pole, with a little dry laugh at her own joke. But, like many people who think they have made a severe and sarcastic speech, which yet is clever of its kind, she began to relax in her grimness from the moment when she made this allusion to the surgery; and we turned to speculate on the way in which Mrs Jamieson would receive the news. The person whom she had left in charge of her house to keep off followers from her maids to set up a follower of her own! And that follower a man whom Mrs Jamieson had tabooed as vulgar, and inadmissible to Cranford society, not merely on account of his name, but because of his voice, his complexion, his boots, smelling of the stable,[166] and himself, smelling of drugs. Had he ever been to see Lady Glenmire at Mrs Jamieson's? Chloride of lime would not purify the house in its owner's estimation if he had. Or had their interviews been confined to the occasional meetings in the chamber of the poor sick conjuror, to whom, with all our sense of the *mésalliance*,[167] we could not help allowing that they had both been exceedingly kind? And now it turned out that a servant of Mrs Jamieson's had been ill, and Mr Hoggins had been attending her for some weeks. So the wolf had got into the fold, and now he was carrying off the shepherdess. What would Mrs Jamieson say? We looked into the darkness of futurity as a child gazes after a rocket up in the cloudy sky, full of wondering expectation of the rattle, the discharge, and the brilliant shower of sparks and light. Then we brought ourselves down to earth and the present time by questioning each other (being all equally ignorant, and all equally without the slightest data to build any conclusions upon) as to when it would take place? Where? How much a year Mr Hoggins had? Whether she would drop her title? And how Martha and the other correct servants in Cranford would ever be brought to announce a married couple as Lady Glenmire and Mr Hoggins? But would they be visited? Would Mrs Jamieson let us? Or must we choose between the Honourable Mrs Jamieson and the degraded Lady Glenmire? We all liked Lady Glenmire the best. She was bright, and kind, and sociable, and agreeable; and Mrs Jamieson was dull, and inert, and pompous, and tiresome. But we had acknowledged the sway of the latter so long, that it seemed like a kind of disloyalty now even to meditate disobedience to the prohibition we anticipated.

Mrs Forrester surprised us in our darned caps and patched collars; and we forgot all about them in our eagerness to see how she would bear the information, which we honourably left to Miss Pole to impart, although, if we had been inclined to take unfair advantage, we might have rushed in ourselves, for she had a most out-of-place fit of coughing for five minutes after Mrs Forrester entered the room. I shall never forget the imploring expression of her eyes, as she looked at us over her pocket-handkerchief. They said, as plain as words could speak: 'Don't let Nature deprive me of the treasure which is mine, although for a time I can make no use of it.' And we did not.

Mrs Forrester's surprise was equal to ours; and her sense of injury rather greater, because she had to feel for her Order, and saw more fully than we could do how such conduct brought stains on the aristocracy.

When she and Miss Pole left us we endeavoured to subside into calmness; but Miss Matty was really upset by the intelligence she had heard. She reckoned it up, and it was more than fifteen years since she had heard of any of her acquaintance going to be married, with the one exception of Miss Jessie Brown; and, as she said, it gave her quite a shock, and made her feel as if she could not think what would happen next.

I don't know whether it is a fancy of mine, or a real fact, but I have noticed that, just after the announcement of an engagement in any set, the unmarried ladies in that set flutter out in an unusual gaiety and newness of dress, as much as to say, in a tacit and unconscious manner: 'We also are spinsters.' Miss Matty and Miss Pole talked and thought more about bonnets, gowns, caps, and shawls, during the fortnight that succeeded this call, than I had known them do for years before. But it might be the spring weather, for it was a warm and pleasant March; and merinoes and beavers,[168] and woollen materials of all sorts were but ungracious receptacles of the bright sun's glancing rays. It had not been Lady Glenmire's dress that had won Mr Hoggins's heart, for she went about on her errands of kindness more shabby than ever. Although in the hurried glimpses I caught of her at church or elsewhere she appeared rather to shun meeting any of her friends, her face seemed to have almost something of the flush of youth in it; her lips looked redder and more trembling full than in their old compressed state, and her eyes dwelt on all things with a lingering light, as if she was learning to love Cranford and its belongings. Mr Hoggins looked broad and radiant, and creaked up the middle aisle at church in a brand-new pair of top-boots – an audible, as well as visible, sign of his purposed change of state; for the tradition went, that the boots he had worn till now were the identical pair in which he first set out on his rounds in Cranford twenty-five years ago; only they had been new-pieced, high and low, top and bottom, heel and sole, black leather and brown leather, more times than anyone could tell.

None of the ladies in Cranford chose to sanction the marriage by congratulating either of the parties. We wished to ignore the whole affair until our liege lady, Mrs Jamieson, returned. Till she came back to give us our cue, we felt that it would be better to consider the engagement in the same light as the Queen of Spain's legs[169] – facts which certainly existed, but the less said about the better. This restraint upon our tongues – for, you see, if we did not speak about it to any of the parties concerned, how could we get answers to the questions that we longed to ask? – was beginning to be irksome, and our idea of the dignity of silence was paling before our curiosity, when another direction was given to our thoughts, by an announcement on the part of the principal shopkeeper of Cranford, who ranged the trades from grocer and cheesemonger to man-milliner, as occasion required, that the spring fashions were arrived, and would be exhibited on the following Tuesday at his rooms in High Street. Now Miss Matty had been only waiting for this before buying herself a new silk gown. I had offered, it is true, to send to Drumble for patterns, but she had rejected my proposal, gently implying that she had not forgotten her disappointment about the sea-green turban. I was thankful that I was on the spot now, to counteract the dazzling fascination of any yellow or scarlet silk.

I must say a word or two here about myself. I have spoken of my father's old friendship for the Jenkyns family; indeed, I am not sure if there was not some distant relationship. He had willingly allowed me to remain all the winter at Cranford, in consideration of a letter which Miss Matty had written to him about the time of the panic, in which I suspect she had exaggerated my powers and my bravery as a defender of the house. But now that the days were longer and more cheerful, he was beginning to urge the necessity of my return; and I only delayed in a sort of odd forlorn hope that if I could obtain any clear information, I might make the account given by the signora of the Aga Jenkyns tally with that of 'poor Peter', his appearance and disappearance, which I had winnowed out of the conversation of Miss Pole and Mrs Forrester.

CHAPTER 12

Stopped Payment

THE VERY TUESDAY MORNING on which Mr Johnson was going to show the fashions, the post-woman brought two letters to the house. I say the post-woman, but I should say the postman's wife. He was a lame shoemaker, a very clean, honest man, much respected in the town; but he never brought the letters round except on unusual occasions, such as Christmas Day or Good Friday; and on those days the letters, which should have been delivered at eight in the morning, did not make their appearance until two or three in the afternoon, for everyone liked poor Thomas, and gave him a welcome on these festive occasions. He used to say, 'He was welly stawed wi' eating, for there were three or four houses where nowt would serve 'em but he must share in their breakfast'; and by the time he had done his last breakfast, he came to some other friend who was beginning dinner; but come what might in the way of temptation, Tom was always sober, civil, and smiling; and, as Miss Jenkyns used to say, it was a lesson in patience, that she doubted not would call out that precious quality in some minds, where, but for Thomas, it might have lain dormant and undiscovered. Patience was certainly very dormant in Miss Jenkyns's mind. She was always expecting letters, and always drumming on the table till the post-woman had called or gone past. On Christmas Day and Good Friday she drummed from breakfast till church, from church-time till two o'clock – unless when the fire wanted stirring, when she invariably knocked down the fire-irons, and scolded Miss Matty for it. But equally certain was the hearty welcome and the good dinner for Thomas; Miss Jenkyns standing over him like a bold dragoon, questioning him as to his children – what they were doing – what school they went to; upbraiding him if another was likely to make its appearance, but sending even the little babies the shilling and the mince-pie which was her gift to all the children, with half a crown in addition for both father and mother. The post was not half of so much consequence to dear Miss Matty; but not for the world would she have diminished Thomas's welcome and his dole, though I could see that she felt rather shy over the ceremony, which had been regarded by Miss Jenkyns as a glorious opportunity for giving advice and benefiting her fellow creatures. Miss Matty would steal the money all in a lump into his hand, as if she were ashamed of herself. Miss Jenkyns gave him each individual coin separate, with a 'There! that's for yourself; that's for Jenny,' etc. Miss Matty would even beckon Martha out of the kitchen while he ate his food: and once, to my knowledge, winked at its rapid disappearance into a blue cotton pocket-handkerchief. Miss Jenkyns almost scolded him if he did not leave a clean plate, however heaped it might have been, and gave an injunction with every mouthful.

I have wandered a long way from the two letters that awaited us on the breakfast-table that Tuesday morning. Mine was from my father. Miss Matty's was printed. My father's was just a man's letter; I mean it was very dull, and gave no information beyond that he was well, that they had had a good deal of rain, that trade was very stagnant, and there were many disagreeable rumours afloat. He then asked me if I knew whether Miss Matty still retained her shares in the Town and County Bank, as there were very unpleasant reports about it; though nothing more than he had always foreseen, and had prophesied to Miss Jenkyns years ago, when she would invest their little property in it – the only unwise step that clever woman had ever taken, to his knowledge (the only time she ever acted against his advice, I knew). However, if anything had gone wrong, of course I was not to think of leaving Miss Matty while I could be of any use, etc.

'Who is your letter from, my dear? Mine is a very civil invitation, signed "Edwin Wilson", asking me to attend an important meeting of the shareholders of the Town and County Bank, to be held in Drumble, on Thursday the twenty-first. I am sure, it is very attentive of them to remember me.'

I did not like to hear of this 'important meeting', for, though I did not know much about business, I feared it confirmed what my father said: however, I thought, ill news always came fast enough, so I resolved to say nothing about my alarm, and merely told her that my father was well, and sent his kind regards to her. She kept turning over and admiring her letter. At last she spoke: 'I remember their sending one to Deborah just like this; but that I did not wonder at, for everybody knew she was so clear-headed. I am afraid I could not help them much; indeed, if they came to accounts I should be quite in the way, for I never could do sums in my head. Deborah, I know, rather wished to go, and went so far as to order a new bonnet for the occasion: but when the time came she had a bad cold; so they sent her a very polite account of what they had done. Chosen a director, I think it was. Do you think they want me to help them to choose a director? I am sure I should choose your father at once.'

'My father has no shares in the bank,' said I.

'Oh, no! I remember. He objected very much to Deborah's buying any, I believe. But she was quite the woman of business, and always judged for herself; and here, you see, they have paid eight per cent all these years.'

It was a very uncomfortable subject to me, with my half-knowledge; so I thought I would change the conversation, and I asked at what time she thought we had better go and see the fashions. 'Well, my dear,' she said, 'the thing is this: it is not etiquette to go till after twelve; but then, you see, all Cranford will be there, and one does not like to be too curious about dress and trimmings and caps with all the world looking on. It is never genteel to be over-curious on these occasions. Deborah had the knack of always looking as if the latest fashion was nothing new to her; a manner she had caught from Lady Arley, who did see all the new modes in London, you know. So I thought we would just slip down this morning, soon after breakfast – for I do want half a pound of tea – and then we could go up and examine the things at our leisure, and see exactly how my new silk gown must be made; and then, after twelve, we could go with our minds disengaged, and free from thoughts of dress.'

We began to talk of Miss Matty's new silk gown. I discovered that it would be really the first time in her life that she had had to choose anything of consequence for herself: for Miss Jenkyns had always been the more decided character, whatever her taste might have been; and it is astonishing how such people carry the world before them by the mere force of will. Miss Matty anticipated the sight of the glossy folds with as much delight as if the five sovereigns, set apart for the purchase, could buy all the silks in the shop; and (remembering my own loss of two hours in a toy shop before I could tell on what wonder to spend a silver threepence) I was very glad that we were going early, that dear Miss Matty might have leisure for the delights of perplexity.

If a happy sea-green could be met with, the gown was to be sea-green: if not, she inclined to maize, and I to silver grey; and we discussed the requisite number of breadths until we arrived at the shop-door. We were to buy the tea, select the silk, and then clamber up the iron corkscrew stairs that led into what was once a loft, though now a fashion showroom.

The young men at Mr Johnson's had on their best looks, and their best cravats, and pivoted themselves over the counter with surprising activity. They wanted to show us upstairs at once; but on the principle of business first and pleasure afterwards, we stayed to purchase the tea. Here Miss Matty's absence of mind betrayed itself. If she was made aware that she had been drinking green tea[170] at any time, she always thought it her duty to lie awake half through the night afterward (I have known her take it in ignorance many a time without such effects), and consequently green tea was prohibited the house; yet today she herself asked for the obnoxious article, under the impression that she was talking about the silk. However, the mistake was soon rectified; and then the silks were unrolled in good truth. By this time the shop was pretty well filled, for it was Cranford market-day, and many of the farmers and country people from the neighbourhood round came in, sleeking down their hair, and glancing shyly about, from under their eyelids, as anxious to take back some notion of the unusual gaiety to the mistress or the lasses at home, and yet feeling that they were out of place among the smart shopmen and gay shawls and summer prints. One honest-looking man, however, made his way up to the counter at which we stood, and boldly asked to look at a shawl or two. The other country folk confined themselves to the grocery side; but our neighbour was evidently too full of some kind intention towards mistress, wife, or daughter, to be shy; and it soon became a question with me, whether he or Miss Matty would keep their shopmen the longest time. He thought each shawl more beautiful than the last; and, as for Miss Matty, she smiled and sighed over each fresh bale that was brought out; one colour set off another, and the heap together would, as she said, make even the rainbow look poor.

'I am afraid,' said she, hesitating, 'whichever I choose I shall wish I had taken another. Look at this lovely crimson! it would be so warm in winter. But spring is coming on, you know. I wish I could have a gown for every season,' said she, dropping her voice – as we all did in Cranford whenever we talked of anything we wished for but could not afford. 'However,' she continued in a louder and more cheerful tone, 'it would give me a great deal of trouble to take care of them if I had them; so, I think, I'll only take one. But which must it be, my dear?'

And now she hovered over a lilac with yellow spots, while I pulled out a quiet sage-green that had faded into insignificance under the more brilliant colours, but which was nevertheless a good silk in its humble way. Our attention was called off to our neighbour. He had chosen a shawl of about thirty shillings' value; and his face looked broadly happy, under the anticipation, no doubt, of the pleasant surprise he would give to some Molly or Jenny at home; he had tugged a leathern purse out of his breeches pocket, and had offered a five-pound note in payment[171] for the shawl, and for some parcels which had been brought round to him from the grocery counter; and it was just at this point that he attracted our notice. The shopman was examining the note with a puzzled, doubtful air.

'Town and County Bank! I am not sure, sir, but I believe we have received a warning against notes issued by this bank only this morning. I will just step and ask Mr Johnson, sir; but I'm afraid I must trouble you for payment in cash, or in a note of a different bank.'

I never saw a man's countenance fall so suddenly into dismay and bewilderment. It was almost piteous to see the rapid change.

'Dang it!' said he, striking his fist down on the table, as if to try which was the harder, 'the chap talks as if notes and gold were to be had for the picking up.'

Miss Matty had forgotten her silk gown in her interest for the man. I don't think she had caught the name of the bank, and in my nervous cowardice I was anxious that she should not; and so I began admiring the yellow-spotted lilac gown that I had been utterly condemning only a minute before. But it was of no use.

'What bank was it? I mean, what bank did your note belong to?'

'Town and County Bank.'

'Let me see it,' said she quietly to the shopman, gently taking it out of his hand, as he brought it back to return it to the farmer.

Mr Johnson was very sorry, but, from information he had received, the notes issued by that bank were little better than waste paper.

'I don't understand it,' said Miss Matty to me in a low voice. 'That is our bank, is it not? – the Town and County Bank?'

'Yes,' said I. 'This lilac silk will just match the ribbons in your new cap, I believe,' I continued, holding up the folds so as to catch the light, and wishing that the man would make haste and be gone, and yet having a new wonder, that had only just sprung up, how far it was wise or right in me to allow Miss Matty to make this expensive purchase, if the affairs of the bank were really so bad as the refusal of the note implied.

But Miss Matty put on the soft dignified manner peculiar to her, rarely used, and yet which became her so well, and laying her hand gently on mine, she said: 'Never mind the silks for a few minutes, dear. I don't understand you, sir,' turning now to the shopman, who had been attending to the farmer. 'Is this a forged note?'

'Oh, no, ma'am. It is a true note of its kind; but you see, ma'am, it is a joint-stock bank, and there are reports out that it is likely to break. Mr Johnson is only doing his duty, ma'am, as I am sure Mr Dobson knows.'

But Mr Dobson could not respond to the appealing bow by any answering smile. He was turning the note absently over in his fingers, looking gloomily enough at the parcel containing the lately chosen shawl.

'It's hard upon a poor man,' said he, 'as earns every farthing with the sweat of his brow. However, there's no help for it. You must take back your shawl, my man; Lizzie must go on with her cloak for a while. And yon figs for the little ones – I promised them to 'em – I'll take them; but the 'bacco, and the other things – '

'I will give you five sovereigns for your note, my good man,' said Miss Matty. 'I think there is some great mistake about it, for I am one of the shareholders, and I'm sure they would have told me if things had not been going on right.'

The shopman whispered a word or two across the table to Miss Matty. She looked at him with a dubious air.

'Perhaps no,' said she. 'But I don't pretend to understand business; I only know that if it is going to fail, and if honest people are to lose their money because they have taken our notes – I can't explain myself,' said she, suddenly becoming aware that she had got into a long sentence with four people for audience; 'only I would rather exchange my gold for the note, if you please,' turning to the farmer, 'and then you can take your wife the shawl. It is only going without my gown a few days longer,' she continued, speaking to me. 'Then, I have no doubt, everything will be cleared up.'

'But if it is cleared up the wrong way?' said I.

'Why, then it will only have been common honesty in me, as a shareholder, to have given this good man the money. I am quite clear about it in my own mind; but, you know, I can never speak quite as comprehensibly as others can, only you must give me your note, Mr Dobson, if you please, and go on with your purchases with these sovereigns.'

The man looked at her with silent gratitude – too awkward to put his thanks into words; but he hung back for a minute or two, fumbling with his note.

'I'm loth to make another one lose instead of me, if it is a loss; but, you see, five pounds is a deal of money to a man with a family; and, as you say, ten to one in a day or two the note will be as good as gold again.'

'No hope of that, my friend,' said the shopman.

'The more reason why I should take it,' said Miss Matty quietly. She pushed her sovereigns towards the man, who slowly laid his note down in exchange. 'Thank you. I will wait a day or two before I purchase any of these silks; perhaps you will then have a greater choice. My dear, will you come upstairs?'

We inspected the fashions with as minute and curious an interest as if the gown to be made after them had been bought. I could not see that the little event in the shop below had in the least damped Miss Matty's curiosity as to the make of sleeves or the sit of skirts. She once or twice exchanged congratulations with me on our private and leisurely view of the bonnets and shawls; but I was, all the time, not so sure that our examination was so utterly private, for I caught glimpses of a figure dodging behind the cloaks and mantles; and, by a dexterous move, I came face to face with Miss Pole, also in morning costume (the principal feature of which was her being without teeth, and wearing a veil to conceal the deficiency), come on the same errand as ourselves. But she quickly took her departure, because as she said, she had a bad headache, and did not feel herself up to conversation.

As we came down through the shop, the civil Mr Johnson was awaiting us; he had been informed of the exchange of the note for gold, and with much good feeling and real kindness, but with a little want of tact, he wished to condole with Miss Matty, and impress upon her the true state of the case. I could only hope that he had heard an exaggerated rumour, for he said that her shares were worse than nothing, and that the bank could not pay a shilling in the pound. I was glad that Miss Matty seemed still a little incredulous; but I could not tell how much of this was real or assumed, with that self-control which seemed habitual to ladies of Miss Matty's standing in Cranford, who would have thought their dignity compromised by the slightest expression of surprise, dismay, or any similar feeling to an inferior in station, or in a public shop. However, we walked home very silently. I am ashamed to say, I believe I was rather vexed and annoyed at Miss Matty's conduct in taking the note to herself so decidedly. I had so set my heart upon her having a new silk gown, which she wanted sadly; in general she was so undecided anybody might turn her round; in this case I had felt that it was no use attempting it, but I was not the less put out at the result.

Somehow, after twelve o'clock, we both acknowledged to a sated curiosity about the fashions, and to a certain fatigue of body (which was, in fact, depression of mind) that indisposed us to go out again. But still we never spoke of the note; till, all at once, something possessed me to ask Miss Matty if she would think it her duty to offer sovereigns for all the notes of the Town and County Bank she met with? I could have bitten my tongue out the minute I had said it. She looked up rather sadly and as if I had thrown a new perplexity into her already distressed mind; and for a minute or two she did not speak. Then she said – my own dear Miss Matty – without a shade of reproach in her voice: 'My dear, I never feel as if my mind was what people call very strong; and it's often hard enough work for me to settle what I ought to do with the case right before me. I was very thankful to – I was very thankful, that I saw my duty this morning, with the poor man standing by me; but it's rather a strain upon me to keep thinking and thinking what I should do if such and such a thing happened; and, I believe, I had rather wait and see what really does come; and I don't doubt I shall be helped then if I don't fidget myself, and get too anxious beforehand. You know, love, I'm not like Deborah. If Deborah had lived, I've no doubt she would have seen after them, before they had got themselves into this state.'

We had neither of us much appetite for dinner, though we tried to talk cheerfully about indifferent things. When we returned into the drawing-room, Miss Matty unlocked her desk and began to look over her account-books. I was so penitent for what I had said in the morning, that I did not choose to take upon myself the presumption to suppose that I could assist her; I rather left her alone, as, with puzzled brow, her eye followed her pen up and down the ruled page. By and by she shut the book, locked the desk, and came and drew a chair to mine, where I sat in moody sorrow over the fire. I stole my hand into hers; she clasped it, but did not speak a word. At last she said, with forced composure in her voice: 'If that bank goes wrong, I shall lose one hundred and forty-nine pounds thirteen shillings and four pence a year; I shall only have thirteen pounds a year left.' I squeezed her hand hard and tight. I did not know what to say. Presently (it was too dark to see her face) I felt her fingers work convulsively in my grasp; and I knew she was going to speak again. I heard the sobs in her voice as she said: 'I hope it's not wrong – not wicked – but, oh! I am so glad poor Deborah is spared this. She could not have borne to come down in the world – she had such a noble, lofty spirit.'

This was all she said about the sister who had insisted upon investing their little property in that unlucky bank. We were later in lighting the candle than usual that night, and until that light shamed us into speaking, we sat together very silently and sadly.

However, we took to our work after tea with a kind of forced cheerfulness (which soon became real as far as it went), talking of that never-ending wonder, Lady Glenmire's engagement. Miss Matty was almost coming round to think it a good thing.

'I don't mean to deny that men are troublesome in a house. I don't judge from my own experience, for my father was neatness itself, and wiped his shoes on coming in as carefully as any woman; but still a man has a sort of knowledge of what should be done in difficulties, that it is very pleasant to have one at hand ready to lean upon. Now, Lady Glenmire, instead of being tossed about, and wondering where she is to settle, will be certain of a home among pleasant and kind people, such as our good Miss Pole and Mrs Forrester. And Mr Hoggins is really a very personable man; and as for his manners, why, if they are not very polished, I have known people with very good hearts and very clever minds too, who were not what some people reckoned refined, but who were both true and tender.'

She fell off into a soft reverie about Mr Holbrook, and I did not interrupt her, I was so busy maturing a plan I had had in my mind for some days, but which this threatened failure of the bank had brought to a crisis. That night, after Miss Matty went to bed, I treacherously lighted the candle again, and sat down in the drawing-room to compose a letter to the Aga Jenkyns, a letter which should affect him if he were Peter, and yet seem a mere statement of dry facts if he were a stranger. The church clock pealed out two before I had done.

The next morning news came, both official and otherwise, that the Town and County Bank had stopped payment. Miss Matty was ruined.

She tried to speak quietly to me; but when she came to the actual fact that she would have but about five shillings a week to live upon, she could not restrain a few tears.

'I am not crying for myself, dear,' said she, wiping them away; 'I believe I am crying for the very silly thought of how my mother would grieve if she could know; she always cared for us so much more than for herself. But many a poor person has less, and I am not very extravagant, and, thank God, when the neck of mutton, and Martha's wages, and the rent are paid, I have not a farthing owing. Poor Martha! I think she'll be sorry to leave me.'

Miss Matty smiled at me through her tears, and she would fain have had me see only the smile, not the tears.

CHAPTER 14

Friends in Need

It was an example to me, and I fancy it might be to many others, to see how immediately Miss Matty set about the retrenchment which she knew to be right under her altered circumstances. While she went down to speak to Martha, and break the intelligence to her, I stole out with my letter to the Aga Jenkyns, and went to the signor's lodgings to obtain the exact address. I bound the signora to secrecy; and indeed her military manners had a degree of shortness and reserve in them which made her always say as little as possible, except when under the pressure of strong excitement. Moreover (which made my secret doubly sure), the signor was now so far recovered as to be looking forward to travelling and conjuring again in the space of a few days, when he, his wife, and little Phoebe would leave Cranford. Indeed, I found him looking over a great black-and-red placard, in which the Signor Brunoni's accomplishments were set forth, and to which only the name of the town where he would next display them was wanting. He and his wife were so much absorbed in deciding where the red letters would come in with most effect (it might have been the Rubric[172] for that matter), that it was some time before I could get my question asked privately, and not before I had given several decisions, the wisdom of which I questioned afterwards with equal sincerity as soon as the signor threw in his doubts and reasons on the important subject. At last I got the address, spelt by sound, and very queer it looked. I dropped it in the post on my way home, and then for a minute I stood looking at the wooden pane with a gaping slit which divided me from the letter but a moment ago in my hand. It was gone from me like life, never to be recalled. It would get tossed about on the sea, and stained with sea-waves perhaps, and be carried among palm-trees, and scented with all tropical fragrance; the little piece of paper, but an hour ago so familiar and commonplace, had set out on its race to the strange wild countries beyond the Ganges! But I could not afford to lose much time on this speculation. I hastened home, that Miss Matty might not miss me. Martha opened the door to me, her face swollen with crying. As soon as she saw me she burst out afresh, and taking hold of my arm she pulled me in, and banged the door to, in order to ask me if indeed it was all true that Miss Matty had been saying.

'I'll never leave her! No; I won't. I telled her so, and said I could not think how she could find in her heart to give me warning. I could not have had the face to do it, if I'd been her. I might ha' been just as good for nothing as Mrs Fitz-Adam's Rosy, who struck for wages after living seven years and a half in one place. I said I was not one to go and serve Mammon at that rate; that I knew when I'd got a good missus, if she didn't know when she'd got a good servant – '

'But, Martha,' said I, cutting in while she wiped her eyes.

'Don't "but Martha" me,' she replied to my deprecatory tone.

'Listen to reason – '

'I'll not listen to reason,' she said, now in full possession of her voice, which had been rather choked with sobbing. 'Reason always means what someone else has got to say. Now I think what I've got to say is good enough reason; but reason or not, I'll say it, and I'll stick to it. I've money in the Savings Bank, and I've a good stock of clothes, and I'm not going to leave Miss Matty. No, not if she gives me warning every hour in the day!'

She put her arms akimbo, as much as to say she defied me; and, indeed, I could hardly tell how to begin to remonstrate with her, so much did I feel that Miss Matty, in her increasing infirmity, needed the attendance of this kind and faithful woman.

'Well – ' said I at last.

'I'm thankful you begin with "well"! If you'd ha' begun with "but", as you did afore, I'd not ha' listened to you. Now you may go on.'

'I know you would be a great loss to Miss Matty, Martha – '

'I telled her so. A loss she'd never cease to be sorry for,' broke in Martha triumphantly.

'Still, she will have so little – so very little – to live upon, that I don't see just now how she could find you food – she will even be pressed for her own. I tell you this, Martha, because I feel you are like a friend to dear Miss Matty, but you know she might not like to have it spoken about.'

Apparently this was even a blacker view of the subject than Miss Matty had presented to her, for Martha just sat down on the first chair that came to hand, and cried out loud (we had been standing in the kitchen).

At last she put her apron down, and looking me earnestly in the face, asked: 'Was that the reason Miss Matty wouldn't order a pudding today? She said she had no great fancy for sweet things, and you and she would just have a mutton chop. But I'll be up to her. Never you tell, but I'll make her a pudding, and a pudding she'll like, too, and I'll pay for it myself; so mind you see she eats it. Many a one has been comforted in their sorrow by seeing a good dish come upon the table.'

I was rather glad that Martha's energy had taken the immediate and practical direction of pudding-making, for it staved off the quarrelsome discussion as to whether she should or should not leave Miss Matty's service. She began to tie on a clean apron, and otherwise prepare herself for going to the shop for the butter, eggs, and what else she might require. She would not use a scrap of the articles already in the house for her cookery, but went to an old teapot in which her private store of money was deposited, and took out what was wanted.

I found Miss Matty very quiet, and not a little sad; but by and by she tried to smile for my sake. It was settled that I was to write to my father, and ask him to come over and hold a consultation, and as soon as this letter was dispatched we began to talk over future plans. Miss Matty's idea was to take a single room, and retain as much of her furniture as would be necessary to fit up this, and sell the rest, and there to quietly exist upon what would remain after paying the rent. For my part, I was more ambitious and less contented. I thought of all the things by which a woman, past middle age, and with the education common to ladies fifty years ago, could earn or add to a living without materially losing caste; but at length I put even this last clause on one side, and wondered what in the world Miss Matty could do.

Teaching was, of course, the first thing that suggested itself. If Miss Matty could teach children anything, it would throw her among the little elves in whom her soul delighted. I ran over her accomplishments. Once upon a time I had heard her say she could play 'Ah! vous dirai-je, maman?'[173] on the piano, but that was long, long ago; that faint shadow of musical acquirement had died out years before. She had also once been able to trace out patterns very nicely for muslin embroidery, by dint of placing a piece of silver paper over the design to be copied, and holding both against the window-pane while she marked the scollop and eyelet-holes. But that was her nearest approach to the accomplishment of drawing, and I did not think it would go very far. Then again, as to the branches of a solid English education – fancy work and the use of the globes – such as the mistress of the Ladies' Seminary,[174] to which all the tradespeople in Cranford sent their daughters, professed to teach; Miss Matty's eyes were failing her, and I doubted if she could discover the number of threads in a worsted-work pattern, or rightly appreciate the different shades required for Queen Adelaide's face in the loyal wool-work[175] now fashionable in Cranford. As for the use of the globes, I had never been able to find it out myself, so perhaps I was not a good judge of Miss Matty's capability of instructing in this branch of education; but it struck me that equators and tropics, and such mystical circles, were very imaginary lines indeed to her, and that she looked upon the signs of the Zodiac as so many remnants of the Black Art.

What she piqued herself upon, as arts in which she excelled, was making candle-lighters, or 'spills' (as she preferred calling them), of coloured paper, cut so as to resemble feathers, and knitting garters in a variety of dainty stitches. I had once said, on receiving a present of an elaborate pair, that I should feel quite tempted to drop one of them in the street, in order to have it admired; but I found this little joke (and it was a very little one) was such a distress to her sense of propriety, and was taken with such anxious, earnest alarm, lest the temptation might some day prove too strong for me, that I quite regretted having ventured upon it. A present of these delicately wrought garters, a bunch of gay 'spills', or a set of cards on which sewing-silk was wound in a mystical manner, were the well-known tokens of Miss Matty's favour. But would anyone pay to have their children taught these arts? or, indeed, would Miss Matty sell, for filthy lucre, the knack and the skill with which she made trifles of value to those who loved her?

I had to come down to reading, writing, and arithmetic; and, in reading the chapter[176] every morning, she always coughed before coming to long words. I doubted her power of getting through a genealogical chapter, with any number of coughs. Writing she did well and delicately – but spelling! She seemed to think that the more out-of-the-way this was, and the more trouble it cost her, the greater the compliment she paid to her correspondent; and words that she would spell quite correctly in her letters to me became perfect enigmas when she wrote to my father.

No! there was nothing she could teach to the rising generation of Cranford, unless they had been quick learners and ready imitators of her patience, her humility, her sweetness, her quiet contentment with all that she could not do. I pondered and pondered until dinner was announced by Martha, with a face all blubbered and swollen with crying.

Miss Matty had a few little peculiarities which Martha was apt to regard as whims below her attention, and appeared to consider as childish fancies of which an old lady of fifty-eight should try and cure herself. But today everything was attended to with the most careful regard. The bread was cut to the imaginary pattern of excellence that existed in Miss Matty's mind, as being the way which her mother had preferred, the curtain was drawn so as to exclude the dead brick wall of a neighbour's stable, and yet left so as to show every tender leaf of the poplar which was bursting into spring beauty. Martha's tone to Miss Matty was just such as that good, rough-spoken servant usually kept sacred for little children, and which I had never heard her use to any grown-up person.

I had forgotten to tell Miss Matty about the pudding, and I was afraid she might not do justice to it, for she had evidently very little appetite this day; so I seized the opportunity of letting her into the secret while Martha took away the meat. Miss Matty's eyes filled with tears, and she could not speak, either to express surprise or delight, when Martha returned bearing it aloft, made in the most wonderful representation of a lion *couchant*[177] that ever was moulded. Martha's face gleamed with triumph as she set it down before Miss Matty with an exultant 'There!' Miss Matty wanted to speak her thanks, but could not; so she took Martha's hand and shook it warmly, which set Martha off crying, and I myself could hardly keep up the necessary composure. Martha burst out of the room, and Miss Matty had to clear her voice once or twice before she could speak. At last she said: 'I should like to keep this pudding under a glass shade, my dear!' and the notion of the lion *couchant*, with his currant eyes, being hoisted up to the place of honour on a mantelpiece, tickled my hysterical fancy, and I began to laugh, which rather surprised Miss Matty.

'I am sure, dear, I have seen uglier things under a glass shade before now,' said she.

So had I, many a time and oft, and I accordingly composed my countenance (and now I could hardly keep from crying), and we both fell to upon the pudding, which was indeed excellent – only every morsel seemed to choke us, our hearts were so full.

We had too much to think about to talk much that afternoon. It passed over very tranquilly. But when the tea-urn was brought in a new thought came into my head. Why should not Miss Matty sell tea – be an agent to the East India Tea Company which then existed? I could see no objections to this plan, while the advantages were many – always supposing that Miss Matty could get over the degradation of condescending to anything like trade. Tea was neither greasy nor sticky – grease and stickiness being two of the qualities which Miss Matty could not endure. No shop-window would be required. A small, genteel notification of her being licensed to sell tea would, it is true, be necessary, but I hoped that it could be placed where no one would see it. Neither was tea a heavy article, so as to tax Miss Matty's fragile strength. The only thing against my plan was the buying and selling involved.

While I was giving but absent answers to the questions Miss Matty was putting – almost as absently – we heard a clumping sound on the stairs, and a whispering outside the door, which indeed once opened and shut as if by some invisible agency. After a little while Martha came in, dragging after her a great tall young man, all crimson with shyness, and finding his only relief in perpetually sleeking down his hair.

'Please, ma'am, he's only Jem Hearn,' said Martha, by way of an introduction; and so out of breath was she that I imagine she had had some bodily struggle before she could overcome his reluctance to be presented on the courtly scene of Miss Matilda Jenkyns's drawing-room.

'And please, ma'am, he wants to marry me off-hand. And please, ma'am, we want to take a lodger – just one quiet lodger, to make our two ends meet; and we'd take any house conformable; and, oh dear Miss Matty, if I may be so bold, would you have any objections to lodging with us? Jem wants it as much as I do.' [To Jem:] – 'You great oaf! why can't you back me! – But he does want it all the same, very bad – don't you, Jem? – only, you see, he's dazed at being called on to speak before quality.'

'It's not that,' broke in Jem. 'It's that you've taken me all on a sudden, and I didn't think for to get married so soon – and such quick words does flabbergast a man. It's not that I'm against it, ma'am' (addressing Miss Matty), 'only Martha has such quick ways with her when once she takes a thing into her head; and marriage, ma'am – marriage nails a man, as one may say. I dare say I shan't mind it after it's once over.'

'Please, ma'am,' said Martha – who had plucked at his sleeve, and nudged him with her elbow, and otherwise tried to interrupt him all the time he had been speaking – 'don't mind him, he'll come to; 'twas only last night he was an-axing me, and an-axing me, and all the more because I said I could not think of it for years to come, and now he's only taken aback with the suddenness of the joy; but you know, Jem, you are just as full as me about wanting a lodger.' (Another great nudge.)

'Ay! if Miss Matty would lodge with us – otherwise I've no mind to be cumbered with strange folk in the house,' said Jem, with a want of tact which I could see enraged Martha, who was trying to represent a lodger as the great object they wished to obtain, and that, in fact, Miss Matty would be smoothing their path and conferring a favour, if she would only come and live with them.

Miss Matty herself was bewildered by the pair; their, or rather Martha's sudden resolution in favour of matrimony staggered her, and stood between her and the contemplation of the plan which Martha had at heart. Miss Matty began: 'Marriage is a very solemn thing, Martha.'

'It is indeed, ma'am,' quoth Jem. 'Not that I've no objections to Martha.'

'You've never let me a-be for asking me for to fix when I would be married,' said Martha – her face all afire, and ready to cry with vexation – 'and now you're shaming me before my missus and all.'

'Nay, now! Martha, don't ee! don't ee! only a man likes to have breathing-time,' said Jem, trying to possess himself of her hand, but in vain. Then seeing that she was more seriously hurt than he had imagined, he seemed to try to rally his scattered faculties, and with more straightforward dignity than, ten minutes before, I should have thought it possible for him to assume, he turned to Miss Matty, and said: 'I hope, ma'am, you know that I am bound to respect everyone who has been kind to Martha. I always looked on her as to be my wife – some time; and she has often and often spoken of you as the kindest lady that ever was; and though the plain truth is, I would not like to be troubled with lodgers of the common run, yet if, ma'am, you'd honour us by living with us, I'm sure Martha would do her best to make you comfortable; and I'd keep out of your way as much as I could, which I reckon would be the best kindness such an awkward chap as me could do.'

Miss Matty had been very busy with taking off her spectacles, wiping them, and replacing them; but all she could say was: 'Don't let any thought of me hurry you into marriage: pray don't. Marriage is such a very solemn thing!'

'But Miss Matilda will think of your plan, Martha,' said I, struck with the advantages that it offered, and unwilling to lose the opportunity of considering about it. 'And I'm sure neither she nor I can ever forget your kindness; nor yours either, Jem.'

'Why, yes, ma'am! I'm sure I mean kindly, though I'm a bit fluttered by being pushed straight ahead into matrimony, as it were, and mayn't express myself conformable. But I'm sure I'm willing enough, and give me time to get accustomed; so, Martha, wench, what's the use of crying so, and slapping me if I come near?'

This last was *sotto voce*, and had the effect of making Martha bounce out of the room, to be followed and soothed by her lover. Whereupon Miss Matty sat down and cried very heartily, and accounted for it by saying that the thought of Martha being married so soon gave her quite a shock, and that she should never forgive herself if she thought she was hurrying the poor creature. I think my pity was more for Jem, of the two; but both Miss Matty and I appreciated to the full the kindness of the honest couple, although we said little about this, and a good deal about the chances and dangers of matrimony.

The next morning, very early, I received a note from Miss Pole, so mysteriously wrapped up, and with so many seals on it to secure secrecy, that I had to tear the paper before I could unfold it. And when I came to the writing I could hardly understand the meaning, it was so involved and oracular. I made out, however, that I was to go to Miss Pole's at eleven o'clock; the number *eleven* being written in full length as well as in numerals, and a.m. twice dashed under, as if I were very likely to come at eleven at night, when all Cranford was usually abed and asleep by ten. There was no signature except Miss Pole's initials reversed, P. E.; but as Martha had given me the note, 'with Miss Pole's kind regards', it needed no wizard to find out who sent it; and if the writer's name was to be kept secret, it was very well that I was alone when Martha delivered it.

I went as requested to Miss Pole's. The door was opened to me by her little maid Lizzy in Sunday trim, as if some grand event was impending over this workday. And the drawing-room upstairs was arranged in accordance with this idea. The table was set out with the best green card-cloth, and writing materials upon it. On the little chiffonier was a tray with a newly decanted bottle of cowslip wine, and some ladies'-finger biscuits. Miss Pole herself was in solemn array, as if to receive visitors, although it was only eleven o'clock. Mrs Forrester was there, crying quietly and sadly, and my arrival seemed only to call forth fresh tears. Before we had finished our greetings, performed with lugubrious mystery of demeanour, there was another rat-tat-tat, and Mrs Fitz-Adam appeared, crimson with walking and excitement. It seemed as if this was all the company expected; for now Miss Pole made several demonstrations of being about to open the business of the meeting, by stirring the fire, opening and shutting the door, and coughing and blowing her nose. Then she arranged us all round the table, taking care to place me opposite to her; and last of all, she enquired of me if the sad report was true, as she feared it was, that Miss Matty had lost all her fortune?

Of course, I had but one answer to make; and I never saw more unaffected sorrow depicted on any countenances than I did there on the three before me.

'I wish Mrs Jamieson was here!' said Mrs Forrester at last; but to judge from Mrs Fitz-Adam's face, she could not second the wish.

'But without Mrs Jamieson,' said Miss Pole, with just a sound of offended merit in her voice, 'we, the ladies of Cranford, in my drawing-room assembled, can resolve upon something. I imagine we are none of us what may be called rich, though we all possess a genteel competency, sufficient for tastes that are elegant and refined, and would not, if they could, be vulgarly ostentatious.' (Here I observed Miss Pole refer to a small card concealed in her hand, on which I imagine she had put down a few notes.)

'Miss Smith,' she continued, addressing me (familiarly known as 'Mary' to all the company assembled, but this was a state occasion), 'I have conversed in private – I made it my business to do so yesterday afternoon – with these ladies on the misfortune which has happened to our friend, and one and all of us have agreed that while we have a superfluity, it is not only a duty, but a pleasure – a true pleasure, Mary!' – her voice was rather choked just here, and she had to wipe her spectacles before she could go on – 'to give what we can to assist her – Miss Matilda Jenkyns. Only in consideration of the feelings of delicate independence existing in the mind of every refined female – ' I was sure she had got back to the card now – 'we wish to contribute our mites in a secret and concealed manner, so as not to hurt the feelings I have referred to. And our object in requesting you to meet us this morning is that, believing you are the daughter – that your father is, in fact, her confidential adviser, in all pecuniary matters, we imagined that, by consulting with him, you might devise some mode in which our contribution could be made to appear the legal due which Miss Matilda Jenkyns ought to receive from —. Probably your father, knowing her investments, can fill up the blank.'

Miss Pole concluded her address, and looked round for approval and agreement.

'I have expressed your meaning, ladies, have I not? And while Miss Smith considers what reply to make, allow me to offer you some little refreshment.'

I had no great reply to make: I had more thankfulness at my heart for their kind thoughts than I cared to put into words; and so I only mumbled out something to the effect 'that I would name what Miss Pole had said to my father, and that if anything could be arranged for dear Miss Matty' – and here I broke down utterly, and had to be refreshed with a glass of cowslip wine before I could check the crying which had been repressed for the last two or three days. The worst was, all the ladies cried in concert. Even Miss Pole cried, who had said a hundred times that to betray emotion before anyone was a sign of weakness and want of self-control. She recovered herself into a slight degree of impatient anger, directed against me, as having set them all off; and, moreover, I think she was vexed that I could not make a speech back in return for hers; and if I had known beforehand what was to be said, and had a card on which to express the probable feelings that would rise in my heart, I would have tried to gratify her. As it was, Mrs Forrester was the person to speak when we had recovered our composure.

'I don't mind, among friends, stating that I – no! I'm not poor exactly, but I don't think I'm what you may call rich; I wish I were, for dear Miss Matty's sake – but, if you please, I'll write down in a sealed paper what I can give. I only wish it was more; my dear Mary, I do indeed.'

Now I saw why paper, pens, and ink were provided. Every lady wrote down the sum she could give annually, signed the paper, and sealed it mysteriously. If their proposal was acceded to, my father was to be allowed to open the papers, under pledge of secrecy. If not, they were to be returned to their writers.

When the ceremony had been gone through, I rose to depart; but each lady seemed to wish to have a private conference with me. Miss Pole kept me in the drawing-room to explain why, in Mrs Jamieson's absence, she had taken the lead in this 'movement', as she was pleased to call it, and also to inform me that she had heard from good sources that Mrs Jamieson was coming home directly in a state of high displeasure against her sister-in-law, who was forthwith to lease her house, and was, she believed, to return to Edinburgh that very afternoon. Of course this piece of intelligence could not be communicated before Mrs Fitz-Adam, more especially as Miss Pole was inclined to think that Lady Glenmire's engagement to Mr Hoggins could not possibly hold against the blaze of Mrs Jamieson's displeasure. A few hearty enquiries after Miss Matty's health concluded my interview with Miss Pole.

On coming downstairs I found Mrs Forrester waiting for me at the entrance to the dining-parlour; she drew me in, and when the door was shut, she tried two or three times to begin on some subject, which was so unapproachable apparently, that I began to despair of our ever getting to a clear understanding. At last out it came; the poor old lady trembling all the time as if it were a great crime which she was exposing to daylight, in telling me how very, very little she had to live upon; a confession which she was brought to make from a dread lest we should think that the small contribution named in her paper bore any proportion to her love and regard for Miss Matty. And yet that sum which she so eagerly relinquished was, in truth, more than a twentieth part of what she had to live upon, and keep house, and a little serving-maid, all as became one born a Tyrrell. And when the whole income does not nearly amount to a hundred pounds, to give up a twentieth of it will necessitate many careful economies, and many pieces of self-denial, small and insignificant in the world's account, but bearing a different value in another account-book that I have heard of. She did so wish she was rich, she said, and this wish she kept repeating, with no thought of herself in it, only with a longing, yearning desire to be able to heap up Miss Matty's measure of comforts.

It was some time before I could console her enough to leave her; and then, on quitting the house, I was waylaid by Mrs Fitz-Adam, who had also her confidence to make of pretty nearly the opposite description. She had not liked to put down all that she could afford and was ready to give. She told me she thought she never could look Miss Matty in the face again if she presumed to be giving her so much as she should like to do. 'Miss Matty!' continued she, 'that I thought was such a fine young lady when I was nothing but a country girl, coming to market with eggs and butter and suchlike things. For my father, though well-to-do, would always make me go on as my mother had done before me, and I had to come into Cranford every Saturday, and see after sales, and prices, and what not. And one day, I remember, I met Miss Matty in the lane that leads to Combehurst; she was walking on the footpath, which, you know, is raised a good way above the road, and a gentleman rode beside her, and was talking to her, and she was looking down at some primroses she had gathered, and pulling them all to pieces, and I do believe she was crying. But after she had passed, she turned round and ran after me to ask – oh, so kindly – about my poor mother, who lay on her deathbed; and when I cried she took hold of my hand to comfort me – and the gentleman waiting for her all the time – and her poor heart very full of something, I am sure; and I thought it such an honour to be spoken to in that pretty way by the rector's daughter, who visited at Arley Hall. I have loved her ever since, though perhaps I'd no right to do it; but if you can think of any way in which I might be allowed to give a little more without anyone knowing it, I should be so much obliged to you, my dear. And my brother would be delighted to doctor her for nothing – medicines, leeches, and all. I know that he and her ladyship (my dear, I little thought in the days I was telling you of that I should ever come to be sister-in-law to a ladyship!) would do anything for her. We all would.'

I told her I was quite sure of it, and promised all sorts of things in my anxiety to get home to Miss Matty, who might well be wondering what had become of me – absent from her two hours without being able to account for it. She had taken very little note of time, however, as she had been occupied in numberless little arrangements preparatory to the great step of giving up her house. It was evidently a relief to her to be doing something in the way of retrenchment, for, as she said, whenever she paused to think, the recollection of the poor fellow with his bad five-pound note came over her, and she felt quite dishonest; only if it made her so uncomfortable, what must it not be doing to the directors of the bank, who must know so much more of the misery consequent upon this failure? She almost made me angry by dividing her sympathy between these directors (whom she imagined overwhelmed by self-reproach for the mismanagement of other people's affairs) and those who were suffering like her. Indeed, of the two, she seemed to think poverty a lighter burden than self-reproach; but I privately doubted if the directors would agree with her.

Old hoards were taken out and examined as to their money value, which luckily was small, or else I don't know how Miss Matty would have prevailed upon herself to part with such things as her mother's wedding-ring, the strange, uncouth brooch with which her father had disfigured his shirt-frill, etc. However, we arranged things a little in order as to pecuniary estimation, and were all ready for my father when he came the next morning.

I am not going to weary you with the details of all the business we went through; and one reason for not telling about them is, that I did not understand what we were doing at the time, and cannot recollect it now. Miss Matty and I sat assenting to accounts, and schemes, and reports, and documents, of which I do not believe we either of us understood a word; for my father was clear-headed and decisive, and a capital man of business, and if we made the slightest enquiry, or expressed the slightest want of comprehension, he had a sharp way of saying: 'Eh? eh? it's as clear as daylight. What's your objection?' And as we had not comprehended anything of what he had proposed, we found it rather difficult to shape our objections; in fact, we never were sure if we had any. So presently Miss Matty got into a nervously acquiescent state, and said 'Yes,' and 'Certainly,' at every pause, whether required or not; but when I once joined in as chorus to a 'Decidedly,' pronounced by Miss Matty in a tremblingly dubious tone, my father fired round at me and asked me 'What there was to decide?' And I am sure to this day I have never known. But, in justice to him, I must say he had come over from Drumble to help Miss Matty when he could ill spare the time, and when his own affairs were in a very anxious state.

While Miss Matty was out of the room giving orders for luncheon – and sadly perplexed between her desire of honouring my father by a delicate, dainty meal, and her conviction that she had no right, now that all her money was gone, to indulge this desire – I told him of the meeting of the Cranford ladies at Miss Pole's the day before. He kept brushing his hand before his eyes as I spoke – and when I went back to Martha's offer the evening before, of receiving Miss Matty as a lodger, he fairly walked away from me to the window, and began drumming with his fingers upon it. Then he turned abruptly round, and said: 'See, Mary, how a good, innocent life makes friends all round. Confound it! I could make a good lesson out of it if I were a parson; but, as it is, I can't get a tail to my sentences – only I'm sure you feel what I want to say. You and I will have a walk after lunch and talk a bit more about these plans.'

The lunch – a hot savoury mutton-chop, and a little of the cold lion sliced and fried – was now brought in. Every morsel of this last dish was finished, to Martha's great gratification. Then my father bluntly told Miss Matty he wanted to talk to me alone, and that he would stroll out and see some of the old places, and then I could tell her what plan we thought desirable. Just before we went out, she called me back and said: 'Remember, dear, I'm the only one left – I mean, there's no one to be hurt by what I do. I'm willing to do anything that's right and honest; and I don't think, if Deborah knows where she is, she'll care so very much if I'm not genteel; because, you see, she'll know all, dear. Only let me see what I can do, and pay the poor people as far as I'm able.'

I gave her a hearty kiss, and ran after my father. The result of our conversation was this. If all parties were agreeable, Martha and Jem were to be married with as little delay as possible, and they were to live on in Miss Matty's present abode; the sum which the Cranford ladies had agreed to contribute annually being sufficient to meet the greater part of the rent, and leaving Martha free to appropriate what Miss Matty should pay for her lodgings to any little extra comforts required. About the sale, my father was dubious at first. He said the old rectory furniture, however carefully used and reverently treated, would fetch very little; and that little would be but as a drop in the sea of the debts of the Town and County Bank. But when I represented how Miss Matty's tender conscience would be soothed by feeling that she had done what she could, he gave way; especially after I had told him the five-pound note adventure, and he had scolded me well for allowing it. I then alluded to my idea that she might add to her small income by selling tea; and, to my surprise (for I had nearly given up the plan), my father grasped at it with all the energy of a tradesman. I think he reckoned his chickens before they were hatched, for he immediately ran up the profits of the sales that she could effect in Cranford to more than twenty pounds a year. The small dining-parlour was to be converted into a shop, without any of its degrading characteristics; a table was to be the counter; one window was to be retained unaltered, and the other changed into a glass door. I evidently rose in his estimation for having made this bright suggestion. I only hoped we should not both fall in Miss Matty's.

But she was patient and content with all our arrangements. She knew, she said, that we should do the best we could for her; and she only hoped, only stipulated, that she should pay every farthing that she could be said to owe, for her father's sake, who had been so respected in Cranford. My father and I had agreed to say as little as possible about the bank, indeed never to mention it again, if it could be helped. Some of the plans were evidently a little perplexing to her; but she had seen me sufficiently snubbed in the morning for want of comprehension to venture on too many enquiries now; and all passed over well, with a hope on her part that no one would be hurried into marriage on her account. When we came to the proposal that she should sell tea, I could see it was rather a shock to her; not on account of any personal loss of gentility involved, but only because she distrusted her own powers of action in a new line of life, and would timidly have preferred a little more privation to any exertion for which she feared she was unfitted. However, when she saw my father was bent upon it, she sighed, and said she would try; and if she did not do well, of course she might give it up. One good thing about it was, she did not think men ever bought tea; and it was of men particularly she was afraid. They had such sharp loud ways with them; and did up accounts, and counted their change so quickly! Now, if she might only sell comfits to children, she was sure she could please them!

CHAPTER 15

A Happy Return

Before I left Miss Matty at Cranford everything had been comfortably arranged for her. Even Mrs Jamieson's approval of her selling tea had been gained. That oracle had taken a few days to consider whether by so doing Miss Matty would forfeit her right to the privileges of society in Cranford. I think she had some little idea of mortifying Lady Glenmire by the decision she gave at last; which was to this effect: that whereas a married woman takes her husband's rank by the strict laws of precedence, an unmarried woman retains the station her father occupied. So Cranford was allowed to visit Miss Matty; and, whether allowed or not, it intended to visit Lady Glenmire.

But what was our surprise – our dismay – when we learnt that Mr and *Mrs Hoggins* were returning on the following Tuesday! Mrs Hoggins! Had she absolutely dropped her title, and so, in a spirit of bravado, cut the aristocracy to become a Hoggins! She, who might have been called Lady Glenmire to her dying day! Mrs Jamieson was pleased. She said it only convinced her of what she had known from the first, that the creature had a low taste. But 'the creature' looked very happy on Sunday at church; nor did we see it necessary to keep our veils down on that side of our bonnets on which Mr and Mrs Hoggins sat, as Mrs Jamieson did; thereby missing all the smiling glory of his face, and all the becoming blushes of hers. I am not sure if Martha and Jem looked more radiant in the afternoon, when they, too, made their first appearance. Mrs Jamieson soothed the turbulence of her soul by having the blinds of her windows drawn down, as if for a funeral, on the day when Mr and Mrs Hoggins received callers; and it was with some difficulty that she was prevailed upon to continue the *St James's Chronicle*, so indignant was she with its having inserted the announcement of the marriage.

Miss Matty's sale went off famously. She retained the furniture of her sitting-room and bedroom; the former of which she was to occupy till Martha could meet with a lodger who might wish to take it; and into this sitting-room and bedroom she had to cram all sorts of things, which were (the auctioneer assured her) bought in for her at the sale by an unknown friend. I always suspected Mrs Fitz-Adam of this; but she must have had an accessory, who knew what articles were particularly regarded by Miss Matty on account of their associations with her early days. The rest of the house looked rather bare, to be sure; all except one tiny bedroom, of which my father allowed me to purchase the furniture for my occasional use in case of Miss Matty's illness.

I had expended my own small store in buying all manner of comfits and lozenges, in order to tempt the little people whom Miss Matty loved so much to come about her. Tea in bright green canisters, and comfits in tumblers – Miss Matty and I felt quite proud as we looked round us on the evening before the shop was to be opened. Martha had scoured the boarded floor to a white cleanness, and it was adorned with a brilliant piece of oilcloth, on which customers were to stand before the table-counter. The wholesome smell of plaster and whitewash pervaded the apartment. A very small 'Matilda Jenkyns, licensed to sell tea', was hidden under the lintel of the new door, and two boxes of tea, with cabalistic inscriptions all over them, stood ready to disgorge their contents into the canisters.

Miss Matty, as I ought to have mentioned before, had had some scruples of conscience at selling tea when there was already Mr Johnson in the town, who included it among his numerous commodities; and, before she could quite reconcile herself to the adoption of her new business, she had trotted down to his shop, unknown to me, to tell him of the project that was entertained, and to enquire if it was likely to injure his business. My father called this idea of hers 'great nonsense', and 'wondered how tradespeople were to get on if there was to be a continual consulting of each other's interests, which would put a stop to all competition directly'. And, perhaps, it would not have done in Drumble, but in Cranford it answered very well; for not only did Mr Johnson kindly put at rest all Miss Matty's scruples and fear of injuring his business, but I have reason to know he repeatedly sent customers to her, saying that the teas he kept were of a common kind, but that Miss Jenkyns had all the choice sorts. And expensive tea is a very favourite luxury with well-to-do tradespeople and rich farmers' wives, who turn up their noses at the Congou and Souchong prevalent at many tables of gentility, and will have nothing else than Gunpowder and Pekoe for themselves.

But to return to Miss Matty. It was really very pleasant to see how her unselfishness and simple sense of justice called out the same good qualities in others. She never seemed to think anyone would impose upon her, because she should be so grieved to do it to them. I have heard her put a stop to the asseverations of the man who brought her coals by quietly saying: 'I am sure you would be sorry to bring me wrong weight'; and if the coals were short measure that time, I don't believe they ever were again. People would have felt as much ashamed of presuming on her good faith as they would have done on that of a child. But my father says 'such simplicity might be very well in Cranford, but would never do in the world'. And I fancy the world must be very bad, for with all my father's suspicion of everyone with whom he has dealings, and in spite of all his many precautions, he lost upwards of a thousand pounds by roguery only last year.

I just stayed long enough to establish Miss Matty in her new mode of life, and to pack up the library, which the rector had purchased. He had written a very kind letter to Miss Matty, saying 'how glad he should be to take a library, so well selected as he knew that the late Mr Jenkyns' must have been, at any valuation put upon them'. And when she agreed to this, with a touch of sorrowful gladness that they would go back to the rectory and be arranged on the accustomed walls once more, he sent word that he feared that he had not room for them all, and perhaps Miss Matty would kindly allow him to leave some volumes on her shelves. But Miss Matty said that she had her Bible and Johnson's *Dictionary*, and should not have much time for reading, she was afraid; still, I retained a few books out of consideration for the rector's kindness.

The money which he had paid, and that produced by the sale, was partly expended in the stock of tea, and part of it was invested against a rainy day – i.e. old age or illness. It was but a small sum, it is true; and it occasioned a few evasions of truth and white lies (all of which I think very wrong indeed – in theory – and would rather not put them in practice), for we knew Miss Matty would be perplexed as to her duty if she were aware of any little reserve fund being made for her while the debts of the bank remained unpaid. Moreover, she had never been told of the way in which her friends were contributing to pay the rent. I should have liked to tell her this, but the mystery of the affair gave a piquancy to their deed of kindness which the ladies were unwilling to give up; and first Martha had to shirk many a perplexed question as to her ways and means of living in such a house, but by and by Miss Matty's prudent uneasiness sank down into acquiescence with the existing arrangement.

I left Miss Matty with a good heart. Her sales of tea during the first two days had surpassed my most sanguine expectations. The whole country round seemed to be all out of tea at once. The only alteration I could have desired in Miss Matty's way of doing business was, that she should not have so plaintively entreated some of her customers not to buy green tea – running it down as a slow poison, sure to destroy the nerves, and produce all manner of evil. Their pertinacity in taking it, in spite of all her warnings, distressed her so much that I really thought she would relinquish the sale of it, and so lose half her custom; and I was driven to my wits' end for instances of longevity entirely attributable to a persevering use of green tea. But the final argument, which settled the question, was a happy reference of mine to the train-oil[178] and tallow candles which the Esquimaux not only enjoy but digest. After that she acknowledged that 'one man's meat might be another man's poison', and contented herself thenceforward with an occasional remonstrance when she thought the purchaser was too young and innocent to be acquainted with the evil effects green tea produced on some constitutions, and an habitual sigh when people old enough to choose more wisely would prefer it.

I went over from Drumble once a quarter at least to settle the accounts, and see after the necessary business letters. And, speaking of letters, I began to be very much ashamed of remembering my letter to the Aga Jenkyns, and very glad I had never named my writing to anyone. I only hoped the letter was lost. No answer came. No sign was made.

About a year after Miss Matty set up shop, I received one of Martha's hieroglyphics, begging me to come to Cranford very soon. I was afraid that Miss Matty was ill, and went off that very afternoon and took Martha by surprise when she saw me on opening the door. We went into the kitchen as usual, to have our confidential conference, and then Martha told me she was expecting her confinement very soon – in a week or two; and she did not think Miss Matty was aware of it, and she wanted me to break the news to her, 'for indeed, miss,' continued Martha, crying hysterically, 'I'm afraid she won't approve of it, and I'm sure I don't know who is to take care of her as she should be taken care of when I am laid up.'

I comforted Martha by telling her I would remain till she was about again, and only wished she had told me her reason for this sudden summons, as then I would have brought the requisite stock of clothes. But Martha was so tearful and tender-spirited, and unlike her usual self, that I said as little as possible about myself, and endeavoured rather to comfort Martha under all the probable and possible misfortunes which came crowding upon her imagination.

I then stole out of the house-door, and made my appearance as if I were a customer in the shop, just to take Miss Matty by surprise, and gain an idea of how she looked in her new situation. It was warm May weather, so only the little half-door was closed; and Miss Matty sat behind the counter, knitting an elaborate pair of garters; elaborate they seemed to me, but the difficult stitch was no weight upon her mind, for she was singing in a low voice to herself as her needles went rapidly in and out. I call it singing, but I dare say a musician would not use that word to the tuneless yet sweet humming of the low worn voice. I found out from the words, far more than from the attempt at the tune, that it was the *Old Hundredth*[179] she was crooning to herself; but the quiet continuous sound told of content, and gave me a pleasant feeling, as I stood in the street just outside the door, quite in harmony with that soft May morning. I went in. At first she did not catch who it was, and stood up as if to serve me; but in another minute watchful pussy had clutched her knitting, which was dropped in eager joy at seeing me. I found, after we had had a little conversation, that it was as Martha said, and that Miss Matty had no idea of the approaching household event. So I thought I would let things take their course, secure that when I went to her with the baby in my arms, I should obtain that forgiveness for Martha which she was needlessly frightening herself into believing that Miss Matty would withhold, under some notion that the new claimant would require attentions from its mother that it would be faithless treason to Miss Matty to render.

But I was right. I think that must be an hereditary quality, for my father says he is scarcely ever wrong. One morning, within a week after I arrived, I went to call Miss Matty, with a little bundle of flannel in my arms. She was very much awestruck when I showed her what it was, and asked for her spectacles off the dressing-table, and looked at it curiously, with a sort of tender wonder at its small perfection of parts. She could not banish the thought of the surprise all day, but went about on tiptoe, and was very silent. But she stole up to see Martha and they both cried with joy, and she got into a complimentary speech to Jem, and did not know how to get out of it again, and was only extricated from her dilemma by the sound of the shop-bell, which was an equal relief to the shy, proud, honest Jem, who shook my hand so vigorously when I congratulated him, that I think I feel the pain of it yet.

I had a busy life while Martha was laid up. I attended on Miss Matty, and prepared her meals; I cast up her accounts, and examined into the state of her canisters and tumblers. I helped her, too, occasionally, in the shop; and it gave me no small amusement, and sometimes a little uneasiness, to watch her ways there. If a little child came in to ask for an ounce of almond comfits (and four of the large kind which Miss Matty sold weighed that much), she always added one more by 'way of make-weight', as she called it, although the scale was handsomely turned before; and when I remonstrated against this, her reply was: 'The little things like it so much!' There was no use in telling her that the fifth comfit weighed a quarter of an ounce, and made every sale into a loss to her pocket. So I remembered the green tea, and winged my shaft with a feather out of her own plumage. I told her how unwholesome almond comfits were, and how ill excess in them might make the little children. This argument produced some effect; for, henceforward, instead of the fifth comfit, she always told them to hold out their tiny palms, into which she shook either peppermint or ginger lozenges, as a preventive to the dangers that might arise from the previous sale. Altogether the lozenge trade, conducted on these principles, did not promise to be remunerative; but I was happy to find she had made more than twenty pounds during the last year by her sales of tea; and, moreover, that now she was accustomed to it, she did not dislike the employment, which brought her into kindly intercourse with many of the people round about. If she gave them good weight, they, in their turn, brought many a little country present to the 'old rector's daughter'; a cream cheese, a few new-laid eggs, a little fresh ripe fruit, a bunch of flowers. The counter was quite loaded with these offerings sometimes, as she told me.

As for Cranford in general, it was going on much as usual. The Jamieson and Hoggins feud still raged, if a feud it could be called, when only one side cared much about it. Mr and Mrs Hoggins were very happy together, and, like most very happy people, quite ready to be friendly; indeed, Mrs Hoggins was really desirous to be restored to Mrs Jamieson's good graces, because of the former intimacy. But Mrs Jamieson considered their very happiness an insult to the Glenmire family, to which she had still the honour to belong, and she doggedly refused and rejected every advance. Mr Mulliner, like a faithful clansman, espoused his mistress's side with ardour. If he saw either Mr or Mrs Hoggins, he would cross the street, and appear absorbed in the contemplation of life in general, and his own path in particular, until he had passed them by. Miss Pole used to amuse herself with wondering what in the world Mrs Jamieson would do, if either she, or Mr Mulliner, or any other member of her household was taken ill; she could hardly have the face to call in Mr Hoggins after the way she had behaved to them. Miss Pole grew quite impatient for some indisposition or accident to befall Mrs Jamieson or her dependants, in order that Cranford might see how she would act under the perplexing circumstances.

Martha was beginning to go about again, and I had already fixed a limit, not very far distant, to my visit, when one afternoon, as I was sitting in the shop parlour with Miss Matty – I remember the weather was colder now than it had been in May, three weeks before, and we had a fire and kept the door fully closed – we saw a gentleman go slowly past the window, and then stand opposite to the door, as if looking out for the name which we had so carefully hidden. He took out a double eye-glass and peered about for some time before he could discover it. Then he came in. And, all on a sudden, it flashed across me that it was the Aga himself! For his clothes had an out-of-the-way foreign cut about them, and his face was deep brown, as if tanned and retanned by the sun. His complexion contrasted oddly with his plentiful snow-white hair, his eyes were dark and piercing, and he had an odd way of contracting them and puckering up his cheeks into innumerable wrinkles when he looked earnestly at objects. He did so to Miss Matty when he first came in. His glance had first caught and lingered a little upon me, but then turned, with the peculiar searching look I have described, to Miss Matty. She was a little fluttered and nervous, but no more so than she always was when any man came into her shop. She thought that he would probably have a note, or a sovereign at least, for which she would have to give change, which was an operation she very much disliked to perform. But the present customer stood opposite to her, without asking for anything, only looking fixedly at her as he drummed upon the table with his fingers, just for all the world as Miss Jenkyns used to do. Miss Matty was on the point of asking him what he wanted (as she told me afterwards), when he turned sharp to me: 'Is your name Mary Smith?'

'Yes!' said I.

All my doubts as to his identity were set at rest, and I only wondered what he would say or do next, and how Miss Matty would stand the joyful shock of what he had to reveal. Apparently he was at a loss how to announce himself, for he looked round at last in search of something to buy, so as to gain time, and, as it happened, his eye caught on the almond comfits, and he boldly asked for a pound of 'those things'. I doubt if Miss Matty had a whole pound in the shop, and, besides the unusual magnitude of the order, she was distressed with the idea of the indigestion they would produce, taken in such unlimited quantities. She looked up to remonstrate. Something of tender relaxation in his face struck home to her heart. She said: 'It is – oh, sir! can you be Peter?' and trembled from head to foot. In a moment he was round the table and had her in his arms, sobbing the tearless cries of old age. I brought her a glass of wine, for indeed her colour had changed so as to alarm me and Mr Peter too. He kept saying: 'I have been too sudden for you, Matty – I have, my little girl.'

I proposed that she should go at once up into the drawing-room and lie down on the sofa there. She looked wistfully at her brother, whose hand she had held tight, even when nearly fainting; but on his assuring her that he would not leave her, she allowed him to carry her upstairs.

I thought that the best I could do was to run and put the kettle on the fire for early tea, and then to attend to the shop, leaving the brother and sister to exchange some of the many thousand things they must have to say. I had also to break the news to Martha, who received it with a burst of tears which nearly infected me. She kept recovering herself to ask if I was sure it was indeed Miss Matty's brother, for I had mentioned that he had grey hair, and she had always heard that he was a very handsome young man. Something of the same kind perplexed Miss Matty at teatime, when she was installed in the great easy-chair opposite to Mr Jenkyns in order to gaze her fill. She could hardly drink for looking at him, and as for eating, that was out of the question.

'I suppose hot climates age people very quickly,' said she, almost to herself. 'When you left Cranford you had not a grey hair in your head.'

'But how many years ago is that?' said Mr Peter, smiling.

'Ah, true! yes, I suppose you and I are getting old. But still I did not think we were so very old! But white hair is very becoming to you, Peter,' she continued – a little afraid lest she had hurt him by revealing how his appearance had impressed her.

'I suppose I forgot dates too, Matty, for what do you think I have brought for you from India? I have an Indian muslin gown and a pearl necklace for you somewhere in my chest at Portsmouth.'[180] He smiled as if amused at the idea of the incongruity of his presents with the appearance of his sister; but this did not strike her all at once, while the elegance of the articles did. I could see that for a moment her imagination dwelt complacently on the idea of herself thus attired; and instinctively she put her hand up to her throat – that little delicate throat which (as Miss Pole had told me) had been one of her youthful charms; but the hand met the touch of folds of soft muslin in which she was always swathed up to her chin, and the sensation recalled a sense of the unsuitableness of a pearl necklace to her age. She said: 'I'm afraid I'm too old; but it was very kind of you to think of it. They are just what I should have liked years ago – when I was young.'

'So I thought, my little Matty. I remembered your tastes; they were so like my dear mother's.' At the mention of that name the brother and sister clasped each other's hands yet more fondly, and, although they were perfectly silent, I fancied they might have something to say if they were unchecked by my presence, and I got up to arrange my room for Mr Peter's occupation that night, intending myself to share Miss Matty's bed. But at my movement, he started up. 'I must go and settle about a room at the George. My carpetbag is there too.'

'No!' said Miss Matty, in great distress – 'you must not go; please, dear Peter – pray, Mary – oh! you must not go!'

She was so much agitated that we both promised everything she wished. Peter sat down again and gave her his hand, which for better security she held in both of hers, and I left the room to accomplish my arrangements.

Long, long into the night, far, far into the morning, did Miss Matty and I talk. She had much to tell me of her brother's life and adventures, which he had communicated to her as they had sat alone. She said all was thoroughly clear to her; but I never quite understood the whole story; and when in after days I lost my awe of Mr Peter enough to question him myself, he laughed at my curiosity, and told me stories that sounded so very much like Baron Munchausen's,[181] that I was sure he was making fun of me. What I heard from Miss Matty was that he had been a volunteer at the siege of Rangoon;[182] had been taken prisoner by the Burmese; and somehow obtained favour and eventual freedom from knowing how to bleed the chief of the small tribe in some case of dangerous illness; that on his release from years of captivity he had had his letters returned from England with the ominous word 'Dead' marked upon them; and, believing himself to be the last of his race, he had settled down as an indigo planter, and had proposed to spend the remainder of his life in the country to whose inhabitants and modes of life he had become habituated, when my letter had reached him; and, with the odd vehemence which characterised him in age as it had done in youth, he had sold his land and all his possessions to the first purchaser, and come home to the poor old sister, who was more glad and rich than any princess when she looked at him. She talked me to sleep at last, and then I was awakened by a slight sound at the door, for which she begged my pardon as she crept penitently into bed; but it seems that when I could no longer confirm her belief that the long-lost was really here – under the same roof – she had begun to fear lest it was only a waking dream of hers; that there never had been a Peter sitting by her all that blessed evening – but that the real Peter lay dead far away beneath some wild sea-wave, or under some strange eastern tree. And so strong had this nervous feeling of hers become, that she was fain to get up and go and convince herself that he was really there by listening through the door to his even, regular breathing – I don't like to call it snoring, but I heard it myself through two closed doors – and by and by it soothed Miss Matty to sleep.

I don't believe Mr Peter came home from India as rich as a

nabob;[183] he even considered himself poor, but neither he nor Miss Matty cared much about that. At any rate, he had enough to live upon 'very genteelly' at Cranford; he and Miss Matty together. And a day or two after his arrival, the shop was closed, while troops of little urchins gleefully awaited the shower of comfits and lozenges that came from time to time down upon their faces as they stood up-gazing at Miss Matty's drawing-room windows. Occasionally Miss Matty would say to them (half-hidden behind the curtains): 'My dear children, don't make yourselves ill'; but a strong arm pulled her back, and a more rattling shower than ever succeeded. A part of the tea was sent in presents to the Cranford ladies; and some of it was distributed among the old people who remembered Mr Peter in the days of his frolicsome youth. The Indian muslin gown was reserved for darling Flora Gordon (Miss Jessie Brown's daughter). The Gordons had been on the Continent for the last few years, but were now expected to return very soon; and Miss Matty, in her sisterly pride, anticipated great delight in the joy of showing them Mr Peter. The pearl necklace disappeared; and about that time many handsome and useful presents made their appearance in the households of Miss Pole and Mrs Forrester; and some rare and delicate Indian ornaments graced the drawing-rooms of Mrs Jamieson and Mrs Fitz-Adam. I myself was not forgotten. Among other things, I had the handsomest-bound and best edition of Dr Johnson's works that could be procured; and dear Miss Matty, with tears in her eyes, begged me to consider it as a present from her sister as well as herself. In short, no one was forgotten; and, what was more, everyone, however insignificant, who had shown kindness to Miss Matty at any time, was sure of Mr Peter's cordial regard.

CHAPTER 16

Peace to Cranford

It was not surprising that Mr Peter became such a favourite at Cranford. The ladies vied with each other who should admire him most; and no wonder, for their quiet lives were astonishingly stirred up by the arrival from India – especially as the person arrived told more wonderful stories than Sindbad the Sailor; and, as Miss Pole said, was quite as good as an Arabian Night any evening. For my own part, I had vibrated all my life between Drumble and Cranford, and I thought it was quite possible that all Mr Peter's stories might be true, although wonderful; but when I found that, if we swallowed an anecdote of tolerable magnitude one week, we had the dose considerably increased the next, I began to have my doubts; especially as I noticed that when his sister was present the accounts of Indian life were comparatively tame; not that she knew more than we did, perhaps less. I noticed also that when the rector came to call, Mr Peter talked in a different way about the countries he had been in. But I don't think the ladies in Cranford would have considered him such a wonderful traveller if they had only heard him talk in the quiet way he did to him. They liked him the better, indeed, for being what they called 'so very Oriental'.

One day, at a select party in his honour, which Miss Pole gave, and from which, as Mrs Jamieson honoured it with her presence, and had even offered to send Mr Mulliner to wait, Mr and Mrs Hoggins and Mrs Fitz-Adam were necessarily excluded – one day at Miss Pole's, Mr Peter said he was tired of sitting upright against the hard-backed uneasy chairs, and asked if he might not indulge himself in sitting cross-legged. Miss Pole's consent was eagerly given, and down he went with the utmost gravity. But when Miss Pole asked me, in an audible whisper, 'if he did not remind me of the Father of the Faithful?'[184] I could not help thinking of poor Simon Jones, the lame tailor, and while Mrs Jamieson slowly commented on the elegance and convenience of the attitude, I remembered how we had all followed that lady's lead in condemning Mr Hoggins for vulgarity because he simply crossed his legs as he sat still on his chair. Many of Mr Peter's ways of eating were a little strange amongst such ladies as Miss Pole, and Miss Matty, and Mrs Jamieson, especially when I recollected the untasted green peas and two-pronged forks at poor Mr Holbrook's dinner.

The mention of that gentleman's name recalls to my mind a conversation between Mr Peter and Miss Matty one evening in the summer after he returned to Cranford. The day had been very hot, and Miss Matty had been much oppressed by the weather, in the heat of which her brother revelled. I remember that she had been unable to nurse Martha's baby, which had become her favourite employment of late, and which was as much at home in her arms as in its mother's, as long as it remained a lightweight, portable by one so fragile as Miss Matty. This day to which I refer, Miss Matty had seemed more than usually feeble and languid, and only revived when the sun went down, and her sofa was wheeled to the open window, through which, although it looked into the principal street of Cranford, the fragrant smell of the neighbouring hayfields came in every now and then, borne by the soft breezes that stirred the dull air of the summer twilight, and then died away. The silence of the sultry atmosphere was lost in the murmuring noises which came in from many an open window and door; even the children were abroad in the street, late as it was (between ten and eleven), enjoying the game of play for which they had not had spirits during the heat of the day. It was a source of satisfaction to Miss Matty to see how few candles were lighted, even in the apartments of those houses from which issued the greatest signs of life. Mr Peter, Miss Matty, and I had all been quiet, each with a separate reverie, for some little time, when Mr Peter broke in: 'Do you know, little Matty, I could have sworn you were on the high road to matrimony when I left England that last time! If anybody had told me you would have lived and died an old maid then, I should have laughed in their faces.'

Miss Matty made no reply, and I tried in vain to think of some subject which should effectually turn the conversation; but I was very stupid; and before I spoke he went on: 'It was Holbrook, that fine manly fellow who lived at Woodley, that I used to think would carry off my little Matty. You would not think it now, I dare say, Mary; but this sister of mine was once a very pretty girl – at least, I thought so, and so I've a notion did poor Holbrook. What business had he to die before I came home to thank him for all his kindness to a good-for-nothing cub as I was? It was that that made me first think he cared for you; for in all our fishing expeditions it was Matty, Matty, we talked about. Poor Deborah! What a lecture she read me on having asked him home to lunch one day, when she had seen the Arley carriage in the town, and thought that my lady might call. Well, that's long years ago; more than half a lifetime, and yet it seems like yesterday! I don't know a fellow I should have liked better as a brother-in-law. You must have played your cards badly, my little Matty, somehow or another – wanted your brother to be a good go-between, eh, little one?' said he, putting out his hand to take hold of hers as she lay on the sofa. 'Why, what's this? you're shivering and shaking, Matty, with that confounded open window. Shut it, Mary, this minute!'

I did so, and then stooped down to kiss Miss Matty, and see if she really were chilled. She caught at my hand, and gave it a hard squeeze – but unconsciously, I think – for in a minute or two she spoke to us quite in her usual voice, and smiled our uneasiness away, although she patiently submitted to the prescriptions we enforced of a warm bed and a glass of weak negus.[185] I was to leave Cranford the next day, and before I went I saw that all the effects of the open window had quite vanished. I had superintended most of the alterations necessary in the house and household during the latter weeks of my stay. The shop was once more a parlour; the empty resounding rooms again furnished up to the very garrets.

There had been some talk of establishing Martha and Jem in another house, but Miss Matty would not hear of this. Indeed, I never saw her so much roused as when Miss Pole had assumed it to be the most desirable arrangement. As long as Martha would remain with Miss Matty, Miss Matty was only too thankful to have her about her; yes, and Jem too, who was a very pleasant man to have in the house, for she never saw him from week's end to week's end. And as for the probable children, if they would all turn out such little darlings as her goddaughter, Matilda, she should not mind the number, if Martha didn't. Besides, the next was to be called Deborah – a point which Miss Matty had reluctantly yielded to Martha's stubborn determination that her first-born was to be Matilda. So Miss Pole had to lower her colours, and even her voice, as she said to me that, as Mr and Mrs Hearn were still to go on living in the same house with Miss Matty, we had certainly done a wise thing in hiring Martha's niece as an auxiliary.

I left Miss Matty and Mr Peter most comfortable and contented; the only subject for regret to the tender heart of the one, and the social friendly nature of the other, being the unfortunate quarrel between Mrs Jamieson and the plebeian Hogginses and their following. In joke, I prophesied one day that this would only last until Mrs Jamieson or Mr Mulliner were ill, in which case they would only be too glad to be friends with Mr Hoggins; but Miss Matty did not like my looking forward to anything like illness in so light a manner, and before the year was out all had come round in a far more satisfactory way.

I received two Cranford letters on one auspicious October morning. Both Miss Pole and Miss Matty wrote to ask me to come over and meet the Gordons, who had returned to England alive and well with their two children, now almost grown up. Dear Jessie Brown had kept her old kind nature, although she had changed her name and station; and she wrote to say that she and Major Gordon expected to be in Cranford on the fourteenth, and she hoped and begged to be remembered to Mrs Jamieson (named first, as became her honourable station), Miss Pole and Miss Matty – could she ever forget their kindness to her poor father and sister? – Mrs Forrester, Mr Hoggins (and here again came in an allusion to kindness shown to the dead long ago), his new wife, who as such must allow Mrs Gordon to desire to make her acquaintance, and who was, moreover, an old Scotch friend of her husband's. In short, everyone was named, from the rector – who had been appointed to Cranford in the interim between Captain Brown's death and Miss Jessie's marriage, and was now associated with the latter event – down to Miss Betty Barker. All were asked to the luncheon; all except Mrs Fitz-Adam, who had come to live in Cranford since Miss Jessie Brown's days, and whom I found rather moping on account of the omission. People wondered at Miss Betty Barker's being included in the honourable list; but, then, as Miss Pole said, we must remember the disregard of the genteel proprieties of life in which the poor captain had educated his girls, and for his sake we swallowed our pride. Indeed, Mrs Jamieson rather took it as a compliment, as putting Miss Betty (formerly *her* maid)[186] on a level with 'those Hogginses'.

But when I arrived in Cranford, nothing was as yet ascertained of Mrs Jamieson's own intentions; would the honourable lady go, or would she not? Mr Peter declared that she should and she would; Miss Pole shook her head and desponded. But Mr Peter was a man of resources. In the first place, he persuaded Miss Matty to write to Mrs Gordon, and to tell her of Mrs Fitz-Adam's existence, and to beg that one so kind, and cordial, and generous, might be included in the pleasant invitation. An answer came back by return of post, with a pretty little note for Mrs Fitz-Adam, and a request that Miss Matty would deliver it herself and explain the previous omission. Mrs Fitz-Adam was as pleased as could be, and thanked Miss Matty over and over again. Mr Peter had said: 'Leave Mrs Jamieson to me'; so we did; especially as we knew nothing that we could do to alter her determination if once formed.

I did not know, nor did Miss Matty, how things were going on, until Miss Pole asked me, just the day before Mrs Gordon came, if I thought there was anything between Mr Peter and Mrs Jamieson in the matrimonial line, for that Mrs Jamieson was really going to the lunch at the George. She had sent Mr Mulliner down to desire that there might be a footstool put to the warmest seat in the room, as she meant to come, and knew that their chairs were very high. Miss Pole had picked this piece of news up, and from it she conjectured all sorts of things, and bemoaned yet more. 'If Peter should marry, what would become of poor dear Miss Matty? And Mrs Jamieson, of all people!' Miss Pole seemed to think there were other ladies in Cranford who would have done more credit to his choice, and I think she must have had someone who was unmarried in her head, for she kept saying: 'It was so wanting in delicacy in a widow to think of such a thing.'

When I got back to Miss Matty's I really did begin to think that Mr Peter might be thinking of Mrs Jamieson for a wife, and I was as unhappy as Miss Pole about it. He had the proof sheet of a great placard in his hand. 'Signor Brunoni, Magician to the King of Delhi, the Rajah of Oude, and the great Lama of Tibet', etc., was going to 'perform in Cranford for one night only', the very next night; and Miss Matty, exultant, showed me a letter from the Gordons, promising to remain over this gaiety, which Miss Matty said was entirely Peter's doing. He had written to ask the signor to come, and was to be at all the expenses of the affair. Tickets were to be sent gratis to as many as the room would hold. In short, Miss Matty was charmed with the plan, and said that tomorrow Cranford would remind her of the Preston Guild,[187] to which she had been in her youth – a luncheon at the George, with the dear Gordons, and the signor in the Assembly Room in the evening. But I – I looked only at the fatal words: '*Under the Patronage of the Honourable Mrs Jamieson*'.

She, then, was chosen to preside over this entertainment of Mr Peter's; she was perhaps going to displace my dear Miss Matty in his heart, and make her life lonely once more! I could not look forward to the morrow with any pleasure; and every innocent anticipation of Miss Matty's only served to add to my annoyance.

So, angry and irritated, and exaggerating every little incident which could add to my irritation, I went on till we were all assembled in the great parlour at the George. Major and Mrs Gordon and pretty Flora and Mr Ludovic were all as bright and handsome and friendly as could be; but I could hardly attend to them for watching Mr Peter, and I saw that Miss Pole was equally busy. I had never seen Mrs Jamieson so roused and animated before; her face looked full of interest in what Mr Peter was saying. I drew near to listen. My relief was great when I caught that his words were not words of love, but that, for all his grave face, he was at his old tricks. He was telling her of his travels in India, and describing the wonderful height of the Himalaya mountains: one touch after another added to their size, and each exceeded the former in absurdity; but Mrs Jamieson really enjoyed all in perfect good faith. I suppose she required strong stimulants to excite her to come out of her apathy. Mr Peter wound up his account by saying that, of course, at that altitude there were none of the animals to be found that existed in the lower regions; the game – everything was different. Firing one day at some flying creature, he was very much dismayed when it fell, to find that he had shot a cherubim! Mr Peter caught my eye at this moment, and gave me such a funny twinkle, that I felt sure he had no thoughts of Mrs Jamieson as a wife from that time. She looked uncomfortably amazed: 'But, Mr Peter, shooting a cherubim – don't you think – I am afraid that was sacrilege!'

Mr Peter composed his countenance in a moment, and appeared shocked at the idea, which, as he said truly enough, was now presented to him for the first time; but then Mrs Jamieson must remember that he had been living for a long time among savages – all of whom were heathens – some of them, he was afraid, were downright Dissenters.[188] Then, seeing Miss Matty draw near, he hastily changed the conversation, and after a little while, turning to me, he said: 'Don't be shocked, prim little Mary, at all my wonderful stories. I consider Mrs Jamieson fair game, and besides I am bent on propitiating her, and the first step towards it is keeping her well awake. I bribed her here by asking her to let me have her name as patroness for my poor conjuror this evening; and I don't want to give her time enough to get up her rancour against the Hogginses, who are just coming in. I want everybody to be friends, for it harasses Matty so much to hear of these quarrels. I shall go at it again by and by, so you need not look shocked. I intend to enter the Assembly Room tonight with Mrs Jamieson on one side, and my lady, Mrs Hoggins, on the other. You see if I don't.'

Somehow or another he did; and fairly got them into conversation together. Major and Mrs Gordon helped at the good work with their perfect ignorance of any existing coolness between any of the inhabitants of Cranford.

Ever since that day there has been the old friendly sociability in Cranford society; which I am thankful for, because of my dear Miss Matty's love of peace and kindliness. We all love Miss Matty, and I somehow think we are all of us better when she is near us.

NOTES TO *CRANFORD*

I have been able to profit from consulting the following previous editions of *Cranford:* Knutsford Edition of *Works* (Vol. 2, A. W. Ward, 1906); Penguin English Library (Peter Keating, 1976); Everyman Library (Graham Handley, 1995); Oxford World's Classics (Elizabeth Porges Watson, 1972; with Charlotte Mitchell, 1998).

Abbreviations used in the Notes (details given in the Bibliography)

ECG Elizabeth Cleghorn Gaskell

EGEY John Chapple, *Elizabeth Gaskell: The Early Years*, 1997

GSJ *Gaskell Society Journal*

Green Henry Green, *Knutsford*, 1859

Letters *The Letters of Mrs Gaskell*, Chapple and Pollard (eds), 1966

Payne George A. Payne, *Mrs Gaskell and Knutsford*, 2nd edn, 1905

1 (p. 25) *Amazons* women warriors (Greek): this ironic usage not uncommon

2 (p. 25) *Drumble* Manchester is to the north of Knutsford.

3 (p. 25) *surgeon* here a general practitioner. See Marie Fitzwilliam, ' "Mr Harrison's Confessions": A Study of the General Practitioner's Social and Professional Disease', *GSJ*, 12, 1998, pp. 28–30.

4 (p. 25) *geese* Flocks were kept just opposite ECG's Aunt Hannah Lumb's house (Payne, p. 40).

5 (p. 26) *cleanly memory* Robert Southey's eccentric aunt, who would not allow him to 'dirt himself'; Ward (ed.), *Works*, II, p. xii

6 (p. 26) *gigot* 'leg of mutton' sleeve, narrow at wrist

7 (p. 26) *Tinwald Mount* The Tynwald Court is now the Manx Parliament.

8 (p. 26) *Spartans* Greeks noted for their endurance

9 (p. 27) *esprit de corps* pride in one's group (French)

10 (p. 27) *pattens* raised wooden soles to protect shoes

11 (p. 27) *elegant economy* Mitchell cites 'The Elegant Economist's Pudding' in Eliza Acton's *Modern Cookery* (1845). See also *Letters*, p. 174.

12 (p. 28) *Alderney cow* The Gaskells acquired a half-breed Alderney in 1851 (*Letters*, p. 173).

13 (p. 29) *lime-pit* a pit from which marl or clay containing calcite had been dug for fertiliser; a true story about a Miss Harker (Green, p. 114)

14 (p. 29) *Miss Brown* the Christian name of the oldest daughter usually omitted

15 (p. 30) *'Preference'* card game like whist; the dealer sits out

16 (p. 31) *Jock of Hazeldean* Walter Scott's version of an old ballad

17 (p. 32) *rector* parish clergyman entitled to tithes (a tax)

18 (p. 32) *swarry* evening party of Bath footmen, satirised in Chapter 37 of *The Pickwick Papers* (1836–7)

19 (p. 32) *Rasselas* serious moral fable by Samuel Johnson. Cf. p. 34, 'light and agreeable fiction'.

20 (p. 32) *Mr Boz* a pseudonym used by Dickens

21 (p. 33) *Rambler* Johnson's twice-weekly periodical essays (1750–2), 'written in haste', Boswell reports

22 (p. 33) *forte* strong point (French)

23 (p. 33) *sotto voce* in an undertone (Italian)

24 (p. 34) *bakehouse* bakers would cook private meals

25 (p. 35) *Brutus wig* close or curly style, like Roman statues

26 (p. 35) *au fait* in touch (French)

27 (p. 35) *Flint's* well-known London haberdasher

28 (p. 35) *Miss Jenkyns . . . equal to men.* See Uglow, *Elizabeth Gaskell*, pp. 310–16.

29 (p. 36) *quondam* former (Latin)

30 (p. 36) *'plumed wars'* *Othello*, 3, 3, 353: 'plumed troops, and the big wars'

31 (p. 36) *Angel Hotel* Knutsford inn (Green, p. 146)

32 (p. 36) *'the feast of reason and the flow of soul'* Pope, *Imitations of Horace*, Satire II, i, 128

33 (p. 36) *'the pure wells of English undefiled'* Spenser, *Faerie Queene*, IV, ii, stanza 32

34 (p. 39) *three-piled sentence* *Love's Labour's Lost*, 5, 2, 407: 'Three-pil'd hyperboles'

35 (p. 42) *Mary! he has gone before you to the place where the weary are at rest* Jessie quotes from Job 3: 17, and Job 13: 15 below.

36 (p. 44) *Galignani* popular English-language newspaper published in Paris

37 (p. 45) *Old Poz* Lucy is the heroine of Maria Edgeworth's play, acted at Knutsford in 1810. See *EGEY*, p. 165.

38 (p. 45) *Christmas Carol* by Dickens, published December 1843

39 (p. 45) *Hortus Siccus* dry garden (Latin)

40 (p. 46) *father's shirts* Ladies saw to the making of shirts and house linen from shop-bought materials.

41 (p. 49) *screen* a hand-screen to keep off heat of fire, etc.

42 (p. 49) *invalid wife* European sickness rates were very high.

43 (p. 50) *Blue Beard* folk-tale murderer of his wives

44 (p. 50) *Leave me, leave me to repose* Thomas Gray, 'The Descent of Odin', l. 50; cf. *Letters*, p. 192

45 (p. 50) *yeoman* ECG's grandfather at Sandlebridge farm was variously 'grazier' and 'gentleman' in legal documents.

46 (p. 51) *'pride which apes humility'* Watson cites Coleridge and Southey, 'The Devil's Thoughts' (1799).

47 (p. 51) *Thomas Holbrook* a Gaskell family name

48 (p. 51) *Cranford and Misselton* Sandlebridge is between Knutsford and Chelford.

49 (p. 52) *mousseline-de-laine* fine wool material (French)

50 (p. 52) *Don Quixote-looking* ressembling the eccentric Spanish hero of a comic novel (1605, 1615) by Cervantes

51 (p. 52) *black sarsenet* soft, thin silk

52 (p. 53) *fly* light carriage for hire

53 (p. 54) *George Herbert* a favourite poet (1593–1633) of Mrs Gaskell

54 (p. 54) *Goethe* See *GSJ*, 7, 1993, pp. 40–1; 8, 1994, pp. 111–12.

55 (p. 54) *Turkey carpet* of motley-coloured wool, with thick pile cut to resemble velvet

56 (p. 54) *flag floor* paved with stone slabs

57 (p. 55) *feast with the Ghoul* in *The Arabian Nights*. They had fed on corpses.

58 (p. 56) *unbecoming calashes* protective hoods

59 (p. 56) *'The cedar spreads his dark-green layers of shade'* Tennyson, 'The Gardener's Daughter', l. 115; also wrote 'Locksley Hall', both published in 1842

60 (p. 56) *Blackwood* monthly magazine to which Elizabeth Gaskell (in 1837) and her father had contributed

61 (p. 60) *benefit society* Knutsford's Female Benefit Society (1806–1921) was founded by a Mrs Holland and other ladies (*EGEY*, p. 132 and n.)

62 (p. 60) *Arley Hall* near Knutsford, family seat of the Warburtons

63 (p. 61) *To think of . . . having revolutions* as in 1789, 1830 and 1848

64 (p. 61) *But she wears widows' caps* white muslin caps that cover the hair

65 (p. 62) *Though Miss Matty . . . Fate and Love* mock-heroic turn of phrase

66 (p. 62) *fractions of pennies* farthings and halfpennies

67 (p. 62) *Joint-Stock Bank* with capital contributed by shareholders, jointly liable for debts. Cf. Note 171.

68 (p. 62) *Envelopes . . . came in* about 1840 (penny-post reform). ECG's letters of the 1830s are folded and sealed

69 (p. 63) *'keep blind man's holiday'* proverbial. Cousins Mary, Bessie and Lucy Holland claimed that they were economical with candles, tea and clothes. See *EGEY*, pp. 301–3.

70 (p. 64) *Tonquin beans* large scented seeds from South America

71 (p. 64) *gown, cassock, and bands* a long tunic under an academic gown; collar of two falling white strips or bands

72 (p. 64) *assize time* From about 1760, itinerant judges held courts in Knutsford Sessions House (Green, p. 72).

73 (p. 65) *Paduasoy* thick corded silk

74 (p. 66) *J. and J. Rivingtons* specialist theological publishing firm

75 (p. 66) *dum . . . regit artus* Virgil, *Aeneid*, IV, 336 (*hos* omitted): 'While I have memory of myself, while breath controls [these] limbs.'

76 (p. 66) *carmen* poem or song (Latin)

77 (p. 67) *Gentleman's Magazine* Samuel Johnson was an early contributor.

78 (p. 67) *M. T. Ciceronis Epistolae* *Letters* of Marcus Tullius Cicero (Latin)

79 (p. 67) *'a vale of tears'* Mitchell cites translation of Psalm 84.

80 (p. 68) *Mrs Chapone* Mrs Hester Chapone, *Letters on the Improvement of the Mind, Addressed to a Young Lady* (1773–4)

81 (p. 68) *Epictetus* Elizabeth Carter translated the Greek philosopher Epictetus in 1758.

82 (p. 68) *I canna be fashed!* I cannot be bothered

83 (p. 68) *The paper . . . his horn* half-folio sheet, with blind stamp in top left-hand corner

84 (p. 68) *great round red wafer* In Maria Edgeworth's *Patronage* (1814), a duke rejects a note sealed with a wafer, which unlike a wax seal had to be licked.

85 (p. 68) *franks were in great request . . . members of Parliament* Members of Parliament needed only to write their name on the letter for free postage.

86 (p. 68) *crossing* writing at an angle over earlier text to save paper. Letters were then expensively charged by weight.

87 (p. 69) *I think it was in 1805 . . . near Newcastle-upon-Tyne* Britain was again at war with France from May 1803.

88 (p. 69) *salt mines* ECG's uncle Peter Holland was partner in a salt mine at nearby Wilton, *c.*1800. The Cheshire rock-salt mines were very spacious (*EGEY*, p. 145).

89 (p. 69) *Apollyon and Abaddon* names for the angel of the bottomless pit

90 (p. 70) *show letters* ECG's cousin Henry Holland's precocious early letters fit this description (*EGEY*, p. 149).

91 (p. 70) *Bonus Bernardus non videt omnia* Good Bernard does not see all (proverbial).

92 (p. 71) *a living* a benefice, to which a clergyman is presented by its patron

93 (p. 73) *shovel-hat* with broad brim turned up at each side

94 (p. 73) *rhododendron* Watson states that the vogue for these plants came later, in the 1850s.

95 (p. 74) *Queen Esther and King Ahasuerus* See Esther 2: 8.

96 (p. 77) *Don* 'Dor' (Deborah?) in *Household Words* text

97 (p. 77) *race time* Races were held at Knutsford from about 1730 (Green, p. 71).

98 (p. 78) *he was ordered off to India* The First Burmese War began on the Burmese frontier in 1824 (*EGEY*, p. 267); cf. Note 182.

99 (p. 81) *Queen Adelaide* consort of William IV, king 1830–7

100 (p. 81) *she that had been maid to Mrs Jamieson* Cf. Note 186. Miss Betty's sister was maid to Miss Jamieson.

101 (p. 81) *gig* a light carriage. Mitchell notes Thomas Carlyle's sarcastic coinage of 'gigman' in 1832.

102 (p. 83) *Hoggins* A Sarah Hoggins married Henry Cecil, who was created Marquess of Exeter after her death.

103 (p. 83) *bombazine* black, corded material, used for mourning

104 (p. 84) *the spinster daughter of an earl had resided in it* Brook House was taken by a partner of Peter Holland by 1828. Lady Jane Stanley, daughter of the 11th Earl of Derby, lived there from 1780 to 1803 (*EGEY*, pp. 127, 148 and 207).

105 (p. 84) *American war* of Independence, 1776–83. Lady *Charlotte* Stanley married General John Burgoyne.

106 (p. 84) *King William the Fourth* William IV's illegitimate children by Mrs Jordan were called Fitz-Clarence.

107 (p. 84) *ci-devant* the former (French); noble, in France

108 (p. 86) *Spadille from Manille* Watson identifies as ace of spades and second-best trump card.

109 (p. 87) *basting* making fewer tricks than bid; punningly, beaten (Watson)

110 (p. 88) *mandarins* nodding toy figures

111 (p. 88) *Mrs Jamieson had the sedan-chair* Lady Jane Stanley's survived (Green, p. 143).

112 (p. 90) *'county' families* landed nobility or gentry

113 (p. 90) *widow . . . the House of Lords* Only sixteen representative Scotch peers had this right.

114 (p. 93) *stomacher* old-fashioned bodice with point at waist

115 (p. 94) *a large house just outside the town* Cf. Note 104. Brook House (Payne, p. 36) or perhaps Heath House (*EGEY*, p. 108)

116 (p. 95) *Louis Quatorze* Louis XIV, 'the Sun King' (1638–1715)

117 (p. 95) *puzzle-cards* cards with questions, answers and riddles (Handley)

118 (p. 95) *'A Lord and No Lord'* anonymous old ballad

119 (p. 98) *Catholic Emancipation Bill* 1829 repeal of certain legal disabilities

120 (p. 99) *I found pussy on the table . . . pussy's inside* anecdote baldly told in 'The Last Generation in England' (Introduction, p. 8)

121 (p. 99) *Francis Moore's astrological predictions* best known as *Old Moore's Almanac*

122 (p. 100) *Wombwell's lions* George Wombwell's travelling circus

123 (p. 102) *the George* Knutsford's Royal George and its eighteenth-century assembly rooms

124 (p. 102) *minuets de la cour* old-fashioned court minuets

125 (p. 102) *Thaddeus of Warsaw . . . The Hungarian Brothers . . . Santo Sebastiani*; novels by Jane Porter (1803), Anna Maria Porter (1807) and, probably, Catherine Cuthbertson (*The Young Protector, or Santo Sebastiano*, 1806). See *Letters*, pp. 167 and 265 n.

126 (p. 103) *If she was not the rose . . . she had been near it* Watson cites an 1806 translation from Persian by Francis Gladwin.

127 (p. 103) *Witch of Endor* See I Samuel 28.

128 (p. 104) *Gunnings* Maria and Elizabeth Gunning, famous eighteenth-century beauties

129 (p. 104) *And a pretty bargain. . . were true* The painter John Astley (*c.* 1730–89) married Lady Daniel, owner of an Over Tabley estate, which he had to sell in 1780 (Green, pp. 136–7).

130 (p. 105) *chapeau bras* fashionable hat that could be folded

131 (p. 105) *the old tapestry story* E. E. Duncan-Jones proposes Shakespeare's 'Rape of Lucrece', II, 1382–4. See *Notes & Queries*, 27, 1980, pp. 210–11.

132 (p. 107) *National School* Church of England school for poor children

133 (p. 107) *chinks* or kinks: convulsive fits

134 (p. 109) *the French in Spain* Peninsula War, 1808–14. Cf. Note 105 above for 'the American war'.

135 (p. 109) *Madame de Staël* French author (1766–1817). See esp. *Letters*, p. 213.

136 (p. 109) *Mr Denon* Baron (1747–1825) who accompanied Napoleon to Egypt. Watson notes a self-portrait of him in Oriental gown.

137 (p. 111) *till poor Philomel dropped down dead* In classical myth, Philomela, raped by Tereus, was changed into a nightingale. Keating notes a version in Mary R. Mitford, *Our Village* (1824).

138 (p. 111) *One of the stories . . . to the gaieties* a common folk-tale. See Easson, *Elizabeth Gaskell*, p. 108 and n.

139 (p. 111) *Italian irons* round-ended irons used for lace, frills, etc.

140 (p. 112) *'where nae men should be'* Scottish ballad, 'Our goodman came home at e'en'

141 (p. 114) *elf-locks* tangled by Queen Mab (*Romeo & Juliet*, 1, 4, 90)

142 (p. 115) *Over Place* probably Cross Town (Payne, p. 42)

143 (p. 116) *Darkness Lane* perhaps Hollow Lane

144 (p. 116) *videlicet* namely (Latin)

145 (p. 117) *cold-pigged* water from a pig or vessel thrown over him

146 (p. 117) *Dr Ferrier and Dr Hibbert* John Ferrier and Samuel Hibbert wrote on apparitions.

147 (p. 121) *The Rising Sun* perhaps Mainwaring Arms (Payne, p. 42)

148 (p. 121) *fig's up* anything small or worthless; phrase used in playing cards (cribbage)

149 (p. 121) *Mr Hoggins . . . to the Royal Family* ECG's cousin Henry Holland was so appointed in 1852; baronet in 1853

150 (p. 121) *Lord Chesterfield's Letters* gentlemanly guidance in *Letters to His Son* (1774)

151 (p. 122) *a Tyrrell . . . shot King Rufus* supposed to have murdered William II in 1100

152 (p. 122) *murdered the little princes in the Tower* Sir James Tyrrell murdered Edward V and his brother Richard, *c.* 1483.

153 (p. 125) *write his charges* instructions to clergy of his district

154 (p. 127) *pice* smallest Indian coin

155 (p. 127) *near the Avon* ECG's school was on its bank (*EGEY*, p. 241).

156 (p. 127) *station* military settlement

157 (p. 127) *that round shape* Raphael's 'Madonna della Sedia' (*Letters*, p. 218)

158 (p. 128) *Aga* courtesy title, from Turkish for lord

159 (p. 128) *pièce de résistance* main dish at a meal (French)

160 (p. 129) *a passage in Dickens* *Pickwick Papers*, Chapter 32

161 (p. 129) *'Lalla Rookh'* Oriental poem by Thomas Moore, 1817

162 (p. 129) *Rowlands' Kalydor* popular cosmetic

163 (p. 129) *Peruvian bonds* issued to cover loans to Peruvian government

164 (p. 130) *'surveying mankind from China to Peru'* Johnson, *Vanity of Human Wishes* (1749), l. 2

165 (p. 132) *Tibbie Fowler* traditional Scottish song

166 (p. 132) *smelling of the stable* A doctor's rounds were often made on horseback.

167 (p. 132) *mésalliance* marriage beneath one (French)

168 (p. 134) *merinoes and beavers* wool cloths used for coats

169 (p. 134) *Queen of Spain's legs* Mitchell cites Madame D'Aulnoy's *Mémoires* (1690), Chapter 1.

170 (p. 138) *green tea* unfermented tea.

171 (p. 139) *a five-pound note in payment* See Ward (ed.), *Works*, II, xv, for bank failures at Macclesfield (1823) and Manchester (1842).

172 (p. 144) *Rubric* church-service directions printed in red

173 (p. 147) *'Ah! vous dirai-je, maman?'* simple French song, on which Mozart composed variations (K265, 1778)

174 (p. 147) *Ladies' Seminary* probably Heath House (Payne, p. 43)

175 (p. 147) *loyal wool-work* embroidery depicting the royal family

176 (p. 147) *reading the chapter* from Old Testament

177 (p. 148) *couchant* heraldic French: lying, resting

178 (p. 161) *train-oil* oil from whale blubber

179 (p. 162) *Old Hundredth* tune used for Psalm 100

180 (p. 166) *Portsmouth* ECG's brother sailed from Portsmouth as a 'free mariner' of the East India Company (*EGEY*, p. 228).

181 (p. 167) *Baron Munchausen* R. E. Raspe, *Baron Munchausen's Narrative of His Marvellous Travels* (1785)

182 (p. 167) *siege of Rangoon* ECG's brother was involved in the siege of Rangoon, 1824 (EGEY, p. 269); cf. Note 98.

183 (p. 168) *nabob* European who made a fortune in India (Samuel Foote play, *The Nabob*, 1772)

184 (p. 169) *if he did not remind me of the Father of the Faithful?* Watson suggests Abraham.

185 (p. 171) *negus* hot water, wine and spices

186 (p. 172) *Miss Betty (formerly her maid)* Cf. Note 100. Miss Betty's sister has been maid to Mrs Jamieson.

187 (p. 173) *Preston Guild* Festivals were held every five years

188 (p. 174) *Dissenters* ECG was a Unitarian, therefore not a member of the established Church of England.

SELECTED SHORT STORIES

INTRODUCTION TO SELECTED SHORT STORIES

Elizabeth Gaskell was a prolific writer of stories. Her energy never ceases to amaze. Despite an almost frantic family and social life, her writing demon proved insatiable. An atmospheric historical piece, 'Clopton Hall', bears signs that it might have been written whilst she was still a girl at school. She was a great traveller, and every time she visited a new place her imagination caught fire. It seems that she could only relieve her mind of the flood of new experiences by turning them into fiction. Thus in July 1827, when she was only sixteen, her father suggested that she should keep a journal about a holiday trip to relations in Wales. She did more than this. She made a 'very pretty story' out of the rescue of a cousin from a quicksand in Cardigan Bay, according to her brother John in the following year.

Despite the astonishing variety of her tales, many of which are long enough to be called novellas, there are some common themes. She was fascinated by the bearing of the past upon the present, especially as it surfaced in families but also as it affected little societies. She deeply appreciated the ties that bound communities together, but was aware of how these very ties can fail individuals in times of need or stress. She knew from her own experience how young people can feel utterly trapped in their home lives, and how painful can be the processes of escape, growth and change. Playing upon such individual emotions, she develops many of her short stories in a compact, intense and poetic manner. Others plainly show the irrepressible vitality and sense of fun for which she was noted amongst her friends.

Mr Harrison's Confessions (1851)

In this early story, set in a little country town called Duncombe, a young man joins the medical practice of a Mr Morgan. Gaskell knew the medical apprentices of her uncle Peter Holland, surgeon of Knutsford,[1] as well as Charlotte Brontë knew her father's curates, and was

1 Cf. 'Mr Gleeson the Irish assistant', who used to plague her uncle's partner,

just as ready to make use of them in fiction. The arrival of the bachelor Mr Harrison in a society full of widows and unmarried ladies has predictable consequences. Romantic traps are laid for him by determined matrons, who take unfair advantage of a festive picnic in the grounds of an old hall in the neighbourhood, a setting well known to the author in real life.[2] Beneath Mr Harrison's naïve account of his adventures, ironically called 'confessions', Gaskell is anatomising characters and behaviour in a place where 'small sayings were the seeds of great events'.

The constant distortions of gossip (the malicious scandal of Miss Horsman provides an unpleasant instance) ensure that misunderstandings flourish. A ludicrous dialogue in Chapter 17 between the deaf Mrs Munton and Mrs Rose, yearning to be married again, is a typical comic triumph. All this material is cleverly moulded into a series of dramatic scenes. Before long, Mr Harrison finds himself engaged to three ladies at the same time, and regarded as a heartless philanderer though he himself is unaware that he has paid court to any of them. Contretemps multiply, eventually ending with remarkable speed in several pairings-off, a convention of stage comedy. Even Mr Morgan, also a bachelor, conveniently rescues Mr Harrison from Mrs Rose by marrying her himself.

Not everything is simply entertaining. The possible amputation of John Brouncker's arm is designed to raise suspense and evoke strong emotions of pity and terror, far more likely in those days than now. The practice of anaesthesia had only just begun in the mid-1840s. Joseph Lister did not publish on antisepsis until 1867. Unfortunate patients often died under the knife. A new letter of 1853 betrays Gaskell's fascinated horror at what she termed the '*wilfulness* in operating' of a London surgeon (*Further Letters*, p. 95). In this instance, despite religious scruples, she was even ready to consider recommending a cure by mesmerism. The conflict of opinions in Duncombe over amputation is therefore entirely believable. Nor was the death of the vicar's little son from the childhood ailment croup improbable. Cholera, typhus, whooping cough, scarlet fever

---

Dr Richard Deane (*Further Letters*, p. 30). For full details of this and other references, see the Bibliography at the end of this Introduction.

2 Cf. Gaskell's visits to Tabley Hall with friends, the musical ones warbling like birds in 'old crazy boats' on the lake or singing ballads in the deserted old hall (*Letters*, p. 15).

and a host of dangerous diseases were agonising possibilities for all families, even the wealthiest.[3]

The alternation of comic and tragic episodes in this story is, however, somewhat mechanical. *Cranford*, which began to appear later in 1851 as a serial for Dickens, this time with a more detached female narrator, achieved remarkable integration by the time it was concluded in 1853. Duncombe's Miss Tomkinson and her sister Caroline, though an entertaining pair, are not as well characterised as Miss Jenkyns and her sister Matty in *Cranford*. Gaskell's artistry was on a swiftly rising curve during these early years of her public literary career.

The Doom of the Griffiths (1858)

Although this tale did not appear in print until January 1858, Elizabeth Gaskell told a friend that it was 'an old rubbishy one, – begun when Marianne was a baby, – the only merit whereof is that it is founded on fact'.[4] Her self-deprecation is misplaced, because it is by no means rubbishy. The sheer density of her recreated setting in the far north-west of Wales indicates one source of her inspiration. It was in those days relatively isolated, difficult to reach and, culturally, quite alien. On earlier visits to her uncle Samuel Holland's comfortable house above Traeth Mawr, a broad, sandy estuary, she could look across and survey wild country between Criccieth and Porthmadog.

Between the two towns lies Moel-y-Gest, a rocky hill rising steeply above broad water-meadows, on the side of which she places the long, low cottage of Ellis Pritchard. She portrays in rapid strokes the 'rough abundance' of his way of life. She notes the old parochial church of Ynyscynhaearn, now disused and even more desolate than it was in those days, lying along a causeway over marshy ground. A small and solid Elizabethan manor house a little to the east in the direction of Criccieth, Ystumllyn, could have been the Bodowen of Squire Griffith's family, in social terms far above the humble cottage of Pritchard, farmer and fisherman. Even so, the heir to Bodowen,

3 The Gaskells' own baby son had died from scarlet fever on 10 August 1845 (*Further Letters*, pp. 29, n. 1, 34–6).

4 See *Letters*, p. 488; *Further Letters*, pp. 9, 175, 178. (Marianne was born in September 1834.) I am grateful to Michael Lewis and Dewi Williams for their invaluable help in Welsh matters.

increasingly neglected after the death of his mother, made a secret marriage to Pritchard's beautiful daughter, Nest.

The passionate nature of the Welsh characters is stressed: a son becomes locked in irreconcilable conflict with his father, a beautiful, vicious stepmother and her malicious son. Gaskell stresses the universality of this provincial conflict by invoking the spirit of 'old Greek dramas which treat of a family foredoomed by an avenging Fate'. Also, when Gaskell visited Haworth in September 1853, Charlotte Brontë told her 'such wild tales of the ungovernable families' who had lived on the moors above Haworth 'that Wuthering Heights even seemed tame comparatively' (*Letters*, p. 244). And when Gaskell came to revise this Welsh story in October 1857, she had spent much of the previous summer being forced to censor her biography of her dead friend for a new edition, in order to eliminate hearsay accounts of Patrick Brontë's eccentric behaviour – firing pistols out of the back door of the parsonage to release his volcanic rage and deliberately burning the hearthrug or sawing the legs off chairs.[5]

The fanciful historical introduction about the curse of the Griffiths is soon forgotten. We are caught up in the more down-to-earth power of the human story she has to tell. A mile or so away from Moel-y-Gest, on the road that sweeps around Tremadog cliffs, lies the village of Pen-Morfa. In its Goat Inn, drovers and locals drink and dance to the music of a famous harper and Owen Griffiths meets his fate, Nest Pritchard. Welsh names, greetings, songs and proverbs abound. There is even a triad in the Welsh language, providing much more than local colour in its brutal allusion to a 'fine woman without reputation'.

On this hinge turn Owen's father's belief that the son of the flighty Nest Pritchard must be 'the child of another' and his furious action in flinging the child from him, inadvertently causing its death. Gaskell's religion would not allow her to believe in all seriousness that the supernatural force of an ancient curse could then have driven Owen to kill his father in revenge. She makes it clear that the father's death was an accident.[6] Her success lies in establishing the human motivation of her principal characters in that particular time and place. She is especially sensitive to the 'almost feminine' tenderness

5 See especially *The Life of Charlotte Brontë*, ed. Angus Easson, Oxford University Press, 1996, pp. 469–70; *Further Letters*, p. 178; *Letters*, pp. 455, 467.

6 She and her cousin Anne Holland once had the idea of writing 'a history of *crimes* of *innocent* people' (*Further Letters*, p. 9).

displayed by the squire to his infant son. But the mildness of both father and son is overlain by dumb pride and easily obliterated by sudden spasms of violence. In the climactic moments of the drowning and the concealment of the squire's body, Gaskell's narrative control is almost faultless.

Lois the Witch (1859)

This fine story is even more remote – in time, space, thought and feeling. The witch trials of 1692 at a special court in Salem Town, Massachusetts, were by no means the first in New England; scores of people had been indicted in earlier years. But hundreds were named at Salem, and about nineteen actually put to death. One source she used is entitled *Lectures on Witchcraft, Comprising a History of the Delusion in Salem, in 1692*, published in 1831 by Charles Upham, a latter-day Unitarian minister there. It was both a history and an enlightened analysis of the historical phenomenon. He provided the information about the Reverend Cotton Mather (although Mather was not actually present in Salem), together with many other details, such as the story of the young man who rescued his poor mother from her prison and hid her in 'the Blueberry swamp' until the whole persecution was over.[7]

The witchcraft trials of Salem seemed deep in a shameful past for the sophisticated nineteenth-century believer in the progress of the humanitarian spirit, and were intellectually inconceivable for Unitarian rationalists in particular. Yet, in the early 1850s, Gaskell had stayed in the home of a magistrate in Essex who had had to intervene when ignorant villagers suspected an old woman of being a witch. It made a deep impression upon her, as her family testified.

An immensely practical and sensible woman, she nevertheless responded strongly to tales of terror and was well known as a virtuoso teller of ghost stories. In July 1856 a friend told Nathaniel Hawthorne her story about the skeleton of a young woman, bones lit with lambent flames, appearing in, of all places, the office of *The Times* in Printing House Square. On at least two occasions she only just missed meeting Hawthorne, who for a time was American consul in Liverpool, and she knew a good deal about his writings.

7 See Sharps, pp. 316–17; Easson, p. 215, adds necessary emphasis. For Unitarian connections between New England, Liverpool and Manchester, see Chapple, *Gaskell: The Early Years*, pp. 392–3, 422.

He, like her good friend William Story, had actually been born in Salem. A direct ancestor, John Hathorne, had been a hanging judge at the witch trials. In 1850 Hawthorne produced with customary ambiguity his own evocation of guilt and isolation, diabolism and passion in Puritan New England, *The Scarlet Letter*, one of the great novels of the nineteenth century.[8]

Lacking such ancestral connections, Gaskell was like her heroine Lois sailing into unvisited waters of time and space. Historical accounts of painted Indians with war knives and settler youths with guns, Canadian-French pirates raiding the coast and committing atrocities, together with superstitious assertions that they were devils in disguise, are cast plausibly enough into the form of conversations in Widow Smith's house. But the strength of her tale (like Hawthorne's) lies in its evocation of the perverted cast of mind of the people. 'Salem was, as it were, snowed up, and left to prey upon itself', she wrote in perhaps the most memorable phrase of a brilliant passage. This raging outbreak of delusion had numerous roots, ranging from all-too-human jealousy, envy and fear, through male insistence on maintaining social authority and control, right up to an absolute belief in the supernatural reality of 'diabolical possession'. The author's historical imagination is perceptibly under stress. Telling the tale tested the limits of her sympathetic understanding, and must have found deep echoes within her subconscious self.

The very heart of a Puritan household is shown in an extremity of affliction. The upright and religious Grace Hickson is so distorted by mother love that she conceals the fact her son Manasseh had been mad long before Lois arrived in America. She allows people to believe that the innocent girl had been the cause of his derangement. Her daughter Faith is eaten up with jealous love for Pastor Nolan, her other daughter Prudence is a hyperactive, malignant girl of twelve, not unlike Hawthorne's Pearl in *The Scarlet Letter*. Nattee, the old Indian servant, always finds an audience for weird and lurid legends of her tribe, intensifying the evil, death-laden atmosphere. 'There ran through these stories always a ghastly, unexpressed suggestion of some human sacrifice being needed,' Gaskell comments, and they give Nattee 'a strange, unconscious pleasure in her power over her hearers – young girls of the oppressing race'.

8 Gaskell was having a copy rebound as early as January 1851 (*Letters*, p. 142). For a summary of her connection with Hawthorne, see Chapple, *Gaskell: A Portrait*, pp. 133–4.

But it is Gaskell's characterisation of Grace's son Manasseh that is most spine-chilling: a slow, sinister, furtive and obsessive visionary; ugly and ungainly, with lank black hair and coarse grey skin, he is convinced that his sexual desires are the Lord's will and that Lois has no right to stand against them. Lois is even brought to think for a moment that she herself might be a witch, a final turn of the screw as she is transformed in the deranged imagination of a fatalistic society which showed 'no mercy towards anyone whom they believed to be in league with the Evil One'.

Gaskell was now fast approaching the summit of her powers as a writer, apprehending a terrible delusion from within and able to reveal the interconnections of distorted sex, power and religion in action. In the characterisation of Pastor Nolan, for instance, tormented as he is by the natural impulses of 'a carnal man' unexpectedly meeting a 'pretty stranger', and dawningly aware of 'his own spiritual need and spiritual failings', there is a fine acting part. The literary tact of Gaskell's ending, too, is noteworthy, balancing the belated recantation of the jurors in Lois's trial against the pathetic truth of Ralph Lucy's cry, 'All their repentance will avail nothing to my Lois, nor will it bring her back her life.'

Curious, if True (1860)

Elizabeth Gaskell here allowed her imagination to take a holiday, buoyed up whilst writing by the realisation that though a short tale it could easily turn out to be one of her best.[9] Despite its equivocal title, it begins deceptively, with sober realism. A young Englishman, believing he might be related to the severe Protestant theologian John Calvin, travels to France to examine family papers. Lost in a dark wood near Tours, he stumbles upon a château and crosses its threshold into another realm of existence, characterised by its aura of fantastic realism. Gaskell's narrative moves like a comet into and through the orbits of familiar fairy tales, providing a splendid demonstration of playful intertextual whimsy.

Fairy tales, fantasies and legends were everywhere available to her. Translations of *contes des fées* by French authors like Madame d'Aulnoy and Madame Leprince de Beaumont were frequently

9 'I do want to make it as good as I can, & so only to write at it in my best moments' (*Letters*, p. 595), she told her publisher George Smith, who had just started a superior new periodical, the *Cornhill Magazine*.

reprinted. The tales of the Brothers Grimm followed early in the nineteenth century. Mary Howitt translated Hans Andersen in 1846, the year before Gaskell's first published stories appeared in *Howitt's Magazine*. Charles Kingley's *The Water Babies* and Lewis Carroll's *Alice in Wonderland* belong to the 1860s. Appropriately, however, Gaskell's one definite reference is to 'Le Petit Poucet', a tiny man clever enough to defeat an ogre. A brilliant and influential French author, Charles Perrault, had towards the end of the seventeenth century rewritten a number of tales told by his son's nurse. Gaskell, who was fluent in French, used them as her principal source in 'Curious, if True'.[10]

We think of fairy tales as transcending time, their essential details endlessly told in what she happily called the 'voices of generations'. Yet from the moment when her English hero Richard Whittingham is mistaken for Dick Whittington and asked about the absence of 'Monsieur le Géanquilleur', Gaskell is ingeniously revising the texts we know so well. In a *salon* suffused with a pale, mysterious light, Richard meets a sweet-faced but old and fat Cinderella, ironically with feet too swollen to let her walk. A cat-like groom, wearing grey whiskers and fur-trimmed clothes, clatters along in 'boots halfway up his ridiculously small legs'. A sleeping beauty is shaken to wakefulness, not to find the prince she thinks she sees but a peevishly bored husband instead.

These comical variations culminate in a lady bewailing the loss of her first and 'best of husbands', standing before a picture of him grasping her by the hair and threatening her with a scimitar, but also showing cavaliers rushing in to rescue her in the nick of time. What she believes to be their mistaken zeal makes her a widow, with nothing but a hank of hair from his beard kept in a clasp of pearls. It has a bluish tint. Only little Red Riding Hood remains what she has always been. She survives *outside* the château, an image in the popular imagination of unchanging simplicity, trust and innocence.

Six Weeks at Heppenheim (1862)

During visits to Germany in autumn 1858 and summer 1860, Mrs Gaskell was inspired by a picture-book little town called Heppenheim.

10 See Philip Yarrow, 'Mrs Gaskell and France', *Gaskell Society Journal*, 7 (1993), p. 35, n. 34; John Chapple, 'Charles Perrault, Madame D'Aulnoy, and "Curious, if True" ', *Gaskell Society Newsletter*, 31 (2001).

She sketches its appearance, laws, customs and usages, and even its linguistic peculiarities, with a sure professional hand. At first it seems as timelessly idyllic as the Rhineland town Goethe described in his *Hermann und Dorothea*, a narrative poem that seems to have influenced her strongly. But it turns out to be a tale of perplexed instability. She sensitively traces the difficult course of the relationship between Fritz Müller, a widower with two little children, and Thekla, the servant in his inn, engaged at the beginning to a feckless young man. Gaskell writes with deliberate indirection, using an Oxford graduate as narrator, portraying him deep in a fever when a walking tour has brought him to the *Halbmond*, a village inn amongst the vineyards of the Hessische Bergstrasse. He gradually returns to consciousness, but is weak, febrile and dependent upon others. Sights, sounds, tones and moods sometimes waver across boundaries of consciousness, as he displays a slow, sympathetic apprehension of conflicting human feelings mingled with equally human failures of full comprehension.

The luscious description of the famous garden of the *Halbmond* is an example of the prose-poetry of Arcady. It bears an uncanny resemblance to Goethe's description of a garden and vineyard – a passage in canto 4 of *Hermann und Dorothea* once quoted in a book by her friend William Howitt.[11] But it suddenly modulates back into the style of formal realism. 'Why is there a rope with a bunch of straw tied in it stretched across the opening of the garden into the vineyard?' the narrator demands. Historically, the law of the grand duchy used to forbid public entrance to vineyards until harvest-time, when the whole community took part in gathering the grapes. Symbolically, the removal of the rope is a prelude to the resolution of human perplexities.

When the innkeeper's son, little Max, falls seriously ill, the narrator too sinks into in a dream about rustic carts 'which held little coffins instead of baskets of grapes', as if attached by empathic bonds to those who were haunted by the prospect of a child's death. However, he awakens to broad daylight. Max survives, and the ending draws near with a key scene of Fritz Müller feeding Thekla because her hands are occupied holding his child. Gaskell can be seen as reacting against a contemporary Victorian style of assertive masculinity. In the perspective of her writing lifetime, she herself moved away to some

11 See William Howitt, *The Rural and Domestic Life of Germany* (1842), p. 54; *Letters*, pp. 424; *Further Letters*, p. 43.

extent from what has been termed 'optimistic paternalism' but never lost her vision of the caring man.[12]

Thekla, with some difficulty, decides to forsake her faithless lover and marry the innkeeper. Community life again continues along its ancient paths. The pains and sorrows of existence are transcended, subsumed into a larger order of being with roots running deep into work and social life, symbolised by the bareheaded prayer of the workers on the *Weinberg* and their harvest hymn of thanksgiving. The German hymn parallels the psalm sung in the English stubble field in 'Cousin Phillis', for which the often neglected 'Six Weeks at Heppenheim' could be regarded as an admirable trial run.[13]

Cousin Phillis (1863–4)

This is a tale of love and loss. Gradually and calmly, Gaskell focuses on the complex inevitability of suffering that befalls a young woman. Her narrator, Paul Manning, is surprisingly brisk in comparison with the Oxford graduate, as we can tell from his jaunty beginning ('It is a great thing for a lad, when he is first turned into the independence of lodgings'), though his tone deepens considerably as the story proceeds. Thekla's irregular, weather-beaten features were emphasised almost at the outset of 'Six Weeks at Heppenheim', for Gaskell was there assimilating the classical tradition of pastoral idyll to the norms of English realistic fiction. Phillis, in contrast, is entirely beautiful, 'her golden hair, her dazzling complexion, lighting up the corner of the vine-shadowed room'. Like Perdita in *The Winter's Tale*, she seems a 'queen of curds and cream'.

Gaskell never loses sight of the spiritual centre of her vision, but is impelled by her particular genius to recast pastoral idyll for a modern age. Thekla's first lover, travelling to gain hotel experience before coming back to run the family inn, follows a strong tradition, which survives to this day. Edward Holdsworth is a new kind of character in fiction, a railway engineer. Elizabeth Gaskell had first-hand knowledge of great men of this type: George Stephenson and James Nasmyth, for example, men at the forefront of Victorian

12 Stoneman, p. 53. According to Catherine Winkworth, Elizabeth Gaskell praised her husband to Charlotte Brontë in May 1854 for being 'a good sick nurse'.

13 See Peter Skrine's sensitive analysis in his 'Elizabeth Gaskell and Her German Stories', *Gaskell Society Journal*, 12 (1998), pp. 7–13.

technological advance, whose driving enterprise not only transformed the face of the country but altered human relations inescapably. The consequences of industrialisation in the North were appalling, as she underlined in her novel *North and South*. In its hero John Thornton, however, she could not help but portray the excitement and restless dynamism of the male drive to control and to initiate change.

'Oh! that Life would make a stand-still in this happy place,' she had once cried on a visit to the Holland family's farm at Sandlebridge near Knutsford, the model for Heathbridge. Yet nostalgia does not prevent her from realising that the way of life could not remain unchanged. If the Reverend Ebenezer Holman, farmer and minister, at first seems so complete in both his patriarchal roles, he turns out to be strangely unsettled. He knows the farming techniques described by Virgil in the *Georgics* ('vain babbling and profane heathenism', splutters a puritanical fellow-minister), but still hankers after modern knowledge, to the extent of trying to read stiff books on mechanics that he had not the mathematics to understand. He craves for Holdsworth's wealth of information about foreign wonders.[14] It is as addictive as 'dram-drinking'.

Similarly, young Paul soon comes to terms with the realisation that Phillis could never love him. His golden-haired cousin, with long dark eyelashes and round, white pillar of a throat, is both far better educated and taller than he is. This is a nice joke, but Elizabeth Gaskell shrewdly makes him say to his match-making father that he would rather his wife 'think a deal' of her husband; as she writes elsewhere, 'husbands do not dislike such a tribute to their Jupitership'. But Paul had already thought it odd that Phillis, 'so old, so full-grown as she was, should wear a pinafore over her gown'. Her parents kept her emotionally in a state of childhood, though she was seventeen years old: 'a stately, gracious young woman, in the dress, and with the simplicity, of a child'.

Gaskell duplicates Goethe's treatment of his stately heroine Dorothea, continually freezing the narrative to present eloquent pictures – Phillis in the 'slanting stream of light' from the westering sun or sitting quietly at her mending work with bended head. The

14 He appears to combine the qualities of two successive owners of Sandlebridge, Elizabeth Gaskell's philosophical, pipe-smoking grandfather and her polymath cousin Henry. See *Letters*, pp. 8, 75–6; Chapple, *Elizabeth Gaskell: The Early Years*, pp. 54–5, 149–51.

climax comes when she stands with her back to Paul and Holdsworth, holding her basket high in the air over her leaping, barking dog's head. With that Victorian sensuousness which hints at so much more, Gaskell makes her colour all over when she realises she has been seen and hurry away, 'Rover still curving in sinuous lines about her as she walked.' 'I should like to have sketched her,' says Holdsworth, the connoisseur of female beauty. He soon does; not as herself but as the corn-goddess Ceres, with hair loosely flowing. The real young woman could not bear the intentness of his gaze on this occasion, just as she later shrinks from the 'unmistakable look of love in his black eyes'.

Tragedy is inevitable as the seasons change to winter. When Holdsworth leaves for Canada, Phillis falls into a decline, growing pale and wasted, a ghost of her former self, convulsively lacing and unlacing her fingers 'till the compressed flesh became perfectly white'. Paul, so sensitive to her needs, loving her as a brother, then commits the fatal error of telling her that Holdsworth had admitted he loved her just before he left. (The 'scream and whistle of the engine, ready down at the sheds' sounds like an omen.) Elizabeth Gaskell now exerts all her considerable powers to realise the joy of Phillis's second blooming, the dreadful blasting of her hopes by news of Holdsworth's marriage, the suffering that leads to her complete collapse and her near-recovery brought about by the blunt reproaches of their old servant Betty.

There is a great deal more in this richly detailed fiction that deserves patient, thoughtful attention, but the way in which it ends demands a special comment. Gaskell juxtaposes Phillis's assurance that they will all 'go back to the peace of the old days' with Paul's (and the reader's) belief that this is impossible. Their life can never be the same again. It seems a perfect point of balance. Yet we now know that in the middle of composition she had intended to extend her story. In December 1863 she wrote to her publisher George Smith, who had asked her to bring her story to a close, that she wanted to show Phillis, still unmarried years afterwards, nursing cases of fever after an outbreak of typhus, adopting orphans, and 'making practical use of the knowledge she had learnt from Holdsworth and, with the help of common labourers, levelling & draining the undrained village' (*Further Letters*, pp. 259–60).

Can the unexpected independence of her heroine be connected with a letter Elizabeth Gaskell had not long before sent to the indefatigable Florence Nightingale, in which she praises her report on the insanitary conditions of the army and quotes the verdict of a reviewer that it was 'not a literary work, but a great action'? However, even if Nightingale's eminently pragmatic example was recalled when Gaskell was brooding over a continuation of 'Cousin Phillis', we should also notice a startling sentence in the very same letter. Confessing how full her heart has been over the marriage of her 'little daughter Florence', she explains, 'The parting from a child *stuns* one; and it is very strange and difficult to turn back to the home-life and feel that she will never be there as before – as one's own *possession*' (*Further Letters*, p. 258).[15]

15 For a Biographical Note on the author, see page 19.

BIBLIOGRAPHY

'Mr Harrison's Confessions' appeared in the *Ladies' Companion and Monthly Magazine*, Vol. 3, February–April 1851; reprinted in *Lizzie Leigh and Other Tales*, Chapman and Hall, 1855

'The Doom of the Griffiths' appeared in an American periodical, *Harper's New Monthly Magazine*, Vol. 16, January 1858; reprinted as part of *Round the Sofa*, Sampson Low, Son & Co., 1859

'Lois the Witch' appeared in *All the Year Round*, Vol. 1, pp. 8–22 October 1859; reprinted in *Right at Last and Other Tales*, Sampson Low, Son & Co., 1860

'Curious, if True' appeared in the *Cornhill Magazine*, Vol. 1, February 1860; reprinted in *The Grey Woman and Other Tales*, Smith, Elder and Co., 1865

'Six Weeks at Heppenheim' appeared in the *Cornhill Magazine*, Vol. 5, May 1862; reprinted in *The Grey Woman and Other Tales* , Smith, Elder and Co., 1865

Cousin Phillis first appeared in the *Cornhill Magazine*, Vols 8 and 9, November 1863–February 1864; reprinted by Harper & Brothers, New York, 1864

See Walter E. Smith, *Elizabeth Gaskell: A Bibliographical Catalogue of First and Early Editions*, Heritage Bookshop, Los Angeles, 1998

General

Elizabeth Gaskell: The Critical Heritage, Angus Easson (ed.), Routledge, London and New York, 1991; important collection of reviews, opinions and significant judgments up to 1910

John Geoffrey Sharps, *Mrs Gaskell's Observation and Invention: A Study of Her Non-Biographic Works*, Linden Press, Fontwell, Sussex, 1970; a detailed Introduction to each work in turn, based on extensive and original research

Linda K. Hughes and Michael Lund, *Victorian Publishing and Mrs Gaskell's Work*, Virginia University Press, Charlottesville & London, 1999; places her writing in context

Amanda Vickery, *The Gentleman's Daughter: Women's Lives in Georgian England*, Yale University Press, New Haven and London, 1998

Nancy S. Weyant, *Elizabeth Gaskell: An Annotated Bibliography of English-Language Sources, 1976–1991*, Scarecrow Press, Metuchen, NJ and London, 1994; *Guide 1992–2001*, Lanham (Maryland), Toronto, Oxford, 2004

Witch-Hunting in Seventeenth-Century New England: A Documentary History, 1638–1693, edited and introduced by David D. Hall, Northeastern University Press, 1991, 2nd edn Boston, 1999; has good selective bibliography

The Oxford Companion to Fairy Tales, edited by Jack Zipes, Oxford University Press, 2000; standard reference work

Graham Handley, *Elizabeth Gaskell: A Chronology*, Palgrave Macmillan, 2005

Letters

The Letters of Mrs Gaskell, J. A. V. Chapple and Arthur Pollard (eds), Manchester University Press, 1966; Mandolin, 1997

Further Letters of Mrs Gaskell, John Chapple and Alan Shelston (eds), Manchester University Press, 2000; supplementary volume

J. A. V. Chapple (assisted by J. G. Sharps), *Elizabeth Gaskell: A Portrait in Letters*, Manchester University Press, 1980; a selection of letters with interlinking commentary

Selected Biography and Criticism (in chronological order)

A. B. Hopkins, *Elizabeth Gaskell: Her Life and Work*, John Lehmann, 1952; an early and well-researched study

Arthur Pollard, *Mrs Gaskell: Novelist and Biographer*, Manchester University Press, 1965; introduction to the life and works by a pioneer scholar

Margaret Ganz, *Elizabeth Gaskell: The Artist in Conflict*, Twayne Publishers, New York, 1969; clear and cogent critical appraisal

Winifred Gérin, *Elizabeth Gaskell: A Biography*, Clarendon Press, Oxford, 1976; fluent and readable

Angus Easson, *Elizabeth Gaskell*, Routledge and Kegan Paul, London, Boston and Henley, 1979; acute and independent survey of Gaskell's life and times, with a chapter on the short stories

Patsy Stoneman, *Elizabeth Gaskell*, Harvester Press, Brighton, 1987; exceptionally clear and informative feminist analysis

Sechs Wochen in Heppenheim, German translation, edited and introduced by Maria Deidrich, with historical contributions by Werner Werth, Kreistadt Heppenheim, 1991; illustrated with engravings from Gaskell's time and more recent photographs

Felicia Bonaparte, *The Gypsy Bachelor of Manchester: The Life of Mrs Gaskell's Demon*, Virginia University Press, Charlottesville and London, 1992; unusual but engaging psychological study

Jenny Uglow, *Elizabeth Gaskell: A Habit of Stories*, Faber and Faber, London and Boston, 1993; the most stimulating book to date and a substantial critical study of Gaskell's life, times and works

Terence Wright, *Elizabeth Gaskell 'We are not angels': Realism, Gender, Values*, Macmillan, Basingstoke, 1995; close, sensitive textual analysis and criticism

Anna Unsworth, *Elizabeth Gaskell: An Independent Woman*, Minerva Press, Montreux, London and Washington, 1996; useful for German, French and Italian influences

John Chapple, *Elizabeth Gaskell: The Early Years*, Manchester University Press, Manchester and New York, 1997; contains much new information about ECG's family, background and life up to 1832, derived from hitherto unused documentary sources

Shirley Foster, *Elizabeth Gaskell: A Literary Life*, Palgrave Macmillan, 2002

The Works of Elizabeth Gaskell, Joanne Shattock (general editor), Pickering and Chatto, London, 10 vols – in progress. Five volumes of this scholarly, collected edition have been published (2005).

The Gaskell Society Journal (published annually from 1987). Volumes 5, 10, 11–13, 2003 and 2005 are especially useful for Gaskell's tales.

Professor Mitsuharu Matsuoka's 'The Gaskell Web' (http://lang.nagoya-u.ac.jp/~matsuoka/Gaskell.html) is a valuable and exceptionally comprehensive resource for Gaskell texts and studies. I am happy to acknowledge his generous help.

MR HARRISON'S CONFESSIONS

Chapter 1

THE FIRE was burning gaily. My wife had just gone upstairs to put baby to bed. Charles sat opposite to me, looking very brown and handsome. It was pleasant enough that we should feel sure of spending some weeks under the same roof, a thing which we had never done since we were mere boys. I felt too lazy to talk, so I ate walnuts and looked into the fire. But Charles grew restless.

'Now that your wife is gone upstairs, Will,[1] you must tell me what I've wanted to ask you ever since I saw her this morning. Tell me all about the wooing and winning. I want to have the receipt for getting such a charming little wife of my own. Your letters only gave the barest details. So set to, man, and tell me every particular.'

'If I tell you all, it will be a long story.'

'Never fear. If I get tired, I can go to sleep, and dream that I am back again, a lonely bachelor, in Ceylon; and I can waken up when you have done, to know that I am under your roof. Dash away, man! "Once upon a time, a gallant young bachelor" – There's a beginning for you!'

'Well, then: "Once upon a time, a gallant young bachelor" was sorely puzzled where to settle, when he had completed his education as a surgeon – I must speak in the first person; I cannot go on as a gallant young bachelor. I had just finished walking the hospitals when you went to Ceylon, and, if you remember, I wanted to go abroad like you, and thought of offering myself as a ship-surgeon; but I found I should rather lose caste in my profession; so I hesitated, and, while I was hesitating, I received a letter from my father's cousin, Mr Morgan – that old gentleman who used to write such long letters of good advice to my mother, and who tipped me a five-pound note when I agreed to be bound apprentice to Mr Howard, instead of going to sea. Well, it seems the old gentleman had all along thought of taking me as his partner, if I turned out pretty well; and, as he heard a good account of me from an old friend of his, who was a surgeon at Guy's,[2] he wrote to propose this arrangement: I was to have a third of the profits for five years; after that, half; and eventually I was to succeed to the whole. It was no bad offer for a penniless man like me, as Mr Morgan had a capital country practice, and, though I did not know him personally, I had formed a pretty good idea of him, as an honourable, kind-hearted, fidgety, meddlesome old bachelor; and a very correct notion it was, as I found out in the very first half-hour of seeing him. I had had some idea that I was to live in his house, as he was a bachelor and a kind of family friend, and I think he was afraid that I should expect this arrangement; for, when I walked up to his door, with the porter carrying my portmanteau, he met me on the steps, and while he held my hand and shook it, he said to the porter, "Jerry, if you'll wait a moment, Mr Harrison will be ready to go with you to his lodgings, at Jocelyn's, you know"; and then, turning to me, he addressed his first words of welcome. I was a little inclined to think him inhospitable, but I got to understand him better afterwards. "Jocelyn's," said he, "is the best place I have been able to hit upon in a hurry, and there is a good deal of fever about, which made me desirous that you should come this month – a low kind of typhoid, in the oldest part of the town. I think you'll be comfortable there for a week or two. I have taken the liberty of desiring my housekeeper to send down one or two things which give the place a little more of a home aspect – an easy-chair, a beautiful case of preparations, and one or two little matters in the way of eatables; but, if you'll take my advice, I've a plan in my head which we will talk about tomorrow morning. At present, I don't like to keep you standing out on the steps here; so I'll not detain you from your lodgings, where I rather think my housekeeper is gone to get tea ready for you."

'I thought I understood the old gentleman's anxiety for his own health, which he put upon care for mine; for he had on a kind of loose grey coat, and no hat on his head. But I wondered that he did not ask me indoors, instead of keeping me on the steps. I believe, after all, I made a mistake in supposing he was afraid of taking cold; he was only afraid of being seen in dishabille. And for his apparent inhospitality, I had not been long in Duncombe before I understood the comfort of having one's house considered as a castle into which no one might intrude, and saw good reason for the practice Mr Morgan had established of coming to his door to speak to everyone. It was only the effect of habit that made him receive me so. Before long, I had the free run of his house.

'There was every sign of kind attention and forethought on the part of someone, whom I could not doubt to be Mr Morgan, in my lodgings. I was too lazy to do much that evening, and sat in the little bow-window which projected over Jocelyn's shop, looking up and down the street. Duncombe calls itself a town, but I should call it a village. Really, looking from Jocelyn's, it is a very picturesque place. The houses are anything but regular; they may be mean in their details; but altogether they look well; they have not that flat unrelieved front, which many towns of far more pretensions present. Here and there a bow-window – every now and then a gable, cutting up against the sky – occasionally a projecting upper storey – throws good effect of light and shadow along the street; and they have a queer fashion of their own of colouring the whitewash of some of the houses with a sort of pink blotting-paper tinge, more like the stone of which Mayence[3] is built than anything else. It may be very bad taste, but to my mind it gives a rich warmth to the colouring. Then, here and there a dwelling-house has a court in front, with a grass-plot on each side of the flagged walk, and a large tree or two – limes or horse-chestnuts – which send their great projecting upper branches over into the street, making round dry places of shelter on the pavement in the times of summer showers.

'While I was sitting in the bow-window, thinking of the contrast between this place and the lodgings in the heart of London, which I had left only twelve hours before – the window open here, and, although in the centre of the town, admitting only scents from the mignonette boxes on the sill, instead of the dust and smoke of — Street – the only sound heard in this, the principal street, being the voices of mothers calling their playing children home to bed, and the eight o'clock bell of the old parish church bimbomming in remembrance of the curfew: while I was sitting thus idly, the door opened, and the little maidservant, dropping a courtesy, said: "Please, sir, Mrs Munton's compliments, and she would be glad to know how you are after your journey."

'There! was not that hearty and kind? Would even the dearest chum I had at Guy's have thought of doing such a thing? while Mrs Munton, whose name I had never heard of before, was doubtless suffering anxiety till I could relieve her mind by sending back word that I was pretty well.

' "My compliments to Mrs Munton, and I am pretty well: much obliged to her." It was as well to say only "pretty well", for "very well" would have destroyed the interest Mrs Munton evidently felt in me. Good Mrs Munton! Kind Mrs Munton! Perhaps, also, young – handsome – rich – widowed Mrs Munton! I rubbed my hands with delight and amusement, and, resuming my post of observation, began to wonder at which house Mrs Munton lived.

'Again the little tap, and the little maidservant: "Please, sir, the

Miss Tomkinsons' compliments, and they would be glad to know how you feel yourself after your journey."

'I don't know why, but the Miss Tomkinsons' name had not such a halo about it as Mrs Munton's. Still it was very pretty in the Miss Tomkinsons to send and enquire. I only wished I did not feel so perfectly robust. I was almost ashamed that I could not send word I was quite exhausted by fatigue, and had fainted twice since my arrival. If I had but had a headache, at least! I heaved a deep breath: my chest was in perfect order; I had caught no cold; so I answered again: "Much obliged to the Miss Tomkinsons; I am not much fatigued; tolerably well: my compliments."

'Little Sally could hardly have got downstairs, before she returned, bright and breathless: "Mr and Mrs Bullock's compliments, sir, and they hope you are pretty well after your journey."

'Who would have expected such kindness from such an unpromising name? Mr and Mrs Bullock were less interesting, it is true, than their predecessors; but I graciously replied: "My compliments; a night's rest will perfectly recruit me."

'The same message was presently brought up from one or two more unknown kind hearts. I really wished I were not so ruddy-looking. I was afraid I should disappoint the tender-hearted town when they saw what a hale young fellow I was. And I was almost ashamed of confessing to a great appetite for supper when Sally came up to enquire what I would have. Beefsteaks were so tempting; but perhaps I ought rather to have water-gruel, and go to bed. The beefsteak carried the day, however. I need not have felt such a gentle elation of spirits, as this mark of the town's attention is paid to everyone when they arrive after a journey. Many of the same people have sent to enquire after you – great, hulking, brown fellow as you are – only Sally spared you the infliction of devising interesting answers.

Chapter 2

'THE NEXT MORNING Mr Morgan came before I had finished breakfast. He was the most dapper little man I ever met. I see the affection with which people cling to the style of dress that was in vogue when they were beaux and belles, and received the most admiration. They are unwilling to believe that their youth and beauty are gone, and think that the prevailing mode is unbecoming. Mr Morgan will inveigh by the hour together against frock-coats, for instance, and whiskers. He keeps his chin close shaven, wears a black dress-coat, and dark-grey pantaloons; and in his morning round to his town patients, he invariably wears the brightest and blackest of Hessian[4] boots, with dangling silk tassels on each side. When he goes home, about ten o'clock, to prepare for his ride to see his country patients, he puts on the most dandy top-boots I ever saw, which he gets from some wonderful bootmaker a hundred miles off. His appearance is what one calls "jemmy"; there is no other word that will do for it. He was evidently a little discomfited when he saw me in my breakfast costume, with the habits which I brought with me from the fellows at Guy's; my feet against the fireplace, my chair balanced on its hind legs (a habit of sitting which I afterwards discovered he particularly abhorred); slippers on my feet (which, also, he considered a most ungentlemanly piece of untidiness "out of a bedroom"); in short, from what I afterwards learned, every prejudice he had was outraged by my appearance on this first visit of his. I put my book down, and sprang up to receive him. He stood, hat and cane in hand.

' "I came to enquire if it would be convenient for you to accompany me on my morning's round, and to be introduced to a few of our friends." I quite detected the little tone of coldness, induced by his disappointment at my appearance, though he never imagined that it was in any way perceptible. "I will be ready directly, sir," said I; and bolted into my bedroom, only too happy to escape his scrutinising eye.

'When I returned, I was made aware, by sundry indescribable little coughs and hesitating noises, that my dress did not satisfy him. I stood ready, hat and gloves in hand; but still he did not offer to set off on our round. I grew very red and hot. At length he said: "Excuse me, my dear young friend, but may I ask if you have no other coat besides that – 'cut-away', I believe you call them? We are rather sticklers for propriety, I believe, in Duncombe; and much depends on a first impression. Let it be professional, my dear sir. Black is the garb of our profession. Forgive my speaking so plainly; but I consider myself *in loco parentis*".[5]

'He was so kind, so bland, and, in truth, so friendly, that I felt it would be most childish to take offence; but I had a little resentment in my heart at this way of being treated. However, I mumbled, "Oh, certainly, sir, if you wish it"; and returned once more to change my coat – my poor cut-away.

'"Those coats, sir, give a man rather too much of a sporting appearance, not quite befitting the learned professions; more as if you came down here to hunt than to be the Galen or Hippocrates[6] of the neighbourhood." He smiled graciously, so I smothered a sigh; for, to tell you the truth, I had rather anticipated – and, in fact, had boasted at Guy's of – the runs I hoped to have with the hounds; for Duncombe was in a famous hunting district.[7] But all these ideas were quite dispersed when Mr Morgan led me to the inn-yard, where there was a horse-dealer on his way to a neighbouring fair, and "strongly advised me" – which in our relative circumstances was equivalent to an injunction – to purchase a little, useful, fast-trotting, brown cob, instead of a fine showy horse, "who would take any fence I put him to", as the horse-dealer assured me. Mr Morgan was evidently pleased when I bowed to his decision, and gave up all hopes of an occasional hunt.

'He opened out a great deal more after this purchase. He told me his plan of establishing me in a house of my own, which looked more respectable, not to say professional, than being in lodgings; and then he went on to say that he had lately lost a friend, a brother surgeon in a neighbouring town, who had left a widow[8] with a small income, who would be very glad to live with me, and act as mistress to my establishment; thus lessening the expense.

'"She is a ladylike woman," said Mr Morgan, "to judge from the little I have seen of her; about forty-five or so; and may really be of some help to you in the little etiquettes of our profession – the slight delicate attentions which every man has to learn, if he wishes to get on in life. This is Mrs Munton's, sir," said he, stopping short at a very unromantic-looking green door, with a brass knocker,

'I had no time to say, "Who is Mrs Munton?" before we had heard Mrs Munton was at home, and were following the tidy elderly servant up the narrow carpeted stairs into the drawing-room. Mrs Munton was the widow of a former vicar, upwards of sixty, rather deaf; but, like all the deaf people I have ever seen, very fond of talking; perhaps because she then knew the subject, which passed out of her grasp when another began to speak. She was ill of a chronic complaint, which often incapacitated her from going out; and the kind people of the town were in the habit of coming to see her and sit with her, and of bringing her the newest, freshest, titbits of news; so that her room was the centre of the gossip of Duncombe – not of scandal, mind; for I make a distinction between gossip and scandal. Now you can fancy the discrepancy between the ideal and the real Mrs Munton. Instead of any foolish notion of a beautiful blooming widow, tenderly anxious about the health of the stranger, I saw a homely, talkative, elderly person, with a keen observant eye, and marks of suffering on her face; plain in manner and dress, but still unmistakably a lady.

She talked to Mr Morgan, but she looked at me; and I saw that nothing I did escaped her notice. Mr Morgan annoyed me by his anxiety to show me off; but he was kindly anxious to bring out every circumstance to my credit in Mrs Munton's hearing, knowing well that the town-crier had not more opportunities to publish all about me than she had.

'"What was that remark you repeated to me of Sir Astley Cooper's?" asked he. It had been the most trivial speech in the world that I had named as we walked along, and I felt ashamed of having to repeat it: but it answered Mr Morgan's purpose, and before night all the town had heard that I was a favourite pupil of Sir Astley's (I had never seen him but twice in my life); and Mr Morgan was afraid that as soon as he knew my full value I should be retained by Sir Astley to assist him in his duties as surgeon to the Royal Family.[9] Every little circumstance was pressed into the conversation which could add to my importance.

'"As I once heard Sir Robert Peel[10] remark to Mr Harrison, the father of our young friend here – The moons in August are remarkably full and bright." – If you remember, Charles, my father was always proud of having sold a pair of gloves to Sir Robert, when he was staying at the Grange, near Biddicombe, and I suppose good Mr Morgan had paid his only visit to my father at the time; but Mrs Munton evidently looked at me with double respect after this incidental remark, which I was amused to meet with, a few months afterwards, disguised in the statement that my father was an intimate friend of the Premier's, and had, in fact, been the adviser of most of the measures taken by him in public life. I sat by, half indignant and half amused. Mr Morgan looked so complacently pleased at the whole effect of the conversation, that I did not care to mar it by explanations; and, indeed, I had little idea at the time how small sayings were the seeds of great events in the town of Duncombe. When we left Mrs Munton's, he was in a blandly communicative mood.

'"You will find it a curious statistical fact, but five-sixths of our householders of a certain rank in Duncombe are women.[11] We have widows and old maids in rich abundance. In fact, my dear sir, I believe that you and I are almost the only gentlemen in the place –

Mr Bullock, of course, excepted. By gentlemen, I mean professional men. It behoves us to remember, sir, that so many of the female sex rely upon us for the kindness and protection which every man who is worthy of the name is always so happy to render."

'Miss Tomkinson, on whom we next called, did not strike me as remarkably requiring protection from any man. She was a tall, gaunt, masculine-looking woman, with an air of defiance about her, naturally; this, however, she softened and mitigated, as far as she was able, in favour of Mr Morgan. He, it seemed to me, stood a little in awe of the lady, who was very *brusque* and plain-spoken, and evidently piqued herself on her decision of character and sincerity of speech.

' "So this is the Mr Harrison we have heard so much of from you, Mr Morgan? I must say, from what I had heard, that I had expected something a little more – hum – hum! But he's young yet; he's young. We have been all anticipating an Apollo, Mr Harrison, from Mr Morgan's description, and an Esculapius[12] combined in one; or, perhaps I might confine myself to saying Apollo, as he, I believe, was the god of medicine!"

'How could Mr Morgan have described me without seeing me? I asked myself.

'Miss Tomkinson put on her spectacles, and adjusted them on her Roman nose. Suddenly relaxing from her severity of inspection, she said to Mr Morgan – "But you must see Caroline. I had nearly forgotten it; she is busy with the girls, but I will send for her. She had a bad headache yesterday, and looked very pale; it made me very uncomfortable."

'She rang the bell, and desired the servant to fetch Miss Caroline.

'Miss Caroline was the younger sister – younger by twenty years; and so considered as a child by Miss Tomkinson, who was fifty-five, at the very least. If she was considered as a child, she was also petted and caressed, and cared for as a child; for she had been left as a baby to the charge of her elder sister; and when the father died, and they had to set up a school, Miss Tomkinson took upon herself every difficult arrangement, and denied herself every pleasure, and made every sacrifice in order that "Carry" might not feel the change in their circumstances. My wife tells me she once knew the sisters purchase a piece of silk, enough, with management, to have made two gowns; but Carry wished for flounces, or some such fal-lals; and, without a word, Miss Tomkinson gave up her gown to have the whole made up as Carry wished, into one handsome one; and wore an old shabby affair herself as cheerfully as if it were Genoa velvet.

That tells the sort of relationship between the sisters as well as anything, and I consider myself very good to name it thus early; for it was long before I found out Miss Tomkinson's real goodness, and we had a great quarrel first. Miss Caroline looked very delicate and die-away when she came in; she was as soft and sentimental as Miss Tomkinson was hard and masculine; and had a way of saying, "Oh, sister, how can you?" at Miss Tomkinson's startling speeches, which I never liked – especially as it was accompanied by a sort of protesting look at the company present, as if she wished to have it understood that she was shocked at her sister's *outré*[13] manners. Now, that was not faithful between sisters. A remonstrance in private might have done good – though, for my own part, I have grown to like Miss Tomkinson's speeches and ways; but I don't like the way some people have of separating themselves from what may be unpopular in their relations. I know I spoke rather shortly to Miss Caroline when she asked me whether I could bear the change from "the great metropolis" to a little country village. In the first place, why could not she call it "London", or "town", and have done with it? And, in the next place, why should she not love the place that was her home well enough to fancy that everyone would like it when they came to know it as well as she did?

'I was conscious I was rather abrupt in my conversation with her, and I saw that Mr Morgan was watching me, though he pretended to be listening to Miss Tomkinson's whispered account of her sister's symptoms. But when we were once more in the street, he began, "My dear young friend – "

'I winced; for all the morning I had noticed that when he was going to give a little unpalatable advice, he always began with "My dear young friend". He had done so about the horse.

' "My dear young friend, there are one or two hints I should like to give you about your manner. The great Sir Everard Home used to say, 'A general practitioner should either have a very good manner, or a very bad one.' Now, in the latter case, he must be possessed of talents and acquirements sufficient to ensure his being sought after, whatever his manner might be. But the rudeness will give notoriety to these qualifications. Abernethy[14] is a case in point. I rather, myself, question the taste of bad manners. I, therefore, have studied to acquire an attentive, anxious politeness, which combines ease and grace with a tender regard and interest. I am not aware whether I have succeeded (few men do) in coming up to my ideal; but I recommend you to strive after this manner, peculiarly befitting our profession. Identify yourself with your patients, my dear sir. You have sympathy in your good heart, I am sure, to really feel pain when listening to their account of their sufferings, and it soothes them to see the expression of this feeling in your manner. It is, in fact, sir, manners that make the man in our profession. I don't set myself up as an example – far from it; but – This is Mr Hutton's, our vicar; one of the servants is indisposed, and I shall be glad of the opportunity of introducing you. We can resume our conversation at another time."

'I had not been aware that we had been holding a conversation, in which, I believe, the assistance of two persons is required. Why had not Mr Hutton sent to ask after my health the evening before, according to the custom of the place? I felt rather offended.

Chapter 3

'The vicarage was on the north side of the street, at the end opening towards the hills. It was a long low house, receding behind its neighbours; a court was between the door and the street, with a flag-walk and an old stone cistern on the right-hand side of the door; Solomon's seal growing under the windows. Someone was watching from behind the window-curtain; for the door opened, as if by magic, as soon as we reached it; and we entered a low room, which served as hall, and was matted all over, with deep old-fashioned window-seats, and Dutch tiles in the fireplace; altogether it was very cool and refreshing, after the hot sun in the white and red street.

' "Bessie is not so well, Mr Morgan," said the sweet little girl of eleven or so, who had opened the door. "Sophy wanted to send for you; but papa said he was sure you would come soon this morning, and we were to remember that there were other sick people wanting you."

' "Here's Mr Morgan, Sophy," said she, opening the door into an inner room, to which we descended by a step, as I remember well; for I was nearly falling down it, I was so caught by the picture within. It was like a picture – at least, seen through the door frame. A sort of mixture of crimson and sea-green in the room, and a sunny garden beyond; a very low casement window, open to the amber air; clusters of white roses peeping in; and Sophy sitting on a cushion on the ground, the light coming from above on her head, and a little sturdy round-eyed brother kneeling by her, to whom she was teaching the alphabet. It was a mighty relief to him when we came in, as I could see; and I am much mistaken if he was easily caught again to say his lesson, when he was once sent off to find papa. Sophy rose quietly; and of course we were just introduced, and that was all, before she took Mr Morgan upstairs to see her sick servant. I was left to myself in the room. It looked so like a home that it at once made me know the full charm of the word. There were books and work about, and tokens of employment; there was a child's plaything on the floor, and against the sea-green walls there hung a likeness or two, done in watercolours; one, I was sure, was that of Sophy's mother. The chairs and sofa were covered with chintz, the same as the curtains – a little pretty red rose on a white ground. I don't know where the crimson came from, but I am sure there was crimson somewhere; perhaps in the carpet. There was a glass door besides the window, and you went up a step into the garden. This was, first, a grass plot, just under the windows, and, beyond that, straight gravel walks, with box-borders and narrow flower-beds on each side, most brilliant and gay at the end of August, as it was then; and behind the flower-borders were fruit trees trained over woodwork, so as to shut out the beds of kitchen-garden within.

'While I was looking round, a gentleman came in, who, I was sure, was the Vicar. It was rather awkward, for I had to account for my presence there.

' "I came with Mr Morgan; my name is Harrison," said I, bowing. I could see he was not much enlightened by this explanation, but we sat down and talked about the time of year, or some such matter, till Sophy and Mr Morgan came back. Then I saw Mr Morgan to advantage. With a man whom he respected, as he did the Vicar, he lost the prim, artificial manner he had in general, and was calm and dignified; but not so dignified as the Vicar. I never saw anyone like him. He was very quiet and reserved, almost absent at times; his personal appearance was not striking; but he was altogether a man you would talk to with your hat off whenever you met him. It was his character that produced this effect – character that he never thought about, but that appeared in every word, and look, and motion.

' "Sophy," said he, "Mr Morgan looks very warm; could you not gather a few jargonelle pears off the south wall? I fancy there are some ripe there. Our jargonelle pears are remarkably early this year."

'Sophy went into the sunny garden, and I saw her take a rake and tilt at the pears, which were above her reach, apparently. The parlour had become chilly (I found out afterwards it had a flag floor, which accounts for its coldness), and I thought I should like to go into the warm sun. I said I would go and help the young lady; and, without waiting for an answer, I went into the warm scented garden, where the bees were rifling the flowers, and making a continual busy sound. I think Sophy had begun to despair of getting the fruit, and was glad of my assistance. I thought I was very senseless to have knocked them down so soon, when I found we were to go in as soon as they were gathered. I should have liked to have walked round the garden, but Sophy walked straight off with the pears, and I could do nothing but follow her. She took up her needlework while we ate them: they were very soon finished, and, when the Vicar had ended his conversation with Mr Morgan about some poor people, we rose up to come away. I was thankful that Mr Morgan had said so little about me. I could not have endured that he should have introduced Sir Astley Cooper or Sir Robert Peel at the vicarage; nor yet could I have brooked much mention of my "great opportunities for acquiring a thorough knowledge of my profession", which I had heard him describe to Miss Tomkinson, while her sister was talking to me. Luckily, however, he spared me all this at the Vicar's. When we left, it was time to mount our horses and go the country rounds, and I was glad of it.

Chapter 4

'By and by the inhabitants of Duncombe began to have parties in my honour. Mr Morgan told me it was on my account, or I don't think I should have found it out. But he was pleased at every fresh invitation, and rubbed his hands, and chuckled, as if it was a compliment to himself, as in truth it was.

'Meanwhile, the arrangement with Mrs Rose had been brought to a conclusion. She was to bring her furniture, and place it in a house, of which I was to pay the rent. She was to be the mistress, and, in return, she was not to pay anything for her board. Mr Morgan took the house, and delighted in advising and settling all my affairs. I was partly indolent, and partly amused, and was altogether passive. The house he took for me was near his own: it had two sitting-rooms downstairs, opening into each other by folding-doors, which were, however, kept shut in general. The back room was my consulting-room ("the library", he advised me to call it), and he gave me a skull to put on the top of my bookcase, in which the medical books were all ranged on the conspicuous shelves; while Miss Austen, Dickens, and Thackeray were, by Mr Morgan himself, skilfully placed in a careless way, upside down or with their backs turned to the wall. The front parlour was to be the dining-room, and the room above was furnished with Mrs Rose's drawing-room chairs and table, though I found she preferred sitting downstairs in the dining-room close to the window, where, between every stitch, she could look up and see what was going on in the street. I felt rather queer to be the master of this house, filled with another person's furniture, before I had even seen the lady whose property it was.

'Presently she arrived. Mr Morgan met her at the inn where the coach stopped, and accompanied her to my house. I could see them out of the drawing-room window, the little gentleman stepping daintily along, flourishing his cane, and evidently talking away. She was a little taller than he was, and in deep widow's mourning; such veils and falls, and capes and cloaks, that she looked like a black crape haycock. When we were introduced, she put up her thick veil, and looked around and sighed.

' "Your appearance and circumstances, Mr Harrison, remind me forcibly of the time when I was married to my dear husband, now at rest. He was then, like you, commencing practice as a surgeon. For twenty years I sympathised with him, and assisted him by every means in my power, even to making up pills when the young man was out. May we live together in like harmony for an equal length of time! May the regard between us be equally sincere, although, instead of being conjugal, it is to be maternal and filial!"

'I am sure she had been concocting this speech in the coach, for she afterwards told me she was the only passenger. When she had ended, I felt as if I ought to have had a glass of wine in my hand to drink, after the manner of toasts. And yet I doubt if I should have done it heartily, for I did not hope to live with her for twenty years; it had rather a dreary sound. However, I only bowed and kept my thoughts to myself. I asked Mr Morgan, while Mrs Rose was upstairs taking off her things, to stay to tea; to which he agreed, and kept rubbing his hands with satisfaction, saying: "Very fine woman, sir; very fine woman! And what a manner! How she will receive patients, who may wish to leave a message during your absence. Such a flow of words to be sure!"

'Mr Morgan could not stay long after tea, as there were one or two cases to be seen. I would willingly have gone, and had my hat on, indeed, for the purpose, when he said it would not be respectful, "not the thing", to leave Mrs Rose the first evening of her arrival.

' "Tender deference to the sex – to a widow in the first months of her loneliness – requires a little consideration, my dear sir. I will leave that case at Miss Tomkinson's for you; you will perhaps call early tomorrow morning. Miss Tomkinson is rather particular, and is apt to speak plainly if she does not think herself properly attended to."

'I had often noticed that he shuffled off the visits to Miss Tomkinson's on me, and I suspect he was a little afraid of the lady.

'It was rather a long evening with Mrs Rose. She had nothing to do, thinking it civil, I suppose, to stop in the parlour, and not go upstairs and unpack. I begged I might be no restraint upon her if she wished to do so; but (rather to my disappointment) she smiled in a measured, subdued way, and said it would be a pleasure to her to become better acquainted with me. She went upstairs once, and my heart misgave me when I saw her come down with a clean folded pocket-handkerchief. Oh, my prophetic soul! – she was no sooner seated, than she began to give me an account of her late husband's illness, and symptoms, and death. It was a very common case, but she evidently seemed to think it had been peculiar. She had just a smattering of medical knowledge, and used the technical terms so very *mal-àpropos*[15] that I could hardly keep from smiling; but I would not have done it for the world, she was evidently in such deep and sincere distress. At last she said: "I have the 'dognoses' of my dear husband's complaint in my desk, Mr Harrison, if you would like to draw up the case for the *Lancet*.[16] I think he would have felt gratified, poor fellow, if he had been told such a compliment would be paid to his remains, and that his case should appear in those distinguished columns."

'It was rather awkward; for the case was of the very commonest, as I said before. However, I had not been even this short time in practice without having learnt a few of those noises which do not compromise one, and yet may bear a very significant construction if the listener chooses to exert a little imagination.

'Before the end of the evening, we were such friends that she brought me down the late Mr Rose's picture to look at. She told me she could not bear herself to gaze upon the beloved features; but that, if I would look upon the miniature, she would avert her face. I offered to take it into my own hands, but she seemed wounded at the proposal, and said she never, never could trust such a treasure out of her own possession; so she turned her head very much over her left shoulder, while I examined the likeness held by her extended right arm.

'The late Mr Rose must have been rather a good-looking jolly man; and the artist had given him such a broad smile, and such a twinkle about the eyes, that it really was hard to help smiling back at him. However, I restrained myself.

'At first Mrs Rose objected to accepting any of the invitations which were sent her to accompany me to the tea-parties in the town. She was so good and simple that I was sure she had no other reason than the one which she alleged – the short time that had elapsed since her husband's death; or else, now that I had had some experience of the entertainments which she declined so pertinaciously, I might have suspected that she was glad of the excuse. I used sometimes to wish that I was a widow. I came home tired from a hard day's riding, and, if I had but felt sure that Mr Morgan would not come in, I should certainly have put on my slippers and my loose morning coat, and have indulged in a cigar in the garden. It seemed a cruel sacrifice to society to dress myself in tight boots, and a stiff coat, and go to a five-o'clock tea. But Mr Morgan read me such lectures upon the necessity of cultivating the goodwill of the people among whom I was settled, and seemed so sorry, and almost hurt, when I once complained of the dulness of these parties, that I felt I could not be so selfish as to decline more than one out of three. Mr Morgan, if he found that I had an invitation for the evening, would often take the longer round, and the more distant visits. I suspected him at first of the design, which I confess I often entertained, of shirking the parties; but I soon found out he was really making a sacrifice of his inclinations for what he considered to be my advantage.

Chapter 5

'There was one invitation which seemed to promise a good deal of pleasure. Mr Bullock (who is the attorney of Duncombe) was married a second time to a lady from a large provincial town; she wished to lead the fashion – a thing very easy to do, for everyone was willing to follow her. So, instead of giving a tea-party in my honour, she proposed a picnic to some old hall in the neighbourhood; and really the arrangements sounded tempting enough. Every patient we had seemed full of the subject – both those who were invited and those who were not. There was a moat round the house, with a boat on it; and there was a gallery in the hall, from which music sounded delightfully.[17] The family to whom the place belonged were abroad, and lived at a newer and grander mansion when they were at home; there were only a farmer and his wife in the old hall, and they were to have the charge of the preparations. The little kind-hearted town was delighted when the sun shone bright on the October morning of our picnic; the shopkeepers and cottagers all looked pleased as they saw the cavalcade gathering at Mr Bullock's door. We were somewhere about twenty in number; a "silent few", she called us; but I thought we were quite enough. There were the Miss Tomkinsons, and two of their young ladies – one of them belonged to a "county family",[18] Mrs Bullock told me in a whisper; then came Mr and Mrs and Miss Bullock, and a tribe of little children, the offspring of the present wife. Miss Bullock was only a stepdaughter. Mrs Munton had accepted the invitation to join our party, which was rather unexpected by the host and hostess, I imagine, from little remarks that I overheard; but they made her very welcome. Miss Horsman (a maiden lady who had been on a visit from home till last week) was another. And last, there were the Vicar and his children. These, with Mr Morgan and myself, made up the party. I was very much pleased to see something more of the Vicar's family. He had come in occasionally to the evening parties, it is true; and spoken kindly to us all; but it was not his habit to stay very long at them. And his daughter was, he said, too young to visit. She had had the charge of her little sisters and brother since her mother's death, which took up a good deal of her time, and she was glad of the evenings to pursue her own studies. But today the case was different; and Sophy, and Helen, and Lizzie, and even little Walter, were all there, standing at Mrs Bullock's door; for we none of us could be patient enough to sit still in the parlour with Mrs Munton and the elder ones, quietly waiting for the two chaises and the spring-cart, which were to have been there by two o'clock, and now it was nearly a quarter past. "Shameful! the brightness of the day would be gone." The sympathetic shopkeepers, standing at their respective doors with their hands in their pockets, had, one and all, their heads turned in the direction from which the carriages (as Mrs Bullock called them) were to come. There was a rumble along the paved street; and the shopkeepers turned and smiled, and bowed their heads congratulatingly to us; all the mothers and all the little children of the place stood clustering round the door to see us set off. I had my horse waiting; and, meanwhile, I assisted people into their vehicles. One sees a good deal of management on such occasions. Mrs Munton was handed first into one of the chaises; then there was a little hanging back, for most of the young people wished to go in the cart – I don't know why. Miss Horsman, however, came forward, and, as she was known to be the intimate friend of Mrs Munton, so far it was satisfactory. But who was to be third – bodkin[19] with two old ladies, who liked the windows shut? I saw Sophy speaking to Helen; and then she came forward and offered to be the third. The two old ladies looked pleased and glad (as everyone did near Sophy); so that chaise-full was arranged. Just as it was going off, however, the servant from the vicarage came running with a note for her master. When he had read it, he went to the chaise door, and I suppose told Sophy, what I afterwards heard him say to Mrs Bullock, that the clergyman of a neighbouring parish was ill, and unable to read the funeral service for one of his parishioners, who was to be buried that afternoon. The Vicar was, of course, obliged to go, and said he should not return home that night. It seemed a relief to some, I perceived, to be without the little restraint of his dignified presence. Mr Morgan came up just at the moment, having ridden hard all the morning to be in time to join our party; so we were resigned, on the whole, to the Vicar's absence. His own family regretted him the most, I noticed, and I liked them all the better for it. I believe that I came next in being sorry for his departure; but I respected and admired him, and felt always the better for having been in his company. Miss Tomkinson, Mrs Bullock, and the "county" young lady, were in the next chaise. I think the last would rather have been in the cart with the younger and merrier set, but I imagine that was considered *infra dig.*[20] The remainder of the party were to ride and tie;[21] and a most riotous laughing set they were. Mr Morgan and I were on horseback; at least I led my horse, with little Walter riding on him; his fat, sturdy legs standing stiff out on each side of my cob's broad back. He was a little darling, and chattered all the way, his sister Sophy being the heroine of all his stories. I found he owed this day's excursion entirely to her begging papa to let him come; nurse was strongly against it – "cross old nurse!" he called her once, and then said, "No, not cross; kind nurse; Sophy tells Walter not to say cross nurse." I never saw so young a child so brave. The horse shied at a log of wood. Walter looked very red, and grasped the mane, but sat upright like a little man, and never spoke all the time the horse was dancing. When it was over he looked at me, and smiled: "You would not let me be hurt, Mr Harrison, would you?" He was the most winning little fellow I ever saw.

'There were frequent cries to me from the cart, "Oh, Mr Harrison! do get us that branch of blackberries; you can reach it with your whip handle." "Oh, Mr Harrison! there were such splendid nuts on the other side of that hedge; would you just turn back for them?" Miss Caroline Tomkinson was once or twice rather faint with the motion of the cart, and asked me for my smelling-bottle, as she had forgotten hers. I was amused at the idea of my carrying such articles about with me. Then she thought she should like to walk, and got out, and came on my side of the road; but I found little Walter the pleasanter companion, and soon set the horse off into a trot, with which pace her tender constitution could not keep up.

'The road to the old hall was along a sandy lane, with high hedge-banks; the wych-elms almost met overhead. "Shocking farming!" Mr Bullock called out; and so it might be, but it was very pleasant and picturesque-looking. The trees were gorgeous, in their orange and crimson hues, varied by great dark green holly trees, glistening in the autumn sun. I should have thought the colours too vivid, if I had seen them in a picture, especially when we wound up the brow, after crossing the little bridge over the brook – (what laughing and screaming there was as the cart splashed through the sparkling water!) – and I caught the purple hills beyond. We could see the old hall, too, from that point, with its warm rich woods billowing up behind, and the blue waters of the moat lying still under the sunlight.

'Laughing and talking is very hungry work, and there was a universal petition for dinner when we arrived at the lawn before the hall, where it had been arranged that we were to dine. I saw Miss Carry take Miss Tomkinson aside, and whisper to her; and presently the elder sister came up to me, where I was busy, rather apart, making a seat of hay, which I had fetched from the farmer's loft for my little friend Walter, who, I had noticed, was rather hoarse, and for whom I was afraid of a seat on the grass, dry as it appeared to be.

' "Mr Harrison, Caroline tells me she has been feeling very faint, and she is afraid of a return of one of her attacks. She says she has more confidence in your medical powers than in Mr Morgan's. I should not be sincere if I did not say that I differ from her; but, as it is so, may I beg you to keep an eye upon her? I tell her she had better not have come if she did not feel well; but, poor girl, she had set her heart upon this day's pleasure. I have offered to go home with her; but she says, if she can only feel sure you are at hand, she would rather stay."

'Of course I bowed, and promised all due attendance on Miss Caroline; and in the meantime, until she did require my services, I thought I might as well go and help the Vicar's daughter, who looked so fresh and pretty in her white muslin dress, here, there, and everywhere, now in the sunshine, now in the green shade, helping everyone to be comfortable, and thinking of everyone but herself.

'Presently, Mr Morgan came up.

' "Miss Caroline does not feel quite well. I have promised your services to her sister."

' "So have I, sir. But Miss Sophy cannot carry this heavy basket."

'I did not mean her to have heard this excuse; but she caught it up and said: "Oh, yes, I can! I can take the things out one by one. Go to poor Miss Caroline, pray, Mr Harrison."

'I went; but very unwillingly, I must say. When I had once seated myself by her, I think she must have felt better. It was, probably, only a nervous fear, which was relieved when she knew she had assistance near at hand; for she made a capital dinner. I thought she would never end her modest requests for "just a little more pigeon-pie, or a merry-thought[22] of chicken". Such a hearty meal would, I hope, effectually revive her; and so it did; for she told me she thought she could manage to walk round the garden, and see the old peacock yews, if I would kindly give her my arm. It was very provoking; I had so set my heart upon being with the Vicar's children. I advised Miss Caroline strongly to lie down a little, and rest before tea, on the sofa in the farmer's kitchen; you cannot think how persuasively I begged her to take care of herself. At last she consented, thanking me for my tender interest; she should never forget my kind attention to her. She little knew what was in my mind at the time. However, she was safely consigned to the farmer's wife, and I was rushing out in search of a white gown and a waving figure, when I encountered Mrs Bullock at the door of the hall. She was a fine, fierce-looking woman. I thought she had appeared a little displeased at my (unwilling) attentions to Miss Caroline at dinner-time; but now, seeing me alone, she was all smiles.

' "Oh, Mr Harrison, all alone! How is that? What are the young ladies about to allow such churlishness? And, by the way, I have left a young lady who will be very glad of your assistance, I am sure – my daughter, Jemima (her stepdaughter, she meant). Mr Bullock is so particular, and so tender a father, that he would be frightened to death at the idea of her going into the boat on the moat unless she was with someone who could swim. He is gone to discuss the new wheel-plough with the farmer (you know agriculture is his hobby, although law, horrid law, is his business). But the poor girl is pining on the bank, longing for my permission to join the others, which I dare not give unless you will kindly accompany her, and promise, if any accident happens, to preserve her safe."

'Oh, Sophy, why was no one anxious about you?

Chapter 6

'MISS BULLOCK was standing by the waterside, looking wistfully, as I thought, at the water party; the sound of whose merry laughter came pleasantly enough from the boat, which lay off (for, indeed, no one knew how to row, and she was of a clumsy flat-bottomed build) about a hundred yards, "weather-bound", as they shouted out, among the long stalks of the water-lilies.

'Miss Bullock did not look up till I came close to her; and then, when I told her my errand, she lifted up her great, heavy, sad eyes, and looked at me for a moment. It struck me, at the time, that she expected to find some expression on my face which was not there, and that its absence was a relief to her. She was a very pale, unhappy-looking girl, but very quiet, and, if not agreeable in manner, at any rate not forward or offensive. I called to the party in the boat, and they came slowly enough through the large, cool, green lily-leaves towards us. When they got near, we saw there was no room for us, and Miss Bullock said she would rather stay in the meadow and saunter about, if I would go into the boat; and I am certain from the look on her countenance that she spoke the truth; but Miss Horsman called out, in a sharp voice, while she smiled in a very disagreeable knowing way: "Oh, mamma will be displeased if you don't come in, Miss Bullock, after all her trouble in making such a nice arrangement."

'At this speech the poor girl hesitated, and at last, in an undecided way, as if she was not sure whether she was doing right, she took Sophy's place in the boat. Helen and Lizzie landed with their sister, so that there was plenty of room for Miss Tomkinson, Miss Horsman, and all the little Bullocks; and the three vicarage girls went off strolling along the meadow side, and playing with Walter, who was in a high state of excitement. The sun was getting low, but the declining light was beautiful upon the water; and, to add to the charm of the time, Sophy and her sisters, standing on the green lawn in front of the hall, struck up the little German canon,[23] which I had never heard before, "O wie wohl ist mir am Abend," etc. At last we were summoned to tug the boat to the landing-steps on the lawn, tea and a blazing wood fire being ready for us in the hall. I was offering my arm to Miss Horsman, as she was a little lame, when she said again, in her peculiar disagreeable way, "Had you not better take Miss Bullock, Mr Harrison? It will be more satisfactory."

'I helped Miss Horsman up the steps, however, and then she repeated her advice; so, remembering that Miss Bullock was in fact the daughter of my entertainers, I went to her; but, though she accepted my arm, I could perceive that she was sorry that I had offered it.

'The hall was lighted by the glorious wood fire in the wide old grate; the daylight was dying away in the west; and the large windows admitted but little of what was left, through their small leaded frames, with coats of arms emblazoned upon them. The farmer's wife had set out a great long table, which was piled with good things; and a huge black kettle sang on the glowing fire, which sent a cheerful warmth through the room as it crackled and blazed. Mr Morgan (who I found had been taking a little round in the neighbourhood among his patients) was there, smiling and rubbing his hands as usual. Mr Bullock was holding a conversation with the farmer at the garden-door on the nature of different manures, in which it struck me that, if Mr Bullock had the fine names and the theories on his side, the farmer had all the practical knowledge and the experience, and I know which I would have trusted. I think Mr Bullock rather liked to talk about Liebig[24] in my hearing; it sounded well, and was knowing. Mrs Bullock was not particularly placid in her mood. In the first place, I wanted to sit by the Vicar's daughter, and Miss Caroline as decidedly wanted to sit on my other side, being afraid of her fainting fits, I imagine. But Mrs Bullock called me to a place near her daughter. Now, I thought I had done enough civility to a girl who was evidently annoyed rather than pleased by my attentions, and I pretended to be busy stooping under the table for Miss Caroline's gloves, which were missing; but it was of no avail; Mrs Bullock's fine severe eyes were awaiting my reappearance, and she summoned me again.

' "I am keeping this place on my right hand for you, Mr Harrison. Jemima, sit still!"

'I went up to the post of honour and tried to busy myself with pouring out coffee to hide my chagrin; but, on my forgetting to empty the water put in ("to warm the cups", Mrs Bullock said), and omitting to add any sugar, the lady told me she would dispense with my services, and turn me over to my neighbour on the other side.

' "Talking to the younger lady was, no doubt, more Mr Harrison's vocation than assisting the elder one." I dare say it was only the manner that made the words seem offensive. Miss Horsman sat opposite to me, smiling away. Miss Bullock did not speak, but seemed more depressed than ever. At length, Miss Horsman and Mrs Bullock got to a war of innuendoes, which were completely unintelligible to me, and I was very much displeased with my situation; while, at the bottom of the table, Mr Morgan and Mr Bullock were making the young ones laugh most heartily. Part of the joke was Mr Morgan insisting upon making tea at the end; and Sophy and Helen were busy contriving every possible mistake for him. I thought honour was a very good thing, but merriment a better. Here was I in the place of distinction, hearing nothing but cross words. At last the time came for us to go home. As the evening was damp, the seats in the chaises were the best and most to be desired. And now Sophy offered to go in the cart; only she seemed anxious, and so was I, that Walter should be secured from the effects of the white wreaths of fog rolling up from the valley; but the little violent, affectionate fellow would not be separated from Sophy. She made a nest for him on her knee in one corner of the cart, and covered him with her own shawl; and I hoped that he would take no harm. Miss Tomkinson, Mr Bullock, and some of the young ones walked; but I seemed chained to the windows of the chaise, for Miss Caroline begged me not to leave her, as she was dreadfully afraid of robbers; and Mrs Bullock implored me to see that the man did not overturn them in the bad roads, as he had certainly had too much to drink.

'I became so irritable before I reached home, that I thought it was the most disagreeable day of pleasure I had ever had, and could hardly bear to answer Mrs Rose's never-ending questions. She told me, however, that from my account the day was so charming that she thought she should relax in the rigour of her seclusion, and mingle a little more in the society of which I gave so tempting a description. She really thought her dear Mr Rose would have wished it; and his will should be law to her after his death, as it had ever been during his life. In compliance, therefore, with his wishes, she would even do a little violence to her own feelings.

'She was very good and kind; not merely attentive to everything which she thought could conduce to my comfort, but willing to take any trouble in providing the broths and nourishing food which I often found it convenient to order, under the name of kitchen-physic, for my poorer patients; and I really did not see the use of her shutting herself up, in mere compliance with an etiquette, when she began to wish to mix in the little quiet society of Buncombe. Accordingly I urged her to begin to visit, and, even when applied to as to what I imagined the late Mr Rose's wishes on that subject would have been, answered for that worthy gentleman, and assured his widow that I was convinced he would have regretted deeply her giving way to immoderate grief, and would have been rather grateful than otherwise at seeing her endeavour to divert her thoughts by a few quiet visits. She cheered up, and said, "As I really thought so, she would sacrifice her own inclinations, and accept the very next invitation that came."

Chapter 7

'I WAS ROUSED from my sleep in the middle of the night by a messenger from the vicarage. Little Walter had got the croup,[25] and Mr Morgan had been sent for into the country. I dressed myself hastily, and went through the quiet little street. There was a light burning upstairs at the vicarage. It was in the nursery. The servant, who opened the door the instant I knocked, was crying sadly, and could hardly answer my enquiries as I went upstairs, two steps at a time, to see my little favourite.

'The nursery was a great large room. At the farther end it was lighted by a common candle, which left the other end, where the door was, in shade; so I suppose the nurse did not see me come in, for she was speaking very crossly.

' "Miss Sophy!" said she, "I told you over and over again it was not fit for him to go, with the hoarseness that he had; and you would take him. It will break your papa's heart, I know; but it's none of my doing."

'Whatever Sophy felt, she did not speak in answer to this. She was on her knees by the warm bath, in which the little fellow was struggling to get his breath, with a look of terror on his face that I have often noticed in young children when smitten by a sudden and violent illness. It seems as if they recognised something infinite and invisible, at whose bidding the pain and the anguish come, from which no love can shield them. It is a very heart-rending look to observe, because it comes on the faces of those who are too young to receive comfort from the words of faith, or the promises of religion. Walter had his arms tight round Sophy's neck, as if she, hitherto his paradise-angel, could save him from the grave shadow of Death. Yes! of Death! I knelt down by him on the other side, and examined him. The very robustness of his little frame gave violence to the disease, which is always one of the most fearful by which children of his age can be attacked.

' "Don't tremble, Watty," said Sophy, in a soothing tone; "it's Mr Harrison, darling, who let you ride on his horse." I could detect the quivering in the voice, which she tried to make so calm and soft to quiet the little fellow's fears. We took him out of the bath, and I went for leeches.[26] While I was away, Mr Morgan came. He loved the vicarage children as if he were their uncle; but he stood still and aghast at the sight of Walter – so lately bright and strong – and now hurrying along to the awful change – to the silent mysterious land, where, tended and cared for as he had been on earth, he must go – alone. The little fellow! the darling!

'We applied the leeches to his throat. He resisted at first; but Sophy, God bless her! put the agony of her grief on one side, and thought only of him, and began to sing the little songs he loved. We were all still. The gardener had gone to fetch the Vicar; but he was twelve miles off, and we doubted if he would come in time. I don't know if they had any hope; but, the first moment Mr Morgan's eyes met mine, I saw that he, like me, had none. The ticking of the house clock sounded through the dark quiet house. Walter was sleeping now, with the black leeches yet hanging to his fair, white throat. Still Sophy went on singing little lullabies, which she had sung under far different and happier circumstances. I remember one verse, because it struck me at the time as strangely applicable.

> ' "Sleep, baby, sleep!
> Thy rest shall angels keep;
> While on the grass the lamb shall feed,
> And never suffer want or need.
> Sleep, baby, sleep."[27]

'The tears were in Mr Morgan's eyes. I do not think either he or I could have spoken in our natural tones; but the brave girl went on clear though low. She stopped at last, and looked up.

' "He is better, is he not, Mr Morgan?"

' "No, my dear. He is – ahem" – he could not speak all at once. Then he said – "My dear! he will be better soon. Think of your mamma, my dear Miss Sophy. She will be very thankful to have one of her darlings safe with her, where she is."

'Still she did not cry. But she bent her head down on the little face, and kissed it long and tenderly.

' "I will go for Helen and Lizzie. They will be sorry not to see him again." She rose up and went for them. Poor girls, they came in, in their dressing-gowns, with eyes dilated with sudden emotion, pale with terror, stealing softly along, as if sound could disturb him. Sophy comforted them by gentle caresses. It was over soon.

'Mr Morgan was fairly crying like a child. But he thought it necessary to apologise to me, for what I honoured him for. "I am a little overdone by yesterday's work, sir. I have had one or two bad nights, and they rather upset me. When I was your age I was as strong and manly as anyone, and would have scorned to shed tears."

'Sophy came up to where we stood.

' "Mr Morgan! I am so sorry for papa. How shall I tell him?" She was struggling against her own grief for her father's sake. Mr Morgan offered to await his coming home; and she seemed thankful for the proposal. I, new friend, almost a stranger, might stay no longer. The street was as quiet as ever; not a shadow was changed; for it was not yet four o'clock. But during the night a soul had departed.

'From all I could see, and all I could learn, the Vicar and his daughter strove which should comfort the other the most. Each thought of the other's grief – each prayed for the other rather than for themselves. We saw them walking out, countrywards; and we heard of them in the cottages of the poor. But it was some time before I happened to meet either of them again. And then I felt, from something indescribable in their manner towards me, that I was one of the "Peculiar people, whom Death had made dear".[28]

'That one day at the old hall had done this. I was, perhaps, the last person who had given the poor little fellow any unusual pleasure. Poor Walter! I wish I could have done more to make his short life happy!

Chapter 8

'There was a little lull, out of respect to the Vicar's grief, in the visiting. It gave time to Mrs Rose to soften down the anguish of her weeds.

'At Christmas, Miss Tomkinson sent out invitations for a party. Miss Caroline had once or twice apologised to me because such an event had not taken place before; but, as she said, "the avocations of their daily life prevented their having such little *réunions* except in the vacations". And, sure enough, as soon as the holidays began, came the civil little note: "The Misses Tomkinson request the pleasure of Mrs Rose's and Mr Harrison's company at tea, on the evening of Monday, the 23rd inst. Tea at five o'clock."

'Mrs Rose's spirit roused, like a warhorse at the sound of the trumpet, at this. She was not of a repining disposition, but I do think she believed the party-giving population of Duncombe had given up inviting her, as soon as she had determined to relent, and accept the invitations, in compliance with the late Mr Rose's wishes.

'Such snippings of white love-ribbon as I found everywhere, making the carpet untidy! One day, too, unluckily, a small box was brought to me by mistake. I did not look at the direction, for I never doubted it was some hyoscyamus[29] which I was expecting from London; so I tore it open, and saw inside a piece of paper, with "No more grey hair", in large letters, upon it. I folded it up in a hurry, and sealed it afresh, and gave it to Mrs Rose; but I could not refrain from asking her, soon after, if she could recommend me anything to keep my hair from turning grey, adding that I thought prevention was better than cure. I think she made out the impression of my seal on the paper after that; for I learned that she had been crying, and that she talked about there being no sympathy left in the world for her since Mr Rose's death; and that she counted the days until she could rejoin him in the better world. I think she counted the days to Miss Tomkinson's party, too; she talked so much about it.

'The covers were taken off Miss Tomkinson's chairs, and curtains, and sofas; and a great jar full of artificial flowers was placed in the centre of the table, which, as Miss Caroline told me, was all her doing, as she doted on the beautiful and artistic in life. Miss Tomkinson stood, erect as a grenadier, close to the door, receiving her friends, and heartily shaking them by the hands as they entered; she said she was truly glad to see them. And so she really was.

'We had just finished tea, and Miss Caroline had brought out a little pack of conversation cards – sheaves of slips of cardboard, with intellectual or sentimental questions on one set, and equally intellectual and sentimental answers on the other; and, as the answers were fit to any and all the questions, you may think they were a characterless and "wersh"[30] set of things. I had just been asked by Miss Caroline: "*Can you tell what those dearest to you think of you at this present time?*" and had answered: "*How can you expect me to reveal such a secret to the present company!*" when the servant announced that a gentleman, a friend of mine, wished to speak to me downstairs.

' "Oh, show him up, Martha; show him up!" said Miss Tomkinson, in her hospitality.

' "Any friend of our friend is welcome," said Miss Caroline, in an insinuating tone.

'I jumped up, however, thinking it might be someone on business; but I was so penned in by the spider-legged tables, stuck out on every side, that I could not make the haste I wished; and, before I could prevent it, Martha had shown up Jack Marshland, who was on his road home for a day or two at Christmas.

'He came up in a hearty way, bowing to Miss Tomkinson, and explaining that he had found himself in my neighbourhood, and had come over to pass a night with me, and that my servant had directed him where I was.

'His voice, loud at all times, sounded like Stentor's[31] in that little room, where we all spoke in a kind of purring way. He had no swell in his tones; they were *forte* from the beginning. At first it seemed like the days of my youth come back again, to hear full manly speaking; I felt proud of my friend, as he thanked Miss Tomkinson for her kindness in asking him to stay the evening. By and by he came up to me, and I dare say he thought he had lowered his voice, for he looked as if speaking confidentially, while in fact the whole room might have heard him.

' "Frank, my boy, when shall we have dinner at this good old lady's? I'm deuced hungry."

' "Dinner! Why, we had had tea an hour ago." While he yet spoke, Martha came in with a little tray, on which was a single cup of coffee and three slices of wafer bread-and-butter. His dismay, and his evident submission to the decrees of Fate, tickled me so much, that I thought he should have a further taste of the life I led from month's end to month's end, and I gave up my plan of taking him home at once, and enjoyed the anticipation of the hearty laugh we should have together at the end of the evening. I was famously punished for my determination.

' "Shall we continue our game?" asked Miss Caroline, who had never relinquished her sheaf of questions.

'We went on questioning and answering, with little gain of information to either party.

' "No such thing as heavy betting in this game, eh, Frank?" asked Jack, who had been watching us. "You don't lose ten pounds at a sitting, I guess, as you used to do at Short's. Playing for love, I suppose you call it?"

'Miss Caroline simpered, and looked down. Jack was not thinking of her. He was thinking of the days we had had "at the Mermaid".[32] Suddenly he said, "Where were you this day last year, Frank?"

' "I don't remember!" said I.

' "Then I'll tell you. It's the 23rd – the day you were taken up for knocking down the fellow in Long Acre, and that I had to bail you out ready for Christmas Day. You are in more agreeable quarters tonight."

'He did not intend this reminiscence to be heard, but was not in the least put out when Miss Tomkinson, with a face of dire surprise, asked: "Mr Harrison taken up, sir?"

' "Oh, yes, ma'am; and you see it was so common an affair with him to be looked up that he can't remember the dates of his different imprisonments."

'He laughed heartily; and so should I have done, but that I saw the impression it made. The thing was, in fact, simple enough, and capable of easy explanation. I had been made angry by seeing a great hulking fellow, out of mere wantonness, break the crutch from under a cripple; and I struck the man more violently than I intended, and down he went, yelling out for the police, and I had to go before the magistrate to be released. I disdained giving this explanation at the time. It was no business of theirs what I had been doing a year ago; but still Jack might have held his tongue. However, that unruly member of his was set a-going, and he told me afterwards he was resolved to let the old ladies into a little of life; and accordingly he remembered every practical joke we had ever had, and talked and laughed, and roared again. I tried to converse with Miss Caroline – Mrs Munton – anyone; but Jack was the hero of the evening, and everyone was listening to him.

' "Then he has never sent any hoaxing letters since he came here, has he? Good boy! He has turned over a new leaf. He was the deepest dog at that I ever met with. Such anonymous letters as he used to send! Do you remember that to Mrs Walbrook, eh, Frank? That was too bad!" (the wretch was laughing all the time). "No; I won't tell about it – don't be afraid. Such a shameful hoax!" (laughing again).

' "Pray do tell," I called out; for he made it seem far worse than it was.

' "Oh no, no; you've established a better character – I would not for the world nip your budding efforts. We'll bury the past in oblivion."

'I tried to tell my neighbours the story to which he alluded; but they were attracted by the merriment of Jack's manner, and did not care to hear the plain matter of fact.

'Then came a pause; Jack was talking almost quietly to Miss Horsman. Suddenly he called across the room – "How many times have you been out with the hounds? The hedges were blind very late this year, but you must have had some good mild days since."

' "I have never been out," said I shortly.

' "Never! – whew! – Why, I thought that was the great attraction to Duncombe."

'Now was not he provoking! He would condole with me, and fix the subject in the minds of everyone present.

'The supper trays were brought in, and there was a shuffling of situations. He and I were close together again.

' "I say, Frank, what will you lay me that I don't clear that tray before people are ready for their second helping? I'm as hungry as a hound."

' "You shall have a round of beef and a raw leg of mutton when you get home. Only do behave yourself here."

' "Well, for your sake; but keep me away from those trays, or I'll not answer for myself. 'Hould me, or I'll fight,' as the Irishman said. I'll go and talk to that little old lady in blue, and sit with my back to those ghosts of eatables."

'He sat down by Miss Caroline, who would not have liked his description of her; and began an earnest, tolerably quiet conversation. I tried to be as agreeable as I could, to do away with the impression he had given of me; but I found that everyone drew up a little stiffly at my approach, and did not encourage me to make any remarks.

'In the middle of my attempts, I heard Miss Caroline beg Jack to take a glass of wine, and I saw him help himself to what appeared to be port; but in an instant he set it down from his lips, exclaiming, "Vinegar, by Jove!" He made the most horribly wry face: and Miss Tomkinson came up in a severe hurry to investigate the affair. It turned out it was some blackcurrant wine, on which she particularly piqued herself; I drank two glasses of it to ingratiate myself with her, and can testify to its sourness. I don't think she noticed my exertions, she was so much engrossed in listening to Jack's excuses for his *mal-àpropos* observation. He told her, with the gravest face, that he had been a teetotaller so long that he had but a confused recollection of the distinction between wine and vinegar, particularly eschewing the latter, because it had been twice fermented; and that he had imagined Miss Caroline had asked him to take toast-and-water, or he should never have touched the decanter.

Chapter 9

'As we were walking home, Jack said, "Lord, Frank! I've had such fun with the little lady in blue. I told her you wrote to me every Saturday, telling me the events of the week. She took it all in." He stopped to laugh; for he bubbled and chuckled so that he could not laugh and walk. "And I told her you were deeply in love" (another laugh); "and that I could not get you to tell me the name of the lady, but that she had light brown hair – in short, I drew from life, and gave her an exact description of herself; and that I was most anxious to see her, and implore her to be merciful to you, for that you were a most timid, faint-hearted fellow with women." He laughed till I thought he would have fallen down. "I begged her, if she could guess who it was from my description – I'll answer for it she did – I took care of that; for I said you described a mole on the left cheek, in the most poetical way, saying Venus had pinched it out of envy at seeing anyone more lovely – oh, hold me up, or I shall fall – laughing and hunger make me so weak; – well, I say, I begged her, if she knew who your fair one could be, to implore her to save you. I said I knew one of your lungs had gone after a former unfortunate love-affair, and that I could not answer for the other if the lady here were cruel. She spoke of a respirator;[33] but I told her that might do very well for the odd lung; but would it minister to a heart diseased?[34] I really did talk fine. I have found out the secret of eloquence – it's believing what you've got to say; and I worked myself well up with fancying you married to the little lady in blue."

'I got to laughing at last, angry as I had been; his impudence was irresistible. Mrs Rose had come home in the sedan, and gone to bed; and he and I sat up over the round of beef and brandy-and-water till two o'clock in the morning.

'He told me I had got quite into the professional way of mousing about a room, and mewing and purring according as my patients were ill or well. He mimicked me, and made me laugh at myself. He left early the next morning.

'Mr Morgan came at his usual hour; he and Marshland would never have agreed, and I should have been uncomfortable to see two friends of mine disliking and despising each other.

'Mr Morgan was ruffled; but with his deferential manner to women, he smoothed himself down before Mrs Rose – regretted that he had not been able to come to Miss Tomkinson's the evening before, and consequently had not seen her in the society she was so well calculated to adorn. But when we were by ourselves, he said: "I was sent for to Mrs Munton's this morning – the old spasms. May I ask what is this story she tells me about – about prison, in fact? I trust, sir, she has made some little mistake, and that you never were – that it is an unfounded report." He could not get it out – "that you were in Newgate[35] for three months!" I burst out laughing; the story had grown like a mushroom indeed. Mr Morgan looked grave. I told him the truth. Still he looked grave. "I've no doubt, sir, that you acted rightly; but it has an awkward sound. I imagined from your hilarity just now that there was no foundation whatever for the story. Unfortunately, there is."

' "I was only a night at the police-station. I would go there again for the same cause, sir."

' "Very fine spirit, sir – quite like Don Quixote; but don't you see you might as well have been to the hulks[36] at once?"

' "No, sir; I don't."

' "Take my word, before long, the story will have grown to that. However, we won't anticipate evil. *Mens conscia recti*,[37] you remember, is the great thing. The part I regret is, that it may require some short time to overcome a little prejudice which the story may excite against you. However, we won't dwell on it. *Mens conscia recti!* Don't think about it, sir."

'It was clear he was thinking a good deal about it.

Chapter 10

'TWO OR THREE DAYS before this time, I had had an invitation from the Bullocks to dine with them on Christmas Day. Mrs Rose was going to spend the week with friends in the town where she formerly lived; and I had been pleased at the notion of being received into a family, and of being a little with Mr Bullock, who struck me as a bluff, good-hearted fellow.

'But this Tuesday before Christmas Day, there came an invitation from the Vicar to dine there; there were to be only their own family and Mr Morgan. "Only their own family". It was getting to be all the world to me. I was in a passion with myself for having been so ready to accept Mr Bullock's invitation – coarse and ungentlemanly as he was; with his wife's airs of pretension and Miss Bullock's stupidity. I turned it over in my mind. No! I could not have a bad headache, which should prevent me going to the place I did not care for, and yet leave me at liberty to go where I wished. All I could do was to join the vicarage girls after church, and walk by their side in a long country ramble. They were quiet; not sad, exactly; but it was evident that the thought of Walter was in their minds on this day. We went through a copse where there were a good number of evergreens planted as covers for game. The snow was on the ground; but the sky was clear and bright, and the sun glittered on the smooth holly-leaves. Lizzie asked me to gather her some of the very bright red berries, and she was beginning a sentence with: "Do you remember" – when Helen said "*Hush*," and looked towards Sophy, who was walking a little apart, and crying softly to herself. There was evidently some connection between Walter and the holly-berries, for Lizzie threw them away at once when she saw Sophy's tears. Soon we came to a stile which led to an open breezy common, half-covered with gorse. I helped the little girls over it, and set them to run down the slope; but I took Sophy's arm in mine, and, though I could not speak, I think she knew how I was feeling for her. I could hardly bear to bid her goodbye at the vicarage gate; it seemed as if I ought to go in and spend the day with her.

Chapter 11

'I VENTED MY ILL-HUMOUR in being late for the Bullocks' dinner. There were one or two clerks, towards whom Mr Bullock was patronising and pressing. Mrs Bullock was decked out in extraordinary finery. Miss Bullock looked plainer than ever; but she had on some old gown or other, I think, for I heard Mrs Bullock tell her she was always making a figure of herself. I began today to suspect that the mother would not be sorry if I took a fancy to the step-daughter. I was again placed near her at dinner, and, when the little ones came in to dessert, I was made to notice how fond of children she was – and, indeed, when one of them nestled to her, her face did brighten; but, the moment she caught this loud-whispered remark, the gloom came back again, with something even of anger in her look; and she was quite sullen and obstinate when urged to sing in the drawing-room. Mrs Bullock turned to me: "Some young ladies won't sing unless they are asked by gentlemen." She spoke very crossly. "If you ask Jemima, she will probably sing. To oblige me, it is evident she will not."

'I thought the singing, when we got it, would probably be a great bore; however, I did as I was bid, and went with my request to the young lady, who was sitting a little apart. She looked up at me with eyes full of tears, and said, in a decided tone (which, if I had not seen her eyes, I should have said was as cross as her mamma's), "No, sir, I will not." She got up, and left the room. I expected to hear Mrs Bullock abuse her for her obstinacy. Instead of that, she began to tell me of the money that had been spent on her education; of what each separate accomplishment had cost. "She was timid," she said, "but very musical. Wherever her future home might be, there would be no want of music." She went on praising her till I hated her. If they thought I was going to marry that great lubberly girl, they were mistaken. Mr Bullock and the clerks came up. He brought out Liebig, and called me to him.

' "I can understand a good deal of this agricultural chemistry," said he, "and have put it in practice – without much success, hitherto, I confess. But these unconnected letters puzzle me a little. I suppose they have some meaning, or else I should say it was mere book-making to put them in."

'"I think they give the page a very ragged appearance," said Mrs Bullock, who had joined us. "I inherit a little of my late father's taste for books, and must say I like to see a good type, a broad margin, and an elegant binding. My father despised variety; how he would have held up his hands aghast at the cheap literature of these times! He did not require many books, but he would have twenty editions of those that he had; and he paid more for binding than he did for the books themselves. But elegance was everything with him. He would not have admitted your Liebig, Mr Bullock; neither the nature of the subject, nor the common type, nor the common way in which your book is got up, would have suited him."

'"Go and make tea, my dear, and leave Mr Harrison and me to talk over a few of these manures."

'We settled to it; I explained the meaning of the symbols, and the doctrine of chemical equivalents. At last he said, "Doctor! you're giving me too strong a dose of it at one time. Let's have a small quantity taken '*hodie*';[38] that's professional, as Mr Morgan would call it. Come in and call, when you have leisure, and give me a lesson in my alphabet. Of all you've been telling me I can only remember that C means carbon and O oxygen; and I see one must know the meaning of all these confounded letters before one can do much good with Liebig."

'"We dine at three," said Mrs Bullock. "There will always be a knife and fork for Mr Harrison. Bullock! don't confine your invitation to the evening!"

'"Why, you see, I've a nap always after dinner; so I could not be learning chemistry then."

'"Don't be so selfish, Mr B. Think of the pleasure Jemima and I shall have in Mr Harrison's society."

'I put a stop to the discussion by saying I would come in in the evenings occasionally, and give Mr Bullock a lesson, but that my professional duties occupied me invariably until that time.

'I liked Mr Bullock. He was simple, and shrewd; and to be with a man was a relief, after all the feminine society I went through every day.

Chapter 12

'The next morning I met Miss Horsman.

' "So you dined at Mr Bullock's yesterday, Mr Harrison? Quite a family party, I hear. They are quite charmed with you, and your knowledge of chemistry. Mr Bullock told me so, in Hodgson's shop, just now. Miss Bullock is a nice girl, eh, Mr Harrison?" She looked sharply at me. Of course, whatever I thought, I could do nothing but assent. "A nice little fortune, too – three thousand pounds, Consols,[39] from her own mother."

'What did I care? She might have three millions for me. I had begun to think a good deal about money, though, but not in connection with her. I had been doing up our books ready to send out our Christmas bills, and had been wondering how far the Vicar would consider three hundred a year, with a prospect of increase, would justify me in thinking of Sophy. Think of her I could not help; and, the more I thought of how good, and sweet, and pretty she was, the more I felt that she ought to have far more than I could offer. Besides, my father was a shopkeeper, and I saw the Vicar had a sort of respect for family. I determined to try and be very attentive to my profession. I was as civil as could be to everyone; and wore the nap off the brim of my hat by taking it off so often.

'I had my eyes open to every glimpse of Sophy. I am overstocked with gloves now that I bought at that time, by way of making errands into the shops where I saw her black gown. I bought pounds upon pounds of arrowroot, till I was tired of the eternal arrowroot puddings Mrs Rose gave me. I asked her if she could not make bread of it, but she seemed to think that would be expensive; so I took to soap as a safe purchase. I believe soap improves by keeping.

Chapter 13

'The more I knew of Mrs Rose, the better I liked her. She was sweet, and kind, and motherly, and we never had any rubs. I hurt her once or twice, I think, by cutting her short in her long stories about Mr Rose. But I found out that when she had plenty to do she did not think of him quite so much; so I expressed a wish for Corazza shirts,[40] and, in the puzzle of devising how they were to be cut out, she forgot Mr Rose for some time. I was still more pleased by her way about some legacy her elder brother left her. I don't know the amount, but it was something handsome, and she might have set up housekeeping for herself; but, instead, she told Mr Morgan (who repeated it to me), that she should continue with me, as she had quite an elder sister's interest in me.

'The "county young lady", Miss Tyrrell, returned to Miss Tomkinson's after the holidays. She had an enlargement of the tonsils, which required to be frequently touched with caustic, so I often called to see her. Miss Caroline always received me, and kept me talking in her washed-out style, after I had seen my patient. One day she told me she thought she had a weakness about the heart, and would be glad if I would bring my stethoscope the next time, which I accordingly did! and, while I was on my knees listening to the pulsations, one of the young ladies came in. She said: "Oh dear! I never! I beg your pardon, ma'am," and scuttled out. There was not much the matter with Miss Caroline's heart: a little feeble in action or so, a mere matter of weakness and general languor. When I went down I saw two or three of the girls peeping out of the half-closed schoolroom door, but they shut it immediately, and I heard them laughing. The next time I called, Miss Tomkinson was sitting in state to receive me.

' "Miss Tyrrell's throat does not seem to make much progress. Do you understand the case, Mr Harrison, or should we have further advice? I think Mr Morgan would probably know more about it."

'I assured her it was the simplest thing in the world; that it always implied a little torpor in the constitution, and that we preferred working through the system, which of course was a slow process; and that the medicine the young lady was taking (iodide of iron) was sure to be successful, although the progress would not be rapid. She bent her head, and said, "It might be so; but she confessed she had more confidence in medicines which had some effect."

'She seemed to expect me to tell her something; but I had nothing to say, and accordingly I bade her goodbye. Somehow, Miss Tomkinson always managed to make me feel very small, by a succession of snubbings; and, whenever I left her I had always to comfort myself under her contradictions by saying to myself, "Her saying it is so does not make it so." Or I invented good retorts which I might have made to her brusque speeches, if I had but thought of them at the right time.

But it was provoking that I had not had the presence of mind to recollect them just when they were wanted.

Chapter 14

'ON THE WHOLE, things went on smoothly. Mr Holden's legacy came in just about this time; and I felt quite rich. Five hundred pounds would furnish the house, I thought, when Mrs Rose left and Sophy came. I was delighted, too, to imagine that Sophy perceived the difference of my manner to her from what it was to anyone else, and that she was embarrassed and shy in consequence, but not displeased with me for it. All was so flourishing that I went about on wings instead of feet. We were very busy, without having anxious cares. My legacy was paid into Mr Bullock's hands, who united a little banking business to his profession of law. In return for his advice about investments (which I never meant to take, having a more charming, if less profitable, mode in my head), I went pretty frequently to teach him his agricultural chemistry. I was so happy in Sophy's blushes that I was universally benevolent, and desirous of giving pleasure to everyone. I went, at Mrs Bullock's general invitation, to dinner there one day unexpectedly: but there was such a fuss of ill-concealed preparation consequent upon my coming, that I never went again. Her little boy came in, with an audibly given message from the cook, to ask: "If this was the gentleman as she was to send in the best dinner-service and dessert for?"

'I looked deaf, but determined never to go again.

'Miss Bullock and I, meanwhile, became rather friendly. We found out that we mutually disliked each other, and were contented with the discovery. If people are worth anything, this sort of non-liking is a very good beginning of friendship. Every good quality is revealed naturally and slowly, and is a pleasant surprise. I found out that Miss Bullock was sensible, and even sweet-tempered, when not irritated by her stepmother's endeavours to show her off. But she would sulk for hours after Mrs Bullock's offensive praise of her good points. And I never saw such a black passion as she went into, when she suddenly came into the room when Mrs Bullock was telling me of all the offers she had had.

'My legacy made me feel up to extravagance. I scoured the country for a glorious nosegay of camellias, which I sent to Sophy on

Valentine's Day. I durst not add a line; but I wished the flowers could speak, and tell her how I loved her.

'I called on Miss Tyrrell that day. Miss Caroline was more simpering and affected than ever, and full of allusions to the day.

' "Do you affix much sincerity of meaning to the little gallantries of this day, Mr Harrison?" asked she, in a languishing tone. I thought of my camellias, and how my heart had gone with them into Sophy's keeping; and I told her I thought one might often take advantage of such a time to hint at feelings one dared not fully express.

'I remembered afterwards the forced display she made, after Miss Tyrrel left the room, of a valentine. But I took no notice at the time; my head was full of Sophy.

'It was on that very day that John Brouncker, the gardener to all of us who had small gardens to keep in order, fell down and injured his wrist severely (I don't give you the details of the case, because they would not interest you, being too technical; if you've any curiosity, you will find them in the *Lancet* of August in that year). We all liked John, and this accident was felt like a town's misfortune. The gardens, too, just wanted doing up. Both Mr Morgan and I went directly to him. It was a very awkward case, and his wife and children were crying sadly. He himself was in great distress at being thrown out of work. He begged us to do something that would cure him speedily, as he could not afford to be laid up, with six children depending on him for bread. We did not say much before him; but we both thought the arm would have to come off, and it was his right arm. We talked it over when we came out of the cottage. Mr Morgan had no doubt of the necessity. I went back at dinner-time to see the poor fellow. He was feverish and anxious. He had caught up some expression of Mr Morgan's in the morning, and had guessed the measure we had in contemplation. He bade his wife leave the room, and spoke to me by myself.

' "If you please, sir, I'd rather be done for at once than have my arm taken off, and be a burden to my family. I'm not afraid of dying; but I could not stand being a cripple for life, eating bread, and not able to earn it."

'The tears were in his eyes with earnestness. I had all along been more doubtful about the necessity of the amputation than Mr Morgan. I knew the improved treatment in such cases. In his days there was much more of the rough and ready in surgical practice;[41] so I gave the poor fellow some hope.

'In the afternoon I met Mr Bullock.

' "So you're to try your hand at an amputation, tomorrow, I hear. Poor John Brouncker! I used to tell him he was not careful enough about his ladders. Mr Morgan is quite excited about it. He asked me to be present, and see how well a man from Guy's could operate; he says he is sure you'll do it beautifully. Pah! no such sights for me, thank you."

'Ruddy Mr Bullock went a shade or two paler at the thought.

' "Curious, how professionally a man views these things! Here's Mr Morgan, who has been all along as proud of you as if you were his own son, absolutely rubbing his hands at the idea of this crowning glory, this feather in your cap! He told me just now he knew he had always been too nervous to be a good operator, and had therefore preferred sending for White[42] from Chesterton. But now anyone might have a serious accident who liked, for you would be always at hand."

'I told Mr Bullock, I really thought we might avoid the amputation; but his mind was preoccupied with the idea of it, and he did not care to listen to me. The whole town was full of it. That is a charm in a little town, everybody is so sympathetically full of the same events. Even Miss Horsman stopped me to ask after John Brouncker with interest; but she threw cold water upon my intention of saving the arm.

' "As for the wife and family, we'll take care of them. Think what a fine opportunity you have of showing off, Mr Harrison!"

'That was just like her. Always ready with her suggestions of ill-natured or interested motives.

'Mr Morgan heard my proposal of a mode of treatment by which I thought it possible that the arm might be saved.

' "I differ from you, Mr Harrison," said he. "I regret it; but I differ *in toto*[43] from you. Your kind heart deceives you in this instance. There is no doubt that amputation must take place – not later than tomorrow morning, I should say. I have made myself at liberty to attend upon you, sir; I shall be happy to officiate as your assistant. Time was when I should have been proud to be principal; but a little trembling in my arm incapacitates me."

'I urged my reasons upon him again; but he was obstinate. He had, in fact, boasted so much of my acquirements as an operator that he was unwilling I should lose this opportunity of displaying my skill. He could not see that there would be greater skill evinced in saving the arm; nor did I think of this at the time. I grew angry at his old-fashioned narrow-mindedness, as I thought it; and I became dogged in my resolution to adhere to my own course. We parted very coolly;

and I went straight off to John Brouncker to tell him I believed that I could save the arm, if he would refuse to have it amputated. When I calmed myself a little, before going in and speaking to him, I could not help acknowledging that we should run some risk of lockjaw; but, on the whole, and after giving most earnest conscientious thought to the case, I was sure that my mode of treatment would be best.

'He was a sensible man. I told him the difference of opinion that existed between Mr Morgan and myself. I said that there might be some little risk attending the non-amputation, but that I should guard against it; and I trusted that I should be able to preserve his arm.

' "Under God's blessing," said he reverently. I bowed my head. I don't like to talk too frequently of the dependence which I always felt on that holy blessing, as to the result of my efforts; but I was glad to hear that speech of John's, because it showed a calm and faithful heart; and I had almost certain hopes of him from that time.

'We agreed that he should tell Mr Morgan the reason of his objections to the amputation, and his reliance on my opinion. I determined to recur to every book I had relating to such cases, and to convince Mr Morgan, if I could, of my wisdom. Unluckily, I found out afterwards that he had met Miss Horsman in the time that intervened before I saw him again at his own house that evening; and she had more than hinted that I shrunk from performing the operation, "for very good reasons, no doubt. She had heard that the medical students in London were a bad set, and were not remarkable for regular attendance in the hospitals. She might be mistaken; but she thought it was, perhaps, quite as well poor John Brouncker had not his arm cut off by – Was there not such a thing as mortification coming on after a clumsy operation? It was, perhaps, only a choice of deaths!"

'Mr Morgan had been stung at all this. Perhaps I did not speak quite respectfully enough: I was a good deal excited. We only got more and more angry with each other; though he, to do him justice, was as civil as could be all the time, thinking that thereby he concealed his vexation and disappointment. He did not try to conceal his anxiety about poor John. I went home weary and dispirited. I made up and took the necessary applications to John; and, promising to return with the dawn of day (I would fain have stayed, but I did not wish him to be alarmed about himself), I went home, and resolved to sit up and study the treatment of similar cases.

'Mrs Rose knocked at the door.

' "Come in!" said I sharply.

'She said she had seen I had something on my mind all day, and she could not go to bed without asking if there was nothing she could do. She was good and kind; and I could not help telling her a little of the truth. She listened pleasantly; and I shook her warmly by the hand, thinking that though she might not be very wise, her good heart made her worth a dozen keen, sharp, hard people, like Miss Horsman.

'When I went at daybreak, I saw John's wife for a few minutes outside of the door. She seemed to wish her husband had been in Mr Morgan's hands rather than mine; but she gave me as good an account as I dared to hope for of the manner in which her husband had passed the night. This was confirmed by my own examination.

'When Mr Morgan and I visited him together later on in the day, John said what we had agreed upon the day before; and I told Mr Morgan openly that it was by my advice that amputation was declined. He did not speak to me till we had left the house. Then he said – "Now, sir, from this time, I consider this case entirely in your hands. Only remember the poor fellow has a wife and six children. In case you come round to my opinion, remember that Mr White could come over, as he has done before, for the operation."

'So Mr Morgan believed I declined operating because I felt myself incapable! Very well! I was much mortified.

'An hour after we parted, I received a note to this effect:

> DEAR SIR – I will take the long round today, to leave you at liberty to attend to Brouncker's case, which I feel to be a very responsible one.
>
> J. MORGAN

'This was kindly done. I went back, as soon as I could, to John's cottage. While I was in the inner room with him, I heard the Miss Tomkinsons' voices outside. They had called to enquire. Miss Tomkinson came in, and evidently was poking and snuffing about. (Mrs Brouncker told her that I was within; and within I resolved to be till they had gone.)

' "What is this close smell?" asked she. "I am afraid you are not cleanly. Cheese! – cheese in this cupboard! No wonder there is an unpleasant smell. Don't you know how particular you should be about being clean when there is illness about?"

'Mrs Brouncker was exquisitely clean in general, and was piqued at these remarks.

' "If you please, ma'am, I could not leave John yesterday to do any housework, and Jenny put the dinner things away. She is but eight years old."

'But this did not satisfy Miss Tomkinson, who was evidently pursuing the course of her observations.

' "Fresh butter, I declare! Well now, Mrs Brouncker, do you know I don't allow myself fresh butter at this time of the year? How can you save, indeed, with such extravagance!"

' "Please, ma'am," answered Mrs Brouncker, "you'd think it strange, if I was to take such liberties in your house as you're taking here."

'I expected to hear a sharp answer. No! Miss Tomkinson liked true plain-speaking. The only person in whom she would tolerate round-about ways of talking was her sister.

' "Well, that's true," she said. "Still, you must not be above taking advice. Fresh butter is extravagant at this time of the year. However, you're a good kind of woman, and I've a great respect for John. Send Jenny for some broth as soon as he can take it. Come, Caroline, we have got to go on to Williams's."

'But Miss Caroline said that she was tired, and would rest where she was till Miss Tomkinson came back. I was a prisoner for some time, I found. When she was alone with Mrs Brouncker, she said: "You must not be hurt by my sister's abrupt manner. She means well. She has not much imagination or sympathy, and cannot understand the distraction of mind produced by the illness of a worshipped husband." I could hear the loud sigh of commiseration which followed this speech. Mrs Brouncker said: "Please, ma'am, I don't worship my husband. I would not be so wicked."

' "Goodness! You don't think it wicked, do you? For my part, if . . . I should worship, I should adore him." I thought she need not imagine such improbable cases. But sturdy Mrs Brouncker said again: "I hope I know my duty better. I've not learned my Commandments for nothing. I know Whom I ought to worship."

'Just then the children came in, dirty and unwashed, I have no doubt. And now Miss Caroline's real nature peeped out. She spoke sharply to them, and asked them if they had no manners, little pigs as they were, to come brushing against her silk gown in that way? She sweetened herself again, and was as sugary as love when Miss Tomkinson returned for her, accompanied by one whose voice, "like winds in summer sighing", I knew to be my dear Sophy's.

'She did not say much; but what she did say, and the manner in which she spoke, was tender and compassionate in the highest degree; and she came to take the four little ones back with her to the vicarage, in order that they might be out of their mother's way; the older two might help at home. She offered to wash their hands and faces; and when I emerged from my inner chamber, after the Miss Tomkinsons had left, I found her with a chubby child on her knees, bubbling and spluttering against her white wet hand, with a face bright, rosy, and merry under the operation. Just as I came in, she said to him, "There, Jemmy, now I can kiss you with this nice clean face."

'She coloured when she saw me. I liked her speaking, and I liked her silence. She was silent now, and I "lo'ed her a' the better". I gave my directions to Mrs Brouncker, and hastened to overtake Sophy and the children; but they had gone round by the lanes, I suppose, for I saw nothing of them.

'I was very anxious about the case. At night I went again. Miss Horsman had been there; I believe she was really kind among the poor, but she could not help leaving a sting behind her everywhere. She had been frightening Mrs Brouncker about her husband, and had been, I have no doubt, expressing her doubts of my skill; for Mrs Brouncker began: "Oh, please, sir, if you'll only let Mr Morgan take off his arm, I will never think the worse of you for not being able to do it."

'I told her it was from no doubt of my own competency to perform the operation that I wished to save the arm; but that he himself was anxious to have it spared.

' "Ay, bless him! he frets about not earning enough to keep us, if he's crippled; but, sir, I don't care about that. I would work my fingers to the bone, and so would the children; I'm sure we'd be proud to do for him, and keep him; God bless him! it would be far better to have him only with one arm, than to have him in the churchyard, Miss Horsman says – "

' "Confound Miss Horsman!" said I.

' "Thank you, Mr Harrison," said her well-known voice behind me. She had come out, dark as it was, to bring some old linen to Mrs Brouncker; for, as I said before, she was very kind to all the poor people of Duncombe.

' "I beg your pardon"; for I really was sorry for my speech – or rather that she had heard it.

' "There is no occasion for any apology," she replied, drawing herself up, and pinching her lips into a very venomous shape.

'John was doing pretty well; but of course the danger of lockjaw was not over. Before I left, his wife entreated me to take off the arm; she wrung her hands in her passionate entreaty. "Spare him to me, Mr Harrison," she implored. Miss Horsman stood by. It was mortifying enough; but I thought of the power which was in my hands, as I firmly believed, of saving the limb; and I was inflexible.

'You cannot think how pleasantly Mrs Rose's sympathy came in on my return. To be sure she did not understand one word of the case, which I detailed to her; but she listened with interest, and, as long as she held her tongue, I thought she was really taking it in; but her first remark was as *mal-àpropos* as could be.

' "You are anxious to save the tibia – I see completely how difficult that will be. My late husband had a case exactly similar, and I remember his anxiety; but you must not distress yourself too much, my dear Mr Harrison; I have no doubt it will end well."

'I knew she had no grounds for this assurance, and yet it comforted me.

'However, as it happened, John did fully as well as I could have hoped for; of course, he was long in rallying his strength; and, indeed, sea-air was evidently so necessary for his complete restoration, that I accepted with gratitude Mrs Rose's proposal of sending him to Highport for a fortnight or three weeks. Her kind generosity in this matter made me more desirous than ever of paying her every mark of respect and attention.

Chapter 15

'ABOUT THIS TIME there was a sale at Ashmeadow, a pretty house in the neighbourhood of Duncombe. It was likewise an easy walk, and the spring days tempted many people thither, who had no intention of buying anything, but who liked the idea of rambling through the woods, gay with early primroses and wild daffodils, and of seeing the gardens and house, which till now had been shut up from the ingress of the townspeople. Mrs Rose had planned to go, but an unlucky cold prevented her. She begged me to bring her a very particular account, saying she delighted in details, and always questioned Mr Rose as to the side-dishes of the dinners to which he went. The late Mr Rose's conduct was always held up as a model to me, by the way. I walked to Ashmeadow, pausing or loitering with different parties of townspeople, all bound in the same direction. At last I found the Vicar and Sophy, and with them I stayed. I sat by Sophy and talked and listened. A sale is a very pleasant gathering after all. The auctioneer, in a country place, is privileged to joke from his rostrum, and, having a personal knowledge of most of the people, can sometimes make a very keen hit at their circumstances, and turn the laugh against them. For instance, on the present occasion, there was a farmer present, with his wife, who was notoriously the grey mare.[44] The auctioneer was selling some horse-cloths, and called out to recommend the article to her, telling her, with a knowing look at the company, that they would make her a dashing pair of trousers, if she was in want of such an article. She drew herself up with dignity, and said, "Come, John, we've had enough of this." Whereupon there was a burst of laughter, and in the midst of it John meekly followed his wife out of the place. The furniture in the sitting-rooms was, I believe, very beautiful, but I did not notice it much. Suddenly I heard the auctioneer speaking to me, "Mr Harrison, won't you give me a bid for this table?"

'It was a very pretty little table of walnut-wood. I thought it would go into my study very well, so I gave him a bid. I saw Miss Horsman bidding against me, so I went off with full force, and at last it was knocked down to me. The auctioneer smiled, and congratulated me.

' "A most useful present for Mrs Harrison, when that lady comes."

'Everybody laughed. They like a joke about marriage; it is so easy of comprehension. But the table which I had thought was for writing, turned out to be a work-table, scissors and thimble complete. No wonder I looked foolish. Sophy was not looking at me, that was one comfort. She was busy arranging a nosegay of wood-anemone and wild sorrel.

'Miss Horsman came up, with her curious eyes.

' "I had no idea things were far enough advanced for you to be purchasing a work-table, Mr Harrison."

'I laughed off my awkwardness.

' "Did not you, Miss Horsman? You are very much behindhand. You have not heard of my piano, then?"

' "No, indeed," she said, half uncertain whether I was serious or not. "Then it seems there is nothing wanting but the lady."

' "Perhaps she may not be wanting either," said I; for I wished to perplex her keen curiosity.

Chapter 16

'When I got home from my round, I found Mrs Rose in some sorrow.

' "Miss Horsman called after you left," said she. "Have you heard how John Brouncker is at Highport?"

' "Very well," replied I. "I called on his wife just now, and she had just got a letter from him. She had been anxious about him, for she had not heard for a week. However, all's right now; and she has pretty well enough of work, at Mrs Munton's, as her servant is ill. Oh, they'll do, never fear."

' "At Mrs Munton's? Oh, that accounts for it, then. She is so deaf, and makes such blunders."

' "Accounts for what?" asked I.

' "Oh, perhaps I had better not tell you," hesitated Mrs Rose.

' "Yes, tell me at once. I beg your pardon, but I hate mysteries."

' "You are so like my poor dear Mr Rose. He used to speak to me just in that sharp, cross way. It is only that Miss Horsman called. She had been making a collection for John Brouncker's widow and – "

' "But the man's alive!" said I.

' "So it seems. But Mrs Munton had told her that he was dead. And she has got Mr Morgan's name down at the head of the list, and Mr Bullock's."

'Mr Morgan and I had got into a short, cool way of speaking to each other ever since we had differed so much about the treatment of Brouncker's arm; and I had heard once or twice of his shakes of the head over John's case. He would not have spoken against my method for the world, and fancied that he concealed his fears.

' "Miss Horsman is very ill-natured, I think," sighed forth Mrs Rose.

'I saw that something had been said of which I had not heard, for the mere fact of collecting money for the widow was good-natured, whoever did it; so I asked, quietly, what she had said.

' "Oh, I don't know if I should tell you. I only know she made me cry; for I'm not well, and I can't bear to hear anyone that I live with abused."

'Come! this was pretty plain.

' "What did Miss Horsman say of me?" asked I, half laughing, for I knew there was no love lost between us.

' "Oh, she only said she wondered you could go to sales, and spend your money there, when your ignorance had made Jane Brouncker a widow, and her children fatherless."

' "Pooh! pooh! John's alive, and likely to live as long as you or I, thanks to you, Mrs Rose."

'When my work-table came home, Mrs Rose was so struck with its beauty and completeness, and I was so much obliged to her for her identification of my interests with hers, and the kindness of her whole conduct about John, that I begged her to accept of it. She seemed very much pleased; and, after a few apologies, she consented to take it, and placed it in the most conspicuous part of the front parlour, where she usually sat. There was a good deal of morning calling in Duncombe after the sale, and during this time the fact of John being alive was established to the conviction of all except Miss Horsman, who, I believe, still doubted. I myself told Mr Morgan, who immediately went to reclaim his money; saying to me, that he was thankful for the information; he was truly glad to hear it; and he shook me warmly by the hand for the first time for a month.

Chapter 17

'A FEW DAYS AFTER THE SALE, I was in the consulting-room. The servant must have left the folding-doors a little ajar, I think. Mrs Munton came to call on Mrs Rose; and the former being deaf, I heard all the speeches of the latter lady, as she was obliged to speak very loud in order to be heard. She began: "This is a great pleasure, Mrs Munton, so seldom as you are well enough to go out."

'Mumble, mumble, mumble, through the door.

' "Oh, very well, thank you. Take this seat, and then you can admire my new work-table, ma'am; a present from Mr Harrison."

'Mumble, mumble.

' "Who could have told you, ma'am? Miss Horsman? Oh, yes, I showed it Miss Horsman."

'Mumble, mumble.

' "I don't quite understand you, ma'am."

'Mumble, mumble.

' "I'm not blushing, I believe. I really am quite in the dark as to what you mean."

'Mumble, mumble.

' "Oh, yes, Mr Harrison and I are most comfortable together. He reminds me so of my dear Mr Rose – just as fidgety and anxious in his profession."

'Mumble, mumble.

' "I'm sure you are joking now, ma'am." Then I heard a pretty loud: "Oh, no"; mumble, mumble, mumble, for a long time.

' "Did he really? Well, I'm sure I don't know. I should be sorry to think he was doomed to be unfortunate in so serious an affair; but you know my undying regard for the late Mr Rose."

'Another long mumble.

' "You're very kind, I'm sure. Mr Rose always thought more of my happiness than his own " – a little crying – "but the turtledove has always been my ideal, ma'am."

'Mumble, mumble.

' "No one could have been happier than I. As you say, it is a compliment to matrimony."

'Mumble.

' "Oh, but you must not repeat such a thing! Mr Harrison would not like it. He can't bear to have his affairs spoken about."

'Then there was a change of subject; an enquiry after some poor person, I imagine. I heard Mrs Rose say: "She has got a mucous membrane, I'm afraid, ma'am."

'A commiserating mumble.

' "Not always fatal. I believe Mr Rose knew some cases that lived for years after it was discovered that they had a mucous membrane." A pause. Then Mrs Rose spoke in a different tone.

' "Are you sure, ma'am, there is no mistake about what he said?"

'Mumble.

' "Pray don't be so observant, Mrs Munton; you find out too much. One can have no little secrets."

'The call broke up; and I heard Mrs Munton say in the passage, "I wish you joy, ma'am, with all my heart. There's no use denying it; for I've seen all along what would happen."

'When I went in to dinner, I said to Mrs Rose: "You've had Mrs Munton here, I think. Did she bring any news?" To my surprise, she bridled and simpered, and replied, "Oh, you must not ask, Mr Harrison; such foolish reports!"

'I did not ask, as she seemed to wish me not, and I knew there were silly reports always about. Then I think she was vexed that I did not ask. Altogether she went on so strangely that I could not help looking at her; and then she took up a hand-screen, and held it between me and her. I really felt rather anxious.

' "Are you not feeling well?" said I innocently.

' "Oh, thank you, I believe I'm quite well; only the room is rather warm, is it not?"

' "Let me put the blinds down for you? the sun begins to have a good deal of power." I drew down the blinds.

' "You are so attentive, Mr Harrison. Mr Rose himself never did more for my little wishes than you do."

' "I wish I could do more – I wish I could show you how much I feel" – her kindness to John Brouncker, I was going on to say; but I was just then called out to a patient. Before I went I turned back, and said: "Take care of yourself, my dear Mrs Rose; you had better rest a little."

' "For your sake, I will," said she tenderly.

'I did not care for whose sake she did it. Only I really thought she was not quite well, and required rest. I thought she was more affected than usual at teatime; and could have been angry with her nonsensical ways once or twice, but that I knew the real goodness of her heart. She said she wished she had the power to sweeten my life as she could my tea. I told her what a comfort she had been during my late time of anxiety; and then I stole out to try if I could hear the evening singing at the vicarage, by standing close to the garden-wall.

Chapter 18

'THE NEXT MORNING I met Mr Bullock by appointment to talk a little about the legacy which was paid into his hands. As I was leaving his office, feeling full of my riches, I met Miss Horsman. She smiled rather grimly, and said: "Oh! Mr Harrison, I must congratulate you, I believe. I don't know whether I ought to have known, but as I do, I must wish you joy. A very nice little sum, too. I always said you would have money."

'So she had found out my legacy, had she? Well, it was no secret, and one likes the reputation of being a person of property. Accordingly I smiled, and said I was much obliged to her; and, if I could alter the figures to my liking, she might congratulate me still more.

'She said, "Oh, Mr Harrison, you can't have everything. It would be better the other way, certainly. Money is the great thing, as you've found out. The relation died most opportunely, I must say."

' "He was no relative," said I; "only an intimate friend."

' "Dear-ah-me! I thought it had been a brother! Well, at any rate, the legacy is safe."

'I wished her good-morning, and passed on. Before long I was sent for to Miss Tomkinson's.

'Miss Tomkinson sat in severe state to receive me. I went in with an air of ease, because I always felt so uncomfortable.

' "Is this true that I hear?" asked she, in an inquisitorial manner.

'I thought she alluded to my five hundred pounds; so I smiled, and said that I believed it was.

' "Can money be so great an object with you, Mr Harrison?" she asked again.

'I said I had never cared much for money, except as an assistance to any plan of settling in life; and then, as I did not like her severe way of treating the subject, I said that I hoped everyone was well; though of course I expected someone was ill, or I should not have been sent for.

'Miss Tomkinson looked very grave and sad. Then she answered: "Caroline is very poorly – the old palpitations at the heart; but of course that is nothing to you."

'I said I was very sorry. She had a weakness there, I knew. Could I see her? I might be able to order something for her.

'I thought I heard Miss Tomkinson say something in a low voice about my being a heartless deceiver. Then she spoke up. "I was always distrustful of you, Mr Harrison. I never liked your looks. I begged Caroline again and again not to confide in you. I foresaw how it would end. And now I fear her precious life will be a sacrifice."

'I begged her not to distress herself, for in all probability there was very little the matter with her sister. Might I see her?

' "No!" she said shortly, standing up as if to dismiss me. "There has been too much of this seeing and calling. By my consent, you shall never see her again."

'I bowed. I was annoyed, of course. Such a dismissal might injure my practice just when I was most anxious to increase it.

' "Have you no apology, no excuse to offer?"

'I said I had done my best; I did not feel that there was any reason to offer an apology. I wished her good-morning. Suddenly she came forwards.

' "Oh, Mr Harrison," said she, "if you have really loved Caroline, do not let a little paltry money make you desert her for another."

'I was struck dumb. Loved Miss Caroline! I loved Miss Tomkinson a great deal better, and yet I disliked her. She went on: "I have saved nearly three thousand pounds. If you think you are too poor to marry without money, I will give it all to Caroline. I am strong, and can go on working; but she is weak, and this disappointment will kill her." She sat down suddenly, and covered her face with her hands. Then she looked up.

' "You are unwilling, I see. Don't suppose I would have urged you if it had been for myself; but she has had so much sorrow." And now she fairly cried aloud. I tried to explain; but she would not listen, but kept saying, "Leave the house, sir! leave the house!" But I would be heard.

' "I have never had any feeling warmer than respect for Miss Caroline, and I have never shown any different feeling. I never for an instant thought of making her my wife, and she has had no cause in my behaviour to imagine I entertained any such intention."

' "This is adding insult to injury," said she. "Leave the house, sir, this instant!"

Chapter 19

'I WENT, and sadly enough. In a small town such an occurrence is sure to be talked about, and to make a great deal of mischief. When I went home to dinner I was so full of it, and foresaw so clearly that I should need some advocate soon to set the case in its right light, that I determined on making a confidante of good Mrs Rose. I could not eat. She watched me tenderly, and sighed when she saw my want of appetite.

' "I am sure you have something on your mind, Mr Harrison. Would it be – would it not be – a relief to impart it to some sympathising friend?"

'It was just what I wanted to do.

' "My dear kind Mrs Rose," said I, "I must tell you, if you will listen."

'She took up the fire-screen, and held it, as yesterday, between me and her.

' "The most unfortunate misunderstanding has taken place. Miss Tomkinson thinks that I have been paying attentions to Miss Caroline; when, in fact – may I tell you, Mrs Rose? – my affections are placed elsewhere. Perhaps you have found it out already?" for indeed I thought I had been too much in love to conceal my attachment to Sophy from anyone who knew my movements as well as Mrs Rose.

'She hung down her head, and said she believed she had found out my secret.

' "Then only think how miserably I am situated. If I have any hope – oh, Mrs Rose, do you think I have any hope – "

'She put the hand-screen still more before her face, and after some hesitation she said she thought "If I persevered – in time – I might have hope." And then she suddenly got up, and left the room.

Chapter 20

'That afternoon I met Mr Bullock in the street. My mind was so full of the affair with Miss Tomkinson that I should have passed him without notice, if he had not stopped me short, and said that he must speak to me; about my wonderful five hundred pounds, I supposed. But I did not care for that now.

' "What is this I hear," said he severely, "about your engagement with Mrs Rose?"

' "With Mrs Rose!" said I, almost laughing, although my heart was heavy enough.

' "Yes! with Mrs Rose!" said he sternly.

' "I'm not engaged to Mrs Rose," I replied. "There is some mistake."

' "I'm glad to hear it, sir," he answered, "very glad. It requires some explanation, however. Mrs Rose has been congratulated, and has acknowledged the truth of the report. It is confirmed by many facts. The work-table you bought, confessing your intention of giving it to your future wife, is given to her. How do you account for these things, sir?"

'I said I did not pretend to account for them. At present a good deal was inexplicable; and, when I could give an explanation, I did not think that I should feel myself called upon to give it to him.

' "Very well, sir; very well," replied he, growing very red. "I shall take care and let Mr Morgan know the opinion I entertain of you. What do you think that man deserves to be called who enters a family under the plea of friendship, and takes advantage of his intimacy to win the affections of the daughter, and then engages himself to another woman?"

'I thought he referred to Miss Caroline. I simply said I could only say that I was not engaged; and that Miss Tomkinson had been quite mistaken in supposing I had been paying any attentions to her sister beyond those dictated by mere civility.

' "Miss Tomkinson! Miss Caroline! I don't understand to what you refer. Is there another victim to your perfidy? What I allude to are the attentions you have paid to my daughter, Miss Bullock."

'Another! I could but disclaim, as I had done in the case of Miss Caroline; but I began to be in despair. Would Miss Horsman, too, come forward as a victim to my tender affections? It was all Mr Morgan's doing, who had lectured me into this tenderly deferential manner. But, on the score of Miss Bullock, I was brave in my innocence. I had positively disliked her; and so I told her father, though in more civil and measured terms, adding that I was sure the feeling was reciprocal.

'He looked as if he would like to horsewhip me. I longed to call him out.

' "I hope my daughter has had sense enough to despise you; I hope she has, that's all. I trust my wife may be mistaken as to her feelings."

'So, he had heard all through the medium of his wife. That explained something, and rather calmed me. I begged he would ask Miss Bullock if she had ever thought I had any ulterior object in my intercourse with her, beyond mere friendliness (and not so much of that, I might have added). I would refer it to her.

' "Girls," said Mr Bullock, a little more quietly, "do not like to acknowledge that they have been deceived and disappointed. I consider my wife's testimony as likely to be nearer the truth than my daughter's, for that reason. And she tells me she never doubted but that, if not absolutely engaged, you understood each other perfectly. She is sure Jemima is deeply wounded by your engagement to Mrs Rose."

' "Once for all, I am not engaged to anybody. Till you have seen your daughter, and learnt the truth from her, I will wish you farewell."

'I bowed in a stiff, haughty manner, and walked off homewards. But when I got to my own door, I remembered Mrs Rose, and all that Mr Bullock had said about her acknowledging the truth of the report of my engagement to her. Where could I go to be safe? Mrs Rose, Miss Bullock, Miss Caroline – they lived as it were at the three points of an equilateral triangle; here was I in the centre. I would go to Mr Morgan's, and drink tea with him. There, at any rate, I was secure from anyone wanting to marry me; and I might be as professionally bland as I liked, without being misunderstood. But there, too, a *contretemps*[45] awaited me.

Chapter 21

'MR MORGAN was looking grave. After a minute or two of humming and hawing, he said, "I have been sent for to Miss Caroline Tomkinson, Mr Harrison. I am sorry to hear of this. I am grieved to find that there seems to have been some trifling with the affections of a very worthy lady. Miss Tomkinson, who is in sad distress, tells me that they had every reason to believe that you were attached to her sister. May I ask if you do not intend to marry her?"

'I said, nothing was farther from my thoughts.

' "My dear sir," said Mr Morgan, rather agitated, "do not express yourself so strongly and vehemently. It is derogatory to the sex to speak so. It is more respectful to say, in these cases, that you do not venture to entertain a hope; such a manner is generally understood, and does not sound like such positive objection."

' "I cannot help it, sir; I must talk in my own natural manner. I would not speak disrespectfully of any woman; but nothing should induce me to marry Miss Caroline Tomkinson; not if she were Venus herself, and Queen of England into the bargain. I cannot understand what has given rise to the idea."

' "Indeed, sir; I think that is very plain. You have a trifling case to attend to in the house, and you invariably make it a pretext for seeing and conversing with the lady."

' "That was her doing, not mine!" said I vehemently.

' "Allow me to go on. You are discovered on your knees before her – a positive injury to the establishment, as Miss Tomkinson observes; a most passionate valentine is sent; and, when questioned, you acknowledge the sincerity of meaning which you affix to such things." He stopped; for in his earnestness he had been talking more quickly than usual, and was out of breath. I burst in with my explanations: "The valentine I know nothing about."

' "It is in your handwriting," said he coldly. "I should be most deeply grieved to – in fact, I will not think it possible of your father's son. But I must say, it is in your handwriting."

'I tried again, and at last succeeded in convincing him that I had been only unfortunate, not intentionally guilty of winning Miss Caroline's affections. I said that I had been endeavouring, it was true, to practise the manner he had recommended, of universal sympathy, and recalled to his mind some of the advice he had given me. He was a good deal hurried.

' "But, my dear sir, I had no idea that you would carry it out to such consequences. 'Philandering', Miss Tomkinson called it. That is a hard word, sir. My manner has been always tender and sympathetic; but I am not aware that I ever excited any hopes; there never was any report about me. I believe no lady was ever attached to me. You must strive after this happy medium, sir."

'I was still distressed. Mr Morgan had only heard of one, but there were three ladies (including Miss Bullock) hoping to marry me. He saw my annoyance.

' "Don't be too much distressed about it, my dear sir; I was sure you were too honourable a man, from the first. With a conscience like yours, I would defy the world."

'He became anxious to console me, and I was hesitating whether I would not tell him all my three dilemmas, when a note was brought in to him. It was from Mrs Munton. He threw it to me, with a face of dismay.

> 'My dear Mr Morgan – I most sincerely congratulate you on the happy matrimonial engagement I hear you have formed with Miss Tomkinson. All previous circumstances, as I have just been remarking to Miss Horsman, combine to promise you felicity. And I wish that every blessing may attend your married life. – Most sincerely yours,
>
> 'Jane Munton

'I could not help laughing, he had been so lately congratulating himself that no report of the kind had ever been circulated about himself. He said: "Sir! this is no laughing matter; I assure you it is not."

'I could not resist asking, if I was to conclude that there was no truth in the report.

' "Truth, sir! it's a lie from beginning to end. I don't like to speak too decidedly about any lady; and I've a great respect for Miss Tomkinson; but I do assure you, sir, I'd as soon marry one of Her Majesty's Life Guards. I would rather; it would be more suitable. Miss Tomkinson is a very worthy lady; but she's a perfect grenadier."

'He grew very nervous. He was evidently insecure. He thought it not impossible that Miss Tomkinson might come and marry him, *vi et armis*.[46] I am sure he had some dim idea of abduction in his mind. Still, he was better off than I was; for he was in his own house, and report had only engaged him to one lady; while I stood, like Paris, among three contending beauties. Truly, an apple of discord[47] had been thrown into our little town. I suspected at the time, what I know now, that it was Miss Horsman's doing; not intentionally, I will do her the justice to say. But she had shouted out the story of my behaviour to Miss Caroline up Mrs Munton's trumpet; and that lady, possessed with the idea that I was engaged to Mrs Rose, had imagined the masculine pronoun to relate to Mr Morgan, whom she had seen only that afternoon tête-à-tête with Miss Tomkinson, condoling with her in some tender deferential manner, I'll be bound.

Chapter 22

'I WAS VERY COWARDLY. I positively dared not go home; but at length I was obliged to. I had done all I could to console Mr Morgan, but he refused to be comforted. I went at last. I rang at the bell. I don't know who opened the door, but I think it was Mrs Rose. I kept a handkerchief to my face, and, muttering something about having a dreadful toothache, I flew up to my room and bolted the door. I had no candle; but what did that signify. I was safe. I could not sleep; and when I did fall into a sort of doze, it was ten times worse wakening up. I could not remember whether I was engaged or not. If I was engaged, who was the lady? I had always considered myself as rather plain than otherwise; but surely I had made a mistake. Fascinating I certainly must be; but perhaps I was handsome. As soon as day dawned, I got up to ascertain the fact at the looking-glass. Even with the best disposition to be convinced, I could not see any striking beauty in my round face, with an unshaven beard and a nightcap like a fool's cap at the top. No! I must be content to be plain, but agreeable. All this I tell you in confidence. I would not have my little bit of vanity known for the world. I fell asleep towards morning. I was awakened by a tap at my door. It was Peggy: she put in a hand with a note. I took it.

' "It is not from Miss Horsman?" said I, half in joke, half in very earnest fright.

' "No, sir; Mr Morgan's man brought it."

'I opened it. It ran thus:

'My dear Sir – It is now nearly twenty years since I have had a little relaxation, and I find that my health requires it. I have also the utmost confidence in you, and I am sure this feeling is shared by our patients. I have, therefore, no scruple in putting in execution a hastily-formed plan, and going to Chesterton to catch the early train on my way to Paris. If your accounts are good, I shall remain away probably a fortnight. Direct to Meurice's.[48]

'Yours most truly,

'J. Morgan

'P.S. – Perhaps it may be as well not to name where I am gone, especially to Miss Tomkinson.

'He had deserted me. He – with only one report – had left me to stand my ground with three.

' "Mrs Rose's kind regards, sir, and it's nearly nine o'clock. Breakfast has been ready this hour, sir."

' "Tell Mrs Rose I don't want any breakfast. Or stay" (for I was very hungry), "I will take a cup of tea and some toast up here."

'Peggy brought the tray to the door.

' "I hope you're not ill, sir?" said she kindly.

' "Not very. I shall be better when I get into the air."

' "Mrs Rose seems sadly put about," said she; "she seems so grieved like."

'I watched my opportunity, and went out by the side-door in the garden.

Chapter 23

'I had intended to ask Mr Morgan to call at the vicarage, and give his parting explanation before they could hear the report. Now I thought that, if I could see Sophy, I would speak to her myself; but I did not wish to encounter the Vicar. I went along the lane at the back of the vicarage, and came suddenly upon Miss Bullock. She coloured, and asked me if I would allow her to speak to me. I could only be resigned; but I thought I could probably set one report at rest by this conversation.

'She was almost crying.

' "I must tell you, Mr Harrison, I have watched you here in order to speak to you. I heard with the greatest regret of papa's conversation with you yesterday." She was fairly crying. "I believe Mrs Bullock finds me in her way, and wants to have me married. It is the only way in which I can account for such a complete misrepresentation as she had told papa. I don't care for you, in the least, sir. You never paid me any attentions. You've been almost rude to me; and I have liked you the better. That's to say, I never have liked you."

' "I am truly glad to hear what you say," answered I. "Don't distress yourself. I was sure there was some mistake."

'But she cried bitterly.

' "It is so hard to feel that my marriage – my absence – is desired so earnestly at home. I dread every new acquaintance we form with any gentleman. It is sure to be the beginning of a series of attacks on him, of which everybody must be aware, and to which they may think I am a willing party. But I should not much mind if it were not for the conviction that she wishes me so earnestly away. Oh, my own dear mamma, you would never – "

'She cried more than ever. I was truly sorry for her, and had just taken her hand, and began – "My dear Miss Bullock" – when the door in the wall of the vicarage garden opened. It was the Vicar letting out Miss Tomkinson, whose face was all swelled with crying. He saw me; but he did not bow, or make any sign. On the contrary, he looked down as from a severe eminence, and shut the door hastily. I turned to Miss Bullock.

' "I am afraid the Vicar has been hearing something to my disadvantage from Miss Tomkinson, and it is very awkward" – She finished my sentence – "To have found us here together. Yes; but, as long as we understand that we do not care for each other, it does not signify what people say."

' "Oh, but to me it does," said I. "I may, perhaps, tell you – but do not mention it to a creature – I am attached to Miss Hutton."

' "To Sophy! Oh, Mr Harrison, I am so glad; she is such a sweet creature. Oh, I wish you joy."

' "Not yet; I have never spoken about it."

' "Oh, but it is certain to happen." She jumped with a woman's rapidity to a conclusion. And then she began to praise Sophy. Never was a man yet who did not like to hear the praises of his mistress. I walked by her side; we came past the front of the vicarage together. I looked up, and saw Sophy there, and she saw me.

'That afternoon she was sent away – sent to visit her aunt ostensibly; in reality, because of the reports of my conduct, which were showered down upon the Vicar, and one of which he saw confirmed by his own eyes.

Chapter 24

'I HEARD OF SOPHY'S DEPARTURE as one heard of everything, soon after it had taken place. I did not care for the awkwardness of my situation, which had so perplexed and amused me in the morning. I felt that something was wrong; that Sophy was taken away from me. I sank into despair. If anybody liked to marry me, they might. I was willing to be sacrificed. I did not speak to Mrs Rose. She wondered at me, and grieved over my coldness, I saw; but I had left off feeling anything. Miss Tomkinson cut me in the street; and it did not break my heart. Sophy was gone away; that was all I cared for. Where had they sent her to? Who was her aunt that she should go and visit her? One day I met Lizzie, who looked as though she had been told not to speak to me; but I could not help doing so.

' "Have you heard from your sister?" said I.

' "Yes."

' "Where is she? I hope she is well."

' "She is at the Leoms." – I was not much wiser. "Oh yes, she is very well. Fanny says she was at the Assembly last Wednesday, and danced all night with the officers."

'I thought I would enter myself a member of the Peace Society[49] at once. She was a little flirt, and a hard-hearted creature. I don't think I wished Lizzie goodbye.

Chapter 25

'WHAT MOST PEOPLE would have considered a more serious evil than Sophy's absence, befell me. I found that my practice was falling off. The prejudice of the town ran strongly against me. Mrs Munton told me all that was said. She heard it through Miss Horsman. It was said – cruel little town – that my negligence or ignorance had been the cause of Walter's death; that Miss Tyrrell had become worse under my treatment; and that John Brouncker was all but dead, if he was not quite, from my mismanagement. All Jack Marshland's jokes and revelations, which had, I thought, gone to oblivion, were raked up to my discredit. He himself, formerly, to my astonishment, rather a favourite with the good people of Duncombe, was spoken of as one of my disreputable friends.

'In short, so prejudiced were the good people of Duncombe that I believe a very little would have made them suspect me of a brutal highway robbery, which took place in the neighbourhood about this time. Mrs Munton told me, *à propos* of the robbery, that she had never yet understood the cause of my year's imprisonment in Newgate; she had no doubt, from what Mr Morgan had told her, there was some good reason for it; but if I would tell her the particulars, she should like to know them.

'Miss Tomkinson sent for Mr White, from Chesterton, to see Miss Caroline; and, as he was coming over, all our old patients seemed to take advantage of it, and send for him too.

'But the worst of all was the Vicar's manner to me. If he had cut me, I could have asked him why he did so. But the freezing change in his behaviour was indescribable, though bitterly felt. I heard of Sophy's gaiety from Lizzie. I thought of writing to her. Just then Mr Morgan's fortnight of absence expired. I was wearied out by Mrs Rose's tender vagaries, and took no comfort from her sympathy, which indeed I rather avoided. Her tears irritated, instead of grieving, me. I wished I could tell her at once that I had no intention of marrying her.

Chapter 26

'Mr Morgan had not been at home above two hours before he was sent for to the vicarage. Sophy had come back, and I had never heard of it. She had come home ill and weary, and longing for rest: and the *rest* seemed approaching with awful strides. Mr Morgan forgot all his Parisian adventures, and all his terror of Miss Tomkinson, when he was sent for to see her. She was ill of a fever, which made fearful progress. When he told me, I wished to force the vicarage door, if I might but see her. But I controlled myself; and only cursed my weak indecision, which had prevented my writing to her. It was well I had no patients: they would have had but a poor chance of attention. I hung about Mr Morgan, who might see her, and did see her. But, from what he told me, I perceived that the measures he was adopting were powerless to check so sudden and violent an illness. Oh! if they would but let me see her! But that was out of the question. It was not merely that the Vicar had heard of my character as a gay Lothario,[50] but that doubts had been thrown out of my medical skill. The accounts grew worse. Suddenly my resolution was taken. Mr Morgan's very regard for Sophy made him more than usually timid in his practice. I had my horse saddled, and galloped to Chesterton. I took the express train to town. I went to Dr —. I told him every particular of the case. He listened; but shook his head. He wrote down a prescription, and recommended a new preparation, not yet in full use – a preparation of a poison, in fact.

' "It may save her," said he. "It is a chance, in such a state of things as you describe. It must be given on the fifth day, if the pulse will bear it. Crabbe makes up the preparation most skilfully. Let me hear from you, I beg."

'I went to Crabbe's; I begged to make it up myself; but my hands trembled, so that I could not weigh the quantities. I asked the young man to do it for me. I went, without touching food, to the station, with my medicine and my prescription in my pocket. Back we flew through the country. I sprang on Bay Maldon, which my groom had in waiting, and galloped across the country to Duncombe.

'But I drew bridle when I came to the top of the hill – the hill above the old hall, from which we catch the first glimpse of the town, for I thought within myself that she might be dead; and I dreaded to come near certainty. The hawthorns were out in the woods, the young lambs were in the meadows, the song of the thrushes filled the air; but it only made the thought the more terrible.

' "What if, in this world of hope and life, she lies dead!" I heard the church bells soft and clear. I sickened to listen. Was it the passing bell? No! it was ringing eight o'clock. I put spurs to my horse, down hill as it was. We dashed into the town. I turned him, saddle and bridle, into the stable-yard, and went off to Mr Morgan's.

' "Is she – " said I. "How is she?"

' "Very ill. My poor fellow, I see how it is with you. She may live – but I fear. My dear sir, I am very much afraid."

'I told him of my journey and consultation with Dr —, and showed him the prescription. His hands trembled as he put on his spectacles to read it.

' "This is a very dangerous medicine, sir," said he, with his finger under the name of the poison.

' "It is a new preparation," said I. "Dr — relies much upon it."

' "I dare not administer it," he replied. "I have never tried it. It must be very powerful. I dare not play tricks in this case."

'I believe I stamped with impatience; but it was all of no use. My journey had been in vain. The more I urged the imminent danger of the case requiring some powerful remedy, the more nervous he became.

'I told him I would throw up the partnership. I threatened him with that, though, in fact, it was only what I felt I ought to do, and had resolved upon before Sophy's illness, as I had lost the confidence of his patients. He only said: "I cannot help it, sir. I shall regret it for your father's sake; but I must do my duty. I dare not run the risk of giving Miss Sophy this violent medicine – a preparation of a deadly poison."

'I left him without a word. He was quite right in adhering to his own views, as I can see now; but at the time I thought him brutal and obstinate.

Chapter 27

'I WENT HOME. I spoke rudely to Mrs Rose, who awaited my return at the door. I rushed past, and locked myself in my room. I could not go to bed.

'The morning sun came pouring in, and enraged me, as everything did since Mr Morgan refused. I pulled the blind down so violently that the string broke. What did it signify? The light might come in. What was the sun to me? And then I remembered that that sun might be shining on her – dead.

'I sat down and covered my face. Mrs Rose knocked at the door. I opened it. She had never been in bed, and had been crying too.

' "Mr Morgan wants to speak to you, sir."

'I rushed back for my medicine, and went to him. He stood at the door, pale and anxious.

' "She's alive, sir," said he, "but that's all. We have sent for Dr Hamilton. I'm afraid he will not come in time. Do you know, sir, I think we should venture – with Dr —'s sanction – to give her that medicine. It is but a chance; but it is the only one, I'm afraid." He fairly cried before he had ended.

' "I've got it here," said I, setting off to walk; but he could not go so fast.

' "I beg your pardon, sir," said he, "for my abrupt refusal last night."

' "Indeed, sir," said I; "I ought much rather to beg your pardon. I was very violent."

' "Oh! never mind! never mind! Will you repeat what Dr — said?"

'I did so; and then I asked, with a meekness that astonished myself, if I might not go in and administer it.

' "No, sir," said he, "I'm afraid not. I am sure your good heart would not wish to give pain. Besides, it might agitate her, if she has any consciousness before death. In her delirium she has often mentioned your name; and, sir, I'm sure you won't name it again, as it may, in fact, be considered a professional secret; but I did hear our good Vicar speak a little strongly about you; in fact, sir, I did hear him curse you. You see the mischief it might make in the parish, I'm sure, if this were known."

'I gave him the medicine, and watched him in, and saw the door shut. I hung about the place all day. Poor and rich all came to enquire. The county people drove up in their carriages – the halt and the lame came on their crutches. Their anxiety did my heart good. Mr Morgan told me that she slept, and I watched Dr Hamilton into the house. The night came on. She slept. I watched round the house. I saw the light high up, burning still and steady. Then I saw it moved. It was the crisis, in one way or other.

Chapter 28

'Mr Morgan came out. Good old man! The tears were running down his cheeks: he could not speak; but kept shaking my hands. I did not want words. I understood that she was better.

' "Dr Hamilton says, it was the only medicine that could have saved her. I was an old fool, sir. I beg your pardon. The Vicar shall know all. I beg your pardon, sir, if I was abrupt."

'Everything went on brilliantly from this time.

'Mr Bullock called to apologise for his mistake, and consequent upbraiding. John Brouncker came home, brave and well.

'There was still Miss Tomkinson in the ranks of the enemy; and Mrs Rose too much, I feared, in the ranks of the friends.

Chapter 29

'One night she had gone to bed, and I was thinking of going. I had been studying in the back room, where I went for refuge from her in the present position of affairs – (I read a good number of surgical books about this time, and also *Vanity Fair*[51]) – when I heard a loud, long-continued knocking at the door, enough to waken the whole street. Before I could get to open it, I heard that well-known bass of Jack Marshland's – once heard, never to be forgotten – pipe up the negro song – "Who's dat knocking at de door?"[52] Though it was raining hard at the time, and I stood waiting to let him in, he would finish his melody in the open air; loud and clear along the street it sounded. I saw Miss Tomkinson's night-capped head emerge from a window. She called out "Police! police!"

'Now there were no police, only a rheumatic constable, in the town; but it was the custom of the ladies, when alarmed at night, to call an imaginary police, which had, they thought, an intimidating effect; but, as everyone knew the real state of the unwatched town, we did not much mind it in general. Just now, however, I wanted to regain my character. So I pulled Jack in, quavering as he entered.

' "You've spoilt a good shake," said he, "that's what you have. I'm nearly up to Jenny Lind;[53] and you see I'm a nightingale, like her."

'We sat up late; and I don't know how it was, but I told him all my matrimonial misadventures.

' "I thought I could imitate your hand pretty well," said he. "My word! it was a flaming valentine! No wonder she thought you loved her!"

' "So that was your doing, was it? Now I'll tell you what you shall do to make up for it. You shall write me a letter confessing your hoax – a letter that I can show."

' "Give me pen and paper, my boy! you shall dictate. 'With a deeply penitent heart' – Will that do for a beginning?"

'I told him what to write; a simple, straightforward confession of his practical joke. I enclosed it in a few lines of regret that, unknown to me, any of my friends should have so acted.

Chapter 30

'ALL THIS TIME I knew that Sophy was slowly recovering. One day I met Miss Bullock, who had seen her.

' "We have been talking about you," said she, with a bright smile; for, since she knew I disliked her, she felt quite at her ease, and could smile very pleasantly. I understood that she had been explaining the misunderstanding about herself to Sophy; so that, when Jack Marshland's note had been sent to Miss Tomkinson's, I thought myself in a fair way to have my character established in two quarters. But the third was my dilemma. Mrs Rose had really so much of my true regard for her good qualities, that I disliked the idea of a formal explanation, in which a good deal must be said on my side to wound her. We had become very much estranged ever since I had heard of this report of my engagement to her. I saw that she grieved over it. While Jack Marshland stayed with us, I felt at my ease in the presence of a third person. But he told me confidentially he durst not stay long, for fear some of the ladies should snap him up, and marry him. Indeed I myself did not think it unlikely that he would snap one of them up if he could. For when we met Miss Bullock one day, and heard her hopeful, joyous account of Sophy's progress (to whom she was a daily visitor), he asked me who that bright-looking girl was? And when I told him she was the Miss Bullock of whom I had spoken to him, he was pleased to observe that he thought I had been a great fool, and asked me if Sophy had anything like such splendid eyes. He made me repeat about Miss Bullock's unhappy circumstances at home, and then became very thoughtful – a most unusual and morbid symptom in his case.

'Soon after he went, by Mr Morgan's kind offices and explanations, I was permitted to see Sophy. I might not speak much; it was prohibited, for fear of agitating her. We talked of the weather and the flowers; and we were silent. But her little white thin hand lay in mine; and we understood each other without words. I had a long interview with the Vicar afterwards, and came away glad and satisfied.

'Mr Morgan called in the afternoon, evidently anxious, though he made no direct enquiries (he was too polite for that), to hear the result of my visit at the vicarage. I told him to give me joy. He shook me warmly by the hand, and then rubbed his own together. I thought

I would consult him about my dilemma with Mrs Rose, who, I was afraid, would be deeply affected by my engagement.

' "There is only one awkward circumstance," said I – "about Mrs Rose." I hesitated how to word the fact of her having received congratulations on her supposed engagement with me, and her manifest attachment; but, before I could speak, he broke in: "My dear sir, you need not trouble yourself about that; she will have a home. In fact, sir," said he, reddening a little, "I thought it would, perhaps, put a stop to those reports connecting my name with Miss Tomkinson's, if I married someone else. I hoped it might prove an efficacious contradiction. And I was struck with admiration for Mrs Rose's undying memory of her late husband. Not to be prolix, I have this morning obtained Mrs Rose's consent to – to marry her, in fact, sir!" said he, jerking out the climax.

'Here was an event! Then Mr Morgan had never heard the report about Mrs Rose and me. (To this day, I think she would have taken me, if I had proposed.) So much the better.

'Marriages were in the fashion that year. Mr Bullock met me one morning, as I was going to ride with Sophy. He and I had quite got over our misunderstanding, thanks to Jemima, and were as friendly as ever. This morning he was chuckling aloud as he walked.

' "Stop, Mr Harrison!" he said, as I went quickly past. "Have you heard the news? Miss Horsman has just told me Miss Caroline has eloped with young Hoggins! She is ten years older than he is! How can her gentility like being married to a tallow-chandler?[54] It is a very good thing for her, though," he added, in a more serious manner; "old Hoggins is very rich; and, though he's angry just now, he will soon be reconciled."

'Any vanity I might have entertained on the score of the three ladies who were, at one time, said to be captivated by my charms, was being rapidly dispersed. Soon after Mr Hoggins's marriage, I met Miss Tomkinson face to face, for the first time since our memorable conversation. She stopped me, and said: "Don't refuse to receive my congratulations, Mr Harrison, on your most happy engagement to Miss Hutton. I owe you an apology, too, for my behaviour when I last saw you at our house. I really did think Caroline was attached to you then; and it irritated me, I confess, in a very wrong and unjustifiable way. But I heard her telling Mr Hoggins only yesterday that she had been attached to him for years; ever since he was in pinafores, she dated it from; and when I asked her afterwards how she could say so, after her distress on hearing that false report about you and Mrs Rose, she cried, and said I never had understood her; and that the hysterics which alarmed me so much were simply caused by eating pickled cucumber. I am very sorry for my stupidity and improper way of speaking; but I hope we are friends now, Mr Harrison, for I should wish to be liked by Sophy's husband."

'Good Miss Tomkinson, to believe the substitution of indigestion for disappointed affection! I shook her warmly by the hand; and we have been all right ever since. I think I told you she is baby's godmother.

Chapter 31

'I HAD SOME DIFFICULTY in persuading Jack Marshland to be groomsman; but, when he heard all the arrangements, he came. Miss Bullock was bridesmaid. He liked us all so well, that he came again at Christmas, and was far better behaved than he had been the year before. He won golden opinions[55] indeed. Miss Tomkinson said he was a reformed young man. We dined all together at Mr Morgan's (the Vicar wanted us to go there; but, from what Sophy told me, Helen was not confident of the mincemeat, and rather dreaded so large a party). We had a jolly day of it. Mrs Morgan was as kind and motherly as ever. Miss Horsman certainly did set out a story that the Vicar was thinking of Miss Tomkinson for his second; or else, I think, we had no other report circulated in consequence of our happy, merry Christmas Day; and it is a wonder, considering how Jack Marshland went on with Jemima.'

Here Sophy came back from putting baby to bed; and Charles wakened up.

THE DOOM OF THE GRIFFITHS

Chapter 1

I HAVE ALWAYS BEEN much interested by the traditions which are scattered up and down North Wales relating to Owen Glendower[56] (Owain Glendwr is the national spelling of the name), and I fully enter into the feeling which makes the Welsh peasant still look upon him as the hero of his country. There was great joy among many of the inhabitants of the principality, when the subject of the Welsh prize poem at Oxford, some fifteen or sixteen years ago, was announced to be 'Owain Glendwr'. It was the most proudly national subject that had been given for years.

Perhaps some may not be aware that this redoubted chieftain is, even in the present days of enlightenment, as famous among his illiterate countrymen for his magical powers as for his patriotism. He says himself – or Shakespeare says it for him, which is much the same thing:

> 'At my nativity
> The front of heaven was full of fiery shapes
> Of burning cressets . . .
> . . . I can call spirits from the vasty deep.'

And few among the lower orders in the principality would think of asking Hotspur's irreverent question in reply.[57]

Among other traditions preserved relative to this part of the Welsh hero's character, is the old family prophecy which gives title to this tale. When Sir David Gam, 'as black a traitor as if he had been born in Builth',[58] sought to murder Owen at Machynlleth, there was one with him whose name Glendwr little dreamed of having associated with his enemies. Rhys ap Gryfydd, his 'old familiar friend', his relation, his more than brother, had consented unto his blood. Sir David Gam[59] might be forgiven, but one whom he had loved, and who had betrayed him, could never be forgiven. Glendwr was too deeply read in the human heart to kill him. No, he let him live on, the loathing and scorn of his compatriots, and the victim of bitter remorse. The mark of Cain was upon him.

But before he went forth – while he yet stood a prisoner, cowering beneath his conscience before Owain Glendwr – that chieftain passed a doom upon him and his race: 'I doom thee to live, because I know thou wilt pray for death. Thou shalt live on beyond the natural term of the life of man, the scorn of all good men. The very children shall point to thee with hissing tongue, and say, "There goes one who would have shed a brother's blood!" For I loved thee more than a brother, O Rhys ap Gryfydd! Thou shalt live on to see all of thy house, except the weakling in arms, perish by the sword. Thy race shall be accursed. Each generation shall see their lands melt away like snow; yea, their wealth shall vanish, though they may labour night and day to heap up gold. And when nine generations have passed from the face of the earth, thy blood shall no longer flow in the veins of any human being. In those days the last male of thy race shall avenge me. The son shall slay the father.'

Such was the traditionary account of Owain Glendwr's speech to his once-trusted friend. And it was declared that the doom had been fulfilled in all things; that, live in as miserly a manner as they would, the Griffiths never were wealthy and prosperous – indeed, that their worldly stock diminished without any visible cause.

But the lapse of many years had almost deadened the wonder-inspiring power of the whole curse. It was only brought forth from the hoards of Memory when some untoward event happened to the Griffiths family; and in the eighth generation the faith in the prophecy was nearly destroyed, by the marriage of the Griffiths of that day to a Miss Owen, who, unexpectedly, by the death of a brother, became an heiress – to no considerable amount, to be sure, but enough to make the prophecy appear reversed. The heiress and her husband removed from his small patrimonial estate in Merionethshire, to her heritage in Caernarvonshire, and for a time the prophecy lay dormant.

If you go from Tremadoc to Criccaeth, you pass by the parochial church of Ynysynhanarn, situated in a boggy valley running from the mountains, which shoulder up to the Rivals, down to Cardigan Bay. This tract of land has every appearance of having been redeemed at no distant period of time from the sea, and has all the desolate rankness often attendant upon such marshes. But the valley beyond, similar in character, had yet more of gloom at the time of which I write. In the higher part there were large plantations of firs, set too closely to attain any size, and remaining stunted in height and scrubby in appearance. Indeed, many of the smaller and more weakly had died, and the bark had fallen down on the brown soil neglected and unnoticed. These trees had a ghastly appearance, with their white trunks, seen by the dim light which struggled through the thick boughs above. Nearer to the sea, the valley assumed a more open, though hardly a more cheerful character; it looked dark and was overhung by sea-fog through the greater part of the year; and even a farmhouse, which usually imparts something of cheerfulness to a landscape, failed to do so here. This valley formed the greater part of the estate to which Owen Griffiths became entitled by right of his wife. In the higher part of the valley was situated the family mansion, or rather dwelling-house; for 'mansion' is too grand a word to apply to the clumsy, but substantially-built Bodowen. It was square and heavy-looking, with just that much pretension to ornament necessary to distinguish it from the mere farmhouse.

In this dwelling Mrs Owen Griffiths bore her husband two sons – Llewellyn, the future Squire, and Robert, who was early destined for the Church. The only difference in their situation, up to the time when Robert was entered at Jesus College, was that the elder was invariably indulged by all around him, while Robert was thwarted and indulged by turns; that Llewellyn never learned anything from the poor Welsh parson, who was nominally his private tutor; while occasionally Squire Griffiths made a great point of enforcing Robert's diligence, telling him that, as he had his bread to earn, he must pay attention to his learning. There is no knowing how far the very irregular education he had received would have carried Robert through his college examinations; but, luckily for him in this respect, before such a trial of his learning came round, he heard of the death of his elder brother, after a short illness, brought on by a hard drinking-bout. Of course, Robert was summoned home; and it seemed quite as much of course, now that there was no necessity for him to 'earn his bread by his learning', that he should not return to Oxford. So the half-educated, but not unintelligent, young man continued at home, during the short remainder of his parents' lifetime.

His was not an uncommon character. In general he was mild, indolent, and easily managed; but once thoroughly roused, his passions were vehement and fearful. He seemed, indeed, almost afraid of himself, and in common hardly dared to give way to justifiable anger – so much did he dread losing his self-control. Had he been judiciously educated, he would, probably, have distinguished himself in those branches of literature which call for taste and imagination, rather than for any exertion of reflection or judgement. As it was, his literary taste showed itself in making collections of Cambrian antiquities of every description, till his stock of Welsh manuscripts would have excited the envy of Dr Pugh[60] himself, had he been alive at the time of which I write.

There is one characteristic of Robert Griffiths which I have omitted to note, and which was peculiar among his class. He was no hard drinker; whether it was that his head was easily affected, or that his partially-refined taste led him to dislike intoxication and its attendant circumstances, I cannot say; but at five-and-twenty Robert Griffiths was habitually sober – a thing so rare in Llyn,[61] that he was almost shunned as a churlish, unsociable being, and passed much of his time in solitude.

About this time, he had to appear in some case that was tried at the Caernarvon assizes and, while there, was a guest at the house of his agent, a shrewd, sensible Welsh attorney, with one daughter, who had charms enough to captivate Robert Griffiths. Though he remained only a few days at her father's house, they were sufficient to decide his affections, and short was the period allowed to elapse before he brought home a mistress to Bodowen. The new Mrs Griffiths was a gentle, yielding person, full of love toward her husband, of whom, nevertheless, she stood something in awe, partly arising from the difference in their ages, partly from his devoting much time to studies of which she could understand nothing.

She soon made him the father of a blooming little daughter, called Angharad after her mother. Then there came several uneventful years in the household of Bodowen; and, when the old women had one and all declared that the cradle would not rock again, Mrs Griffiths bore the son and heir. His birth was soon followed by his mother's death: she had been ailing and low-spirited during her pregnancy, and she seemed to lack the buoyancy of body and mind requisite to bring her round after her time of trial. Her husband, who loved her all the more from having few other claims on his affections, was deeply grieved by her early death, and his only comforter was the sweet little boy whom she had left behind. That part of the squire's character, which was so tender, and almost feminine, seemed called forth by the helpless situation of the little infant, who stretched out his arms to his father with the same earnest cooing that happier children make use of to their mother alone. Angharad was almost neglected, while the little Owen was king of the house; still, next to his father, none tended him so lovingly as his sister. She was so accustomed to give way to him that it was no longer a hardship. By night and by day Owen was the constant companion of his father, and increasing years seemed only to confirm the custom. It was an unnatural life for the child, seeing no bright little faces peering into his own (for Angharad was, as I said before, five or six years older, and her face, poor motherless girl! was often anything but bright), hearing no din of clear ringing voices, but day after day sharing the otherwise solitary hours of his father, whether in the dim room surrounded by wizard-like antiquities, or pattering his little feet to keep up with his 'tada' in his mountain rambles or shooting excursions. When the pair came to some little foaming brook, where the stepping-stones were far and wide, the father carried his little boy across with the tenderest care; when the lad was weary, they rested, he cradled in his father's arms, or the Squire would lift him up and carry him to his home again. The boy was indulged (for his father felt flattered by the desire) in his wish of sharing his meals and keeping the same hours. All this indulgence did not render Owen unamiable, but it made him wilful, and not a happy child. He had a thoughtful look, not common to the face of a young boy. He knew no games, no merry sports; his information was of an imaginative and speculative character. His father delighted to interest him in his own studies, without considering how far they were healthy for so young a mind.

Of course Squire Griffiths was not unaware of the prophecy which was to be fulfilled in his generation. He would occasionally refer to it when among his friends, with sceptical levity; but in truth it lay nearer to his heart than he chose to acknowledge. His strong imagination rendered him peculiarly impressionable on such subjects; while his judgement, seldom exercised or fortified by severe thought, could not prevent his continually recurring to it. He used to gaze on the half-sad countenance of the child, who sat looking up into his face with his large dark eyes, so fondly yet so enquiringly, till the old legend swelled around his heart, and became too painful for him not to require sympathy. Besides, the overpowering love he bore to the child seemed to demand fuller vent than tender words; it made him like, yet dread, to upbraid its object for the fearful contrast foretold. Still Squire Griffiths told the legend, in a half-jesting manner, to his little son, when they were roaming over the wild heaths in the autumn days, 'the saddest of the year', or while they sat in the oak-wainscoted room, surrounded by mysterious relics that gleamed strangely forth by the flickering firelight. The legend was wrought into the boy's mind, and he would crave, yet tremble, to hear it told over and over again, while the words were intermingled with caresses and questions as to his love. Occasionally his loving words and actions were cut short by his father's light yet bitter speech – 'Get thee away, my lad; thou knowest not what is to come of all this love.'

When Angharad was seventeen, and Owen eleven or twelve, the rector of the parish in which Bodowen was situated endeavoured to prevail on Squire Griffiths to send the boy to school. Now, this rector had many tastes in common with his parishioner, and was his only intimate; and, by repeated arguments, he succeeded in convincing the Squire that the unnatural life Owen was leading was in every way injurious. Unwillingly was the father brought to part from his son; but he did at length send him to the Grammar School at Bangor,[62] then under the management of an excellent classic. Here Owen showed that he had more talents than the rector had given him credit for, when he affirmed that the lad had been completely stupefied by the life he led at Bodowen. He bade fair to do credit to the school in the peculiar branch of learning for which it was famous. But he was not popular among his schoolfellows. He was wayward, though, to a certain degree, generous and unselfish; he was reserved but gentle, except when the tremendous bursts of passion (similar in character to those of his father) forced their way.

On his return from school one Christmas-time, when he had been a year or so at Bangor, he was stunned by hearing that the undervalued Angharad was about to be married to a gentleman of South Wales, residing near Aberystwyth. Boys seldom appreciate their sisters; but Owen thought of the many slights with which he had requited the patient Angharad, and he gave way to bitter regrets, which, with a selfish want of control over his words, he kept expressing to his father, until the Squire was thoroughly hurt and chagrined at the repeated exclamations of 'What shall we do when Angharad is gone?' 'How dull we shall be when Angharad is married!' Owen's holidays were prolonged a few weeks, in order that he might be present at the wedding; and when all the festivities were over, and the bride and bridegroom had left Bodowen, the boy and his father really felt how much they missed the quiet, loving Angharad. She had performed so many thoughtful, noiseless little offices, on which their daily comfort depended; and, now she was gone, the household seemed to miss the spirit that peacefully kept it in order; the servants roamed about in search of commands and directions; the rooms had no longer the unobtrusive ordering of taste to make them cheerful; the very fires burned dim, and were always sinking down into dull heaps of grey ashes. Altogether Owen did not regret his return to Bangor, and this also the mortified parent perceived. Squire Griffiths was a selfish parent.

Letters in those days were a rare occurrence. Owen usually received one during his half-yearly absences from home, and occasionally his father paid him a visit. This half-year the boy had no visit, nor even a letter, till very near the time of his leaving school, and then he was astounded by the intelligence that his father was married again.

Then came one of his paroxysms of rage; the more disastrous in its effects upon his character because it could find no vent in action. Independently of slight to the memory of his first wife, which children are so apt to fancy such an action implies, Owen had hitherto considered himself (and with justice) the first object of his father's life. They had been so much to each other; and now a shapeless, but too real, something had come between him and his father for ever. He felt as if his permission should have been asked, as if he should have been consulted. Certainly he ought to have been told of the intended event. So the Squire felt, and hence his constrained letter, which had so much increased the bitterness of Owen's feelings.

With all this anger, when Owen saw his stepmother, he thought he had never seen so beautiful a woman for her age; for she was no longer in the bloom of youth, being a widow when his father married her. Her manners, to the Welsh lad, who had seen little of female grace among the families of the few antiquarians with whom his father visited, were so fascinating that he watched her with a sort of breathless admiration. Her measured grace, her faultless movements, her tones of voice, sweet, till the ear was sated with their sweetness, made Owen less angry at his father's marriage. Yet he felt, more than ever, that the cloud was between him and his father; that the hasty letter he had sent in answer to the announcement of his wedding was not forgotten, although no allusion was ever made to it. He was no longer his father's confidant – hardly ever his father's companion; for the newly-married wife was all in all to the Squire, and his son felt himself almost a cipher, where he had so long been everything. The lady herself had ever the softest consideration for her stepson; almost too obtrusive was the attention paid to his wishes; but still he fancied that the heart had no part in the winning advances. There was a watchful glance of the eye that Owen once or twice caught when she had imagined herself unobserved, and many other nameless little circumstances, that gave him a strong feeling of want of sincerity in his stepmother. Mrs Owen brought with her into the family her little child by her first husband, a boy nearly three years old. He was one of those selfish, observant, mocking children, over whose feelings you seem to have no control: agile and mischievous, his little practical jokes, at first performed in ignorance of the pain he gave, but afterward proceeding to a malicious pleasure in suffering, really seemed to afford some ground to the superstitious notion of some of the common people that he was a fairy changeling.

Years passed on; and as Owen grew older he became more observant. He saw, even in his occasional visits at home (for from school he had passed on to college), that a great change had taken place in the outward manifestations of his father's character; and, by degrees, Owen traced this change to the influence of his stepmother; so slight, so imperceptible to the common observer, yet so resistless in its effects. Squire Griffiths caught up his wife's humbly advanced opinions, and, unawares to himself, adopted them as his own, defying all argument and opposition. It was the same with her wishes; they met their fulfilment, from the extreme and delicate art with which she insinuated them into her husband's mind as his own. She sacrificed the show of authority for the power. At last, when Owen perceived some oppressive act in his father's conduct towards his dependants, or some unaccountable thwarting of his own wishes, he fancied he saw his stepmother's secret influence thus displayed, however much she might regret the injustice of his father's actions in her conversations with him when they were alone. His father was fast losing his temperate habits, and frequent intoxication soon took its usual effect upon the temper. Yet even here was the spell of his wife upon him. Before her he placed a restraint upon his passion, yet she was perfectly aware of his irritable disposition, and directed it hither and thither with the same apparent ignorance of the tendency of her words.

Meanwhile Owen's situation became peculiarly mortifying to a youth whose early remembrances afforded such a contrast to his present state. As a child, he had been elevated to the consequence of a man before his years gave any mental check to the selfishness which such conduct was likely to engender; he could remember when his will was law to the servants and dependants, and his sympathy necessary to his father: now he was as a cipher in his father's house; and the Squire, estranged in the first instance by a feeling of the injury he had done his son in not sooner acquainting him with his purposed marriage, seemed rather to avoid than to seek him as a companion, and too frequently showed the most utter indifference to the feelings and wishes which a young man of a high and independent spirit might be supposed to indulge.

Perhaps Owen was not fully aware of the force of all these circumstances; for an actor in a family drama is seldom unimpassioned enough to be perfectly observant. But he became moody and soured; brooding over his unloved existence, and craving with a human heart after sympathy.

This feeling took more full possession of his mind when he had left college, and returned home to lead an idle and purposeless life. As the heir, there was no worldly necessity for exertion: his father was too much of a Welsh squire to dream of the moral necessity; and he himself had not sufficient strength of mind to decide at once upon abandoning a place and mode of life which abounded in daily mortifications. Yet to this course his judgement was slowly tending, when some circumstances occurred to detain him at Bodowen.

It was not to be expected that harmony would long be preserved, even in appearance, between an unguarded and soured young man, such as Owen, and his wary stepmother, when he had once left college, and come, not as a visitor, but as the heir, to his father's house. Some cause of difference occurred, where the woman subdued her hidden anger sufficiently to become convinced that Owen was not entirely the dupe she had believed him to be. Henceforward there was no peace between them. Not in vulgar altercations did this show itself; but in moody reserve on Owen's part, and in undisguised and contemptuous pursuance of her own plans by his stepmother. Bodowen was no longer a place where, if Owen was not loved or attended to, he could at least find peace and care for himself: he was thwarted at every step, and in every wish, by his father's desire, apparently, while the wife sat by with a smile of triumph on her beautiful lips.

So Owen went forth at the early day-dawn, sometimes roaming about on the shore or the upland, shooting or fishing, as the season might be, but oftener 'stretched in indolent repose'[63] on the short, sweet grass, indulging in gloomy and morbid reveries. He would fancy that this mortified state of existence was a dream, a horrible dream, from which he should awake and find himself again the sole object and darling of his father. And then he would start up and strive to shake off the incubus. There was the molten sunset of his childish memory; the gorgeous crimson piles of glory in the west, fading away into the cold calm light of the rising moon, while here and there a cloud floated across the western heaven, like a seraph's wing, in its flaming beauty; the earth was the same as in his childhood's days, full of gentle evening sounds, and the harmonies of twilight – the breeze came sweeping low over the heather and blue-bells by his side, and the turf was sending up its evening incense of perfume. But life, and heart, and hope were changed for ever since those bygone days!

Or he would seat himself in a favourite niche of the rocks on Moel Gêst, hidden by a stunted growth of the whitty, or mountain-ash, from general observation, with a rich-tinted cushion of stone-crop for his feet, and a straight precipice of rock rising just above. Here would he sit for hours, gazing idly at the bay below with its background of purple hills, and the little fishing-sail on its bosom, showing white in the sunbeam, and gliding on in such harmony with the quiet beauty of the glassy sea; or he would pull out an old school-volume, his companion for years, and in morbid accordance with the dark legend that still lurked in the recesses of his mind – a shape of gloom in those innermost haunts awaiting its time to come forth in distinct outline – would he turn to the old Greek dramas which treat of a family foredoomed by an avenging Fate. The worn page opened of itself at the play of the Oedipus Tyrannus,[64] and Owen dwelt with the craving disease upon the prophecy so nearly resembling that which concerned himself. With his consciousness of neglect, there was a sort of self-flattery in the consequence which the legend gave him. He almost wondered how they durst, with slights and insults, thus provoke the Avenger.[65]

The days drifted onward. Often he would vehemently pursue some sylvan sport, till thought and feeling were lost in the violence of bodily exertion. Occasionally his evenings were spent at a small public-house, such as stood by the unfrequented wayside, where the welcome – hearty, though bought – seemed so strongly to contrast with the gloomy negligence of home – unsympathising home.

One evening (Owen might be four- or five-and-twenty), wearied with a day's shooting on the Clenneny Moors, he passed by the open door of the Goat at Penmorfa. The light and the cheeriness within tempted him, poor self-exhausted man! as it has done many a one more wretched in worldly circumstances, to step in, and take his evening meal where at least his presence was of some consequence. It was a busy day in that little hostel. A flock of sheep, amounting to some hundreds, had arrived at Penmorfa, on their road to England, and thronged the space before the house. Inside was the shrewd, kind-hearted hostess, bustling to and fro, with merry greetings for every tired drover who was to pass the night in her house, while the sheep were penned in a field close by. Ever and anon, she kept attending to the second crowd of guests, who were celebrating a rural wedding in her house. It was busy work to Martha Thomas, yet her smile never flagged; and when Owen Griffiths had finished his evening meal she was there, ready with a hope that it had done him good, and was to his mind, and a word of intelligence that the wedding-folk were about to dance in the kitchen, and the harper was the famous Edward of Corwen.

Owen, partly from good-natured compliance with his hostess's implied wish, and partly from curiosity, lounged to the passage which led to the kitchen – not the everyday, working, cooking kitchen, which was behind, but a good-sized room, where the mistress sat when her work was done, and where the country people were commonly entertained at such merry-makings as the present. The lintels of the door formed a frame for the animated picture which Owen saw within, as he leaned against the wall in the dark passage. The red light of the fire, with every now and then a falling piece of turf sending forth a fresh blaze, shone full upon four young men who were dancing a measure something like a Scotch reel, keeping admirable time in their rapid movements to the capital tune the harper was playing. They had their hats on when Owen first took his stand, but as they grew more and more animated they flung them away, and presently their shoes were kicked off with like disregard to the spot where they might happen to alight. Shouts of applause followed any remarkable exertion of agility, in which each seemed to try to excel his companions. At length, wearied and exhausted, they sat down, and the harper gradually changed to one of those wild, inspiring national airs for which he was so famous. The thronged audience sat earnest and breathless, and you might have heard a pin drop, except when some maiden passed hurriedly, with flaring candle and busy look, through to the real kitchen beyond. When he had finished his beautiful theme of 'The March of the Men of Harlech', he changed the measure again to 'Tri chant o' bunnan' (Three hundred pounds), and immediately a most unmusical-looking man began chanting 'Pennillion', or a sort of recitative stanzas, which were soon taken up by another; and this amusement lasted so long that Owen grew weary, and was thinking of retreating from his post by the door, when some little bustle was occasioned, on the opposite side of the room, by the entrance of a middle-aged man, and a young girl, apparently his daughter. The man advanced to the bench occupied by the seniors of the party, who welcomed him with the usual pretty Welsh greeting, '*Pa sut mae dy galon?*' (How is thy heart?) and drinking his health passed on to him the cup of excellent *cwrw*.[66] The girl, evidently a village belle, was as warmly greeted by the young men, while the girls eyed her rather askance with a half-jealous look, which Owen set down to the score of her extreme prettiness. Like most Welsh women, she was of middle size as to height, but beautifully made, with the most perfect yet delicate roundness in every limb. Her little mob-cap was carefully adjusted to a face which was excessively pretty, though it never could be called handsome. It also was round, with the slightest tendency to the oval shape, richly coloured, though somewhat olive in complexion, with dimples in cheek and chin, and the most scarlet lips Owen had ever seen, that were too short to meet over the small pearly teeth. The nose was the most defective feature; but the eyes were splendid. They were so long, so lustrous, yet at times so very soft under their thick fringe of eyelash! The nut-brown hair was carefully braided beneath the border of delicate lace: it was evident the little village beauty knew how to make the most of all her attractions, for the gay colours which were displayed in her neckerchief were in complete harmony with the complexion.

Owen was much attracted, while yet he was amused, by the evident coquetry the girl displayed, collecting around her a whole bevy of young fellows, for each of whom she seemed to have some gay speech, some attractive look or action. In a few minutes young Griffiths of Bodowen was at her side, brought thither by a variety of idle motives, and as her undivided attention was given to the Welsh heir, her admirers, one by one, dropped off, to seat themselves by some less fascinating but more attentive fair one. The more Owen conversed with the girl, the more he was taken; she had more wit and talent than he had fancied possible; a self-abandon and thoughtfulness, to boot, that seemed full of charms; and then her voice was so clear and sweet, and her actions so full of grace, that Owen was fascinated before he was well aware, and kept looking into her bright, blushing face, till her uplifted flashing eye fell beneath his earnest gaze.

While it thus happened that they were silent – she from confusion at the unexpected warmth of his admiration, he from an unconsciousness of anything but the beautiful changes in her flexile countenance – the man whom Owen took for her father came up and addressed some observation to his daughter, from whence he glided into some commonplace though respectful remark to Owen; and at length, engaging him in some slight, local conversation, he led the way to the account of a spot on the peninsula of Penthryn, where teal abounded, and concluded with begging Owen to allow him to show him the exact place, saying that whenever the young Squire felt so inclined, if he would honour him by a call at his house, he would take him across in his boat. While Owen listened, his attention was not so much absorbed as to be unaware that the little beauty at his side was refusing one or two who endeavoured to draw her from her place by invitations to dance. Flattered by his own construction of her refusals, he again directed all his attention to her, till she was called away by her father, who was leaving the scene of festivity. Before he left he reminded Owen of his promise, and added: 'Perhaps, sir, you do not know me. My name is Ellis Pritchard, and I live at Ty Glas, on this side of Moel Gêst; anyone can point it out to you.'

When the father and daughter had left, Owen slowly prepared for his ride home; but, encountering the hostess, he could not resist asking a few questions relative to Ellis Pritchard and his pretty daughter. She answered shortly but respectfully, and then said, rather hesitatingly: 'Master Griffiths, you know the triad,[67] "*Tri pheth tebyg y naill i'r llall, ysgnbwr heb yd, mail deg heb ddiawd, a merch deg heb ei geirda*" (Three things are alike: a fine barn without corn, a fine cup without drink, a fine woman without her reputation).' She hastily quitted him, and Owen rode slowly to his unhappy home.

Ellis Pritchard, half farmer and half fisherman, was shrewd, and keen, and worldly; yet he was good-natured, and sufficiently generous to have become rather a popular man among his equals. He had been struck with the young Squire's attention to his pretty daughter, and was not insensible to the advantages to be derived from it. Nest[68] would not be the first peasant-girl, by any means, who had been transplanted to a Welsh manor-house as its mistress; and, accordingly, her father had shrewdly given the admiring young man some pretext for further opportunities of seeing her.

As for Nest herself, she had somewhat of her father's worldliness, and was fully alive to the superior station of her new admirer, and quite prepared to slight all her old sweethearts on his account. But then she had something more of feeling in her reckoning; she had not been insensible to the earnest yet comparatively refined homage which Owen paid her; she had noticed his expressive and occasionally handsome countenance with admiration, and was flattered by his so immediately singling her out from her companions. As to the hint which Martha Thomas had thrown out, it is enough to say that Nest was very giddy, and that she was motherless. She had high spirits and a great love of admiration, or, to use a softer term, she loved to please; men, women, and children, all, she delighted to gladden with her smile and voice. She coquetted, and flirted, and went to the extreme lengths of Welsh courtship, till the seniors of the village shook their heads, and cautioned their daughters against her acquaintance. If not absolutely guilty, she had too frequently been on the verge of guilt.

Even at the time, Martha Thomas's hint made but little impression on Owen, for his senses were otherwise occupied; but in a few days the recollection thereof had wholly died away, and one warm glorious summer's day he bent his steps toward Ellis Pritchard's with a beating heart; for, except some very slight flirtations at Oxford, Owen had never been touched; his thoughts, his fancy, had been otherwise engaged.

Ty Glas was built against one of the lower rocks of Moel Gêst, which, indeed, formed a side to the low, lengthy house. The materials of the cottage were the shingly stones which had fallen from above, plastered rudely together, with deep recesses for the small oblong windows. Altogether, the exterior was much ruder than Owen had expected; but inside there seemed no lack of comforts. The house was divided into two apartments, one large, roomy, and dark, into which Owen entered immediately; and, before the blushing Nest came from the inner chamber (for she had seen the young Squire coming, and hastily gone to make some alteration in her dress), he had had time to look around him, and note the various little particulars of the room. Beneath the window (which commanded a magnificent view) was an oaken dresser, replete with drawers and cupboards, and brightly polished to a rich dark colour. In the farther part of the room Owen could at first distinguish little, entering as he did from the glaring sunlight; but he soon saw that there were two oaken beds, closed up after the manner of the Welsh: in fact, the dormitories of Ellis Pritchard and the man who served under him, both on sea and on land. There was the large wheel used for spinning wool, left standing on the middle of the floor, as if in use only a few minutes before; and around the ample chimney hung flitches of bacon, dried kids'-flesh, and fish, that was in process of smoking for winter's store.

Before Nest had shyly dared to enter, her father, who had been mending his nets down below, and seen Owen winding up to the house, came in and gave him a hearty yet respectful welcome; and then Nest, downcast and blushing, full of the consciousness which her father's advice and conversation had not failed to inspire, ventured to join them. To Owen's mind this reserve and shyness gave her new charms.

It was too bright, too hot, too anything to think of going to shoot teal till later in the day, and Owen was delighted to accept a hesitating invitation to share the noonday meal. Some ewe-milk cheese, very hard and dry, oatcake, slips of the dried kid's-flesh broiled, after having been previously soaked in water for a few minutes, delicious butter and fresh buttermilk, with a liquor called '*diod griafol*' (made from the berries of the *Sorbus aucuparia*,[69] infused in water and then fermented), composed the frugal repast; but there was something so clean and neat, and withal such a true welcome, that Owen had seldom enjoyed a meal so much. Indeed, at that time of day the Welsh squires differed from the farmers more in the plenty and rough abundance of their manner of living than in the refinement of style of their table.

At the present day, down in Llyn, the Welsh gentry are not a wit behind their Saxon equals in the expensive elegances of life; but then (when there was but one pewter-service in all Northumberland) there was nothing in Ellis Pritchard's mode of living that grated on the young Squire's sense of refinement.

Little was said by that young pair of wooers during the meal; the father had all the conversation to himself, apparently heedless of the ardent looks and inattentive mien of his guest. As Owen became more serious in his feelings, he grew more timid in their expression, and at night, when they returned from their shooting-excursion, the caress he gave Nest was almost as bashfully offered as received.

This was but the first of a series of days devoted to Nest in reality, though at first he thought some little disguise of his object was necessary. The past, the future, was all forgotten in those happy days of love.

And every worldly plan, every womanly wile was put in practice by Ellis Pritchard and his daughter, to render his visits agreeable and alluring. Indeed, the very circumstance of his being welcome was enough to attract the poor young man, to whom the feeling so produced was new and full of charms. He left a home where the certainty of being thwarted made him chary in expressing his wishes; where no tones of love ever fell on his ear, save those addressed to others; where his presence or absence was a matter of utter indifference; and when he entered Ty Glas, all, down to the little cur which, with clamorous barkings, claimed a part of his attention, seemed to rejoice. His account of his day's employment found a willing listener in Ellis; and when he passed on to Nest, busy at her wheel or at her churn, the deepened colour, the conscious eye, and the gradual yielding of herself up to his lover-like caress, had worlds of charms. Ellis Pritchard was a tenant on the Bodowen estate, and therefore had reasons in plenty for wishing to keep the young Squire's visits secret; and Owen, unwilling to disturb the sunny calm of these halcyon days by any storm at home, was ready to use all the artifice which Ellis suggested as to the mode of his calls at Ty Glas. Nor was he unaware of the probable, nay, the hoped-for termination of these repeated days of happiness. He was quite conscious that the father wished for nothing better than the marriage of his daughter to the heir of Bodowen; and when Nest had hidden her face in his neck, which was encircled by her clasping arms, and murmured into his ear her acknowledgement of love, he felt only too desirous of finding someone to love him for ever. Though not highly principled, he would not have tried to obtain Nest on other terms save those of marriage: he did so pine after enduring love, and fancied he should have bound her heart for evermore to his, when they had taken the solemn oaths of matrimony.

There was no great difficulty attending a secret marriage at such a place and at such a time. One gusty autumn day, Ellis ferried them round Penthryn to Llandutrwyn, and there saw his little Nest become future Lady of Bodowen.

How often do we see giddy, coquetting, restless girls become sobered by marriage? A great object in life is decided, one on which their thoughts have been running in all their vagaries; and they seem to verify the beautiful fable of Undine.[70] A new soul beams out in the gentleness and repose of their future lives. An indescribable softness and tenderness takes the place of the wearying vanity of their former endeavours to attract admiration. Something of this sort happened to Nest Pritchard. If at first she had been anxious to attract the young Squire of Bodowen, long before her marriage this feeling had merged into a truer love than she had ever felt before; and now that he was her own, her husband, her whole soul was bent toward making him amends, as far as in her lay, for the misery which, with a woman's tact, she saw that he had to endure at his home. Her greetings were abounding in delicately-expressed love; her study of his tastes unwearying, in the arrangement of her dress, her time, her very thoughts.

No wonder that he looked back on his wedding-day with a

thankfulness which is seldom the result of unequal marriages. No wonder that his heart beat aloud as formerly when he wound up the little path to Ty Glas, and saw – keen though the winter's wind might be – that Nest was standing out at the door to watch for his dimly-seen approach, while the candle flared in the little window as a beacon to guide him aright.

The angry words and unkind actions of home fell deadened on his heart; he thought of the love that was surely his, and of the new promise of love that a short time would bring forth; and he could almost have smiled at the impotent efforts to disturb his peace.

A few more months, and the young father was greeted by a feeble little cry, when he hastily entered Ty Glas, one morning early, in consequence of a summons conveyed mysteriously to Bodowen; and the pale mother, smiling, and feebly holding up her babe to its father's kiss, seemed to him even more lovely than the bright, gay Nest who had won his heart at the little inn of Penmorfa.

But the curse was at work! The fulfilment of the prophecy was nigh at hand!

Chapter 2

It was the autumn after the birth of their boy; it had been a glorious summer, with bright, hot, sunny weather; and now the year was fading away as seasonably into mellow days, with mornings of silver mists and clear frosty nights. The blooming look of the time of flowers was past and gone; but instead there were even richer tints abroad in the sun-coloured leaves, the lichens, the golden-blossomed furze; if it was the time of fading, there was a glory in the decay.

Nest, in her loving anxiety to surround her dwelling with every charm for her husband's sake, had turned gardener, and the little corners of the rude court before the house were filled with many a delicate mountain-flower, transplanted more for its beauty than its rarity. The sweetbrier bush may even yet be seen, old and grey, which she and Owen planted, a green slipling, beneath the window of her little chamber. In those moments Owen forgot all besides the present; all the cares and griefs he had known in the past, and all that might await him of woe and death in the future. The boy, too, was as lovely a child as the fondest parent was ever blessed with, and crowed with delight, and clapped his little hands, as his mother held him in her arms at the cottage door to watch his father's ascent up the rough path that led to Ty Glas, one bright autumnal morning; and, when the three entered the house together, it was difficult to say which was the happiest. Owen carried his boy, and tossed and played with him, while Nest sought out some little article of work, and seated herself on the dresser beneath the window, where, now busily plying the needle, and then again looking at her husband, she eagerly told him the little pieces of domestic intelligence, the winning ways of the child, the result of yesterday's fishing, and such of the gossip of Penmorfa as came to the ears of the now retired Nest. She noticed that, when she mentioned any little circumstance which bore the slightest reference to Bodowen, her husband appeared chafed and uneasy, and at last avoided anything that might in the least remind him of home. In truth, he had been suffering much of late from the irritability of his father, shown in trifles to be sure, but not the less galling on that account.

While they were thus talking, and caressing each other and the child, a shadow darkened the room, and before they could catch a glimpse of the object that had occasioned it, it vanished, and Squire Griffiths lifted the door-latch, and stood before them. He stood and looked – first on his son, so different, in his buoyant expression of content and enjoyment, with his noble child in his arms, like a proud and happy father, as he was, from the depressed, moody young man he too often appeared at Bodowen; then on Nest – poor, trembling, sickened Nest! – who dropped her work, but yet durst not stir from her seat on the dresser, while she looked to her husband as if for protection from his father.

The Squire was silent, as he glared from one to the other, his features white with restrained passion. When he spoke, his words came most distinct in their forced composure. It was to his son he addressed himself: 'That woman! who is she?'

Owen hesitated one moment, and then replied, in a steady, yet quiet, voice: 'Father, that woman is my wife.'

He would have added some apology for the long concealment of his marriage; have appealed to his father's forgiveness; but the foam flew from Squire Owen's lips as he burst forth with invective against Nest: 'You have married her! It is as they told me! Married Nest Pritchard, *yr buten*![71] And you stand there as if you had not disgraced yourself for ever and ever with your accursed wiving! And the fair harlot sits there, in her mocking modesty, practising the mimming airs that will become her state as future Lady of Bodowen. But I will move heaven and earth before that false woman darken the doors of my father's house as mistress!'

All this was said with such rapidity that Owen had no time for the words that thronged to his lips. 'Father!' (he burst forth at length) 'Father, whosoever told you that Nest Pritchard was a harlot told you a lie as false as hell! Ay! a lie as false as hell!' he added, in a voice of thunder, while he advanced a step or two nearer to the Squire. And then, in a lower tone, he said: 'She is as pure as your own wife; nay, God help me! as the dear, precious mother who brought me forth, and then left me – with no refuge in a mother's heart – to struggle on through life alone. I tell you Nest is as pure as that dear, dead mother!'

'Fool – poor fool!'

At this moment the child – the little Owen – who had kept gazing from one countenance to the other, and with earnest look, trying to understand what had brought the fierce glare into the face where till now he had read nothing but love, in some way attracted the Squire's attention, and increased his wrath.

'Yes,' he continued, 'poor, weak fool that you are, hugging the child of another as if it were your own offspring!' Owen involuntarily caressed the affrighted child, and half smiled at the implication of his father's words. This the Squire perceived, and raising his voice to a scream of rage, he went on: 'I bid you, if you call yourself my son, to cast away that miserable, shameless woman's offspring; cast it away this instant – this instant!'

In this ungovernable rage, seeing that Owen was far from complying with his command, he snatched the poor infant from the loving arms that held it, and throwing it to his mother, left the house inarticulate with fury.

Nest – who had been pale and still as marble during this terrible dialogue, looking on and listening as if fascinated by the words that smote her heart – opened her arms to receive and cherish her precious babe; but the boy was not destined to reach the white refuge of her breast. The furious action of the Squire had been almost without aim, and the infant fell against the sharp edge of the dresser down on to the stone floor.

Owen sprang up to take the child, but he lay so still, so motionless, that the awe of death came over the father, and he stooped down to gaze more closely. At that moment, the upturned, filmy eyes rolled convulsively – a spasm passed along the body – and the lips, yet warm with kissing, quivered into everlasting rest.

A word from her husband told Nest all. She slid down from her seat, and lay by her little son as corpse-like as he, unheeding all the agonising endearments and passionate adjurations of her husband. And that poor, desolate husband and father! Scarce one little quarter of an hour, and he had been so blessed in his consciousness of love! the bright promise of many years on his infant's face, and the new, fresh soul beaming forth in its awakened intelligence. And there it was: the little clay image, that would never more gladden up at the sight of him, nor stretch forth to meet his embrace; whose inarticulate, yet most eloquent cooings might haunt him in his dreams, but would never more be heard in waking life again! And by the dead babe, almost as utterly insensate, the poor mother had fallen in a merciful faint – the slandered, heart-pierced Nest! Owen struggled against the sickness that came over him, and busied himself in vain attempts at her restoration.

It was now near noonday, and Ellis Pritchard came home, little dreaming of the sight that awaited him; but, though stunned, he was able to take more effectual measures for his poor daughter's recovery than Owen had done.

By and by she showed symptoms of returning sense, and was placed in her own little bed in a darkened room, where, without ever waking to complete consciousness, she fell asleep. Then it was that her husband, suffocated by pressure of miserable thought, gently drew his hand from her tightened clasp and, printing one long soft kiss on her white waxen forehead, hastily stole out of the room, and out of the house.

Near the base of Moel Gêst – it might be a quarter of a mile from Ty Glas – was a little neglected solitary copse, wild and tangled with the trailing branches of the dog-rose and the tendrils of the white bryony. Toward the middle of this thicket lay a deep crystal pool – a clear mirror for the blue heavens above – and round the margin floated the broad green leaves of the water-lily; and, when the regal sun shone down in his noonday glory, the flowers arose from their cool depths to welcome and greet him. The copse was musical with many sounds; the warbling of birds rejoicing in its shades, the ceaseless hum of the insects that hovered over the pool, the chime of the distant waterfall, the occasional bleating of the sheep from the mountain-top, were all blended into the delicious harmony of nature.

It had been one of Owen's favourite resorts when he had been a lonely wanderer – a pilgrim in search of love in the years gone by. And thither he went, as if by instinct, when he left Ty Glas; quelling the uprising agony till he should reach that little solitary spot.

It was the time of day when a change in the aspect of the weather so frequently takes place, and the little pool was no longer the reflection of a blue and sunny sky; it sent back the dark and slaty clouds above; and, every now and then, a rough gust shook the painted autumn leaves from their branches, and all other music was lost in the sound of the wild winds piping down from the moorlands, which lay up and beyond the clefts in the mountain-side. Presently the rain came on and beat down in torrents.

But Owen heeded it not. He sat on the dank ground, his face buried in his hands, and his whole strength, physical and mental, employed in quelling the rush of blood which rose and boiled and gurgled in his brain, as if it would madden him.

The phantom of his dead child rose ever before him, and seemed to cry aloud for vengeance. And, when the poor young man thought upon the victim whom he required in his wild longing for revenge, he shuddered, for it was his father!

Again and again he tried not to think; but still the circle of thought came round, eddying through his brain. At length he mastered his passions, and they were calm; then he forced himself to arrange some plan for the future.

He had not, in the passionate hurry of the moment, seen that his father had left the cottage before he was aware of the fatal accident that befell the child. Owen thought he had seen all; and once he planned to go to the Squire and tell him of the anguish of heart he had wrought, and awe him, as it were, by the dignity of grief. But then again he durst not – he distrusted his self-control – the old prophecy rose up in its horror – he dreaded his doom.

At last he determined to leave his father for ever; to take Nest to some distant country where she might forget her first-born, and where he himself might gain a livelihood by his own exertions.

But when he tried to descend to the various little arrangements which were involved in the execution of this plan, he remembered that all his money (and in this respect Squire Griffiths was no niggard) was locked up in his escritoire at Bodowen. In vain he tried to do away with this matter-of-fact difficulty; go to Bodowen he must; and his only hope – nay, his determination – was to avoid his father.

He rose and took a by-path to Bodowen. The house looked even more gloomy and desolate than usual in the heavy down-pouring rain; yet Owen gazed on it with something of regret – for, sorrowful as his days in it had been, he was about to leave it for many many years, if not for ever. He entered by a side door opening into a passage that led to his own room, where he kept his books, his guns, his fishing-tackle, his writing materials, *et cetera*.

Here he hurriedly began to select the few articles he intended to take; for, besides the dread of interruption, he was feverishly anxious to travel far that very night, if only Nest was capable of performing the journey. As he was thus employed, he tried to conjecture what his father's feelings would be on finding that his once-loved son was gone away for ever. Would he then awaken to regret for the conduct which had driven him from home, and bitterly think on the loving and caressing boy who haunted his footsteps in former days? Or, alas! would he only feel that an obstacle to his daily happiness – to his contentment with his wife, and his strange, doting affection for the child – was taken away? Would they make merry over the heir's departure? Then he thought of Nest – the young childless mother, whose heart had not yet realised her fulness of desolation. Poor Nest! so loving as she was, so devoted to her child – how should he console her? He pictured her away in a strange land, pining for her native mountains, and refusing to be comforted because her child was not.

Even this thought of the homesickness that might possibly beset Nest hardly made him hesitate in his determination; so strongly had the idea taken possession of him, that only by putting miles and leagues between him and his father could he avert the doom which seemed blending itself with the very purposes of his life, as long as he stayed in proximity with the slayer of his child.

He had now nearly completed his hasty work of preparation, and was full of tender thoughts of his wife, when the door opened, and the elfish Robert peered in, in search of some of his brother's possessions. On seeing Owen he hesitated, but then came boldly forward, and laid his hand on Owen's arm, saying: '*Nesta yr buten!* How is Nest *yr buten?*'

He looked maliciously into Owen's face to mark the effect of his words, but was terrified at the expression he read there. He started off and ran to the door, while Owen tried to check himself, saying continually, 'He is but a child. He does not understand the meaning of what he says. He is but a child!' Still Robert, now in fancied security, kept calling out his insulting words, and Owen's hand was on his gun, grasping it as if to restrain his rising fury.

But, when Robert passed on daringly to mocking words relating to the poor dead child, Owen could bear it no longer; and, before the boy was well aware, Owen was fiercely holding him in an iron clasp with one hand, while he struck him hard with the other.

In a minute he checked himself. He paused, relaxed his grasp, and, to his horror, he saw Robert sink to the ground; in fact, the lad was half-stunned, half-frightened, and thought it best to assume insensibility.

Owen – miserable Owen – seeing him lie there prostrate, was bitterly repentant, and would have dragged him to the carved settle, and done all he could to restore him to his senses; but at this instant the Squire came in.

Probably, when the household at Bodowen rose that morning, there was but one among them ignorant of the heir's relation to Nest Pritchard and her child; for, secret as he tried to make his visits to Ty Glas, they had been too frequent not to be noticed, and Nest's altered conduct – no longer frequenting dances and merry-makings – was a strongly corroborative circumstance. But Mrs Griffiths's influence reigned paramount, if unacknowledged, at Bodowen; and, till she sanctioned the disclosure, none would dare to tell the Squire.

Now, however, the time drew near when it suited her to make her husband aware of the connection his son had formed; so, with many tears, and much seeming reluctance, she broke the intelligence to him – taking good care, at the same time, to inform him of the light character Nest had borne. Nor did she confine this evil reputation to her conduct before her marriage, but insinuated that even to this day she was a 'woman of the grove and brake' – for centuries the Welsh term of opprobrium for the loosest female characters.

Squire Griffiths easily tracked Owen to Ty Glas; and, without any aim but the gratification of his furious anger, followed him to upbraid him as we have seen. But he left the cottage even more enraged against his son than he had entered it, and returned home to hear the evil suggestions of the stepmother. He had heard a slight scuffle in which he caught the tones of Robert's voice, as he passed along the hall, and an instant afterwards he saw the apparently lifeless body of his little favourite dragged along by the culprit Owen – the marks of strong passion yet visible on his face. Not loud, but bitter and deep, were the evil words which the father bestowed on the son; and, as Owen stood proudly and sullenly silent, disdaining all exculpation of himself in the presence of one who had wrought him so much graver – so fatal – an injury, Robert's mother entered the room. At sight of her natural emotion the wrath of the Squire was redoubled, and his wild suspicions that this violence of Owen's to Robert was a premeditated act appeared like the proven truth through the mists of rage. He summoned domestics, as if to guard his own and his wife's life from the attempts of his son; and the servants stood wondering around – now gazing at Mrs Griffiths, alternately scolding and sobbing, while she tried to restore the lad from his really bruised and half-unconscious state; now at the fierce and angry Squire; and now at the sad and silent Owen. And he – he was hardly aware of their looks of wonder and terror; his father's words fell on a deadened ear; for before his eyes there rose a pale dead babe, and in that lady's violent sounds of grief he heard the wailing of a more sad, more hopeless mother. For by this time the lad Robert had opened his eyes, and, though evidently suffering a good deal from the effects of Owen's blows, was fully conscious of all that was passing around him.

Had Owen been left to his own nature, his heart would have worked itself to love doubly the boy whom he had injured; but he was stubborn from injustice, and hardened by suffering. He refused to vindicate himself; he made no effort to resist the imprisonment the Squire had decreed, until a surgeon's opinion of the real extent of Robert's injuries was made known. It was not until the door was locked and barred, as if upon some wild and furious beast, that the recollection of poor Nest, without his comforting presence, came into his mind. Oh! thought he, how she would be wearying, pining for his tender sympathy; if, indeed, she had recovered from the shock of mind sufficiently to be sensible of consolation! What would she think of his absence? Could she imagine he believed his father's words, and had left her in this her sore trouble and bereavement? The thought maddened him, and he looked around for some mode of escape.

He had been confined in a small unfurnished room on the first floor, wainscoted, and carved all round, with a massy door, calculated to resist the attempts of a dozen strong men, even had he afterward been able to escape from the house unseen, unheard. The window was placed (as is common in old Welsh houses) over the fireplace;[72] with branching chimneys on either hand, forming a sort of projection on the outside. By this outlet his escape was easy, even had he been less determined and desperate than he was. And when he had descended, with a little care, a little winding, he might elude all observation and pursue his original intention of going to Ty Glas.

The storm had abated, and watery sunbeams were gilding the bay, as Owen descended from the window, and, stealing along in the broad afternoon shadows, made his way to the little plateau of green turf in the garden at the top of a steep precipitous rock, down the abrupt face of which he had often dropped, by means of a well-secured rope, into the small sailing-boat (his father's present, alas! in days gone by) which lay moored in the deep sea-water below. He had always kept his boat there, because it was the nearest available spot to the house; but before he could reach the place – unless, indeed, he crossed a broad sun-lighted piece of ground in full view of the windows on that side of the house, and without the shadow of a single sheltering tree or shrub – he had to skirt round a rude semicircle of underwood, which would have been considered as a shrubbery, had anyone taken pains with it. Step by step he stealthily moved along – hearing voices now; again seeing his father and step-mother in no distant walk, the Squire evidently caressing and consoling his wife, who seemed to be urging some point with great vehemence; again forced to crouch down to avoid being seen by the cook, returning from the rude kitchen-garden with a handful of herbs. This was the way the doomed heir of Bodowen left his ancestral house for ever, and hoped to leave behind him his doom. At length he reached the plateau – he breathed more freely. He stooped to discover the hidden coil of rope, kept safe and dry in a hole under a great round flat piece of rock; his head was bent down; he did not see his father approach, nor did he hear his footstep for the rush of blood to his head in the stooping effort of lifting the stone. The Squire had grappled with him before he rose up again, before he fully knew whose hands detained him, now, when his liberty of person and action seemed secure. He made a vigorous struggle to free himself; he wrestled with his father for a moment – he pushed him hard, and drove him on to the great displaced stone, all unsteady in its balance.

Down went the Squire, down into the deep waters below – down after him went Owen, half consciously, half unconsciously; partly compelled by the sudden cessation of any opposing body, partly from a vehement irrepressible impulse to rescue his father. But he had instinctively chosen a safer place in the deep sea-water pool than that into which his push had sent his father. The Squire had hit his head with much violence against the side of the boat, in his fall; it is, indeed, doubtful whether he was not killed before ever he sank into the sea. But Owen knew nothing save that the awful doom seemed even now present. He plunged down; he dived below the water in search of the body, which had none of the elasticity of life to buoy it up; he saw his father in those depths; he clutched at him; he brought him up and cast him, a dead weight, into the boat; and, exhausted by the effort, he had begun himself to sink again before he instinctively strove to rise and climb into the rocking boat. There lay his father, with a deep dent in the side of his head where the skull had been fractured by his fall; his face blackened by the arrested course of the blood. Owen felt his pulse, his heart – all was still. He called him by his name.

'Father, father!' he cried, 'come back! come back! You never knew how I loved you! how I could love you still – if – Oh, God!'

And the thought of his little child rose before him. 'Yes, father,' he cried afresh, 'you never knew how he fell – how he died! Oh, if I had but had patience to tell you! If you would but have borne with me and listened! And now it is over! Oh, father! father!'

Whether she had heard this wild wailing voice, or whether it was only that she missed her husband and wanted him for some little everyday question, or, as was perhaps more likely, she had discovered Owen's escape, and come to inform her husband of it, I do not know – but on the rock, right above his head, as it seemed, Owen heard his stepmother calling her husband.

He was silent, and softly pushed the boat right under the rock till the sides grated against the stones; and the overhanging branches concealed him and it from all on a level with the water. Wet as he was, he lay down by his dead father, the better to conceal himself; and, somehow, the action recalled those early days of childhood – the first in the Squire's widowhood – when Owen had shared his father's bed, and used to waken him in the morning in order to hear one of the old Welsh legends. How long he lay thus – body chilled, and brain hard-working through the heavy pressure of a reality as terrible as a nightmare – he never knew; but at length he roused himself up to think of Nest.

Drawing out a great sail, he covered up the body of his father with it where he lay in the bottom of the boat. Then with his numbed hands he took the oars, and pulled out into the more open sea toward Criccaeth. He skirted along the coast till he found a shadowed cleft in the dark rocks; to that point he rowed, and anchored his boat close inland. Then he mounted, staggering, half longing to fall into the dark waters and be at rest – half instinctively finding out the surest footrests on that precipitous face of rock, till he was high up, safe landed on the turfy summit. He ran off, as if pursued, towards Penmorfa; he ran with maddened energy. Suddenly he paused, turned, ran again with the same speed, and threw himself prone on the summit, looking down into his boat with straining eyes to see if there had been any movement of life – any displacement of a fold of sailcloth. It was all quiet deep down below, but as he gazed the shifting light gave the appearance of a slight movement. Owen ran to a lower part of the rock, stripped, plunged into the water, and swam to the boat. When there, all was still – awfully still! For a minute or two, he dared not lift up the cloth. Then, reflecting that the same terror might beset him again – of leaving his father unaided while yet a spark of life lingered – he removed the shrouding cover. The eyes looked into his with a dead stare! He closed the lids and bound up the jaw. Again he looked. This time, he raised himself out of the water and kissed the brow.

'It was my doom, father! It would have been better if I had died at my birth!'

Daylight was fading away. Precious daylight! He swam back, dressed, and set off afresh for Penmorfa. When he opened the door of Ty Glas, Ellis Pritchard looked at him reproachfully from his seat in the darkly-shadowed chimney-corner.

'You're come at last,' said he. 'One of our kind' (*i.e.*, station) 'would not have left his wife to mourn by herself over her dead child; nor would one of our kind have let his father kill his own true son. I've a good mind to take her from you for ever.'

'I did not tell him,' cried Nest, looking piteously at her husband; 'he made me tell him part, and guessed the rest.'

She was nursing her babe on her knee as if it was alive. Owen stood before Ellis Pritchard.

'Be silent,' said he quietly. 'Neither words nor deeds but what are decreed can come to pass. I was set to do my work, this hundred years and more. The time waited for me, and the man waited for me. I have done what was foretold of me for generations!'

Ellis Pritchard knew the old tale of the prophecy, and believed in it in a dull, dead kind of way, but somehow never thought it would come to pass in his time. Now, however, he understood it all in a moment, though he mistook Owen's nature so much as to believe that the deed was intentionally done, out of revenge for the death of his boy; and, viewing it in this light, Ellis thought it little more than a just punishment for the cause of all the wild despairing sorrow he had seen his only child suffer during the hours of this long afternoon. But he knew the law[73] would not so regard it. Even the lax Welsh law of those days could not fail to examine into the death of a man of Squire Griffiths's standing. So the acute Ellis thought how he could conceal the culprit for a time.

'Come,' said he; 'don't look so scared! It was your doom, not your fault'; and he laid a hand on Owen's shoulder.

'You're wet,' said he suddenly. 'Where have you been? Nest, your husband is dripping, drookit[74] wet. That's what makes him look so blue and wan.'

Nest softly laid her baby in its cradle; she was half stupefied with crying, and had not understood to what Owen alluded, when he spoke of his doom being fulfilled, if indeed she had heard the words.

Her touch thawed Owen's miserable heart.

'Oh, Nest!' said he, clasping her in his arms; 'do you love me still – can you love me, my own darling?'

'Why not?' asked she, her eyes filling with tears. 'I only love you more than ever, for you were my poor baby's father!'

'But, Nest – Oh, tell her, Ellis! *you* know.'

'No need, no need!' said Ellis. 'She's had enough to think on. Bustle, my girl, and get out my Sunday clothes.'

'I don't understand,' said Nest, putting her hand up to her head. 'What is to tell? and why are you so wet? God help me for a poor crazed thing; for I cannot guess at the meaning of your words and your strange looks! I only know my baby is dead!' and she burst into tears.

'Come, Nest! go and fetch him a change, quick!' and, as she meekly obeyed, too languid to strive further to understand, Ellis said rapidly to Owen, in a low, hurried voice: 'Are you meaning that the Squire is dead? Speak low, lest she hear? Well, well, no need to talk about how he died. It was sudden, I see; and we must all of us die; and he'll have to be buried. It's well the night is near. And I should not wonder now if you'd like to travel for a bit; it would do Nest a power of good; and then – there's many a one goes out of his own house and never comes back again; and – I trust he's not lying in his own house – and there's a stir for a bit, and a search, and a wonder – and, by and by, the heir just steps in, as quiet as can be. And that's what you'll do, and bring Nest to Bodowen after all. Nay, child, better stockings nor those; find the blue woollens I bought at Llanrwst fair. Only don't lose heart. It's done now and can't be helped. It was the piece of work set you to do from the days of the Tudors, they say. And he deserved it. Look in yon cradle. So tell us where he is, and I'll take heart of grace and see what can be done for him.'

But Owen sat wet and haggard, looking into the peat fire as if for visions of the past, and never heeding a word Ellis said. Nor did he move when Nest brought the armful of dry clothes.

'Come, rouse up, man!' said Ellis, growing impatient.

But he neither spoke nor moved.

'What is the matter, father?' asked Nest, bewildered.

Ellis kept on watching Owen for a minute or two, till on his daughter's repetition of the question, he said: 'Ask him yourself, Nest.'

'Oh, husband, what is it?' said she, kneeling down and bringing her face to a level with his.

'Don't you know?' said he heavily. 'You won't love me when you do know. And yet it was not my doing: it was my doom.'

'What does he mean, father?' asked Nest, looking up; but she caught a gesture from Ellis urging her to go on questioning her husband.

'I will love you, husband, whatever has happened. Only let me know the worst.'

A pause, during which Nest and Ellis hung breathless.

'My father is dead, Nest.'

Nest caught her breath with a sharp gasp.

'God forgive him!' said she, thinking on her babe.

'God forgive *me*!' said Owen.

'You did not – ' Nest stopped.

'Yes, I did. Now you know it. It was my doom. How could I help it? The devil helped me – he placed the stone so that my father fell. I jumped into the water to save him. I did, indeed, Nest. I was nearly drowned myself. But he was dead – dead – killed by the fall!'

'Then he is safe at the bottom of the sea?' said Ellis, with hungry eagerness.

'No, he is not; he lies in my boat,' said Owen, shivering a little, more at the thought of his last glimpse at his father's face than from cold.

'Oh, husband, change your wet clothes!' pleaded Nest, to whom the death of the old man was simply a horror with which she had nothing to do, while her husband's discomfort was a present trouble.

While she helped him to take off the wet garments which he would never have had energy enough to remove of himself, Ellis was busy preparing food, and mixing a great tumbler of spirits and hot water. He stood over the unfortunate young man and compelled him to eat and drink, and made Nest, too, taste some mouthfuls – all the while planning in his own mind how best to conceal what had been done, and who had done it; not altogether without a certain feeling of vulgar triumph in the reflection that Nest, as she stood there, carelessly dressed, dishevelled in her grief, was in reality the mistress of Bodowen, than which Ellis Pritchard had never seen a grander house, though he believed such might exist.

By dint of a few dexterous questions he found out all he wanted to know from Owen, as he ate and drank. In fact, it was almost a relief to Owen to dilute the horror by talking about it. Before the meal was done, if meal it could be called, Ellis knew all he cared to know.

'Now, Nest, on with your cloak and haps. Pack up what needs to go with you, for both you and your husband must be halfway to Liverpool by tomorrow's morn. I'll take you past Rhyl Sands in my fishing-boat, with yours in tow; and, once over the dangerous part, I'll return with my cargo of fish, and learn how much stir there is at Bodowen. Once safe hidden in Liverpool, no one will know where you are, and you may stay quiet till your time comes for returning.'

'I will never come home again,' said Owen doggedly. 'The place is accursed!'

'Hoot! be guided by me, man. Why, it was but an accident, after all! And we'll land at the Holy Island, at the Point of Llyn; there is an old cousin of mine, the parson, there – for the Pritchards have known better days, Squire – and we'll bury him there. It was but an accident, man. Hold up your head! You and Nest will come home yet and fill Bodowen with children, and I'll live to see it.'

'Never!' said Owen. 'I am the last male of my race, and the son has murdered his father!'

Nest came in laden and cloaked. Ellis was for hurrying them off. The fire was extinguished, the door was locked.

'Here, Nest, my darling, let me take your bundle while I guide you down the steps.' But her husband bent his head, and spoke never a word. Nest gave her father the bundle (already loaded with such things as he himself had seen fit to take), but clasped another softly and tightly.

'No one shall help me with this,' said she, in a low voice.

Her father did not understand her; her husband did, and placed his strong helping arm round her waist, and blessed her.

'We will all go together, Nest,' said he. 'But where?' and he looked up at the storm-tossed clouds coming up from windward.

'It is a dirty night,' said Ellis, turning his head round to speak to his companions at last. 'But never fear, we'll weather it.' And he made for the place where his vessel was moored. Then he stopped and thought a moment.

'Stay here!' said he, addressing his companions. 'I may meet folk, and I shall, maybe, have to hear and to speak. You wait here till I come back for you.' So they sat down close together in a corner of the path.

'Let me look at him, Nest!' said Owen.

She took her little dead son out from under her shawl; they looked at his waxen face long and tenderly; kissed it, and covered it up reverently and softly.

'Nest,' said Owen, at last, 'I feel as though my father's spirit had been near us, and as if it had bent over our poor little one. A strange, chilly air met me as I stooped over him. I could fancy the spirit of our pure, blameless child guiding my father's safe over the paths of the sky to the gates of heaven, and escaping those accursed dogs of hell that were darting up from the north in pursuit of souls not five minutes since.'

'Don't talk so, Owen,' said Nest, curling up to him in the darkness of the copse. 'Who knows what may be listening?'

The pair were silent, in a kind of nameless terror, till they heard Ellis Pritchard's loud whisper. 'Where are ye? Come along, soft and steady. There were folk about even now, and the Squire is missed, and madam in a fright.'

They went swiftly down to the little harbour, and embarked on board Ellis's boat. The sea heaved and rocked even there; the torn clouds went hurrying overhead in a wild tumultuous manner.

They put out into the bay; still in silence, except when some word of command was spoken by Ellis, who took the management of the vessel. They made for the rocky shore, where Owen's boat had been moored. It was not there. It had broken loose and disappeared.

Owen sat down and covered his face. This last event, so simple and natural in itself, struck on his excited and superstitious mind in an extraordinary manner. He had hoped for a certain reconciliation, so to say, by laying his father and his child both in one grave. But now it appeared to him as if there was to be no forgiveness; as if his father revolted even in death against any such peaceful union. Ellis took a practical view of the case. If the Squire's body was found drifting about in a boat known to belong to his son, it would create terrible suspicion as to the manner of his death. At one time in the evening, Ellis had thought of persuading Owen to let him bury the Squire in a sailor's grave; or, in other words, to sew him up in a spare sail, and, weighting it well, sink it for ever. He had not broached the subject, from a certain fear of Owen's passionate repugnance to the plan; otherwise, if he had consented, they might have returned to Penmorfa, and passively awaited the course of events, secure of Owen's succession to Bodowen, sooner or later; or, if Owen was too much overwhelmed by what had happened, Ellis would have advised him to go away for a short time, and return when the buzz and the talk was over.

Now it was different. It was absolutely necessary that they should leave the country for a time. Through those stormy waters they must plough their way that very night. Ellis had no fear – would have had no fear, at any rate, with Owen as he had been a week, a day ago; but with Owen wild, despairing, helpless, fate-pursued, what could he do?

They sailed into the tossing darkness, and were never more seen of men.

The house of Bodowen has sunk into damp, dark ruins; and a Saxon stranger holds the lands of the Griffiths.

You cannot think how kindly Mrs Dawson thanked Miss Duncan for writing and reading this story. She shook my poor, pale governess so tenderly by the hand that the tears came into her eyes, and the colour into her cheeks.

'I thought you had been so kind; I liked hearing about Lady Ludlow; I fancied, perhaps, I could do something to give a little pleasure,' were the half-finished sentences Miss Duncan stammered out. I am sure it was the wish to earn similar kind words from Mrs Dawson, that made Mrs Preston try and rummage through her memory to see if she could not recollect some fact, or event, or history, which might interest Mrs Dawson and the little party that gathered round her sofa. Mrs Preston it was who told us the following tale – 'Half a Lifetime ago'.

LOIS THE WITCH

Chapter 1

In the year 1691, Lois Barclay stood on a little wooden pier, steadying herself on the stable land, in much the same manner as, eight or nine weeks ago, she had tried to steady herself on the deck of the rocking ship which had carried her across from Old to New England. It seemed as strange now to be on solid earth as it had been, not long ago, to be rocked by the sea both by day and by night; and the aspect of the land was equally strange. The forests which showed in the distance all around, and which, in truth, were not very far from the wooden houses forming the town of Boston, were of different shades of green, and different, too, in shape of outline to those which Lois Barclay knew well in her old home in Warwickshire. Her heart sank a little as she stood alone, waiting for the captain of the good ship *Redemption*, the kind, rough old sailor, who was her only known friend in this unknown continent. Captain Holdernesse was busy, however, as she saw, and it would probably be some time before he would be ready to attend to her; so Lois sat down on one of the casks that lay about, and wrapped her grey duffle cloak tight around her, and sheltered herself under her hood, as well as might be, from the piercing wind, which seemed to follow those whom it had tyrannised over at sea with a dogged wish of still tormenting them on land. Very patiently did Lois sit there, although she was weary, and shivering with cold; for the day was severe for May, and the *Redemption*, with store of necessaries and comforts for the Puritan colonists of New England, was the earliest ship that had ventured across the seas.

How could Lois help thinking of the past, and speculating on the future, as she sat on Boston pier, at this breathing-time of her life? In the dim sea mist which she gazed upon with aching eyes (filled, against her will, with tears, from time to time), there rose the little village church of Barford[75] (not three miles from Warwick – you may see it yet), where her father[76] had preached ever since 1661, long before she was born. He and her mother both lay dead in Barford churchyard; and the old low grey church could hardly come before her vision without her seeing the old parsonage too, the cottage covered with Austrian roses and yellow jessamine, where she had been born, sole child of parents already long past the prime of youth. She saw the path, not a hundred yards long, from the parsonage to the vestry door: that path which her father trod daily; for the vestry was his study, and the sanctum where he pored over the ponderous tomes of the Fathers,[77] and compared their precepts with those of the authorities of the Anglican Church of that day – the day of the later Stuarts; for Barford Parsonage, at that time, scarcely exceeded in size and dignity the cottages by which it was surrounded: it only contained three rooms on a floor, and was but two storeys high. On the first or ground-floor, were the parlour, kitchen, and back- or working-kitchen; upstairs, Mr and Mrs Barclay's room, that belonging to Lois, and the maidservant's room. If a guest came, Lois left her own chamber, and shared old Clemence's bed. But those days were over. Never more should Lois see father or mother on earth; they slept, calm and still, in Barford churchyard, careless of what became of their orphan child, as far as earthly manifestations of care or love went. And Clemence lay there too, bound down in her grassy bed by withes of the briar-rose, which Lois had trained over those three precious graves before leaving England for ever.

There were some who would fain have kept her there; one who swore in his heart a great oath unto the Lord that he would seek her, sooner or later, if she was still upon the earth. But he was the rich heir and only son of the Miller Lucy, whose mill stood by the Avon side in the grassy Barford meadows; and his father looked higher for him than the penniless daughter of Parson Barclay (so low were clergymen esteemed in those days!); and the very suspicion of Hugh Lucy's attachment to Lois Barclay made his parents think it more prudent not to offer the orphan a home, although none other of the parishioners had the means, even if they had the will, to do so.

So Lois swallowed her tears down till the time came for crying, and acted upon her mother's words: 'Lois, thy father is dead of this terrible fever, and I am dying. Nay, it is so; though I am easier from pain for these few hours, the Lord be praised! The cruel men of the Commonwealth have left thee very friendless. Thy father's only brother was shot down at Edgehill.[78] I, too, have a brother, though thou hast never heard me speak of him, for he was a schismatic;[79] and thy father and me had words, and he left for that new country beyond the seas, without ever saying farewell to us. But Ralph was a kind lad until he took up these new-fangled notions; and for the old days' sake he will take thee in, and love thee as a child, and place thee among his children. Blood is thicker than water. Write to him as soon as I am gone – for, Lois, I am going; and I bless the Lord that has letten me join my husband again so soon.' Such was the selfishness of conjugal love; she thought little of Lois's desolation in comparison with her rejoicing over her speedy reunion with her dead husband! 'Write to thine uncle, Ralph Hickson, Salem, New England (put it down, child, on thy tablets), and say that I, Henrietta Barclay, charge him, for the sake of all he holds dear in heaven or on earth – for his salvation's sake, as well as for the sake of the old home at Lester Bridge – for the sake of the father and mother that gave us birth, as well as for the sake of the six little children who lie dead between him and me – that he take thee into his home as if thou wert his own flesh and blood, as indeed thou art. He has a wife and children of his own, and no one need fear having thee, my Lois, my darling, my baby, among his household. O Lois, would that thou wert dying with me! The thought of thee makes death sore!' Lois comforted her mother more than herself, poor child, by promises to obey her dying wishes to the letter, and by expressing hopes she dared not feel of her uncle's kindness.

'Promise me' – the dying woman's breath came harder and harder – 'that thou wilt go at once. The money our goods will bring – the letter thy father wrote to Captain Holdernesse, his old schoolfellow – thou knowest all I would say – my Lois, God bless thee!'

Solemnly did Lois promise; strictly she kept her word. It was all the more easy, for Hugh Lucy met her, and told her, in one great burst of love, of his passionate attachment, his vehement struggles with his father, his impotence at present, his hopes and resolves for the future. And, intermingled with all this, came such outrageous threats and expressions of uncontrolled vehemence, that Lois felt that in Barford she must not linger to be a cause of desperate quarrel between father and son, while her absence might soften down matters, so that either the rich old miller might relent, or – and her heart ached to think of the other possibility – Hugh's love might cool, and the dear playfellow of her childhood learn to forget. If not – if Hugh were to be trusted in one tithe of what he said – God might permit him to fulfil his resolve of coming to seek her out, before many years were over. It was all in God's hands; and that was best, thought Lois Barclay.

She was aroused out of her trance of recollections by Captain Holdernesse, who, having done all that was necessary in the way of orders and directions to his mate, now came up to her, and, praising her for her quiet patience, told her that he would now take her to the Widow Smith's, a decent kind of house, where he and many other sailors of the better order were in the habit of lodging during their stay on the New England shores. Widow Smith, he said, had a parlour for herself and her daughters, in which Lois might sit, while he went about the business that, as he had told her, would detain him in Boston for a day or two, before he could accompany her to her uncle's at Salem. All this had been to a certain degree arranged on shipboard; but Captain Holdernesse, for want of anything else that he could think of to talk about, recapitulated it, as he and Lois walked along. It was his way of showing sympathy with the emotion that made her grey eyes full of tears, as she started up from the pier at the sound of his voice. In his heart he said, 'Poor wench! poor wench! it's a strange land to her, and they are all strange folks, and, I reckon, she will be feeling desolate. I'll try and cheer her up.' So he talked on about hard facts, connected with the life that lay before her, until they reached Widow Smith's; and perhaps Lois was more brightened by this style of conversation, and the new ideas it presented to her, than she would have been by the tenderest woman's sympathy.

'They are a queer set, these New Englanders,' said Captain Holdernesse. 'They are rare chaps for praying; down on their knees at every turn of their life. Folk are none so busy in a new country, else they would have to pray like me, with a "Yo-hoy!" on each side of my prayer, and a rope cutting like fire through my hand. Yon pilot was for calling us all to thanksgiving for a good voyage, and lucky escape from the pirates; but I said I always put up my thanks on dry land, after I had got my ship into harbour. The French colonists, too, are vowing vengeance for the expedition against Canada, and the people here are raging like heathens – at least, as like as godly folk can be – for the loss of their charter.[80] All that is the news the pilot told me; for, for all he wanted us to be thanksgiving instead of casting the lead, he was as down in the mouth as could be about the state of the country. But here we are at Widow Smith's! Now, cheer up, and show the godly a pretty smiling Warwickshire lass!'

Anybody would have smiled at Widow Smith's greeting. She was a comely, motherly woman, dressed in the primmest fashion in vogue twenty years before in England, among the class to which she belonged. But, somehow, her pleasant face gave the lie to her dress; were it as brown and sober-coloured as could be, folk remembered it bright and cheerful, because it was a part of Widow Smith herself.

She kissed Lois on both cheeks, before she rightly understood who the stranger maiden was, only because she was a stranger and looked sad and forlorn; and then she kissed her again, because Captain Holdernesse commended her to the widow's good offices. And so she led Lois by the hand into her rough, substantial log-house, over the door of which hung a great bough of a tree, by way of sign of entertainment for man and horse. Yet not all men were received by Widow Smith. To some she could be as cold and reserved as need be, deaf to all enquiries save one – where else they could find accommodation? To this question she would give a ready answer, and speed the unwelcome guest on his way. Widow Smith was guided in these matters by instinct: one glance at a man's face told her whether or not she chose to have him as an inmate of the same house as her daughters; and her promptness of decision in these matters gave her manner a kind of authority which no one liked to disobey, especially as she had stalwart neighbours within call to back her, if her assumed deafness in the first instance, and her voice and gesture in the second, were not enough to give the would-be guest his dismissal. Widow Smith chose her customers merely by their physical aspect; not one whit with regard to their apparent worldly circumstances. Those who had been staying at her house once always came again; for she had the knack of making everyone beneath her roof comfortable and at his ease. Her daughters, Prudence and Hester, had somewhat of their mother's gifts, but not in such perfection. They reasoned a little upon a stranger's appearance, instead of knowing at the first moment whether they liked him or no; they noticed the indications of his clothes, the quality and cut thereof, as telling somewhat of his station in society; they were more reserved; they hesitated more than their mother; they had not her prompt authority, her happy power. Their bread was not so light; their cream went sometimes to sleep, when it should have been turning into butter; their hams were not always 'just like the hams of the old country'; as their mother's were invariably pronounced to be – yet they were good, orderly, kindly girls, and rose and greeted Lois with a friendly shake of the hand, as their mother, with her arm round the stranger's waist, led her into the private room which she called her parlour. The aspect of this room was strange in the English girl's eyes. The logs of which the house was built showed here and there through the mud-plaster, although before both plaster and logs were hung the skins of many curious animals – skins presented to the widow by many a trader of her acquaintance, just as her sailor-guests brought her another description of gifts – shells, strings of wampum-beads,[81] sea-birds' eggs, and presents from the old country. The room was more like a small museum of natural history of these days than a parlour; and it had a strange, peculiar, but not unpleasant smell about it, neutralised in some degree by the smoke from the enormous trunk of pine wood which smouldered on the hearth.

The instant their mother told them that Captain Holdernesse was in the outer room, the girls began putting away their spinning-wheel and knitting needles, and preparing for a meal of some kind; what meal, Lois, sitting there and unconsciously watching, could hardly tell. First, dough was set to rise for cakes; then came out of a corner-cupboard – a present from England – an enormous square bottle of a cordial called Gold-Wasser;[82] next, a mill for grinding chocolate – a rare, unusual treat anywhere at that time; then a great Cheshire cheese. Three venison-steaks were cut ready for broiling, fat cold pork sliced up and treacle poured over it; a great pie, something like a mince-pie, but which the daughters spoke of with honour as the 'punken-pie',[83] fresh and salt-fish brandered,[84] oysters cooked in various ways. Lois wondered where would be the end of the provisions for hospitably receiving the strangers from the old country. At length everything was placed on the table, the hot food smoking; but all was cool, not to say cold, before Elder[85] Hawkins (an old neighbour of much repute and standing, who had been invited in by Widow Smith to hear the news) had finished his grace, into which was embodied thanksgiving for the past, and prayers for the future, lives of every individual present, adapted to their several cases, as far as the elder could guess at them from appearances. This grace might not have ended so soon as it did, had it not been for the somewhat impatient drumming of his knife-handle on the table, with which Captain Holdernesse accompanied the latter half of the elder's words.

When they first sat down to their meal, all were too hungry for much talking; but, as their appetites diminished, their curiosity increased, and there was much to be told and heard on both sides. With all the English intelligence Lois was, of course, well acquainted; but she listened with natural attention to all that was said about the new country, and the new people among whom she had come to live. Her father had been a Jacobite, as the adherents of the Stuarts were beginning at this time to be called. His father, again, had been a follower of Archbishop Laud;[86] so Lois had hitherto heard little of the conversation, and seen little of the ways of the Puritans. Elder Hawkins was one of the strictest of the strict, and evidently his presence kept the two daughters of the house considerably in awe.

But the widow herself was a privileged person; her known goodness of heart (the effects of which had been experienced by many) gave her the liberty of speech which was tacitly denied to many, under penalty of being esteemed ungodly, if they infringed certain conventional limits. And Captain Holdernesse and his mate spoke out their minds, let who would be present. So that, on this first landing in New England, Lois was, as it were, gently let down into the midst of the Puritan peculiarities; and yet they were sufficient to make her feel very lonely and strange.

The first subject of conversation was the present state of the colony – Lois soon found out that, although at the beginning she was not a little perplexed by the frequent reference to names of places which she naturally associated with the old country. Widow Smith was speaking: 'In county of Essex the folk are ordered to keep four scouts, or companies of minute-men;[87] six persons in each company; to be on the look-out for the wild Indians, who are for ever stirring about in the woods, stealthy brutes as they are! I am sure, I got such a fright the first harvest-time after I came over to New England, I go on dreaming, now near twenty years after Lothrop's business,[88] of painted Indians, with their shaven scalps and their war-streaks, lurking behind the trees, and coming nearer and nearer with their noiseless steps.'

'Yes,' broke in one of her daughters; 'and, mother, don't you remember how Hannah Benson told us how her husband had cut down every tree near his house at Deerbrook, in order that no one might come near him, under cover; and how one evening she was a-sitting in the twilight, when all her family were gone to bed, and her husband gone off to Plymouth on business, and she saw a log of wood, just like a trunk of a felled tree, lying in the shadow, and thought nothing of it, till, on looking again a while after, she fancied it was come a bit nearer to the house; and how her heart turned sick with fright; and how she dared not stir at first, but shut her eyes while she counted a hundred, and looked again, and the shadow was deeper, but she could see that the log was nearer; so she ran in and bolted the door, and went up to where her eldest lad lay. It was Elijah, and he was but sixteen then; but he rose up at his mother's words, and took his father's long duck-gun down; and he tried the loading, and spoke for the first time to put up a prayer that God would give his aim good guidance, and went to a window that gave a view upon the side where the log lay, and fired; and no one dared to look what came of it; but all the household read the Scriptures, and prayed the whole night long; till morning came and showed a long stream of blood lying on the grass close by the log – which the full sunlight showed to be no log at all, but just a Red Indian covered with bark, and painted most skilfully, with his war-knife by his side.'

All were breathless with listening; though to most the story, or others like it, were familiar. Then another took up the tale of horror: 'And the pirates[89] have been down at Marblehead, since you were here, Captain Holdernesse. 'Twas only the last winter they landed – French Papist pirates; and the people kept close within their houses, for they knew not what would come of it; and they dragged folk ashore. There was one woman among those folk – prisoners from some vessel, doubtless – and the pirates took them by force to the inland marsh; and the Marblehead folk kept still and quiet, every gun loaded, and every ear on the watch, for who knew but what the wild sea-robbers might take a turn on land next; and, in the dead of the night, they heard a woman's loud and pitiful outcry from the marsh, "Lord Jesu! have mercy on me! Save me from the power of man, O Lord Jesu!" And the blood of all who heard the cry ran cold with terror; till old Nance Hickson, who had been stone-deaf and bedridden for years, stood up in the midst of the folk all gathered together in her grandson's house, and said, that, as they, the dwellers in Marblehead, had not had brave hearts or faith enough to go and succour the helpless, that cry of a dying woman should be in their ears, and in their children's ears, till the end of the world. And Nance dropped down dead as soon as she had made an end of speaking, and the pirates set sail from Marblehead at morning dawn; but the folk there hear the cry still, shrill and pitiful, from the waste marshes, "Lord Jesu! have mercy on me! Save me from the power of man, O Lord Jesu!" '

'And, by token,'[90] said Elder Hawkins's deep bass voice, speaking with the strong nasal twang of the Puritans (who, says Butler, 'Blasphemed custard through the nose')[91] 'godly Mr Noyes ordained a fast at Marblehead, and preached a soul-stirring discourse on the words, "Inasmuch as ye did it not unto one of the least of these, my brethen, ye did it not unto me."[92] But it has been borne in upon me at times, whether the whole vision of the pirates and the cry of the woman was not a device of Satan's to sift the Marblehead folk, and see what fruit their doctrine bore, and so to condemn them in the sight of the Lord. If it were so, the enemy had a great triumph; for assuredly it was no part of Christian men to leave a helpless woman unaided in her sore distress.'

'But, Elder,' said Widow Smith, 'it was no vision; they were real living men who went ashore, men who broke down branches and left their footmarks on the ground.'

'As for that matter, Satan hath many powers, and, if it be the day when he is permitted to go about like a roaring lion,[93] he will not stick at trifles, but make his work complete. I tell you, many men are spiritual enemies in visible forms, permitted to roam about the waste places[94] of the earth. I myself believe that these Red Indians are indeed the evil creatures of whom we read in Holy Scripture; and there is no doubt that they are in league with those abominable Papists, the French people in Canada. I have heard tell, that the French pay the Indians so much gold for every dozen scalps of Englishmen's heads.'

'Pretty cheerful talk this!' said Captain Holdernesse to Lois, perceiving her blanched cheek and terror-stricken mien. 'Thou art thinking that thou hadst better have stayed at Barford, I'll answer for it, wench. But the devil is not so black as he is painted.'

'Ho! there again!' said Elder Hawkins. 'The devil is painted, it hath been said so from old times; and are not these Indians painted, even like unto their father?'

'But is it all true?' asked Lois, aside, of Captain Holdernesse, letting the Elder hold forth unheeded by her, though listened to with the utmost reverence by the two daughters of the house.

'My wench,' said the old sailor, 'thou hast come to a country where there are many perils, both from land and from sea. The Indians hate the white men. Whether other white men' (meaning the French away to the north) 'have hounded-on the savages, or whether the English have taken their lands and hunting-grounds without due recompense, and so raised the cruel vengeance of the wild creatures – who knows? But it is true that it is not safe to go far into the woods, for fear of the lurking painted savages; nor has it been safe to build a dwelling far from a settlement; and it takes a brave heart to make a journey from one town to another; and folk do say the Indian creatures rise up out of the very ground to waylay the English! and then others affirm they are all in league with Satan to affright the Christians out of the heathen country, over which he has reigned so long. Then, again, the seashore is infested by pirates, the scum of all nations: they land, and plunder, and ravage, and burn, and destroy. Folk get affrighted of the real dangers, and in their fright imagine, perchance, dangers that are not. But who knows? Holy Scripture speaks of witches and wizards, and of the power of the Evil One in desert places; and, even in the old country, we have heard tell of those who have sold their souls for ever for the little power they get for a few years on earth.'

By this time the whole table was silent, listening to the captain; it was just one of those chance silences that sometimes occur, without any apparent reason, and often without any apparent consequence. But all present had reason, before many months had passed over, to remember the words which Lois spoke in answer, although her voice was low, and she only thought, in the interest of the moment, of being heard by her old friend the captain.

'They are fearful creatures, the witches! and yet I am sorry for the poor old women, whilst I dread them. We had one in Barford, when I was a little child. No one knew whence she came, but she settled herself down in a mud-hut by the common-side; and there she lived, she and her cat.'[95] (At the mention of the cat, Elder Hawkins shook his head long and gloomily.) 'No one knew how she lived, if it were not on nettles and scraps of oatmeal and suchlike food, given her more for fear than for pity. She went double, and always talking and muttering to herself. Folk said she snared birds and rabbits in the thicket that came down to her hovel. How it came to pass I cannot say, but many a one fell sick in the village, and much cattle died one spring, when I was near four years old. I never heard much about it, for my father said it was ill talking about such things; I only know I got a sick fright one afternoon, when the maid had gone out for milk and had taken me with her, and we were passing a meadow where the Avon, circling, makes a deep round pool, and there was a crowd of folk, all still – and a still, breathless crowd makes the heart beat worse than a shouting, noisy one. They were all gazing towards the water, and the maid held me up in her arms, to see the sight above the shoulders of the people; and I saw old Hannah in the water, her grey hair all streaming down her shoulders, and her face bloody and black with the stones and mud they had been throwing at her, and her cat tied round her neck.[96] I hid my face, I know, as soon as I saw the fearsome sight, for her eyes met mine as they were glaring with fury – poor, helpless, baited creature! – and she caught the sight of me, and cried out, "Parson's wench, parson's wench, yonder, in thy nurse's arms, thy dad hath never tried for to save me; and none shall save thee, when thou art brought up for a witch." Oh! the words rang in my ears, when I was dropping asleep, for years after. I used to dream that I was in that pond; that all men hated me with their eyes because I was a witch: and, at times, her black cat used to seem living again, and say over those dreadful words.'

Lois stopped: the two daughters looked at her excitement with a kind of shrinking surprise, for the tears were in her eyes. Elder Hawkins shook his head, and muttered texts from Scripture; but cheerful Widow Smith, not liking the gloomy turn of the conversation, tried to give it a lighter cast by saying, 'And I don't doubt but what the parson's bonny lass has bewitched many a one since, with her dimples and her pleasant ways – eh, Captain Holdernesse? It's you must tell us tales of the young lass's doings in England.'

'Ay, ay,' said the captain; 'there's one under her charms in Warwickshire who will never get the better of it, I'm thinking.'

Elder Hawkins rose to speak; he stood leaning on his hands, which were placed on the table: 'Brethren,' said he, 'I must upbraid you if ye speak lightly; charms and witchcraft are evil things; I trust this maiden hath had nothing to do with them, even in thought. But my mind misgives me at her story. The hellish witch might have power from Satan to infect her mind, she being yet a child, with the deadly sin. Instead of vain talking, I call upon you all to join with me in prayer for this stranger in our land, that her heart may be purged from all iniquity. Let us pray.'

'Come, there's no harm in that,' said the captain; 'but, Elder Hawkins, when you are at work, just pray for us all; for I am afeared there be some of us need purging from iniquity a good deal more than Lois Barclay, and a prayer for a man never does mischief.'

Captain Holdernesse had business in Boston which detained him there for a couple of days; and during that time Lois remained with the Widow Smith, seeing what was to be seen of the new land that contained her future home. The letter of her dying mother was sent off to Salem, meanwhile, by a lad going thither, in order to prepare her Uncle Ralph Hickson for his niece's coming, as soon as Captain Holdernesse could find leisure to take her; for he considered her given into his own personal charge, until he could consign her to her uncle's care. When the time came for going to Salem, Lois felt very sad at leaving the kindly woman under whose roof she had been staying, and looked back as long as she could see anything of Widow Smith's dwelling. She was packed into a rough kind of country-cart, which just held her and Captain Holdernesse, beside the driver. There was a basket of provisions under their feet, and behind them hung a bag of provender for the horse; for it was a good day's journey to Salem, and the road was reputed so dangerous that it was ill tarrying a minute longer than necessary for refreshment. English roads were bad enough at that period, and for long after; but in

America the way was simply the cleared ground of the forest – the stumps of the felled trees still remaining in the direct line, forming obstacles which it required the most careful driving to avoid; and in the hollows, where the ground was swampy, the pulpy nature of it was obviated by logs of wood laid across the boggy part. The deep green forest, tangled into heavy darkness even thus early in the year, came within a few yards of the road all the way, though efforts were regularly made by the inhabitants of the neighbouring settlements to keep a certain space clear on each side, for fear of the lurking Indians, who might otherwise come upon them unawares. The cries of strange birds, the unwonted colour of some of them, all suggested to the imaginative or unaccustomed traveller the idea of war-whoops and painted deadly enemies. But at last they drew near to Salem, which rivalled Boston in size in those days, and boasted the names of one or two streets, although to an English eye they looked rather more like irregularly built houses, clustered round the meeting-house, or rather one of the meeting-houses, for a second was in process of building. The whole place was surrounded with two circles of stockades; between the two were the gardens and grazing-ground for those who dreaded their cattle straying into the woods, and the consequent danger of reclaiming them.

The lad who drove them flogged his spent horse into a trot, as they went through Salem to Ralph Hickson's house. It was evening, the leisure-time for the inhabitants, and their children were at play before the houses. Lois was struck by the beauty of one wee, toddling child, and turned to look after it; it caught its little foot in a stump of wood, and fell with a cry that brought the mother out in affright. As she ran out, her eye caught Lois's anxious gaze, although the noise of the heavy wheels drowned the sound of her words of enquiry as to the nature of the hurt the child had received. Nor had Lois time to think long upon the matter; for, the instant after, the horse was pulled up at the door of a good, square, substantial wooden house, plastered over into a creamy white, perhaps as handsome a house as any in Salem; and there she was told by the driver that her uncle, Ralph Hickson, lived. In the flurry of the moment she did not notice, but Captain Holdernesse did, that no one came out at the unwonted sound of wheels, to receive and welcome her. She was lifted down by the old sailor, and led into a large room, almost like the hall of some English manor-house as to size. A tall, gaunt young man of three- or four-and-twenty sat on a bench by one of the windows, reading a great folio by the fading light of day. He did not rise when they came in, but looked at them with surprise, no gleam of intelligence coming into his stern, dark face. There was no woman in the house-place. Captain Holdernesse paused a moment, and then said: 'Is this house Ralph Hickson's?'

'It is,' said the young man, in a slow, deep voice. But he added no word further.

'This is his niece, Lois Barclay,' said the captain, taking the girl's arm, and pushing her forwards. The young man looked at her steadily and gravely for a minute; then rose, and carefully marking the page in the folio, which hitherto had laid open upon his knee, said, still in the same heavy, indifferent manner, 'I will call my mother; she will know.'

He opened a door which looked into a warm bright kitchen, ruddy with the light of the fire, over which three women were apparently engaged in cooking something, while a fourth, an old Indian woman, of a greenish-brown colour, shrivelled-up and bent with apparent age, moved backwards and forwards, evidently fetching the others the articles they required.

'Mother!' said the young man; and, having arrested her attention, he pointed over his shoulder to the newly-arrived strangers and returned to the study of his book, from time to time, however, furtively examining Lois from beneath his dark shaggy eyebrows.

A tall, largely-made woman, past middle life, came in from the kitchen, and stood reconnoitring the strangers.

Captain Holdernesse spoke: 'This is Lois Barclay, master Ralph Hickson's niece.'

'I know nothing of her,' said the mistress of the house in a deep voice, almost as masculine as her son's.

'Master Hickson received his sister's letter, did he not? I sent it off myself by a lad named Elias Wellcome, who left Boston for this place yester morning.'

'Ralph Hickson has received no such letter. He lies bedridden in the chamber beyond. Any letters for him must come through my hands; wherefore I can affirm with certainty that no such letter has been delivered here. His sister Barclay, she that was Henrietta Hickson, and whose husband took the oaths to Charles Stuart, and stuck by his living[97] when all godly men left theirs – '

Lois, who had thought her heart was dead and cold, a minute before, at the ungracious reception she had met with, felt words come up into her mouth at the implied insult to her father, and spoke out, to her own and the captain's astonishment: 'They might be godly men who left their churches on that day of which you speak, madam; but they alone were not the godly men, and no one has a right to limit true godliness for mere opinion's sake.'

'Well said, lass,' spoke out the captain, looking round upon her with a kind of admiring wonder, and patting her on the back.

Lois and her aunt gazed into each other's eyes unflinchingly, for a minute or two of silence; but the girl felt her colour coming and going, while the elder woman's never varied; and the eyes of the young maiden were filling fast with tears, while those of Grace Hickson kept on their stare, dry and unwavering.

'Mother,' said the young man, rising up with a quicker motion than anyone had yet used in this house, 'it is ill speaking of such matters when my cousin comes first among us. The Lord may give her grace hereafter; but she has travelled from Boston city today, and she and this seafaring man must need rest and food.'

He did not attend to see the effect of his words, but sat down again, and seemed to be absorbed in his book in an instant. Perhaps he knew that his word was law with his grim mother; for he had hardly ceased speaking before she had pointed to a wooden settle; and, smoothing the lines on her countenance, she said: 'What Manasseh says is true. Sit down here, while I bid Faith and Nattee get food ready; and meanwhile I will go tell my husband that one who calls herself his sister's child is come over to pay him a visit.'

She went to the door leading into the kitchen, and gave some directions to the elder girl, whom Lois now knew to be the daughter of the house. Faith stood impassive, while her mother spoke, scarcely caring to look at the newly-arrived strangers. She was like her brother Manasseh in complexion, but had handsomer features, and large, mysterious-looking eyes, as Lois saw, when once she lifted them up, and took in, as it were, the aspect of the sea-captain and her cousin with one swift, searching look. About the stiff, tall, angular mother, and the scarce less pliant figure of the daughter, a girl of twelve years old, or thereabouts, played all manner of impish antics, unheeded by them, as if it were her accustomed habit to peep about, now under their arms, now at this side, now at that, making grimaces all the while at Lois and Captain Holdernesse, who sat facing the door, weary, and somewhat disheartened by their reception. The captain pulled out tobacco, and began to chew it by way of consolation; but in a moment or two his usual elasticity of spirit came to his rescue, and he said in a low voice to Lois: 'That scoundrel Elias, I will give it him! If the letter had but been delivered, thou wouldst have had a different kind of welcome; but, as soon as I have had some victuals, I will go out and find the lad, and bring back the letter, and that will make all right, my wench. Nay, don't be downhearted, for I cannot stand women's tears. Thou'rt just worn-out with the shaking and the want of food.'

Lois brushed away her tears, and, looking round to try and divert her thoughts by fixing them on present objects, she caught her cousin Manasseh's deep-set eyes furtively watching her. It was with no unfriendly gaze; yet it made Lois uncomfortable, particularly as he did not withdraw his looks, after he must have seen that she observed him. She was glad when her aunt called her into an inner room to see her uncle, and she escaped from the steady observance of her gloomy, silent cousin.

Ralph Hickson was much older than his wife, and his illness made him look older still. He had never had the force of character that Grace, his spouse, possessed; and age and sickness had now rendered him almost childish at times. But his nature was affectionate; and, stretching out his trembling arms from where he lay bedridden, he gave Lois an unhesitating welcome, never waiting for the confirmation of the missing letter before he acknowledged her to be his niece.

'Oh! 'tis kind in thee to come all across the sea to make acquaintance with thine uncle; kind in sister Barclay to spare thee!'

Lois had to tell him, there was no one living to miss her at home in England; that, in fact, she had no home in England, no father nor mother left upon earth; and that she had been bidden by her mother's last words to seek him out and ask him for a home. Her words came up, half-choked from a heavy heart, and his dulled wits could not take in their meaning without several repetitions; and then he cried like a child, rather at his own loss of a sister whom he had not seen for more than twenty years, than at that of the orphan's, standing before him, trying hard not to cry, but to start bravely in this new strange home. What most of all helped Lois in her self-restraint was her aunt's unsympathetic look. Born and bred in New England, Grace Hickson had a kind of jealous dislike to her husband's English relations, which had increased since of late years his weakened mind yearned after them; and he forgot the good reason he had had for his self-exile, and moaned over the decision which had led to it as the great mistake of his life. 'Come,' said she; 'it strikes me that, in all this sorrow for the loss of one who died full of years, ye are forgetting in Whose hands life and death are!'

True words, but ill-spoken at that time. Lois looked up at her with a scarcely disguised indignation; which increased as she heard the contemptuous tone in which her aunt went on talking to Ralph Hickson, even while she was arranging his bed with a regard to his greater comfort.

'One would think thou wert a godless man, by the moan thou art always making over spilt milk; and truth is, thou art but childish in thine old age. When we were wed, thou left all things to the Lord; I would never have married thee else. Nay, lass,' said she, catching the expression on Lois's face, 'thou art never going to browbeat me with thine angry looks. I do my duty as I read it, and there is never a man in Salem that dare speak a word to Grace Hickson about either her works or her faith. Godly Mr Cotton Mather[98] hath said, that even he might learn of me; and I would advise thee rather to humble thyself, and see if the Lord may not convert thee from thy ways, since He has sent thee to dwell, as it were, in Zion,[99] where the precious dew falls daily on Aaron's beard.'[100]

Lois felt ashamed and sorry to find that her aunt had so truly interpreted the momentary expression of her features; she blamed herself a little for the feeling that had caused that expression, trying to think how much her aunt might have been troubled with something, before the unexpected irruption of the strangers, and again hoping that the remembrance of this misunderstanding would soon pass away. So she endeavoured to reassure herself, and not to give way to her uncle's tender trembling pressure of her hand, as, at her aunt's bidding, she wished him 'good-night', and returned into the outer, or keeping-room,[101] where all the family were now assembled, ready for the meal of flour-cakes and venison-steaks which Nattee, the Indian servant, was bringing in from the kitchen. No one seemed to have been speaking to Captain Holdernesse, while Lois had been away. Manasseh sat quiet and silent where he did, with the book open upon his knee; his eyes thoughtfully fixed on vacancy, as if he saw a vision, or dreamed dreams.[102] Faith stood by the table, lazily directing Nattee in her preparations; and Prudence lolled against the door frame, between kitchen and keeping-room, playing tricks on the old Indian woman, as she passed backwards and forwards, till Nattee appeared to be in a state of strong irritation, which she tried in vain to suppress; as, whenever she showed any sign of it, Prudence only seemed excited to greater mischief. When all was ready, Manasseh lifted his right hand and 'asked a blessing', as it was termed; but the grace became a long prayer for abstract spiritual blessings, for strength to combat Satan, and to quench his fiery darts, and at length assumed – so Lois thought – a purely personal character, as if the young man had forgotten the occasion, and even the people present, but was searching into the nature of the diseases that beset his own sick soul, and spreading them out before the Lord. He was brought back by a pluck at the coat from Prudence; he opened his shut eyes, cast an angry glance at the child, who made a face at him for sole reply, and then he sat down, and they all fell to. Grace Hickson would have thought her hospitality sadly at fault, if she had allowed Captain Holdernesse to go out in search of a bed. Skins were spread for him on the floor of the keeping-room; a Bible and a square bottle of spirits were placed on the table to supply his wants during the night; and, in spite of all the cares and troubles, temptations, or sins of the members of that household, they were all asleep before the town clock struck ten.

In the morning, the captain's first care was to go out in search of the boy Elias and the missing letter. He met him bringing it with an easy conscience, for, thought Elias, a few hours sooner or later will make no difference; tonight or the morrow morning will be all the same. But he was startled into a sense of wrong-doing, by a sound box on the ear from the very man who had charged him to deliver it speedily, and whom he believed to be at that very moment in Boston city.

The letter delivered, all possible proof being given that Lois had a right to claim a home from her nearest relations, Captain Holdernesse thought it best to take leave.

'Thou'lt take to them, lass, maybe, when there is no one here to make thee think on the old country. Nay, nay! parting is hard work at all times, and best get hard work done out of hand! Keep up thine heart, my wench, and I'll come back and see thee next spring, if we are all spared till then; and who knows what fine young miller mayn't come with me? Don't go and get wed to a praying Puritan, meanwhile! There, there; I'm off. God bless thee!'

And Lois was left alone in New England.

Chapter 2

It was hard up-hill work for Lois to win herself a place in this family. Her aunt was a woman of narrow, strong affections. Her love for her husband, if ever she had any, was burnt out and dead long ago. What she did for him, she did from duty; but duty was not strong enough to restrain that little member, the tongue; and Lois's heart often bled at the continual flow of contemptuous reproof which Grace constantly addressed to her husband, even while she was sparing no pains or trouble to minister to his bodily ease and comfort. It was more as a relief to herself that she spoke in this way, than with any desire that her speeches should affect him; and he was too deadened by illness to feel hurt by them; or, it may be, the constant repetition of her sarcasms had made him indifferent; at any rate, so that he had his food and his state of bodily warmth attended to, he very seldom seemed to care much for anything else. Even his first flow of affection towards Lois was soon exhausted; he cared for her, because she arranged his pillows well and skilfully, and because she could prepare new and dainty kinds of food for his sick appetite, but no longer for her as his dead sister's child. Still he did care for her, and Lois was too glad of his little hoard of affection to examine how or why it was given. To him she could give pleasure, but apparently to no one else in that household. Her aunt looked askance at her for many reasons: the first coming of Lois to Salem was inopportune; the expression of disapprobation on her face on that evening still lingered and rankled in Grace's memory; early prejudices, and feelings, and prepossessions of the English girl were all on the side of what would now be called Church and State,[103] what was then esteemed in that country a superstitious observance of the directions of a Popish rubric,[104] and a servile regard for the family of an oppressing and irreligious king. Nor is it to be supposed that Lois did not feel, and feel acutely, the want of sympathy that all those with whom she was now living manifested towards the old hereditary loyalty (religious as well as political loyalty) in which she had been brought up. With her aunt and Manasseh it was more than want of sympathy; it was positive, active antipathy to all the ideas Lois held most dear. The very allusion, however incidentally made, to the little old grey church at Barford, where her father had preached so long –

the occasional reference to the troubles in which her own country had been distracted when she left – and the adherence, in which she had been brought up, to the notion that the king could do no wrong,[105] seemed to irritate Manasseh past endurance. He would get up from his reading, his constant employment when at home, and walk angrily about the room after Lois had said anything of this kind, muttering to himself; and once he had even stopped before her, and in a passionate tone bade her not talk so like a fool. Now this was very different to his mother's sarcastic, contemptuous way of treating all poor Lois's little loyal speeches. Grace would lead her on – at least she did at first, till experience made Lois wiser – to express her thoughts on such subjects, till, just when the girl's heart was opening, her aunt would turn round upon her with some bitter sneer that roused all the evil feelings in Lois's disposition by its sting. Now Manasseh seemed, through all his anger, to be so really grieved by what he considered her error, that he went much nearer to convincing her that there might be two sides to a question. Only this was a view that it appeared like treachery to her dead father's memory to entertain.

Somehow, Lois felt instinctively that Manasseh was really friendly towards her. He was little in the house; there was farming, and some kind of mercantile business to be transacted by him, as real head of the house; and, as the season drew on, he went shooting and hunting in the surrounding forests, with a daring which caused his mother to warn and reprove him in private, although to the neighbours she boasted largely of her son's courage and disregard of danger. Lois did not often walk out for the mere sake of walking; there was generally some household errand to be transacted when any of the women of the family went abroad; but once or twice she had caught glimpses of the dreary, dark wood, hemming in the cleared land on all sides – the great wood with its perpetual movement of branch and bough, and its solemn wail, that came into the very streets of Salem when certain winds blew, bearing the sound of the pine trees clear upon the ears that had leisure to listen. And, from all accounts, this old forest, girdling round the settlement, was full of dreaded and mysterious beasts, and still more to be dreaded Indians, stealing in and out among the shadows, intent on bloody schemes against the Christian people: panther-streaked, shaven Indians, in league by their own confession, as well as by the popular belief, with evil powers.

Nattee, the old Indian servant, would occasionally make Lois's blood run cold, as she and Faith and Prudence listened to the wild stories she told them of the wizards of her race. It was often in the kitchen, in the darkening evening, while some cooking process was going on, that the old Indian crone, sitting on her haunches by the bright red wood embers which sent up no flame, but a lurid light reversing the shadows of all the faces around, told her weird stories, while they were awaiting the rising of the dough, perchance, out of which the household bread had to be made. There ran through these stories always a ghastly, unexpressed suggestion of some human sacrifice being needed to complete the success of any incantation to the Evil One; and the poor old creature, herself believing and shuddering as she narrated her tale in broken English, took a strange, unconscious pleasure in her power over her hearers – young girls of the oppressing race, which had brought her down into a state little differing from slavery, and reduced her people to outcasts on the hunting-grounds which had belonged to her fathers.

After such tales, it required no small effort on Lois's part to go out, at her aunt's command, into the common pasture round the town, and bring the cattle home at night. Who knew but what the double-headed snake might start up from each blackberry tree – that wicked, cunning, accursed creature in the service of the Indian wizards, that had such power over all those white maidens who met the eyes placed at either end of his long, sinuous, creeping body, so that, loathe him, loathe the Indian race as they would, off they must go into the forest to seek out some Indian man, and must beg to be taken into his wigwam, adjuring faith and race for ever? Or there were spells – so Nattee said – hidden about the ground by the wizards, which changed that person's nature who found them; so that, gentle and loving as they might have been before, thereafter they took no pleasure but in the cruel torments of others, and had a strange power given to them of causing such torments at their will. Once, Nattee, speaking low to Lois, who was alone with her in the kitchen, whispered out her terrified belief that such a spell had Prudence found; and, when the Indian showed her arms to Lois, all pinched black and blue by the impish child, the English girl began to be afraid of her cousin as of one possessed. But it was not Nattee alone, nor young imaginative girls alone, that believed in these stories. We can afford to smile at them now; but our English ancestors entertained superstitions of much the same character at the same period, and with less excuse, as the circumstances surrounding them were better known, and consequently more explicable by common sense, than the real mysteries of the deep, untrodden forests of New England. The gravest divines not only believed stories similar to that of the double-headed serpent, and other tales of witchcraft, but they made such narrations the subjects of preaching and prayer; and, as cowardice makes us all cruel, men who were blameless in many of the relations of life, and even praiseworthy in some, became, from superstition, cruel persecutors about this time, showing no mercy towards anyone whom they believed to be in league with the Evil One.

Faith was the person with whom the English girl was the most intimately associated in her uncle's house. The two were about the same age, and certain household-employments were shared between them. They took it in turns to call in the cows, to make up the butter which had been churned by Hosea, a stiff, old out-door servant, in whom Grace Hickson placed great confidence; and each lassie had her great spinning-wheel for wool, and her lesser for flax, before a month had elapsed after Lois's coming. Faith was a grave, silent person, never merry, sometimes very sad, though Lois was a long time in even guessing why. She would try, in her sweet, simple fashion, to cheer her cousin up, when the latter was depressed, by telling her old stories of English ways and life. Occasionally, Faith seemed to care to listen; occasionally, she did not heed one word, but dreamed on. Whether of the past or of the future, who could tell?

Stern old ministers came in to pay their pastoral visits. On such occasions, Grace Hickson would put on clean apron and clean cap, and make them more welcome than she was ever seen to do anyone else, bringing out the best provisions of her store, and setting of all before them. Also, the great Bible was brought forth, and Hosea and Nattee summoned from their work, to listen while the minister read a chapter, and, as he read, expounded it at considerable length. After this all knelt, while he, standing, lifted up his right hand, and prayed for all possible combinations of Christian men, for all possible cases of spiritual need; and lastly, taking the individuals before him, he would put up a very personal supplication for each, according to his notion of their wants. At first, Lois wondered at the aptitude of one or two of his prayers of this description to the outward circumstances of each case; but, when she perceived that her aunt had usually a pretty long confidential conversation with the minister in the early part of his visit, she became aware that he received both his impressions and his knowledge through the medium of 'that godly woman, Grace Hickson'; and I am afraid she paid less regard to the prayer 'for the maiden from another land, who hath brought the errors of that land as a seed with her, even across the great ocean, and who is letting even now the little seeds shoot up into an evil tree, in which all unclean creatures may find shelter'.

'I like the prayers of our Church better,' said Lois one day to Faith. 'No clergyman in England can pray his own words; and therefore it is that he does not judge of others so as to fit his prayers to what he esteems to be their case, as Mr Tappau[106] did this morning.'

'I hate Mr Tappau!' said Faith shortly, a passionate flash of light coming out of her dark, heavy eyes.

'Why so, cousin? It seems to me as if he were a good man, although I like not his prayers.'

Faith only repeated her words, 'I hate him!'

Lois was sorry for this strong, bad feeling; instinctively sorry, for she was loving herself, delighted in being loved, and felt a jar run through her at every sign of want of love in others. But she did not know what to say, and was silent at the time. Faith, too, went on turning her wheel with vehemence, but spoke never a word until her thread snapped; and then she pushed the wheel away hastily, and left the room.

Then Prudence crept softly up to Lois's side. This strange child seemed to be tossed about by varying moods: today she was caressing and communicative; tomorrow she might be deceitful, mocking, and so indifferent to the pain or sorrows of others that you could call her almost inhuman.

'So thou dost not like Pastor Tappau's prayers?' she whispered.

Lois was sorry to have been overheard; but she neither would nor could take back her words.

'I like them not so well as the prayers I used to hear at home.'

'Mother says thy home was with the ungodly. Nay, don't look at me so – it was not I that said it. I'm none so fond of praying myself, nor of Pastor Tappau, for that matter. But Faith cannot abide him, and I know why. Shall I tell thee, Cousin Lois?'

'No! Faith did not tell me; and she was the right person to give her own reasons.'

'Ask her where young Mr Nolan[107] is gone to and thou wilt hear. I have seen Faith cry by the hour together about Mr Nolan.'

'Hush, child! hush!' said Lois, for she heard Faith's approaching step, and feared lest she should overhear what they were saying.

The truth was that, a year or two before, there had been a great struggle in Salem village, a great division in the religious body, and Pastor Tappau had been the leader of the more violent, and, ultimately, the successful party. In consequence of this, the less popular minister, Mr Nolan, had had to leave the place. And him Faith Hickson loved with all the strength of her passionate heart, although he never was aware of the attachment he had excited, and her own family were too regardless of manifestations of mere feeling ever to observe the signs of any emotion on her part. But the old Indian servant Nattee saw and observed them all. She knew, as well as if she had been told the reason, why Faith had lost all care about father or mother, brother and sister, about household work and daily occupation; nay, about the observances of religion as well. Nattee read the meaning of the deep smouldering of Faith's dislike to Pastor Tappau aright; the Indian woman understood why the girl (whom alone of all the white people she loved) avoided the old minister – would hide in the wood-stack, sooner than be called in to listen to his exhortations and prayers. With savage, untutored people, it is not 'Love me, love my dog'[108] – they are often jealous of the creature beloved; but it is, 'Whom thou hatest I will hate'; and Nattee's feeling towards Pastor Tappau was even an exaggeration of the mute, unspoken hatred of Faith.

For a long time, the cause of her cousin's dislike and avoidance of the minister was a mystery to Lois; but the name of Nolan remained in her memory, whether she would or no; and it was more from girlish interest in a suspected love affair, than from any indifferent and heartless curiosity, that she could not help piecing together little speeches and actions with Faith's interest in the absent banished minister, for an explanatory clue, till not a doubt remained in her mind. And this without any further communication with Prudence; for Lois declined hearing any more on the subject from her, and so gave deep offence.

Faith grew sadder and duller, as the autumn drew on. She lost her appetite; her brown complexion became sallow and colourless; her dark eyes looked hollow and wild. The first of November was near at hand. Lois, in her instinctive, well-intentioned efforts to bring some life and cheerfulness into the monotonous household, had been telling Faith of many English customs, silly enough, no doubt, and which scarcely lighted up a flicker of interest in the American girl's mind. The cousins were lying awake in their bed, in the great unplastered room, which was in part store-room, in part bedroom. Lois was full of sympathy for Faith that night. For long she had listened to her cousin's heavy, irrepressible sighs, in silence. Faith sighed, because her grief was of too old a date for violent emotion or crying. Lois listened without speaking in the dark, quiet night hours, for a long, long time. She kept quite still, because she thought such vent for sorrow might relieve her cousin's weary heart. But, when at length, instead of lying motionless, Faith seemed to be growing restless, even to convulsive motions of her limbs, Lois began to speak, to talk about England, and the dear old ways at home, without exciting much attention on Faith's part; until at length she fell upon the subject of Hallow-e'en,[109] and told about customs then and long afterwards practised in England, and that have scarcely yet died out in Scotland. As she told of tricks she had often played, of the apple eaten facing a mirror, of the dripping sheet, of the basins of water, of the nuts burning side by side, and many other such innocent ways of divination, by which laughing, trembling English maidens sought to see the form of their future husbands, if husbands they were to have: then Faith listened breathlessly, asking short eager questions, as if some ray of hope had entered into her gloomy heart. Lois went on speaking, telling her of all the stories that would confirm the truth of the second sight[110] vouchsafed to all seekers in the accustomed methods; half-believing, half-incredulous herself, but desiring, above all things, to cheer up poor Faith.

Suddenly, Prudence rose up from her truckle-bed in the dim corner of the room. They had not thought that she was awake; but she had been listening long.

'Cousin Lois may go out and meet Satan by the brookside, if she will; but, if thou goest, Faith, I will tell mother – ay, and I will tell Pastor Tappau, too. Hold thy stories, Cousin Lois; I am afeared of my very life. I would rather never be wed at all, than feel the touch of the creature that would take the apple out of my hand, as I held it over my left shoulder.' The excited girl gave a loud scream of terror at the image her fancy had conjured up. Faith and Lois sprang out towards her, flying across the moonlit room in their white night-gowns. At the same instant, summoned by the same cry, Grace Hickson came to her child.

'Hush! hush!' said Faith, authoritatively.

'What is it, my wench?' asked Grace. While Lois, feeling as if she had done all the mischief, kept silence.

'Take her away, take her away!' screamed Prudence. 'Look over her shoulder – her left shoulder – the Evil One is there now, I see him stretching over for the half-bitten apple.'

'What is it she says?' said Grace austerely.

'She is dreaming,' said Faith; 'Prudence, hold thy tongue.' And she pinched the child severely, while Lois more tenderly tried to soothe

the alarms she felt that she had conjured up.

'Be quiet, Prudence,' said she, 'and go to sleep! I will stay by thee, till thou hast gone off into slumber.'

'No, no! go away!' sobbed Prudence, who was really terrified at first, but was now assuming more alarm than she felt, from the pleasure she received at perceiving herself the centre of attention. 'Faith shall stay by me, not you, wicked English witch!'

So Faith sat by her sister; and Grace, displeased and perplexed, withdrew to her own bed, purposing to enquire more into the matter in the morning. Lois only hoped it might all be forgotten by that time, and resolved never to talk again of such things. But an event happened in the remaining hours of the night to change the current of affairs. While Grace had been absent from her room, her husband had had another paralytic stroke: whether he, too, had been alarmed by that eldritch[111] scream no one could ever know. By the faint light of the rush-candle burning at the bedside, his wife perceived that a great change had taken place in his aspect on her return: the irregular breathing came almost like snorts – the end was drawing near. The family were roused, and all help given that either the doctor or experience could suggest. But before the late November morning-light, all was ended for Ralph Hickson.

The whole of the ensuing day, they sat or moved in darkened rooms, and spoke few words, and those below their breath. Manasseh kept at home, regretting his father, no doubt, but showing little emotion. Faith was the child that bewailed her loss most grievously; she had a warm heart, hidden away somewhere under her moody exterior, and her father had shown her far more passive kindness than ever her mother had done; for Grace made distinct favourites of Manasseh, her only son, and Prudence, her youngest child. Lois was about as unhappy as any of them; for she had felt strongly drawn towards her uncle as her kindest friend, and the sense of his loss renewed the old sorrow she had experienced at her own parent's death. But she had no time and no place to cry in. On her devolved many of the cares which it would have seemed indecorous in the nearer relatives to interest themselves in enough to take an active part: the change required in their dress, the household preparations for the sad feast of the funeral – Lois had to arrange all under her aunt's stern direction.

But, a day or two afterwards – the last day before the funeral – she went into the yard to fetch in some faggots for the oven; it was a solemn, beautiful, starlit evening, and some sudden sense of desolation in the midst of the vast universe thus revealed touched Lois's heart, and she sat down behind the wood-stack, and cried very plentiful tears.

She was startled by Manasseh, who suddenly turned the corner of the stack, and stood before her.

'Lois crying!'

'Only a little,' she said, rising up, and gathering her bundle of faggots; for she dreaded being questioned by her grim, impassive cousin. To her surprise, he laid his hand on her arm, and said: 'Stop one minute. Why art thou crying, cousin?'

'I don't know,' she said, just like a child questioned in like manner; and she was again on the point of weeping.

'My father was very kind to thee, Lois; I do not wonder that thou grievest after him. But the Lord who taketh away can restore tenfold. I will be as kind as my father – yea, kinder. This is not a time to talk of marriage and giving in marriage. But after we have buried our dead, I wish to speak to thee.'

Lois did not cry now; but she shrank with affright. What did her cousin mean? She would far rather that he had been angry with her for unreasonable grieving, for folly.

She avoided him carefully – as carefully as she could, without seeming to dread him – for the next few days. Sometimes, she thought it must have been a bad dream; for, if there had been no English lover in the case, no other man in the whole world, she could never have thought of Manasseh as her husband; indeed, till now, there had been nothing in his words or actions to suggest such an idea. Now it had been suggested, there was no telling how much she loathed him. He might be good, and pious – he doubtless was – but his dark, fixed eyes, moving so slowly and heavily, his lank, black hair, his grey, coarse skin, all made her dislike him now – all his personal ugliness and ungainliness struck on her senses with a jar, since those few words spoken behind the haystack.

She knew that, sooner or later, the time must come for further discussion of this subject; but, like a coward, she tried to put it off by clinging to her aunt's apron-string, for she was sure that Grace Hickson had far different views for her only son. As, indeed, she had; for she was an ambitious, as well as a religious, woman; and, by an early purchase of land in Salem village, the Hicksons had become wealthy people, without any great exertions of their own – partly, also, by the silent process of accumulation; for they had never cared to change their manner of living, from the time when it had been suitable to a far smaller income than that which they at present enjoyed. So much for worldly circumstances. As for their worldly character, it stood as high. No one could say a word against any of their habits or actions. Their righteousness and godliness were patent to everyone's eyes. So Grace Hickson thought herself entitled to pick and choose among the maidens, before she should meet with one fitted to be Manasseh's wife. None in Salem came up to her imaginary standard. She had it in her mind even at this very time, so soon after her husband's death, to go to Boston, and take counsel with the leading ministers there, with worthy Mr Cotton Mather at their head, and see if they could tell her of a well-favoured and godly young maiden in their congregations worthy of being the wife of her son. But, besides good looks and godliness, the wench must have good birth and good wealth, or Grace Hickson would have put her contemptuously on one side. When once this paragon was found, and the ministers had approved, Grace anticipated no difficulty on her son's part. So Lois was right in feeling that her aunt would dislike any speech of marriage between Manasseh and herself.

But the girl was brought to bay one day, in this wise. Manasseh had ridden forth on some business, which everyone said would occupy him the whole day; but, meeting the man with whom he had to transact his affairs, he returned earlier than anyone expected. He missed Lois from the keeping-room, where his sisters were spinning, almost immediately. His mother sat by at her knitting; he could see Nattee in the kitchen through the open door. He was too reserved to ask where Lois was; but he quietly sought till he found her, in the great loft, already piled with winter stores of fruit and vegetables. Her aunt had sent her there to examine the apples one by one, and pick out such as were unsound for immediate use. She was stooping down, and intent upon this work, and was hardly aware of his approach, until she lifted up her head and saw him standing close before her. She dropped the apple she was holding, went a little paler than her wont, and faced him in silence.

'Lois,' he said, 'thou rememberest the words that I spoke while we yet mourned over my father. I think that I am called to marriage now, as the head of this household. And I have seen no maiden so pleasant in my sight as thou art, Lois!' He tried to take her hand. But she put it behind her with a childish shake of her head, and, half-crying, said: 'Please, Cousin Manasseh, do not say this to me! I dare say you ought to be married, being the head of the household now; but I don't want to be married. I would rather not.'

'That is well spoken,' replied he; frowning a little, nevertheless. 'I should not like to take to wife an over-forward maiden, ready to jump at wedlock. Besides, the congregation might talk, if we were to be married too soon after my father's death. We have, perchance, said enough, even now. But I wished thee to have thy mind set at ease as to thy future well-doing. Thou wilt have leisure to think of it, and to bring thy mind more fully round to it.' Again he held out his hand. This time she took hold of it with a free, frank gesture.

'I owe you somewhat for your kindness to me ever since I came, Cousin Manasseh; and I have no way of paying you but by telling you truly I can love you as a dear friend, if you will let me, but never as a wife.'

He flung her hand away, but did not take his eyes off her face, though his glance was lowering and gloomy. He muttered something which she did not quite hear; and so she went on bravely, although she kept trembling a little, and had much ado to keep from crying.

'Please, let me tell you all! There was a young man in Barford – nay, Manasseh, I cannot speak if you are so angry; it is hard work to tell you anyhow – he said that he wanted to marry me; but I was poor, and his father would have none of it; and I do not want to marry anyone; but, if I did, it would be' – Her voice dropped, and her blushes told the rest. Manasseh stood looking at her with sullen, hollow eyes, that had a gathering touch of wildness in them; and then he said: 'It is borne in[112] upon me – verily, I see it as in a vision – that thou must be my spouse, and no other man's. Thou canst not escape what is fore-doomed. Months ago, when I set myself to read the old godly books in which my soul used to delight until thy coming; I saw no letter of printer's ink marked on the page, but I saw a gold and ruddy type of some unknown language, the meaning whereof was whispered into my soul; it was, "Marry Lois! marry Lois!" And, when my father died, I knew it was the beginning of the end. It is the Lord's will, Lois, and thou canst not escape from it.' And again he would have taken her hand, and drawn her towards him. But this time she eluded him with ready movement.

'I do not acknowledge it to be the Lord's will, Manasseh,' said she. 'It is not "borne in upon me", as you Puritans call it, that I am to be your wife. I am none so set upon wedlock as to take you, even though there be no other chance for me. For I do not care for you as I ought to care for my husband. But I could have cared for you very much as a cousin – as a kind cousin.'

She stopped speaking; she could not choose the right words with which to speak to him of her gratitude and friendliness, which yet could never be any feeling nearer and dearer, no more than two parallel lines can ever meet.

But he was so convinced by what he considered the spirit of prophecy, that Lois was to be his wife, that he felt rather more indignant at what he considered to be her resistance to the pre-ordained decree, than really anxious as to the result. Again he tried to convince her that neither he nor she had any choice in the matter, by saying: 'The voice said unto me "Marry Lois"; and I said, "I will, Lord." '

'But,' Lois replied, 'the voice, as you call it, has never spoken such a word to me.'

'Lois,' he answered solemnly, 'it will speak. And then wilt thou obey, even as Samuel[113] did?'

'No; indeed I cannot!' she answered briskly. 'I may take a dream to be the truth, and hear my own fancies, if I think about them too long. But I cannot marry anyone from obedience.'

'Lois, Lois, thou art as yet unregenerate; but I have seen thee in a vision as one of the elect,[114] robed in white. As yet thy faith is too weak for thee to obey meekly; but it shall not always be so. I will pray that thou mayest see thy preordained course. Meanwhile, I will smooth away all worldly obstacles.'

'Cousin Manasseh! Cousin Manasseh!' cried Lois after him, as he was leaving the room, 'come back! I cannot put it in strong enough words. Manasseh, there is no power in heaven or earth that can make me love thee enough to marry thee, or to wed thee without such love. And this I say solemnly, because it is better that this should end at once.'

For a moment he was staggered; then he lifted up his hands, and said: 'God forgive thee thy blasphemy! Remember Hazael, who said, "Is thy servant a dog, that he should do this great thing?"[115] and went straight and did it, because his evil courses were fixed and appointed for him from before the foundation of the world. And shall not thy paths be laid out among the godly, as it hath been foretold to me?'

He went away; and for a minute or two Lois felt as if his words must come true, and that, struggle as she would, hate her doom as she would, she must become his wife; and, under the circumstances, many a girl would have succumbed to her apparent fate. Isolated from all previous connections, hearing no word from England, living in the heavy, monotonous routine of a family with one man for head, and this man esteemed a hero by most of those around him, simply because he was the only man in the family – these facts alone would have formed strong presumptions that most girls would have yielded to the offers of such a one. But, besides this, there was much to tell upon the imagination in those days, in that place and time. It was prevalently believed that there were manifestations of spiritual influence – of the direct influence both of good and bad spirits – constantly to be perceived in the course of men's lives. Lots were drawn,[116] as guidance from the Lord; the Bible was opened, and the leaves allowed to fall apart; and the first text the eye fell upon was supposed to be appointed from above as a direction. Sounds were heard that could not be accounted for; they were made by the evil spirits not yet banished from the desert-places of which they had so long held possession. Sights, inexplicable and mysterious, were dimly seen – Satan, in some shape, seeking whom he might devour.[117] And, at the beginning of the long winter season, such whispered tales, such old temptations and hauntings, and devilish terrors, were supposed to be peculiarly rife. Salem was, as it were, snowed up, and left to prey upon itself. The long, dark evenings; the dimly-lighted rooms; the creaking passages, where heterogeneous articles were piled away, out of the reach of the keen-piercing frost, and where occasionally, in the dead of night, a sound was heard, as of some heavy falling body, when, next morning, everything appeared to be in its right place (so accustomed are we to measure noises by comparison with themselves, and not with the absolute stillness of the night-season); the white mist, coming nearer and nearer to the windows every evening in strange shapes, like phantoms – all these, and many other circumstances: such as the distant fall of mighty trees in the mysterious forests girdling them round; the faint whoop and cry of some Indian seeking his camp, and unwittingly nearer to the white men's settlement than either he or they would have liked, could they have chosen; the hungry yells of the wild beasts approaching the cattle-pens – these were the things which made that winter life in Salem, in the memorable time of 1691–2, seem strange, and haunted, and terrific to many; peculiarly weird and awful to the English girl, in her first year's sojourn in America.

And now, imagine Lois worked upon perpetually by Manasseh's conviction that it was decreed that she should be his wife, and you will see that she was not without courage and spirit to resist as she did, steadily, firmly, and yet sweetly. Take one instance out of many, when her nerves were subjected to a shock – slight in relation, it is true; but then remember that she had been all day, and for many days, shut up within doors, in a dull light that at midday was almost dark with a long-continued snowstorm. Evening was coming on, and the wood fire was more cheerful than any of the human beings surrounding it; the monotonous whirr of the smaller spinning-wheels had been going on all day, and the store of flax downstairs was nearly exhausted: when Grace Hickson bade Lois fetch down some more from the store-room, before the light so entirely waned away that it could not be found without a candle, and a candle it would be dangerous to carry into that apartment full of combustible materials, especially at this time of hard frost, when every drop of water was locked up and bound in icy hardness. So Lois went, half-shrinking from the long passage that led to the stairs leading up into the store-room; for it was in this passage that the strange night-sounds were heard, which everyone had begun to notice, and speak about in lowered tones. She sang, however, as she went, 'to keep her courage up', in a subdued voice, the evening hymn she had so often sung in Barford church – 'Glory to Thee, my God, this night';[118] and so it was, I suppose, that she never heard the breathing or motion of any creature near her, till, just as she was loading herself with flax to carry down, she heard someone – it was Manasseh – say close to her ear: 'Has the voice spoken yet? Speak, Lois! Has the voice spoken yet to thee – that speaketh to me day and night, "Marry Lois"?'

She started and turned a little sick, but spoke almost directly in a brave, clear manner: 'No, Cousin Manasseh! And it never will.'

'Then I must wait yet longer,' he replied hoarsely, as if to himself. 'But all submission – all submission.'

At last, a break came upon the monotony of the long, dark winter. The parishioners once more raised the discussion whether – the parish extending as it did – it was not absolutely necessary for Pastor Tappau to have help. This question had been mooted once before; and then Pastor Tappau had acquiesced in the necessity, and all had gone on smoothly for some months after the appointment of his assistant; until a feeling had sprung up on the part of the elder minister, which might have been called jealousy of the younger, if so godly a man as Pastor Tappau could have been supposed to entertain so evil a passion. However that might be, two parties were speedily formed; the younger and more ardent being in favour of Mr Nolan, the elder and more persistent – and, at the time, the more numerous – clinging to the old, grey-headed, dogmatic Mr Tappau, who had married them, baptised their children, and was to them, literally, as a 'pillar of the church'. So Mr Nolan left Salem, carrying away with him, possibly, more hearts than that of Faith Hickson's; but certainly she had never been the same creature since.

But now – Christmas, 1691 – one or two of the older members of the congregation being dead, and some who were younger men having come to settle in Salem – Mr Tappau being also older, and, some charitably supposed, wiser – a fresh effort had been made, and Mr Nolan was returning to labour in ground apparently smoothed over. Lois had taken a keen interest in all the proceedings for Faith's sake – far more than the latter did for herself, any spectator would have said. Faith's wheel never went faster or slower, her thread never broke, her colour never came, her eyes were never uplifted with sudden interest, all the time these discussions respecting Mr Nolan's return were going on. But Lois, after the hint given by Prudence, had found a clue to many a sigh and look of despairing sorrow, even without the help of Nattee's improvised songs, in which, under strange allegories, the helpless love of her favourite was told to ears heedless of all meaning, except those of the tender-hearted and sympathetic Lois. Occasionally, she heard a strange chant of the old Indian woman's – half in her own language, half in broken English – droned over some simmering pipkin,[119] from which the smell was, to say the least, unearthly. Once, on perceiving this odour in the keeping-room, Grace Hickson suddenly exclaimed: 'Nattee is at her heathen ways again; we shall have some mischief unless she is stayed.'

But Faith, moving quicker than ordinary, said something about putting a stop to it, and so forestalled her mother's evident intention of going into the kitchen. Faith shut the door between the two rooms, and entered upon some remonstrance with Nattee; but no one could hear the words used. Faith and Nattee seemed more bound together by love and common interest than any other two among the self-contained individuals comprising this household. Lois sometimes felt as if her presence, as a third, interrupted some confidential talk between her cousin and the old servant. And yet she was fond of Faith, and could almost think that Faith liked her more than she did either mother, brother, or sister; for the first two were indifferent as to any unspoken feelings, while Prudence delighted in discovering them, only to make an amusement to herself out of them.

One day, Lois was sitting by herself at her sewing-table, while

Faith and Nattee were holding one of their secret conclaves, from which Lois felt herself to be tacitly excluded: when the outer door opened, and a tall, pale young man, in the strict professional habit of a minister, entered. Lois sprang up with a smile and a look of welcome for Faith's sake; for this must be the Mr Nolan whose name had been on the tongue of everyone for days, and who was, as Lois knew, expected to arrive the day before.

He seemed half-surprised at the glad alacrity with which he was received by this stranger: possibly, he had not heard of the English girl who was an inmate in the house where formerly he had seen only grave, solemn, rigid, or heavy faces, and had been received with a stiff form of welcome, very different from the blushing, smiling, dimpled looks that innocently met him with the greeting almost of an old acquaintance. Lois, having placed a chair for him, hastened out to call Faith, never doubting but that the feeling which her cousin entertained for the young pastor was mutual, although it might be unrecognised in its full depth by either.

'Faith!' said she, bright and breathless. 'Guess – No,' checking herself to an assumed unconsciousness of any particular importance likely to be affixed to her words; 'Mr Nolan, the new pastor, is in the keeping-room. He has asked for my aunt and Manasseh. My aunt is gone to the prayer-meeting at Pastor Tappau's, and Manasseh is away.' Lois went on speaking, to give Faith time; for the girl had become deadly white at the intelligence, while, at the same time, her eyes met the keen, cunning eyes of the old Indian with a peculiar look of half-wondering awe; while Nattee's looks expressed triumphant satisfaction.

'Go,' said Lois, smoothing Faith's hair, and kissing the white, cold cheek, 'or he will wonder why no one comes to see him, and perhaps think he is not welcome.' Faith went without another word into the keeping-room, and shut the door of communication. Nattee and Lois were left together. Lois felt as happy as if some piece of good fortune had befallen herself. For the time, her growing dread of Manasseh's wild, ominous persistence in his suit, her aunt's coldness, her own loneliness, were all forgotten, and she could almost have danced with joy. Nattee laughed aloud, and talked and chuckled to herself – 'Old Indian woman great mystery. Old Indian woman sent hither and thither; go where she is told, where she hears with her ears. But old Indian woman' – and here she drew herself up, and the expression of her face quite changed – 'know how to call, and then white man must come; and old Indian woman have spoken never a word, and white man have heard nothing with his ears.' So the old crone muttered.

All this time, things were going on very differently in the keeping-room to what Lois imagined. Faith sat stiller even than usual; her eyes downcast, her words few. A quick observer might have noticed a certain tremulousness about her hands, and an occasional twitching throughout all her frame. But Pastor Nolan was not a keen observer upon this occasion; he was absorbed with his own little wonders and perplexities. His wonder was that of a carnal man – who that pretty stranger might be, who had seemed, on his first coming, so glad to see him, but had vanished instantly, apparently not to reappear. And, indeed, I am not sure if his perplexity was not that of a carnal man rather than that of a godly minister, for this was his dilemma. It was the custom of Salem (as we have already seen) for the minister, on entering a household for the visit which, among other people and in other times, would have been termed a 'morning call', to put up a prayer for the eternal welfare of the family under whose roof-tree he was. Now this prayer was expected to be adapted to the individual character, joys, sorrows, wants, and failings of every member present; and here was he, a young pastor, alone with a young woman; and he thought – vain thoughts, perhaps, but still very natural – that the implied guesses at her character, involved in the minute supplications above described, would be very awkward in a tête-à-tête prayer; so, whether it was his wonder or his perplexity, I do not know, but he did not contribute much to the conversation for some time, and at last, by a sudden burst of courage and impromptu hit, he cut the Gordian knot[120] by making the usual proposal for prayer, and adding to it a request that the household might be summoned. In came Lois, quiet and decorous; in came Nattee, all one impassive, stiff piece of wood – no look of intelligence or trace of giggling near her countenance. Solemnly recalling each wandering thought, Pastor Nolan knelt in the midst of these three to pray. He was a good and truly religious man, whose name here is the only thing disguised, and played his part bravely in the awful trial to which he was afterwards subjected; and if, at the time, before he went through his fiery persecutions, the human fancies which beset all young hearts came across his, we at this day know that these fancies are no sin. But now he prays in earnest, prays so heartily for himself, with such a sense of his own spiritual need and spiritual failings, that each one of his hearers feels as if a prayer and a supplication had gone up for each of them. Even Nattee muttered the few words she knew of the Lord's

Prayer; gibberish though the disjointed nouns and verbs might be, the poor creature said them because she was stirred to unwonted reverence. As for Lois, she rose up comforted and strengthened, as no special prayers of Pastor Tappau had ever made her feel. But Faith was sobbing, sobbing aloud, almost hysterically, and made no effort to rise, but lay on her outstretched arms spread out upon the settle. Lois and Pastor Nolan looked at each other for an instant. Then Lois said: 'Sir, you must go. My cousin has not been strong for some time, and doubtless she needs more quiet than she has had today.'

Pastor Nolan bowed, and left the house; but in a moment he returned. Half-opening the door, but without entering, he said: 'I come back to ask, if perchance I may call this evening to enquire how young Mistress Hickson finds herself?'

But Faith did not hear this; she was sobbing louder than ever.

'Why did you send him away, Lois? I should have been better directly, and it is so long since I have seen him.'

She had her face hidden as she uttered these words, and Lois could not hear them distinctly. She bent her head down by her cousin's on the settle, meaning to ask her to repeat what she had said. But in the irritation of the moment, and prompted possibly by some incipient jealousy, Faith pushed Lois away so violently that the latter was hurt against the hard, sharp corner of the wooden settle. Tears came into her eyes; not so much because her cheek was bruised, as because of the surprised pain she felt at this repulse from the cousin towards whom she was feeling so warmly and kindly. Just for the moment, Lois was as angry as any child could have been; but some of the words of Pastor Nolan's prayer yet rang in her ears, and she thought it would be a shame if she did not let them sink into her heart. She dared not, however, stoop again to caress Faith, but stood quietly by her, sorrowfully waiting; until a step at the outer door caused Faith to rise quickly, and rush into the kitchen, leaving Lois to bear the brunt of the new-comer. It was Manasseh, returned from hunting. He had been two days away, in company with other young men belonging to Salem. It was almost the only occupation which could draw him out of his secluded habits. He stopped suddenly at the door on seeing Lois, and alone; for she had avoided him of late in every possible way.

'Where is my mother?'

'At a prayer-meeting at Pastor Tappau's. She has taken Prudence. Faith has left the room this minute. I will call her.' And Lois was going towards the kitchen, when he placed himself between her and the door.

'Lois,' said he, 'the time is going by, and I cannot wait much longer. The visions come thick upon me, and my sight grows clearer and clearer. Only this last night, camping out in the woods, I saw in my soul, between sleeping and waking, the spirit come and offer thee two lots; and the colour of the one was white, like a bride's, and the other was black and red, which is, being interpreted, a violent death. And, when thou didst choose the latter, the spirit said unto me, "Come!" and I came, and did as I was bidden. I put it on thee with mine own hands, as it is pre-ordained, if thou wilt not hearken unto the voice and be my wife. And when the black and red dress fell to the ground, thou wert even as a corpse three days old. Now, be advised, Lois, in time! Lois, my cousin, I have seen it in a vision, and my soul cleaveth unto thee – I would fain spare thee.'

He was really in earnest – in passionate earnest; whatever his visions, as he called them, might be, he believed in them, and this belief gave something of unselfishness to his love for Lois. This she felt at this moment, if she had never done so before; and it seemed like a contrast to the repulse she had just met with from his sister. He had drawn near her, and now he took hold of her hand, repeating in his wild, pathetic, dreamy way: 'And the voice said unto me, "Marry Lois!" ' And Lois was more inclined to soothe and reason with him than she had ever been before, since the first time of his speaking to her on the subject – when Grace Hickson and Prudence entered the room from the passage. They had returned from the prayer-meeting by the back-way, which had prevented the sound of their approach from being heard.

But Manasseh did not stir or look round; he kept his eyes fixed on Lois, as if to note the effect of his words. Grace came hastily forwards and, lifting up her strong right arm, smote their joined hands in twain, in spite of the fervour of Manasseh's grasp.

'What means this?' said she, addressing herself more to Lois than to her son, anger flashing out of her deep-set eyes.

Lois waited for Manasseh to speak. He seemed, but a few minutes before, to be more gentle and less threatening than he had been of late on this subject, and she did not wish to irritate him. But he did not speak, and her aunt stood angrily waiting for an answer.

'At any rate,' thought Lois, 'it will put an end to the thought in his mind, when my aunt speaks out about it.'

'My cousin seeks me in marriage,' said Lois.

'Thee!' and Grace struck out in the direction of her niece with a gesture of supreme contempt. But now Manasseh spoke forth: 'Yea!

it is pre-ordained. The voice has said it, and the spirit has brought her to me as my bride.'

'Spirit! an evil spirit then! A good spirit would have chosen out for thee a godly maiden of thine own people, and not a prelatist[121] and a stranger like this girl. A pretty return, Mistress Lois, for all our kindness!'

'Indeed, Aunt Hickson, I have done all I could – Cousin Manasseh knows it – to show him I can be none of his. I have told him,' said she, blushing, but determined to say the whole out at once, 'that I am all but troth-plight[122] to a young man of our own village at home; and even putting all that on one side, I wish not for marriage at present.'

'Wish rather for conversion and regeneration! Marriage is an unseemly word in the mouth of a maiden. As for Manasseh, I will take reason with him in private; and, meanwhile, if thou hast spoken truly, throw not thyself in his path, as I have noticed thou hast done but too often of late.'

Lois's heart burnt within her at this unjust accusation, for she knew how much she had dreaded and avoided her cousin, and she almost looked to him to give evidence that her aunt's last words were not true. But, instead, he recurred to his one fixed idea, and said: 'Mother, listen! If I wed not Lois, both she and I die within the year. I care not for life; before this, as you know, I have sought for death' (Grace shuddered, and was for a moment subdued by some recollection of past horror); 'but, if Lois were my wife, I should live, and she would be spared from what is the other lot. That whole vision grows clearer to me, day by day. Yet, when I try to know whether I am one of the elect, all is dark. The mystery of Free-Will and Fore-Knowledge is a mystery of Satan's devising, not of God's.'[123]

'Alas, my son! Satan is abroad among the brethren even now; but let the old vexed topics rest! Sooner than fret thyself again, thou shalt have Lois to be thy wife, though my heart was set far differently for thee.'

'No, Manasseh,' said Lois. 'I love you well as a cousin, but wife of yours I can never be. Aunt Hickson, it is not well to delude him so. I say, if ever I marry man, I am troth-plight to one in England.'

'Tush, child! I am your guardian in my dead husband's place. Thou thinkest thyself so great a prize that I could clutch at thee whether or no, I doubt not. I value thee not, save as a medicine for Manasseh, if his mind get disturbed again, as I have noted signs of late.'

This, then, was the secret explanation of much that had alarmed her in her cousin's manner: and, if Lois had been a physician of modern times, she might have traced somewhat of the same temperament in his sisters as well – in Prudence's lack of natural feeling and impish delight in mischief, in Faith's vehemence of unrequited love. But, as yet, Lois did not know, any more than Faith, that the attachment of the latter to Mr Nolan was not merely unreturned, but even unperceived, by the young minister.

He came, it is true – came often to the house, sat long with the family, and watched them narrowly, but took no especial notice of Faith. Lois perceived this, and grieved over it; Nattee perceived it, and was indignant at it, long before Faith slowly acknowledged it to herself, and went to Nattee the Indian woman, rather than to Lois her cousin, for sympathy and counsel.

'He cares not for me,' said Faith. 'He cares more for Lois's little finger than for my whole body,' the girl moaned out, in the bitter pain of jealousy.

'Hush thee, hush thee, prairie-bird! How can he build a nest, when the old bird has got all the moss and the feathers? Wait till the Indian has found means to send the old bird flying far away.' This was the mysterious comfort Nattee gave.

Grace Hickson took some kind of charge over Manasseh that relieved Lois of much of her distress at his strange behaviour. Yet, at times, he escaped from his mother's watchfulness, and in such opportunities he would always seek Lois, entreating her, as of old, to marry him – sometimes pleading his love for her, oftener speaking wildly of his visions and the voices which he heard, foretelling a terrible futurity.

We have now to do with events which were taking place in Salem, beyond the narrow circle of the Hickson family; but, as they only concern us in as far as they bore down in their consequences on the future of those who formed part of it, I shall go over the narrative very briefly. The town of Salem had lost by death, within a very short time preceding the commencement of my story, nearly all its venerable men and leading citizens – men of ripe wisdom and sound counsel. The people had hardly yet recovered from the shock of their loss, as one by one the patriarchs of the primitive little community had rapidly followed each other to the grave. They had been beloved as fathers, and looked up to as judges in the land. The first bad effect of their loss was seen in the heated dissension which sprang up between Pastor Tappau and the candidate Nolan. It had been apparently healed over; but Mr Nolan had not been many weeks in Salem, after his second coming, before the strife broke out afresh, and alienated many for life who had till then been bound together by the ties of friendship or relationship. Even in the Hickson family something of this feeling soon sprang up; Grace being a vehement partisan of the elder pastor's more gloomy doctrines, while Faith was a passionate, if a powerless, advocate of Mr Nolan. Manasseh's growing absorption in his own fancies, and imagined gift of prophecy, making him comparatively indifferent to all outward events, did not tend to either the fulfilment of his visions, or the elucidation of the dark mysterious doctrines over which he had pondered too long for the health either of his mind or body; while Prudence delighted in irritating everyone by her advocacy of the views of thinking to which they were most opposed, and relating every gossiping story to the person most likely to disbelieve, and to be indignant at, what she told with an assumed unconsciousness of any such effect to be produced. There was much talk of the congregational difficulties and dissensions being carried up to the general court; and each party naturally hoped that, if such were the course of events, the opposing pastor and that portion of the congregation which adhered to him might be worsted in the struggle.

Such was the state of things in the township, when, one day towards the end of the month of February, Grace Hickson returned from the weekly prayer-meeting, which it was her custom to attend at Pastor Tappau's house, in a state of extreme excitement. On her entrance into her own house she sat down, rocking her body backwards and forwards, and praying to herself. Both Faith and Lois stopped their spinning, in wonder at her agitation, before either of them ventured to address her. At length Faith rose, and spoke: 'Mother, what is it? Hath anything happened of any evil nature?'

The brave, stern old woman's face was blenched, and her eyes were almost set in horror, as she prayed; the great drops running down her cheeks.

It seemed almost as if she had to make a struggle to recover her sense of the present homely accustomed life, before she could find words to answer: 'Evil nature! Daughters, Satan is abroad – is close to us; I have this very hour seen him afflict two innocent children, as of old he troubled those who were possessed by him in Judea. Hester and Abigail Tappau have been contorted and convulsed by him and his servants into such shapes as I am afeared to think on; and when their father, godly Mr Tappau, began to exhort and to pray, their howlings were like the wild beasts of the field. Satan is of a truth let loose among us. The girls kept calling upon him, as if he were even then present among us. Abigail screeched out that he stood at my very back in the guise of a black man; and truly, as I turned round at her words, I saw a creature like a shadow vanishing, and turned all of a cold sweat. Who knows where he is now? Faith, lay straws across on the door-sill!'

'But, if he be already entered in,' asked Prudence, 'may not that make it difficult for him to depart?'

Her mother, taking no notice of her question, went on rocking herself, and praying, till again she broke out into narration: 'Reverend Mr Tappau says, that only last night he heard a sound as of a heavy body dragged all through the house by some strong power; once it was thrown against his bedroom door, and would, doubtless, have broken it in, if he had not prayed fervently and aloud at that very time; and a shriek went up at his prayer that made his hair stand on end; and this morning all the crockery in the house was found broken and piled up in the middle of the kitchen floor; and Pastor Tappau says that, as soon as he began to ask a blessing on the morning's meal, Abigail and Hester cried out, as if someone was pinching them. Lord, have mercy upon us all! Satan is of a truth let loose.'

'They sound like the old stories I used to hear in Barford,' said Lois, breathless with affright.

Faith seemed less alarmed; but then her dislike to Pastor Tappau was so great, that she could hardly sympathise with any misfortunes that befell him or his family.

Towards evening Mr Nolan came in. In general, so high did party spirit run, Grace Hickson only tolerated his visits, finding herself often engaged at such hours, and being too much abstracted in thought to show him the ready hospitality which was one of her most prominent virtues. But today, both as bringing the latest intelligence of the new horrors sprung up in Salem, and as being one of the Church militant[124] (or what the Puritans considered as equivalent to the Church militant) against Satan, he was welcomed by her in an unusual manner.

He seemed oppressed with the occurrences of the day; at first it appeared to be almost a relief to him to sit still, and cogitate upon them, and his hosts were becoming almost impatient for him to say something more than mere monosyllables, when he began: 'Such a day as this I pray that I may never see again. It is as if the devils, whom our Lord banished into the herd of swine,[125] had been permitted to come again upon the earth. And I would it were only the lost spirits who were tormenting us; but I much fear that certain of those whom we have esteemed as God's people have sold their souls to Satan, for the sake of a little of his evil power, whereby they may afflict others for a time. Elder Sherringham hath lost this very day a good and valuable horse, wherewith he used to drive his family to meeting.'

'Perchance,' said Lois, 'the horse died of some natural disease.'

'True,' said Pastor Nolan; 'but I was going on to say, that, as he entered into his house, full of dolour at the loss of his beast, a mouse ran in before him so sudden that it almost tripped him up, though an instant before there was no such thing to be seen; and he caught at it with his shoe and hit it, and it cried out like a human creature in pain, and straight ran up the chimney, caring nothing for the hot flame and smoke.'

Manasseh listened greedily to all this story; and, when it was ended he smote his breast, and prayed aloud for deliverance from the power of the Evil One; and he continually went on praying at intervals through the evening, with every mark of abject terror on his face and in his manner – he, the bravest, most daring hunter in all the settlement. Indeed, all the family huddled together in silent fear, scarcely finding any interest in the usual household occupations. Faith and Lois sat with arms entwined, as in days before the former had become jealous of the latter; Prudence asked low, fearful questions of her mother and of the pastor as to the creatures that were abroad, and the ways in which they afflicted others; and, when Grace besought the minister to pray for her and her household, he made a long and passionate supplication that none of that little flock might ever so far fall away into hopeless perdition as to be guilty of the sin without forgiveness[126] – the Sin of Witchcraft.

Chapter 3

'The Sin of Witchcraft'. We read about it, we look on it from the outside; but we can hardly realise the terror it induced. Every impulsive or unaccustomed action, every little nervous affection, every ache or pain was noticed, not merely by those around the sufferer, but by the person himself, whoever he might be, that was acting, or being acted upon, in any but the most simple and ordinary manner. He or she (for it was most frequently a woman or girl that was the supposed subject) felt a desire for some unusual kind of food – some unusual motion or rest – her hand twitched, her foot was asleep, or her leg had the cramp; and the dreadful question immediately suggested itself, 'Is anyone possessing an evil power over me; by the help of Satan?' and perhaps they went on to think, 'It is bad enough to feel that my body can be made to suffer through the power of some unknown evil-wisher to me; but what if Satan gives them still further power, and they can touch my soul, and inspire me with loathful thoughts leading me into crimes which at present I abhor?' and so on, till the very dread of what might happen, and the constant dwelling of the thoughts, even with horror, upon certain possibilities, or what were esteemed such, really brought about the corruption of imagination at last, which at first they had shuddered at. Moreover, there was a sort of uncertainty as to who might be infected – not unlike the overpowering dread of the plague, which made some shrink from their best-beloved with irrepressible fear. The brother or sister, who was the dearest friend of their childhood and youth, might now be bound in some mysterious deadly pact with evil spirits of the most horrible kind – who could tell? And in such a case it became a duty, a sacred duty, to give up the earthly body which had been once so loved, but which was now the habitation of a soul corrupt and horrible in its evil inclinations. Possibly, terror of death might bring on confession, and repentance, and purification. Or if it did not, why, away with the evil creature, the witch, out of the world, down to the kingdom of the master, whose bidding was done on earth in all manner of corruption and torture of God's creatures! There were others who, to these more simple, if more ignorant, feelings of horror at witches and witchcraft, added the desire, conscious or unconscious, of revenge on those whose conduct had been in any way displeasing to them. Where evidence takes a supernatural character, there is no disproving it. This argument comes up: 'You have only the natural powers; I have supernatural. You admit the existence of the supernatural by the condemnation of this very crime of witchcraft. You hardly know the limits of the natural powers; how, then, can you define the supernatural? I say that in the dead of night, when my body seemed to all present to be lying in quiet sleep, I was, in the most complete and wakeful consciousness, present in my body at an assembly of witches and wizards, with Satan at their head; that I was by them tortured in my body, because my soul would not acknowledge him as its king; and that I witnessed such and such deeds. What the nature of the appearance was that took the semblance of myself, sleeping quietly in my bed, I know not; but, admitting, as you do, the possibility of witchcraft, you cannot disprove my evidence.' The evidence might be given truly or falsely, as the person witnessing believed it or not; but everyone must see what immense and terrible power was abroad for revenge. Then, again, the accused themselves ministered to the horrible panic abroad. Some, in dread of death, confessed from cowardice to the imaginary crimes of which they were accused, and of which they were promised a pardon on confession. Some, weak and terrified, came honestly to believe in their own guilt, through the diseases of imagination which were sure to be engendered at such a time as this.

Lois sat spinning with Faith. Both were silent, pondering over the stories that were abroad. Lois spoke first.

'Oh, Faith! this country is worse than ever England was, even in the days of Master Matthew Hopkinson,[127] the witch-finder. I grow frightened of everyone, I think. I even get afeared sometimes of Nattee!'

Faith coloured a little. Then she asked: 'Why? What should make you distrust the Indian woman?'

'Oh! I am ashamed of my fear as soon as it arises in my mind. But, you know, her look and colour were strange to me when I first came; and she is not a christened woman; and they tell stories of Indian wizards; and I know not what the mixtures are which she is sometimes stirring over the fire, nor the meaning of the strange chants she sings to herself. And once I met her in the dusk, just close by Pastor Tappau's house, in company with Hota, his servant – it was just before we heard of the sore disturbance in his house – and I have wondered if she had aught to do with it.'

Faith sat very still, as if thinking. At last she said: 'If Nattee has powers beyond what you and I have, she will not use them for evil; at least not evil to those whom she loves.'

'That comforts me but little,' said Lois. 'If she has powers beyond what she ought to have, I dread her, though I have done her no evil; nay, though I could almost say she bore me a kindly feeling. But such powers are only given by the Evil One; and the proof thereof is, that, as you imply, Nattee would use them on those who offend her.'

'And why should she not?' asked Faith, lifting her eyes, and flashing heavy fire out of them, at the question.

'Because,' said Lois, not seeing Faith's glance, 'we are told to pray for them that despitefully use us, and to do good to them that persecute us. But poor Nattee is not a christened woman. I would that Mr Nolan would baptise her: it would, maybe, take her out of the power of Satan's temptations.'

'Are you never tempted?' asked Faith half-scornfully; 'and yet I doubt not you were well baptised!'

'True,' said Lois sadly; 'I often do very wrong; but, perhaps, I might have done worse, if the holy form had not been observed.'

They were again silent for a time.

'Lois,' said Faith, 'I did not mean any offence. But do you never feel as if you would give up all that future life, of which the parsons talk, and which seems so vague and so distant, for a few years of real, vivid blessedness, to begin tomorrow – this hour – this minute? Oh! I could think of happiness for which I would willingly give up all those misty chances of heaven – '

'Faith, Faith!' cried Lois in terror, holding her hand before her cousin's mouth, and looking around in fright. 'Hush! you know not who may be listening; you are putting yourself in his power.'

But Faith pushed her hand away, and said, 'Lois, I believe in him no more than I believe in heaven. Both may exist; but they are so far away that I defy them. Why all this ado about Mr Tappau's house – promise me never to tell living creature, and I will tell you a secret.'

'No!' said Lois, terrified. 'I dread all secrets. I will hear none. I will do all that I can for you, Cousin Faith, in any way; but just at this time, I strive to keep my life and thoughts within the strictest bounds of godly simplicity, and I dread pledging myself to aught that is hidden and secret.'

'As you will, cowardly girl, full of terrors, which, if you had listened to me, might have been lessened, if not entirely done away with.' And Faith would not utter another word, though Lois tried meekly to entice her into conversation on some other subject.

The rumour of witchcraft was like the echo of thunder among the hills. It had broken out in Mr Tappau's house, and his two little daughters were the first supposed to be bewitched; but round about, from every quarter of the town, came in accounts of sufferers by witchcraft. There was hardly a family without one of these supposed victims. Then arose a growl and menaces of vengeance from many a household – menaces deepened, not daunted, by the terror and mystery of the suffering that gave rise to them.

At length a day was appointed when, after solemn fasting and prayer, Mr Tappau invited the neighbouring ministers and all godly people to assemble at his house, and unite with him in devoting a day to solemn religious services, and to supplication for the deliverance of his children, and those similarly afflicted, from the power of the Evil One. All Salem poured out towards the house of the minister. There was a look of excitement on all their faces; eagerness and horror were depicted on many, while stern resolution, amounting to determined cruelty, if the occasion arose, was seen on others.

In the midst of the prayer, Hester Tappau, the younger girl, fell into convulsions; fit after fit came on, and her screams mingled with the shrieks and cries of the assembled congregation. In the first pause, when the child was partially recovered, when the people stood around, exhausted and breathless, her father, the Pastor Tappau, lifted his right hand, and adjured her, in the name of the Trinity, to say who tormented her. There was a dead silence; not a creature stirred of all those hundreds. Hester turned wearily and uneasily, and moaned out the name of Hota, her father's Indian servant. Hota was present, apparently as much interested as anyone; indeed, she had been busying herself much in bringing remedies to the suffering child. But now she stood aghast, transfixed, while her name was caught up and shouted out in tones of reprobation and hatred by all the crowd around her. Another moment, and they would have fallen upon the trembling creature and torn her limb from limb – pale, dusky, shivering Hota, half guilty-looking from her very bewilderment. But Pastor Tappau, that gaunt, grey man, lifting himself to his utmost height, signed to them to go back, to keep still while he addressed them; and then he told them that instant vengeance was not just, deliberate punishment; that there would be need of conviction, perchance of confession; he hoped for some redress for his suffering children from her revelations, if she were brought to confession. They must leave the culprit in his hands, and in those of his brother ministers, that they might wrestle with Satan before delivering her up to the civil power. He spoke well; for he spoke from the heart of a father seeing his children exposed to dreadful and mysterious suffering, and firmly believing that he now held the clue in his hand which should ultimately release them and their fellow-sufferers. And the congregation moaned themselves into unsatisfied submission, and listened to his long, passionate prayer, which he uplifted even while the hapless Hota stood there, guarded and bound by two men, who glared at her like bloodhounds ready to slip,[128] even while the prayer ended in the words of the merciful Saviour.

Lois sickened and shuddered at the whole scene; and this was no intellectual shuddering at the folly and superstition of the people, but tender moral shuddering at the sight of guilt which she believed in, and at the evidence of men's hatred and abhorrence, which, when shown even to the guilty, troubled and distressed her merciful heart. She followed her aunt and cousins out into the open air, with downcast eyes and pale face. Grace Hickson was going home with a feeling of triumphant relief at the detection of the guilty one. Faith alone seemed uneasy and disturbed beyond her wont; for Manasseh received the whole transaction as the fulfilment of a prophecy, and Prudence was excited by the novel scene into a state of discordant high spirits.

'I am quite as old as Hester Tappau,' said she; 'her birthday is in September and mine in October.'

'What has that to do with it?' said Faith sharply.

'Nothing; only she seemed such a little thing for all those grave ministers to be praying for, and so many folk come from a distance; some from Boston, they said, all for her sake, as it were. Why, didst thou see, it was godly Mr Henwick that held her head when she wriggled so, and old Madam Holbrook had herself helped up on a chair to see the better? I wonder how long I might wriggle, before great and godly folk would take so much notice of me? But, I suppose, that comes of being a pastor's daughter. She'll be so set up, there'll be no speaking to her now. Faith! thinkest thou that Hota really had bewitched her? She gave me corn-cakes the last time I was at Pastor Tappau's, just like any other woman, only, perchance, a trifle more good-natured; and to think of her being a witch after all!'

But Faith seemed in a hurry to reach home, and paid no attention to Prudence's talking. Lois hastened on with Faith; for Manasseh was walking alongside of his mother, and she kept steady to her plan of avoiding him, even though she pressed her company upon Faith, who had seemed of late desirous of avoiding her.

That evening the news spread through Salem, that Hota had confessed her sin – had acknowledged that she was a witch. Nattee was the first to hear the intelligence. She broke into the room where the girls were sitting with Grace Hickson, solemnly doing nothing, because of the great prayer-meeting in the morning, and cried out, 'Mercy, mercy, mistress, everybody! take care of poor Indian Nattee, who never do wrong, but for mistress and the family! Hota one bad, wicked witch; she say so herself; oh, me! oh, me!' and, stooping over Faith, she said something in a low, miserable tone of voice, of which

Lois only heard the word 'torture'. But Faith heard all, and, turning very pale, half-accompanied, half-led Nattee back to her kitchen.

Presently, Grace Hickson came in. She had been out to see a neighbour: it will not do to say that so godly a woman had been gossiping; and, indeed, the subject of the conversation she had held was of too serious and momentous a nature for me to employ a light word to designate it. There was all the listening to, and repeating of, small details and rumours, in which the speakers have no concern, that constitutes gossiping; but, in this instance, all trivial facts and speeches might be considered to bear such dreadful significance, and might have so ghastly an ending, that such whispers were occasionally raised to a tragic importance. Every fragment of intelligence that related to Mr Tappau's household was eagerly snatched at: how his dog howled all one long night through, and could not be stilled; how his cow suddenly failed in her milk, only two months after she had calved; how his memory had forsaken him one morning, for a minute or two, in repeating the Lord's Prayer, and he had even omitted a clause thereof in his sudden perturbation; and how all these forerunners of his children's strange illness might now be interpreted and understood – this had formed the staple of the conversation between Grace Hickson and her friends. There had arisen a dispute among them at last, as to how far these subjections to the power of the Evil One were to be considered as a judgment upon Pastor Tappau for some sin on his part; and if so, what? It was not an unpleasant discussion, although there was considerable difference of opinion; for, as none of the speakers had had their families so troubled, it was rather a proof that they had none of them committed any sin. In the midst of this talk, one, entering in from the street, brought the news that Hota had confessed all – had owned to signing a certain little red book which Satan had presented to her – had been present at impious sacraments – had ridden through the air to Newbury Falls – and, in fact, had assented to all the questions which the elders and magistrates, carefully reading over the confessions of the witches who had formerly been tried in England, in order that they might not omit a single enquiry, had asked of her. More she had owned to, but things of inferior importance, and partaking more of the nature of earthly tricks than of spiritual power. She had spoken of carefully-adjusted strings, by which all the crockery in Pastor Tappau's house could be pulled down or disturbed; but of such intelligible malpractices the gossips of Salem took little heed. One of them said that such an action showed Satan's prompting; but they all preferred to listen to the grander guilt of the blasphemous sacraments and supernatural rides. The narrator ended with saying that Hota was to be hung the next morning, in spite of her confession, even although her life had been promised to her if she acknowledged her sin; for it was well to make an example of the first-discovered witch, and it was also well that she was an Indian, a heathen, whose life would be no great loss to the community. Grace Hickson on this spoke out. It was well that witches should perish off the face of the earth, Indian or English, heathen or, worse, a baptised Christian who had betrayed the Lord, even as Judas did, and had gone over to Satan. For her part, she wished that the first-discovered witch had been a member of a godly English household, that it might be seen of all men that religious folk were willing to cut off the right hand, and pluck out the right eye,[129] if tainted with the devilish sin. She spoke sternly and well. The last comer said that her words might be brought to the proof, for it had been whispered that Hota had named others, and some from the most religious families of Salem, whom she had seen among the unholy communicants at the sacraments of the Evil One. And Grace replied that she would answer for it, all godly folk would stand the proof, and quench all natural affection rather than that such a sin should grow and spread among them. She herself had a weak bodily dread of witnessing the violent death even of an animal; but she would not let that deter her from standing amidst those who cast the accursed creature out from among them on the morrow morning.

Contrary to her wont, Grace Hickson told her family much of this conversation. It was a sign of her excitement on the subject that she thus spoke, and the excitement spread in different forms through her family. Faith was flushed and restless, wandering between the keeping-room and the kitchen, and questioning her mother particularly as to the more extraordinary parts of Hota's confession, as if she wished to satisfy herself that the Indian witch had really done those horrible and mysterious deeds.

Lois shivered and trembled with affright at the narration, and at the idea that such things were possible. Occasionally she found herself wandering off into sympathetic thought for the woman who was to die, abhorred of all men, and unpardoned by God, to whom she had been so fearful a traitor, and who was now, at this very time – when Lois sat among her kindred by the warm and cheerful firelight, anticipating many peaceful, perchance happy, morrows – solitary, shivering, panic-stricken, guilty, with none to stand by her and exhort her, shut up in darkness between the cold walls of the town prison. But Lois almost shrank from sympathising with so loathsome an accomplice of Satan, and prayed for forgiveness for her charitable thought; and yet, again, she remembered the tender spirit of the Saviour, and allowed herself to fall into pity, till at last her sense of right and wrong became so bewildered that she could only leave all to God's disposal, and just ask that he would take all creatures and all events into His hands.

Prudence was as bright as if she were listening to some merry story – curious as to more than her mother would tell her – seeming to have no particular terror of witches or witchcraft, and yet to be especially desirous to accompany her mother the next morning to the hanging. Lois shrank from the cruel, eager face of the young girl, as she begged her mother to allow her to go. Even Grace was disturbed and perplexed by her daughter's pertinacity.

'No,' said she. 'Ask me no more! Thou shalt not go. Such sights are not for the young. I go, and I sicken at the thoughts of it. But I go to show that I, a Christian woman, take God's part against the devil's. Thou shalt not go, I tell thee. I could whip thee for thinking of it.'

'Manasseh says Hota was well whipped by Pastor Tappau ere she was brought to confession,' said Prudence, as if anxious to change the subject of discussion.

Manasseh lifted up his head from the great folio Bible, brought by his father from England, which he was studying. He had not heard what Prudence said, but he looked up at the sound of his name. All present were startled at his wild eyes, his bloodless face. But he was evidently annoyed at the expression of their countenances.

'Why look ye at me in that manner?' asked he. And his manner was anxious and agitated. His mother made haste to speak: 'It was but that Prudence said something that thou hast told her – that Pastor Tappau defiled his hands by whipping the witch Hota. What evil thought has got hold of thee? Talk to us, and crack not thy skull against the learning of man.'

'It is not the learning of man that I study; it is the Word of God. I would fain know more of the nature of this sin of witchcraft, and whether it be, indeed, the unpardonable sin against the Holy Ghost.[130] At times I feel a creeping influence coming over me, prompting all evil thoughts and unheard-of deeds, and I question within myself, "Is not this the power of witchcraft?" and I sicken, and loathe all that I do or say; and yet some evil creature hath the mastery over me, and I must needs do and say what I loathe and dread. Why wonder you, mother, that I, of all men, strive to learn the exact nature of witchcraft, and for that end study the Word of God? Have you not seen me when I was, as it were, possessed with a devil?'

He spoke calmly, sadly, but as under deep conviction. His mother rose to comfort him.

'My son,' she said, 'no one ever saw thee do deeds, or heard thee utter words, which anyone could say were prompted by devils. We have seen thee, poor lad, with thy wits gone astray for a time; but all thy thoughts sought rather God's will in forbidden places, than lost the clue to them for one moment in hankering after the powers of darkness. Those days are long past; a future lies before thee. Think not of witches, or of being subject to the power of witchcraft. I did evil to speak of it before thee. Let Lois come and sit by thee, and talk to thee.'

Lois went to her cousin, grieved at heart for his depressed state of mind, anxious to soothe and comfort him, and yet recoiling more than ever from the idea of ultimately becoming his wife – an idea to which she saw her aunt reconciling herself unconsciously day by day, as she perceived the English girl's power of soothing and comforting her cousin, even by the very tones of her sweet cooing voice.

He took Lois's hand.

'Let me hold it! It does me good,' said he. 'Ah, Lois, when I am by you, I forget all my troubles – will the day never come when you will listen to the voice that speaks to me continually?'

'I never hear it, Cousin Manasseh,' she said softly; 'but do not think of the voices. Tell me of the land you hope to enclose from the forest – what manner of trees grow on it?'

Thus, by simple questions on practical affairs, she led him back, in her unconscious wisdom, to the subjects on which he had always shown strong practical sense. He talked on these, with all due discretion, till the hour for family prayer came round, which was early in those days. It was Manasseh's place to conduct it, as head of the family; a post which his mother had always been anxious to assign to him since her husband's death. He prayed extempore, and tonight his supplications wandered off into wild, unconnected fragments of prayer, which all those kneeling around began, each according to her anxiety for the speaker, to think would never end. Minutes elapsed, and grew to quarters of an hour, and his words only became more emphatic and wilder, praying for himself alone, and laying bare the recesses of his heart. At length his mother rose, and took Lois by the hand; for she had faith in Lois's power over her son, as being akin to that which the shepherd David, playing on his harp, had over king Saul sitting on his throne.[131] She drew her towards him, where he knelt facing into the circle, with his eyes upturned, and the tranced agony of his face depicting the struggle of the troubled soul within.

'Here is Lois,' said Grace, almost tenderly; 'she would fain go to her chamber.' (Down the girl's face the tears were streaming.) 'Rise, and finish thy prayer in thy closet.'

But at Lois's approach he sprang to his feet – sprang aside.

'Take her away, mother! Lead me not into temptation! She brings me evil and sinful thoughts. She overshadows me, even in the presence of my God. She is no angel of light, or she would not do this. She troubles me with the sound of a voice bidding me marry her, even when I am at my prayers. Avaunt! Take her away!'

He would have struck at Lois, if she had not shrunk back, dismayed and affrighted. His mother, although equally dismayed, was not affrighted. She had seen him thus before, and understood the management of his paroxysm.

'Go, Lois! the sight of thee irritates him, as once that of Faith did. Leave him to me!'

And Lois rushed away to her room, and threw herself on her bed, like a panting, hunted creature. Faith came after her slowly and heavily.

'Lois,' said she, 'wilt thou do me a favour? It is not much to ask. Wilt thou arise before daylight, and bear this letter from me to Pastor Nolan's lodgings? I would have done it myself; but mother has bidden me to come to her, and I may be detained until the time when Hota is to be hung; and the letter tells of matters pertaining to life and death. Seek out Pastor Nolan, wherever he may be, and have speech of him after he has read the letter.'

'Cannot Nattee take it?' asked Lois.

'No!' Faith answered fiercely. 'Why should she?'

But Lois did not reply. A quick suspicion darted through Faith's mind, sudden as lightning. It had never entered there before.

'Speak, Lois! I read thy thoughts. Thou would'st fain not be the bearer of this letter?'

'I will take it,' said Lois meekly. 'It concerns life and death, you say?'

'Yes!' said Faith, in quite a different tone of voice. But, after a pause of thought, she added: 'Then, as soon as the house is still, I will write what I have to say, and leave it here on this chest; and thou wilt promise me to take it before the day is fully up, while there is yet time for action.'

'Yes; I promise,' said Lois. And Faith knew enough of her to feel sure that the deed would be done, however reluctantly.

The letter was written – laid on the chest; and, ere day dawned, Lois was astir, Faith watching her from between her half-closed eyelids – eyelids that had never been fully closed in sleep the livelong night. The instant Lois, cloaked and hooded, left the room, Faith sprang up, and prepared to go to her mother, whom she heard already stirring. Nearly everyone in Salem was awake and up on this awful morning, though few were out-of-doors, as Lois passed along the streets. Here was the hastily-erected gallows, the black shadow of which fell across the street with ghastly significance; now she had to pass the iron-barred gaol, through the unglazed windows of which she heard the fearful cry of a woman, and the sound of many footsteps. On she sped, sick almost to faintness, to the widow woman's where Mr Nolan lodged. He was already up and abroad, gone, his hostess believed, to the gaol. Thither Lois, repeating the words 'for life and for death!' was forced to go. Retracing her steps, she was thankful to see him come out of those dismal portals, rendered more dismal for being in heavy shadow, just as she approached. What his errand had been she knew not; but he looked grave and sad, as she put Faith's letter into his hands, and stood before him quietly waiting until he should read it, and deliver the expected answer. But, instead of opening it, he hid it in his hand, apparently absorbed in thought. At last he spoke aloud, but more to himself than to her: 'My God! and is she, then, to die in this fearful delirium? It must be – can be – only delirium, that prompts such wild and horrible confessions. Mistress Barclay, I come from the presence of the Indian woman appointed to die. It seems, she considered herself betrayed last evening by her sentence not being respited, even after she had made confession of sin enough to bring down fire from heaven; and, it seems to me, the passionate, impotent anger of this helpless creature has turned to madness, for she appals me by the additional revelations she has made to the keepers during the night – to me this morning. I could almost fancy that she thinks, by deepening the guilt she confesses, to escape this last dread punishment of all; as if, were a tithe of what she says true, one could suffer such a sinner to live! Yet to send her to death in such a state of mad terror! What is to be done?'

'Yet Scripture says that we are not to suffer witches in the land,'[132] said Lois slowly.

'True; I would but ask for a respite, till the prayers of God's people had gone up for His mercy. Some would pray for her, poor wretch as she is. You would, Mistress Barclay, I am sure?' But he said it in a questioning tone.

'I have been praying for her in the night many a time,' said Lois, in a low voice. 'I pray for her in my heart at this moment; I suppose they are bidden to put her out of the land, but I would not have her entirely God-forsaken. But, sir, you have not read my cousin's letter. And she bade me bring back an answer with much urgency.'

Still he delayed. He was thinking of the dreadful confession he came from hearing. If it were true, the beautiful earth was a polluted place, and he almost wished to die, to escape from such pollution, into the white innocence of those who stood in the presence of God.

Suddenly his eyes fell on Lois's pure, grave face, upturned and watching his. Faith in earthly goodness came over his soul in that instant, 'and he blessed her unaware'.[133]

He put his hand on her shoulder, with an action half paternal – although the difference in their ages was not above a dozen years – and, bending a little towards her, whispered, half to himself, 'Mistress Barclay, you have done me good.'

'I!' said Lois, half-affrighted; 'I done you good! How?'

'By being what you are. But, perhaps, I should rather thank God, who sent you at the very moment when my soul was so disquieted.'

At this instant, they were aware of Faith standing in front of them, with a countenance of thunder. Her angry look made Lois feel guilty. She had not enough urged the pastor to read his letter, she thought; and it was indignation at this delay in what she had been commissioned to do with the urgency of life or death, that made her cousin lower at her so from beneath her straight black brows. Lois explained how she had not found Mr Nolan at his lodgings, and had had to follow him to the door of the gaol. But Faith replied, with obdurate contempt: 'Spare thy breath, Cousin Lois! It is easy seeing on what pleasant matters thou and the Pastor Nolan were talking. I marvel not at thy forgetfulness. My mind is changed. Give me back my letter, sir; it was about a poor matter – an old woman's life. And what is that compared to a young girl's love?'

Lois heard but for an instant; did not understand that her cousin, in her jealous anger, could suspect the existence of such a feeling as love between her and Mr Nolan. No imagination as to its possibility had ever entered her mind; she had respected him, almost revered him – nay, had liked him as the probable husband of Faith. At the thought that her cousin could believe her guilty of such treachery, her grave eyes dilated, and fixed themselves on the flaming countenance of Faith. That serious, unprotesting manner of perfect innocence must have told on her accuser, had it not been that, at the same instant, the latter caught sight of the crimsoned and disturbed countenance of the pastor, who felt the veil rent off the unconscious secret of his heart. Faith snatched her letter out of his hands, and said: 'Let the witch hang! What care I? She has done harm enough with her charms and her sorcery on Pastor Tappau's girls. Let her die, and let all other witches look to themselves; for there be many kinds of witchcraft abroad. Cousin Lois, thou wilt like best to stop with Pastor Nolan, or I would pray thee to come back with me to breakfast.'

Lois was not to be daunted by jealous sarcasm. She held out her hand to Pastor Nolan, determined to take no heed of her cousin's mad words, but to bid him farewell in her accustomed manner. He hesitated before taking it; and, when he did, it was with a convulsive squeeze that almost made her start. Faith waited and watched all, with set lips and vengeful eyes. She bade no farewell; she spake no word; but, grasping Lois tightly by the back of the arm, she almost drove her before her down the street till they reached their home.

The arrangement for the morning was this: Grace Hickson and her son Manasseh were to be present at the hanging of the first witch executed in Salem, as pious and godly heads of a family. All the other members were strictly forbidden to stir out, until such time as the low-tolling bell announced that all was over in this world for Hota, the Indian witch. When the execution was ended, there was to be a solemn prayer-meeting of all the inhabitants of Salem; ministers had come from a distance to aid by the efficacy of their prayers in these efforts to purge the land of the devil and his servants. There was reason to think that the great old meeting-house would be crowded; and, when Faith and Lois reached home, Grace Hickson was giving her directions to Prudence, urging her to be ready for an early start to that place. The stern old woman was troubled in her mind at the anticipation of the sight she was to see, before many minutes were over, and spoke in a more hurried and incoherent manner than was her wont. She was dressed in her Sunday best; but her face was very grey and colourless, and she seemed afraid to cease speaking about household affairs, for fear she should have time to think. Manasseh stood by her, perfectly, rigidly still; he also was in his Sunday clothes.

His face, too, was paler than its wont; but it wore a kind of absent, rapt expression, almost like that of a man who sees a vision. As Faith entered, still holding Lois in her fierce grasp, Manasseh started and smiled, but still dreamily. His manner was so peculiar that even his mother stayed her talking to observe him more closely; he was in that state of excitement which usually ended in what his mother and certain of her friends esteemed a prophetic revelation. He began to speak, at first very low, and then his voice increased in power.

'How beautiful is the land of Beulah, far over the sea, beyond the mountains! Thither the angels carry her, lying back in their arms like one fainting. They shall kiss away the black circle of death, and lay her down at the feet of the Lamb.[134] I hear her pleading there for those on earth who consented to her death. O Lois! pray also for me, pray for me, miserable!'

When he uttered his cousin's name all their eyes turned towards her. It was to her that his vision related! She stood among them, amazed, awestricken, but not like one affrighted or dismayed. She was the first to speak: 'Dear friends, do not think of me; his words may or may not be true. I am in God's hands all the same, whether he have the gift of prophecy or not. Besides, hear you not that I end where all would fain end? Think of him, and of his needs! Such times as these always leave him exhausted and weary, and he comes out of them.'

And she busied herself in cares for his refreshment, aiding her aunt's trembling hands to set before him the requisite food, as he now sat tired and bewildered, gathering together with difficulty his scattered senses.

Prudence did all she could to assist and speed their departure. But Faith stood apart, watching in silence with her passionate, angry eyes.

As soon as they had set out on their solemn, fatal errand, Faith left the room. She had not tasted food or touched drink. Indeed, they all felt sick at heart. The moment her sister had gone upstairs, Prudence sprang to the settle on which Lois had thrown down her cloak and hood: 'Lend me your muffles and mantle, Cousin Lois. I never yet saw a woman hanged, and I see not why I should not go. I will stand on the edge of the crowd; no one will know me, and I will be home long before my mother.'

'No!' said Lois, 'that may not be. My aunt would be sore displeased. I wonder at you, Prudence, seeking to witness such a sight.' And as she spoke she held fast her cloak, which Prudence vehemently struggled for.

Faith returned, brought back possibly by the sound of the struggle. She smiled – a deadly smile.

'Give it up, Prudence. Strive no more with her. She has bought success in this world, and we are but her slaves.'

'Oh, Faith!' said Lois, relinquishing her hold of the cloak, and turning round with passionate reproach in her look and voice, 'what have I done that you should speak so of me: you, that I have loved as I think one loves a sister?'

Prudence did not lose her opportunity, but hastily arrayed herself in the mantle, which was too large for her, and which she had, therefore, considered as well adapted for concealment; but, as she went towards the door, her feet became entangled in the unusual length, and she fell, bruising her arm pretty sharply.

'Take care, another time, how you meddle with a witch's things,' said Faith, as one scarcely believing her own words, but at enmity with all the world in her bitter jealousy of heart. Prudence rubbed her arm, and looked stealthily at Lois.

'Witch Lois! Witch Lois!' said she at last, softly, pulling a childish face of spite at her.

'Oh, hush, Prudence! Do not bandy such terrible words! Let me look at thine arm! I am sorry for thy hurt; only glad that it has kept thee from disobeying thy mother.'

'Away, away!' said Prudence, springing from her. 'I am afeared of her in very truth, Faith. Keep between me and the witch, or I will throw a stool at her.'

Faith smiled – it was a bad and wicked smile – but she did not stir to calm the fears she had called up in her young sister. Just at this moment, the bell began to toll. Hota, the Indian witch, was dead. Lois covered her face with her hands. Even Faith went a deadlier pale than she had been, and said, sighing, 'Poor Hota! But death is best.'

Prudence alone seemed unmoved by any thoughts connected with the solemn, monotonous sound. Her only consideration was, that now she might go out into the street and see the sights, and hear the news, and escape from the terror which she felt at the presence of her cousin. She flew upstairs to find her own mantle, ran down again, and past Lois, before the English girl had finished her prayer, and was speedily mingled among the crowd going to the meeting-house. There also Faith and Lois came in due course of time, but separately, not together. Faith so evidently avoided Lois that she, humbled and grieved, could not force her company upon her cousin, but loitered a little behind – the quiet tears stealing down her face, shed for the many causes that had occurred this morning.

The meeting-house was full to suffocation; and, as it sometimes happens on such occasions, the greatest crowd was close about the doors, from the fact that few saw, on their first entrance, where there might be possible spaces into which they could wedge themselves. Yet they were impatient of any arrivals from the outside, and pushed and hustled Faith, and after her Lois, till the two were forced on to a conspicuous place in the very centre of the building, where there was no chance of a seat, but still space to stand in. Several stood around, the pulpit being in the middle, and already occupied by two ministers in Geneva bands and gowns,[135] while other ministers, similarly attired, stood holding on to it, almost as if they were giving support instead of receiving it. Grace Hickson and her son sat decorously in their own pew, thereby showing that they had arrived early from the execution. You might almost have traced out the number of those who had been at the hanging of the Indian witch, by the expression of their countenances. They were awestricken into terrible repose; while the crowd pouring in, still pouring in, of those who had not attended the execution, looked all restless, and excited, and fierce. A buzz went round the meeting that the stranger minister who stood along with Pastor Tappau in the pulpit was no other than Dr Cotton Mather himself, come all the way from Boston to assist in purging Salem of witches.

And now Pastor Tappau began his prayer, extempore, as was the custom. His words were wild and incoherent, as might be expected from a man who had just been consenting to the bloody death of one who was, but a few days ago, a member of his own family; violent and passionate, as was to be looked for in the father of children, whom he believed to suffer so fearfully from the crime he would denounce before the Lord. He sat down at length from pure exhaustion. Then Dr Cotton Mather stood forward; he did not utter more than a few words of prayer, calm in comparison with what had gone before, and then he went on to address the great crowd before him in a quiet, argumentative way, but arranging what he had to say with something of the same kind of skill which Antony used in his speech to the Romans after Caesar's murder.[136] Some of Dr Mather's words have been preserved to us, as he afterwards wrote them down in one of his works. Speaking of those 'unbelieving Sadducees'[137] who doubted the existence of such a crime, he said: 'Instead of their apish shouts and jeers at blessed Scripture, and histories which have such undoubted confirmation as that no man that has breeding enough to regard the common laws of human society will offer to doubt of them, it becomes us rather to adore the goodness of God, who from the mouths of babes and sucklings has ordained truth, and by the means of the sore-afflicted children of your godly pastor, has revealed the fact that the devils have with most horrid operations broken in upon your neighbourhood. Let us beseech Him that their power may be restrained, and that they go not so far in their evil machinations as they did but four years ago in the city of Boston, where I was the humble means, under God, of loosing from the power of Satan the four children of that religious and blessed man, Mr Goodwin.[138] These four babes of grace were bewitched by an Irish witch; there is no end of the narration of the torments they had to submit to. At one time they would bark like dogs, at another purr like cats; yea, they would fly like geese, and be carried with an incredible swiftness, having but just their toes now and then upon the ground, sometimes not once in twenty feet, and their arms waved like those of a bird. Yet, at other times, by the hellish devices of the woman who had bewitched them, they could not stir without limping; for, by means of an invisible chain, she hampered their limbs, or sometimes, by means of a noose, almost choked them. One, in special, was subjected by this woman of Satan to such heat as of an oven, that I myself have seen the sweat drop from off her, while all around were moderately cold and well at ease. But not to trouble you with more of my stories, I will go on to prove that it was Satan himself that held power over her. For a very remarkable thing it was, that she was not permitted by that evil spirit to read any godly or religious book, speaking the truth as it is in Jesus. She could read Popish books well enough, while both sight and speech seemed to fail her, when I gave her the Assembly's Catechism.[139] Again, she was fond of that prelatical Book of Common Prayer, which is but the Roman mass-book in an English and ungodly shape. In the midst of her sufferings, if one put the Prayer-book into her hands, it relieved her. Yet, mark you, she could never be brought to read the Lord's Prayer, whatever book she met with it in, proving thereby distinctly that she was in league with the devil. I took her into my own house, that I, even as Dr Martin Luther[140] did, might wrestle with the devil, and have my fling at him. But, when I called my household to prayer, the devils that possessed her caused her to whistle, and sing, and yell in a discordant and hellish fashion.'

At this very instant a shrill, clear whistle pierced all ears. Dr Mather stopped for a moment: 'Satan is among you!' he cried. 'Look to yourselves!' And he prayed with fervour, as if against a present and threatening enemy; but no one heeded him. Whence came that ominous, unearthly whistle? Every man watched his neighbour. Again the whistle, out of their very midst! And then a bustle in a corner of the building; three or four people stirring, without any cause immediately perceptible to those at a distance; the movement spread; and, directly after, a passage even in that dense mass of people was cleared for two men, who bore forwards Prudence Hickson, lying rigid as a log of wood, in the convulsive position of one who suffered from an epileptic fit. They laid her down among the ministers who were gathered round the pulpit. Her mother came to her, sending up a wailing cry at the sight of her distorted child. Dr Mather came down from the pulpit and stood over her, exorcising the devil in possession, as one accustomed to such scenes. The crowd pressed forward in mute horror. At length her rigidity of form and feature gave way, and she was terribly convulsed – torn by the devil, as they called it. By and by, the violence of the attack was over, and the spectators began to breathe once more; though still the former horror brooded over them, and they listened as if for the sudden ominous whistle again, and glanced fearfully around, as if Satan were at their backs picking out his next victim.

Meanwhile, Dr Mather, Pastor Tappau, and one or two others, were exhorting Prudence to reveal, if she could, the name of the person, the witch, who, by influence over Satan, had subjected the child to such torture as that which they had just witnessed. They bade her speak in the name of the Lord. She whispered a name in the low voice of exhaustion. None of the congregation could hear what it was. But the Pastor Tappau, when he heard it, drew back in dismay, while Dr Mather, knowing not to whom the name belonged, cried out, in a clear, cold voice: 'Know ye one Lois Barclay; for it is she who hath bewitched this poor child?'

The answer was given rather by action than by word, although a low murmur went up from many. But all fell back, as far as falling back in such a crowd was possible, from Lois Barclay, where she stood – and looked on her with surprise and horror. A space of some feet, where no possibility of space had seemed to be not a minute before, left Lois standing alone, with every eye fixed upon her in hatred and dread. She stood like one speechless, tongue-tied, as if in a dream. She a witch! accursed as witches were in the sight of God and man! Her smooth, healthy face became contracted into shrivel and pallor; but she uttered not a word, only looked at Dr Mather with her dilated terrified eyes.

Someone said, 'She is of the household of Grace Hickson, a God-fearing woman.' Lois did not know if the words were in her favour or not. She did not think about them, even; they told less on her than on any person present. She a witch! and the silver glittering Avon, and the drowning woman she had seen in her childhood at Barford – at home in England – was before her, and her eyes fell before her doom. There was some commotion – some rustling of papers; the magistrates of the town were drawing near the pulpit and consulting with the ministers. Dr Mather spoke again: 'The Indian woman, who was hung this morning, named certain people, whom she deposed to having seen at the horrible meetings for the worship of Satan; but there is no name of Lois Barclay down upon the paper, although we are stricken at the sight of the names of some – '

An interruption – a consultation. Again Dr Mather spoke: 'Bring the accused witch, Lois Barclay, near to this poor suffering child of Christ.'

They rushed forward to force Lois to the place where Prudence lay. But Lois walked forward of herself: 'Prudence,' she said, in such a sweet, touching voice, that, long afterwards, those who heard it that day spoke of it to their children, 'have I ever said an unkind word to you, much less done you an ill turn? Speak, dear child! You did not know what you said just now, did you?'

But Prudence writhed away from her approach, and screamed out, as if stricken with fresh agony: 'Take her away! take her away! Witch Lois! Witch Lois, who threw me down only this morning, and turned my arm black and blue.' And she bared her arm, as if in confirmation of her words. It was sorely bruised.

'I was not near you, Prudence!' said Lois sadly. But that was only reckoned fresh evidence of her diabolical power.

Lois's brain began to get bewildered. 'Witch Lois'! She a witch, abhorred of all men! yet she would try to think, and make one more effort.

'Aunt Hickson,' she said, and Grace came forwards. 'Am I a witch, Aunt Hickson?' she asked; for her aunt, stern, harsh, unloving as she might be, was truth itself; and Lois thought – so near to delirium had she come – if her aunt condemned her, it was possible she might indeed be a witch.

Grace Hickson faced her unwillingly.

'It is a stain upon our family for ever,' was the thought in her mind.

'It is for God to judge whether thou art a witch or not. Not for me.'

'Alas, alas!' moaned Lois; for she had looked at Faith, and learnt that no good word was to be expected from her gloomy face and averted eyes. The meeting-house was full of eager voices, repressed, out of reverence for the place, into tones of earnest murmuring that seemed to fill the air with gathering sounds of anger; and those who had first fallen back from the place where Lois stood were now pressing forwards and round about her, ready to seize the young friendless girl, and bear her off to prison. Those who might have been, who ought to have been, her friends, were either averse or indifferent to her; though only Prudence made any open outcry upon her. That evil child cried out perpetually that Lois had cast a devilish spell upon her, and bade them keep the witch away from her; and, indeed, Prudence was strangely convulsed, when once or twice Lois's perplexed and wistful eyes were turned in her direction. Here and there, girls, women, uttering strange cries, and apparently suffering from the same kind of convulsive fit as that which had attacked Prudence, were centres of a group of agitated friends, who muttered much and savagely of witchcraft, and the list which had been taken down only the night before from Hota's own lips. They demanded to have it made public, and objected to the slow forms of the law. Others, not so much or so immediately interested in the sufferers, were kneeling around, and praying aloud for themselves and their own safety, until the excitement should be so much quelled as to enable Dr Cotton Mather to be again heard in prayer and exhortation.

And where was Manasseh? What said he? You must remember that the stir of the outcry, the accusation, the appeals of the accused, all seemed to go on at once, amid the buzz and din of the people who had come to worship God, but remained to judge and upbraid their fellow-creature. Till now, Lois had only caught a glimpse of Manasseh, who was apparently trying to push forwards, but whom his mother was holding back with word and action, as Lois knew she would hold him back; for it was not for the first time that she was made aware how carefully her aunt had always shrouded his decent reputation among his fellow-citizens from the least suspicion of his seasons of excitement and incipient insanity. On such days, when he himself imagined that he heard prophetic voices and saw prophetic visions, his mother would do much to prevent any besides his own family from seeing him; and now Lois, by a process swifter than reasoning, felt certain, from her one look at his face when she saw it, colourless and deformed by intensity of expression, among a number of others, all simply ruddy and angry, that he was in such a state that his mother would in vain do her utmost to prevent his making himself conspicuous. Whatever force or argument Grace used, it was of no avail. In another moment, he was by Lois's side, stammering with excitement, and giving vague testimony, which would have been of little value in a calm court of justice, and was only oil to the smouldering fire of that audience.

'Away with her to gaol!' 'Seek out the witches!' 'The sin has spread into all households!' 'Satan is in the very midst of us!' 'Strike and spare not!' In vain Dr Cotton Mather raised his voice in loud prayers, in which he assumed the guilt of the accused girl; no one listened, all were anxious to secure Lois, as if they feared she would vanish from before their very eyes: she, white, trembling, standing quite still in the tight grasp of strange, fierce men, her dilated eyes only wandering a little now and then in search of some pitiful face – some pitiful face that, among all those hundreds, was not to be found. While some fetched cords to bind her, and others, by low questions, suggested new accusations to the distempered brain of Prudence, Manasseh obtained a hearing once more. Addressing Dr Cotton Mather, he said, evidently anxious to make clear some new argument that had just suggested itself to him: 'Sir, in this matter, be she witch or not, the end has been foreshown to me by the spirit of prophecy. Now, reverend sir, if the event be known to the spirit, it must have been foredoomed[141] in the counsels of God. If so, why punish her for doing that in which she had no free-will?'

'Young man,' said Dr Mather, bending down from the pulpit and looking very severely upon Manasseh, 'take care! you are trenching on blasphemy.'

'I do not care. I say it again. Either Lois Barclay is a witch, or she is not. If she is, it has been foredoomed for her, for I have seen a vision of her death as a condemned witch for many months past – and the voice has told me there was but one escape for her – Lois – the voice you know' – In his excitement he began to wander a little; but it was touching to see how conscious he was, that by giving way he would lose the thread of the logical argument by which he hoped to prove that Lois ought not to be punished, and with what an effort he wrenched his imagination away from the old ideas, and strove to concentrate all his mind upon the plea that, if Lois was a witch, it had been shown him by prophecy: and, if there was prophecy, there must be foreknowledge; if foreknowledge, no freedom; if no freedom, no exercise of free-will; and, therefore, that Lois was not justly amenable to punishment.

On he went, plunging into heresy, caring not – growing more and more passionate every instant, but directing his passion into keen argument, desperate sarcasm, instead of allowing it to excite his imagination. Even Dr Mather felt himself on the point of being worsted in the very presence of this congregation, who, but a short half-hour ago, looked upon him as all but infallible. Keep a good heart, Cotton Mather! your opponent's eye begins to glare and flicker with a terrible, yet uncertain, light – his speech grows less coherent, and his arguments are mixed up with wild glimpses at wilder revelations made to himself alone. He has touched on the limits – he has entered the borders – of blasphemy; and, with an awful cry of horror and reprobation, the congregation rise up, as one man, against the blasphemer. Dr Mather smiled a grim smile; and the people were ready to stone Manasseh, who went on, regardless, talking and raving.

'Stay, stay!' said Grace Hickson – all the decent family shame which prompted her to conceal the mysterious misfortune of her only son from public knowledge done away with by the sense of the immediate danger to his life. 'Touch him not! He knows not what he is saying. The fit is upon him. I tell you the truth before God. My son, my only son, is mad.'

They stood aghast at the intelligence. The grave young citizen, who had silently taken his part in life close by them in their daily lives – not mixing much with them, it was true, but looked up to, perhaps, all the more – the student of abstruse books on theology, fit to converse with the most learned ministers that ever came about those parts – was he the same with the man now pouring out wild words to Lois the witch, as if he and she were the only two present? A solution of it all occurred to them. He was another victim. Great was the power of Satan! Through the arts of the devil, that white statue of a girl had mastered the soul of Manasseh Hickson. So the word spread from mouth to mouth. And Grace heard it. It seemed a healing balsam for her shame. With wilful, dishonest blindness, she would not see – not even in her secret heart would she acknowledge – that Manasseh had been strange, and moody, and violent long before the English girl had reached Salem. She even found some specious reason for his attempt at suicide long ago. He was recovering from a fever – and though tolerably well in health, the delirium had not finally left him. But since Lois came, how headstrong he had been at times! how unreasonable! How moody! What a strange delusion was that which he was under, of being bidden by some voice to marry her! How he followed her about, and clung to her, as under some compulsion of affection! And over all reigned the idea that, if he were indeed suffering from being bewitched, he was not mad, and might again assume the honourable position he had held in the congregation and in the town, when the spell by which he was held was destroyed. So Grace yielded to the notion herself, and encouraged it in others, that Lois Barclay had bewitched both Manasseh and Prudence. And the consequence of this belief was, that Lois was to be tried, with little chance in her favour, to see whether she was a witch or no; and if a witch, whether she would confess, implicate others, repent, and live a life of bitter shame, avoided by all men, and cruelly treated by most; or die, impenitent, hardened, denying her crime upon the gallows.[142]

And so they dragged Lois away from the congregation of Christians to the gaol, to await her trial. I say 'dragged her': because, although she was docile enough to have followed them whither they would, she was now so faint as to require extraneous force – poor Lois! who should have been carried and tended lovingly in her state of exhaustion; but, instead, was so detested by the multitude, who looked upon her as an accomplice of Satan in all his evil doings, that they cared no more how they treated her than a careless boy minds how he handles the toad that he is going to throw over the wall.

When Lois came to her full senses, she found herself lying on a short, hard bed in a dark, square room, which she at once knew must be a part of the city gaol. It was about eight feet square; it had stone walls on every side, and a grated opening high above her head, letting in all the light and air that could enter through about a square foot of aperture. It was so lonely, so dark to that poor girl, when she came slowly and painfully out of her long faint. She did so want human help in that struggle which always supervenes after a swoon; when the effort is to clutch at life, and the effort seems too much for the will. She did not at first understand where she was, did not understand how she came to be there; nor did she care to understand. Her physical instinct was to lie still and let the hurrying pulses have time to calm. So she shut her eyes once more. Slowly, slowly the recollection of the scene in the meeting-house shaped itself into a kind of picture before her. She saw within her eyelids, as it were, that sea of loathing faces all turned towards her, as towards something unclean and hateful. And you must remember, you who in the nineteenth century read this account, that witchcraft was a real terrible sin to her, Lois Barclay, two hundred years ago. The look on their faces, stamped on heart and brain, excited in her a sort of strange sympathy. Could it, O God! – could it be true, that Satan had obtained the terrific power over her and her will of which she had heard and read? Could she indeed be possessed by a demon and be indeed a witch, and yet till now have been unconscious of it? And her excited imagination recalled, with singular vividness, all she had ever heard on the subject – the horrible midnight sacrament, the very presence and power of Satan. Then, remembering every angry thought against her neighbour, against the impertinences of Prudence, against the overbearing authority of her aunt, against the persevering crazy suit of Manasseh, her indignation – only that morning, but such ages off in real time – at Faith's injustice: oh, could such evil thoughts have had devilish power given to them by the father of evil, and, all unconsciously to herself, have gone forth as active curses into the world? And so the ideas went on careering wildly through the poor girl's brain, the girl thrown inward upon herself. At length, the sting of her imagination forced her to start up impatiently. What was this? A weight of iron on her legs – a weight stated afterwards, by the gaoler of Salem prison, to have been 'not more than eight pounds'. It was well for Lois it was a tangible ill, bringing her back from the wild, illimitable desert in which her imagination was wandering. She took hold of the iron, and saw her torn stocking, her bruised ankle, and began to cry pitifully, out of strange compassion with herself. They feared, then, that even in that cell she would find a way to escape! Why, the utter, ridiculous impossibility of the thing convinced her of her own innocence and ignorance of all supernatural power; and the heavy iron brought her strangely round from the delusions that seemed to be gathering about her.

No! she never could fly out of that deep dungeon; there was no escape, natural or supernatural, for her, unless by man's mercy. And what was man's mercy in such times of panic? Lois knew that it was nothing; instinct, more than reason, taught her that panic calls out cowardice, and cowardice cruelty. Yet she cried, cried freely, and for the first time, when she found herself ironed and chained. It seemed so cruel, so much as if her fellow-creatures had really learnt to hate and dread her – her, who had had a few angry thoughts, which God forgive! but whose thoughts had never gone into words, far less into actions. Why, even now she could love all the household at home, if they would but let her; yes, even yet, though she felt that it was the open accusation of Prudence and the withheld justifications of her aunt and Faith that had brought her to her present strait. Would they ever come and see her? Would kinder thoughts of her – who had shared their daily bread for months and months – bring them to see her, and ask her whether it were really she who had brought on the illness of Prudence, the derangement of Manasseh's mind?

No one came. Bread and water were pushed in by someone, who hastily locked and unlocked the door, and cared not to see if he put them within his prisoner's reach, or perhaps thought that that physical fact mattered little to a witch. It was long before Lois could reach them; and she had something of the natural hunger of youth left in her still, which prompted her, lying her length on the floor, to weary herself with efforts to obtain the bread. After she had eaten some of it, the day began to wane, and she thought she would lay her down and try to sleep. But before she did so, the gaoler heard her singing the Evening Hymn – 'Glory to Thee, my God, this night, for all the blessings of the light!' And a dull thought came into his dull mind, that she was thankful for few blessings, if she could tune up her voice to sing praises after this day of what, if she were a witch, was shameful detection in abominable practices, and if not – Well, his mind stopped short at this point in his wondering contemplation. Lois knelt down and said the Lord's Prayer, pausing just a little before one clause, that she might be sure that in her heart of hearts she did forgive. Then she looked at her ankle, and the tears came into her eyes once again; but not so much because she was hurt, as because men must have hated her so bitterly before they could have treated her thus. Then she lay down and fell asleep.

The next day, she was led before Mr Hathorn and Mr Curwin,[143] justices of Salem, to be accused legally and publicly of witchcraft. Others were with her, under the same charge. And when the prisoners were brought in, they were cried out at by the abhorrent crowd. The two Tappaus, Prudence, and one or two other girls of the same age were there, in the character of victims of the spells of the accused. The prisoners were placed about seven or eight feet from the justices, and the accusers between the justices and them; the former were then ordered to stand right before the justices. All this Lois did at their bidding, with something of the wondering docility of a child, but not with any hope of softening the hard, stony look of detestation that was on all the countenances around her, save those that were distorted by more passionate anger. Then an officer was bidden to hold each of her hands, and Justice Hathorn bade her keep her eyes continually fixed on him, for this reason – which, however, was not told to her – lest, if she looked on Prudence, the girl might either fall into a fit, or cry out that she was suddenly or violently hurt. If any heart could have been touched in that cruel multitude, they would have felt some compassion for the sweet young face of the English girl, trying so meekly to do all that she was ordered, her face quite white, yet so full of sad gentleness, her grey eyes, a little dilated by the very solemnity of her position, fixed with the intent look of innocent maidenhood on the stern face of Justice Hathorn. And thus they stood in silence, one breathless minute. Then they were bidden to say the Lord's Prayer. Lois went through it as if alone in her cell; but, as she had done alone in her cell the night before, she made a little pause, before the prayer to be forgiven as she forgave. And at this instant of hesitation – as if they had been on the watch for it – they all cried out upon her for a witch; and, when the clamour ended, the justices bade Prudence Hickson come forward. Then Lois turned a little to one side, wishing to see at least one familiar face; but, when her eyes fell upon Prudence, the girl stood stock-still, and answered no questions, nor spoke a word, and the justices declared that she was struck dumb by witchcraft. Then some behind took Prudence under the arms, and would have forced her forwards to touch Lois, possibly esteeming that as a cure for her being bewitched. But Prudence had hardly been made to take three steps, before she struggled out of their arms and fell down writhing, as in a fit, calling out with shrieks, and entreating Lois to help her, and save her from her torment. Then all the girls began 'to tumble down like swine' (to use the words of an eye-witness) and to cry out upon Lois and her fellow-prisoners. These last were now ordered to stand with their hands stretched out, it being imagined that, if the bodies of the witches were arranged in the form of a cross, they would lose their evil power. By and by, Lois felt her strength going, from the unwonted fatigue of such a position, which she had borne patiently until the pain and weariness had forced both tears and sweat down her face; and she asked, in a low, plaintive voice, if she might not rest her head for a few moments against the wooden partition. But Justice Hathorn told her she had strength enough to torment others, and should have strength enough to stand. She sighed a little, and bore on, the clamour against her and the other accused increasing every moment; the only way she could keep herself from utterly losing consciousness was by distracting herself from present pain and danger, and saying to herself verses of the Psalms as she could remember them, expressive of trust in God. At length, she was ordered back to gaol, and dimly understood that she and others were sentenced to be hanged for witchcraft. Many people now looked eagerly at Lois, to see if she would weep at this doom. If she had had strength to cry, it might – it was just possible that it might – have been considered a plea in her favour, for witches could not shed tears; but she was too exhausted and dead. All she wanted was to lie down once more on her prison-bed, out of the reach of men's cries of abhorrence, and out of shot of their cruel eyes. So they led her back to prison, speechless and tearless.

But rest gave her back her power of thought and suffering. Was it indeed true that she was to die? She, Lois Barclay, only eighteen, so well, so young, so full of love and hope as she had been, till but these few days past! What would they think of it at home – real, dear home at Barford, in England? There they had loved her; there she had gone about singing and rejoicing, all the day long, in the pleasant meadows by the Avon side. Oh, why did father and mother die, and leave her their bidding to come here to this cruel New England shore, where no one had wanted her, no one had cared for her, and where now they were going to put her to a shameful death as a witch? And there would be no one to send kindly messages by, to those she should never see more. Never more! Young Lucy was living, and joyful – probably thinking of her, and of his declared intention of coming to fetch her home to be his wife this very spring. Possibly he had forgotten her; no one knew. A week before, she would have been indignant at her own distrust in thinking for a minute that he could forget. Now, she doubted all men's goodness for a time; for those around her were deadly, and cruel, and relentless.

Then she turned round, and beat herself with angry blows (to speak in images) for ever doubting her lover. Oh! if she were but with him! Oh! if she might but be with him! He would not let her die, but would hide her in his bosom from the wrath of this people, and carry her back to the old home at Barford. And he might even now be sailing on the wide blue sea, coming nearer, nearer every moment; and yet be too late after all.

So the thoughts chased each other through her head all that feverish night, till she clung almost deliriously to life, and wildly prayed that she might not die; at least, not just yet, and she so young!

Pastor Tappau and certain elders roused her up from a heavy sleep, late on the morning of the following day. All night long, she had trembled and cried, till morning light had come peering in through the square grating up above. It soothed her, and she fell asleep, to be awakened, as I have said, by Pastor Tappau.

'Arise!' said he, scrupling to touch her, from his superstitious idea of her evil powers. 'It is noonday.'

'Where am I?' said she, bewildered at this unusual wakening and the array of severe faces, all gazing upon her with reprobation.

'You are in Salem gaol, condemned for a witch.'

'Alas! I had forgotten for an instant,' said she, dropping her head upon her breast.

'She has been out on a devilish ride all night long, doubtless, and is weary and perplexed this morning,' whispered one in so low a voice that he did not think she could hear; but she lifted up her eyes, and looked at him, with mute reproach.

'We are come,' said Pastor Tappau, 'to exhort you to confess your great and manifold sin.'

'My great and manifold sin!' repeated Lois to herself, shaking her head.

'Yea, your sin of witchcraft. If you will confess, there may yet be balm in Gilead.'[144]

One of the elders, struck with pity at the young girl's wan, shrunken look, said that if she confessed and repented, and did penance, possibly her life might yet be spared.

A sudden flash of light came into her sunk, dulled eye. Might she yet live? Was it yet in her power? Why, no one knew how soon Ralph Lucy might be here, to take her away for ever into the peace of a new home! Life! Oh, then, all hope was not over – perhaps she might still live, and not die. Yet the truth came once more out of her lips, almost without exercise of her will.

'I am not a witch,' she said.

Then Pastor Tappau blindfolded her, all unresisting, but with languid wonder in her heart as to what was to come next. She heard people enter the dungeon softly, and heard whispering voices; then her hands were lifted up and made to touch someone near, and in an instant she heard a noise of struggling, and the well-known voice of Prudence shrieking out in one of her hysterical fits, and screaming to be taken away and out of that place. It seemed to Lois as if some of her judges must have doubted of her guilt, and demanded yet another test. She sat down heavily on her bed, thinking she must be in a horrible dream, so compassed about with dangers and enemies did she seem. Those in the dungeon – and, by the oppression of the air, she perceived that there were many – kept on eager talking in low voices. She did not try to make out the sense of the fragments of sentences that reached her dulled brain, till, all at once, a word or two made her understand they were discussing the desirableness of applying the whip or the torture to make her confess, and reveal by what means the spell she had cast upon those whom she had bewitched could be dissolved. A thrill of affright ran through her; and she cried out beseechingly: 'I beg you, sirs, for God's mercy sake, that you do not use such awful means. I may say anything – nay, I may accuse anyone – if I am subjected to such torment as I have heard tell about. For I am but a young girl, and not very brave, or very good, as some are.'

It touched the hearts of one or two to see her standing there; the tears streaming down from below the coarse handkerchief, tightly bound over her eyes; the clanking chain fastening the heavy weight to the slight ankle; the two hands held together, as if to keep down a convulsive motion.

'Look!' said one of these. 'She is weeping. They say no witch can weep tears.'

But another scoffed at this test, and bade the first remember how those of her own family, the Hicksons even, bore witness against her.

Once more, she was bidden to confess. The charges, esteemed by all men (as they said) to have been proven against her, were read over to her, with all the testimony borne against her in proof thereof. They told her that, considering the godly family to which she belonged, it had been decided by the magistrates and ministers of Salem that she should have her life spared, if she would own her guilt, make reparation, and submit to penance; but that, if not, she and others convicted of witchcraft along with her, were to be hung in Salem market-place on the next Thursday morning (Thursday being market-day). And when they had thus spoken, they waited silently for her answer. It was a minute or two before she spoke. She had sat down again upon the bed meanwhile; for indeed she was very weak. She asked, 'May I have this handkerchief unbound from my eyes; for indeed, sirs, it hurts me?'

The occasion for which she was blindfolded being over, the bandage was taken off, and she was allowed to see. She looked pitifully at the stern faces around her, in grim suspense as to what her answer would be. Then she spoke: 'Sirs, I must choose death with a quiet conscience, rather than life to be gained by a lie. I am not a witch. I know not hardly what you mean, when you say I am. I have done many, many things very wrong in my life; but I think God will forgive me them for my Saviour's sake.'

'Take not His name on your wicked lips,' said Pastor Tappau, enraged at her resolution of not confessing, and scarcely able to keep himself from striking her. She saw the desire he had, and shrank away in timid fear. Then Justice Hathorn solemnly read the legal condemnation of Lois Barclay to death by hanging, as a convicted witch. She murmured something which nobody heard fully, but which sounded like a prayer for pity and compassion on her tender years and friendless estate. Then they left her to all the horrors of that solitary, loathsome dungeon, and the strange terror of approaching death.

Outside the prison-walls, the dread of the witches, and the excitement against witchcraft, grew with fearful rapidity. Numbers of women, and men, too, were accused, no matter what their station of life and their former character had been. On the other side, it is alleged that upwards of fifty persons were grievously vexed by the devil, and those to whom he had imparted of his power for vile and wicked considerations. How much of malice – distinct, unmistakable, personal malice – was mixed up with these accusations, no one can now tell. The dire statistics of this time tell us, that fifty-five escaped death by confessing themselves guilty; one hundred and fifty were in prison; more than two hundred accused; and upwards of twenty suffered death, among whom was the minister I have called Nolan, who was traditionally esteemed to have suffered through hatred of his co-pastor. One old man, scorning the accusation, and refusing to plead at his trial, was, according to the law, pressed to death for his contumacy.[145] Nay, even dogs were accused of witchcraft, suffered the legal penalties, and are recorded among the subjects of capital punishment. One young man found means to effect his mother's escape from confinement, fled with her on horseback, and secreted her in the Blueberry Swamp, not far from Taplay's Brook, in the Great Pasture; he concealed her here in a wigwam which he built for her shelter, provided her with food and clothing, and comforted and sustained her, until after the delusion had passed away. The poor creature must, however, have suffered dreadfully; for one of her arms was fractured in the all but desperate effort of getting her out of prison.

But there was no one to try and save Lois. Grace Hickson would fain have ignored her altogether. Such a taint did witchcraft bring upon a whole family, that generations of blameless life were not at that day esteemed sufficient to wash it out. Besides, you must remember that Grace, along with most people of her time, believed most firmly in the reality of the crime of witchcraft. Poor, forsaken Lois believed in it herself; and it added to her terror, for the gaoler, in an unusually communicative mood, told her that nearly every cell was now full of witches, and it was possible he might have to put one, if more came, in with her. Lois knew that she was no witch herself; but not the less did she believe that the crime was abroad, and largely shared in by evil-minded persons who had chosen to give up their souls to Satan; and she shuddered with terror at what the gaoler said, and would have asked him to spare her this companionship, if it were possible. But, somehow, her senses were leaving her; and she could not remember the right words in which to form her request, until he had left the place.

The only person who yearned after Lois – who would have befriended her if he could – was Manasseh, poor, mad Manasseh. But he was so wild and outrageous in his talk, that it was all his mother could do to keep his state concealed from public observation. She had for this purpose given him a sleeping potion; and, while he lay heavy and inert under the influence of the poppy-tea, his mother bound him with cords to the ponderous, antique bed in which he slept. She looked broken-hearted, while she did this office and thus acknowledged the degradation of her first-born – him of whom she had ever been so proud.

Late that evening, Grace Hickson stood in Lois's cell, hooded and cloaked up to her eyes. Lois was sitting quite still, playing idly with a bit of string which one of the magistrates had dropped out of his pocket that morning. Her aunt was standing by her for an instant or two in silence, before Lois seemed aware of her presence. Suddenly, she looked up and uttered a little cry, shrinking away from the dark figure. Then, as if her cry had loosened Grace's tongue, she began: 'Lois Barclay, did I ever do you any harm?' Grace did not know how often her want of loving-kindness had pierced the tender heart of the stranger under her roof; nor did Lois remember it against her now. Instead, Lois's memory was filled with grateful thoughts of how much that might have been left undone, by a less conscientious person, her aunt had done for her; and she half-stretched out her arms as to a friend in that desolate place, while she answered: 'Oh no, no! you were very good! very kind!'

But Grace stood immovable.

'I did you no harm, although I never rightly knew why you came to us.'

'I was sent by my mother on her deathbed,' moaned Lois, covering her face. It grew darker every instant. Her aunt stood, still and silent.

'Did any of mine ever wrong you?' she asked, after a time.

'No, no; never, till Prudence said – Oh, aunt, do you think I am a witch?' And now Lois was standing up, holding by Grace's cloak, and trying to read her face. Grace drew herself, ever so little, away from the girl, whom she dreaded, and yet sought to propitiate.

'Wiser than I, godlier than I, have said it. But, oh, Lois, Lois! he was my first-born. Loose him from the demon, for the sake of Him whose name I dare not name in this terrible building, filled with them who have renounced the hopes of their baptism; loose Manasseh from his awful state, if ever I or mine did you a kindness.'

'You ask me for Christ's sake,' said Lois. 'I can name that holy name – for oh, aunt! indeed, and in holy truth, I am no witch! and yet I am to die – to be hanged! Aunt, do not let them kill me! I am so young, and I never did anyone any harm that I know of.'

'Hush! for very shame! This afternoon I have bound my first-born with strong cords, to keep him from doing himself or us a mischief – he is so frenzied. Lois Barclay, look here!' and Grace knelt down at her niece's feet, and joined her hands, as if in prayer. 'I am a proud woman, God forgive me! and I never thought to kneel to any save to Him. And now I kneel at your feet, to pray you to release my children, more especially my son Manasseh, from the spells you have put upon them. Lois, hearken to me, and I will pray to the Almighty for you, if yet there may be mercy.'

'I cannot do it; I never did you or yours any wrong. How can I undo it? How can I?' And she wrung her hands, in intensity of conviction of the inutility of aught she could do.

Here Grace got up, slowly, stiffly, and sternly. She stood aloof from the chained girl, in the remote corner of the prison-cell near the door, ready to make her escape as soon as she had cursed the witch, who would not, or could not, undo the evil she had wrought. Grace lifted up her right hand, and held it up on high, as she doomed Lois to be accursed for ever, for her deadly sin, and her want of mercy even at this final hour. And, lastly, she summoned her to meet her at the judgment seat,[146] and answer for this deadly injury, done to both souls and bodies of those who had taken her in, and received her when she came to them an orphan and a stranger.

Until this last summons, Lois had stood as one who hears her sentence and can say nothing against it, for she knows all would be in vain. But she raised her head when she heard her aunt speak of the judgment-seat, and at the end of Grace's speech she, too, lifted up her right hand, as if solemnly pledging herself by that action, and replied: 'Aunt! I will meet you there. And there you will know my innocence of this deadly thing. God have mercy on you and yours!'

Her calm voice maddened Grace; and, making a gesture as if she plucked up a handful of dust off the floor and threw it at Lois, she cried: 'Witch! witch! ask mercy for thyself – I need not your prayers. Witches' prayers are read backwards. I spit at thee, and defy thee!' And so she went away.

Lois sat moaning that whole night through. 'God comfort me! God strengthen me!' was all she could remember to say. She just felt that want, nothing more – all other fears and wants seemed dead within her. And, when the gaoler brought in her breakfast the next morning, he reported her as 'gone silly'; for, indeed, she did not seem to know him, but kept rocking herself to and fro, and whispering softly to herself, smiling a little from time to time.

But God did comfort her, and strengthen her too. Late on that Wednesday afternoon they thrust another 'witch' into her cell, bidding the two, with opprobrious words, keep company together. The new-comer fell prostrate with the push given her from without; and Lois, not recognising anything but an old ragged woman, lying helpless on her face on the ground, lifted her up; and lo! it was Nattee – dirty, filthy indeed, mud-pelted, stone-bruised, beaten, and all astray in her wits with the treatment she had received from the mob outside. Lois held her in her arms, and softly wiped the old brown wrinkled face with her apron, crying over it, as she had hardly yet cried over her own sorrows. For hours she tended the old Indian woman – tended her bodily woes; and, as the poor scattered senses of the savage creature came slowly back, Lois gathered her infinite dread of the morrow, when she, too, as well as Lois, was to be led out to die, in face of all that infuriated crowd. Lois sought in her own mind for some source of comfort for the old woman, who shook like one in the shaking-palsy at the dread of death – and such a death!

When all was quiet through the prison, in the deep dead midnight, the gaoler outside the door heard Lois telling, as if to a young child, the marvellous and sorrowful story of One who died on the cross for us and for our sakes. As long as she spoke, the Indian woman's terror seemed lulled; but, the instant she paused for weariness, Nattee cried out afresh, as if some wild beast were following her close through the dense forests in which she had dwelt in her youth. And then Lois went on, saying all the blessed words she could remember, and comforting the helpless Indian woman with the sense of the presence of a Heavenly Friend. And, in comforting her, Lois was comforted; in strengthening her, Lois was strengthened.

The morning came, and the summons to come forth and die came. They who entered the cell found Lois asleep, her face resting on the slumbering old woman, whose head she still held in her lap. She did not seem clearly to recognise where she was, when she awakened; the 'silly' look had returned to her wan face; all she appeared to know was that, somehow or another, through some peril or another, she had to protect the poor Indian woman. She smiled faintly, when she saw the bright light of the April day; and put her arm round Nattee, and tried to keep the Indian quiet with hushing, soothing words of broken meaning, and holy fragments of the Psalms. Nattee tightened her hold upon Lois, as they drew near the gallows, and the outrageous crowd below began to hoot and yell. Lois redoubled her efforts to calm and encourage Nattee, apparently unconscious that any of the opprobrium, the hootings, the stones, the mud, was directed towards her herself. But, when they took Nattee from her arms, and led her out to suffer first, Lois seemed all at once to recover her sense of the present terror. She gazed wildly around, stretched out her arms as if to some person in the distance, who was yet visible to her, and cried out once, with a voice that thrilled through all who heard it, 'Mother!' Directly afterwards, the body of Lois the Witch swung in the air; and everyone stood with hushed breath, with a sudden wonder, like a fear of deadly crime, fallen upon them.

The stillness and the silence were broken by one crazed and mad, who came rushing up the steps of the ladder, and caught Lois's body in his arms, and kissed her lips with wild passion. And then, as if it were true what the people believed, that he was possessed by a demon, he sprang down, and rushed through the crowd, out of the bounds of the city, and into the dark dense forest; and Manasseh Hickson was no more seen of Christian man.

The people of Salem had awakened from their frightful delusion before the autumn, when Captain Holdernesse and Ralph Lucy came to find out Lois, and bring her home to peaceful Barford, in the pleasant country of England. Instead, they led them to the grassy grave where she lay at rest, done to death by mistaken men. Ralph

Lucy shook the dust off his feet in quitting Salem, with a heavy, heavy heart, and lived a bachelor all his life long for her sake.

Long years afterwards, Captain Holdernesse sought him out, to tell him some news that he thought might interest the grave miller of the Avon-side. Captain Holdernesse told him, that in the previous year – it was then 1713 – the sentence of excommunication against the witches of Salem was ordered, in godly sacramental meeting of the church, to be erased and blotted out, and that those who met together for this purpose 'humbly requested the merciful God would pardon whatsoever sin, error, or mistake was in the application of justice, through our merciful High Priest, who knoweth how to have compassion on the ignorant, and those that are out of the way'. He also said, that Prudence Hickson – now woman grown – had made a most touching and pungent declaration of sorrow and repentance before the whole church, for the false and mistaken testimony she had given in several instances, among which she particularly mentioned that of her cousin Lois Barclay. To all which Ralph Lucy only answered: 'No repentance of theirs can bring her back to life.'

Then Captain Holdernesse took out a paper and read the following humble and solemn declaration of regret on the part of those who signed it, among whom Grace Hickson was one:

> 'We, whose names are undersigned, being, in the year 1692, called to serve as jurors in the court of Salem, on trial of many who were by some suspected guilty of doing acts of witchcraft upon the bodies of sundry persons: we confess that we ourselves were not capable to understand, nor able to withstand, the mysterious delusions of the powers of darkness, and prince of the air, but were, for want of knowledge in ourselves, and better information from others, prevailed with to take up with such evidence against the accused, as, on further consideration, and better information, we justly fear was insufficient for the touching the lives of any (Deut. 17:6), whereby we feel we have been instrumental, with others, though ignorantly and unwittingly, to bring upon ourselves and this people of the Lord the guilt of innocent blood; which sin, the Lord saith in Scripture, he would not pardon (2 Kings 24:4), that is, we suppose, in regard of his temporal judgments.[147] We do, therefore, signify to all in general (and to the surviving sufferers in special) our deep sense of, and sorrow for, our errors, in acting on such evidence to the condemning of any person; and do hereby declare, that we justly fear that we were

sadly deluded and mistaken, for which we are much disquieted and distressed in our minds, and do therefore humbly beg forgiveness, first of God for Christ's sake, for this our error; and pray that God would not impute the guilt of it to ourselves nor others; and we also pray that we may be considered candidly and aright by the living sufferers, as being then under the power of a strong and general delusion, utterly unacquainted with, and not experienced in, matters of that nature.

'We do heartily ask forgiveness of you all, whom we have justly offended; and do declare, according to our present minds, we would none of us do such things again on such grounds for the whole world; praying you to accept of this in way of satisfaction for our offence, and that you would bless the inheritance of the Lord, that he may be entreated for the land.

Foreman, Thomas Fisk, &c.'

To the reading of this paper Ralph Lucy made no reply save this, even more gloomily than before: 'All their repentance will avail nothing to my Lois, nor will it bring back her life.'

Then Captain Holdernesse spoke once more, and said that on the day of the general fast, appointed to be held all through New England, when the meeting-houses were crowded, an old, old man, with white hair, had stood up in the place in which he was accustomed to worship, and had handed up into the pulpit a written confession, which he had once or twice essayed to read for himself, acknowledging his great and grievous error in the matter of the witches of Salem, and praying for the forgiveness of God and of His people, ending with an entreaty that all then present would join with him in prayer that his past conduct might not bring down the displeasure of the Most High upon his country, his family, or himself. That old man, who was no other than Justice Sewall,[148] remained standing all the time that his confession was read; and at the end he said, 'The good and gracious God be pleased to save New England and me and my family!' And then it came out that, for years past, Judge Sewall had set apart a day for humiliation and prayer, to keep fresh in his mind a sense of repentance and sorrow for the part he had borne in these trials, and that this solemn anniversary he was pledged to keep as long as he lived, to show his feeling of deep humiliation.

Ralph Lucy's voice trembled as he spoke: 'All this will not bring my Lois to life again, or give me back the hope of my youth.'

But – as Captain Holdernesse shook his head (for what word could he say, or how dispute what was so evidently true?) – Ralph added, 'What is the day, know you, that this justice has set apart?'

'The twenty-ninth of April.'

'Then, on that day, will I, here at Barford in England, join my prayers as long as I live with the repentant judge, that his sin may be blotted out and no more had in remembrance. She would have willed it so.'

CURIOUS, IF TRUE

Extract from a Letter from Richard Whittingham, Esq.

YOU WERE FORMERLY so much amused at my pride in my descent from that sister of Calvin's who married a Whittingham, Dean of Durham, that I doubt if you will be able to enter into the regard for my distinguished relation that has led me to France, in order to examine registers and archives, which I thought might enable me to discover collateral descendants of the great Reformer,[149] whom I might call cousins. I shall not tell you of my troubles and adventures in this research; you are not worthy to hear of them; but something so curious befell me one evening last August, that if I had not been perfectly certain I was wide awake, I might have taken it for a dream.

For the purpose I have named, it was necessary that I should make Tours my headquarters for a time. I had traced descendants of the Calvin family out of Normandy into the centre of France; but I found it was necessary to have a kind of permission from the bishop of the diocese, before I could see certain family papers, which had fallen into the possession of the Church; and, as I had several English friends at Tours,[150] I awaited an answer to my request from Monseigneur de —, at that town. I was ready to accept any invitation; but I received very few, and was sometimes a little at a loss what to do with my evenings. The *table d'hôte*[151] was at five o'clock; I did not wish to go to the expense of a private sitting-room, disliked the dinnery atmosphere of the *salle à manger*,[152] could not play either at pool or billiards, and the aspect of my fellow-guests was unprepossessing enough to make me unwilling to enter into any tête-à-tête[153] gamblings with them. So I usually rose from table early, and tried to make the most of the remaining light of the August evenings in walking briskly off to explore the surrounding country; the middle of the day was too hot for this purpose, and better employed in lounging on a bench in the Boulevards, lazily listening to the distant band, and noticing with equal laziness the faces and figures of the women who passed by.

One Thursday evening – the 18th of August it was, I think – I had gone further than usual in my walk, and I found that it was later than I had imagined when I paused to turn back. I fancied I could make a round; I had enough notion of the direction in which I was to see that, by turning up a narrow straight lane to my left, I should shorten my way back to Tours. And so I believe I should have done, could I have found an outlet at the right place; but field-paths are almost unknown in that part of France, and my lane, stiff and straight as any street, and marked into terribly vanishing perspective by the regular row of poplars on each side, seemed interminable. Of course night came on, and I was in darkness. In England I might have had a chance of seeing a light in some cottage only a field or two off, and asking my way from the inhabitants; but here I could see no such welcome sight; indeed, I believe French peasants go to bed with the summer daylight; so, if there were any habitations in the neighbourhood, I never saw them. At last – I believe I must have walked two hours in the darkness – I saw the dusky outline of a wood on one side of the weariful lane; and, impatiently careless of all forest laws and penalties for trespassers, I made my way to it, thinking that, if the worst came to the worst, I could find some covert – some shelter where I could lie down and rest, until the morning light gave me a chance of finding my way back to Tours. But the plantation, on the outskirts of what appeared to me a dense wood, was of young trees, too closely-planted to be more than slender stems growing up to a good height, with scanty foliage on their summits. On I went towards the thicker forest; and, once there, I slackened my pace, and began to look about me for a good lair. I was as dainty as Lochiel's grandchild, who made his grandsire indignant at the luxury of his pillow of snow:[154] this brake was too full of brambles, that felt damp with dew; there was no hurry, since I had given up all hope of passing the night between four walls; and I went leisurely groping about, and trusting that there were no wolves to be poked up out of their summer drowsiness by my stick – when, all at once, I saw a château before me, not a quarter of a mile off, at the end of what seemed to be an ancient avenue (now overgrown and irregular), which I happened to be crossing, when I looked to my right and saw the welcome sight. Large, stately, and dark was its outline against the dusky night-sky; there were pepper-boxes, and *tourelles*,[155] and what not, fantastically growing up into the dim starlight. And, more to the purpose still, though I could not see the details of the building that I was now facing, it was plain enough that there were lights in many windows, as if some great entertainment was going on.

'They are hospitable people, at any rate,' thought I. 'Perhaps they will give me a bed. I don't suppose French *propriétaires*[156] have traps and horses quite as plentiful as English country-gentlemen; but they are evidently having a large party, and some of their guests may be from Tours, and will give me a cast back to the "Lion d'Or". I am not proud, and I am dog-tired. I am not above hanging on behind, if need be.'

So, putting a little briskness and spirit into my walk, I went up to the door, which was standing open, most hospitably, and showing a large lighted hall, all hung round with spoils of the chase, armour, &c., the details of which I had not time to notice; for the instant I stood on the threshold a huge porter appeared, in a strange, old-fashioned dress – a kind of livery which well befitted the general appearance of the house. He asked me, in French (so curiously pronounced that I thought I had hit upon a new kind of *patois*),[157] my name, and whence I came. I thought he would not be much the wiser – still, it was but civil to give it before I made my request for assistance; so, in reply, I said: ' My name is Whittingham – Richard Whittingham, an English gentleman, staying at —.' To my infinite surprise, a light of pleased intelligence came over the giant's face; he made me a low bow, and said (still in the same curious dialect) that I was welcome, that I was long expected.[158]

'Long expected'! What could the fellow mean? Had I stumbled on a nest of relations by John Calvin's side, who had heard of my genealogical enquiries, and were gratified and interested by them? But I was too much pleased to be under shelter for the night to think it necessary to account for my agreeable reception before I enjoyed it. Just as he was opening the great heavy *battants*[159] of the door that led from the hall to the interior, he turned round and said: 'Apparently Monsieur le Géanquilleur[160] is not come with you?'

'No! I am all alone. I have lost my way' – and I was going on with my explanation, when he, as if quite indifferent to it, led the way up a great stone staircase, as wide as many rooms, and having on each landing-place massive iron wickets in a heavy framework; these the porter unlocked with the solemn slowness of age. Indeed, a strange, mysterious awe of the centuries that had passed away since this château was built, came over me, as I waited for the turning of the ponderous keys in the ancient locks. I could almost have fancied that I heard a mighty rushing murmur (like the ceaseless sound of a distant sea, ebbing and flowing for ever and for ever), coming forth from the great vacant galleries that opened out on each side of the broad staircase, and were to be dimly perceived in the darkness above us. It was as if the voices of generations of men yet echoed and eddied in the silent air. It was strange, too, that my friend the porter going before me, ponderously infirm, with his feeble old hands striving in vain to keep the tall flambeau[161] he held steadily before him – strange, I say, that he was the only domestic I saw in the vast halls and passages, or met with on the grand staircase. At length, we stood before the gilded doors that led into the saloon where the family – or it might be the company, so great was the buzz of voices – was assembled. I would have remonstrated, when I found he was going to introduce me, dusty and travel-smeared, in a morning costume that was not even my best, into this grand *salon*,[162] with nobody knew how many ladies and gentlemen assembled; but the obstinate old man was evidently bent upon taking me straight to his master, and paid no heed to my words.

The doors flew open; and I was ushered into a saloon curiously full of pale light, which did not culminate on any spot, nor proceed from any centre, nor flicker with any motion of the air, but filled every nook and corner, making all things deliciously distinct; different from our light of gas or candle, as is the difference between a clear southern atmosphere and that of our misty England.

At the first moment, my arrival excited no attention, the apartment was so full of people, all intent on their own conversation. But my friend the porter went up to a handsome lady of middle age, richly attired in that antique manner which fashion has brought round again of late years, and, waiting first in an attitude of deep respect till her attention fell upon him, told her my name and something about me, as far as I could guess from the gestures of the one and the sudden glance of the eye of the other.

She immediately came towards me with the most friendly actions of greeting, even before she had advanced near enough to speak. Then – and was it not strange? – her words and accent were those of the commonest peasant of the country. Yet she herself looked high-bred, and would have been dignified, had she been a shade less restless; had her countenance worn a little less lively and inquisitive expression. I had been poking a good deal about the old parts of Tours, and had had to understand the dialect of the people who dwelt in the Marché au Vendredi[163] and similar places; or I really should not have understood my handsome hostess as she offered to present me to her husband, a hen-pecked, gentlemanly man, who was more quaintly attired than she in the very extreme of that style of dress. I thought to myself that in France, as in England, it is the provincials who carry fashion to such an excess as to become ridiculous.

However, he spoke (still in the *patois*) of his pleasure in making my acquaintance, and led me to a strange uneasy easy-chair, much of a piece with the rest of the furniture, which might have taken its place without any anachronism by the side of that in the Hôtel Cluny.[164] Then again began the clatter of French voices, which my arrival had for an instant interrupted, and I had leisure to look about me. Opposite to me sat a very sweet-looking lady, who must have been a great beauty in her youth, I should think, and would be charming in old age, from the sweetness of her countenance.[165] She was, however, extremely fat, and, on seeing her feet laid up before her on a cushion, I at once perceived that they were so swollen as to render her incapable of walking, which probably brought on her excessive *embonpoint*.[166] Her hands were plump and small, but rather coarse-grained in texture, not quite so clean as they might have been, and altogether not so aristocratic-looking as the charming face. Her dress was of superb black velvet, ermine-trimmed, with diamonds thrown all abroad over it.

Not far from her stood the least little man I had ever seen, of such admirable proportions no one could call him a dwarf, because with that word we usually associate something of deformity; but yet with an elfin look of shrewd, hard, worldly wisdom in his face that marred the impression which his delicate regular little features would otherwise have conveyed. Indeed, I do not think he was quite of equal rank with the rest of the company, for his dress was inappropriate to the occasion (and he apparently was an invited, while I was an involuntary, guest); and one or two of his gestures and actions were more like the tricks of an uneducated rustic than anything else. To explain what I mean: his boots had evidently seen much service, and had been re-topped, re-heeled, re-soled to the extent of cobbler's powers. Why should he have come in them if they were not his best – his only pair? And what can be more ungenteel than poverty! Then, again, he had an uneasy trick of putting his hand up to his throat, as if he expected to find something the matter with it; and he had the awkward habit – which I do not think he could have copied from Dr Johnson, because most probably he had never heard of him – of trying always to retrace his steps on the exact boards on which he had trodden to arrive at any particular part of the room.[167] Besides, to settle the question, I once heard him addressed as Monsieur Poucet,[168] without any aristocratic 'de' for a prefix; and nearly everyone else in the room was a marquis, at any rate.

I say 'nearly everyone', for some strange people had the *entrée*;[169] unless, indeed, they were, like me, benighted. One of the guests I should have taken for a servant, but for the extraordinary influence he seemed to have over the man I took for his master, and who never did anything without, apparently, being urged thereto by this follower.[170] The master, magnificently dressed, but ill at ease in his clothes, as if they had been made for someone else, was a weak-looking, handsome man, continually sauntering about, and, I almost guessed, an object of suspicion to some of the gentlemen present; which, perhaps, drove him on the companionship of his follower, who was dressed something in the style of an ambassador's chasseur;[171] yet it was not a chasseur's dress after all; it was something more thoroughly old-world; boots halfway up his ridiculously small legs, which clattered as he walked along, as if they were too large for his little feet; and a great quantity of grey fur, as trimming to coat, court-mantle, boots, cap – everything. You know the way in which certain countenances remind you perpetually of some animal, be it bird or beast! Well, this chasseur (as I will call him, for want of a better name) was exceedingly like the great Tom-cat that you have seen so often in my chambers, and laughed at, almost as often, for his uncanny gravity of demeanour. Grey whiskers has my Tom – grey whiskers had the chasseur; grey hair overshadows the upper lip of my Tom – grey mustachios hid that of the chasseur. The pupils of Tom's eyes dilate and contract as I had thought cats' pupils only could do, until I saw those of the chasseur. To be sure, canny as Tom is, the chasseur had the advantage in the more intelligent expression. He seemed to have obtained most complete sway over his master or patron, whose looks he watched, and whose steps he followed, with a kind of distrustful interest that puzzled me greatly.

There were several other groups in the more distant part of the saloon, all of the stately old school, all grand and noble, I conjectured from their bearing. They seemed perfectly well acquainted with each other, as if they were in the habit of meeting. But I was interrupted in my observations by the tiny little gentleman on the opposite side of the room coming across to take a place beside me. It is no difficult matter to a Frenchman to slide into conversation; and so gracefully did my pigmy friend keep up the character of the nation, that we were almost confidential before ten minutes had elapsed.

Now I was quite aware that the welcome which all had extended to me, from the porter up to the vivacious lady and meek lord of the castle, was intended for some other person. But it required either a degree of moral courage, of which I cannot boast, or the self-reliance and conversational powers of a bolder and cleverer man than I, to undeceive people who had fallen into so fortunate a mistake for me. Yet the little man by my side insinuated himself so much into my confidence that I had half a mind to tell him of my exact situation, and to turn him into a friend and an ally.

'Madame is perceptibly growing older,' said he in the midst of my perplexity, glancing at our hostess.

'Madame is still a very fine woman,' replied I.

'Now, is it not strange,' continued he, lowering his voice, 'how women almost invariably praise the absent, or departed, as if they were angels of light? while, as for the present, or the living' – here he shrugged up his little shoulders and made an expressive pause. 'Would you believe it! Madame is always praising her late husband to monsieur's face; till, in fact, we guests are quite perplexed how to look: for, you know, the late M. de Retz's character was quite notorious[172] – everybody has heard of him.' All the world of Touraine, thought I; but I made an assenting noise.

At this instant, monsieur our host came up to me, and, with a civil look of tender interest (such as some people put on when they enquire after your mother, about whom they do not care one straw), asked if I had heard lately how my cat was? 'How my cat was!' What could the man mean? My cat! Could he mean the tail-less Tom, born in the Isle of Man, and now supposed to be keeping guard against the incursions of rats and mice into my chambers in London?[173] Tom is, as you know, on pretty good terms with some of my friends, using their legs for rubbing-posts without scruple, and highly esteemed by them for his gravity of demeanour, and wise manner of winking his eyes. But could his fame have reached across the Channel? However, an answer must be returned to the enquiry, as monsieur's face was bent down to mine with a look of polite anxiety; so I, in my turn, assumed an expression of gratitude, and assured him that, to the best of my belief, my cat was in remarkably good health.

'And the climate agrees with her?'

'Perfectly,' said I, in a maze of wonder at this deep solicitude in a tail-less cat, who had lost one foot and half an ear in some cruel trap. My host smiled a sweet smile, and, addressing a few words to my little neighbour, passed on.

'How wearisome those aristocrats are!' quoth my neighbour, with a slight sneer. 'Monsieur's conversation rarely extends to more than two sentences to anyone. By that time his faculties are exhausted, and he needs the refreshment of silence. You and I, monsieur, are, at any rate, indebted to our own wits for our rise in the world!'

Here again I was bewildered! As you know, I am rather proud of my descent from families which, if not noble themselves, are allied to nobility; and as to my 'rise in the world' – if I had risen, it would have been rather for balloon-like qualities than for mother-wit, being unencumbered with heavy ballast either in my head or my pockets. However, it was my cue to agree: so I smiled again.

'For my part,' said he, 'if a man does not stick at trifles; if he knows how to judiciously add to, or withhold fact, and is not sentimental in his parade of humanity, he is sure to do well; sure to affix a *de* or *von*[174] to his name, and end his days in comfort. There is an example of what I am saying' – and he glanced furtively at the weak-looking master of the sharp, intelligent servant, whom I have called the chasseur.

'Monsieur le Marquis would never have been anything but a miller's son, if it had not been for the talents of his servant. Of course you know his antecedents?'

I was going to make some remarks on the changes in the order of the peerage since the days of Louis XVI[175] – going, in fact, to be very sensible and historical – when there was a slight commotion among the people at the other end of the room. Lackeys in quaint liveries[176] must have come in from behind the tapestry, I suppose (for I never saw them enter, though I sat right opposite to the doors), and were handing about the slight beverages with slighter viands which are considered sufficient refreshments, but which looked rather meagre to my hungry appetite. These footmen were standing solemnly opposite to a lady – beautiful, splendid as the dawn, but – sound asleep in a magnificent settee.[177] A gentleman, who showed so much irritation at her ill-timed slumbers, that I think he must have been her husband, was trying to awaken her with actions not far removed from shakings. All in vain; she was quite unconscious of his annoyance, or the smiles of the company, or the automatic solemnity of the waiting footman, or the perplexed anxiety of monsieur and madame.

My little friend sat down with a sneer, as if his curiosity was quenched in contempt.

'Moralists would make an infinity of wise remarks on that scene,' said he. 'In the first place, note the ridiculous position into which their superstitious reverence for rank and title puts all these people. Because monsieur is a reigning prince over some minute principality, the exact situation of which no one has as yet discovered, no one must venture to take their glass of *eau sucré*[178] till Madame la Princesse awakens; and, judging from past experience, those poor lackeys may have to stand for a century before that happens. Next – always speaking as a moralist, you will observe – note how difficult it is to break off bad habits acquired in youth!'

Just then the prince succeeded, by what means I did not see, in awaking the beautiful sleeper. But, at first, she did not remember where she was; and, looking up at her husband with loving eyes, she smiled, and said: 'Is it you, my prince?'

But he was too conscious of the suppressed amusement of the spectators, and his own consequent annoyance, to be reciprocally tender, and turned away with some little French expression, best rendered into English by 'Pooh, pooh, my dear!'

After I had had a glass of delicious wine of some unknown quality, my courage was in rather better plight than before, and I told my cynical little neighbour – whom I must say I was beginning to dislike – that I had lost my way in the wood, and had arrived at the château quite by mistake.

He seemed mightily amused at my story; said that the same thing had happened to himself more than once; and told me that I had better luck than he had on one of these occasions, when, from his account, he must have been in considerable danger of his life. He ended his story by making me admire his boots, which he said he still wore, patched though they were, and all their excellent quality lost by patching, because they were of such a first-rate make for long pedestrian excursions. 'Though, indeed,' he wound up by saying, 'the new fashion of railroads would seem to supersede the necessity for this description of boots.'

When I consulted him as to whether I ought to make myself known to my host and hostess as a benighted traveller, instead of the guest whom they had taken me for, he exclaimed, 'By no means! I hate such squeamish morality.' And he seemed much offended by my innocent question, as if it seemed by implication to condemn something in himself. He was offended and silent; and just at this moment I caught the sweet, attractive eyes of the lady opposite – that lady whom I named at first as being no longer in the bloom of youth, but as being somewhat infirm about the feet, which were supported on a raised cushion before her. Her looks seemed to say, 'Come here, and let us have some conversation together'; and, with a bow of silent excuse to my little companion, I went across to the lame old lady. She acknowledged my coming with the prettiest gesture of thanks possible; and, half-apologetically, said – 'It is a little dull to be unable to move about on such evenings as this; but it is a just punishment to me for my early vanities. My poor feet, that were by nature so small, are now taking their revenge for my cruelty in forcing them into such little slippers.[179] Besides, monsieur,' with a pleasant smile, 'I thought it was possible you might be weary of the malicious sayings of your little neighbour. He has not borne the best character in his youth, and such men are sure to be cynical in their old age.'

'Who is he?' asked I, with English abruptness.

'His name is Poucet, and his father was, I believe, a woodcutter, or charcoal-burner, or something of the sort. They do tell sad stories of connivance at murder, ingratitude, and obtaining money on false pretences – but you will think me as bad as he if I go on with my slanders. Rather let us admire the lovely lady coming up towards us, with the roses in her hand – I never see her without roses, they are so closely connected with her past history, as you are doubtless aware. Ah, beauty!'[180] said my companion to the lady drawing near to us, 'it is like you to come to me, now that I can no longer go to you.' Then, turning to me, and gracefully drawing me into the conversation, she said, 'You must know that, although we never met until we were both married, we have been almost like sisters ever since. There have been so many points of resemblance in our circumstances, and I think I may say in our characters. We had each two elder sisters – mine were but half-sisters, though – who were not so kind to us as they might have been.'

'But have been sorry for it since,' put in the other lady.

'Since we have married princes,' continued the same lady, with an arch smile that had nothing of unkindness in it, ' – for we both have married far above our original stations in life – we are both unpunctual in our habits; and, in consequence of this failing of ours, we have both had to suffer mortification and pain.'

'And both are charming,' said a whisper close behind me. 'My lord the marquis, say it – say, "And both are charming." '

'And both are charming,' was spoken aloud by another voice. I turned, and saw the wily, cat-like chasseur prompting his master to make civil speeches.

The ladies bowed, with that kind of haughty acknowledgement which shows that compliments from such a source are distasteful. But our trio of conversation was broken up, and I was sorry for it. The marquis looked as if he had been stirred up to make that one speech, and hoped that he would not be expected to say more; while behind him stood the chasseur, half-impertinent and half-servile in his ways and attitudes. The ladies, who were real ladies, seemed to be sorry for the awkwardness of the marquis, and addressed some trifling questions to him, adapting themselves to the subjects on which he could have no trouble in answering. The chasseur, meanwhile, was talking to himself in a growling tone of voice. I had fallen a little into the background at this interruption in a conversation which promised to be so pleasant, and I could not help hearing his words.

'Really, De Carabas[181] grows more stupid every day. I have a great mind to throw off his boots, and leave him to his fate. I was intended for a court, and to a court I will go, and make my own fortune as I have made his. The emperor[182] will appreciate my talents.'

And such are the habits of the French, or such his forgetfulness of good manners in his anger, that he spat right and left on the parquetted floor.

Just then a very ugly, very pleasant-looking man,[183] came towards the two ladies to whom I had lately been speaking, leading up to them a delicate, fair woman, dressed all in the softest white, as if she were *vouée au blanc*.[184] I do not think there was a bit of colour about her. I thought I had heard her making, as she came along, a little noise of pleasure, not exactly like the singing of a tea-kettle, nor yet like the cooing of a dove, but reminding me of each sound.

'Madame de Mioumiou was anxious to see you,' said he, addressing the lady with the roses, 'so I have brought her across to give you a pleasure!' What an honest, good face! but oh! how ugly! And yet I liked his ugliness better than most persons' beauty. There was a look of pathetic acknowledgement of his ugliness, and a deprecation of your too hasty judgement, in his countenance, that was positively winning. The soft, white lady kept glancing at my neighbour the chasseur, as if they had had some former acquaintance; which puzzled me very much, as they were of such different rank. However, their nerves were evidently strung to the same tune; for at a sound behind the tapestry, which was more like the scuttering of rats and mice than anything else, both Madame de Mioumiou and the chasseur started with the most eager look of anxiety on their countenances, and by their restless movements – madame's panting, and the fiery dilation of his eyes – one might see that commonplace sounds affected them both in a manner very different to the rest of the company. The ugly husband of the lovely lady with the roses now addressed himself to me: 'We are much disappointed,' he said, 'in finding that Monsieur is not accompanied by his countryman – le grand Jean d'Angleterre; I cannot pronounce his name rightly' – and he looked at me to help him out.

' "Le grand Jean d'Angleterre!" ' now, who was "le grand Jean d'Angleterre"? John Bull? John Russell? John Bright?[185]

'Jean – Jean' – continued the gentleman, seeing my embarrassment. 'Ah, these terrible English names – "Jean de Géanquilleur"!'

I was as wise as ever. And yet the name struck me as familiar, but slightly disguised. I repeated it to myself. It was mighty like John the Giant-killer; only his friends always call that worthy 'Jack'. I said the name aloud.

'Ah, that is it!' said he. 'But why has he not accompanied you to our little *réunion*[186] tonight?'

I had been rather puzzled once or twice before, but this serious question added considerably to my perplexity. Jack the Giant-killer had once, it is true, been rather an intimate friend of mine, as far as (printer's) ink and paper can keep up a friendship, but I had not heard his name mentioned for years; and for aught I knew he lay enchanted with King Arthur's knights, who lie entranced, until the blast of the trumpets of four mighty kings shall call them to help at England's need.[187] But the question had been asked in serious earnest by that gentleman, whom I more wished to think well of me than I did any other person in the room. So I answered respectfully, that it was long since I had heard anything of my countryman; but that I was sure it would have given him as much pleasure as it was doing myself to have been present at such an agreeable gathering of friends. He bowed, and then the lame lady took up the word.

'Tonight is the night, when, of all the year, this great old forest surrounding the castle is said to be haunted by the phantom of a little peasant girl[188] who once lived hereabouts; the tradition is that she was devoured by a wolf. In former days I have seen her on this night out of yonder window at the end of the gallery. Will you, *ma belle*, take monsieur to see the view outside by the moonlight (you may possibly see the phantom-child); and leave me to a little tête-à-tête with your husband?'

With a gentle movement the lady with the roses complied with the other's request, and we went to a great window, looking down on the forest, in which I had lost my way. The tops of the far-spreading and leafy trees lay motionless beneath us in that pale, wan light, which shows objects almost as distinct in form, though not in colour, as by day. We looked down on the countless avenues which seemed to converge from all quarters to the great old castle; and suddenly across one, quite near to us, there passed the figure of a little girl with the 'capuchon'[189] on, that takes the place of a peasant girl's bonnet in France. She had a basket on one arm, and by her, on the side to which her head was turned, there went a wolf. I could almost have said it was licking her hand, as if in penitent love, if either penitence or love had ever been a quality of wolves; but though not of living, perhaps it may be of phantom wolves.

'There, we have seen her!' exclaimed my beautiful companion. 'Though so long dead, her simple story of household goodness and trustful simplicity still lingers in the hearts of all who have ever heard of her; and the country-people about here say that seeing the phantom-child on this anniversary brings good luck for the year. Let us hope that we shall share in the traditionary good fortune! Ah! here is Madame de Retz – she retains the name of her first husband, you know, as he was of higher rank than the present.' We were joined by our hostess.

'If monsieur is fond of the beauties of nature and art,' said she, perceiving that I had been looking at the view from the great window, 'he will perhaps take pleasure in seeing the picture.' Here she sighed, with a little affectation of grief. 'You know the picture I allude to?' addressing my companion, who bowed assent and smiled a little maliciously, as I followed the lead of madame.

I went after her to the other end of the saloon, noting by the way with what keen curiosity she caught up what was passing either in word or action on each side of her. When we stood opposite to the end-wall, I perceived a full-length picture of a handsome, peculiar-looking man, with – in spite of his good looks – a very fierce and scowling expression. My hostess clasped her hands together as her arms hung down in front, and sighed once more. Then, half in soliloquy, she said: 'He was the love of my youth; his stern, yet manly character first touched this heart of mine. When – when shall I cease to deplore his loss?'

Not being acquainted with her enough to answer this question (if indeed it were not sufficiently answered by the fact of her second marriage), I felt awkward; and, by way of saying something, I remarked: 'The countenance strikes me as resembling something I have seen before – in an engraving from an historical picture, I think; only, it is there the principal figure in a group; he is holding a lady by her hair, and threatening her with his scimitar,[190] while two cavaliers are rushing up the stairs, apparently only just in time to save her life.'

'Alas, alas!' said she, 'you too accurately describe a miserable passage in my life, which has often been represented in a false light. The best of husbands' – here she sobbed, and became slightly inarticulate with her grief – 'will sometimes be displeased. I was young and curious – he was justly angry with my disobedience – my brothers were too hasty – the consequence is, I became a widow.'

After due respect for her tears, I ventured to suggest some commonplace consolation. She turned round sharply: 'No, monsieur; my only comfort is that I have never forgiven the brothers who interfered so cruelly, in such an uncalled-for manner, between my dear husband and myself. To quote my friend, Monsieur Sganarelle[191] – "Ce sont les petites choses qui sont de temps en temps nécessaires dans l'amitié; et cinq ou six coups d'épée entre gens qui s'aiment ne font que ragaillardir l'affection." You observe, the colouring is not quite what it should be.'

'In this light the beard is of rather a peculiar tint,' said I.

'Yes; the painter did not do it justice. It was most lovely, and gave him such a distinguished air, quite different from the common herd. Stay, I will show you the exact colour, if you will come near this flambeau!' And going near the light, she took off a bracelet of hair, with a magnificent clasp of pearls. It was peculiar, certainly. I did not know what to say. 'His precious, lovely beard!' said she. 'And the pearls go so well with the delicate blue!'

Her husband, who had come up to us, and waited till her eye fell upon him before venturing to speak, now said, 'It is strange Monsieur Ogre is not yet arrived!'

'Not at all strange,' said she tartly. 'He was always very stupid, and constantly falls into mistakes, in which he comes worse off; and it is very well he does, for he is a credulous and cowardly fellow. Not at all strange! If you will' – turning to her husband, so that I hardly heard her words, until I caught – 'Then everybody would have their rights, and we should have no more trouble. Is it not, monsieur?' addressing me.

'If I were in England, I should imagine madame was speaking of the Reform Bill,[192] or the millennium; but I am in ignorance.'

And, just as I spoke, the great folding-doors were thrown open wide; and everyone started to their feet, to greet a little old lady, leaning on a thin black wand – and: 'Madame la Fée-marraine',[193] was announced by a chorus of sweet shrill voices.

And in a moment I was lying in the grass close by a hollow oak tree, with the slanting glory of the dawning day shining full in my face, and thousands of little birds and delicate insects piping and warbling out their welcome to the ruddy splendour.

SIX WEEKS AT HEPPENHEIM

After I left Oxford, I determined to spend some months in travel before settling down in life. My father had left me a few thousands, the income arising from which would be enough to provide for all the necessary requirements of a lawyer's education, such as lodgings in a quiet part of London, and fees in payment to the distinguished barrister with whom I was to read; but there would be small surplus left over for luxuries or amusements; and, as I was rather in debt on leaving college, since I had forestalled my income, and the expenses of my travelling would have to be defrayed out of my capital, I determined that they should not exceed fifty pounds. As long as that sum would last me I would remain abroad; when it was spent my holiday should be over, and I would return and settle down somewhere in the neighbourhood of Russell Square, in order to be near Mr —'s chambers in Lincoln's Inn.[194] I had to wait in London for one day while my passport was being made out, and I went to examine the streets in which I purposed to live; I had picked them out, from studying a map, as desirable, and so they were, if judged entirely by my reason; but their aspect was very depressing to one country-bred, and just fresh from the beautiful street-architecture of Oxford. The thought of living in such a monotonous grey district for years made me the more anxious to prolong my holiday by all the economy which could eke out my fifty pounds. I thought I could make it last for one hundred days at least. I was a good walker, and had no very luxurious tastes in the matter of accommodation or food; I had as fair a knowledge of German and French as any untravelled Englishman can have; and I resolved to avoid expensive hotels such as my own countrymen frequented.

I have stated this much about myself, to explain how I fell in with the little story that I am going to record, but with which I had not much to do – my part in it being little more than that of a sympathising spectator. I had been through France into Switzerland, where I had gone beyond my strength in the way of walking, and I was on my way home; when one evening I came to the village of Heppenheim, on the Bergstrasse.[195] I had strolled about the dirty town of Worms all morning, and dined in a filthy hotel; and after that I had crossed the Rhine, and walked through Lorsch to

Heppenheim. I was unnaturally tired and languid, as I dragged myself up the rough-paved and irregular village street to the inn recommended to me. It was a large building with a green court before it. A cross-looking but scrupulously clean hostess received me, and showed me into a large room with a dinner-table in it, which, though it might have accommodated thirty or forty guests, only stretched down half the length of the eating-room.[196] There were windows at each end of the room; two looked to the front of the house, on which the evening shadows had already fallen; the opposite two were partly doors, opening into a large garden full of trained fruit trees and beds of vegetables, amongst which rose trees and other flowers seemed to grow by permission, not by original intention. There was a stove at each end of the room, which, I suspect, had originally been divided into two. The door by which I had entered was exactly in the middle; and opposite to it was another, leading to a great bedchamber, which my hostess showed me as my sleeping quarters for the night.

If the place had been much less clean and inviting, I should have remained there; I was almost surprised myself at my *vis inertiae*;[197] once seated in the last warm rays of the slanting sun by the garden window, I was disinclined to move, or even to speak. My hostess had taken my orders as to my evening-meal, and had left me. The sun went down, and I grew shivery. The vast room looked cold and bare; the darkness brought out shadows that perplexed me, because I could not fully make out the objects that produced them, after dazzling my eyes by gazing out into the crimson light.

Someone came in; it was the maiden to prepare for my supper. She began to lay the cloth at one end of the large table. There was a smaller one close by me. I mustered up my voice, which seemed a little as if it were getting beyond my control, and called to her: 'Will you let me have my supper here on this table?'

She came near; the light fell on her while I was in shadow. She was a tall young woman, with a fine strong figure, a pleasant face, expressive of goodness and sense, and with a good deal of comeliness about it too, although the fair complexion was bronzed and reddened by weather, so as to have lost much of its delicacy, and the features, as I had afterwards opportunity enough of observing, were anything but regular. She had white teeth, however, and well-opened blue eyes – grave-looking eyes which had shed tears for past sorrow – plenty of light-brown hair, rather elaborately plaited, and fastened up by two great silver pins. That was all – perhaps more than all – I noticed that first night. She began to lay the cloth where I had directed. A shiver passed over me; she looked at me, and then said: 'The gentleman is cold; shall I light the stove?'

Something vexed me – I am not usually so impatient; it was the coming on of serious illness – I did not like to be noticed so closely; I believed that food would restore me, and I did not want to have my meal delayed, as I feared it might be by the lighting of the stove: and most of all I was feverishly annoyed by movement. I answered sharply and abruptly: 'No; bring supper quickly; that is all I want.'

Her quiet, sad eyes met mine for a moment; but I saw no change in their expression, as if I had vexed her by my rudeness; her countenance did not for an instant lose its look of patient sense; and that is pretty nearly all I can remember of Thekla, that first evening at Heppenheim.

I suppose I ate my supper, or tried to do so, at any rate; and I must have gone to bed, for days after I became conscious of lying there, weak as a new-born babe, and with a sense of past pain in all my weary limbs. As is the case in recovering from fever, one does not care to connect facts, much less to reason upon them; so, how I came to be lying in that strange bed, in that large, half-furnished room, in what house that room was, in what town, in what country, I did not take the trouble to recall. It was of much more consequence to me then to discover what was the well-known herb that gave the scent to the clean, coarse sheets in which I lay. Gradually I extended my observations, always confining myself to the present. I must have been well cared for by someone, and that lately too, for the window was shaded, so as to prevent the morning-sun from coming in upon the bed; and there was the crackling of fresh wood in the great white china stove, which must have been newly replenished within a short time.

By and by the door opened slowly. I cannot tell why, but my impulse was to shut my eyes as if I were still asleep. But I could see through my apparently closed eyelids. In came, walking on tip-toe, with a slow care that defeated its object, two men. The first was aged from thirty to forty, in the dress of a Black Forest[198] peasant – old-fashioned coat and knee-breeches of strong blue cloth, but of a thoroughly good quality; he was followed by an older man, whose dress, of more pretension as to cut and colour (it was all black), was, nevertheless, as I had often the opportunity of observing afterwards, worn threadbare.

Their first sentences, in whispered German, told me who they were: the landlord of the inn where I was laying a helpless log, and the village doctor who had been called in. The latter felt my pulse, and nodded his head repeatedly in approbation. I had instinctively known that I was getting better, and hardly cared for this confirmation; but it seemed to give the truest pleasure to the landlord, who shook the hand of the doctor in a pantomime expressive of as much thankfulness as if I had been his brother. Some low-spoken remarks were made, and then some question was asked, to which, apparently, my host was unable to reply. He left the room, and in a minute or two returned, followed by Thekla, who was questioned by the doctor, and replied with a quiet clearness, showing how carefully the details of my illness had been observed by her. Then she left the room, and, as if every minute had served to restore to my brain its power of combining facts, I was suddenly prompted to open my eyes, and ask in the best German I could muster what day of the month it was; not that I clearly remembered the date of my arrival at Heppenheim, but I knew it was about the beginning of September.

Again the doctor conveyed his sense of extreme satisfaction in a series of rapid pantomimic nods, and then replied, in deliberate but tolerable English, to my great surprise: 'It is the 29th of September, my dear sir. You must thank the dear God! Your fever has made its course of twenty-one days. Now patience and care must be practised. The good host and his household will have the care; you must have the patience. If you have relations in England, I will do my endeavours to tell them the state of your health.'

'I have no near relations,' said I, beginning in my weakness to cry, as I remembered, as if it had been a dream, the days when I had father, mother, sister.

'Chut, chut!' said he; then, turning to the landlord, he told him in German to make Thekla bring me one of her good bouillons;[199] after which I was to have certain medicines, and to sleep as undisturbedly as possible. For days, he went on, I should require constant watching and careful feeding; every twenty minutes I was to have something, either wine or soup, in small quantities.

A dim notion came into my hazy mind that my previous husbandry of my fifty pounds, by taking long walks and scanty diet, would prove in the end very bad economy; but I sank into dozing unconsciousness before I could quite follow out my idea. I was roused by the touch of a spoon on my lips; it was Thekla feeding me. Her sweet, grave face had something approaching to a mother's look of tenderness upon it, as she gave me spoonful after spoonful with gentle patience and dainty care; and then I fell asleep once more. When next I wakened, it was night; the stove was lighted, and the burning wood made a pleasant crackle, though I could only see the outlines and edges of red flame through the crevices of the small iron door. The uncurtained window on my left looked into the purple solemn night. Turning a little, I saw Thekla sitting near a table, sewing diligently at some great white piece of household work. Every now and then, she stopped to snuff the candle; sometimes she began to ply her needle again immediately; but once or twice she let her busy hands lie idly in her lap, and looked into the darkness, and thought deeply for a moment or two; these pauses always ended in a kind of sobbing sigh, the sound of which seemed to restore her to self-consciousness, and she took to her sewing even more diligently than before. Watching her had a sort of dreamy interest for me; this diligence of hers was a pleasant contrast to my repose; it seemed to enhance the flavour of my rest. I was too much of an animal just then to have my sympathy, or even my curiosity, strongly excited by her look of sad remembrance, or by her sighs.

After a while she gave a little start, looked at a watch lying by her on the table, and came, shading the candle by her hand, softly to my bedside. When she saw my open eyes, she went to a porringer placed at the top of the stove, and fed me with soup. She did not speak while doing this. I was half aware that she had done it many times since the doctor's visit, although this seemed to be the first time that I was fully awake. She passed her arm under the pillow on which my head rested, and raised me a very little; her support was as firm as a man's could have been. Again back to her work, and I to my slumbers, without a word being exchanged.

It was broad daylight when I wakened again; I could see the sunny atmosphere of the garden outside stealing in through the nicks at the side of the shawl, hung up to darken the room – a shawl which I was sure had not been there when I had observed the window in the night. How gently my nurse must have moved about, while doing her thoughtful act!

My breakfast was brought me by the hostess; she who had received me on my first arrival at this hospitable inn. She meant to do everything kindly, I am sure; but a sickroom was not her place; by a thousand little mal-adroitnesses she fidgeted me past bearing: her shoes creaked, her dress rustled; she asked me questions about myself which it irritated me to answer; she congratulated me on being so much better, while I was faint for want of food which she delayed giving me, in order to talk. My host had more sense in him when he came in, although his shoes creaked as well as hers. By this time I was somewhat revived, and could talk a little; besides, it seemed churlish to be longer without acknowledging so much kindness received.

'I am afraid I have been a great trouble,' said I. 'I can only say that I am truly grateful.'

His good, broad face reddened, and he moved a little uneasily.

'I don't see how I could have done otherwise than I – than we did,' replied he, in the soft German of the district. 'We were all glad enough to do what we could; I don't say it was a pleasure, because it is our busiest time of year – but then,' said he, laughing a little awkwardly, as if he feared his expression might have been misunderstood, 'I don't suppose it has been a pleasure to you either, sir, to be laid up so far from home.'

'No, indeed!'

'I may as well tell you now, sir, that we had to look over your papers and clothes. In the first place, when you were so ill I would fain have let your kinsfolk know, if I could have found a clue; and besides, you needed linen.'

'I am wearing a shirt of yours, though,' said I, touching my sleeve.

'Yes, sir!' said he, again reddening a little. 'I told Thekla to take the finest out of the chest; but I am afraid you find it coarser than your own.'

For all answer, I could only lay my weak hand on the great brown paw resting on the bedside. He gave me a sudden squeeze in return, that I thought would have crushed my bones.

'I beg your pardon, sir,' said he, misinterpreting the sudden look of pain which I could not repress; 'but watching a man come out of the shadow of death into life makes one feel very friendly towards him.'

'No old or true friend that I have had could have done more for me than you, and your wife, and Thekla, and the good doctor.'

'I am a widower,' said he, turning round the great wedding-ring that decked his third finger. 'My sister keeps house for me, and takes care of the children – that is to say, she does it with the help of Thekla, the house-maiden. But I have other servants,' he continued. 'I am well-to-do, the good God be thanked! I have land, and cattle, and vineyards. It will soon be our vintage-time, and then you must go and see my grapes as they come into the village. I have a "*chasse*", too, in the Odenwald; perhaps one day you will be strong enough to go and shoot the "*chevreuil*"[200] with me.'

His good, true heart was trying to make me feel like a welcome guest. Some time afterwards I learnt from the doctor that – my poor fifty pounds being nearly all expended – my host and he had been brought to believe in my poverty, as the necessary examination of my clothes and papers showed so little evidence of wealth. But I myself have but little to do with my story; I only name these things, and repeat these conversations, to show what a true, kind, honest man my host was. By the way, I may as well call him by his name henceforward, Fritz Müller. The doctor's name, Wiedermann.

I was tired enough with this interview with Fritz Müller; but when Dr Wiedermann came he pronounced me to be much better; and through the day much the same course was pursued as on the previous one: being fed, lying still, and sleeping, were my passive and active occupations. It was a hot, sunshiny day, and I craved for air. Fresh air does not enter into the pharmacopoeia[201] of a German doctor; but somehow I obtained my wish. During the morning-hours the window through which the sun streamed – the window looking on to the front court – was opened a little; and through it I heard the sounds of active life, which gave me pleasure and interest enough. The hen's cackle, the cock's exultant call, when he had found the treasure of a grain of corn, the movements of a tethered donkey, and the cooing and whirring of the pigeons which lighted on the window-sill, gave me just subjects enough for interest. Now and then a cart or carriage drove up – I could hear them ascending the rough village street long before they stopped at the Halbmond,[202] the village inn. Then there came a sound of running and haste in the house; and Thekla was always called for in sharp, imperative tones. I heard little children's footsteps, too, from time to time; and once there must have been some childish accident or hurt, for a shrill, plaintive little voice kept calling out, '*Thekla*, *Thekla*, *liebe*[203] *Thekla!*' Yet, after the first early morning-hours, when my hostess attended on my wants, it was always Thekla who came to give me my food or my medicine; who redded up[204] my room; who arranged the degree of light, shifting the temporary curtain with the shifting sun: and always as quietly and deliberately as though her attendance upon me were her sole work. Once or twice, my hostess came into the large eating-room (out of which my room opened), and called Thekla away from whatever was her occupation in my room at the time, in a sharp, injured, imperative whisper. Once I remember it was to say that sheets were wanted for some stranger's bed, and to ask where she, the speaker, could have put the keys, in a tone of irritation, as though Thekla were responsible for Fräulein Müller's own forgetfulness.

Night came on; the sounds of daily life died away into silence; the children's voices were no more heard; the poultry were all gone to roost; the beasts of burden to their stables; and travellers were housed. Then Thekla came in softly and quietly, and took up her appointed place, after she had done all in her power for my comfort. I felt that I was in no state to be left all those weary hours which intervened between sunset and sunrise; but I did feel ashamed that this young woman, who had watched by me all the previous night, and, for aught I knew, for many nights before, and had worked hard, been run off her legs, as English servants would say, all day long, should come and take up her care of me again; and it was with a feeling of relief that I saw her head bend forwards, and finally rest on her arms, which had fallen on the white piece of sewing spread before her on the table. She slept; and I slept. When I wakened dawn was stealing into the room, and making pale the lamplight. Thekla was standing by the stove where she had been preparing the bouillon I should require on wakening. But she did not notice my half-open eyes, although her face was turned towards the bed. She was reading a letter slowly, as if its words were familiar to her, yet as though she were trying afresh to extract some fuller or some different meaning from their construction. She folded it up softly and slowly, and replaced it in her pocket with the quiet movement habitual to her. Then she looked before her; not at me, but at vacancy filled up by memory; and, as the enchanter brought up the scenes and people which she saw, but I could not, her eyes filled with tears – tears that gathered almost imperceptibly to herself as it would seem – for when one large drop fell on her hands (held slightly together before her as she stood) she started a little, and brushed her eyes with the back of her hand, and then came towards the bed to see if I was awake. If I had not witnessed her previous emotion, I could never have guessed that she had any hidden sorrow or pain from her manner, tranquil, self-restrained as usual. The thought of this letter haunted me, especially as more than once I, wakeful or watchful during the ensuing nights, either saw it in her hands, or suspected that she had been recurring to it, from noticing the same sorrowful, dreamy look upon her face when she thought herself unobserved. Most likely, everyone has noticed how inconsistently out of proportion some ideas become, when one is shut up in any place without change of scene or thought. I really grew quite irritated about this letter. If I did not see it, I suspected it lay *perdu*[205] in her pocket. What was in it? Of course it was a love-letter; but, if so, what was going wrong in the course of her love? I became like a spoilt child in my recovery: everyone whom I saw for the time being was thinking only of me, so it was perhaps no wonder that I became my sole object of thought; and at last the gratification of my curiosity about this letter seemed to me a duty that I owed to myself. As long as my fidgety inquisitiveness remained ungratified, I felt as if I could not get well. But, to do myself justice, it was more than inquisitiveness. Thekla had tended me with the gentle, thoughtful care of a sister, in the midst of her busy life. I could often hear the Fräulein's sharp voice outside, blaming her for something that had gone wrong; but I never heard much from Thekla in reply. Her name was called in various tones by different people, more frequently than I could count, as if her services were in perpetual requisition; yet I was never neglected, or even long uncared-for. The doctor was kind and attentive; my host friendly and really generous; his sister subdued her acerbity of manner, when in my room; but Thekla was the one of all to whom I owed my comforts, if not my life. If I could do anything to smooth her path (and a little money goes a great way in these primitive parts of Germany), how willingly would I give it! So, one night, I began – she was no longer needed to watch by my bedside, but she was arranging my room before leaving me for the night: 'Thekla,' said I, 'you don't belong to Heppenheim, do you?'

She looked at me, and reddened a little.

'No. Why do you ask?'

'You have been so good to me that I cannot help wanting to know more about you. I must needs feel interested in one who has been by my side through my illness as you have. Where do your friends live? Are your parents alive?'

All this time I was driving at the letter.

'I was born at Altenahr.[206] My father is an innkeeper there. He owns the Golden Stag. My mother is dead, and he has married again, and has many children.'

'And your stepmother is unkind to you?' said I, jumping to a conclusion.

'Who said so?' asked she, with a shade of indignation in her tone. 'She is a right good woman, and makes my father a good wife.'

'Then why are you here living so far from home?'

Now the look came back to her face which I had seen upon it during the night hours when I had watched her by stealth! a dimming of the grave frankness of her eyes, a light quiver at the corners of her mouth. But all she said was, 'It was better.'

Somehow, I persisted with the wilfulness of an invalid. I am half-ashamed of it now.

'But why better, Thekla? Was there' – How should I put it? I stopped a little, and then rushed blindfold at my object: 'Has not that letter which you read so often something to do with your being here?'

She fixed me with her serious eyes, till I believe I reddened far more than she; and I hastened to pour out, incoherently enough, my conviction that she had some secret care, and my desire to help her if she was in any trouble.

'You cannot help me,' said she, a little softened by my explanation, though some shade of resentment at having been thus surreptitiously watched yet lingered in her manner. 'It is an old story; a sorrow gone by, past; at least it ought to be, only sometimes I am foolish' – her tones were softening now – 'and it is punishment enough that you have seen my folly.'

'If you had a brother here, Thekla, you would let him give you his sympathy if he could not give you his help, and you would not blame yourself if you had shown him your sorrow, would you? I tell you again, let me be as a brother to you!'

'In the first place, sir' – this 'sir' was to mark the distinction between me and the imaginary brother – 'I should have been ashamed to have shown even a brother my sorrow, which is also my reproach and my disgrace.' These were strong words, and I suppose that my face showed that I attributed to them a still stronger meaning than they warranted; but *honi soit qui mal y pense*[207] – for she went on dropping her eyes and speaking hurriedly.

'My shame and my reproach is this: I have loved a man who has not loved me' – she grasped her hands together till the fingers made deep white dents in the rosy flesh – 'and I can't make out whether he ever did, or whether he did once and is changed now; if only he did once love me, I could forgive myself.'

With hasty, trembling hands she began to rearrange the tisane[208] and medicines for the night on the little table at my bedside. But, having got thus far, I was determined to persevere.

'Thekla,' said I, 'tell me all about it, as you would to your mother, if she were alive! There are often misunderstandings which, never set to rights, make the misery and desolation of a lifetime.'

She did not speak at first. Then she pulled out the letter, and said, in a quiet, hopeless tone of voice: 'You can read German writing?[209] Read that, and see if I have any reason for misunderstanding!'

The letter was signed 'Franz Weber', and dated from some small town in Switzerland – I forget what – about a month previous to the time when I read it. It began with acknowledging the receipt of some money which had evidently been requested by the writer, and for which the thanks were almost fulsome; and then, by the quietest transition in the world, he went on to consult her as to the desirability of his marrying some girl in the place from which he wrote, saying that this Anna Somebody was only eighteen, and very pretty, and her father a well-to-do shopkeeper, and adding, with coarse coxcombry, his belief that he was not indifferent to the maiden herself. He wound up by saying that, if this marriage did take place, he should certainly repay the various sums of money which Thekla had lent him at different times.

I was some time in making out all this. Thekla held the candle for me to read it; held it patiently and steadily, not speaking a word till I had folded up the letter again, and given it back to her. Then our eyes met.

'There is no misunderstanding possible, is there, sir?' asked she, with a faint smile.

'No,' I replied; 'but you are well rid of such a fellow.'

She shook her head a little. 'It shows his bad side, sir. We have all our bad sides. You must not judge him harshly; at least, I cannot. But then we were brought up together.'

'At Altenahr?'

'Yes; his father kept the other inn, and our parents, instead of being rivals, were great friends. Franz is a little younger than I, and was a delicate child. I had to take him to school, and I used to be so proud of it and of my charge! Then he grew strong, and was the handsomest lad in the village. Our fathers used to sit and smoke together, and talk of our marriage; and Franz must have heard as much as I. Whenever he was in trouble, he would come to me for what advice I could give him, and he danced twice as often with me as with any other girl at all the dances, and always brought his nosegay to me. Then his father wished him to travel, and learn the ways at the great hotels on the Rhine before he settled down in Altenahr. You know that is the custom in Germany, sir. They go from town to town as journeymen, learning something fresh everywhere, they say.'

'I knew that was done in trades,' I replied.

'Oh, yes; and among innkeepers, too,' she said. 'Most of the waiters at the great hotels in Frankfort, and Heidelberg, and Mayence, and I dare say at all the other places, are the sons of innkeepers in small towns, who go out into the world to learn new ways, and perhaps to pick up a little English and French; otherwise, they say, they should never get on. Franz went off from Altenahr on his journeyings four years ago next May Day, and before he went, he brought me back a ring from Bonn, where he bought his new clothes. I don't wear it now; but I have got it upstairs, and it comforts me to see something that shows me it was not all my silly fancy. I suppose he fell among bad people, for he soon began to play for money – and then he lost more than he could always pay; and sometimes I could help him a little, for we wrote to each other from time to time, as we knew each other's addresses; for the little ones grew around my father's hearth, and I thought that I, too, would go forth into the world and earn my own living, so that – well, I will tell the truth – I thought that by going into service, I could lay by enough for buying a handsome stock of household-linen, and plenty of pans and kettles against – against what will never come to pass now.'

'Do the German women buy the pots and kettles, as you call them, when they are married?' asked I, awkwardly, laying hold of a trivial question, to conceal the indignant sympathy with her wrongs which I did not like to express.

'Oh, yes; the bride furnishes all that is wanted in the kitchen, and all the store of house-linen. If my mother had lived, it would have been laid by for me, as she could have afforded to buy it; but my stepmother will have hard enough work to provide for her own four little girls. However,' she continued, brightening up, 'I can help her, for now shall never marry; and my master here is just and liberal, and pays me sixty florins a year, which is high wages.' (Sixty florins are about five pounds sterling.) 'And now, good-night, sir. This cup to the left holds the tisane, that to the right the acorn-tea.' She shaded the candle, and was leaving the room. I raised myself on my elbow, and called her back.

'Don't go on thinking about this man,' said I. 'He was not good enough for you. You are much better unmarried.'

'Perhaps so,' she answered gravely. 'But you cannot do him justice; you do not know him.'

A few minutes after, I heard her soft and cautious return; she had taken her shoes off, and came in her stockinged feet up to my bedside, shading the light with her hand. When she saw that my eyes were open, she laid down two letters on the table, close by my night-lamp.

'Perhaps, sometime, sir, you would take the trouble to read these letters; you would then see how noble and clever Franz really is. It is I who ought to be blamed, not he.'

No more was said that night.

Sometime the next morning I read the letters. They were filled with vague, inflated, sentimental descriptions of his inner life and feelings; entirely egotistical, and intermixed with quotations from second-rate philosophers and poets. There was, it must be said, nothing in them offensive to good principle or good feeling, however much they might be opposed to good taste. I was to go into the next room that afternoon, for the first time of leaving my sick chamber. All the morning I lay and ruminated. From time to time I thought of Thekla and Franz Weber. She was the strong, good, helpful character, he the weak and vain; how strange it seemed that she should have cared for one so dissimilar; and then I remembered the various happy marriages, when to an outsider it seemed as if one was so inferior to the other that their union would have appeared a subject for despair, if it had been looked at prospectively. My host came in, in the midst of these meditations, bringing a great flowered dressing-gown, lined with flannel, and the embroidered smoking-cap which he evidently considered as belonging to this Indian-looking robe. They had been his father's, he told me; and, as he helped me to dress, he went on with his communications on small family matters. His inn was flourishing; the numbers increased every year of those who came to see the church at Heppenheim – the church which was the pride of the place, but which I had never yet seen. It was built by the great Kaiser Karl.[210] And there was the Castle of Starkenburg,[211] too, which the Abbots of Lorsch had often defended, stalwart churchmen as they were, against the temporal power of the emperors. And Melibocus[212] was not beyond a walk either. In fact, it was the work of one person to superintend the inn alone; but he had his farm and his vineyards beyond, which of themselves gave him enough to do. And his sister was oppressed with the perpetual calls made upon her patience and her nerves in an inn; and would rather go back and live at Worms. And his children wanted so much looking after. By the time he had placed himself in a condition for requiring my full sympathy, I had finished my slow toilette, and I had to interrupt his confidences, and accept the help of his good strong arm to lead me into the great eating-room out of which my chamber opened. I had a dreamy recollection of the vast apartment. But how pleasantly it was changed! There was the bare half of the room, it is true, looking as it had done on that first afternoon, sunless and cheerless, with the long, unoccupied table, and the necessary chairs for the possible visitors; but round the windows that opened on the garden a part of the room was enclosed by the household clothes'-horses, hung with great pieces of the blue homespun cloth of which the dress of the Black Forest peasant is made. This shut-in space was warmed by the lighted stove, as well as by the lowering rays of the October sun. There was a little round walnut table with some flowers upon it, and a great cushioned armchair, placed so as to look out upon the garden and the hills beyond. I felt sure that this was all Thekla's arrangement; I had rather wondered that I had seen so little of her this day. She had come once or twice on necessary errands into my room in the morning, but had appeared to be in great haste, and had avoided meeting my eye. Even when I had returned the letters, which she had entrusted to me with so evident a purpose of placing the writer in my good opinion, she had never enquired as to how far they had answered her design; she had merely taken them with some low word of thanks, and put them hurriedly into her pocket. I suppose she shrank from remembering how fully she had given me her confidence the night before, now that daylight and actual life pressed close around her. Besides, there surely never was anyone in such constant request as Thekla. I did not like this estrangement, though it was the natural consequence of my improved health, which would daily make me less and less require services which seemed so urgently claimed by others. And, moreover, after my host left me – I fear I had cut him a little short in the recapitulation of his domestic difficulties, but he was too thorough and good-hearted a man to bear malice – I wanted to be amused or interested. So I rang my little handbell, hoping that Thekla would answer it, when I could have fallen into conversation with her, without specifying any decided want. Instead of Thekla, the Fräulein came, and I had to invent a wish, for I could not act as a baby, and say that I wanted my nurse. However, the Fräulein was better than no one; so I asked her if I could have some grapes, which had been provided for me on every day but this, and which were especially grateful to my feverish palate. She was a good, kind woman, although, perhaps, her temper was not the best in the world; and she expressed the sincerest regret as she told me that there were no more in the house. Like an invalid, I fretted at my wish not being granted, and spoke out.

'But Thekla told me the vintage was not till the fourteenth; and you have a vineyard close beyond the garden, on the slope of the hill[213] out there, have you not?'

'Yes; and grapes for the gathering. But perhaps the gentleman does not know our laws. Until the vintage – the day of beginning the vintage is fixed by the Grand Duke,[214] and advertised in the public papers – until the vintage, all owners of vineyards may only go on two appointed days in every week to gather their grapes; on those two days (Tuesdays and Fridays, this year) they must gather enough for the wants of their families; and, if they do not reckon rightly, and gather short measure, why, they have to go without. And these two last days the Half-Moon has been besieged by visitors, all of whom have asked for grapes. But tomorrow the gentleman can have as many as he will; it is the day for gathering them.'

'What a strange kind of paternal law!' I grumbled out. 'Why is it so ordained? Is it to secure the owners against pilfering from their unfenced vineyards?'

'I am sure I cannot tell,' she replied. 'Country people in these villages have strange customs in many ways, as I dare say the English gentleman has perceived. If he would come to Worms, he would see a different kind of life.'

'But not a view like this,' I replied, caught by a sudden change of light – some cloud passing away from the sun, or something. Right outside of the windows was, as I have so often said, the garden. Trained plum trees with golden leaves, great bushes of purple Michaelmas daisies, late-flowering roses, apple trees, partly stripped of their rosy fruit, but still with enough left on their boughs to require the props set to support the luxuriant burden; to the left an arbour; covered over with honeysuckle and other sweet-smelling creepers – all bounded by a low grey stone wall which opened out upon the steep vineyard that stretched up the hill beyond, one hill of a series rising higher and higher into the purple distance. 'Why is there a rope with a bunch of straw tied in it stretched across the opening of the garden into the vineyard?' I enquired, as my eye suddenly caught upon the object.

'It is the country way of showing that no one must pass along that path. Tomorrow the gentleman will see it removed; and then he shall have the grapes. Now I will go and prepare his coffee.' With a curtsey, after the fashion of Worms gentility, she withdrew. But an under-servant brought me my coffee, and with her I could not exchange a word; she spoke in such an execrable patois. I went to bed early, weary and depressed. I must have fallen asleep immediately, for I never heard anyone come to arrange my bedside table; yet in the morning I found that every usual want or wish of mine had been attended to.

I was wakened by a tap at my door, and a pretty piping child's voice asking, in broken German, to come in. On giving the usual permission, Thekla entered, carrying a great, lovely boy of two years old, or thereabouts, who had only his little nightshirt on, and was all flushed with sleep. He held tight in his hands a great cluster of noble muscatel grapes. He seemed like a little Bacchus,[215] as she carried him towards me with an expression of pretty loving pride upon her face, as she looked at him. But, when he came close to me – the grim, wasted, unshorn – he turned quick away, and hid his face in her neck, still grasping tight his bunch of grapes. She spoke to him rapidly and softly, coaxing him, as I could tell full well, although I could not follow her words; and in a minute or two the little fellow obeyed her, and turned and stretched himself almost to overbalancing out of her arms, and half-dropped the fruit on the bed by me. Then he clutched at her again, burying his face in her kerchief, and fastening his little fists in her luxuriant hair.

'It is my master's only boy,' said she, disentangling his fingers with quiet patience, only to have them grasp her braids afresh. 'He is my little Max, my heart's delight; only he must not pull so hard. Say his "to-meet-again",[216] and kiss his hand lovingly, and we will go.' The promise of a speedy departure from my dusky room proved irresistible; he babbled out his *Auf Wiederseh'n*, and, kissing his chubby hand, he was borne away joyful and chattering fast in his infantile half-language. I did not see Thekla again until late afternoon, when she brought me in my coffee. She was not like the same creature as the blooming, cheerful maiden whom I had seen in the morning; she looked wan and careworn, older by several years.

'What is the matter, Thekla?' said I, with true anxiety as to what might have befallen my good, faithful nurse.

She looked round before answering. 'I have seen him,' she said. 'He has been here, and the Fräulein has been so angry! She says she will tell my master. Oh, it has been such a day!' The poor young woman, who was usually so composed and self-restrained, was on the point of bursting into tears; but by a strong effort she checked herself, and tried to busy herself with rearranging the white china cup, so as to place it more conveniently to my hand.

'Come, Thekla,' said I, 'tell me all about it. I have heard loud voices talking, and I fancied something had put the Fräulein out; and Lottchen looked flurried when she brought me my dinner. Is Franz here? How has he found you out?'

'He is here. Yes, I am sure it is he; but four years makes such a difference in a man; his whole look and manner seemed so strange to me; but he knew me at once, and called me all the old names which we used to call each other when we were children; and he must needs tell me how it had come to pass that he had not married that Swiss Anna. He said he had never loved her; and that now he was going home to settle, and he hoped that I would come too, and' – There she stopped short.

'And marry him, and live at the inn at Altenahr,' said I, smiling to reassure her, though I felt rather disappointed about the whole affair.

'No,' she replied. 'Old Weber, his father, is dead; he died in debt, and Franz will have no money. And he was always one that needed money. Some are, you know; and, while I was thinking, and he was standing near me, the Fräulein came in; and – and – I don't wonder – for poor Franz is not a pleasant-looking man nowadays – she was very angry, and called me a bold, bad girl, and said she could have no such goings on at the Halbmond, but would tell my master when he came home from the forest.'

'But you could have told her that you were old friends' – I hesitated before saying the word 'lovers'; but, after a pause, out it came.

'Franz might have said so,' she replied, a little stiffly. 'I could not; but he went off as soon as she bade him. He went to the Adler[217] over the way, only saying he would come for my answer tomorrow morning. I think it was he that should have told her what we were – neighbour's children and early friends – not have left it all to me. Oh,' said she, clasping her hands tight together, 'she will make such a story of it to my master!'

'Never mind,' said I; 'tell the master I want to see him, as soon as he comes in from the forest, and trust me to set him right before the Fräulein has the chance to set him wrong!'

She looked up at me gratefully, and went away without any more words. Presently, the fine burly figure of my host stood at the opening to my enclosed sitting-room. He was there, three-cornered hat in hand, looking tired and heated as a man does after a hard day's work, but as kindly and genial as ever; which is not what every man is who is called to business after such a day, before he has had the necessary food and rest.

I had been reflecting a good deal on Thekla's story; I could not quite interpret her manner today to my full satisfaction; but yet, the love which had grown with her growth must assuredly have been called forth by her lover's sudden reappearance; and I was inclined to give him some credit for having broken off an engagement to

Swiss Anna, which had promised so many worldly advantages; and, again, I had considered that, if he was a little weak and sentimental, it was Thekla who would marry him by her own free will, and perhaps she had sense and quiet resolution enough for both. So I gave the heads of the little history I have told you to my good friend and host, adding that I should like to have a man's opinion of this man; but that, if he were not an absolute good-for-nothing, and, if Thekla still loved him, as I believed, I would try and advance them the requisite money towards establishing themselves in the hereditary inn at Altenahr.

Such was the romantic ending to Thekla's sorrows I had been planning and brooding over for the last hour. As I narrated my tale, and hinted at the possible happy conclusion that might be in store, my host's face changed. The ruddy colour faded, and his look became almost stern – certainly very grave in expression. It was so unsympathetic, that I instinctively cut my words short. When I had done, he paused a little, and then said, 'You would wish me to learn all I can respecting this stranger now at the Adler, and give you the impression I receive of the fellow.'

'Exactly so,' said I. 'I want to learn all I can about him for Thekla's sake.'

'For Thekla's sake I will do it,' he gravely repeated.

'And come to me tonight, even if I am gone to bed?'

'Not so,' he replied. 'You must give me all the time you can in a matter like this.'

'But he will come for Thekla's answer in the morning.'

'Before he comes, you shall know all I can learn.'

I was resting during the fatigues of dressing the next day, when my host tapped at my door. He looked graver and sterner than I had ever seen him do before. He sat down almost before I had begged him to do so.

'He is not worthy of her,' he said. 'He drinks brandy right hard; he boasts of his success at play, and' – here he set his teeth hard – 'he boasts of the women who have loved him. In a village like this, sir, there are always those who spend their evenings in the gardens of the inns; and this man, after he had drank his fill, made no secrets. It needed no spying to find out what he was; else I should not have been the one to do it.'

'Thekla must be told of this,' said I. 'She is not the woman to love anyone whom she cannot respect.'

Herr Müller laughed a low, bitter laugh, quite unlike himself. Then he replied: 'As for that matter, sir, you are young; you have had no great experience of women. From what my sister tells me, there can be little doubt of Thekla's feeling towards him. She found them standing together by the window – his arm round Thekla's waist, and whispering in her ear; and, to do the maiden justice, she is not the one to suffer such familiarities from everyone. No,' continued he, still in the same contemptuous tone, 'you'll find she will make excuses for his faults and vices; or else, which is perhaps more likely, she will not believe your story, though I who tell it you can vouch for the truth of every word I say.' He turned short away and left the room. Presently I saw his stalwart figure in the hillside vineyard, before my windows, scaling the steep ascent with long, regular steps, going to the forest beyond. I was otherwise occupied than in watching his progress during the next hour. At the end of that time he re-entered my room, looking heated and slightly tired, as if he had been walking fast or labouring hard; but with the cloud off his brows, and the kindly light shining once again out of his honest eyes.

'I ask your pardon, sir,' he began, 'for troubling you afresh. I believe I was possessed by the devil this morning. I have been thinking it over. One has, perhaps, no right to rule for another person's happiness. To have such a' – here the honest fellow choked a little – 'such a woman as Thekla to love him ought to raise any man. Besides, I am no judge for him or for her. I have found out this morning that I love her myself; and so the end of it is, that if you, sir, who are so kind as to interest yourself in the matter, and if you think it is really her heart's desire to marry this man – which ought to be his salvation both for earth and heaven – I shall be very glad to go halves with you in any plan for setting them up in the inn at Altenahr; only allow me to see that whatever money we advance is well and legally tied up, so that it is secured to her. And be so kind as to take no notice of what I have said about my having found out that I have loved her. I named it as a kind of apology for my hard words this morning, and as a reason why I was not a fit judge of what was best.' He had hurried on so that I could not have stopped his eager speaking, even had I wished to do so; but I was too much interested in the revelation of what was passing in his brave tender heart to desire to stop him. Now, however, his rapid words tripped each other up, and his speech ended in an unconscious sigh.

'But,' I said, 'since you were here Thekla has come to me, and we have had a long talk. She speaks now as openly to me as she would if I were her brother; with sensible frankness, where frankness is wise –

with modest reticence, where confidence would be unbecoming. She came to ask me if I thought it her duty to marry this fellow, whose very appearance, changed for the worse, as she says it is, since she last saw him four years ago, seems to have repelled her.'

'She could let him put his arm round her waist yesterday,' said Herr Müller, with a return of his morning's surliness.

'And she would marry him now, if she could believe it to be her duty. For some reason of his own, this Franz Weber has tried to work upon this feeling of hers. He said it would be the saving of him.'

'As if a man had not strength enough in him – a man who is good for aught – to save himself, but needed a woman to pull him through life!'

'Nay,' I replied, hardly able to keep from smiling, 'you yourself said, not five minutes ago, that her marrying him might be his salvation both for earth and heaven.'

'That was when I thought she loved the fellow,' he answered quick. 'Now – but what did you say to her, sir?'

'I told her, what I believe to be as true as gospel, that, as she owned she did not love him any longer, now his real self had come to displace his remembrance, she would be sinning in marrying him – doing evil that possible good might come. I was clear myself on this point; though I should have been perplexed how to advise, if her love had still continued.'

'And what answer did she make?'

'She went over the history of their lives. She was pleading against her wishes, to satisfy her conscience. She said that all along through her childhood she had been his strength; that, while under her personal influence, he had been negatively good; away from her, he had fallen into mischief – '

'Not to say vice,' put in Herr Müller.

'And now he came to her penitent, in sorrow, desirous of amendment, asking her for the love she seems to have considered as tacitly plighted to him in years gone by – '

'And which he has slighted and insulted. I hope you told her of his words and conduct last night in the Adler gardens?'

'No; I kept myself to the general principle, which, I am sure, is a true one. I repeated it in different forms; for the idea of the duty of self-sacrifice had taken strong possession of her fancy. Perhaps, if I had failed in setting her notion of her duty in the right aspect, I might have had recourse to the statement of facts, which would have pained her severely, but would have proved to her how little his words of penitence and promises of amendment were to be trusted to.'

'And it ended?'

'Ended by her being quite convinced that she would be doing wrong instead of right, if she married a man whom she had entirely ceased to love, and that no real good could come[218] from a course of action based on wrong-doing.'

'That is right and true,' he replied, his face broadening into happiness again.

'But she says she must leave your service, and go elsewhere.'

'Leave my service she shall; go elsewhere she shall not.'

'I cannot tell what you may have the power of inducing her to do; but she seems to me very resolute.'

'Why?' said he, firing round at me, as if I had made her resolute.

'She says your sister spoke to her before the maids of the household, and before some of the townspeople, in a way that she could not stand; and that you yourself, by your manner to her last night, showed how she had lost your respect. She added, with her face of pure maidenly truth, that he had come into such close contact with her only the instant before your sister had entered the room.'

'With your leave, sir,' said Herr Müller, turning towards the door, 'I will go and set all that right at once.'

It was easier said than done. When I next saw Thekla, her eyes were swollen up with crying; but she was silent, almost defiant towards me. A look of resolute determination had settled down upon her face. I learnt afterwards that parts of my conversation with Herr Müller had been injudiciously quoted by him in the talk he had had with her. I thought I would leave her to herself, and wait till she unburdened herself of the feelings of unjust resentment towards me. But it was days before she spoke to me with anything like her former frankness. I had heard all about it from my host long before.

He had gone to her straight on leaving me; and, like a foolish, impetuous lover, had spoken out his mind and his wishes to her in the presence of his sister, who, it must be remembered, had heard no explanation of the conduct which had given her propriety so great a shock the day before. Herr Müller thought to reinstate Thekla in his sister's good opinion by giving her in the Fräulein's very presence the highest possible mark of his own love and esteem. And there in the kitchen, where the Fräulein was deeply engaged in the hot work of making some delicate preserve on the stove, and ordering Thekla about with short, sharp displeasure in her tones, the master had come in, and, possessing himself of the maiden's hand, had, to her infinite surprise – to his sister's infinite indignation – made her the offer of his heart, his wealth, his life; had begged of her to marry him. I could gather from his account that she had been in a state of trembling discomfiture at first; she had not spoken, but had twisted her hand out of his, and had covered her face with her apron. And then the Fräulein had burst forth – 'accursed words', he called her speech. Thekla had uncovered her face, to listen – to listen to the end – to the passionate recrimination between the brother and the sister. And then she had gone up close to the angry Fräulein, and had said, quite quietly, but with a manner of final determination which had evidently sunk deep into her suitor's heart, and depressed him into hopelessness, that the Fräulein had no need to disturb herself; that on this very day she had been thinking of marrying another man, and that her heart was not like a room to let, into which as one tenant went out another might enter. Nevertheless, she felt the master's goodness. He had always treated her well, from the time when she had entered the house as his servant. And she should be sorry to leave him; sorry to leave the children; very sorry to leave little Max; yes, she should even be sorry to leave the Fräulein, who was a good woman, only a little too apt to be hard on other women. But she had already been that very day and deposited her warning at the police office;[219] the busy time would be soon over, and she should be glad to leave their service on All Saints' Day.[220] Then (he thought) she had felt inclined to cry, for she suddenly braced herself up, and said, yes, she should be very glad; for somehow, though they had been kind to her, she had been very unhappy at Heppenheim; and she would go back to her home for a time, and see her old father and kind stepmother, and her nursling half-sister Ida, and be among her own people again.

I could see it was this last part that most of all rankled in Herr Müller's mind. In all probability Franz Weber was making his way back to Altenahr too; and the bad suspicion would keep welling up, that some lingering feeling for her old lover and disgraced playmate was making her so resolute to leave and return to Altenahr.

For some days after this I was the confidant of the whole household, except Thekla. She, poor creature, looked miserable enough; but the hardy, defiant expression was always on her face. Lottchen spoke out freely enough; her place would not be worth having, if Thekla left; it was she who had the head for everything, the patience for everything; who stood between all the under-servants and the

Fräulein's tempers. As for the children, poor motherless children! Lottchen was sure that the master did not know what he was doing when he allowed his sister to turn Thekla away – and all for what? for having a lover, as every girl had who could get one. Why, the little boy Max slept in the room which Lottchen shared with Thekla, and she heard him in the night as quickly as if she was his mother; when she had been sitting up with me, when I was so ill, Lottchen had had to attend to him, and it was weary work after a hard day to have to get up and soothe a teething child; she knew she had been cross enough sometimes; but Thekla was always good and gentle with him, however tired she was. And, as Lottchen left the room, I could hear her repeating that she thought she should leave when Thekla went; for that her place would not be worth having.

Even the Fräulein had her word of regret – regret mingled with self-justification. She thought she had been quite right in speaking to Thekla for allowing such familiarities; how was she to know that the man was an old friend and playmate? He looked like a right profligate good-for-nothing. And to have a servant take up her scolding as an unpardonable offence, and persist in quitting her place, just when she had learnt all her work, and was so useful in the household – so useful that the Fräulein could never put up with any fresh, stupid house-maiden; but, sooner than take the trouble of teaching the new servant where everything was, and how to give out the stores if she was busy, she would go back to Worms. For, after all, housekeeping for a brother was thankless work; there was no satisfying men; and Heppenheim was but a poor ignorant village compared to Worms.

She must have spoken to her brother about her intention of leaving him and returning to her former home; indeed, a feeling of coolness had evidently grown up between the brother and sister during these latter days. When one evening Herr Müller brought in his pipe, and, as his custom had sometimes been, sat down by my stove to smoke, he looked gloomy and annoyed. I let him puff away, and take his own time. At length he began: 'I have rid the village of him at last. I could not bear to have him here, disgracing Thekla with speaking to her, whenever she went to the vineyard or the fountain. I don't believe she likes him a bit.'

'No more do I,' I said. He turned on me: 'Then why did she speak to him at all? Why cannot she like an honest man who likes her? Why is she so bent on going home to Altenahr?'

'She speaks to him, because she has known him from a child, and has a faithful pity for one whom she has known so innocent, and who is now so lost in all good men's regard. As for not liking an honest man (though I may have my own opinion about that), liking goes by fancy, as we say in England; and Altenahr is her home; her father's house is at Altenahr, as you know.'

'I wonder if he will go there,' quoth Herr Müller, after two or three more puffs. 'He was fast at the Adler; he could not pay his score; so he kept on staying here, saying that he should receive a letter from a friend with money in a day or two; lying in wait, too, for Thekla, who is well-known and respected all through Heppenheim: so his being an old friend of hers made him have a kind of standing. I went in this morning and paid his score, on condition that he left the place this day; and he left the village as merrily as a cricket, caring no more for Thekla than for the Kaiser who built our church; for he never looked back at the Halbmond, but went whistling down the road.'

'That is a good riddance,' said I.

'Yes. But my sister says she must return to Worms. And Lottchen has given notice; she says the place will not be worth having, when Thekla leaves. I wish I could give notice too.'

'Try Thekla again!'

'Not I,' said he, reddening. 'It would seem now as if I only wanted her for a housekeeper. Besides, she avoids me at every turn, and will not even look at me. I am sure she bears me some ill-will about that ne'er-do-well.'

There was silence between us for some time, which he at length broke.

'The pastor has a good and comely daughter. Her mother is a famous housewife. They often have asked me to come to the parsonage and smoke a pipe. When the vintage is over, and I am less busy, I think I will go there and look about me.'

'When is the vintage?' asked I. 'I hope it will take place soon, for I am growing so well and strong that I fear I must leave you shortly; but I should like to see the vintage first.'

'Oh, never fear! you must not travel yet awhile; and Government has fixed the grape-gathering to begin on the fourteenth.'

'What a paternal Government! How does it know when the grapes will be ripe? Why cannot every man fix his own time for gathering his own grapes?'

'That has never been our way in Germany. There are people employed by the Government to examine the vines, and report when the grapes are ripe. It is necessary to make laws about it; for, as you must have seen, there is nothing but the fear of the law to protect our vineyards and fruit trees; there are no enclosures along the Bergstrasse, as you tell me you have in England; but, as people are only allowed to go into the vineyards on stated days, no one, under pretence of gathering his own produce, can stray into his neighbour's grounds and help himself, without some of the Grand Duke's foresters seeing him.'

'Well,' said I, 'to each country its own laws.'

I think it was on that very evening that Thekla came in for something. She stopped arranging the tablecloth and the flowers, as if she had something to say, yet did not know how to begin. At length I found that her sore, hot heart wanted some sympathy; her hand was against everyone's, and she fancied everyone had turned against her.[221] She looked up at me, and said, a little abruptly: 'Does the gentleman know that I go on the fifteenth?'

'So soon?' said I, with surprise. 'I thought you were to remain here till All Saints' Day.'

'So I should have done – so I must have done – if the Fräulein had not kindly given me leave to accept of a place – a very good place, too – of housekeeper to a widow lady at Frankfort. It is just the sort of situation I have always wished for. I expect I shall be so happy and comfortable there.'

'Methinks the lady doth protest too much,'[222] came into my mind. I saw she expected me to doubt the probability of her happiness, and was in a defiant mood.

'Of course,' said I, 'you would hardly have wished to leave Heppenheim, if you had been happy here; and every new place always promises fair, whatever its performance may be. But, wherever you go, remember you have always a friend in me!'

'Yes,' she replied, 'I think you are to be trusted. Though, from my experience, I should say that of very few men.'

'You have been unfortunate,' I answered; 'many men would say the same of women.'

She thought a moment, and then said, in a changed tone of voice, 'The Fräulein here has been much more friendly and helpful of these late days than her brother; yet I have served him faithfully, and have cared for his little Max as though he were my own brother. But this morning he spoke to me for the first time for many days; he met me in the passage, and, suddenly stopping, he said he was glad I had met with so comfortable a place, and that I was at full liberty to go whenever I liked; and then he went quickly on, never waiting for my answer.'

'And what was wrong in that? It seems to me he was trying to make you feel entirely at your ease, to do as you thought best, without regard to his own interests.'

'Perhaps so. It is silly, I know,' she continued, turning full on me her grave, innocent eyes; 'but one's vanity suffers a little when everyone is so willing to part with one.'

'Thekla! I owe you a great debt – let me speak to you openly! I know that your master wanted to marry you, and that you refused him. Do not deceive yourself! You are sorry for that refusal now?'

She kept her serious look fixed upon me; but her face and throat reddened all over.

'No,' she said, at length; 'I am not sorry. What can you think I am made of; having loved one man ever since I was a little child until a fortnight ago, and now just as ready to love another? I know you do not rightly consider what you say, or I should take it as an insult.'

'You loved an ideal man; he disappointed you, and you clung to your remembrance of him. He came, and the reality dispelled all illusions.'

'I do not understand philosophy,' said she. 'I only know that I think that Herr Müller has lost all respect for me, from what his sister has told him; and I know that I am going away; and I trust I shall be happier in Frankfort than I have been here of late days.' So saying, she left the room.

I was wakened up on the morning of the fourteenth by the merry ringing of church bells, and the perpetual firing and popping off of guns and pistols. But all this was over by the time I was up and dressed, and seated at breakfast in my partitioned room. It was a perfect October day; the dew not yet off the blades of grass, glistening on the delicate gossamer webs, which stretched from flower to flower in the garden, lying in the morning-shadow of the house. But beyond the garden, on the sunny hillside, men, women, and children were clambering up the vineyards like ants – busy, irregular in movement, clustering together, spreading wide apart – I could hear the shrill, merry voices as I sat – and all along the valley, as far as I could see, it was much the same; for everyone filled his house for the day of the vintage, that great annual festival. Lottchen, who had brought in my breakfast, was all in her Sunday best, having risen early to get her work done and go abroad to gather grapes. Bright colours seemed to abound; I could see dots of scarlet, and crimson, and orange through the fading leaves; it was not a day to languish in the house; and I was on the point of going out by myself, when Herr

Müller came in to offer me his sturdy arm, to help me in walking to the vineyard. We crept through the garden, scented with late flowers and sunny fruit – we passed through the gate I had so often gazed at from the easy-chair, and were in the busy vineyard; great baskets lay on the grass already piled nearly full of purple and yellow grapes. The wine made from these was far from pleasant to my taste; for the best Rhine-wine is made from a smaller grape, growing in closer, harder clusters; but the larger and less profitable grape is by far the most picturesque in its mode of growth, and far the best to eat into the bargain.[223] Wherever we trod, it was on fragrant, crushed vine-leaves; everyone we saw had his hands and face stained with the purple juice. Presently, I sat down on a sunny bit of grass, and my host left me to go further afield, to look after the more distant vineyards. I watched his progress. After he left me, he took off coat and waistcoat, displaying his snowy shirt and gaily-worked braces; and presently he was as busy as anyone. I looked down on the village; the grey and orange and crimson roofs lay glowing in the noonday sun. I could see down into the streets; but they were all empty – even the old people came toiling up the hillside to share in the general festivity. Lottchen had brought up cold dinners for a regiment of men; everyone came and helped himself. Thekla was there, leading the little Karoline, and helping the toddling steps of Max; but she kept aloof from me; for I knew, or suspected, or had probed, too much. She alone looked sad and grave, and spoke so little, even to her friends, that it was evident to see that she was trying to wean herself finally from the place. But I could see that she had lost her short, defiant manner. What she did say was kindly and gently spoken. The Fräulein came out late in the morning, dressed, I suppose, in the latest Worms fashion – quite different to anything I had ever seen before. She came up to me, and talked very graciously to me for some time.

'Here comes the proprietor (squire) and his lady, and their dear children. See, the vintagers have tied bunches of the finest grapes on to a stick, heavier than the children, or even the lady, can carry. Look! look! how he bows! – one can tell he has been an *attaché*[224] at Vienna. That is the Court way of bowing there – holding the hat right down before them, and bending the back at right angles. How graceful! And here is the doctor! I thought he would spare time to come up here! Well, doctor, you will go all the more cheerfully to your next patient for having been up into the vineyards. Nonsense, about grapes making other patients for you! Ah, here is the pastor and his wife, and the Fräulein Anna. Now, where is my brother, I wonder? Up in the far vineyard, I make no doubt. Herr Pastor, the view up above is far finer than what it is here, and the best grapes grow there; shall I accompany you and madame, and the dear Fräulein? The gentleman will excuse me.'

I was left alone. Presently, I thought I would walk a little farther, or at any rate change my position. I rounded a corner in the pathway; and there I found Thekla, watching by little sleeping Max. He lay on her shawl; and over his head she had made an arching canopy of broken vine-branches, so that the great leaves threw their cool, flickering shadows on his face. He was smeared all over with grape-juice; his sturdy fingers grasped a half-eaten bunch even in his sleep. Thekla was keeping Lina quiet, by teaching her how to weave a garland for her head out of field-flowers and autumn-tinted leaves. The maiden sat on the ground, with her back to the valley beyond, the child kneeling by her, watching the busy fingers with eager intentness. Both looked up as I drew near, and we exchanged a few words.

'Where is the master?' I asked. 'I promised to await his return; he wished to give me his arm down the wooden steps; but I do not see him.'

'He is in the higher vineyard,' said Thekla quietly, but not looking round in that direction. 'He will be some time there, I should think. He went with the pastor and his wife; he will have to speak to his labourers and his friends. My arm is strong, and I can leave Max in Lina's care for five minutes. If you are tired, and want to go back, let me help you down the steps; they are steep and slippery.'

I had turned to look up the valley. Three or four hundred yards off, in the higher vineyard, walked the dignified pastor and his homely decorous wife. Behind came the Fräulein Anna, in her short-sleeved Sunday gown, daintily holding a parasol over her luxuriant brown hair. Close behind her came Herr Müller, stopping now to speak to his men – again, to cull out a bunch of grapes to tie on to the Fräulein's stick; and by my feet sat the proud serving-maid in her country dress, waiting for my answer, with serious, upturned eyes, and sad, composed face.

'No, I am much obliged to you, Thekla; and, if I did not feel so strong, I would have thankfully taken your arm. But I only wanted to leave a message for the master, just to say that I have gone home.'

'Lina will give it to the father, when he comes down,' said Thekla.

I went slowly down into the garden. The great labour of the day was over, and the younger part of the population had returned to the village, and were preparing the fireworks and pistol-shootings for the evening. Already one or two of those well-known German carts (in the shape of a V) were standing near the vineyard gates, the patient oxen meekly waiting, while basketful after basketful of grapes were being emptied into the leaf-lined receptacle.

As I sat down in my easy-chair close to the open window through which I had entered, I could see the men and women on the hillside drawing to a centre, and all stand round the pastor, bareheaded, for a minute or so. I guessed that some words of holy thanksgiving were being said, and I wished that I had stayed to hear them, and mark my especial gratitude for having been spared to see that day. Then I heard the distant voices, the deep tones of the men, the shriller pipes of women and children, join in the German harvest-hymn, which is generally sung on such occasions;[225] then silence, while I concluded that a blessing was spoken by the pastor, with outstretched arms; and then they once more dispersed, some to the village, some to finish their labours for the day among the vines. I saw Thekla coming through the garden with Max in her arms, and Lina clinging to her woollen skirts. Thekla made for my open window; it was rather a shorter passage into the house than round by the door. 'I may come through, may I not?' she asked softly. 'I fear Max is not well; I cannot understand his look, and he wakened up so strange!' She paused to let me see the child's face; it was flushed almost to a crimson look of heat, and his breathing was laboured and uneasy, his eyes half-open and filmy.

'Something is wrong, I am sure,' said I. 'I don't know anything about children, but he is not in the least like himself.'

She bent down and kissed the cheek, so tenderly that she would not have bruised the petal of a rose. 'Heart's darling!'[226] she murmured. He quivered all over at her touch, working his fingers in an unnatural kind of way, and ending with a convulsive twitching all over his body. Lina began to cry at the grave, anxious look on our faces.

'You had better call the Fräulein to look at him,' said I. 'I feel sure he ought to have a doctor; I should say he was going to have a fit.'

'The Fräulein and the master are gone to the pastor's for coffee, and Lottchen is in the higher vineyard, taking the men their bread and beer. Could you find the kitchen-girl, or old Karl? he will be in the stables, I think. I must lose no time.' Almost without waiting for my reply, she had passed through the room, and in the empty house I could hear her firm, careful footsteps going up the stair; Lina's pattering beside her; and the one voice wailing, the other speaking low comfort.

I was tired enough; but this good family had treated me too much like one of their own for me not to do what I could, in such a case as this. I made my way out into the street, for the first time since I had come to the house on that memorable evening six weeks ago. I bribed the first person I met to guide me to the doctor's, and sent him straight down to the Halbmond, not staying to listen to the thorough scolding he fell to giving me; then, on to the parsonage, to tell the master and the Fräulein of the state of things at home.

I was sorry to be the bearer of bad news into such a festive chamber as the pastor's. There they sat, resting after heat and fatigue, each in their best gala dress, the table spread with 'Dicke Milch',[227] potato-salad, cakes of various shapes and kinds – all the dainty cates[228] dear to the German palate. The pastor was talking to Herr Müller, who stood near the pretty young Fräulein Anna, in her fresh white chemisette, with her round white arms, and her youthful coquettish airs, as she prepared to pour out the coffee; our Fräulein was talking busily to the Frau Mama; the younger boys and girls of the family filling up the room. A ghost would have startled the assembled party less than I did, and would probably have been more welcome, considering the news I brought. As he listened, the master caught up his hat and went forth, without apology or farewell. Our Fräulein made up for both, and questioned me fully; but now she, I could see, was in haste to go, although restrained by her manners, and the kind-hearted Frau Pastorin[229] soon set her at liberty to follow her inclination. As for me, I was dead beat, and only too glad to avail myself of the hospitable couple's pressing request, that I would stop and share their meal. Other magnates of the village came in presently, and relieved me of the strain of keeping up a German conversation about nothing at all with entire strangers. The pretty Fräulein's face had clouded over a little at Herr Müller's sudden departure; but she was soon as bright as could be, giving private chase and sudden little scoldings to her brothers, as they made raids upon the dainties under her charge. After I was duly rested and refreshed, I took my leave; for I, too, had my quieter anxieties about the sorrow in the Müller family.

The only person I could see at the Halbmond was Lottchen; everyone else was busy about the poor little Max, who was passing from one fit into another. I told Lottchen to ask the doctor to come in and see me before he took his leave for the night; and, tired as I was, I kept up till after his visit, though it was very late before he came;

I could see from his face how anxious he was. He would give me no opinion as to the child's chances of recovery; from which I guessed that he had not much hope. But, when I expressed my fear, he cut me very short.

'The truth is, you know nothing about it; no more do I, for that matter. It is enough to try any man, much less a father, to hear his perpetual moans – not that he is conscious of pain, poor little worm;[230] but, if she stops for a moment in her perpetual carrying him backwards and forwards, he plains so piteously it is enough to – enough to make a man bless the Lord, who never led him into the pit of matrimony. To see the father up there, following her as she walks up and down the room, the child's head over her shoulder, and Müller trying to make the heavy eyes recognise the old familiar ways of play, and the chirruping sounds which he can scarce make for crying! I shall be here tomorrow early, though, before that, either life or death will have come without the old doctor's help.'

All night long I dreamt my feverish dream – of the vineyard – the carts, which held little coffins instead of baskets of grapes – of the pastor's daughter, who would pull the dying child out of Thekla's arms; it was a bad, weary night! I slept long into the morning; the broad daylight filled my room; and yet no one had been near to waken me! Did that mean life or death? I got up and dressed as fast as I could; for I was aching all over with the fatigue of the day before. Out into the sitting-room; the table was laid for breakfast, but no one was there. I passed into the house beyond, up the stairs, blindly seeking for the room where I might know whether it was life or death. At the door of a room I found Lottchen crying; at the sight of me in that unwonted place she started, and began some kind of apology, broken both by tears and smiles, as she told me that the doctor said the danger was over – past, and that Max was sleeping a gentle peaceful slumber in Thekla's arms – arms that had held him all through the livelong night.

'Look at him, sir; only go in softly; it is a pleasure to see the child today; tread softly, sir!'

She opened the chamber-door. I could see Thekla sitting, propped up by cushions and stools, holding her heavy burden, and bending over him with a look of tenderest love. Not far off stood the Fräulein, all disordered and tearful, stirring or seasoning some hot soup, while the master stood by her, impatient. As soon as it was cooled or seasoned enough, he took the basin and went to Thekla, and said something very low; she lifted up her head, and I could see her face;

pale, weary with watching, but with a soft, peaceful look upon it, which it had not worn for weeks. Fritz Müller began to feed her, for her hands were occupied in holding his child; I could not help remembering Mrs Inchbald's pretty description of Dorriforth's anxiety in feeding Miss Milner; she compares it, if I remember rightly, to that of a tender-hearted boy, caring for his darling bird, the loss of which would embitter all the joys of his holidays.[231] We closed the door without noise, so as not to waken the sleeping child. Lottchen brought me my coffee and bread; she was ready either to laugh or to weep on the slightest occasion. I could not tell if it was in innocence or in mischief that she asked me the following question: 'Do you think Thekla will leave today, sir?'

In the afternoon I heard Thekla's step behind my extemporary screen. I knew it quite well. She stopped for a moment, before emerging into my view.

She was trying to look as composed as usual; but, perhaps because her steady nerves had been shaken by her night's watching, she could not help faint touches of dimples at the corners of her mouth, and her eyes were veiled from any inquisitive look by their drooping lids.

'I thought you would like to know that the doctor says Max is quite out of danger now. He will only require care.'

'Thank you, Thekla; Dr — has been in already this afternoon to tell me so, and I am truly glad.'

She went to the window, and looked out for a moment. Many people were in the vineyards again today; although we, in our household anxiety, had paid them but little heed. Suddenly, she turned round into the room, and I saw that her face was crimson with blushes. In another instant Herr Müller entered by the window.

'Has she told you, sir?' said he, possessing himself of her hand, and looking all a-glow with happiness. 'Hast thou told our good friend?' addressing her.

'No. I was going to tell him, but I did not know how to begin.'

'Then I will prompt thee. Say after me – "I have been a wilful, foolish woman – " '

She wrenched her hand out of his, half-laughing – 'I am a foolish woman, for I have promised to marry him. But he is a still more foolish man, for he wishes to marry me. That is what I say.'

'And I have sent Babette to Frankfort with the pastor. He is going there, and will explain all to Frau von Schmidt; and Babette will serve her for a time. When Max is well enough to have the change of air the doctor prescribes for him, thou shalt take him to Altenahr; and thither will I also go, and become known to thy people and thy father. And before Christmas the gentleman here shall dance at our wedding.'

'I must go home to England, dear friends, before many days are over. Perhaps we may travel together as far as Remagen. Another year I will come back to Heppenheim and see you.'

As I planned it, so it was. We left Heppenheim all together on a lovely All Saints' Day. The day before – the day of All Souls[232] – I had watched Fritz and Thekla lead little Lina up to the Acre of God,[233] the Field of Rest, to hang the wreath of immortelles on her mother's grave. Peace be with the dead and the living!

COUSIN PHILLIS

Part One

It is a great thing for a lad, when he is first turned into the independence of lodgings. I do not think I ever was so satisfied and proud in my life as when, at seventeen, I sat down in a little three-cornered room above a pastry-cook's shop in the county-town of Eltham. My father had left me that afternoon, after delivering himself of a few plain precepts, strongly expressed, for my guidance in the new course of life on which I was entering. I was to be a clerk under the engineer who had undertaken to make the little branch line[234] from Eltham to Hornby. My father had got me this situation, which was in a position rather above his own in life; or perhaps I should say, above the station in which he was born and bred; for he was raising himself every year in men's consideration and respect. He was a mechanic by trade; but he had some inventive genius, and a great deal of perseverance, and had devised several valuable improvements in railway machinery. He did not do this for profit, though, as was reasonable, what came in the natural course of things was acceptable; he worked out his ideas, because, as he said, 'until he could put them into shape, they plagued him by night and by day'. But this is enough about my dear father; it is a good thing for a country where there are many like him. He was a sturdy Independent[235] by descent and conviction; and this it was, I believe, which made him place me in the lodgings at the pastry-cook's. The shop was kept by the two sisters of our minister at home; and this was considered as a sort of safeguard to my morals, when I was turned loose upon the temptations of the county-town, with a salary of thirty pounds a year.

My father had given up two precious days, and put on his Sunday clothes, in order to bring me to Eltham, and accompany me, first to the office, to introduce me to my new master (who was under some obligations to my father for a suggestion), and next to take me to call on the Independent minister of the little congregation at Eltham. And then he left me; and, though sorry to part with him, I now began to taste with relish the pleasure of being my own master. I unpacked the hamper that my mother had provided me with, and smelt the pots of preserve with all the delight of a possessor who might break into their contents at any time he pleased. I handled, and weighed in my fancy, the home-cured ham, which seemed to promise me interminable feasts; and, above all, there was the fine savour of knowing that I might eat of these dainties when I liked, at my sole will, not dependent on the pleasure of anyone else, however indulgent. I stowed my eatables away in the little corner cupboard – that room was all corners, and everything was placed in a corner, the fireplace, the window, the cupboard; I myself seemed to be the only thing in the middle, and there was hardly room for me. The table was made of a folding leaf under the window, and the window looked out upon the market-place; so the studies for the prosecution of which my father had brought himself to pay extra for a sitting-room for me ran a considerable chance of being diverted from books to men and women. I was to have my meals with the two elderly Miss Dawsons in the little parlour behind the three-cornered shop downstairs – my breakfasts and dinners at least; for, as my hours in an evening were likely to be uncertain, my tea or supper was to be an independent meal.

Then, after this pride and satisfaction, came a sense of desolation. I had never been from home before, and I was an only child; and, though my father's spoken maxim had been, 'Spare the rod, and spoil the child',[236] yet, unconsciously, his heart had yearned after me, and his ways towards me were more tender than he knew, or would have approved of in himself, could he have known. My mother, who never professed sternness, was far more severe than my father; perhaps my boyish faults annoyed her more; for I remember, now that I have written the above words, how she pleaded for me once in my riper years, when I had really offended against my father's sense of right.

But I have nothing to do with that now. It is about cousin Phillis that I am going to write, and as yet I am far enough from even saying who cousin Phillis was.

For some months after I was settled in Eltham, the new employment in which I was engaged – the new independence of my life – occupied all my thoughts. I was at my desk by eight o'clock, home to dinner at one, back at the office by two. The afternoon work was more uncertain than the morning's; it might be the same, or it might be that I had to accompany Mr Holdsworth, the managing engineer, to some point on the line between Eltham and Hornby. This I always enjoyed, because of the variety, and because of the country we traversed (which was very wild and pretty), and because I was thrown into companionship with Mr Holdsworth, who held the position of hero in my boyish mind. He was a young man of five-and-twenty or so, and was in a station above mine, both by birth and education; and he had travelled on the Continent, and wore mustachios and whiskers of a somewhat foreign fashion. I was proud of being seen with him. He was really a fine fellow, in a good number of ways, and I might have fallen into much worse hands.

Every Saturday I wrote home, telling of my weekly doings – my father had insisted upon this; but there was so little variety in my life that I often found it hard work to fill a letter. On Sundays I went twice to chapel, up a dark narrow entry, to hear droning hymns, and long prayers, and a still longer sermon, preached to a small congregation,[237] of which I was, by nearly a score of years, the youngest member. Occasionally, Mr Peters, the minister, would ask me home to tea after the second service. I dreaded the honour; for I usually sat on the edge of my chair all the evening, and answered solemn questions, put in a deep bass voice, until household prayer-time came, at eight o'clock, when Mrs Peters came in, smoothing down her apron, and the maid-of-all-work followed, and first a sermon, and then a chapter, was read, and a long impromptu prayer followed, till some instinct told Mr Peters that supper-time had come, and we rose from our knees with hunger for our predominant feeling. Over supper, the minister did unbend a little into one or two ponderous jokes, as if to show me that ministers were men, after all. And then, at ten o'clock, I went home, and enjoyed my long-repressed yawns in the three-cornered room before going to bed.

Dinah and Hannah Dawson, so their names were put on the board above the shop-door – I always called them Miss Dawson and Miss Hannah – considered these visits of mine to Mr Peters as the greatest honour a young man could have; and evidently thought that if, after such privileges, I did not work out my salvation, I was a sort of modern Judas Iscariot. On the contrary, they shook their heads over my intercourse with Mr Holdsworth. He had been so kind to me in many ways, that when I cut into my ham, I hovered over the thought of asking him to tea in my room; more especially as the annual fair was being held in Eltham market-place, and the sight of the booths, the merry-go-rounds, the wild-beast shows, and such country pomps, was (as I thought at seventeen) very attractive. But, when I ventured to allude to my wish in even distant terms, Miss Hannah caught me up, and spoke of the sinfulness of such sights, and something about wallowing in the mire, and then vaulted into France, and spoke evil of the nation, and all who had ever set foot therein; till, seeing that her anger was concentrating itself into a point, and that that point was Mr Holdsworth, I thought it would be better to finish my breakfast, and make what haste I could out of the sound of her voice. I rather wondered afterwards to hear her and Miss Dawson counting up their weekly profits with glee, and saying that a pastry-cook's shop in the corner of the market-place, in Eltham-fair week, was no such bad thing. However, I never ventured to ask Mr Holdsworth to my lodgings.

There is not much to tell about this first year of mine at Eltham. But when I was nearly nineteen, and beginning to think of whiskers on my own account, I came to know cousin Phillis, whose very existence had been unknown to me till then. Mr Holdsworth and I had been out to Heathbridge for a day, working hard. Heathbridge was near Hornby, for our line of railway was above half finished. Of course a day's outing was a great thing to tell about in my weekly letters; and I fell to describing the country – a fault I was not often guilty of. I told my father of the bogs, all over wild myrtle and soft moss, and shaking ground, over which we had to carry our line; and how Mr Holdsworth and I had gone for our midday meals – for we had to stay here for two days and a night – to a pretty village hard-by, Heathbridge proper; and how I hoped we should often have to go there, for the shaking, uncertain ground was puzzling our engineers – one end of the line going up as soon as the other was weighted down. (I had no thought for the shareholders' interests, as may be seen; we had to make a new line on firmer ground, before the junction railway was completed.) I told all this at great length, thankful to fill up my paper. By return-letter, I heard that a second cousin of my mother's was married to the Independent minister of Hornby, Ebenezer Holman by name, and lived at Heathbridge[238] proper: the very Heathbridge I had described – or so my mother believed; for she had never seen her cousin Phillis Green, who was something of an heiress (my father believed), being her father's only child; and old Thomas Green had owned an estate of near upon fifty acres, which must have come to his daughter. My mother's feeling of kinship seemed to have been strongly stirred by the mention of Heathbridge; for my father said she desired me, if ever I went thither again, to make enquiry for the Reverend Ebenezer Holman; and, if indeed he lived there, I was further to ask if he had not married one Phillis Green, and, if both these questions were answered in the affirmative, I was to go and introduce myself as the only child of Margaret Manning, born Moneypenny. I was enraged at myself for having named Heathbridge at all, when I found what it was drawing down upon me. One Independent minister, as I said to myself, was enough for any man; and here I knew (that is to say, I had been catechised on Sabbath-mornings by) Mr Hunter, our minister at home; and I had had to be civil to old Peters at Eltham, and behave myself for five hours running, whenever he asked me to tea at his house; and now, just as I felt the free air blowing about me up at Heathbridge, I was to ferret out another minister, and I should perhaps have to be catechised by him, or else asked to tea at his house. Besides, I did not like pushing myself upon strangers, who perhaps had never heard of my mother's name, and, such an odd name as it was – Moneypenny; and, if they had, had never cared more for her than she had for them, apparently, until this unlucky mention of Heathbridge.

Still, I would not disobey my parents in such a trifle, however irksome it might be. So, the next time our business took me to Heathbridge, and we were dining in the little sanded inn-parlour, I took the opportunity of Mr Holdsworth's being out of the room, and asked the questions, which I was bidden to ask, of the rosy-cheeked maid. I was either unintelligible or she was stupid; for she said she did not know, but would ask master; and, of course, the landlord came in to understand what it was I wanted to know; and I had to bring out all my stammering enquiries before Mr Holdsworth, who would never have attended to them, I dare say, if I had not blushed and blundered, and made such a fool of myself.

'Yes,' the landlord said, 'the Hope Farm was in Heathbridge proper, and the owner's name was Holman, and he was an Independent minister, and, as far as the landlord could tell, his wife's Christian name was Phillis; anyhow, her maiden name was Green.'

'Relations of yours?' asked Mr Holdsworth.

'No, sir – only my mother's second cousins. Yes, I suppose they are relations. But I never saw them in my life.'

'The Hope Farm is not a stone's throw from here,' said the officious landlord, going to the window. 'If you carry your eye over yon bed of hollyhocks, over the damson trees in the orchard yonder, you may see a stack of queer-like stone chimneys. Them is the Hope Farm chimneys; it's an old place, though Holman keeps it in good order.'

Mr Holdsworth had risen from the table with more promptitude than I had, and was standing by the window, looking. At the landlord's last words, he turned round, smiling – 'It is not often that parsons know how to keep land in order, is it?'

'Beg pardon, sir, but I must speak as I find; and minister Holman – we call the Church clergyman here "parson", sir; he would be a bit jealous, if he heard a Dissenter called parson – minister Holman knows what he's about, as well as e'er a farmer in the neighbourhood. He gives up five days a week to his own work, and two to the Lord's; and it is difficult to say which he works hardest at. He spends Saturday and Sunday a-writing sermons and a-visiting his flock at Hornby; and at five o'clock on Monday morning he'll be guiding his plough, in the Hope Farm yonder, just as well as if he could neither read nor write. But your dinner will be getting cold, gentlemen.'

So we went back to table. After a while, Mr Holdsworth broke the silence – 'If I were you, Manning, I'd look up these relations of yours. You can go and see what they're like, while we're waiting for Dobson's estimates; and I'll smoke a cigar in the garden meanwhile.'

'Thank you, sir. But I don't know them, and I don't think I want to know them.'

'What did you ask all those questions for, then?' said he, looking quickly up at me. He had no notion of doing or saying things without a purpose. I did not answer; so he continued – 'Make up your mind, and go off and see what this farmer-minister is like, and come back and tell me – I should like to hear.'

I was so in the habit of yielding to his authority, or influence, that I never thought of resisting, but went on my errand; though I remember feeling as if I would rather have had my head cut off. The landlord, who had evidently taken an interest in the event of our discussion, in a way that country landlords have, accompanied me to the house-door and gave me repeated directions, as if I was likely to miss my way in two hundred yards. But I listened to him, for I was glad of the delay, to screw up my courage for the effort of facing unknown people and introducing myself. I went along the lane, I recollect, switching at all the taller roadside weeds; till, after a turn or two, I found myself close in front of the Hope Farm. There was a garden between the house and the shady, grassy lane; I afterwards found that this garden was called the court: perhaps because there was a low wall round it, with an iron railing on the top of the wall, and two great gates, between pillars crowned with stone balls,[239] for a state entrance to the flagged path leading up to the front door. It was not the habit of the place to go in either by these great gates or by the front door; the gates, indeed, were locked, as I found, though the door stood wide open. I had to go round by a side-path, slightly worn, on a broad, grassy way, which led past the court-wall, past a horse-mount, half covered with stonecrop and a little wild yellow fumitory, to another door – 'the curate', as I found it was termed by the master of the house, while the front door, 'handsome and all for show', was termed 'the rector'. I knocked with my hand upon the 'curate' door; a tall girl, about my own age, as I thought, came and opened it, and stood there silent, waiting to know my errand. I see her now – cousin Phillis. The westering sun shone full upon her, and made a slanting stream of light into the room within. She was dressed in dark blue cotton of some kind, up to her throat, down to her wrists, with a little frill of the same, wherever it touched her white skin. And such a white skin as it was! I have never seen the like. She had light hair, nearer yellow than any other colour. She looked me steadily in the face with large, quiet eyes, wondering, but untroubled by the sight of a stranger. I thought it odd that so old, so full-grown as she was, she should wear a pinafore over her gown.

Before I had quite made up my mind what to say in reply to her mute enquiry of what I wanted there, a woman's voice called out, 'Who is it, Phillis? If it is anyone for buttermilk, send them round to the back door.'

I thought I would rather speak to the owner of that voice than to the girl before me; so I passed her, and stood at the entrance of a room, hat in hand; for this side-door opened straight into the hall or house-place, where the family sat when work was done. There was a brisk little woman, of forty or so, ironing some huge muslin cravats under the light of a long vine-shaded casement window. She looked at me distrustfully till I began to speak. 'My name is Paul Manning,' said I; but I saw she did not know the name. 'My mother's name was Moneypenny,' said I – 'Margaret Moneypenny.'

'And she married one John Manning, of Birmingham,' said Mrs Holman eagerly. 'And you'll be her son. Sit down! I am right glad to see you. To think of your being Margaret's son! Why, she was almost a child not so long ago. Well, to be sure, it is five-and-twenty years ago. And what brings you into these parts?'

She sat down herself, as if oppressed by her curiosity as to all the five-and-twenty years that had passed by since she had seen my mother. Her daughter Phillis took up her knitting – a long grey worsted man's-stocking, I remember – and knitted away without looking at her work. I felt that the steady gaze of those deep grey eyes was upon me, though once, when I stealthily raised mine to hers, she was examining something on the wall above my head.

When I had answered all my cousin Holman's questions, she heaved a long breath, and said, 'To think of Margaret Moneypenny's boy being in our house! I wish the minister was here. Phillis, in what field is thy father today?'

'In the five-acre; they are beginning to cut the corn.'

'He'll not like being sent for, then; else I should have liked you to have seen the minister. But the five-acre is a good step off. You shall have a glass of wine and a bit of cake, before you stir from this house, though. You're bound to go, you say; or else the minister comes in mostly when the men have their four o'clock.'

'I must go – I ought to have been off before now.'

'Here, then, Phillis, take the keys.' She gave her daughter some whispered directions, and Phillis left the room.

'She is my cousin, is she not?' I asked. I knew she was; but somehow I wanted to talk of her, and did not know how to begin.

'Yes – Phillis Holman. She is our only child – now.'

Either from that 'now', or from a strange momentary wistfulness in her eyes, I knew that there had been more children, who were now dead.[240]

'How old is cousin Phillis?' said I, scarcely venturing on the new name, it seemed too prettily familiar for me to call her by it; but cousin Holman took no notice of it, answering straight to the purpose.

'Seventeen last May Day;[241] but the minister does not like to hear me calling it "May Day",' said she, checking herself with a little awe. 'Phillis was seventeen on the first day of May last,' she repeated in an emended edition.

'And I am nineteen in another month,' thought I to myself; I don't know why.

Then Phillis came in, carrying a tray with wine and cake upon it.

'We keep a house-servant,' said cousin Holman; 'but it is churning-day,[242] and she is busy.' It was meant as a little proud apology for her daughter's being the handmaiden.

'I like doing it, mother,' said Phillis, in her grave, full voice.

I felt as if I were somebody in the Old Testament – who, I could not recollect – being served and waited upon by the daughter of the host. Was I like Abraham's steward, when Rebekah gave him to drink at the well? I thought Isaac had not gone the pleasantest way to work in winning him a wife.[243] But Phillis never thought about such things. She was a stately, gracious young woman, in the dress, and with the simplicity, of a child.

As I had been taught, I drank to the health of my new-found cousin and her husband; and then I ventured to name my cousin Phillis with a little bow of my head towards her; but I was too awkward to look and see how she took my compliment. 'I must go, now,' said I, rising.

Neither of the women had thought of sharing in the wine; cousin Holman had broken a bit of cake for form's sake.

'I wish the minister had been within,' said his wife, rising too. Secretly I was very glad he was not. I did not take kindly to ministers in those days; and I thought he must be a particular kind of man, by his objecting to the term 'May Day'. But, before I went, cousin Holman made me promise that I would come back on the Saturday following and spend Sunday with them: when I should see something of 'the minister'.

'Come on Friday, if you can,' were her last words as she stood at the curate-door, shading her eyes from the sinking sun with her hand.

Inside the house sat cousin Phillis, her golden hair, her dazzling complexion, lighting up the corner of the vine-shadowed room. She had not risen, when I bade her goodbye; she had looked at me straight, as she said her tranquil words of farewell.

I found Mr Holdsworth down at the line, hard at work superintending. As soon as he had a pause, he said, 'Well, Manning, what are the new cousins like? How do preaching and farming seem to get on together? If the minister turns out to be practical as well as reverend, I shall begin to respect him.'

But he hardly attended to my answer, he was so much more occupied with directing his workpeople. Indeed, my answer did not come very readily; and the most distinct part of it was the mention of the invitation that had been given me.

'Oh! of course you can go – and on Friday, too, if you like; there is no reason why not this week; and you've done a long spell of work this time, old fellow.'

I thought that I did not want to go on Friday; but, when the day came, I found that I should prefer going to staying away; so I availed myself of Mr Holdsworth's permission, and went over to Hope Farm some time in the afternoon, a little later than my last visit. I found the 'curate' open, to admit the soft September air, so tempered by the warmth of the sun that it was warmer out of doors than in, although the wooden log lay smouldering in front of a heap of hot ashes on the hearth. The vine-leaves over the window had a tinge more yellow, their edges were here and there scorched and browned; there was no ironing about, and cousin Holman sat just outside the house, mending a shirt. Phillis was at her knitting indoors: it seemed as if she had been at it all the week. The many-speckled fowls were pecking about in the farmyard beyond, and the milk-cans glittered with brightness, hung out to sweeten. The court was so full of flowers that they crept out upon the low-covered wall and horse-mount, and were even to be found self-sown upon the turf that bordered the path to the back of the house. I fancied that my Sunday coat was scented for days afterwards by the bushes of sweet-briar and the fraxinella that perfumed the air. From time to time, cousin Holman put her hand into a covered basket at her feet, and threw handfuls of corn down for the pigeons that cooed and fluttered in the air around, in expectation of this treat.

I had a thorough welcome, as soon as she saw me. 'Now, this is kind – this is right-down friendly,' shaking my hand warmly. 'Phillis, your cousin Manning is come!'

'Call me Paul, will you?' said I; 'they call me so at home, and Manning in the office.'

'Well; Paul, then. Your room is all ready for you, Paul; for, as I said to the minister, "I'll have it ready, whether he comes o' Friday or not." And the minister said he must go up to the ash-field, whether you were to come or not; but he would come home betimes, to see if you were here. I'll show you to your room; and you can wash the dust off a bit.'

After I came down, I think she did not quite know what to do with me; or she might think that I was dull; or she might have work to do in which I hindered her; for she called Phillis, and bade her put on her bonnet, and go with me to the ash-field, and find father. So we set off, I in a little flutter of a desire to make myself agreeable, but wishing that my companion were not quite so tall; for she was above me in height. While I was wondering how to begin our conversation, she took up the words.

'I suppose, cousin Paul, you have to be very busy at your work all day long, in general?'

'Yes, we have to be in the office at half-past eight; and we have an hour for dinner, and then we go at it again till eight or nine.'

'Then you have not much time for reading?'

'No,' said I, with a sudden consciousness that I did not make the most of what leisure I had.

'No more have I. Father always gets an hour before going a-field in the mornings; but mother does not like me to get up so early.'

'My mother is always wanting me to get up earlier, when I am at home.'

'What time do you get up?'

'Oh! – ah! – sometimes half-past six; not often, though'; for I remembered only twice that I had done so during the past summer.

She turned her head, and looked at me.

'Father is up at three; and so was mother till she was ill. I should like to be up at four.'

'Your father up at three! Why, what has he to do at that hour?'

'What has he not to do? He has his private exercise in his own room; he always rings the great bell which calls the men to milking; he rouses up Betty, our maid; as often as not, he gives the horses their feed before the man is up – for Jem, who takes care of the horses, is an old man; and father is always loth to disturb him; he looks at the calves, and the shoulders, heels, traces, chaff, and corn, before the horses go a-field; he has often to whipcord the plough-whips; he sees the hogs fed; he looks into the swill-tubs, and writes his orders for what is wanted for food for man and beast; yes, and for fuel, too. And then, if he has a bit of time to spare, he comes in and reads with me – but only English; we keep Latin for the evenings, that we may have time to enjoy it; and then he calls in the man to breakfast, and cuts the boys' bread and cheese, and sees their wooden bottles filled, and sends them off to their work; – and by this time it is half-past six, and we have our breakfast. There is father!' she exclaimed, pointing out to me a man in his shirt-sleeves, taller by the head than the other two with whom he was working. We only saw him through the leaves of the ash trees growing in the hedge, and I thought I must be confusing the figures, or mistaken: that man still looked like a very powerful labourer, and had none of the precise demureness of appearance which I had always imagined was the characteristic of a minister. It was the Reverend Ebenezer Holman, however. He gave us a nod as we entered the stubble-field; and I think he would have come to meet us, but that he was in the middle of giving some directions to his men. I could see that Phillis was built more after his type than her mother's. He, like his daughter, was largely made, and of a fair, ruddy complexion, whereas hers was brilliant and delicate. His hair had been yellow or sandy, but now was grizzled. Yet his grey hairs betokened no failure in strength. I never saw a more powerful man – deep chest, lean flanks, well-planted head. By this time we were nearly up to him; and he interrupted himself and stepped forwards, holding out his hand to me, but addressing Phillis.

'Well, my lass, this is cousin Manning, I suppose. Wait a minute, young man, and I'll put on my coat, and give you a decorous and formal welcome. But – Ned Hall, there ought to be a water-furrow across this land: it's a nasty, stiff, clayey, dauby bit of ground, and thou and I must fall to, come next Monday – I beg your pardon, cousin Manning – and there's old Jem's cottage wants a bit of thatch; you can do that job tomorrow, while I am busy.' Then, suddenly changing the tone of his deep bass voice to an odd suggestion of chapels and preachers, he added, 'Now I will give out the psalm: "Come all harmonious tongues," to be sung to "Mount Ephraim" tune.'[244]

He lifted his spade in his hand, and began to beat time with it; the two labourers seemed to know both words and music, though I did not; and so did Phillis: her rich voice followed her father's, as he set the tune; and the men came in with more uncertainty, but still harmoniously. Phillis looked at me once or twice, with a little surprise at my silence; but I did not know the words. There we five stood, bareheaded, excepting Phillis, in the tawny stubble-field, from which all the shocks of corn had not yet been carried – a dark wood on one side, where the wood-pigeons were cooing; blue distance, seen through the ash trees, on the other. Somehow, I think that, if I had known the words, and could have sung, my throat would have been choked up by the feeling of the unaccustomed scene.[245]

The hymn was ended, and the men had drawn off, before I could stir. I saw the minister beginning to put on his coat, and looking at me with friendly inspection in his gaze, before I could rouse myself.

'I dare say you railway gentlemen don't wind up the day with singing a psalm together,' said he; 'but it is not a bad practice – not a bad practice. We have had it a bit earlier today for hospitality's sake – that's all.'

I had nothing particular to say to this, though I was thinking a great deal. From time to time, I stole a look at my companion. His coat was black, and so was his waistcoat; neckcloth he had none, his strong full throat being bare above the snow-white shirt. He wore drab-coloured knee-breeches, grey worsted stockings (I thought I knew the maker), and strong-nailed shoes. He carried his hat in his hand, as if he liked to feel the coming breeze lifting his hair. After a while, I saw that the father took hold of the daughter's hand; and so they, holding each other, went along towards home. We had to cross a lane. In it there were two little children – one lying prone on the grass in a passion of crying; the other standing stock still, with its finger in its mouth, the large tears slowly rolling down its cheeks for sympathy. The cause of their distress was evident; there was a broken brown pitcher, and a little pool of spilt milk on the road.

'Hollo! hollo! What's all this?' said the minister. 'Why, what have you been about, Tommy?' lifting the little petticoated lad, who was lying sobbing, with one vigorous arm. Tommy looked at him with surprise in his round eyes, but no affright – they were evidently old acquaintances.

'Mammy's jug!' said he at last, beginning to cry afresh.

'Well! and will crying piece mammy's jug, or pick up spilt milk? How did you manage it, Tommy?'

'He' (jerking his head at the other) 'and me was running races.'

'Tommy said he could beat me,' put in the other.

'Now, I wonder what will make you two silly lads mind, and not run races again, with a pitcher of milk between you,' said the minister, as if musing. 'I might flog you, and so save mammy the trouble; for I dare say she'll do it, if I don't.' The fresh burst of whimpering from both showed the probability of this. 'Or I might take you to the Hope Farm, and give you some more milk; but then you'd be running races again, and my milk would follow that to the ground, and make another white pool. I think the flogging would be best – don't you?'

'We would never run races no more,' said the elder of the two.

'Then you'd not be boys; you'd be angels.'

'No, we shouldn't.'

'Why not?'

They looked into each other's eyes for an answer to this puzzling question. At length, one said, 'Angels is dead folk.'

'Come; we'll not get too deep into theology. What do you think of my lending you a tin can with a lid, to carry the milk home in? That would not break, at any rate; though I would not answer for the milk not spilling, if you ran races. That's it!'

He had dropped his daughter's hand, and now held out each of his to the little fellows. Phillis and I followed, and listened to the prattle which the minister's companions now poured out to him, and which he was evidently enjoying. At a certain point, there was a sudden burst of the tawny, ruddy evening landscape. The minister turned round, and quoted a line or two of Latin.

'It's wonderful,' said he, 'how exactly Virgil has hit the enduring epithets, nearly two thousand years ago, and in Italy;[246] and yet how it describes to a T what is now lying before us in the parish of Heathbridge, —shire, England.'

'I dare say it does,' said I, all aglow with shame; for I had forgotten the little Latin I ever knew.

The minister shifted his eyes to Phillis's face; it mutely gave him back the sympathetic appreciation that I, in my ignorance, could not bestow.

'Oh! this is worse than the catechism,' thought I; 'that was only remembering words.'

'Phillis, lass, thou must go home with these lads, and tell their mother all about the race and the milk. Mammy must always know the truth,' now speaking to the children. 'And tell her, too, from me that I have got the best birch-rod in the parish; and that, if she ever thinks her children want a flogging, she must bring them to me, and, if I think they deserve it, I'll give it them better than she can.' So Phillis led the children towards the dairy, somewhere in the back-yard; and I followed the minister in through the 'curate' into the house-place.[247]

'Their mother,' said he, 'is a bit of a vixen, and apt to punish her children without rhyme or reason. I try to keep the parish-rod as well as the parish-bull.'

He sat down in the three-cornered chair by the fireside, and looked around the empty room.

'Where's the missus?' said he to himself. But she was there in a minute; it was her regular plan to give him his welcome home – by a look, by a touch, nothing more – as soon as she could after his return, and he had missed her now. Regardless of my presence, he went over the day's doings to her; and then, getting up, he said he must go and make himself 'reverend', and that then we would have a cup of tea in the parlour. The parlour was a large room, with two casemented windows on the other side of the broad flagged passage leading from the rector-door to the wide staircase, with its shallow, polished oaken steps, on which no carpet was ever laid. The parlour-floor was covered in the middle by a homemade carpeting of needlework and list. One or two quaint family pictures of the Holman family hung round the walls; the fire-grate and irons were much ornamented with brass; and on a table against the wall between the windows, a great beau-pot of flowers was placed upon the folio volumes of Matthew Henry's Bible.[248] It was a compliment to me to use this room, and I tried to be grateful for it; but we never had our meals there after that first day, and I was glad of it; for the large house-place, living-room, dining-room, whichever you might like to call it, was twice as comfortable and cheerful. There was a rug in front of the great large fireplace, and an oven by the grate, and a crook, with the kettle hanging from it, over the bright wood-fire; everything that ought to be black and polished in that room was black and polished; and the flags, and window-curtains, and such things as were to be white and clean, were just spotless in their purity. Opposite to the fireplace, extending the whole length of the room, was an oaken shovel-board, with the right incline for a skilful player to send the weights into the prescribed space. There were baskets of white work about, and a small shelf of books hung against the wall – books used for reading, and not for propping up a beau-pot of flowers. I took down one or two of those books once when I was left alone in the house-place on the first evening – Virgil, Caesar, a Greek grammar – oh, dear! ah, me! and Phillis Holman's name in each of them! I shut them up, and put them back in their places, and walked as far away from the bookshelf as I could. Yes, and I gave my cousin Phillis a wide berth, although she was sitting at her work quietly enough, and her hair was looking more golden, her dark eyelashes longer, her round pillar of a throat whiter, than ever. We had done tea, and we had returned into the house-place, that the minister might smoke his pipe without fear of contaminating the drab damask window-curtains of the parlour. He had made himself 'reverend' by putting on one of the voluminous white muslin neckcloths that I had seen cousin Holman ironing, that first visit I had paid to the Hope Farm, and by making one or two other unimportant changes in his dress. He sat looking steadily at me; but whether he saw me or not I cannot tell. At the time, I fancied that he did, and was gauging me in some unknown fashion in his secret mind. Every now and then, he took his pipe out of his mouth, knocked out the ashes, and asked me some fresh question. As long as these related to my acquirements or my reading, I shuffled uneasily and did not know what to answer. By and by, he got round to the more practical subject of railroads, and on this I was more at home. I really had taken an interest in my work; nor would Mr Holdsworth, indeed, have kept me in his employment, if I had not given my mind as well as my time to it; and I was, besides, full of the difficulties which beset us just then, owing to our not being able to find a steady bottom on the Heathbridge moss,[249] over which we wished to carry our line. In the midst of all my eagerness in speaking about this, I could not help being struck with the extreme pertinence of his questions. I do not mean that he did not show ignorance of many of the details of engineering: that was to have been expected; but on the premises he had got hold of he thought clearly and reasoned logically. Phillis – so like him as she was both in body and mind – kept stopping at her work and looking at me, trying to fully understand all that I said. I felt she did; and perhaps it made me take more pains in using clear expressions and arranging my words, than I otherwise should.

'She shall see I know something worth knowing, though it mayn't be her dead-and-gone languages,' thought I.

'I see,' said the minister at length. 'I understand it all. You've a clear, good head of your own, my lad – choose how you came by it.'

'From my father,' said I proudly. 'Have you not heard of his discovery of a new method of shunting? It was in the *Gazette*.[250] It was patented. I thought everyone had heard of Manning's patent winch.'

'We don't know who invented the alphabet,' said he, half-smiling, and taking up his pipe.

'No, I dare say not, sir,' replied I, half-offended; 'that's so long ago.'

Puff – puff – puff.

'But your father must be a notable man. I heard of him once before; and it is not many a one fifty miles away whose fame reaches Heathbridge.'

'My father is a notable man, sir. It is not me that says so; it is Mr Holdsworth, and – and everybody.'

'He is right to stand up for his father,' said cousin Holman, as if she were pleading for me.

I chafed inwardly, thinking that my father needed no one to stand up for him. He was man sufficient for himself.

'Yes – he is right,' said the minister placidly. 'Right, because it comes from his heart – right, too, as I believe, in point of fact. Else, there is many a young cockerel that will stand upon a dunghill and crow about his father, by way of making his own plumage to shine. I should like to know thy father,' he went on, turning straight to me, with a kindly, frank look in his eyes.

But I was vexed, and would take no notice. Presently, having finished his pipe, he got up and left the room. Phillis put her work hastily down, and went after him. In a minute or two she returned, and sat down again. Not long after, and before I had quite recovered my good temper, he opened the door out of which he had passed, and called to me to come to him. I went across a narrow stone passage into a strange, many-cornered room, not ten feet in area, part study, part counting-house, looking into the farmyard; with a desk to sit at, a desk to stand at, a spittoon, a set of shelves with old divinity books upon them; another, smaller, filled with books on farriery, farming, manures, and such subjects, with pieces of paper containing memoranda stuck against the whitewashed walls with wafers,[251] nails, pins, anything that came readiest to hand; a box of carpenter's tools on the floor, and some manuscripts in shorthand on the desk.

He turned round, half-laughing. 'That foolish girl of mine thinks I have vexed you' – putting his large, powerful hand on my shoulder. ' "Nay," says I; "kindly meant is kindly taken" – is it not so?'

'It was not quite, sir,' replied I, vanquished by his manner; 'but it shall be in future.'

'Come, that's right. You and I shall be friends. Indeed, it's not many a one I would bring in here. But I was reading a book this morning, and I could not make it out; it is a book that was left here by mistake one day; I had subscribed to Brother Robinson's sermons; and I was glad to see this instead of them, for, sermons though they be, they're . . . well, never mind! I took 'em both, and made my old coat do a bit longer; but all's fish that comes to my net. I have fewer books than leisure to read them, and I have a prodigious big appetite. Here it is.'

It was a volume of stiff mechanics, involving many technical terms, and some rather deep mathematics. These last, which would have puzzled me, seemed easy enough to him; all that he wanted was the explanation of the technical words, which I could easily give.

While he was looking through the book, to find the places where he had been puzzled, my wandering eye caught on some of the papers on the wall, and I could not help reading one, which has stuck by me ever since. At first, it seemed a kind of weekly diary; but then I saw that the seven days were portioned out for special prayers and intercessions: Monday for his family, Tuesday for enemies, Wednesday for the Independent churches, Thursday for all other churches, Friday for persons afflicted, Saturday for his own soul, Sunday for all wanderers and sinners, that they might be brought home to the fold.

We were called back into the house-place to have supper. A door opening into the kitchen was opened; and all stood up in both rooms, while the minister, tall, large, one hand resting on the spread table, the other lifted up, said, in the deep voice that would have been loud, had it not been so full and rich, but with the peculiar accent or twang that I believe is considered devout by some people, 'Whether we eat or drink, or whatsoever we do, let us do all to the glory of God.'

The supper was an immense meat-pie. We of the house-place were helped first; then the minister hit the handle of his buckhorn carving-knife on the table once, and said – 'Now or never'; which meant, did any of us want any more; and, when we had all declined, either by silence or by words, he knocked twice with his knife on the table, and Betty came in through the open door, and carried off the great dish to the kitchen, where an old man and a young one, and a help-girl, were awaiting their meal.

'Shut the door, if you will,' said the minister to Betty.

'That's in honour of you,' said cousin Holman, in a tone of satisfaction, as the door was shut. 'When we've no stranger with us, the minister is so fond of keeping the door open, and talking to the men and maids, just as much as to Phillis and me.'

'It brings us all together, like a household, just before we meet as a household in prayer,' said he in explanation. 'But to go back to what we were talking about – can you tell me of any simple book on dynamics that I could put in my pocket, and study a little at leisure times in the day?'

' "Leisure times," father?' said Phillis, with a nearer approach to a smile than I had yet seen on her face.

'Yes; leisure times, daughter. There is many an odd minute lost in waiting for other folk; and, now that railroads are coming so near us, it behoves us to know something about them.'

I thought of his own description of his 'prodigious big appetite' for learning. And he had a good appetite of his own for the more material victual before him. But I saw, or fancied I saw, that he had some rule for himself in the matter both of food and drink.

As soon as supper was done, the household assembled for prayer. It was a long impromptu evening prayer; and it would have seemed desultory enough, had I not had a glimpse of the kind of day that preceded it, and so been able to find a clue to the thoughts that preceded the disjointed utterances; for he kept there, kneeling down in the centre of a circle, his eyes shut, his outstretched hands pressed palm to palm – sometimes with a long pause of silence, as if waiting to see if there was anything else he wished to 'lay before the Lord' (to use his own expression) – before he concluded with the blessing. He prayed for the cattle and live creatures, rather to my surprise; for my attention had begun to wander, till it was recalled by the familiar words.

And here I must not forget to name an odd incident at the conclusion of the prayer, and before we had risen from our knees (indeed, before Betty was well awake, for she made a nightly practice of having a sound nap, her weary head lying on her stalwart arms); the minister, still kneeling in our midst, but with his eyes wide open, and his arms dropped by his side, spoke to the elder man, who turned round on his knees to attend. 'John, didst see that Daisy had her warm mash tonight? for we must not neglect the means, John – two quarts of gruel, a spoonful of ginger, and a gill of beer – the poor beast needs it, and I fear it slipped out of my mind to tell thee; and here was I asking a blessing and neglecting the means, which is a mockery,' said he, dropping his voice.

Before we went to bed, he told me he should see little or nothing more of me during my visit, which was to end on Sunday evening, as he always gave up both Saturday and Sabbath to his work in the ministry. I remembered that the landlord at the inn had told me this, on the day when I first enquired about these new relations of mine; and I did not dislike the opportunity which I saw would be afforded me of becoming more acquainted with cousin Holman and Phillis, though I earnestly hoped that the latter would not attack me on the subject of the dead languages.

I went to bed, and dreamed that I was as tall as cousin Phillis, and had a sudden and miraculous growth of whisker, and a still more miraculous acquaintance with Latin and Greek. Alas! I wakened up still a short, beardless lad, with '*tempus fugit*'[252] for my sole remembrance of the little Latin I had once learnt. While I was dressing, a bright thought came over me: I could question cousin Phillis, instead of her questioning me, and so manage to keep the choice of the subjects of conversation in my own power.

Early as it was, everyone had breakfasted, and my basin of bread and milk was put on the oven-top to await my coming down. Everyone was gone about their work. The first to come into the house-place was Phillis, with a basket of eggs. Faithful to my resolution, I asked: 'What are those?'

She looked at me for a moment, and then said gravely: 'Potatoes.'

'No! they are not,' said I. 'They are eggs. What do you mean by saying they are potatoes?'

'What did you mean by asking me what they were, when they were plain to be seen?' retorted she.

We were both getting a little angry with each other.

'I don't know. I wanted to begin to talk to you; and I was afraid you would talk to me about books as you did yesterday. I have not read much; and you and the minister have read so much.'

'I have not,' said she. 'But you are our guest; and mother says I must make it pleasant to you. We won't talk of books. What must we talk about?'

'I don't know. How old are you?'

'Seventeen last May. How old are you?'

'I am nineteen. Older than you by nearly two years,' said I, drawing myself up to my full height.

'I should not have thought you were above sixteen,' she replied, as quietly as if she were not saying the most provoking thing she possibly could. Then came a pause.

'What are you going to do now?' asked I.

'I should be dusting the bedchambers; but mother said I had better stay and make it pleasant to you,' said she, a little plaintively, as if dusting rooms was far the easier task.

'Will you take me to see the livestock? I like animals, though I don't know much about them.'

'Oh, do you? I am so glad. I was afraid you would not like animals, as you did not like books.'

I wondered why she said this. I think it was because she had begun to fancy all our tastes must be dissimilar. We went together all through the farmyard; we fed the poultry, she kneeling down with her pinafore full of corn and meal, and tempting the little timid downy chickens upon it, much to the anxiety of the fussy ruffled hen, their mother. She called to the pigeons, who fluttered down at the sound of her voice. She and I examined the great sleek cart-horses; sympathised in our dislike of pigs; fed the calves; coaxed the sick cow, Daisy; and admired the others out at pasture; and came back tired and hungry and dirty at dinner-time, having quite forgotten that there were such things as dead languages, and consequently capital friends.

Part Two

Cousin Holman gave me the weekly county-newspaper to read aloud to her, while she mended stockings out of a high piled-up basket, Phillis helping her mother. I read and read, unregardful of the words I was uttering, thinking of all manner of other things; of the bright colour of Phillis's hair, as the afternoon sun fell on her bending head; of the silence of the house, which enabled me to hear the double tick of the old clock which stood halfway up the stairs; of the variety of inarticulate noises which cousin Holman made while I read, to show her sympathy, wonder, or horror at the newspaper intelligence. The tranquil monotony of that hour made me feel as if I had lived for ever, and should live for ever, droning out paragraphs in that warm sunny room, with my two quiet hearers, and the curled-up pussy-cat sleeping on the hearthrug, and the clock on the house-stairs perpetually clicking out the passage of the moments. By and by, Betty the servant came to the door into the kitchen, and made a sign to Phillis, who put her half-mended stocking down, and went away to the kitchen without a word. Looking at cousin Holman a minute or two afterwards, I saw that she had dropped her chin upon her breast, and had fallen fast asleep. I put the newspaper down, and was nearly following her example, when a waft of air from some unseen source slightly opened the door of communication with the kitchen, that Phillis must have left unfastened; and I saw part of her figure as she sat by the dresser, peeling apples with quick dexterity of finger, but with repeated turnings of her head towards some book lying on the dresser by her. I softly rose, and as softly went into the kitchen, and looked over her shoulder; before she was aware of my neighbourhood, I had seen that the book was in a language unknown to me, and the running title was *L'Inferno*.[253] Just as I was making out the relationship of this word to 'infernal', she started and turned round, and, as if continuing her thought as she spoke, she sighed out: 'Oh! it is so difficult! Can you help me?' putting her finger below a line.

'Me! I! Not I! I don't even know what language it is in!'

'Don't you see it is Dante?' she replied, almost petulantly; she did so want help.

'Italian, then?' said I dubiously; for I was not quite sure.

'Yes. And I do so want to make it out. Father can help me a little, for he knows Latin; but then he has so little time.'

'You have not much, I should think, if you have often to try and do two things at once, as you are doing now.'

'Oh! that's nothing! Father bought a heap of old books cheap. And I knew something about Dante before; and I have always liked Virgil so much. Paring apples is nothing, if I could only make out this old Italian. I wish you knew it.'

'I wish I did,' said I, moved by her impetuosity of tone. 'If, now, only Mr Holdsworth were here! he can speak Italian like anything, I believe.'

'Who is Mr Holdsworth?' said Phillis, looking up.

'Oh, he's our head-engineer. He's a regular first-rate fellow! He can do anything'; my hero-worship and my pride in my chief all coming into play. Besides, if I was not clever and book-learned myself, it was something to belong to someone who was.

'How is it that he speaks Italian?' asked Phillis.

'He had to make a railway through Piedmont, which is in Italy, I believe; and he had to talk to all the workmen in Italian; and I have heard him say that, for nearly two years, he had only Italian books to read in the queer outlandish places he was in.'

'Oh, dear!' said Phillis; 'I wish' – and then she stopped. I was not quite sure whether to say the next thing that came into my mind; but I said it.

'Could I ask him anything about your book, or your difficulties?'

She was silent for a minute or so, and then she made reply: 'No! I think not. Thank you very much, though. I can generally puzzle a thing out in time. And then, perhaps, I remember it better than if someone had helped me. I'll put it away now, and you must move off, for I've got to make the paste for the pies; we always have a cold dinner on Sabbaths.'

'But I may stay and help you, mayn't I?'

'Oh, yes; not that you can help at all, but I like to have you with me.'

I was both flattered and annoyed at this straightforward avowal. I was pleased that she liked me; but I was young coxcomb enough to have wished to play the lover, and I was quite wise enough to perceive that, if she had any idea of the kind in her head, she would never have spoken out so frankly. I comforted myself immediately, however, by finding out the grapes were sour.[254] A great, tall girl in a pinafore, half-a-head taller than I was, reading books that I had never heard of, and talking about them too, as of far more interest than any mere personal subjects – that was the last day on which I ever thought of my dear cousin Phillis as the possible mistress of my heart and life. But we were all the greater friends for this idea being utterly put away and buried out of sight.

Late in the evening the minister came home from Hornby. He had been calling on the different members of his flock; and unsatisfactory work it had proved to him, it seemed, from the fragments that dropped out of his thoughts into his talk.

'I don't see the men; they are all at their business, their shops, or their warehouses; they ought to be there. I have no fault to find with them; only, if a pastor's teaching or words of admonition are good for anything, they are needed by the men as much as by the women.'

'Cannot you go and see them in their places of business, and remind them of their Christian privileges and duties, minister?' asked cousin Holman, who evidently thought that her husband's words could never be out of place.

'No!' said he, shaking his head. 'I judge them by myself. If there are clouds in the sky, and I am getting in the hay just ready for loading, and rain sure to come in the night, I should look ill upon Brother Robinson if he came into the field to speak about serious things.'

'But, at any rate, father, you do good to the women, and perhaps they repeat what you have said to them to their husbands and children?'

'It is to be hoped they do, for I cannot reach the men directly; but the women are apt to tarry before coming to me, to put on ribbons and gauds; as if they could hear the message I bear to them best in their smart clothes. Mrs Dobson today – Phillis, I am thankful thou dost not care for the vanities of dress!'

Phillis reddened a little as she said, in a low humble voice: 'But I do, father, I'm afraid. I often wish I could wear pretty-coloured ribbons round my throat, like the squire's daughters.'

'It's but natural, minister!' said his wife; 'I'm not above liking a silk gown better than a cotton one myself!'

'The love of dress is a temptation and a snare,' said he, gravely. 'The true adornment is a meek and quiet spirit. And, wife,' said he, as a sudden thought crossed his mind, 'in that matter I, too, have sinned. I wanted to ask you, could we not sleep in the grey room, instead of our own?'

'Sleep in the grey room? – change our room at this time o' day!' cousin Holman asked, in dismay.

'Yes,' said he. 'It would save me from a daily temptation to anger.

Look at my chin!' he continued; 'I cut it this morning – I cut it on Wednesday, when I was shaving; I do not know how many times I have cut it of late, and all from impatience at seeing Timothy Cooper at his work in the yard.'

'He's a downright lazy tyke!' said cousin Holman. 'He's not worth his wage. There's but little he can do; and what he can do, he does badly.'

'True,' said the minister. 'But he is but, so to speak, a half-wit; and yet he has got a wife and children.'

'More shame for him!'

'But that is past change. And, if I turn him off, no one else would take him on. Yet I cannot help watching him of a morning as he goes sauntering about his work in the yard; and I watch, and I watch, till the old Adam[255] rises strong within me at his lazy ways; and someday, I am afraid, I shall go down and send him about his business – let alone the way in which he makes me cut myself while I am shaving – and then his wife and children will starve. I wish we could move to the grey room.'

I do not remember much more of my first visit to the Hope Farm. We went to chapel in Heathbridge, slowly and decorously walking along the lanes, ruddy and tawny with the colouring of the coming autumn. The minister walked a little before us, his hands behind his back, his head bent down, thinking about the discourse to be delivered to his people, cousin Holman said; and we spoke low and quietly, in order not to interrupt his thoughts. But I could not help noticing the respectful greetings which he received from both rich and poor as we went along: greetings which he acknowledged with a kindly wave of his hand, but with no words of reply. As we drew near the town, I could see some of the young fellows we met casting admiring looks on Phillis; and that made me look too. She had on a white gown, and a short black silk cloak, according to the fashion of the day. A straw bonnet, with brown ribbon strings; that was all. But what her dress wanted in colour, her sweet bonny face had. The walk made her cheeks bloom like the rose; the very whites of her eyes had a blue tinge in them, and her dark eyelashes brought out the depth of the blue eyes themselves. Her yellow hair was put away as straight as its natural curliness would allow. If she did not perceive the admiration she excited, I am sure cousin Holman did; for she looked as fierce and as proud as ever her quiet face could look, guarding her treasure, and yet glad to perceive that others could see that it was a treasure. This afternoon I had to return to Eltham, to be ready for the next day's work. I found out afterwards that the minister and his family were all 'exercised in spirit',[256] as to whether they did well in asking me to repeat my visits at the Hope Farm, seeing that of necessity I must return to Eltham on the Sabbath-day. However, they did go on asking me, and I went on visiting them, whenever my other engagements permitted me; Mr Holdsworth being in this case, as in all, a kind and indulgent friend. Nor did my new acquaintances oust him from my strong regard and admiration. I had room in my heart for all, I am happy to say; and, as far as I can remember, I kept praising each to the other in a manner which, if I had been an older man, living more amongst people of the world, I should have thought unwise, as well as a little ridiculous. It was unwise, certainly, as it was almost sure to cause disappointment, if ever they did become acquainted; and perhaps it was ridiculous, though I do not think we any of us thought it so at the time. The minister used to listen to my accounts of Mr Holdsworth's many accomplishments and various adventures in travel with the truest interest, and most kindly good faith; and Mr Holdsworth, in return, liked to hear about my visits to the farm, and description of my cousins' life there – liked it, I mean, as much as he liked anything that was merely narrative, without leading to action.

So I went to the farm certainly, on an average, once a month during that autumn; the course of life there was so peaceful and quiet, that I can only remember one small event,[257] and that was one that I think I took more notice of than anyone else: Phillis left off wearing the pinafores that had always been so obnoxious to me: I do not know why they were banished, but on one of my visits I found them replaced by pretty linen aprons in the morning, and a black silk one in the afternoon. And the blue cotton gown became a brown stuff one as winter drew on; this sounds like some book I once read, in which a migration from the blue bed to the brown was spoken of as a great family event.

Towards Christmas, my dear father came to see me, and to consult Mr Holdsworth about the improvement which has since been known as 'Manning's driving-wheel'. Mr Holdsworth, as I think I have before said, had a very great regard for my father, who had been employed in the same great machine-shop in which Mr Holdsworth had served his apprenticeship; and he and my father had many mutual jokes about one of these gentlemen-apprentices who used to set about his smith's work in white wash-leather gloves, for fear of spoiling his hands.[258] Mr Holdsworth often spoke to me about my father as having the same kind of genius for mechanical invention as that of George Stephenson;[259] and my father had come over now to consult him about several improvements, as well as an offer of partnership. It was a great pleasure to me to see the mutual regard of these two men: Mr Holdsworth, young, handsome, keen, well-dressed, an object of admiration to all the youth of Eltham; my father, in his decent but unfashionable Sunday clothes, his plain, sensible face full of hard lines, the marks of toil and thought – his hands blackened, beyond the power of soap and water, by years of labour in the foundry; speaking a strong Northern dialect, while Mr Holdsworth had a long, soft drawl in his voice, as many of the Southerners have, and was reckoned in Eltham to give himself airs.

Although most of my father's leisure-time was occupied with conversations about the business I have mentioned, he felt that he ought not to leave Eltham without going to pay his respects to the relations who had been so kind to his son. So he and I ran up on an engine along the incomplete line as far as Heathbridge, and went, by invitation, to spend a day at the farm.

It was odd and yet pleasant to me to perceive how these two men, each having led up to this point such totally dissimilar lives, seemed to come together by instinct, after one quiet straight look into each other's faces. My father was a thin, wiry man of five foot seven; the minister was a broad-shouldered, fresh-coloured man of six foot one; they were neither of them great talkers in general – perhaps the minister the most so – but they spoke much to each other. My father went into the fields with the minister; I think I see him now, with his hands behind his back, listening intently to all explanations of tillage, and the different processes of farming; occasionally taking up an implement, as if unconsciously, and examining it with a critical eye, and now and then asking a question, which I could see was considered as pertinent by his companion. Then we returned to look at the cattle, housed and bedded in expectation of the snowstorm hanging black on the western horizon, and my father learned the points of a cow with as much attention as if he meant to turn farmer. He had his little book that he used for mechanical memoranda and measurements in his pocket, and he took it out to write down 'straight back', 'small muzzle', 'deep barrel', and I know not what else, under the head 'cow'. He was very critical on a turnip-cutting machine, the clumsiness of which first incited him to talk; and, when we went into the house, he sat thinking and quiet for a bit, while Phillis and her mother made the last preparations for tea, with a little unheeded apology from cousin Holman, because we were not sitting in the best parlour, which she thought might be chilly on so cold a night. I wanted nothing better than the blazing, crackling fire that sent a glow over all the house-place, and warmed the snowy flags under our feet, till they seemed to have more heat than the crimson rug, right in front of the fire. After tea, as Phillis and I were talking together very happily, I heard an irrepressible exclamation from cousin Holman: 'Whatever is the man about!'

And, on looking round, I saw my father taking a straight burning stick out of the fire; and, after waiting for a minute, and examining the charred end, to see if it was fitted for his purpose, he went to the hardwood dresser, scoured to the last pitch of whiteness and cleanliness, and began drawing with the stick;[260] the best substitute for chalk or charcoal within his reach, for his pocketbook pencil was not strong or bold enough for his purpose. When he had done, he began to explain his new model of a turnip-cutting machine to the minister, who had been watching him in silence all the time. Cousin Holman had, in the meantime, taken a duster out of a drawer, and, under pretence of being as much interested as her husband in the drawing, was secretly trying on an outside mark how easily it would come off, and whether it would leave her dresser as white as before. Then Phillis was sent for the book of dynamics, about which I had been consulted during my first visit; and my father had to explain many difficulties, which he did in language as clear as his mind, making drawings with his stick wherever they were needed as illustrations; the minister sitting with his massive head resting on his hands, his elbows on the table, almost unconscious of Phillis, leaning over and listening greedily, with her hand on his shoulder, sucking in information, like her father's own daughter. I was rather sorry for cousin Holman; I had been so once or twice before; for do what she would, she was completely unable even to understand the pleasure her husband and daughter took in intellectual pursuits, much less to care in the least herself for the pursuits themselves, and was thus unavoidably thrown out of some of their interests. I had once or twice thought she was a little jealous of her own child, as a fitter companion for her husband than she was herself; and I fancied the minister himself was aware of this feeling, for I had noticed an occasional sudden change of subject, and a tenderness of appeal in his voice as he spoke to her, which always made her look contented and peaceful again. I do not think that Phillis ever perceived these little shadows; in the first place, she had such complete reverence for her parents that she listened to them both as if they had been St Peter and St Paul; and, besides, she was always too much engrossed with any matter in hand to think about other people's manners and looks.

This night I could see, though she did not, how much she was winning on my father. She asked a few questions which showed that she had followed his explanations up to that point; possibly, too, her unusual beauty might have something to do with his favourable impression of her; but he made no scruple of expressing his admiration of her to her father and mother in her absence from the room; and from that evening I date a project of his which came out to me, a day or two afterwards, as we sat in my little three-cornered room in Eltham.

'Paul,' he began, 'I never thought to be a rich man; but I think it's coming upon me. Some folk are making a deal of my new machine' (calling it by its technical name); 'and Ellison, of the Borough Green Works, has gone so far as to ask me to be his partner.'[261]

'Mr Ellison, the justice – who lives in King Street? why, he drives his carriage!' said I, doubting, yet exultant.

'Ay, lad, John Ellison. But that's no sign that I shall drive my carriage. Though I should like to save thy mother walking, for she's not so young as she was. But that's a long way off, anyhow. I reckon I should start with a third profit. It might be seven hundred, or it might be more. I should like to have the power to work out some fancies o' mine. I care for that much more than for th' brass. And Ellison has no lads; and by nature the business would come to thee in course o' time. Ellison's lassies are but bits o' things, and are not like to come by husbands just yet; and, when they do, maybe they'll not be in the mechanical line. It will be an opening for thee, lad, if thou art steady. Thou'rt not great shakes, I know, in th' inventing line; but many a one gets on better without having fancies for something he does not see and never has seen. I'm right down glad to see that mother's cousins are such uncommon folk for sense and goodness. I have taken the minister to my heart like a brother, and she is a womanly, quiet sort of a body. And I'll tell you frank, Paul, it will be a happy day for me, if ever you can come and tell me that Phillis Holman is like to be my daughter. I think, if that lass had not a penny, she would be the making of a man; and she'll have yon house and lands, and you may be her match yet in fortune, if all goes well.'

I was growing as red as fire; I did not know what to say, and yet I wanted to say something; but the idea of having a wife of my own at some future day, though it had often floated about in my own head, sounded so strange, when it was thus first spoken about by my father. He saw my confusion, and half-smiling said: 'Well, lad, what dost say to the old father's plans? Thou art but young, to be sure; but when I was thy age, I would ha' given my right hand, if I might ha' thought of the chance of wedding the lass I cared for – '

'My mother?' asked I, a little struck by the change of his tone of voice.

'No! not thy mother. Thy mother is a very good woman – none better. No! the lass I cared for at nineteen ne'er knew how I loved her, and a year or two after and she was dead, and ne'er knew. I think she would ha' been glad to ha' known it, poor Molly; but I had to leave the place where we lived, for to try to earn my bread – and I meant to come back – but, before ever I did, she was dead and gone: I ha' never gone there since. But, if you fancy Phillis Holman, and can get her to fancy you, my lad, it shall go different with you, Paul, to what it did with your father.'

I took counsel with myself very rapidly, and I came to a clear conclusion.

'Father,' said I, 'if I fancied Phillis ever so much, she would never fancy me. I like her as much as I could like a sister; and she likes me as if I were her brother – her younger brother.'

I could see my father's countenance fall a little.

'You see she's so clever – she's more like a man than a woman – she knows Latin and Greek.'

'She'd forget 'em, if she'd a houseful of children,' was my father's comment on this.

'But she knows many a thing besides, and is wise as well as learned: she has been so much with her father. She would never think much of me, and I should like my wife to think a deal of her husband.'

'It is not just book-learning, or the want of it, as makes a wife think much or little of her husband,' replied my father, evidently unwilling to give up a project which had taken deep root in his mind. 'It's a something – I don't rightly know how to call it – if he's manly, and sensible, and straightforward; and I reckon you're that, my boy.'

'I don't think I should like to have a wife taller than I am, father,' said I, smiling; he smiled too, but not heartily.

'Well,' said he, after a pause. 'It's but a few days I've been thinking of it; but I'd got as fond of my notion as if it had been a new engine as I'd been planning out. Here's our Paul, thinks I to myself, a good sensible breed o' lad, as has never vexed or troubled his mother or me; with a good business opening out before him; age nineteen; not so bad-looking, though perhaps not to call handsome; and here's his cousin, not too near a cousin, but just nice, as one may say; aged seventeen; good and true, and well brought up to work with her hands as well as her head; a scholar – but that can't be helped, and is more her misfortune than her fault, seeing she is the only child of a scholar – and as I said afore, once she's a wife and a mother, she'll forget it all, I'll be bound – with a good fortune in land and house, when it shall please the Lord to take her parents to himself; with eyes like poor Molly's for beauty, a colour that comes and goes on a milk-white skin, and as pretty a mouth – '

'Why, Mr Manning, what fair lady are you describing?' asked Mr Holdsworth, who had come quickly and suddenly upon our tête-à-tête, and had caught my father's last words as he entered the room.

Both my father and I felt rather abashed; it was such an odd subject for us to be talking about; but my father, like a straightforward, simple man as he was, spoke out the truth.

'I've been telling Paul of Ellison's offer, and saying how good an opening it made for him – '

'I wish I'd as good,' said Mr Holdsworth. 'But has the business a "pretty mouth"?'

'You're always so full of your joking, Mr Holdsworth,' said my father. 'I was going to say that if he and his cousin Phillis Holman liked to make it up between them, I would put no spoke in the wheel.'

'Phillis Holman!' said Mr Holdsworth. 'Is she the daughter of the minister-farmer out at Heathbridge? Have I been helping on the course of true love, by letting you go there so often? I knew nothing of it.'

'There is nothing to know,' said I, more annoyed than I chose to show. 'There is no more true love in the case than may be between the first brother and sister you may choose to meet. I have been telling father she would never think of me; she's a great deal taller and cleverer; and I'd rather be taller and more learned than my wife when I have one.'

'And it is she, then, that has the pretty mouth your father spoke about? I should think that would be an antidote to the cleverness and learning. But I ought to apologise for breaking in upon your last night; I came upon business to your father.'

And then he and my father began to talk about many things that had no interest for me just then, and I began to go over again my conversation with my father. The more I thought about it, the more I felt that I had spoken truly about my feelings towards Phillis Holman. I loved her dearly as a sister, but I could never fancy her as my wife. Still less could I think of her ever – yes, *condescending*, that is the word – condescending to marry me. I was roused from a reverie on what I should like my possible wife to be, by hearing my father's warm praise of the minister, as a most unusual character; how they had got back from the diameter of driving-wheels to the subject of the Holmans, I could never tell; but I saw that my father's weighty praises were exciting some curiosity in Mr Holdsworth's mind; indeed, he said, almost in a voice of reproach: 'Why, Paul, you never told me what kind of a fellow this minister-cousin of yours was?'

'I don't know that I found out, sir,' said I. 'But if I had, I don't think you'd have listened to me, as you have done to my father.'

'No! most likely not, old fellow,' replied Mr Holdsworth, laughing. And, again and afresh, I saw what a handsome pleasant clear face his was; and, though this evening I had been a bit put out with him – through his sudden coming, and his having heard my father's open-hearted confidence – my hero resumed all his empire over me by his bright merry laugh.

And, if he had not resumed his old place that night, he would have done so the next day: when, after my father's departure, Mr Holdsworth spoke about him with such just respect for his character, such ungrudging admiration of his great mechanical genius, that I was compelled to say, almost unawares: 'Thank you, sir. I am very much obliged to you.'

'Oh, you're not at all. I am only speaking the truth. Here's a Birmingham workman, self-educated, one may say – having never associated with stimulating minds, or had what advantages travel and contact with the world may be supposed to afford – working out his own thoughts into steel and iron, making a scientific name for himself – a fortune, if it pleases him to work for money – and keeping his singleness of heart, his perfect simplicity of manner; it puts me out of patience to think of my expensive schooling, my travels hither and thither, my heaps of scientific books – and I have done nothing to speak of! But it's evidently good blood; there's that Mr Holman, that cousin of yours, made of the same stuff.'

'But he's only cousin because he married my mother's second cousin,' said I.

'That knocks a pretty theory on the head, and twice over, too. I should like to make Holman's acquaintance.'

'I am sure they would be so glad to see you at Hope Farm,' said I eagerly. 'In fact, they've asked me to bring you several times; only I thought you would find it dull.'

'Not at all. I can't go yet though, even if you do get me an invitation; for the — Company want me to go to the — Valley, and look over the ground a bit for them, to see if it would do for a branch line; it's a job which may take me away for some time; but I shall be backwards and forwards, and you're quite up to doing what is needed in my absence; the only work that may be beyond you is keeping old Jevons from drinking.'

He went on giving me directions about the management of the men employed on the line; and no more was said then, or for several months, about his going to Hope Farm. He went off into — Valley, a dark overshadowed dale, where the sun seemed to set behind the hills before four o'clock on midsummer afternoons.

Perhaps it was this that brought on the attack of low fever, which he had soon after the beginning of the new year; he was very ill for many weeks, almost many months; a married sister – his only relation, I think – came down from London to nurse him, and I went over to him when I could, to see him, and give him 'masculine news', as he called it; reports of the progress of the line, which, I am glad to say, I was able to carry on in his absence, in the slow gradual way which suited the company best, while trade was in a languid state and money dear in the market. Of course, with this occupation for my scanty leisure, I did not often go over to Hope Farm. Whenever I did go, I met with a thorough welcome; and many enquiries were made as to Holdsworth's illness, and the progress of his recovery.

At length, in June I think it was, he was sufficiently recovered to come back to his lodgings at Eltham, and resume part at least of his work. His sister, Mrs Robinson, had been obliged to leave him some weeks before, owing to some epidemic amongst her own children. As long as I had seen Mr Holdsworth in the rooms at the little inn at Hensleydale, where I had been accustomed to look upon him as an invalid, I had not been aware of the visible shake his fever had given to his health. But, once back in the old lodgings, where I had always seen him so buoyant, eloquent, decided, and vigorous in former days, my spirits sank at the change in one whom I had always regarded with a strong feeling of admiring affection. He sank into silence and despondency after the least exertion; he seemed as if he could not make up his mind to any action, or else, as if, when it was made up, he lacked strength to carry out his purpose. Of course, it was but the natural state of slow convalescence, after so sharp an illness; but, at the time, I did not know this, and perhaps I represented his state as more serious than it was, to my kind relations at Hope Farm; who, in their grave, simple, eager way, immediately thought of the only help they could give.

'Bring him out here,' said the minister. 'Our air here is good, to a proverb; the June days are fine; he may loiter away his time in the hayfield, and the sweet smells will be a balm in themselves – better than physic.'

'And,' said cousin Holman, scarcely waiting for her husband to finish his sentence, 'tell him there is new milk and fresh eggs to be had for the asking; it's lucky Daisy has just calved, for her milk is always as good as other cows' cream; and there is the plaid-room, with the morning-sun all streaming in.'

Phillis said nothing, but looked as much interested in the project as anyone. I took it up myself. I wanted them to see him and him to know them. I proposed it to him, when I got home. He was too languid, after the day's fatigue, to be willing to make the little exertion of going amongst strangers; and disappointed me by almost declining to accept the invitation I brought. The next morning it was different; he apologised for his ungraciousness of the night before; and told me that he would get all things in train, so as to be ready to go out with me to Hope Farm on the following Saturday.

'For you must go with me, Manning,' said he; 'I used to be as impudent a fellow as need be, and rather liked going amongst strangers and making my way; but since my illness I am almost like a girl, and turn hot and cold with shyness; as they do, I fancy.'

So it was fixed. We were to go out to Hope Farm on Saturday afternoon; and it was also understood that, if the air and the life suited Mr Holdsworth, he was to remain there for a week or ten days, doing what work he could at that end of the line, while I took his place at Eltham to the best of my ability. I grew a little nervous, as the time drew near, and wondered how the brilliant Holdsworth would agree with the quiet quaint family of the minister; how they would like him and many of his half-foreign ways. I tried to prepare him, by telling him, from time to time, little things about the goings-on at Hope Farm.

'Manning,' said he, 'I see you don't think I am half good enough for your friends. Out with it, man!'

'No,' I replied boldly. 'I think you are good; but I don't know if you are quite of their kind of goodness.'

'And you've found out already that there is greater chance of disagreement between two "kinds of goodness", each having its own idea of right, than between a given goodness and a moderate degree of naughtiness – which last often arises from an indifference to right?'

'I don't know. I think you're talking metaphysics;[262] and I am sure that is bad for you.'

' "When a man talks to you in a way that you don't understand about a thing which he does not understand, them's metaphysics." You remember the clown's definition, don't you, Manning?'

'No, I don't,' said I. 'But what I do understand is, that you must go to bed, and tell me at what time we must start tomorrow; that I may go to Hepworth, and get those letters written we were talking about this morning.'

'Wait till tomorrow, and let us see what the day is like,' he answered, with such languid indecision as showed me he was over-fatigued. So I went my way.

The morrow was blue and sunny and beautiful; the very perfection of an early summer's day. Mr Holdsworth was all impatience to be off into the country; morning had brought back his freshness and strength, and consequent eagerness to be going. I was afraid we were going to my cousin's farm rather too early, before they would expect us; but what could I do with such a restless vehement man as Holdsworth was that morning? We came down upon the Hope Farm, before the dew was off the grass on the shady side of the lane; the great house-dog was loose, basking in the sun, near the closed side door. I was surprised at this door being shut, for all summer long it was open from morning to night; but it was only on latch. I opened it; Rover watching me with half-suspicious, half-trustful eyes. The room was empty.

'I don't know where they can be,' said I. 'But come in and sit down, while I go and look for them! You must be tired.'

'Not I. This sweet balmy air is like a thousand tonics. Besides, this room is hot, and smells of those pungent wood-ashes. What are we to do?'

'Go round to the kitchen. Betty will tell us where they are.'

So we went round into the farmyard, Rover accompanying us out of a grave sense of duty. Betty was washing out her milk-pans, in the cold bubbling spring water that constantly trickled in and out of a stone trough. In such weather as this, most of her kitchen-work was done out of doors.

'Eh, dear!' said she, 'the minister and missus is away at Hornby!

They ne'er thought of your coming so betimes! The missus had some errands to do; and she thought as she'd walk with the minister and be back by dinner-time.'

'Did not they expect us to dinner?' said I.

'Well, they did, and they did not, as I may say. Missus said to me, the cold lamb would do well enough, if you did not come; and, if you did, I was to put on a chicken and some bacon to boil; and I'll go do it now, for it is hard to boil bacon enough.'

'And is Phillis gone, too?' Mr Holdsworth was making friends with Rover.

'No! She's just somewhere about. I reckon you'll find her in the kitchen-garden, getting peas.'

'Let us go there,' said Holdsworth, suddenly leaving off his play with the dog.

So I led the way into the kitchen-garden. It was in the first promise of a summer profuse in vegetables and fruits. Perhaps it was not so much cared for as other parts of the property; but it was more attended to than most kitchen-gardens belonging to farmhouses. There were borders of flowers along each side of the gravel-walks; and there was an old sheltering wall on the north side, covered with tolerably choice fruit trees; there was a slope down to the fishpond at the end, where there were great strawberry-beds; and raspberry trees and rose trees grew wherever there was a space; it seemed a chance which had been planted. Long rows of peas stretched at right angles from the main walk; and I saw Phillis stooping down among them, before she saw us. As soon as she heard our cranching steps on the gravel, she stood up, and, shading her eyes from the sun, recognised us. She was quite still for a moment, and then came slowly towards us, blushing a little, from evident shyness. I had never seen Phillis shy before.

'This is Mr Holdsworth, Phillis,' said I, as soon as I had shaken hands with her. She glanced up at him, and then looked down, more flushed than ever at his grand formality of taking his hat off and bowing; such manners had never been seen at Hope Farm before.

'Father and mother are out. They will be so sorry; you did not write, Paul, as you said you would.'

'It was my fault,' said Holdsworth, understanding what she meant, as well as if she had put it more fully into words. 'I have not yet given up all the privileges of an invalid; one of which is indecision. Last night, when your cousin asked me at what time we were to start, I really could not make up my mind.'

Phillis seemed as if she could not make up her mind as to what to do with us. I tried to help her: 'Have you finished getting peas?' taking hold of the half-filled basket she was unconsciously holding in her hand; 'or may we stay and help you?'

'If you would. But perhaps it will tire you, sir?' added she, speaking now to Holdsworth.

'Not a bit,' said he. 'It will carry me back twenty years in my life, when I used to gather peas in my grandfather's garden. I suppose I may eat a few, as I go along?'

'Certainly, sir. But, if you went to the strawberry-beds, you would find some strawberries ripe; and Paul can show you where they are.'

'I am afraid you distrust me. I can assure you, I know the exact fulness at which peas should be gathered. I take great care not to pluck them when they are unripe. I will not be turned off, as unfit for my work.'

This was a style of half-joking talk that Phillis was not accustomed to. She looked for a moment as if she would have liked to defend herself from the playful charge of distrust made against her; but she ended by not saying a word. We all plucked our peas in busy silence for the next five minutes. Then Holdsworth lifted himself up from between the rows, and said, a little wearily: 'I am afraid I must strike work. I am not as strong as I fancied myself.'

Phillis was full of penitence immediately. He did, indeed, look pale; and she blamed herself for having allowed him to help her.

'It was very thoughtless of me. I did not know – I thought, perhaps, you really liked it. I ought to have offered you something to eat, sir! Oh, Paul, we have gathered quite enough; how stupid I was to forget that Mr Holdsworth had been ill!' And in a blushing hurry she led the way towards the house. We went in, and she moved a heavy-cushioned chair forwards, into which Holdsworth was only too glad to sink. Then, with deft and quiet speed, she brought in a little tray – wine, water, cake, homemade bread, and newly-churned butter. She stood by in some anxiety till, after bite and sup, the colour returned to Mr Holdsworth's face, and he would fain have made us some laughing apologies for the fright he had given us. But then Phillis drew back from her innocent show of care and interest, and relapsed into the cold shyness habitual to her when she was first thrown into the company of strangers. She brought out the last week's county-paper (which Mr Holdsworth had read five days ago), and then quietly withdrew; and then he subsided into languor, leaning back and shutting his eyes, as if he would go to sleep. I stole into the kitchen after Phillis; but she had made the round of the corner of the house outside, and I found her sitting on the horse-mount, with her basket of peas, and a basin into which she was shelling them. Rover lay at her feet, snapping now and then at the flies. I went to her, and tried to help her; but somehow the sweet, crisp young peas found their way more frequently into my mouth than into the basket, while we talked together in a low tone, fearful of being overheard through the open casements of the house-place, in which Holdsworth was resting.

'Don't you think him handsome?' asked I.

'Perhaps – yes – I have hardly looked at him,' she replied. 'But is not he very like a foreigner?'

'Yes, he cuts his hair foreign fashion,' said I.

'I like an Englishman to look like an Englishman.'

'I don't think he thinks about it. He says he began that way when he was in Italy, because everybody wore it so, and it is natural to keep it on in England.'

'Not if he began it in Italy, because everybody there wore it so. Everybody here wears it differently.'

I was a little offended with Phillis's logical fault-finding with my friend; and I determined to change the subject.

'When is your mother coming home?'

'I should think she might come any time now; but she had to go and see Mrs Morton, who was ill; and she might be kept, and not be home till dinner. Don't you think you ought to go and see how Mr Holdsworth is going on, Paul? He may be faint again.'

I went at her bidding; but there was no need for it. Mr Holdsworth was up, standing by the window, his hands in his pockets; he had evidently been watching us. He turned away as I entered.

'So that is the girl I found your good father planning for your wife, Paul, that evening when I interrupted you! Are you of the same coy mind still? It did not look like it a minute ago.'

'Phillis and I understand each other,' I replied sturdily. 'We are like brother and sister. She would not have me as a husband, if there was not another man in the world; and it would take a deal to make me think of her – as my father wishes' (somehow I did not like to say 'as a wife'); 'but we love each other dearly.'

'Well, I am rather surprised at it – not at your loving each other in a brother-and-sister kind of way – but at your finding it so impossible to fall in love with such a beautiful woman.'

Woman! beautiful woman! I had thought of Phillis as a comely, but awkward, girl; and I could not banish the pinafore from my mind's eye when I tried to picture her to myself. Now I turned, as Mr Holdsworth had done, to look at her again out of the window: she had just finished her task, and was standing up, her back to us, holding the basket and the basin in it, high in the air, out of Rover's reach, who was giving vent to his delight at the probability of a change of place by glad leaps and barks, and snatches at what he imagined to be a withheld prize. At length she grew tired of their mutual play, and, with a feint of striking him, and a 'Down, Rover! do hush!' she looked towards the window where we were standing, as if to reassure herself that no one had been disturbed by the noise; and seeing us, she coloured all over, and hurried away, with Rover still curving in sinuous lines about her as she walked.

'I should like to have sketched her,' said Mr Holdsworth, as he turned away. He went back to his chair, and rested in silence for a minute or two. Then he was up again.

'I would give a good deal for a book,' said he. 'It would keep me quiet.' He began to look round; there were a few volumes at one end of the shovel-board.

'Fifth volume of Matthew Henry's *Commentary*,' said he, reading their titles aloud. '*Housewife's Complete Manual*;[263] *Berridge on Prayer*;[264] *L'Inferno* – Dante!' in great surprise. 'Why, who reads this?'

'I told you Phillis read it. Don't you remember? She knows Latin and Greek, too.'

'To be sure! I remember! But somehow I never put two and two together. That quiet girl, full of household-work, is the wonderful scholar, then, that put you to rout with her questions, when you first began to come here! To be sure, "Cousin Phillis!" What's here – a paper with the hard obsolete words written out. I wonder what sort of a dictionary she has got. Baretti[265] won't tell her all these words. Stay! I have got a pencil here. I'll write down the most accepted meanings, and save her a little trouble.'

So he took her book and the paper back to the little round table, and employed himself in writing explanations and definitions of the words which had troubled her. I was not sure if he was not taking a liberty; it did not quite please me, and yet I did not know why. He had only just done, and replaced the paper in the book, and put the latter back in its place, when I heard the sound of wheels stopping in the lane; and, looking out, I saw cousin Holman getting out of a neighbour's gig,[266] making her little curtsey of acknowledgement, and then coming towards the house. I went out to meet her.

'Oh, Paul!' said she, 'I am so sorry I was kept; and then Thomas

Dobson said, if I would wait a quarter of an hour, he would – But where's your friend Mr Holdsworth? I hope he is come?'

Just then he came out and, with his pleasant cordial manner, took her hand, and thanked her for asking him to come out here to get strong.

'I'm sure I am very glad to see you, sir. It was the minister's thought. I took it into my head you would be dull in our quiet house, for Paul says you've been such a great traveller; but the minister said that dulness would perhaps suit you while you were but ailing, and that I was to ask Paul to be here as much as he could. I hope you'll find yourself happy with us, I'm sure, sir. Has Phillis given you something to eat and drink, I wonder? there's a deal in eating a little often, if one has to get strong after an illness.' And then she began to question him as to the details of his indisposition, in her simple, motherly way. He seemed at once to understand her, and to enter into friendly relations with her. It was not quite the same in the evening, when the minister came home. Men have always a little natural antipathy to get over when they first meet as strangers. But, in this case, each was disposed to make an effort to like the other; only, each was to each a specimen of an unknown class. I had to leave the Hope Farm on Sunday afternoon, as I had Mr Holdsworth's work as well as my own to look to in Eltham; and I was not at all sure how things would go on during the week that Holdsworth was to remain on his visit; I had been once or twice in hot water already, at the near clash of opinions between the minister and my much-vaunted friend. On the Wednesday I received a short note from Holdsworth; he was going to stay on, and return with me on the following Sunday, and he wanted me to send him a certain list of books, his theodolite, and other surveying instruments, all of which could easily be conveyed down the line to Heathbridge. I went to his lodgings and picked out the books. Italian, Latin, trigonometry; a pretty considerable parcel they made, besides the implements. I began to be curious as to the general progress of affairs at Hope Farm; but I could not go over till the Saturday. At Heathbridge I found Holdsworth, come to meet me. He was looking quite a different man to what I had left him: embrowned; sparkles in his eyes, so languid before. I told him how much stronger he looked.

'Yes!' said he. 'I am fidging-fain[267] to be at work again. Last week, I dreaded the thoughts of my employment; now I am full of desire to begin. This week in the country has done wonders for me.'

'You have enjoyed yourself, then?'

'Oh! it has been perfect in its way. Such a thorough country-life! and yet removed from the dulness which I always used to fancy accompanied country-life, by the extraordinary intelligence of the minister. I have fallen into calling him "the minister", like everyone else.'

'You get on with him, then?' said I. 'I was a little afraid.'

'I was on the verge of displeasing him once or twice, I fear, with random assertions and exaggerated expressions, such as one always uses with other people, and thinks nothing of; but I tried to check myself when I saw how it shocked the good man; and really it is very wholesome exercise, this trying to make one's words represent one's thoughts, instead of merely looking to their effect on others.'

'Then you are quite friends now?' I asked.

'Yes, thoroughly; at any rate as far as I go. I never met a man with such a desire for knowledge. In information, as far as it can be gained from books, he far exceeds me on most subjects; but then I have travelled and seen – Were not you surprised at the list of things I sent for?'

'Yes; I thought it did not promise much rest.'

'Oh, some of the books were for the minister, and some for his daughter. (I call her "Phillis" to myself, but I use a roundabout way of speaking of her to others. I don't like to seem familiar, and yet "Miss Holman" is a term I have never heard used.)'

'I thought the Italian books were for her.'

'Yes! Fancy her trying at Dante for her first book in Italian! I had a capital novel by Manzoni, *I Promessi Sposi*,[268] just the thing for a beginner! and, if she must still puzzle out Dante, my dictionary is far better than hers.'

'Then she found out you had written those definitions on her list of words?'

'Oh! yes' – with a smile of amusement and pleasure. He was going to tell me what had taken place, but checked himself.

'But I don't think the minister will like your having given her a novel to read?'

'Pooh! What can be more harmless? Why make a bugbear of a word! It is as pretty and innocent a tale as can be met with. You don't suppose they take Virgil for gospel?'

By this time we were at the farm. I think Phillis gave me a warmer welcome than usual, and cousin Holman was kindness itself. Yet somehow I felt as if I had lost my place, and that Holdsworth had taken it. He knew all the ways of the house; he was full of little filial attentions to cousin Holman; he treated Phillis with the affectionate condescension of an elder brother; not a bit more; not in any way different. He questioned me about the progress of affairs in Eltham with eager interest.

'Ah!' said cousin Holman, 'you'll be spending a different kind of time next week to what you have done this! I can see how busy you'll make yourself! But, if you don't take care, you'll be ill again, and have to come back to our quiet ways of going on.'

'Do you suppose I shall need to be ill to wish to come back here?' he answered warmly. 'I am only afraid you have treated me so kindly that I shall always be turning up on your hands.'

'That's right,' she replied. 'Only don't go and make yourself ill by over-work. I hope you'll go on with a cup of new milk every morning, for I am sure that is the best medicine; and put a teaspoonful of rum in it, if you like; many a one speaks highly of that, only we had no rum in the house.'

I brought with me an atmosphere of active life which I think he had begun to miss; and it was natural that he should seek my company, after his week of retirement. Once, I saw Phillis looking at us, as we talked together, with a kind of wistful curiosity; but, as soon as she caught my eye, she turned away, blushing deeply.

That evening I had a little talk with the minister. I strolled along the Hornby road to meet him; for Holdsworth was giving Phillis an Italian lesson, and cousin Holman had fallen asleep over her work.

Somehow, and not unwillingly on my part, our talk fell on the friend whom I had introduced to the Hope Farm.

'Yes! I like him!' said the minister, weighing his words a little as he spoke. 'I like him. I hope I am justified in doing it; but he takes hold of me, as it were, and I have almost been afraid lest he carries me away, in spite of my judgement.'

'He is a good fellow; indeed he is,' said I. 'My father thinks well of him; and I have seen a deal of him. I would not have had him come here, if I did not know that you would approve of him.'

'Yes' (once more hesitating), 'I like him, and I think he is an upright man; there is a want of seriousness in his talk at times, but, at the same time, it is wonderful to listen to him! He makes Horace and Virgil living, instead of dead, by the stories he tells me of his sojourn in the very countries where they lived, and where to this day, he says – But it is like dram-drinking. I listen to him, till I forget my duties and am carried off my feet. Last Sabbath-evening, he led us away into talk on profane subjects ill-befitting the day.'

By this time we were at the house, and our conversation stopped. But, before the day was out, I saw the unconscious hold that my friend had got over all the family. And no wonder: he had seen so much and done so much, as compared to them, and he told about it all so easily and naturally, and yet as I never heard anyone else do; and his ready pencil was out in an instant to draw on scraps of paper all sorts of illustrations – modes of drawing up water in Northern Italy, wine-carts, buffaloes, stone-pines, I know not what. After we had all looked at these drawings, Phillis gathered them together, and took them.

It is many years since I have seen thee, Edward Holdsworth, but thou wast a delightful fellow! Ay, and a good one too; though much sorrow was caused by thee!

Part Three

Just after this, I went home for a week's holiday. Everything was prospering there; my father's new partnership gave evident satisfaction to both parties. There was no display of increased wealth in our modest household; but my mother had a few extra comforts provided for her by her husband. I made acquaintance with Mr and Mrs Ellison, and first saw pretty Margaret Ellison, who is now my wife. When I returned to Eltham, I found that a step was decided upon which had been in contemplation for some time: that Holdsworth and I should remove our quarters to Hornby; our daily presence, and as much of our time as possible, being required for the completion of the line at that end.

Of course this led to greater facility of intercourse with the Hope Farm people. We could easily walk out there, after our day's work was done, and spend a balmy evening hour or two, and yet return before the summer's twilight had quite faded away. Many a time, indeed, we would fain have stayed longer – the open air, the fresh and pleasant country, made so agreeable a contrast to the close, hot town lodgings which I shared with Mr Holdsworth; but early hours, both at eve and morn, were an imperative necessity with the minister, and he made no scruple at turning either or both of us out of the house directly after evening prayer, or 'exercise', as he called it. The remembrance of many a happy day, and of several little scenes, comes back upon me as I think of that summer. They rise like pictures to my memory, and in this way I can date their succession; for I know that corn-harvest must have come after haymaking, apple-gathering after corn-harvest.

The removal to Hornby took up some time, during which we had neither of us any leisure to go out to the Hope Farm. Mr Holdsworth had been out there once, during my absence at home. One sultry evening, when work was done, he proposed our walking out and paying the Holmans a visit. It so happened that I had omitted to write my usual weekly letter home in our press of business, and I wished to finish that before going out. Then he said that he would go, and that I could follow him, if I liked. This I did in about an hour; the weather was so oppressive, I remember, that I took off my coat as I walked, and hung it over my arm. All the doors and windows at the farm were open, when I arrived there, and every tiny leaf on the trees was still. The silence of the place was profound; at first I thought it was entirely deserted; but, just as I drew near the door, I heard a weak, sweet voice begin to sing; it was cousin Holman, all by herself in the house-place, piping up a hymn, as she knitted away in the clouded light. She gave me a kindly welcome, and poured out all the small domestic news of the fortnight past upon me; and, in return, I told her about my own people and my visit at home.

'Where were the rest?' at length I asked.

Betty and the men were in the field helping with the last load of hay, for the minister said there would be rain before the morning. Yes, and the minister himself, and Phillis, and Mr Holdsworth, were all there helping. She thought that she herself could have done something; but perhaps she was the least fit for haymaking of any-one; and somebody must stay at home and take care of the house, there were so many tramps about; if I had not had something to do with the railroad, she would have called them navvies.[269] I asked her if she minded being left alone, as I should like to go and help; and, having her full and glad permission to leave her alone, I went off, following her directions: through the farmyard, past the cattle-pond, into the ash-field, beyond into the higher field, with two holly trees in the middle. I arrived there: there was Betty with all the farming men, and a cleared field, and a heavily-laden cart; one man at the top of the great pile, ready to catch the fragrant hay which the others threw up to him with their pitchforks; a little heap of cast-off clothes in a corner of the field (for the heat, even at seven o'clock, was insufferable), a few cans and baskets, and Rover lying by them, panting, and keeping watch. Plenty of loud, hearty, cheerful talking; but no minister, no Phillis, no Mr Holdsworth. Betty saw me first, and, understanding who it was that I was in search of, she came towards me.

'They're out yonder – a-gait[270] wi' them things o' Measter Holds-worth's.'

So 'out yonder' I went; out on to a broad upland common, full of red sandbanks, and sweeps and hollows; bordered by dark firs, purple in the coming shadows, but near at hand all ablaze with flowering gorse, or, as we call it in the south, furze trees, which, seen against the belt of distant trees, appeared brilliantly golden. On this heath, a little way from the field-gate, I saw the three. I counted their heads, joined together in an eager group over Holdsworth's theodolite. He was teaching the minister the practical art of surveying and taking a level. I was wanted to assist, and was quickly set to work to hold the chain. Phillis was as intent as her father; she had hardly time to greet me, so desirous was she to hear some answer to her father's question.

So we went on, the dark clouds still gathering, for perhaps five minutes after my arrival. Then came the blinding lightning and the rumble and quick-following rattling peal of thunder, right over our heads. It came sooner than I expected, sooner than they had looked for: the rain delayed not; it came pouring down; and what were we to do for shelter? Phillis had nothing on but her indoor things – no bonnet, no shawl. Quick as the darting lightning around us, Holdsworth took off his coat and wrapped it round her neck and shoulders, and, almost without a word, hurried us all into such poor shelter as one of the overhanging sandbanks could give. There we were, cowered down, close together, Phillis innermost, almost too tightly-packed to free her arms enough to divest herself of the coat, which she, in her turn, tried to put lightly over Holdsworth's shoulders. In doing so, she touched his shirt.

'Oh, how wet you are!' she cried, in pitying dismay; 'and you've hardly got over your fever! Oh, Mr Holdsworth, I am so sorry!' He turned his head a little, smiling at her.

'If I do catch cold, it is all my fault for having deluded you into staying out here!' But she only murmured again, 'I am so sorry.'

The minister spoke now. 'It is a regular downpour. Please God that the hay is saved! But there is no likelihood of its ceasing, and I had better go home at once, and send you all some wraps; umbrellas will not be safe with yonder thunder and lightning.'

Both Holdsworth and I offered to go instead of him; but he was resolved, although perhaps it would have been wiser if Holdsworth, wet as he already was, had kept himself in exercise. As he moved off, Phillis crept out, and could see on to the storm-swept heath. Part of Holdsworth's apparatus still remained exposed to all the rain. Before we could have any warning, she had rushed out of the shelter and collected the various things, and brought them back in triumph to where we crouched. Holdsworth had stood up, uncertain whether to go to her assistance or not. She came running back, her long lovely hair floating and dripping, her eyes glad and bright, and her colour freshened to a glow of health by the exercise and the rain.

'Now, Miss Holman, that's what I call wilful,' said Holdsworth, as she gave them to him. 'No, I won't thank you' (his looks were thanking her all the time). 'My little bit of dampness annoyed you, because you thought I had got wet in your service; so you were determined to make me as uncomfortable as you were yourself. It was an unchristian piece of revenge!'

His tone of badinage[271] (as the French call it) would have been palpable enough to anyone accustomed to the world; but Phillis was not, and it distressed or rather bewildered her. 'Unchristian' had to her a very serious meaning; it was not a word to be used lightly; and, though she did not exactly understand what wrong it was that she was accused of doing, she was evidently desirous to throw off the imputation. At first, her earnestness to disclaim unkind motives amused Holdsworth; while his light continuance of the joke perplexed her still more; but at last he said something gravely, and in too low a tone for me to hear, which made her all at once become silent, and called out her blushes. After a while, the minister came back, a moving mass of shawls, cloaks, and umbrellas. Phillis kept very close to her father's side on our return to the farm. She appeared to me to be shrinking away from Holdsworth, while he had not the slightest variation in his manner from what it usually was in his graver moods; kind, protecting, and thoughtful towards her. Of course, there was a great commotion about our wet clothes; but I name the little events of that evening now, because I wondered at the time what he had said in that low voice to silence Phillis so effectually, and because, in thinking of their intercourse by the light of future events, that evening stands out with some prominence.

I have said that, after our removal to Hornby, our communications with the farm became almost of daily occurrence. Cousin Holman and I were the two who had least to do with this intimacy. After Mr Holdsworth regained his health, he too often talked above her head in intellectual matters, and too often in his light bantering tone for her to feel quite at her ease with him. I really believe that he adopted this latter tone in speaking to her because he did not know what to talk about to a purely motherly woman, whose intellect had never been cultivated, and whose loving heart was entirely occupied with her husband, her child, her household affairs, and, perhaps, a little with the concerns of the members of her husband's congregation, because they, in a way, belonged to her husband. I had noticed before that she had fleeting shadows of jealousy even of Phillis, when her daughter and her husband appeared to have strong interests and sympathies in things which were quite beyond her comprehension. I had noticed it in my first acquaintance with them, I say, and had admired the delicate tact which made the minister, on such occasions, bring the conversation back to such subjects as those on which his wife, with her practical experience of everyday life, was an authority; while Phillis, devoted to her father, unconsciously followed his lead, totally unaware, in her filial reverence, of his motive for doing so.

To return to Holdsworth. The minister had at more than one time spoken of him to me with slight distrust, principally occasioned by the suspicion that his careless words were not always those of soberness and truth. But it was more as a protest against the fascination which the younger man evidently exercised over the elder one – more, as it were, to strengthen himself against yielding to this fascination – that the minister spoke out to me about this failing of Holdsworth's, as it appeared to him. In return, Holdsworth was subdued by the minister's uprightness and goodness, and delighted with his clear intellect – his strong healthy craving after further knowledge. I never met two men who took more thorough pleasure and relish in each other's society. To Phillis his relation continued that of an elder brother: he directed her studies into new paths; he patiently drew out the expression of many of her thoughts, and perplexities, and unformed theories, scarcely ever now falling into the vein of banter which she was so slow to understand.

One day – harvest-time – he had been drawing on a loose piece of paper – sketching ears of corn, sketching carts drawn by bullocks and laden with grapes – all the time talking with Phillis and me, cousin Holman putting in her not pertinent remarks, when suddenly he said to Phillis: 'Keep your head still; I see a sketch! I have often tried to draw your head from memory, and failed; but I think I can do it now. If I succeed, I will give it to your mother. You would like a portrait of your daughter as Ceres, would you not, ma'am?'

'I should like a picture of her; yes, very much, thank you, Mr Holdsworth; but if you put that straw in her hair' (he was holding some wheat ears above her passive head, looking at the effect with an artistic eye), 'you'll ruffle her hair. Phillis, my dear, if you're to have your picture taken, go upstairs, and brush your hair smooth.'

'Not on any account. I beg your pardon; but I want hair loosely-flowing.'

He began to draw, looking intently at Phillis; I could see this stare of his discomposed her – her colour came and went, her breath quickened with the consciousness of his regard; at last, when he said, 'Please look at me for a minute or two, I want to get in the eyes,' she looked up at him, quivered, and suddenly got up and left the room. He did not say a word, but went on with some other part of the drawing; his silence was unnatural, and his dark cheek blanched a little. Cousin Holman looked up from her work, and put her spectacles down.

'What's the matter? Where is she gone?'

Holdsworth never uttered a word, but went on drawing. I felt obliged to say something; it was stupid enough, but stupidity was better than silence just then.

'I'll go and call her,' said I. So I went into the hall, and to the bottom of the stairs; but just as I was going to call Phillis, she came down swiftly with her bonnet on, and saying, 'I'm going to father in the five-acre,' passed out by the open 'rector', right in front of the house-place windows, and out at the little white side-gate. She had been seen by her mother and Holdsworth as she passed; so there was no need for explanation; only, cousin Holman and I had a long discussion as to whether she could have found the room too hot, or what had occasioned her sudden departure. Holdsworth was very quiet during all the rest of that day; nor did he resume the portrait-taking by his own desire, only, at my cousin Holman's request, the next time that he came; and then he said he should not require any more formal sittings for only such a slight sketch as he felt himself capable of making. Phillis was just the same as ever, the next time I saw her after her abrupt passing me in the hall. She never gave any explanation of her rush out of the room.

So all things went on, at least as far as my observation reached at the time, or memory can recall now, till the great apple-gathering of the year. The nights were frosty, the mornings and evenings were misty, but at midday all was sunny and bright; and it was one midday that, both of us being on the line near Heathbridge, and knowing that they were gathering apples at the farm, we resolved to spend the men's dinner-hour in going over there. We found the great clothes-baskets full of apples, scenting the house and stopping up the way, and an universal air of merry contentment with this the final produce of the year. The yellow leaves hung on the trees, ready to flutter down at the slightest puff of air; the great bushes of Michaelmas daisies in the kitchen-garden were making their last show of flowers. We must needs taste the fruit off the different trees, and pass our judgement as to their flavour; and we went away with our pockets stuffed with those that we liked best. As we had passed to the orchard, Holdsworth had admired and spoken about some flower which he saw; it so happened he had never seen this old-fashioned kind since the days of his boyhood. I do not know whether he had thought anything more about this chance speech of his, but I know I had not – when Phillis, who had been missing just at the last moment of our hurried visit, re-appeared with a little nosegay of this same flower, which she was tying up with a blade of grass. She offered it to Holdsworth as he stood with her father on the point of departure. I saw their faces. I saw for the first time an unmistakable look of love in his black eyes; it was more than gratitude for the little attention; it was tender and beseeching – passionate. She shrank from it in confusion, her glance fell on me; and, partly to hide her emotion, partly out of real kindness at what might appear ungracious neglect of an older friend, she flew off to gather me a few late-blooming China roses. But it was the first time she had ever done anything of the kind for me.

We had to walk fast to be back on the line before the men's return; so we spoke but little to each other, and of course the afternoon was too much occupied for us to have any talk. In the evening we went back to our joint lodgings in Hornby. There, on the table, lay a letter for Holdsworth, which had been forwarded to him from Eltham. As our tea was ready, and I had had nothing to eat since morning, I fell to directly, without paying much attention to my companion as he opened and read his letter. He was very silent for a few minutes; at length he said: 'Old fellow! I'm going to leave you.'

'Leave me!' said I. 'How? When?'

'This letter ought to have come to hand sooner. It is from Greathed the engineer' (Greathed was well known in those days; he is dead now, and his name half-forgotten); 'he wants to see me about some business; in fact, I may as well tell you, Paul, this letter contains a very advantageous proposal for me to go out to Canada, and superintend the making of a line there.'

I was in utter dismay.

'But what will our Company say to that?'

'Oh, Greathed has the superintendence of this line, you know, and he is going to be engineer-in-chief to this Canadian line: many of the shareholders in this Company are going in for the other; so I fancy they will make no difficulty in following Greathed's lead. He says he has a young man ready to put in my place.'

'I hate him,' said I.

'Thank you,' said Holdsworth, laughing.

'But you must not,' he resumed; 'for this is a very good thing for me; and, of course, if no one can be found to take my inferior work, I can't be spared to take the superior. I only wish I had received this letter a day sooner. Every hour is of consequence, for Greathed says they are threatening a rival line. Do you know, Paul, I almost fancy I must go up tonight? I can take an engine back to Eltham, and catch the night train. I should not like Greathed to think me lukewarm.'

'But you'll come back?' I asked, distressed at the thought of this sudden parting.

'Oh, yes! At least I hope so. They may want me to go out by the next steamer; that will be on Saturday.' He began to eat and drink standing, but I think he was quite unconscious of the nature of either his food or his drink.

'I will go tonight. Activity and readiness go a long way in our profession. Remember that, my boy! I hope I shall come back; but, if I don't, be sure and recollect all the words of wisdom that have fallen from my lips. Now, where's the portmanteau? If I can gain half an hour for a gathering up of my things in Eltham, so much the better. I'm clear of debt, anyhow; and what I owe for my lodgings you can pay for me out of my quarter's salary, due November 4th.'

'Then you don't think you will come back?' I said despondingly.

'I will come back sometime, never fear,' said he kindly. 'I may be back in a couple of days, having been found incompetent for the Canadian work; or I may not be wanted to go out so soon as I now anticipate. Anyhow, you don't suppose I am going to forget you, Paul – this work out there ought not to take me above two years, and, perhaps, after that, we may be employed together again.'

Perhaps! I had very little hope. The same kind of happy days never return. However, I did all I could in helping him: clothes, papers, books, instruments; how we pushed and struggled – how I stuffed! All was done in a much shorter time than we had calculated upon, when I had run down to the sheds to order the engine. I was going to drive him to Eltham. We sat ready for a summons. Holdsworth took up the little nosegay he had brought away from the Hope Farm, and had laid on the mantelpiece on first coming into the room. He smelt at it, and caressed it with his lips.

'What grieves me is that I did not know – that I have not said goodbye to – to them.'

He spoke in a grave tone, the shadow of the coming separation falling upon him at last.

'I will tell them,' said I. 'I am sure they will be very sorry.' Then we were silent.

'I never liked any family so much.'

'I knew you would like them.'

'How one's thoughts change – this morning I was full of a hope, Paul.' He paused, and then he said: 'You put that sketch in carefully?'

'That outline of a head?' asked I. But I knew he meant an abortive sketch of Phillis, which had not been successful enough for him to complete it with shading or colouring.

'Yes. What a sweet innocent face it is! and yet so – Oh, dear!'

He sighed and got up, his hands in his pockets, to walk up and down the room in evident disturbance of mind. He suddenly stopped opposite to me.

'You'll tell them how it all was. Be sure and tell the good minister that I was so sorry not to wish him goodbye, and to thank him and his wife for all their kindness. As for Phillis – please God, in two years I'll be back and tell her myself all in my heart.'

'You love Phillis, then?' said I.

'Love her! – Yes, that I do. Who could help it, seeing her as I have done? Her character as unusual and rare as her beauty! God bless her! God keep her in her high tranquillity, her pure innocence! – Two years! It is a long time. But she lives in such seclusion, almost like the sleeping beauty, Paul – ' (he was smiling now, though a minute before I had thought him on the verge of tears) ' – but I shall come back like a prince from Canada, and waken her to my love. I can't help hoping that it won't be difficult; eh, Paul?'

This touch of coxcombry[272] displeased me a little, and I made no answer. He went on, half apologetically: 'You see, the salary they offer me is large; and besides that, this experience will give me a name which will entitle me to expect a still larger in any future undertaking.'

'That won't influence Phillis.'

'No! but it will make me more eligible in the eyes of her father and mother.'

I made no answer.

'You give me your best wishes, Paul,' said he, almost pleading. 'You would like me for a cousin?'

I heard the scream and whistle of the engine, ready down at the sheds.

'Ay, that I should,' I replied, suddenly softened towards my friend, now that he was going away. 'I wish you were to be married tomorrow, and I were to be best man.'

'Thank you, lad. Now for this cursed portmanteau (how the minister would be shocked!) – but it is heavy!' and off we sped into the darkness.

He only just caught the night train at Eltham; and I slept, desolately enough, at my old lodgings at Miss Dawson's, for that night. Of course, the next few days I was busier than ever, doing both his work and my own. Then came a letter from him, very short and affectionate. He was going out in the Saturday steamer, as he had more than half expected; and by the following Monday the man who was to succeed him would be down at Eltham. There was a postscript, with only these words: 'My nosegay goes with me to Canada; but I do not need it to remind me of Hope Farm.'

Saturday came; but it was very late before I could go out to the farm. It was a frosty night; the stars shone clear above me, and the road was crisping beneath my feet. They must have heard my footsteps, before I got up to the house. They were sitting at their usual employments in the house-place, when I went in. Phillis's eyes went beyond me in their look of welcome, and then fell in quiet disappointment on her work.

'And where's Mr Holdsworth?' asked cousin Holman, in a minute or two. 'I hope his cold is not worse – I did not like his short cough.'

I laughed awkwardly; for I felt that I was the bearer of unpleasant news.

'His cold had need be better – for he's gone – gone away to Canada!'

I purposely looked away from Phillis, as I thus abruptly told my news.

'To Canada!' said the minister.

'Gone away!' said his wife.

But no word from Phillis.

'Yes!' said I. 'He found a letter at Hornby, when we got home the other night – when we got home from here; he ought to have got it sooner; he was ordered to go up to London directly, and to see some people about a new line in Canada; and he's gone to lay it down; he has sailed today. He was sadly grieved not to have time to come out and wish you all goodbye; but he started for London within two hours after he got that letter. He bade me thank you most gratefully for all your kindnesses; he was very sorry not to come here once again.'

Phillis got up and left the room with noiseless steps.

'I am very sorry,' said the minister.

'I am sure so am I!' said cousin Holman. 'I was real fond of that lad, ever since I nursed him last June after that bad fever.'

The minister went on asking me questions respecting Holdsworth's future plans, and brought out a large old-fashioned atlas, that he might find out the exact places between which the new railroad was to run. Then supper was ready; it was always on the table as soon as the clock on the stairs struck eight, and down came Phillis – her face white and set, her dry eyes looking defiance at me; for I am afraid I hurt her maidenly pride by my glance of sympathetic interest as she entered the room. Never a word did she say – never a question did she ask about the absent friend; yet she forced herself to talk.

And so it was all the next day. She was as pale as could be, like one who has received some shock; but she would not let me talk to her, and she tried hard to behave as usual. Two or three times I repeated, in public, the various affectionate messages to the family with which I was charged by Holdsworth; but she took no more notice of them than if my words had been empty air. And in this mood I left her on the Sabbath evening.

My new master was not half so indulgent as my old one. He kept up strict discipline as to hours; so that it was sometime before I could again go out, even to pay a call at the Hope Farm.

It was a cold, misty evening in November. The air, even indoors, seemed full of haze; yet there was a great log burning on the hearth, which ought to have made the room cheerful. Cousin Holman and Phillis were sitting at the little round table before the fire, working away in silence. The minister had his books out on the dresser, seemingly deep in study, by the light of his solitary candle; perhaps the fear of disturbing him made the unusual stillness of the room. But a welcome was ready for me from all; not noisy, not demonstrative – that it never was; my damp wrappers were taken off, the next meal was hastened, and a chair placed for me on one side of the fire, so that I pretty much commanded a view of the room. My eye caught on Phillis, looking so pale and weary, and with a sort of aching tone (if I may call it so) in her voice. She was doing all the accustomed things – fulfilling small household duties, but somehow differently – I can't tell you how, for she was just as deft and quick in her movements, only the light spring was gone out of them. Cousin Holman began to question me; even the minister put aside his books, and came and stood on the opposite side of the fireplace, to hear what waft of intelligence I brought. I had first to tell them why I had not been to see them for so long – more than five weeks. The answer was simple enough: business and the necessity of attending strictly to the orders of a new superintendent, who had not yet learned trust, much less indulgence. The minister nodded his approval of my conduct, and said: 'Right, Paul! "Servants, obey in all things your masters according to the flesh".[273] I have had my fears lest you had too much licence under Edward Holdsworth.'

'Ah,' said cousin Holman, 'poor Mr Holdsworth! he'll be on the salt seas by this time!'

'No, indeed,' said I; 'he's landed. I have had a letter from him from Halifax.'

Immediately a shower of questions fell thick upon me. 'When?' 'How?' 'What was he doing?' 'How did he like it?' 'What sort of a voyage?' &c.

'Many is the time we thought of him when the wind was blowing so hard; the old quince tree is blown down, Paul, that on the right hand of the great pear tree; it was blown down last Monday week, and it was that night that I asked the minister to pray in an especial manner for all them that went down in ships upon the great deep; and he said then, that Mr Holdsworth might be already landed; but I said, even if the prayer did not fit him, it was sure to be fitting somebody out at sea, who would need the Lord's care. Both Phillis and I thought he would be a month on the seas.'

Phillis began to speak; but her voice did not come rightly at first. It was a little higher pitched than usual, when she said: 'We thought he would be a month, if he went in a sailing-vessel, or perhaps longer. I suppose he went in a steamer?'[274]

'Old Obadiah Grimshaw was more than six weeks in getting to America,' observed cousin Holman.

'I presume he cannot as yet tell how he likes his new work?' asked the minister.

'No! he is but just landed; it is but one page long. I'll read it to you, shall I?

> ' "Dear Paul – We are safe on shore, after a rough passage. Thought you would like to hear this; but homeward-bound steamer is making signals for letters. Will write again soon. It seems a year since I left Hornby. Longer, since I was at the farm. I have got my nosegay safe. Remember me to the Holmans.
>
> Yours,
>
> "E. H." '

'That's not much, certainly,' said the minister. 'But it's a comfort to know he's on land these blowy nights.'

Phillis said nothing. She kept her head bent down over her work; but I don't think she put a stitch in, while I was reading the letter. I wondered if she understood what nosegay was meant; but I could not tell. When next she lifted up her face, there were two spots of brilliant colour on the cheeks that had been so pale before. After I had spent an hour or two there, I was bound to return back to Hornby. I told them, I did not know when I could come again, as we – by which I mean the Company – had undertaken the Hensleydale line; that branch for which poor Holdsworth was surveying, when he caught his fever.

'But you'll have a holiday at Christmas,' said my cousin. 'Surely, they'll not be such heathens as to work you then?'

'Perhaps the lad will be going home,' said the minister, as if to mitigate his wife's urgency; but, for all that, I believe he wanted me to come. Phillis fixed her eyes on me with a wistful expression, hard to resist. But, indeed, I had no thought of resisting. Under my new master I had no hope of a holiday long enough to enable me to go to Birmingham and see my parents with any comfort; and nothing could be pleasanter to me than to find myself at home at my cousin's for a day or two, then. So it was fixed that we were to meet in Hornby Chapel on Christmas Day, and that I was to accompany them home after service, and, if possible, to stay over the next day.

I was not able to get to chapel till late on the appointed day; and so I took a seat near the door in considerable shame, although it really was not my fault. When the service was ended, I went and stood in the porch, to await the coming-out of my cousins. Some worthy people belonging to the congregation clustered into a group, just where I stood, and exchanged the good wishes of the season. It had just begun to snow; and this occasioned a little delay, and they fell into further conversation. I was not attending to what was not meant for me to hear, till I caught the name of Phillis Holman. And then I listened; where was the harm?

'I never saw anyone so changed!'

'I asked Mrs Holman,' quoth another, ' "Is Phillis well?" and she just said she had been having a cold which had pulled her down; she did not seem to think anything of it.'

'They had best take care of her,' said one of the oldest of the good ladies; 'Phillis comes of a family as is not long-lived. Her mother's sister, Lydia Green, her own aunt as was, died of a decline just when she was about this lass's age.'

This ill-omened talk was broken in upon by the coming-out of the minister, his wife and daughter, and the consequent interchange of Christmas compliments. I had had a shock, and felt heavy-hearted and anxious, and hardly up to making the appropriate replies to the kind greetings of my relations. I looked askance at Phillis. She had certainly grown taller and slighter, and was thinner; but there was a flush of colour on her face which deceived me for a time, and made me think she was looking as well as ever. I only saw her paleness after we had returned to the farm, and she had subsided into silence and quiet. Her grey eyes looked hollow and sad; her complexion was of a dead white. But she went about just as usual; at least, just as she had done the last time I was there, and seemed to have no ailment; and I was inclined to think that my cousin was right, when she had answered the enquiries of the good-natured gossips, and told them that Phillis was suffering from the consequences of a bad cold, nothing more.

I have said that I was to stay over the next day; a great deal of snow had come down, but not all, they said, though the ground was covered deep with the white fall. The minister was anxiously housing his cattle, and preparing all things for a long continuance of the same kind of weather. The men were chopping wood, sending wheat to the mill to be ground before the road should become impassable for a cart and horse. My cousin and Phillis had gone upstairs to the apple-room, to cover up the fruit from the frost. I had been out the greater part of the morning, and came in about an hour before dinner. To my surprise, knowing how she had planned to be engaged, I found Phillis sitting at the dresser, resting her head on her two hands and reading, or seeming to read. She did not look up when I came in, but murmured something about her mother having sent her down out of the cold. It flashed across me that she was crying, but I put it down to some little spurt of temper; I might have known better than to suspect the gentle, serene Phillis of crossness, poor girl; I stooped down, and began to stir and build up the fire, which appeared to have been neglected. While my head was down I heard a noise which made me pause and listen – a sob, an unmistakable, irrepressible sob. I started up.

'Phillis!' I cried, going towards her, with my hand out, to take hers for sympathy with her sorrow, whatever it was. But she was too quick for me; she held her hand out of my grasp, for fear of my detaining her; as she quickly passed out of the house, she said: 'Don't, Paul! I cannot bear it!' and passed me, still sobbing, and went out into the keen, open air.

I stood still and wondered. What could have come to Phillis? The most perfect harmony prevailed in the family; and Phillis especially, good and gentle as she was, was so beloved that, if they had found out that her finger ached, it would have cast a shadow over their hearts. Had I done anything to vex her? No: she was crying before I came in. I went to look at her book – one of those unintelligible Italian books. I could make neither head nor tail of it. I saw some pencil-notes on the margin, in Holdsworth's handwriting.

Could that be it? Could that be the cause of her white looks, her weary eyes, her wasted figure, her struggling sobs? This idea came upon me like a flash of lightning on a dark night, making all things so clear we cannot forget them afterwards, when the gloomy obscurity returns. I was still standing with the book in my hand, when I heard cousin Holman's footsteps on the stairs; and, as I did not wish to speak to her just then, I followed Phillis's example, and rushed out of the house. The snow was lying on the ground; I could track her feet by the marks they had made; I could see where Rover had joined her. I followed on, till I came to a great stack of wood in the orchard – it was built up against the back-wall of the out-buildings – and I recollected then how Phillis had told me, that first day when we strolled about together, that underneath this stack had been her hermitage, her sanctuary, when she was a child; how she used to bring her book to study there, or her work, when she was not wanted in the house; and she had now evidently gone back to this quiet retreat of her childhood, forgetful of the clue given me by her footmarks on the new-fallen snow. The stack was built up very high; but through the interstices of the sticks I could see her figure, although I did not all at once perceive how I could get to her. She was sitting on a log of wood, Rover by her. She had laid her cheek on Rover's head, and had her arm round his neck, partly for a pillow, partly from an instinctive craving for warmth on that bitter cold day. She was making a low moan, like an animal in pain, or perhaps more like the sobbing of the wind. Rover, highly flattered by her caress, and also, perhaps, touched by sympathy, was flapping his heavy tail against the ground, but not otherwise moving a hair, until he heard my approach with his quick erect ears. Then, with a short, abrupt bark of distrust, he sprang up, as if to leave his mistress. Both he and I were immovably still for a moment. I was not sure if what I longed to do was wise; and yet I could not bear to see the sweet serenity of my dear cousin's life so disturbed by a suffering which I thought I could assuage. But Rover's ears were sharper than my breathing was noiseless: he heard me, and sprang out from under Phillis's restraining hand.

'Oh, Rover, don't you leave me too!' she plained out.

'Phillis!' said I, seeing by Rover's exit that the entrance to where she sat was to be found on the other side of the stack. 'Phillis, come out! You have got a cold already; and it is not fit for you to sit there on such a day as this. You know how displeased and anxious it would make them all.'

She sighed, but obeyed; stooping a little, she came out, and stood upright, opposite to me in the lonely, leafless orchard. Her face looked so meek and so sad that I felt as if I ought to beg her pardon for my necessarily authoritative words.

'Sometimes I feel the house so close,' she said; 'and I used to sit under the wood-stack when I was a child. It was very kind of you; but there was no need to come after me. I don't catch cold easily.'

'Come with me into this cow-house, Phillis! I have got something to say to you; and I can't stand this cold, if you can.'

I think she would have fain run away again; but her fit of energy was all spent. She followed me unwillingly enough – that I could see. The place to which I took her was full of the fragrant breath of the cows, and was a little warmer than the outer air. I put her inside, and stood myself in the doorway, thinking how I could best begin. At last I plunged into it.

'I must see that you don't get cold for more reasons than one; if you are ill, Holdsworth will be so anxious and miserable out there' (by which I meant Canada) –

She shot one penetrating look at me, and then turned her face away, with a slightly impatient movement. If she could have run away then, she would; but I held the means of exit in my own power. 'In for a penny, in for a pound,' thought I; and I went on rapidly, anyhow.

'He talked so much about you, just before he left – that night after he had been here, you know – and you had given him those flowers.' She put her hands up to hide her face, but she was listening now – listening with all her ears.

'He had never spoken much about you before; but the sudden going-away unlocked his heart, and he told me how he loved you, and how he hoped on his return that you might be his wife.'

'Don't,' said she, almost gasping out the word, which she had tried once or twice before to speak; but her voice had been choked. Now, she put her hand backwards; she had quite turned away from me, and felt for mine. She gave it a soft lingering pressure; and then she put her arms down on the wooden division, and laid her head on it, and cried quiet tears. I did not understand her at once, and feared lest I had mistaken the whole case, and only annoyed her. I went up to her. 'Oh, Phillis! I am so sorry – I thought you would, perhaps, have cared to hear it; he did talk so feelingly, as if he did love you so much, and somehow I thought it would give you pleasure.'

She lifted up her head and looked at me. Such a look! Her eyes, glittering with tears as they were, expressed an almost heavenly happiness; her tender mouth was curved with rapture – her colour vivid and blushing; but, as if she was afraid her face expressed too much – more than the thankfulness to me she was essaying to speak – she hid it again almost immediately. So it was all right then, and my conjecture was well-founded. I tried to remember something more to tell her of what he had said; but again she stopped me.

'Don't,' she said. She still kept her face covered and hidden. In half a minute she added, in a very low voice, 'Please, Paul, I think I would rather not hear any more – I don't mean but what I have – but what I am very much obliged – Only – only, I think I would rather hear the rest from himself when he comes back.'

And then she cried a little more, in quite a different way. I did not say any more; I waited for her. By and by, she turned towards me – not meeting my eyes, however; and, putting her hand in mine, just as if we were two children, she said: 'We had best go back now – I don't look as if I had been crying, do I?'

'You look as if you had a bad cold,' was all the answer I made.

'Oh! but I am – I am quite well, only cold; and a good run will warm me. Come along, Paul.'

So we ran, hand in hand, till, just as we were on the threshold of the house, she stopped: 'Paul, please, we won't speak about *that* again.'

Part Four

WHEN I WENT OVER on Easter Day, I heard the chapel-gossips complimenting cousin Holman on her daughter's blooming looks, quite forgetful of their sinister prophecies three months before. And I looked at Phillis, and did not wonder at their words. I had not seen her since the day after Christmas Day. I had left the Hope Farm only a few hours after I had told her the news which had quickened her heart into renewed life and vigour. The remembrance of our conversation in the cow-house was vividly in my mind, as I looked at her when her bright healthy appearance was remarked upon. As her eyes met mine, our mutual recollections flashed intelligence from one to the other. She turned away, her colour heightening as she did so. She seemed to be shy of me for the first few hours after our meeting, and I felt rather vexed with her for her conscious avoidance of me after my long absence. I had stepped a little out of my usual line in telling her what I did; not that I had received any charge of secrecy, or given even the slightest promise to Holdsworth that I would not repeat his words. But I had an uneasy feeling sometimes, when I thought of what I had done in the excitement of seeing Phillis so ill and in so much trouble. I meant to have told Holdsworth when I wrote next to him; but, when I had my half-finished letter before me, I sat with my pen in my hand, hesitating. I had more scruple in revealing what I had found out or guessed at of Phillis's secret than in repeating to her his spoken words. I did not think I had any right to say out to him what I believed – namely, that she loved him dearly, and had felt his absence even to the injury of her health. Yet, to explain what I had done in telling her how he had spoken about her that last night, it would be necessary to give my reasons, so I had settled within myself to leave it alone. As she had told me she should like to hear all the details and fuller particulars and more explicit declarations first from him, so he should have the pleasure of extracting the delicious tender secret from her maidenly lips. I would not betray my guesses, my surmises, my all but certain knowledge of the state of her heart. I had received two letters from him after he had settled to his business; they were full of life and energy; but in each there had been a message to the family at the Hope Farm of more than common regard, and a slight but distinct mention of

Phillis herself, showing that she stood single and alone in his memory. These letters I had sent on to the minister; for he was sure to care for them, even supposing he had been unacquainted with their writer, because they were so clever and so picturesquely-worded that they brought, as it were, a whiff of foreign atmosphere into his circumscribed life. I used to wonder what was the trade or business in which the minister would not have thriven, mentally I mean, if it had so happened that he had been called into that state. He would have made a capital engineer, that I know; and he had a fancy for the sea, like many other landlocked men to whom the great deep is a mystery and a fascination. He read law-books with relish; and once, happening to borrow *De Lolme on the British Constitution* (or some such title),[275] he talked about jurisprudence till he was far beyond my depth. But to return to Holdsworth's letters. When the minister sent them back, he also wrote out a list of questions suggested by their perusal, which I was to pass on in my answers to Holdsworth, until I thought of suggesting a direct correspondence between the two. That was the state of things as regarded the absent one when I went to the farm for my Easter visit, and when I found Phillis in that state of shy reserve towards me which I have named before. I thought she was ungrateful; for I was not quite sure if I had done wisely in having told her what I did. I had committed a fault, or a folly, perhaps, and all for her sake; and here was she, less friends with me than she had ever been before. This little estrangement only lasted a few hours. I think that, as soon as she felt pretty sure of there being no recurrence, either by word, look, or allusion, to the one subject that was predominant in her mind, she came back to her old sisterly ways with me. She had much to tell me of her own familiar interests: how Rover had been ill, and how anxious they had all of them been, and how, after some little discussion between her father and her, both equally grieved by the sufferings of the old dog, he had been 'remembered in the household prayers', and how he had begun to get better only the very next day; and then she would have led me into a conversation on the right ends of prayer, and on special providences, and I know not what; only, I 'jibbed' like their old cart-horse, and refused to stir a step in that direction. Then we talked about the different broods of chickens, and she showed me the hens that were good mothers, and told me the characters of all the poultry with the utmost good-faith; and in all good-faith I listened, for I believe there was a great deal of truth in all she said. And then we strolled on into the wood beyond the ash-meadow, and both of us sought for early primroses and the fresh green crinkled leaves. She was not afraid of being alone with me after the first day. I never saw her so lovely, or so happy. I think she hardly knew why she was so happy all the time. I can see her now, standing under the budding branches of the grey trees, over which a tinge of green seemed to be deepening day after day, her sun-bonnet fallen back on her neck, her hands full of delicate wood-flowers, quite unconscious of my gaze, but intent on sweet mockery of some bird in neighbouring bush or tree. She had the art of warbling, and replying to the notes of different birds, and knew their song, their habits and ways, more accurately than anyone else I ever knew. She had often done it at my request the spring before; but this year she really gurgled, and whistled, and warbled, just as they did, out of the very fulness and joy of her heart. She was more than ever the very apple of her father's eye; her mother gave her both her own share of love and that of the dead child who had died in infancy. I have heard cousin Holman murmur, after a long dreamy look at Phillis, and tell herself how like she was growing to Johnnie,[276] and soothe herself with plaintive inarticulate sounds, and many gentle shakes of the head, for the aching sense of loss she would never get over in this world. The old servants about the place had the dumb loyal attachment to the child of the land, common to most agricultural labourers; not often stirred into activity or expression. My cousin Phillis was like a rose that had come to full bloom on the sunny side of a lonely house, sheltered from storms. I have read in some book of poetry:

> 'A maid whom there were none to praise,
> And very few to love.'[277]

And somehow those lines always reminded me of Phillis; yet they were not true of her either. I never heard her praised; and out of her own household there were very few to love her; but, though no one spoke out their approbation, she always did right in her parents' eyes, out of her natural simple goodness and wisdom. Holdsworth's name was never mentioned between us when we were alone; but I had sent on his letters to the minister, as I have said; and more than once he began to talk about our absent friend, when he was smoking his pipe after the day's work was done. Then Phillis hung her head a little over her work, and listened in silence.

'I miss him more than I thought for; no offence to you, Paul! I said once, his company was like dram-drinking; that was before I knew him; and perhaps I spoke in a spirit of judgement. To some men's minds everything presents itself strongly, and they speak accordingly; and so did he. And I thought, in my vanity of censorship, that his were not true and sober words; they would not have been if I had used them, but they were so to a man of his class of perceptions. I thought of the measure which I had been meting[278] out to him, when Brother Robinson was here last Thursday, and told me that a poor little quotation I was making from the *Georgics* savoured of vain babbling and profane heathenism. He went so far as to say that, by learning other languages than our own, we were flying in the face of the Lord's purpose when He had said, at the building of the Tower of Babel, that He would confound their languages so that they should not understand each other's speech. As Brother Robinson was to me, so was I to the quick wits, bright senses, and ready words of Holdsworth.'

The first little cloud upon my peace came in the shape of a letter from Canada, in which there were two or three sentences that troubled me more than they ought to have done, to judge merely from the words employed. It was this: – 'I should feel dreary enough in this out-of-the-way place, if it were not for a friendship I have formed with a French Canadian of the name of Ventadour. He and his family are a great resource to me in the long evenings. I never heard such delicious vocal music as the voices of these Ventadour boys and girls in their part-songs; and the foreign element retained in their characters and manner of living reminds me of some of the happiest days of my life. Lucille, the second daughter, is curiously like Phillis Holman.' In vain I said to myself, that it was probably this likeness that made him take pleasure in the society of the Ventadour family. In vain I told my anxious fancy, that nothing could be more natural than this intimacy, and that there was no sign of its leading to any consequence that ought to disturb me. I had a presentiment, and I was disturbed; and I could not reason it away. I dare say my presentiment was rendered more persistent and keen by the doubts which would force themselves into my mind, as to whether I had done well in repeating Holdsworth's words to Phillis. Her state of vivid happiness this summer was markedly different to the peaceful serenity of former days. If, in my thoughtfulness at noticing this, I caught her eye, she blushed and sparkled all over, guessing that I was remembering our joint secret. Her eyes fell before mine, as if she could hardly bear me to see the revelation of their bright glances. And yet I considered again, and comforted myself by the reflection that, if this change had been anything more than my silly fancy, her father or her mother would have perceived it. But they went on in tranquil unconsciousness and undisturbed peace.

A change in my own life was quickly approaching. In the July of this year my occupation on the — railway and its branches came to an end. The lines were completed; and I was to leave —shire, to return to Birmingham, where there was a niche already provided for me in my father's prosperous business. But, before I left the north, it was an understood thing amongst us all that I was to go and pay a visit of some weeks at the Hope Farm. My father was as much pleased at this plan as I was; and the dear family of cousins often spoke of things to be done, and sights to be shown me, during this visit. My want of wisdom in having told 'that thing' (under such ambiguous words I concealed the injudicious confidence I had made to Phillis) was the only drawback to my anticipations of pleasure.

The ways of life were too simple at the Hope Farm for my coming to them to make the slightest disturbance. I knew my room, like a son of the house. I knew the regular course of their days, and that I was expected to fall into it, like one of the family. Deep summer peace brooded over the place; the warm golden air was filled with the murmur of insects near at hand, the more distant sound of voices out in the fields, the clear far-away rumble of carts over the stone-paved lanes miles away. The heat was too great for the birds to be singing; only now and then one might hear the wood-pigeons in the trees beyond the ash-field. The cattle stood knee-deep in the pond, flicking their tails about to keep off the flies. The minister stood in the hayfield, without hat or cravat, coat or waistcoat, panting and smiling. Phillis had been leading the row of farm-servants, turning the swathes of fragrant hay with measured movement. She went to the end – to the hedge, and then, throwing down her rake, she came to me with her free sisterly welcome. 'Go, Paul!' said the minister. 'We need all hands to make use of the sunshine today. "Whatsoever thine hand findeth to do, do it with all thy might."[279] It will be a healthy change of work for thee, lad; and I find my best rest in change of work.' So off I went, a willing labourer, following Phillis's lead; it was the primitive distinction of rank; the boy who frightened the sparrows off the fruit was the last in our rear. We did not leave off till the red sun was gone down behind the fir trees bordering the common. Then we went home to supper – prayers – to bed; some bird singing far into the night, as I heard it through my open window, and the poultry beginning their clatter and cackle in the earliest morning. I had carried what luggage I immediately needed with me from my lodgings, and the rest was to be sent by the carrier. He brought it to the farm betimes that morning; and along with it he brought a letter or two that had arrived since I had left. I was talking to cousin Holman – about my mother's ways of making bread, I remember; cousin Holman was questioning me, and had got me far beyond my depth – in the house-place, when the letters were brought in by one of the men, and I had to pay the carrier for his trouble before I could look at them. A bill – a Canadian letter! What instinct made me so thankful that I was alone with my dear unobservant cousin? What made me hurry them away into my coat-pocket? I do not know. I felt strange and sick, and made irrelevant answers, I am afraid. Then I went to my room, ostensibly to carry up my boxes. I sat on the side of my bed and opened my letter from Holdsworth. It seemed to me as if I had read its contents before, and knew exactly what he had got to say. I knew he was going to be married to Lucille Ventadour – nay, that he *was* married; for this was the 5th of July, and he wrote word that his marriage was fixed to take place on the 29th of June. I knew all the reasons he gave, all the raptures he went into. I held the letter loosely in my hands, and looked into vacancy; yet I saw a chaffinch's nest on the lichen-covered trunk of an old apple tree opposite my window, and saw the mother-bird come fluttering in to feed her brood – and yet I did not see it, although it seemed to me afterwards as if I could have drawn every fibre, every feather. I was stirred up to action by the merry sound of voices and the clamp of rustic feet coming home for the midday meal. I knew I must go down to dinner; I knew, too, I must tell Phillis; for in his happy egotism, his newfangled foppery, Holdsworth had put in a P.S., saying that he should send wedding-cards[280] to me and some other Hornby and Eltham acquaintances, and 'to his kind friends at Hope Farm'. Phillis had faded away to one among several 'kind friends'. I don't know how I got through dinner that day. I remember forcing myself to eat, and talking hard; but I also recollect the wondering look in the minister's eyes. He was not one to think evil without cause; but many a one would have taken me for drunk. As soon as I decently could, I left the table, saying I would go out for a walk. At first, I must have tried to stun reflection by rapid walking, for I had lost myself on the high moorlands far beyond the familiar gorse-covered common, before I was obliged for very weariness to slacken my pace. I kept wishing – oh! how fervently wishing – I had never committed that blunder; that the one little half-hour's indiscretion could be blotted out. Alternating with this was anger against Holdsworth; unjust enough, I dare say. I suppose I stayed in that solitary place for a good hour or more; and then I turned homewards, resolving to get over the telling Phillis at the first opportunity, but shrinking from the fulfilment of my resolution so much that, when I came into the house (doors and windows open wide in the sultry weather) and saw Phillis alone in the kitchen, I became quite sick with apprehension. She was standing by the dresser, cutting up a great household loaf into hunches of bread for the hungry labourers who might come in any minute, for the heavy thunderclouds were over-spreading the sky. She looked round as she heard my step.

'You should have been in the field, helping with the hay,' said she, in her calm, pleasant voice. I had heard her, as I came near the house, softly chanting some hymn-tune; and the peacefulness of that seemed to be brooding over her now.

'Perhaps I should. It looks as if it was going to rain.'

'Yes, there is thunder about. Mother has had to go to bed with one of her bad headaches. Now you are come in – '

'Phillis,' said I, rushing at my subject and interrupting her, 'I went a long walk to think over a letter I had this morning – a letter from Canada. You don't know how it has grieved me.' I held it out to her as I spoke. Her colour changed a little; but it was more the reflection of my face, I think, than because she formed any definite idea from my words. Still she did not take the letter. I had to bid her read it, before she quite understood what I wished. She sat down rather suddenly as she received it into her hands; and, spreading it on the dresser before her, she rested her forehead on the palms of her hands, her arms supported on the table, her figure a little averted, and her countenance thus shaded. I looked out of the open window; my heart was very heavy. How peaceful it all seemed in the farm-yard! Peace and plenty. How still and deep was the silence of the house! Tick-tick went the unseen clock on the wide staircase. I had heard the rustle once, when she turned over the page of thin paper. She must have read to the end. Yet she did not move, or say a word, or even sigh. I kept on looking out of the window, my hands in my pockets. I wonder how long that time really was? It seemed to me interminable – unbearable. At length I looked round at her. She must have felt my look, for she changed her attitude with a quick sharp movement, and caught my eyes.

'Don't look so sorry, Paul,' she said. 'Don't, please. I can't bear it. There is nothing to be sorry for. I think not, at least. You have not done wrong, at any rate.' I felt that I groaned, but I don't think she heard me. 'And he – there's no wrong in his marrying, is there? I'm sure I hope he'll be happy. Oh! how I hope it!' These last words were like a wail; but I believe she was afraid of breaking down, for she changed the key in which she spoke, and hurried on. 'Lucille – that's our English Lucy, I suppose? Lucille Holdsworth! It's a pretty name; and I hope – I forget what I was going to say. Oh! it was this. Paul, I think we need never speak about this again; only, remember, you are not to be sorry. You have not done wrong; you have been very, *very* kind; and, if I see you looking grieved, I don't know what I might do; – I might break down, you know.'

I think she was on the point of doing so then; but the dark storm came dashing down, and the thundercloud broke right above the house, as it seemed. Her mother, roused from sleep, called out for Phillis; the men and women from the hayfield came running into shelter, drenched through. The minister followed, smiling, and not unpleasantly excited by the war of elements; for, by dint of hard work through the long summer's day, the greater part of the hay was safely housed in the barn in the field. Once or twice in the succeeding bustle I came across Phillis, always busy, and, as it seemed to me, always doing the right thing. When I was alone in my own room at night, I allowed myself to feel relieved: and to believe that the worst was over, and was not so very bad after all. But the succeeding days were very miserable. Sometimes I thought it must be my fancy that falsely represented Phillis to me as strangely changed; for surely, if this idea of mine was well-founded, her parents – her father and mother – her own flesh and blood – would have been the first to perceive it. Yet they went on in their household peace and content; if anything, a little more cheerfully than usual, for the 'harvest of the first fruits', as the minister called it, had been more bounteous than usual, and there was plenty all around, in which the humblest labourer was made to share. After the one thunderstorm, came one or two lovely serene summer days, during which the hay was all carried; and then succeeded long soft rains, filling the ears of corn and causing the mown grass to spring afresh. The minister allowed himself a few more hours of relaxation and home enjoyment than usual during this wet spell: hard earthbound frost was his winter holiday; these wet days, after the hay harvest, his summer holiday. We sat with open windows, the fragrance and the freshness called out by the soft-falling rain filling the house-place; while the quiet ceaseless patter among the leaves outside ought to have had the same lulling effect as all other gentle perpetual sounds, such as mill-wheels and bubbling springs, have on the nerves of happy people. But two of us were not happy. I was sure enough of myself, for one. I was worse than sure – I was wretchedly anxious about Phillis. Ever since that day of the thunderstorm there had been a new, sharp, discordant sound to me in her voice, a sort of jangle in her tone; and her restless eyes had no quietness in them; and her colour came and went, without a cause that I could find out. The minister, happy in ignorance of what most concerned him, brought out his books; his learned volumes and classics. Whether he read and talked to Phillis, or to me, I do not know; but, feeling by instinct that she was not, could not be, attending to the peaceful details, so strange and foreign to the turmoil in her heart, I forced myself to listen, and if possible to understand.

'Look here!' said the minister, tapping the old vellum-bound book he held; 'in the first *Georgic* he speaks of rolling and irrigation; a little further on, he insists on choice of the best seed, and advises us to keep the drains clear. Again, no Scotch farmer could give shrewder advice than to cut light meadows while the dew is on, even though it involve night-work.[281] It is all living truth in these days.' He began beating time with a ruler upon his knee, to some Latin lines he read aloud just then. I suppose the monotonous chant irritated Phillis to some irregular energy, for I remember the quick knotting and breaking of the thread with which she was sewing. I never hear that snap repeated now, without suspecting some sting or stab troubling the heart of the worker. Cousin Holman, at her peaceful knitting, noticed the reason why Phillis had so constantly to interrupt the progress of her seam.

'It is bad thread, I'm afraid,' she said, in a gentle, sympathetic voice. But it was too much for Phillis.

'The thread is bad – everything is bad – I am so tired of it all!' And she put down her work, and hastily left the room. I do not suppose that in all her life Phillis had ever shown so much temper before. In many a family the tone, the manner, would not have been noticed; but here it fell with a sharp surprise upon the sweet, calm atmosphere of home. The minister put down ruler and book, and pushed his spectacles up to his forehead. The mother looked distressed for a moment, and then smoothed her features and said in an explanatory tone – 'It's the weather, I think. Some people feel it different to others. It always brings on a headache with me.' She got up to follow her daughter, but halfway to the door she thought better of it, and came back to her seat. Good mother! she hoped the better to conceal the unusual spirt of temper, by pretending not to take much notice of it. 'Go on, minister,' she said; 'it is very interesting what you are reading about; and, when I don't quite understand it, I like the sound of your voice.' So he went on, but languidly and irregularly, and beat no more time with his ruler to any Latin lines. When the dusk came on, early that July night because of the cloudy sky, Phillis came softly back, making as though nothing had happened. She took up her work, but it was too dark to do many stitches; and she dropped it soon. Then I saw her hand steal into her mother's, and how this latter fondled it with quiet little caresses, while the minister, as fully aware as I was of this tender pantomime, went on talking in a happier tone of voice about things as uninteresting to him, at the time, I verily believe, as they were to me; and that is saying a good deal, and shows how much more real what was passing before him was, even to a farmer, than the agricultural customs of the ancients.

I remember one thing more – an attack which Betty the servant made upon me one day, as I came in through the kitchen where she was churning, and stopped to ask her for a drink of buttermilk.

'I say, cousin Paul' (she had adopted the family habit of addressing me generally as cousin Paul, and always speaking of me in that form), 'something's amiss with our Phillis, and I reckon you've a good guess what it is. She's not one to take up wi' such as you' (not complimentary, but that Betty never was, even to those for whom she felt the highest respect); 'but I'd as lief yon Holdsworth had never come near us. So there you've a bit o' my mind.'

And a very unsatisfactory bit it was. I did not know what to answer to the glimpse at the real state of the case implied in the shrewd woman's speech; so I tried to put her off by assuming surprise at her first assertion.

'Amiss with Phillis! I should like to know why you think anything is wrong with her. She looks as blooming as anyone can do.'

'Poor lad! you're but a big child, after all; and you've likely never heared of a fever-flush. But you know better nor that, my fine fellow! so don't think for to put me off wi' blooms and blossoms and such-like talk. What makes her walk about for hours and hours o' nights, when she used to be abed and asleep? I sleep next room to her, and hear her plain as can be. What makes her come in panting and ready to drop into that chair' – nodding to one close to the door – 'and it's "Oh! Betty, some water, please"? That's the way she comes in now, when she used to come back as fresh and bright as she went out. If yon friend o' yours has played her false, he's a deal for t' answer for: she's a lass who's as sweet and as sound as a nut, and the very apple of her father's eye, and of her mother's too, only wi' her she ranks second to th' minister. You'll have to look after yon chap; for I, for one, will stand no wrong to our Phillis.'

What was I to do, or to say? I wanted to justify Holdsworth, to keep Phillis's secret, and to pacify the woman all in the same breath. I did not take the best course, I'm afraid.

'I don't believe Holdsworth ever spoke a word of – of love to her in all his life. I am sure he didn't.'

'Ay, ay! but there's eyes, and there's hands, as well as tongues; and a man has two o' th' one and but one o' t'other.'

'And she's so young; do you suppose her parents would not have seen it?'

'Well! if you ax me that, I'll say out boldly, "No." They've called her "the child" so long – "the child" is always their name for her when they talk on her between themselves, as if never anybody else had a ewe-lamb before them – that she's grown up to be a woman under their very eyes, and they look on her still as if she were in her long-clothes. And you ne'er heard on a man falling in love wi' a babby in long-clothes!'

'No!' said I, half-laughing. But she went on as grave as a judge.

'Ay! you see you'll laugh at the bare thought on it – and I'll be bound th' minister, though he's not a laughing man, would ha' sniggled at th' notion of falling in love wi' the child. Where's Holdsworth off to?'

'Canada,' said I shortly.

'Canada here, Canada there,' she replied testily. 'Tell me how far he's off, instead of giving me your gibberish. Is he a two days' journey away? or a three? or a week?'

'He's ever so far off – three weeks at the least,' cried I in despair. 'And he's either married, or just going to be. So there!' I expected a fresh burst of anger. But no; the matter was too serious. Betty sat down, and kept silence for a minute or two. She looked so miserable and downcast, that I could not help going on, and taking her a little into my confidence.

'It is quite true what I said. I know he never spoke a word to her. I think he liked her; but it's all over now. The best thing we can do – the best and kindest for her – and I know you love her, Betty – '

'I nursed her in my arms; I gave her little brother his last taste o' earthly food,' said Betty, putting her apron up to her eyes.

'Well! don't let us show her we guess that she is grieving; she'll get over it the sooner. Her father and mother don't even guess at it, and we must make as if we didn't. It's too late now to do anything else.'

'I'll never let on; I know nought. I've known true love mysel', in my day. But I wish he'd been farred[282] before he ever came near this house, with his "Please Betty" this, and "Please Betty" that, and drinking up our new milk as if he'd been a cat. I hate such beguiling ways.'

I thought it was as well to let her exhaust herself in abusing the absent Holdsworth; if it was shabby and treacherous in me, I came in for my punishment directly.

'It's a caution to a man how he goes about beguiling. Some men do it as easy and innocent as cooing doves. Don't you be none of 'em, my lad. Not that you've got the gifts to do it, either; you're no great shakes to look at, neither for figure nor yet for face; and it would need be a deaf adder to be taken in wi' your words, though there may be no great harm in 'em.' A lad of nineteen or twenty is not flattered by such an outspoken opinion even from the oldest and ugliest of her sex; and I was only too glad to change the subject by my repeated injunctions to keep Phillis's secret. The end of our conversation was this speech of hers: 'You great gaupus, for all you're called cousin o' th' minister – many a one is cursed wi' fools for cousins – d'ye think I can't see sense except through your spectacles? I give you leave to cut out my tongue, and nail it up on th' barn-door for a caution to magpies, if I let out on that poor wench, either to herself, or anyone that is hers, as the Bible says. Now you've heard me speak Scripture language, perhaps you'll be content, and leave me my kitchen to myself.'

During all these days, from the 5th of July to the 17th, I must have forgotten what Holdsworth had said about sending cards. And yet I think I could not have quite forgotten; but, once having told Phillis about his marriage, I must have looked upon the after-consequence of cards as of no importance. At any rate, they came upon me as a surprise at last. The penny-post reform,[283] as people call it, had come into operation a short time before; but the never-ending stream of notes and letters which seems now to flow in upon most households had not yet begun its course; at least in those remote parts. There was a post-office at Hornby; and an old fellow, who stowed away the few letters in any or all his pockets, as it best suited him, was the letter-carrier to Heathbridge and the neighbourhood. I have often met him in the lanes thereabouts, and asked him for letters. Sometimes I have come upon him, sitting on the hedge-bank resting; and he has begged me to read him an address, too illegible for his spectacled eyes to decipher. When I used to enquire if he had anything for me, or for Holdsworth (he was not particular to whom he gave up the letters, so that he got rid of them somehow, and could set off homewards), he would say he thought that he had, for such was his invariable safe form of answer; and would fumble in breast-pockets, waistcoat-pockets, breeches-pockets, and, as a last resource, in coat-tail pockets; and at length try to comfort me, if I looked disappointed, by telling me, 'Hoo[284] had missed this toime, but was sure to write tomorrow'; 'hoo' representing an imaginary sweetheart.

Sometimes I had seen the minister bring home a letter which he had found lying for him at the little shop that was the post-office at Heathbridge, or from the grander establishment at Hornby. Once or twice Josiah, the carter, remembered that the old letter-carrier had trusted him with an epistle to 'Measter', as they had met in the lanes. I think it must have been about ten days after my arrival at the farm, and my talk to Phillis cutting bread-and-butter at the kitchen dresser, before the day on which the minister suddenly spoke at the dinner-table, and said: 'By the by, I've got a letter in my pocket. Reach me my coat here, Phillis.' The weather was still sultry, and for coolness and ease the minister was sitting in his shirt-sleeves. 'I went to Heathbridge about the paper they had sent me, which spoils all the pens – and I called at the post-office, and found a letter for me, unpaid – and they did not like to trust it to old Zekiel. Ay! here it is! Now we shall hear news of Holdsworth – I thought I'd keep it till we were all together.' My heart seemed to stop beating, and I hung my head over my plate, not daring to look up. What would come of it now? What was Phillis doing? How was she looking? A moment of suspense – and then he spoke again. 'Why? what's this? Here are two visiting-tickets with his name on; no writing at all. No! it's not his name on both. Mrs Holdsworth. The young man has gone and got married.' I lifted my head at these words; I could not help looking just for one instant at Phillis. It seemed to me as if she had been keeping watch over my face and ways. Her face was brilliantly flushed; her eyes were dry and glittering; but she did not speak; her lips were set together, almost as if she was pinching them tight to prevent words or sounds coming out. Cousin Holman's face expressed surprise and interest.

'Well!' said she, 'who'd ha' thought it? He's made quick work of his wooing and wedding. I'm sure I wish him happy. Let me see' –

counting on her fingers – 'October, November, December, January, February, March, April, May, June, July – at least we're at the 28th – it is nearly ten months after all, and reckon a month each way off – '

'Did you know of this news before?' said the minister, turning sharp round on me, surprised, I suppose, at my silence – hardly suspicious, as yet.

'I knew – I had heard – something. It is to a French Canadian young lady,' I went on, forcing myself to talk. 'Her name is Ventadour.'

'Lucille Ventadour!' said Phillis, in a sharp voice, out of tune.

'Then you knew, too!' exclaimed the minister.

We both spoke at once. I said, 'I heard of the probability of – , and told Phillis.' She said, 'He is married to Lucille Ventadour, of French descent; one of a large family near St Meurice; am not I right?' I nodded. 'Paul told me – that is all we know, is not it? Did you see the Howsons, father, in Heathbridge?' and she forced herself to talk more than she had done for several days; asking many questions; trying, as I could see, to keep the conversation off the one raw surface, on which to touch was agony. I had less self-command; but I followed her lead. I was not so much absorbed in the conversation but what I could see that the minister was puzzled and uneasy; though he seconded Phillis's efforts to prevent her mother from recurring to the great piece of news, and uttering continual exclamations of wonder and surprise. But, with that one exception, we were all disturbed out of our natural equanimity, more or less. Every day, every hour, I was reproaching myself more and more for my blundering officiousness. If only I had held my foolish tongue for that one half-hour; if only I had not been in such impatient haste to do something to relieve pain! I could have knocked my stupid head against the wall in my remorse. Yet all I could do now was to second the brave girl in her efforts to conceal her disappointment and keep her maidenly secret. But I thought that dinner would never, never come to an end. I suffered for her, even more than for myself. Until now, everything which I had heard spoken in that happy household were simple words of true meaning. If we had aught to say, we said it; and if anyone preferred silence, nay, if all did so, there would have been no spasmodic, forced efforts to talk for the sake of talking, or to keep off intrusive thoughts or suspicions.

At length we got up from our places, and prepared to disperse; but two or three of us had lost our zest and interest in the daily labour. The minister stood looking out of the window in silence; and, when he roused himself to go out to the fields where his labourers were working, it was with a sigh; and he tried to avert his troubled face, as he passed us on his way to the door. When he had left us, I caught sight of Phillis's face, as, thinking herself unobserved, her countenance relaxed for a moment or two into sad, woeful weariness. She started into briskness again when her mother spoke, and hurried away to do some little errand at her bidding. When we two were alone, cousin Holman recurred to Holdsworth's marriage. She was one of those people who like to view an event from every side of probability, or even possibility; and she had been cut short from indulging herself in this way during dinner.

'To think of Mr Holdsworth's being married! I can't get over it, Paul. Not but what he was a very nice young man! I don't like her name, though; it sounds foreign. Say it again, my dear. I hope she'll know how to take care of him, English fashion. He is not strong; and, if she does not see that his things are well aired, I should be afraid of the old cough.'

'He always said he was stronger than he had ever been before, after that fever.'

'He might think so; but I have my doubts. He was a very pleasant young man; but he did not stand nursing very well. He got tired of being coddled, as he called it. I hope they'll soon come back to England, and then he'll have a chance for his health. I wonder, now, if she speaks English; but, to be sure, he can speak foreign tongues like anything, as I've heard the minister say.'

And so we went on for some time, till she became drowsy over her knitting, on the sultry summer afternoon; and I stole away for a walk, for I wanted some solitude in which to think over things, and, alas! to blame myself with poignant stabs of remorse.

I lounged lazily as soon as I got to the wood. Here and there, the bubbling, brawling brook circled round a great stone, or a root of an old tree, and made a pool; otherwise it coursed brightly over the gravel and stones. I stood by one of these for more than half an hour, or, indeed, longer, throwing bits of wood or pebbles into the water, and wondering what I could do to remedy the present state of things. Of course all my meditation was of no use; and, at length, the distant sound of the horn employed to tell the men far afield to leave off work warned me that it was six o'clock, and time for me to go home. Then I caught wafts of the loud-voiced singing of the evening psalm. As I was crossing the ash-field, I saw the minister at some distance talking to a man. I could not hear what they were saying; but I saw an impatient or dissentient (I could not tell which) gesture on the part of the former, who walked quickly away, and was apparently absorbed in his thoughts; for, though he passed within twenty yards of me, as both our paths converged towards home, he took no notice of me. We passed the evening in a way which was even worse than dinner-time. The minister was silent, depressed, even irritable. Poor cousin Holman was utterly perplexed by this unusual frame of mind and temper in her husband; she was not well herself, and was suffering from the extreme and sultry heat, which made her less talkative than usual. Phillis, usually so reverently tender to her parents, so soft, so gentle, seemed now to take no notice of the unusual state of things, but talked to me – to anyone – on indifferent subjects, regardless of her father's gravity, of her mother's piteous looks of bewilderment. But once my eyes fell upon her hands, concealed under the table, and I could see the passionate, convulsive manner in which she laced and interlaced her fingers perpetually, wringing them together from time to time, wringing till the compressed flesh became perfectly white. What could I do? I talked with her, as I saw she wished; her grey eyes had dark circles round them, and a strange kind of dark light in them; her cheeks were flushed, but her lips were white and wan. I wondered that others did not read these signs as clearly as I did. But perhaps they did; I think, from what came afterwards, the minister did.

Poor cousin Holman! she worshipped her husband; and the outward signs of his uneasiness were more patent to her simple heart than were her daughter's. After a while, she could bear it no longer. She got up, and, softly laying her hand on his broad stooping shoulder, she said: 'What is the matter, minister? Has anything gone wrong?'

He started as if from a dream. Phillis hung her head, and caught her breath in terror at the answer she feared. But he, looking round with a sweeping glance, turned his broad, wise face up to his anxious wife, and forced a smile, and took her hand in a reassuring manner.

'I am blaming myself, dear. I have been overcome with anger this afternoon. I scarcely knew what I was doing, but I turned away Timothy Cooper. He has killed the Ribstone pippin at the corner of the orchard; gone and piled the quicklime for the mortar for the new stable-wall against the trunk of the tree – stupid fellow! killed the tree outright – and it loaded with apples!'

'And Ribstone pippins are so scarce,' said sympathetic cousin Holman.

'Ay! But Timothy is but a half-wit; and he has a wife and children. He had often put me to it sore, with his slothful ways; but I had laid it before the Lord, and striven to bear with him. But I will not stand it any longer; it's past my patience. And he has notice to find another place. Wife, we won't talk more about it.' He took her hand gently off his shoulder; touched it with his lips; but relapsed into a silence as profound, if not quite so morose in appearance, as before. I could not tell why, but this bit of talk between her father and mother seemed to take all the factitious spirits out of Phillis. She did not speak now, but looked out of the open casement at the calm large moon, slowly moving through the twilight sky. Once I thought her eyes were filling with tears; but, if so, she shook them off, and arose with alacrity when her mother, tired and dispirited, proposed to go to bed immediately after prayers. We all said good-night in our separate ways to the minister, who still sat at the table with the great Bible open before him, not much looking up at any of our salutations, but returning them kindly. But when I, last of all, was on the point of leaving the room, he said, still scarcely looking up: 'Paul, you will oblige me by staying here a few minutes. I would fain have some talk with you.'

I knew what was coming, all in a moment. I carefully shut-to the door, put out my candle, and sat down to my fate. He seemed to find some difficulty in beginning, for, if I had not heard that he wanted to speak to me, I should never have guessed it, he seemed so much absorbed in reading a chapter to the end. Suddenly he lifted his head up and said: 'It is about that friend of yours, Holdsworth! Paul, have you any reason for thinking he has played tricks upon Phillis?'

I saw that his eyes were blazing with such a fire of anger at the bare idea, that I lost all my presence of mind, and only repeated: 'Played tricks on Phillis!'

'Ay! you know what I mean: made love to her, courted her, made her think that he loved her, and then gone away and left her. Put it as you will; only give me an answer of some kind or another – a true answer, I mean – and don't repeat my words, Paul.'

He was shaking all over, as he said this. I did not delay a moment in answering him: 'I do not believe that Edward Holdsworth ever played tricks on Phillis, ever made love to her; he never, to my knowledge, made her believe that he loved her.'

I stopped; I wanted to nerve up my courage for a confession, yet I wished to save the secret of Phillis's love for Holdsworth, as much as I could; that secret which she had so striven to keep sacred and safe; and I had need of some reflection, before I went on with what I had to say.

He began again, before I had quite arranged my manner of speech. It was almost as if to himself – 'She is my only child; my little daughter! She is hardly out of childhood; I have thought to gather her under my wings for years to come; her mother and I would lay down our lives to keep her from harm and grief.' Then, raising his voice, and looking at me, he said, 'Something has gone wrong with the child; and it seems to me to date from the time she heard of that marriage. It is hard to think that you may know more of her secret cares and sorrows than I do – but perhaps you do, Paul, perhaps you do – only, if it be not a sin, tell me what I can do to make her happy again; tell me!'

'It will not do much good, I am afraid,' said I; 'but I will own how wrong I did; I don't mean wrong in the way of sin, but in the way of judgement. Holdsworth told me just before he went that he loved Phillis, and hoped to make her his wife; and I told her.'

There! it was out; all my part in it, at least; and I set my lips tight together, and waited for the words to come. I did not see his face; I looked straight at the wall opposite; but I heard him once begin to speak, and then turn over the leaves in the book before him. How awfully still that room was! The air outside, how still it was! The open window let in no rustle of leaves, no twitter or movement of birds – no sound whatever. The clock on the stairs – the minister's hard breathing – was it to go on for ever? Impatient beyond bearing at the deep quiet, I spoke again: 'I did it for the best, as I thought.'

The minister shut the book to hastily, and stood up. Then I saw how angry he was.

'For the best, do you say? It was best, was it, to go and tell a young girl what you never told a word of to her parents, who trusted you like a son of their own?'

He began walking about, up and down the room, close under the open windows, churning up his bitter thoughts of me.

'To put such thoughts into the child's head!' continued he; 'to spoil her peaceful maidenhood with talk about another man's love; and such love, too!' – he spoke scornfully now – 'a love that is ready for any young woman! Oh, the misery in my poor little daughter's face today at dinner – the misery, Paul! I thought you were one to be trusted – your father's son too, to go and put such thoughts into the child's mind; you two talking together about that man wishing to marry her!'

I could not help remembering the pinafore, the childish garment which Phillis wore so long, as if her parents were unaware of her progress towards womanhood. Just in the same way, the minister spoke and thought of her now, as a child, whose innocent peace I had spoiled by vain and foolish talk. I knew that the truth was different, though I could hardly have told it now; but, indeed, I never thought of trying to tell; it was far from my mind to add one iota to the sorrow which I had caused. The minister went on walking, occasionally stopping to move things on the table, or articles of furniture, in a sharp, impatient, meaningless way, then he began again: 'So young, so pure from the world! how could you go and talk to such a child, raising hopes, exciting feelings – all to end thus; and best so, even though I saw her poor piteous face look as it did? I can't forgive you, Paul; it was more than wrong – it was wicked – to go and repeat that man's words.'

His back was now to the door; and, in listening to his low angry tones, he did not hear it slowly open, nor did he see Phillis, standing just within the room, until he turned round; then he stood still. She must have been half undressed; but she had covered herself with a dark winter cloak, which fell in long folds to her white, naked, noiseless feet. Her face was strangely pale; her eyes heavy in the black circles round them. She came up to the table very slowly, and leant her hand upon it, saying mournfully: 'Father, you must not blame Paul. I could not help hearing a great deal of what you were saying. He did tell me, and perhaps it would have been wiser not, dear Paul! But – oh, dear! oh, dear! I am so sick with shame! He told me out of his kind heart, because he saw – that I was so very unhappy at *his* going away.'

She hung her head, and leant more heavily than before on her supporting hand.

'I don't understand,' said her father; but he was beginning to understand. Phillis did not answer, till he asked her again. I could have struck him now for his cruelty; but, then, I knew all.

'I loved him, father!' she said at length, raising her eyes to the minister's face.

'Had he ever spoken of love to you? Paul says not!'

'Never.' She let fall her eyes, and drooped more than ever. I almost thought she would fall.

'I could not have believed it,' said he, in a hard voice, yet sighing the moment he had spoken. A dead silence for a moment. 'Paul! I was unjust to you. You deserved blame, but not all that I said.' Then again a silence. I thought I saw Phillis's white lips moving, but it might be the flickering of the candlelight – a moth had flown in through the open casement, and was fluttering round the flame; I might have saved it, but I did not care to do so, my heart was too full of other things. At any rate, no sound was heard for long endless minutes. Then he said – 'Phillis! did we not make you happy here? Have we not loved you enough?'

She did not seem to understand the drift of this question; she looked up as if bewildered, and her beautiful eyes dilated with a painful, tortured expression. He went on, without noticing the look on her face; he did not see it, I am sure.

'And yet you would have left us, left your home, left your father and your mother, and gone away with this stranger, wandering over the world!'

He suffered, too; there were tones of pain in the voice in which he uttered this reproach. Probably, the father and daughter were never so far apart in their lives, so unsympathetic. Yet some new terror came over her, and it was to him she turned for help. A shadow came over her face, and she tottered towards her father; falling down, her arms across his knees, and moaning out: 'Father, my head! my head!' and then she slipped through his quick-enfolding arms, and lay on the ground at his feet.

I shall never forget his sudden look of agony while I live; never! We raised her up; her colour had strangely darkened; she was insensible. I ran through the back-kitchen to the yard-pump, and brought back water. The minister had her on his knees, her head against his breast, almost as though she were a sleeping child. He was trying to rise up with his poor precious burden; but the momentary terror had robbed the strong man of his strength, and he sank back in his chair with sobbing breath.

'She is not dead, Paul! is she?' he whispered, hoarse, as I came near him.

I, too, could not speak, but I pointed to the quivering of the muscles round her mouth. Just then cousin Holman, attracted by some unwonted sound, came down. I remember I was surprised at the time at her presence of mind: she seemed to know so much better what to do than the minister, in the midst of the sick affright which blanched her countenance, and made her tremble all over. I think now that it was the recollection of what had gone before; the miserable thought that possibly his words had brought on this attack, whatever it might be, that so unmanned the minister. We carried her upstairs; and, while the women were putting her to bed, still unconscious, still slightly convulsed, I slipped out, and saddled one of the horses, and rode as fast as the heavy-trotting beast could go, to Hornby, to find the doctor there, and bring him back. He was out; might be detained the whole night. I remember saying, 'God help us all!' as I sat on my horse, under the window, through which the apprentice's head had appeared to answer my furious tugs at the night-bell. He was a good-natured fellow. He said: 'He may be home in half an hour, there's no knowing; but I dare say he will. I'll send him out to the Hope Farm directly he comes in. It's that good-looking young woman, Holman's daughter, that's ill, isn't it?'

'Yes.'

'It would be a pity if she was to go. She's an only child, isn't she? I'll get up, and smoke a pipe in the surgery, ready for the governor's coming home. I might go to sleep if I went to bed again.'

'Thank you, you're a good fellow!' and I rode back almost as quickly as I came.

It was a brain-fever. The doctor said so, when he came in the early summer morning. I believe we had come to know the nature of the illness in the night-watches that had gone before. As to hope of ultimate recovery, or even evil prophecy of the probable end, the cautious doctor would be entrapped into neither. He gave his directions, and promised to come again: so soon, that this one thing showed his opinion of the gravity of the case.

By God's mercy, she recovered; but it was a long, weary time first. According to previously made plans, I was to have gone home at the beginning of August. But all such ideas were put aside now, without a word being spoken. I really think that I was necessary in the house, and especially necessary to the minister at this time; my father was the last man in the world, under such circumstances, to expect me home.

I say, I think I was necessary in the house. Every person (I had almost said every creature, for all the dumb beasts seemed to know and love Phillis) about the place went grieving and sad, as though a cloud was over the sun. They did their work, each striving to steer clear of the temptation to eye-service,[285] in fulfilment of the trust reposed in them by the minister. For, the day after Phillis had been taken ill, he had called all the men employed on the farm into the empty barn; and there he had entreated their prayers for his only child; and, then and there, he had told them of his present incapacity for thought about any other thing in this world but his little daughter, lying nigh unto death, and he had asked them to go on with their daily labours as best they could, without his direction. So, as I say, these honest men did their work to the best of their ability; but they slouched along with sad and careful faces, coming one by one in the dim mornings to ask news of the sorrow that overshadowed the house, and receiving Betty's intelligence, always rather darkened by passing through her mind, with slow shakes of the head, and a dull wistfulness of sympathy. But, poor fellows, they were hardly fit to be trusted with hasty messages; and here my poor services came in. One time, I was to ride hard to Sir William Bentinck's, and petition for ice out of his ice-house, to put on Phillis's head. Another, it was to Eltham I must go, by train, horse, anyhow, and bid the doctor there come for a consultation; for fresh symptoms had appeared, which Mr Brown, of Hornby, considered unfavourable. Many an hour have I sat on the window-seat, halfway up the stairs, close by the old clock, listening in the hot stillness of the house for the sounds in the sick-room. The minister and I met often, but spoke together seldom. He looked so old – so old! He shared the nursing with his wife; the strength that was needed seemed to be given to them both in that day. They required no one else about their child. Every office about her was sacred to them; even Betty only went into the room for the most necessary purposes. Once I saw Phillis through the open door; her pretty golden hair had been cut off long before; her head was covered with wet cloths, and she was moving it backwards and forwards on the pillow, with weary, never-ending motion, her poor eyes shut, trying in the old-accustomed way to croon out a hymn tune, but perpetually breaking it up into moans of pain. Her mother sat by her, tearless, changing the cloths upon her head with patient solicitude. I did not see the minister at first; but there he was, in a dark corner, down upon his knees, his hands clasped together in passionate prayer. Then the door shut, and I saw no more.

One day he was wanted; and I had to summon him. Brother Robinson and another minister, hearing of his 'trial', had come to see him. I told him this upon the stair-landing in a whisper. He was strangely troubled.[286]

'They will want me to lay bare my heart. I cannot do it. Paul, stay with me! They mean well; but as for spiritual help at such a time – it is God only, God only, who can give it.'

So I went in with him. They were two ministers from the neighbourhood; both older than Ebenezer Holman, but evidently inferior to him in education and worldly position. I thought they looked at me as if I were an intruder; but, remembering the minister's words, I held my ground, and took up one of poor Phillis's books (of which I could not read a word) to have an ostensible occupation. Presently I was asked to 'engage in prayer'; and we all knelt down, Brother Robinson 'leading', and quoting largely, as I remember, from the Book of Job. He seemed to take for his text, if texts are ever taken for prayers, 'Behold, thou hast instructed many; but now it is come upon thee, and thou faintest; it toucheth thee, and thou art troubled.' When we others rose up, the minister continued for some minutes on his knees. Then he too got up, and stood facing us, for a moment, before we all sat down in conclave. After a pause Robinson began: 'We grieve for you, Brother Holman, for your trouble is great. But we would fain have you remember you are as a light set on a hill; and the congregations are looking at you with watchful eyes. We have been talking as we came along on the two duties required of you in this strait, Brother Hodgson and me. And we have resolved to exhort you on these two points. First, God has given you the opportunity of showing forth an example of resignation.' Poor Mr Holman visibly winced at this word. I could fancy how he had tossed aside such brotherly preachings in his happier moments; but now his whole system was unstrung, and 'resignation' seemed a term which presupposed that the dreaded misery of losing Phillis was inevitable. But good, stupid Mr Robinson went on. 'We hear on all sides that there are scarce any hopes of your child's recovery; and it may be well to bring you to mind of Abraham; and how he was willing to kill his only child when the Lord commanded. Take example by him, Brother Holman. Let us hear you say, "The Lord giveth and the Lord taketh away. Blessed be the name of the Lord!" '[287]

There was a pause of expectancy. I verily believe the minister tried to feel it; but he could not. Heart of flesh was too strong. Heart of stone he had not.

'I will say it to my God, when He gives me strength – when the day comes,' he spoke at last.

The other two looked at each other, and shook their heads. I think the reluctance to answer as they wished was not quite unexpected. The minister went on: 'There are hopes yet,' he said, as if to himself. 'God has given me a great heart for hoping, and I will not look forward beyond the hour.' Then, turning more to them, and speaking louder, he added: 'Brethren, God will strengthen me when the time comes, when such resignation as you speak of is needed. Till then I cannot feel it; and what I do not feel I will not express, using words as if they were a charm.' He was getting chafed, I could see.

He had rather put them out by these speeches of his; but after a short time and some more shakes of the head, Robinson began again: 'Secondly, we would have you listen to the voice of the rod, and ask yourself for what sins this trial has been laid upon you: whether you may not have been too much given up to your farm and your cattle; whether this world's learning has not puffed you up to vain conceit and neglect of the things of God; whether you have not made an idol of your daughter?'

'I cannot answer – I will not answer!' exclaimed the minister. 'My sins I confess to God. But if they were scarlet – and they are so in His sight,' he added humbly – 'I hold with Christ that afflictions are not sent by God in wrath as penalties for sin.'

'Is that orthodox, Brother Robinson?' asked the third minister, in a deferential tone of enquiry.

Despite the minister's injunction not to leave him, I thought matters were getting so serious that a little homely interruption would be more to the purpose than my continued presence, and I went round to the kitchen to ask for Betty's help.

' 'Od rot 'em!' said she; 'they're always a-coming at inconvenient times; and they have such hearty appetites, they'll make nothing of what would have served master and you since our poor lass has been ill. I've but a bit of cold beef in th' house; but I'll do some ham and eggs, and that'll rout 'em from worrying the minister. They're a deal quieter after they've had their victual. Last time as old Robinson came, he was very reprehensible upon master's learning, which he couldn't compass to save his life, so he needn't have been afeared of that temptation, and used words long enough to have knocked a body down; but after me and missus had given him his fill of victual, and he'd had some good ale and a pipe, he spoke just like any other man, and could crack a joke with me.'

Their visit was the only break in the long weary days and nights. I do not mean that no other enquiries were made. I believe that all the neighbours hung about the place daily, till they could learn from some out-comer how Phillis Holman was. But they knew better than to come up to the house; for the August weather was so hot that every door and window was kept constantly open, and the least sound outside penetrated all through. I am sure the cocks and hens had a sad time of it; for Betty drove them all into an empty barn, and kept them fastened up in the dark for several days, with very little effect as regarded their crowing and clacking. At length came a sleep which was the crisis, and from which she wakened up with a new faint life. Her slumber had lasted many, many hours. We scarcely dared to breathe or move during the time; we had striven to hope so long, that we were sick at heart, and durst not trust in the favourable signs: the even breathing, the moistened skin, the slight return of delicate colour into the pale, wan lips. I recollect stealing out that evening in the dusk, and wandering down the grassy lane, under the shadow of the over-arching elms to the little bridge at the foot of the hill, where the lane to the Hope Farm joined another road to Hornby. On the low parapet of that bridge I found Timothy Cooper, the stupid, half-witted labourer, sitting, idly throwing bits of mortar into the brook below. He just looked up at me as I came near, but gave me no greeting, either by word or gesture. He had generally made some sign of recognition to me; but this time I thought he was sullen at being dismissed. Nevertheless, I felt as if it would be a relief to talk a little to someone, and I sat down by him. While I was thinking how to begin, he yawned wearily.

'You are tired, Tim,' said I.

'Ay,' said he. 'But I reckon I may go home now.'

'Have you been sitting here long?'

'Welly all day long. Leastways sin' seven i' th' morning.'

'Why, what in the world have you been doing?'

'Nought.'

'Why have you been sitting here, then?'

'T' keep carts off.' He was up now, stretching himself, and shaking his lubberly limbs.

'Carts! what carts?'

'Carts as might ha' wakened yon wench! It's Hornby market-day. I reckon yo're no better nor a half-wit yoursel'.' He cocked his eye at me, as if he were gauging my intellect.

'And have you been sitting here all day to keep the lane quiet?'

'Ay. I've nought else to do. Th' minister has turned me adrift. Have yo' heard how th' lass is faring tonight?'

'They hope she'll waken better for this long sleep. Good-night to you, and God bless you, Timothy!' said I.

He scarcely took any notice of my words, as he lumbered across a stile that led to his cottage. Presently, I went home to the farm. Phillis had stirred, had spoken two or three faint words. Her mother was with her, dropping nourishment into her scarce conscious mouth. The rest of the household were summoned to evening prayer, for the first time for many days. It was a return to the daily habits of happiness and health. But in these silent days our very lives had been an unspoken prayer. Now, we met in the house-place, and looked at each other with strange recognition of the thankfulness on all our faces. We knelt down; we waited for the minister's voice. He did not begin as usual. He could not; he was choking. Presently we heard the strong man's sob. Then old John turned round on his knees, and said: 'Minister, I reckon we have blessed the Lord wi' all our souls though we've ne'er talked about it; and maybe He'll not need spoken words this night. God bless us all, and keep our Phillis safe from harm! Amen.'

Old John's impromptu prayer was all we had that night.

'Our Phillis', as he had called her, grew better day by day from that time. Not quickly; I sometimes grew desponding, and feared that she would never be what she had been before; no more she has, in some ways.

I seized an early opportunity to tell the minister about Timothy Cooper's unsolicited watch on the bridge during the long summer's day.

'God forgive me!' said the minister. 'I have been too proud in my own conceit. The first steps I take out of this house shall be to Cooper's cottage.'

I need hardly say Timothy was reinstated in his place on the farm; and I have often since admired the patience with which his master tried to teach him how to do the easy work which was henceforward carefully adjusted to his capacity.

Phillis was carried downstairs, and lay for hour after hour quite silent on the great sofa, drawn up under the windows of the house-place. She seemed always the same – gentle, quiet, and sad. Her energy did not return with her bodily strength. It was sometimes pitiful to see her parents' vain endeavours to rouse her to interest. One day the minister brought her a set of blue ribbons, reminding her with a tender smile of a former conversation, in which she had owned to a love of such feminine vanities. She spoke gratefully to him; but, when he was gone, she laid them on one side, and languidly shut her eyes. Another time I saw her mother bring her the Latin and Italian books that she had been so fond of before her illness – or, rather, before Holdsworth had gone away. That was worst of all. She turned her face to the wall, and cried as soon as her mother's back was turned. Betty was laying the cloth for the early dinner. Her sharp eyes saw the state of the case.

'Now, Phillis!' said she, coming up to the sofa; 'we ha' done a' we can for you, and th' doctors has done a' they can for you, and I think the Lord has done a' He can for you, and more than you deserve, too, if you don't do something for yourself. If I were you, I'd rise up and snuff the moon, sooner than break your father's and your mother's hearts wi' watching and waiting, till it pleases you to fight your own way back to cheerfulness. There, I never favoured long preachings, and I've said my say.'

A day or two after, Phillis asked me, when we were alone, if I thought my father and mother would allow her to go and stay with them for a couple of months. She blushed a little, as she faltered out her wish for change of thought and scene.

'Only for a short time, Paul! Then – we will go back to the peace of the old days. I know we shall; I can, and I will!'

NOTES TO THE SHORT STORIES

I am indebted to A. W. Ward's Introductions to the standard Knutsford Edition of 1906 and to previous editions of selected Gaskell stories by Angus Easson, Graham Handley, Laura Kranzler, Suzanne Lewis, Jenny Uglow and Edgar Wright.

Abbreviations used in the Notes (details given in the Bibliography)

ECG	Elizabeth Cleghorn Gaskell
EGEY	John Chapple, *Elizabeth Gaskell: The Early Years*, 1997
Letters	*The Letters of Mrs Gaskell*, Chapple and Pollard (eds), 1966
Further Letters	*Further Letters of Mrs Gaskell*, Chapple and Shelston (eds), 2000
Sharps	John Geoffrey Sharps, *Mrs Gaskell's Observation and Invention*, 1970

Mr Harrison's Confessions (February–April 1851)

1 (p. 205) *Will* later called Frank
2 (p. 205) *Guy's* Guy's Hospital, London
3 (p. 207) *Mayence* French for Mainz, in the Rhineland-Palatinate
4 (p. 209) *Hessian* fashionable military high boot from the grand duchy of Hesse, Germany
5 (p. 209) *in loco parentis* 'in a parent's place' (Latin)
6 (p. 210) *Galen or Hippocrates* ancient Greek medical authorities
7 (p. 210) *Duncombe was in a famous hunting district* Cf. Cheshire in *Further Letters*, p. 234.
8 (p. 210) *widow* ECG's first cousin Susan (1811–89), lost her husband, Richard Deane, in January 1851; he had been a medical partner of her father, Peter Holland (*EGEY*, p. 126).
9 (p. 211) *surgeon to the Royal Family* Henry Holland became one of their physicians extraordinary in 1837 (see *EGEY*, pp. 148–

151). Sir Astley Cooper (1768–1841) was a famous surgeon at Guy's Hospital in London.

10 (p. 211) *Sir Robert Peel* Conservative Prime Minister 1834–5, 1841–6

11 (p. 211) *You will find . . . women* Cf. Cranford: 'in possession of the Amazons'.

12 (p. 212) *Esculapius* god of healing and son of Apollo (Greek mythology)

13 (p. 213) *outré* unusual or improper (French)

14 (p. 213) *Abernethy* Sir Everard Home (1756–1832) and John Abernethy (1764–1831) were famous surgeons, the latter noted for irritability.

15 (p. 218) *mal-àpropos* French: 'inappropriately'

16 (p. 218) *Lancet* major medical journal, which contains diagnoses and accounts of medical experiments

17 (p. 220) *there was a gallery. . . delightfully* Tabley old hall, which has not survived, had a singing gallery (*Letters*, p. 15; *EGEY*, pp. 209–12).

18 (p. 220) *county family* belonging to the nobility or gentry

19 (p. 221) *bodkin* like a long thin needle

20 (p. 221) *infra dig* *infra dignitatem* – beneath one's dignity (Latin)

21 (p. 221) *ride and tie* with two people sharing one horse

22 (p. 223) *merry-thought* wishbone

23 (p. 225) *German canon* traditional German part-song: 'How well I am in the evening . . . ', translated by E. P. Prentiss (Wright)

24 (p. 225) *Liebig* Justus von Liebig (1803–73), famous German chemist who proved that plants absorb minerals and water from the soil

25 (p. 227) *croup* inflammation of the throat and windpipe, a very serious condition for children in earlier times

26 (p. 228) *leeches* to suck blood; then a very common medical practice

27 (p. 228) *Sleep . . . sleep* Cf. Tyrolese folk-song: 'Still, still, still, weil's Kindlein schlafen will . . . '

28 (p. 229) *'Peculiar people, whom Death had made dear'* 'peculiar people' is an allusion to 1 Peter 2:9: 'an holy nation, a peculiar people'. Cf. ECG's attitude to Barbara Fergusson after the death of her baby son, Willie (*Further Letters*, pp. 34–6).

29 (p. 230) *hyoscyamus* drug found in henbane and related plants

30 (p. 231) *wersh* dialect: 'tasteless' or 'insipid'

31 (p. 231) *Stentor* Greek herald in Homer's *Iliad*

32 (p. 232) *Mermaid* a famous London tavern. 'What things have we seen, / Done at the Mermaid!' (Francis Beaumont, 'Letter to Ben Jonson')

33 (p. 234) *respirator* protective mask, invented in 1835 by Julius Jeffreys

34 (p. 234) *diseased* Cf. *Macbeth*, 5, 3, 41: 'minister to a mind diseased'.

35 (p. 235) *Newgate* London prison, demolished in 1902

36 (p. 235) *hulks* moored prison ships

37 (p. 235) *Mens conscia recti* Virgil, *Aeneid* I, l. 604: 'a mind conscious of its own virtue'

38 (p. 238) *hodie* today (Latin); a term used in medical prescriptions

39 (p. 239) *Consols* British government securities, bearing interest

40 (p. 240) *Corazza shirts* Italian revolutionary-style shirts

41 (p. 242) *surgical practice* Cf. 'stories wh[ic]h amounted to absolute cruelty' (*Further Letters*, p. 95).

42 (p. 243) *White* Peter Holland had been apprenticed to Charles White (1728–1813) of Manchester, who introduced 'conservative' surgery (*DNB*; *EGEY*, p. 145)

43 (p. 243) *in toto* in all respects (Latin)

44 (p. 249) *grey mare* 'The grey mare is the better horse' (proverbial).

45 (p. 257) *contretemps* setback or awkward situation (French)

46 (p. 259) *vi et armis* by force of arms (Latin)

47 (p. 260) *an apple of discord* Paris preferred Aphrodite to Hera and Athena, awarding her the golden apple as prize for beauty (Greek mythology).

48 (p. 261) *Meurice's* hotel in rue de Rivoli, Paris

49 (p. 263) *Peace Society* ECG lived 'in the very midst of . . . the Peace party (*Further Letters*, p. 192).

50 (p. 265) *Lothario* proverbial: libertine character in Nicholas Rowe, *The Fair Penitent* (1703)

51 (p. 268) *Vanity Fair* W. M. Thackeray's novel of 1848

52 (p. 268) 'Who's dat knocking at de door?' In 1846, E. P. Christy, an American showman, established the Christy Minstrels; their songs became immensely popular.

53 (p. 268) *Jenny Lind* Jenny Lind (1820–87), popular singer, called 'the Swedish Nightingale'. Cf. *Further Letters*, p. 42 n. 3.

54 (p. 270) *tallow-chandler* maker or seller of candles. Hoggins is a deliberately coarse-sounding name, also used in *Cranford*.

55 (p. 271) *He won golden opinions* See *Macbeth*, 1, 7, 32–3: 'I have bought / Golden opinions from all sorts of people.

The Doom of the Griffiths (January 1858)

56 (p. 275) *Owen Glendower* a Welsh nationalist leader who defeated Henry IV, 1400–02; styled himself Prince of Wales, 1404; died *c.*1416
57 (p. 275) *And few . . . in reply* 'But will they come when you do call for them?' (*1 Henry IV*, 3, 1, 52).
58 (p. 275) *Builth* referring to the killing of Prince Llewelyn at Builth Wells in 1282. (Welsh spellings are variable; obvious misprints have been silently corrected.)
59 (p. 275) *Sir David Gam* There is no evidence that Dafydd Gam (d. 1415) attempted to kill Glendower at the 1404 Parliament (Sharps, p. 268).
60 (p. 278) *Dr Pugh* William Owen Pughe (1759–1835)
61 (p. 278) *Llyn* the Lleyn peninsula
62 (p. 280) *Grammar School at Bangor* the Friars' School
63 (p. 283) *'stretched in indolent repose'* James Thomson, *The Castle of Indolence* (1748), canto 2, stanza 50: 'Renown is not the child of indolent repose.'
64 (p. 284) *Oedipus Tyrannus* or *Oedipus Rex*, a Greek tragedy by Sophocles, in which a son kills his father unknowingly
65 (p. 284) *Avenger* the Greek god Ate
66 (p. 286) *cwrw* ale (Welsh)
67 (p. 287) *triad* bardic literary form (slightly inaccurately quoted)
68 (p. 287) *Nest* name of an ancient Welsh princess
69 (p. 289) *Sorbus aucuparia* mountain ash tree (Latin)
70 (p. 290) *Undine* tragedy of a water nymph who married a mortal
71 (p. 292) *yr buten* the harlot (Welsh)
72 (p. 298) *fireplace* This is true of Plas yn Penrhyn, her uncle Samuel Holland's house, where ECG might have begun her tale. (It was inherited by his son Samuel in 1851.) See also Sharps, p. 267.
73 (p. 299) *law* Cf. *Further Letters*, p. 9.
74 (p. 300) *drookit* soaked (dialect)

'Lois the Witch' (1859)

75 (p. 309) *Barford* town upon the river Avon. ECG was at school there 1821–4 (*EGEY*, pp. 238–40).
76 (p. 309) *father* a fictitious clergyman (Sharps, p. 319)
77 (p.310) *Fathers* early writers on Christian doctrine
78 (p. 310) *Edgehill* in Warwickshire; first battle (1642) of the Civil War between Cavaliers and Roundheads

79 (p. 310) *schismatic* one who left the Church of England

80 (p. 312) *charter* King Charles II abrogated the Massachusetts charter in 1684.

81 (p. 314) *wampum-beads* shells strung together that Indians used for money

82 (p. 314) *Gold-Wasser* gold-water (German), spirits (*Mary Barton*, Ch. 31)

83 (p. 314) *punkenpie* pumpkin pie (US dialect)

84 (p. 314) *brandered* Northern dialect: cooked on the gridiron

85 (p. 314) *Elder* lay officer in some Protestant churches

86 (p. 314) *Archbishop Laud* High Church Archbishop of Canterbury from 1633, a supporter of King Charles I who persecuted Puritans

87 (p. 315) *minute-men* ready to fight with little notice

88 (p. 315) *Lothrop's business* Thomas Lothrop and his men had been killed by Indians in 1675.

89 (p. 316) *pirates* Catholic French from Canada

90 (p. 316) *by token* by association

91 (p. 316) *'Blasphemed . . . the nose'* Samuel Butler, *Hudibras*, Part 1 (1663), canto 1, line 230, satirising Puritan condemnation of religious festivals

92 (p. 316) *Inasmuch . . . unto me* negative variant of Matthew 25:40

93 (p. 317) *roaring lion* 1 Peter 5:8: '. . . the devil, as a roaring lion, walketh about, seeking whom he may devour.'

94 (p. 317) *waste places* Matthew 4:1: 'Then was Jesus led up of the Spirit into the wilderness to be tempted of the devil.'

95 (p. 318) *cat* supposed to be a familiar evil spirit

96 (p. 318) *They were . . . neck* ordeal by immersion in the ducking-pond for those presumed to be witches

97 (p. 321) *took the oaths . . . living* Many clergymen were ejected from Anglican Church livings in 1662 for refusing to swear an oath of loyalty to King Charles II.

98 (p. 324) *Mr Cotton Mather* 1663–1728, leading Puritan minister at Boston, author of books on the witch trials

99 (p. 324) *Zion* hill of Jerusalem, representing the heavenly city

100 (p. 324) *Aaron's beard* Psalm 133: 'like the precious ointment on the head, that ran down upon the beard, even Aaron's beard . . . '

101 (p. 324) *keeping-room* living-room. *Oxford English Dictionary* cites H. B. Stowe, *Uncle Tom's Cabin* (1852), Chapter 15.

102 (p. 324) *dreamed dreams* Acts 2:17: '. . . your young men shall see visions, and your old men shall dream dreams.'

103 (p. 326) *Church and State* the Church of England and the Government
104 (p. 326) *Popish rubric* the Church of England's Book of Common Prayer (1662), thought to be Roman Catholic by Puritans
105 (p. 327) *the king could do no wrong* a principle of the English constitution, according to Sir William Blackstone's *Commentaries upon the Laws of England*
106 (p. 330) *Mr Tappau* based on the Revd Samuel Parris, minister at Salem Village, driven out in 1696
107 (p. 330) *Mr Nolan* based on the Revd George Burroughs, at Salem Village 1680–3, indicted for witchcraft and executed 1692
108 (p. 331) *'Love me, love my dog'* proverb quoted in Latin by St Bernard of Clairvaux
109 (p. 332) *Hallow-e'en* 31 October, the eve of All Hallows or Saints, the night of the witches
110 (p. 332) *second sight* supposed power to see future happenings or things at a distance
111 (p. 333) *eldritch* weird or unearthly
112 (p. 334) *borne in* impressed with force upon the mind
113 (p. 335) *Samuel* 1 Samuel 3:18: 'It is the Lord . . . that has spoken; let him do His will.'
114 (p. 335) *elect* those chosen or preordained by God to receive salvation
115 (p. 335) *Is thy servant a dog . . . great thing?* 2 Kings 8:13
116 (p. 338) *Lots were drawn* random selection of a straw or stick, etc. from its fellows
117 (p. 338) *Satan . . . devour* 1 Peter 5:8 – see Note 93 above.
118 (p. 339) *Glory . . . night* Thomas Ken's 'Evening Hymn'. See J. R. Watson, *The English Hymn: A Critical and Historical Study*, Oxford, 1999, pp. 93–7.
119 (p. 340) *pipkin* small cooking vessel
120 (p. 342) *Gordian knot* solved a problem; from the Greek legend of a complicated knot that Alexander the Great cut with his sword
121 (p. 345) *prelatist* believer in Church government by bishops, etc.
122 (p. 345) *troth-plight* engaged
123 (p. 345) *The mystery . . . God's* Followers of John Calvin believed that God had inescapably chosen 'the elect'; others believed that an eternal God knew who they were but allowed humans freedom of choice in their lifetime. Cf. ECG's antipathy to 'the Calvinistic or Low Church creed' (*Letters*, p. 648).
124 (p. 348) *Church militant* Church on earth

125 (p. 349) *herd of swine* See Matthew 8:28–32: Jesus, meeting two people possessed by devils, ordered them to leave, 'And when they were come out, they went into the herd of swine.'
126 (p. 349) *forgiveness* blasphemy against the Holy Spirit (Matthew 12:31–2). Witchcraft was associated with heresy, but cf. Note 142 below.
127 (p. 351) *Matthew Hopkinson* i.e., Hopkins, author of *The Discovery of Witches* (1647) and persecutor of women. He was himself executed for witchcraft.
128 (p. 353) *slip* to be let loose
129 (p. 356) *seen of all men . . . eye* see Matthew 18:8–9: 'Wherefore if thy hand or thy foot offend thee, cut them off . . . And if thine eye offend thee, pluck it out . . . '
130 (p. 357) *Holy Ghost* Cf. Note 126 above.
131 (p. 359) *Saul . . . throne* See 1 Samuel 16:14–23.
132 (p. 361) *Yet Scripture . . . land* Exodus 22:18: 'Thou shalt not suffer a witch to live.'
133 (p. 361) *he blessed her unaware* S. T. Coleridge, 'The Ancient Mariner', Part IV, ll. 284–5: 'A spring of love gushed from my heart / And I blessed them unaware.'
134 (p. 363) *Lamb* i.e., Christ. For *Beulah* or *Zion*, see Isaiah 62:4 and Note 99 above.
135 (p. 365) *Geneva bands and gowns* dress worn by Swiss Calvinist clergy
136 (p. 365) *Caesar's murder* See Shakespeare, *Julius Caesar*, 3, 2.
137 (p. 365) *'unbelieving Sadducees'* ancient Jewish sect that denied the existence of spirits
138 (p. 366) *Mr Goodwin* Boston mason, whose Irish wife had been executed as a witch in 1688 (account in Mather's *Memorable Providences*, 1689)
139 (p. 366) *Assembly's Catechism* published by Puritan Church Assembly
140 (p. 366) *Dr Martin Luther* an allusion to the story that Martin Luther (1483–1546) flung his ink-pot at the devil
141 (p. 370) *foredoomed* as opposed to foreseen
142 (p. 372) *gallows* Witchcraft was a civil felony in Massachusetts, punishable by death (Hall, p. 11).
143 (p. 374) *Mr Hathorn and Mr Curwin* Jonathan Corwin and John Hathorn (1641–1717). There are similarities to the trial and execution of Rebecca Nurse, though she was seventy-one and the mother of eight children.

144 (p. 377) *balm in Gilead* Jeremiah 8:22: 'Is there no balm in Gilead?' (i. e., no forgiveness)
145 (p. 379) *contumacy* resistance to authority, the refusal to plead by Giles Corey
146 (p. 381) *judgment seat* of God in Heaven
147 (p. 384) *temporal judgments* i.e., on earth
148 (p. 385) *Justice Sewall* Samuel Sewall (1652–1730), special commissioner appointed by the Governor

Curious, if True (February 1860)

149 (p. 389) *the great Reformer* John Calvin (1509–64) of Geneva
150 (p. 389) *Tours* French city in the valley of the Loire
151 (p. 389) *table-d'hôte* supper for residents (French)
152 (p. 389) *salle à manger* dining-room (French)
153 (p. 389) *tête-à-tête* head-to-head – private conversation (French)
154 (p. 390) *pillow of snow* anecdote in Walter Scott, *Tales of a Grandfather* (Easson)
155 (p. 390) *tourelles* turrets (French)
156 (p. 391) *propriétaires* property owners (French)
157 (p. 391) *patois* dialect (French)
158 (p. 391) *Richard Whittingham . . . expected* 'Whittingham' misheard; cf. the English legend 'Dick Whittington and His Cat'. Richard Whittington (d. 1423) was mayor of London.
159 (p. 391) *battants* hinged sections of a double door (French)
160 (p. 391) *Monsieur le Géanquilleur* 'Giantkiller'. Possibly French *patois*, but the absence of *t* suggests that ECG was using French spelling to imitate French pronunciation of English. 'Jack and the Giants' is a British tale from the eighteenth century.
161 (p. 392) *flambeau* torch (French)
162 (p. 392) *salon* drawing-room (French)
163 (p. 392) *Marché au Vendredi* Friday market-place (French)
164 (p. 393) *Hôtel Cluny* major museum in Paris for medieval arts and crafts
165 (p. 393) *countenance* Cinderella (Charles Perrault's 'Cendrillon')
166 (p. 393) *embonpoint* stoutness, plumpness (French)
167 (p. 394) *awkward habit . . . room* Boswell saw Johnson do this whenever his private ceremonies seemed to have gone wrong (*Life of Johnson*, new ed. J. D. Fleeman, Oxford University Press, 1970, p. 342).
168 (p. 394) *Monsieur Poucet* Little Thumb, from Perrault's *Histoires*

ou Contes du temps passé (1697; *Contes*, Gallimard, 1999). Poucet used pebbles to retrace his steps when deserted in a forest, deceived an ogre into cutting the throats of his own daughters and stole his seven-league boots.

169 (p. 394) *entrée* admission (French)

170 (p. 394) *follower* Puss in Boots (Perrault's 'Le Chat botté'); his master was a miller's son pretending to be a marquis.

171 (p. 394) *chasseur* groom (French)

172 (p. 395) *M. de Retz's . . . notorious* Gilles de Rais (Rays or Retz), executed in 1440 for multiple murders. He became associated with Perrault's story of Bluebeard ('La Barbe bleu'), a wife-murderer.

173 (p. 395) *My cat! . . . in London* Dick Whittington's cat. Manx cats are naturally almost tail-less.

174 (p. 396) *de or von* French and German indications of nobility

175 (p. 396) *Louis XVI* King of France from 1774, guillotined in 1793. Many nobles emigrated.

176 (p. 396) *quaint liveries* servants in the distinctive uniforms of their lords

177 (p. 396) *sound asleep in a magnificent settee* the Sleeping Beauty (Perrault's 'La Belle au bois dormant')

178 (p. 397) *eau sucré[e]* sugared water (French)

179 (p. 398) *such little slippers* Cinderella's slippers of glass

180 (p. 398) *Rather let us . . . beauty!* from the tale of 'Beauty and the Beast', who became a prince in the 1756 version by Jean-Marie Leprince de Beaumont

181 (p. 399) *De Carabas* name given to miller's son. See Note 170 above.

182 (p. 399) *emperor* Napoleon III (1808–73), who was not a favourite of Gaskell. See *Further Letters*, pp. 61–2, 229.

183 (p. 399) *pleasant-looking man* the Beast (Perrault's 'Riquet' is similar)

184 (p. 399) *voueé au blanc* devoted to white (French). From 'La Chatte blanche' (1698) by Marie-Catherine Comtesse d'Aulnoy. ECG makes extensive use of 'The White Cat' in her 'Company Manners' (1854).

185 (p. 400) *John Bull . . . John Bright* allusions to John Bull, nick-name for an Englishman, and two British politicians: 1st Earl Russell (1792–1878), then Foreign Minister, and John Bright (1811–1889), reformer and Liberal parliamentarian known to ECG.

186 (p. 400) *réunion* French: 'social gathering'
187 (p. 400) *King Arthur . . . England's need* legendary British hero, for ECG buried at Alderley Edge (*Letters*, p. 32)
188 (p. 400) *peasant-girl* probably Red Riding Hood (Perrault's 'Le Petit Chaperon rouge')
189 (p. 401) *capuchon* hood (French)
190 (p. 402) *scimitar* Persian *shamshir*, a sword with strongly curved blade
191 (p. 402) *Monsieur Sganarelle* character in Molière's *Le Médicin malgré lui* (1666), who quarrelled with his wife, then claimed, 'These are the little things that from time to time are necessary in a friendship, and five or six blows of a sword between people who love each other can only renew their affection.' (Original text: *coups de baton*, i. e. 'stick')
192 (p. 402) *Reform Bill* The Reform Bill, extending the right to vote in parliamentary elections, was passed in 1832; the second Act was not passed until 1870.
193 (p. 403) *Madame la Fée-marraine* Fairy godmother (French), a character in Perrault's 'Cinderella'.

Six Weeks at Heppenheim (May 1862)

194 (p. 407) *Lincoln's Inn* one of the four Inns of Court in London, where barristers took pupils
195 (p. 407) *Bergstrasse* mountain road (German). The Hessische Bergstrasse is a wine-growing region running north-south along the edge of the Odenwald hills between Darmstadt and Heidelberg, parallel to and about twelve miles east of the Rhine.
196 (p. 408) *eating-room* Cf. German *Esszimmer*
197 (p. 408) *vis inertiae* inactivity (Latin)
198 (p. 409) *Black Forest* mountainous area to the south of the Bergstrasse
199 (p. 410) *bouillons* clear meat soup (French)
200 (p. 412) *chasse . . . chevreuil* a right to hunt game, such as the roe deer (French). French influence was strong in the Rhineland states.
201 (p. 413) *pharmacopoeia* list of medicinal drugs
202 (p. 413) *Halbmond* an inn that still exists, the *Halber Mond* (Half-Moon – German). One of its landlords had been left a widower with a baby son and six-year-old daughter.
203 (p. 413) *liebe* dear (German)

204 (p. 413) *redded up* tidied
205 (p. 414) *perdu* hidden, lost (French)
206 (p. 415) *Altenahr* town about one hundred miles to the north-west, in the state of Westphalia
207 (p. 416) *honi soit qui mal y pense* shame be to him who thinks evil of it (French) – motto of the Order of the Garter, Britain's highest honour
208 (p. 416) *tisane* infusion of leaves or flowers (French)
209 (p. 416) *German writing* an old-fashioned cursive Gothic script
210 (p. 419) *Kaiser Karl* The original church was said to have been founded by Charlemagne.
211 (p. 419) *Castle of Starkenburg* a ruined castle above the town
212 (p. 419) *Melibocus* the highest hill of the Odenwald
213 (p. 420) *hill* the *Weinberg* ('wine-hill') called Steinkopf, where picking actually began on 14 October in 1858. The garden (illustrated in *Sechs Wochen*, p. 14) was some distance from the vineyard.
214 (p. 421) *Grand Duke* Louis III. The grand duchy of Hesse-Darmstadt was in Gaskell's time the smallest of the Rhineland states.
215 (p. 422) *Bacchus* classical god of wine
216 (p. 422) *to-meet-again* auf Weidersehen (German)
217 (p. 423) *Adler* Eagle (German) – another inn
218 (p. 427) *no real good . . . come* Romans 3:8. See Uglow, p. 446, for ECG's daughter Meta's reluctantly breaking off an engagement in August 1858.
219 (p. 428) *deposited her warning at the police office* She did not belong to the state of Hesse-Darmstadt.
220 (p. 429) *All Saints' Day* 1 November
221 (p. 431) *At length . . . against her* variant of Genesis 16:12
222 (p. 431) *Methinks the lady doth protest too much* *Hamlet*, 3, 2, 225 ('profess too much' in *Cornhill* text)
223 (p. 433) *The wine made . . . the bargain* then Traminer and red Burgunder grapes, and the superior white Riesling variety
224 (p. 433) *attaché* member of embassy staff
225 (p. 435) *the German harvest-hymn . . . such occasions* ECG's footnote here quotes a hymn by Matthias Claudius (1740–1815), set to music by Peter Schulz (1747–1800)

> Wir pflügen und wir streuen
> Den Saamen auf das Land;

Das Wachsen und Gedeihen
Steht in des Höchsten Hand.
Er sendet Thau und Regen,
Und Sonn- und Mondenschein;
Von Ihn kommt aller Segen,
Von unserm Gott allein.
Alle gute Gabe kommt her
Von Gott dem Herrn,
Drum dankt und hofft auf Ihn!

We plough and we sow seeds on the land; growth and thriving lie in the highest hand. He sends dew and rain, and sunshine and moonshine. From Him comes all blessing, from our God alone. All good gifts come to us from the Lord God, therefore thank and hope in Him.

Professor Peter Skrine notes that Jane Montgomery Campbell published a verse translation in 1861, which later became famous from its appearance in *Hymns Ancient and Modern* in 1868.

226 (p. 435) *Heart's darling!* Herzblättchen (German)
227 (p. 436) *Dicke Milch* sour milk curds
228 (p. 436) *cates* foodstuffs
229 (p. 436) *Frau Pastorin* pastor's wife (German)
230 (p. 437) *poor little worm* *armes Worm* – poor worm (German idiom)
231 (p. 438) *holidays* near-quotation from Elizabeth Inchbald, *A Simple Story* (1791), Vol. II, Chapter 6. A story set, however, amongst the English Catholic aristocracy.
232 (p. 439) *All Souls* November 2nd, the day *after* All Saints (November 1st)
233 (p. 439) *Acre of God* *Gottesacker* – churchyard (German)

Cousin Phillis (November 1863–February 1864)

234 (p. 443) *branch line* The first line was publicly opened at Knutsford (Eltham) in 1862.
235 (p. 443) *Independent* Protestants who left the Anglican Church in the seventeenth century, becoming Baptists, Congregationalists, Presbyterians and Unitarians
236 (p. 444) *'Spare the rod, and spoil the child'* Samuel Butler, 2 *Hudibras* (1664), canto 1, line 843
237 (p. 445) *small congregation* The 'old dissenting chapel' attended by ECG as a girl had about forty families.

238 (p. 446) *Heathbridge* Sandlebridge farm, the home of ECG's mother

239 (p. 448) *stone balls* as at Sandlebridge farm (see *Letters*, pp. 75–6)

240 (p. 450) *I knew . . . now dead* ECG had lost three of her own seven children.

241 (p. 450) *May Day* a day for traditional country revelry

242 (p. 450) *churning-day* a day for butter-making

243 (p. 450) *Was I like Abraham's steward . . . wife* See Genesis 24. Paul is like the steward sent to find a wife for Abraham's son Isaac. He found Rebekah, who became Isaac's wife.

244 (p. 454) *'Mount Ephraim' tune* from *Hymns and Spiritual Songs* (1707, etc.), by Isaac Watts, set by Benjamin Milgrove. See Watson, pp. 133, 148.

245 (p. 454) *unaccustomed scene* Cf. *Six Weeks at Heppenheim* (Note 225 – *occasions* – above).

246 (p. 456) *Italy* perhaps 'Illic sera rubens accendit lumina Vesper' (I, line 251), from Virgil's *Georgics*

247 (p. 456) *house-place* living-room, like that at Sandlebridge (*EGEY*, pp. 54, 199)

248 (p. 456) *Matthew Henry's Bible* standard for non-conformists. Matthew Henry's 'exposition' or commentaries on the Bible date from 1708–10.

249 (p. 457) *Heathbridge moss* a bog or swamp. The line from Manchester to Liverpool over Chat Moss (opened 1830) was an early triumph of railway engineering.

250 (p. 458) *Gazette* perhaps the *Railway Gazette* (1846–72)

251 (p. 459) *wafers* small, sticky discs of flour and gum

252 (p. 461) *tempus fugit* time flies (Latin)

253 (p. 463) *L'Inferno* Hell (Italian), the first section of Dante's early-fourteenth-century poem, *The Divine Comedy*

254 (p. 464) *the grapes were sour* a fox rejects grapes that in fact he could not reach (fable).

255 (p. 466) *old Adam* human being without regenerating grace from God

256 (p. 467) *exercised in spirit* considering the morality of their actions

257 (p. 467) *one small event* See Chapter 1 of Oliver Goldsmith, *The Vicar of Wakefield* (1766).

258 (p. 467) *Mr Holdsworth . . . his hands* ECG's friend, the inventor James Nasmyth of Patricroft Foundry near Manchester, held this view.

259 (p. 468) *George Stephenson* 1781–1848, engineer of the Liverpool–Manchester railway

260 (p. 469) *stick* James Nasmyth (1808–90) used a sooty forefinger.

261 (p. 470) *his partner* Nasmyth's commercial partner until 1850 was Holbrook Gaskell, a relation of ECG's husband.

262 (p. 476) *metaphysics* here, abstract or subtle discussion

263 (p. 480) *Housewife's Complete Manual* *A Housekeeper's Manual* appeared in 1759.

264 (p. 480) *On Prayer* by John Berridge (1716–93), voluminous author

265 (p. 480) *Baretti* Giuseppi Baretti, *Dictionary* (1760)

266 (p. 480) *gig* light carriage

267 (p. 481) *fidging-fain* restlessly eager (Northern dialect)

268 (p. 482) *I Promessi Sposi* Alessandro Manzoni, *I Promessi Sposi* (*The Betrothed*) (1825–27), patriotic Italian classic

269 (p. 486) *navvies* labourers who used to dig canals, railway cuttings, etc.

270 (p. 486) *a-gait* in action (Northern dialect)

271 (p. 488) *badinage* playful banter (French)

272 (p. 493) *coxcombry* conceitedness

273 (p. 496) *'Servants . . . flesh'* Ephesians 6:5

274 (p. 496) *steamer* From 1838 Brunel's *Great Western* used to take fifteen days to reach New York (*Further Letters*, p. 26, n. 9).

275 (p. 503) *On the British Constitution* (or some such title) Jean Louis de Lolme's translation of *The Constitution of England* (1775, etc.)

276 (p. 504) *Johnnie* ECG's son Willie had died aged ten months

277 (p. 504) *A maid . . . love* a Wordsworth Lucy poem, 'She dwelt among th'untrodden ways . . . '

278 (p. 505) *the measure . . . meting* St Mark 4:24: 'With what measure ye meet, it shall be measured to you.'

279 (p. 506) *'Whatsoever . . . might'* Ecclesiastes 9:10

280 (p. 507) *wedding-cards* two cards, one bearing the bride's name and the other the groom's

281 (p. 510) *in the first Georgic . . . night-work* Virgil, *Georgics* I, *c.* lines 178–290

282 (p. 513) *farred* old verb surviving in dialect: 'put far off'

283 (p. 513) *the penny-post reform* instigated by Rowland Hill, in 1840 for the UK

284 (p. 514) *Hoo* representation of Northern dialect 'she'

285 (p. 522) *eye-service* working hard only when under their employer's eye

286 (p. 523) *He was strangely troubled* Job 4:3–5

287 (p. 524) *The Lord giveth . . . Lord* Genesis 22:10; Job 1:21